Sparkles

Sparkles

Louise Bagshawe

headline
review

First published in Great Britain in 2006 by Review
An imprint of HEADLINE BOOK PUBLISHING

This paperback published in 2006 by Review
An imprint of HEADLINE BOOK PUBLISHING

1

ISBN 0 7553 0429 2 (hardback)
ISBN 0 7553 0430 6 (trade paperback)

Typeset in Meridien by Avon DataSet Ltd,
Bidford-on-Avon, Warwickshire

Printed and bound in Great Britain by
Clays Ltd, St Ives plc

Headline's policy is to use papers that are natural, renewable and
recyclable products and made from wood grown in sustainable
forests. The logging and manufacturing processes are expected to
conform to the environmental regulations of the country of origin.

HEADLINE BOOK PUBLISHING
A division of Hodder Headline
338 Euston Road
London NW1 3BH

www.headline.co.uk
www.hodderheadline.com

To my friend Jacob Rees-Mogg

Please visit Louise online at www.louise-bagshawe.com
– and don't forget the dash!

Acknowledgements

As ever, I must begin with my friend and agent Michael Sissons, who signed me as an unpublished hopeful twelve years ago and who has made breaking authors from scratch look effortless. I am also extremely grateful to the entire team at Headline, especially my editor Harrie Evans, who gave me a novella's worth of notes on this book and improved the final result immeasurably. My additional thanks go to Kerr MacRae, Martin Neild, Jane Morpeth, Georgina Moore, Catherine Cobain, James Horobin, Kate Burke, Amy Johnson, Poppy Shirlaw, Emily Kennedy, Barbara Ronan, Katherine Rhodes, Paul Erdpresser and the entire sales force. Extra special thanks to the Board and to all occupants of the Comfy Chairs.

Most of all, of course, I'm grateful to every one of my readers, and hope you will visit me at www.louise-bagshawe.com.

Prologue

'Ten million dollars. US,' Pierre Massot said.

The other man grunted; there was a crackle on the line. He hoped it wouldn't go dead all of a sudden. Telecommunications were shoddy over there.

'Twenty.'

'I don't have it.' He spoke with calm assurance. 'Twelve. It's the best I can do. Plus the equipment. Take it or leave it.'

There was a pause; Massot felt his destiny hanging on the reply.

'Very well.'

He forced himself not to exhale. It was his habit not to show weakness.

'You must be here soon, though.'

'I leave tonight.' Pierre smiled. 'I will see you shortly.'

He hung up. Excellent . . . excellent. For the first time, he felt a quiver of excitement. Not the shallow thrills of a rich man, the ones he sought and obtained daily, but the real thing. That passion, that sizzle in the blood. Something Pierre had not felt for a long time. Not since the birth of Thomas. And before that . . . Long before that . . .

He glanced around his huge corner office in the eighteenth-century building. It was elegant, but a little nondescript; an ideal place to do serious business. At the heart of Paris, he had once thought of himself as a spider; his diamonds and gems sparkling like dewdrops on a web, enticing in the prey.

Once you gained all you desired, though, you got fat and lazy. Pierre, who still did a hundred push-ups a day, did not want that.

And now a window had opened to a whole new level. One that could only be bought at great personal risk. Paris belonged to him; soon it would be the world. Like Tiffany's. Or better – De Beers . . .

House Massot sold great jewellery. But Pierre wanted more. The raw materials.

Diamonds.

He walked over to his desk and opened the secret drawer with the tiny gold key he wore around his neck. On their bed of dark green baize, the samples nestled.

Pierre drew them out and laid them in his hand. Breathtaking. They sparkled in the fading light of the evening, like tiny chips of ice glittering on his skin; as though moonlight could be captured and placed into cool, dazzling stones. One in particular caught his eye; it was blushing a rosy pink, like dawn over his château. A natural fancy pink, excellent clarity and rich colour saturation. At least three carats. It alone was worth at least ten million francs . . .

When he returned from that otherworldly place, he decided, he would take all these stones and have them set in a necklace. It would be a collar of diamonds in twenty-four-carat gold, the rose-pink pear shape nestling in the centre. He would hang it around the neck of his wife, Sophie; for she, like the diamonds . . . like the mines . . . like everything . . . belonged to him.

His telephone rang.

'Yes?'

'Excuse me, sir.' It was his secretary, cool and efficient in the office, eager to please out of it, when he was in the mood. 'It's Mlle Judy on the phone.' Her dislike showed; Pierre was amused by her jealousy. 'Shall I put her through?'

He considered it. It might be a week, maybe two, before he was back. There might not be sufficient women on the journey. Young Judy was so slavishly adoring . . . so lithe, so fit; he had not been worshipped that way since Natasha, and he enjoyed her . . .

But no, not tonight. He did not want the distractions. He would conserve his energy, as he always did at important times.

'No; I am busy.' He added cruelly, 'I am returning to the château for dinner with my wife and son.'

The minute sigh at the end of the receiver showed that the barb had gone home. He liked to remind his mistresses of their situation, at times; it prevented any unpleasantness, any foolish expectations.

'Certainly, sir. Good evening, sir.'

He wondered if he should visit his deputy, Gregoire Lazard. But he thought not. Lazard already knew too much. He would discover Pierre had left tomorrow; and in the meantime, he would have crossed the French border. The less anyone knew of his movements, the better.

Pierre Massot remained a loner.

He wanted to see his son and heir. Without speaking to anyone, he secured the sample diamonds, retrieved his coat, and stepped into his private elevator, the one that led directly to the garage.

No farewells; no complications. He liked it that way.

It was half-past eight when his car reached the château. This was one of his favourite times of day – early evening, with his son playing in the bath, and Sophie, his little bride, waiting with a cocktail; he preferred a Tom Collins, and enjoyed her slight air of nervousness almost as much as the drink. Sophie was not the child-bride she had once been; she was thirty-two now, but still with that milky English skin, those high cheek-bones – a beauty that would last well into her fifties. Pierre had made that particular calculation early.

She was not quite so gauche these days, not quite so grateful and nervous. His vast wealth had ceased to overawe her. But yet, she was still anxious around him, off-balance; timid with the master of the house and her mother-in-law, the formidable and distant Katherine, who still withheld all approval and warmth.

Sophie poured herself into Tom, which was precisely what Pierre intended she should do. She was loyal, stylish, and polite. A wonderful hostess, a loving mother; a decorative and obedient wife.

3

Not all that thrilling, perhaps. But he sought excitement elsewhere. The qualities he wanted in a spouse were the exact opposite of those he looked for in a mistress.

Well, there were plenty of women in the world. No one of them could be all things to Pierre.

He walked briskly across the gravel drive towards the pillared entrance of his château. Sercourt, his butler, was there waiting; he silently took Pierre's coat.

'Is Master Thomas still in the bath?'

'I believe so, monsieur. Mme is with him in the east wing . . .'

Pierre did not wait to hear the rest of the sentence; he bounded upstairs towards his son's bathroom suite.

'Papa!'

Tom recognised his father's tread; Pierre heard the hasty splashing as the taps were turned off. The door swung open; Sophie was there, smiling softly at him.

'You're early, *chéri,*' she said. 'I'm sorry – I haven't got your drink ready . . .'

'That's quite all right, my dear.' Pierre kissed her coolly on the cheek. 'It's Tom's bath time.' He grinned at his naked son. 'We always keep to our schedule, *n'est-ce pas*?'

'I'll get out!' Tom said eagerly. He jumped up and grabbed a thick, fluffy towel. Pierre gazed, fascinatedly, at his son. Tom had his features, and it was strange – endlessly so – to see the joy that was written there, the love; like watching himself as a child, in an alternate universe, where his father had loved him.

Tom was himself, altered – different, better. He wanted to believe it. The one corner of his heart that was not wholly closed he had given to his son.

'You're all red. Like a Breton lobster,' Sophie said, and kissed him; Tom shrugged away, pretending to be annoyed, but his eyes lit up.

'Papa,' he said eagerly. 'Papa, will you read to me before bed?'

'Of course, my darling. I'd love to.' He bent down and gathered the boy in his arms, towel and all; to his wife, he said, 'I'll meet you in the drawing room.'

'Very well. God bless, sweetheart.' Sophie kissed Tom's wet cheek, and then vanished noiselessly from the room.

'Come on.' Pierre held out one hand to the boy. 'What should it be? Dumas perhaps. The man in the Iron Mask.'

When his son was asleep, he came downstairs to find Sophie waiting. As he had expected, she had changed; she was wearing a pleasant dress of canary-yellow silk with a pattern of green and white across the skirt, and some yellow South Sea pearl earrings he had given her for Easter. She hurried across the room to hand him his drink, but he set it aside. Alcohol had no place in his plans for the evening.

'How are you, darling? How was your day?'

'Fine.' He smiled at her, but without warmth. 'Is all as it should be, in the house?'

She shrank back slightly, as ever, fearful of his disapproval. 'Darling – what do you mean?'

He shrugged. 'The gardeners. The grounds . . . the servants . . .'

'Everything is perfect – exactly what you wanted.' Sophie looked worried. 'Why, have you noticed anything wrong?'

He shook his head. Yes, he could safely leave her in charge. She would change nothing.

'Have you visited my mother lately?'

'I went to see her this morning, for tea,' Sophie answered, promptly. Pierre knew how she hated the visits to Katherine, but she kept them up all the same; she understood the concept of family. That pleased him.

He came over to her and kissed her on the cheek; his wife looked up at him, surprised.

'Come to the door with me. See me off,' Pierre said.

'See you off? But where are you going?'

'Back to Paris.' He pressed her hand. 'I have a couple of things to do; I may stay in the city for a few days.'

'We'll miss you,' Sophie said. 'Come back soon.'

He turned on his heel and walked back to his car; the lovely evening light was now fading over his pear orchard.

Pierre Massot climbed into his car and drove away. And Sophie stood there, watching until he disappeared.

Chapter One

'So,' the old lady said. 'You have come at last.'

'Just so, madame,' said Sophie, nervously.

Her mother-in-law shook her head and made a little moue of annoyance with her thin lips.

'Speak English, girl, for heaven's sake,' she snapped. 'You were never any good at French.'

The maid was still hovering, pouring the tea, but Katherine Massot paid no notice. Of course she would snap at Sophie in front of a servant; in Katherine's world, servants were invisible. They simply didn't count.

'I wanted you to understand my decision,' Sophie said, trying to keep her voice from trembling. She had always been nervous of the older woman. There had never been any warmth from Katherine, not when she and Pierre were first married, not even when Tom had been conceived.

'I can see your decision with my own eyes.' Her paper-thin claw of a hand gestured angrily at Sophie's dress. It was perfectly chic; Givenchy, gathered at the waist, falling to just below the knee, with a tailored jacket, and severe Christian Louboutin court shoes.

But the elegance didn't matter today. The colour mattered. And the colour was black.

'You are giving up on my son,' the elder Mme Massot said.

Sophie flushed. It was as close to emotion as she had ever seen Katherine come, and Sophie had no desire to hurt anybody. There had already been so much pain.

For a second she didn't say anything. They sat together, silently, in the sumptuous parlour of the dower house, the

7

Earl Grey rapidly cooling in front of them in its bone china cups. Sophie wished she could bolt. The excessive richness of the Louis XIV furniture, the antique silk Chinese wallpaper, it all seemed oppressive.

'I could never give up on Pierre. But it has been seven years.'

'Seven years and two days.'

Sophie nodded. Of course she kept exact count; she was his mother.

'We've heard nothing,' she pointed out. 'Not a word, not a sign.'

'There were reports that he was seen,' Mme Massot said stubbornly.

'We investigated all those,' Sophie reminded her. 'They came to nothing.'

She glanced outside the tall, narrow windows of the eighteenth-century house. They afforded a beautiful view of the park, across the lake, all the way up to the main house, Château des Étoiles. The Castle of the Stars. Pierre's house. And now, hers.

'If I had the slightest hope that he was alive . . .'

'I have not the slightest doubt he is,' the old lady said, fiercely.

'Based on what?' Sophie asked. 'Have you some new information?'

Oh, how she hoped she did. Then she would not have to go through all this. Then she could retreat to the familiar comfort of the château, and go on doing what she was good at, being Pierre's patient, obedient wife, keeping the home fires burning, and their son's hope alive.

Instead of having to face everything. Starting, but by no means ending, with Katherine Massot.

'I have not felt it. When a man like Pierre dies, you know, you sense it. Men like him do not pass unmarked.'

She looked at Sophie scornfully, as though to ask, for the millionth time, what Pierre had been doing to unite himself to such a mouse.

'I understand. It is a mother's love,' Sophie said.

The old lady turned away in a rustle of silk.

'What do you know of love,' she said.

'I loved Pierre.'

'I wonder,' said her mother-in-law.

Sophie felt anger for the first time, but it was drowned out by her fear. Katherine scared her; she always had. It had taken weeks, months even, to screw up enough courage to do this. And of course, she would take whatever Katherine threw at her. In this, as in everything else, Sophie would behave as Pierre had demanded she do. With impeccable dignity; with the bearing Sophie hadn't acquired by birth, but which she had been aping for so long it was now part of her.

And besides – this was Pierre's mother. And she was in pain. Imagine if it were Tom, and I were hearing this from Tom's wife, she thought.

'This is a dreadful thing for you,' Sophie said, kindly. 'I hope you will come and see me in a few days. And Tom,' she added, trying to sweeten the deal with the promise of her grandson. 'He should be over from Oxford for the weekend.'

'What does Thomas think of what you are doing?' Katherine demanded.

She pronounced the name in the French way, just to let Sophie know what Pierre would have wanted.

Sophie's face paled a little.

'He is very fond of his father. And, like you, he still hopes.'

'He disapproves,' Katherine said, triumphantly.

Sophie sighed. 'It has been too long. It is time to put an end to it. As much for Tom's sake as anything. He must learn to move on, to have his chance to grieve.'

Katherine stared at her, then gave a brittle laugh.

'You are very naïve,' she said, 'if you don't think life gives one plenty of chances to do that.'

Sophie looked down. Naïve. Stupid. Passive. Yes, well; she knew what Katherine thought, what they all thought. She, middle-class, uneducated Sophie Roberts, picked, against all likelihood, by the great Pierre Massot when she was nineteen, to be his wife. And the mother to his one child, thankfully, a son. What had she done, all these years, except learn how to dress, and behave, and host parties?

She rose. 'I had to inform you myself.'

'Yes. Thank you for that.' Katherine's bony claw picked up the papers, neatly folded, and extended them towards Sophie. She reached to take them, but for a moment the old woman held on to them.

'Amazing,' she said. 'You need only sign. And you will control eighty million euros.'

Sophie hesitated, then gently took the documents from her mother-in-law's hand.

'Pierre would never have wanted us to quarrel.'

'And all you have to do to get them,' Katherine said, as though she hadn't spoken, 'is declare that he is dead.'

'Because he is dead,' Sophie said, helplessly. 'It's been so many years.'

Katherine Massot sighed and turned her face away, as though she were just too weary to deal with Sophie any more.

Sophie waited a moment, then noiselessly rose, and left the house. Outside, on the raked gravel of the driveway, her car and driver were waiting. As he stepped out and opened the back door for her, and Sophie slid gracefully inside – knees together, ankles lifted in one catlike movement – she breathed out. Not so much in relief. There was too much to do for her to be relieved. But at least in respite.

The car pulled silently away, following the winding road back to the main house. It was late May, and a glorious spring evening, the warm, fading light bright with the promise of summer. The topiary hedges cast long shadows over the smooth lawns, and the lake sparkled brilliantly in the setting sun.

It was an evening very like that one just over seven years ago, when her husband, Pierre Massot, kissed her on the cheek and told her he had to see to some business in the city. Nothing important, he had told her.

He had walked out of the front porch, and she never saw him again.

Chapter Two

'And the Oscar goes to . . .'

The superstar comic paused for a second to give the moment its required suspense. In the glittering ballroom, Hugh heard the intake of breath all around him. Everybody was waiting, eyes fixed on the giant screen.

He was not nervous. He felt perfectly calm. His heart was pulsing at a steady sixty beats per minute, an athlete's pace.

'Jill Calvert!'

The comic's plastic smile was drowned in the sounds of whoops and cheering as the screen split from five beautiful faces, four of them pretending to be pleased, to the one who really was. She lifted one arched eyebrow, placed her manicured fingers to her throat, as if to ask, 'Me?'

The camera loved it. It lingered for a second on the creamy skin. And, of course, the deliciously avant-garde necklace that surrounded it.

There was a fresh explosion of cheering. Hugh now permitted himself just the faintest of smiles. Hands were slapping his back, his shoulders. Ah, he thought with satisfaction, you just wait.

Jill swept regally up to the stage in her dress, a twenties-style flapper thing made of millions of tiny sequins. A heavy fabric that clung to her skin, black and sleek like an otter. Sexy, but very simple. The perfect backdrop for jewellery. And what jewellery! Hugh had chosen these pieces himself. Gems for a rebel. Great chunks of citrine, one of the cheapest, most plentiful semi-precious stones in the world, strung on wires of yellow eighteen-carat gold; but along those wires, glittering like tiny suns, were bezel-set canary diamonds.

It was perfect. Nobody had ever seen anything like it. Mixing the cheap and the incredibly costly, the delicate and the spiky. Matching wire earrings dangled from her perfect lobes, silhouetted against her jet-black Louise Brooks bob.

Hugh Montfort had won the designers' lottery. A fresh young star had just received her first Oscar, wearing a design by Mayberry, his firm. A firm which Hugh Montfort, the youngest CEO in its history, had led out of the fusty, half-forgotten backwaters of St James's to international prominence as the number one house for the freshest, funkiest pieces money could buy. He had followed his hunches and worked – slaved, even – to get Mayberry gems round the necks and fingers of every hot young thing who ever graced the cover of a hip magazine. Indeed, such had been his success that Jill Calvert's people had called him.

He briefly imagined the faces of his rivals in New York, Paris and London. Cursing. Montfort had pulled it off yet again. Yes, he thought; perfect. A brief surge of pleasure at a job well done washed over him. He lived for these moments, when his successes enabled him to forget.

'Perfect!' Pete Stockton, the chairman of the Mayberry board, exploded next to him.

Hugh nodded towards the screen. 'Watch.'

He had another surprise up his sleeve; one he had suggested to a surprised, and instantly grateful, Miss Calvert, who could see at once what it would do for her. How it would take her from just another worthy actress into instant superstardom. Fame was the currency, Hugh thought. For her; for him, as well. An Oscar was nice, but it didn't necessarily make you huge by itself. Who remembered Marisa Tomei? Or Roberto Benigni?

Jill Calvert smiled, bowed, shook her beautiful head. The citrine and diamond earrings sparkled like raindrops in sunlight. Around Hugh there were sighs of envy and pleasure.

On the screens in front of them, Miss Calvert lifted her golden Oscar aloft and kissed it. More cheering. She smiled radiantly and said, 'Thanks.'

And then she turned and left the stage.

The superstar comic stared.

There was a horrible pause, before the band leader, caught utterly by surprise, started to play, his muzak barely drowning out the murmurs of the crowd. And then, as Hugh watched, there were smiles . . . smiles of amusement, and smiles of jealousy. Every man and woman sitting there was an old media hand, and each one of them realised at once what Jill Calvert had just done. The only thing that would be talked about the next morning. On a show where weeping, ten-minute speeches thanking everybody from God to a star's dog-walker were the norm, she had made the shortest Oscar speech ever.

And it couldn't be beaten, either, because it was precisely one word long.

Jill Calvert would be everywhere tomorrow. And in the months to come. Endless pieces would be written about that moment. Analysing everything, talking about her image. And the sleek black dress, and the wild, flashing jewellery would be a part of that.

Montfort smiled. When the exchanges opened tomorrow, Mayberry stock would be up. He thought possibly as much as 5 or 6 per cent.

The crowd broke around him, applauding him, as though he were a movie star himself. These were Mayberry executives and salespeople, the front-line troops in the L.A. office. Most of whom owned a little stock in the company, and all of whom were thinking about their wallets.

Montfort glanced at his watch, a discreet gold Patek Philippe. Mayberry made watches, but he never wore them; nor his firm's cufflinks, for that matter. Funky was not his style. He was an old-fashioned Englishman with a horror of ostentation, and would rather have been shot dead than caught wearing any of Mayberry's jewellery for men. He had inherited several pairs of cufflinks and a signet ring from his father, Sir Richard, and that was all the ornamentation he required. Early on Pete Stockton had suggested Hugh switch to Mayberry products, but a single look had been enough to warn him that that was a deal-breaker.

And they had wanted Montfort, while he had not particularly cared about going to work for them. Mayberry's was an interesting challenge, nothing more. He had been born rich, the son of a baronet, and didn't need the money.

Working at the firm was only about one thing to Hugh Montfort. Winning. That was it. And that was enough.

It was ten-thirty. By the time his limousine had arrived at the Governor's Ball, dinner would have started. Even in Hollywood, where it was fashionable, Montfort hated to be late. It seemed undisciplined.

'I should go,' he said quietly.

'Go, go,' Pete said, slapping him on the back again. 'Damn good job, Hugh. What is it you Brits say? Good show.'

Montfort smiled thinly. 'Can I give you a lift somewhere?'

Pete Stockton shrugged. 'I'm OK. I'll probably just head back to the hotel.' His eyes, hooded in the fleshy face, flickered over the crowd, settling on a couple of salesgirls. Both blondes, one of them pneumatic. They smiled warmly at his corpulent boss.

Montfort tried not to let his distaste register. No, Pete Stockton would not care to party tonight. Too many people about that knew his wife, Claudia, a regular on the L.A. charity circuit. And Stockton did not really care about stars or mingling. Just the bottom line. He knew perfectly well that was served best when their dashing CEO did the meet and greet.

'See you later,' Stockton said. He stared at the girl with the tits. She simpered and tossed her fountain of blonde hair.

Montfort nodded. 'I believe we have a board meeting in June,' he said. An implicit rebuke. He had no intention of seeing Pete Stockton again until he absolutely had to. Stockton waddled off in the direction of the salesgirl, and Montfort, diligently avoiding all congratulations with murmurs of thanks, made directly for the door, and his limo.

The signature red and white stripes of the Mayberry awning hung over the illuminated showroom, newly leased at great expense, but well worth it. In L.A., if you weren't directly on Rodeo, forget it, Hugh thought. He would drive by here tomorrow on his way to the airport, just to see the crowds that would be thronging around the door, clamouring for a glimpse of the new collection. He made a note to himself to raise the starting price on every piece a thousand dollars. Tonight. An imperceptible nod, and his driver pulled into position.

'The Dorothy Chandler Pavilion,' he said, once he was seated inside.

'Yes, your honour,' said the driver, respectfully.

Montfort lifted his head; grinned. The first genuine smile to have crossed his lips for some time. That was funny. The man had evidently looked up the passenger name – the Hon. Hugh Montfort – and thought he was some kind of a judge. But he wouldn't dream of correcting him. He tried never to make people uncomfortable, if business wasn't involved.

'Big party tonight, sir,' said the driver.

'I'd rather be in bed with a book,' Montfort said, completely honestly.

The man laughed. Hugh swallowed a sigh and looked out of his tinted windows at the L.A. traffic streaming through the night. This was the part of the job he most loathed, but he would do it to the best of his ability, all the same. Glad-handing celebrities, networking with agents. Fending off the attentions of the minor starlets, delicately, so that none of them took offence. That was hard; some of them were very persistent.

Hugh Montfort had everything a millionaire actress could want. Chiselled good looks of the non-plastic kind. A military background he never discussed. Money of his own. Success that would never compete with hers. A sort-of title. And a castle in Ireland. It was a distinguished list, and not one that was overlooked. But he had no interest in actresses, even very beautiful ones, except as walking billboards for Mayberry jewels. He supposed there would be lots of offers tonight, both business and personal. Especially once the rumours started; that he had advised Jill Calvert, not only on what to wear, but on what to say.

But he would disengage himself gently. Appear at as many parties as possible, and head for home, what, about 3 a.m.

A great weariness swept over him. He was already jet-lagged and exhausted. And he took an engineer's care with the

15

machine that was his body; no stimulants other than coffee, and not too much of that. He would not be fuelled by coke or uppers, or whatever designer drug the rich were into these days, to ease the pain of having nothing important to do.

Montfort balled his fist, summoning forth reserves of adrenaline. When much younger, in the Marines, he had learned how to do with very little sleep, and how to concentrate in much worse conditions than this. A raw second lieutenant, barely twenty-one, crawling through sodden, freezing fields on his belly. Trying to take an Argentine position. Praying he didn't get anyone shot. Yes; that was suffering. Not going to a dull party, even ten dull parties.

He thought of the war whenever he felt depressed, or the urge to quit reared its persistent head. It was better to think of that than his real sorrow, the one he fought day and night not to dwell on. And it put the present trouble back in perspective; as something trivial, not worth his consideration. That attitude, he knew, had helped him become the powerhouse of his business that he was tonight. No covers of *Fortune* or *Forbes*; not yet. But Hugh Montfort had something better. His rivals, to a man, knew him. And feared him. He had taken Mayberry from nothing, from just another fussy, small marque eternally obsessing over Cartier, to the leaders of young style, and the brink of worldwide dominance.

But the brink was not good enough. Montfort wanted to go all the way. To establish a brand so big, so impressive, that people would pay tens, even hundreds of times what a piece was worth just because it came packaged in red and white stripes. He knew it could be done. Tiffany's had done it.

Mayberry was going to be next.

The limousine pulled up and Hugh prepared himself for the next round of congratulations. He smiled in the back seat. Preparing his charm like the weapon it was.

This was business, he reminded himself. And he lived for business.

There was certainly nothing else to live for.

Chapter Three

'*Voilà*, mademoiselle,' said the waiter. He placed Judy's breakfast down in front of her with a flourish, together with the cheque.

She smiled. '*Merci.*'

Judy sighed with pleasure. This was absolutely her favourite moment of the day, and her favourite time of the year. Breakfast in a little café along the banks of the Seine, 8 a.m. on one of those warm mornings as spring faded into summer, with the light golden and warm, and the breezes not cool enough to be chilly. She was surrounded by tourists, but she didn't care. Her *café au lait* smelled heavenly, as did her croissant, and they were guilt-free, because she had finished her morning run. Three miles a day, without fail, all weather. It kept her figure slim, her eyes bright, her energy up. And it worked. Sometimes, like today, waiters still called her mademoiselle and not madame.

She was trying to learn not to hate that word so much. There was no point in hating aging. I need to keep my energies for things I can change, Judy thought. She was proud of that attitude. Fifteen years in France had not knocked all the American out of her yet. She took a sip of milky, sweet coffee – only the French really did coffee quite this well – and stared out at the river, glittering in the morning sunlight. Soon it would be warm enough to switch to an outside table.

Her reflection gazed back at her from the window. Judy approved of it. She was thirty-six, five-seven and a hundred and twenty-five carefully monitored pounds. Today she had chosen a particularly chic little outfit; a red dress, with an A-line skirt, a cream cardigan and purse, and cream shoes with a red piping trim. She wore simple earrings, pearl studs, and a small, but very fine, solitaire ruby set in rose gold on her right hand. Both Massot pieces. Even with an employee discount, Judy had saved three months to afford each of them. But she had never regretted it. That was something else she had learned in France. It is so much better to have a very few, costly and classic pieces, in both clothes and jewels, than a crowded wardrobe full of junk. One was both better dressed and better off, shopping that way. This cardigan had cost her almost three thousand francs, three hundred euros in the new and less romantic money. But she had been wearing it every spring for five years, and thought she would be able to use it for another five, at least.

Yes; it was an elegant outfit. Judy had no doubt M. Lazard would approve. She buttered her croissant and ate it with relish. She was going to ask for – no, demand – a promotion today, and she had no doubt at all that she would be successful. It had been seven years, and she was due.

Ever since Pierre had left, disappeared, Judy's career had been on hold. Naturally. He had helped his young lover rise rapidly through the ranks, making her a director of publicity just before he disappeared – walked out of her life, and everybody's. Even now, when she thought of him, there was a wince of pain. Pierre. A playboy, a dazzler of a man. He had blinded her when she first knew him; the smooth good looks, the endless money, the status. Everything hungry young Judy had aspired to have and to be. And he had offered to take her along for the ride. How eagerly she had jumped on board.

But then, once he left, and didn't come back, and all the police investigations and missing persons reports came to nothing, nobody had known what to do with her. In the end they didn't do anything. And Judy, for want of better choices, had put her head down and worked.

Of course M. Lazard, the new CEO, knew. Everybody in the office knew. But he did not seem to object on principle. And at first, of course, everybody thought that Pierre might some day just turn up. Nobody would dare to sack his girl.

Or one of his girls, as she now knew she had been.

I ought to hate him, she thought, but then shook the thought away. Dwelling on the past was unproductive. No, years of patient, cautious work, running parties, entertaining journalists, and they had finally made her a vice-president. Judy had grown to love her work. The day she got that title, she felt some of the pain seep out of her. Pain from the loss of Pierre, first, and then pain from the loss of who she thought Pierre was. But anyway . . . she had received that title entirely on her own merit. Nobody could say she had earned it on her back.

Judy threw down a few euros and left the restaurant. She would walk to the Massot offices, a quiet eighteenth-century building on the rue Tricot, almost a mile from the nearest glittering Massot showroom. She had asked M. Lazard to see her at nine precisely, and she didn't want to be late.

She smiled in anticipation as her pace quickened. Senior Vice-President, with the money to follow. Two hundred and fifty thousand a year. Yes! Judy wanted all that. She wanted to upgrade her smart little flat to a townhouse, wanted a few more outfits like the one she was wearing. Some classic Vuitton luggage, maybe a shopping spree in New York. She had learned the hard way she could only rely on herself in this world. And her career, not a man, was going to give her everything she wanted.

There had not been a man for a long time.

Judy pulled her cardigan around her. What had it been, three years now? There was that unfortunate one-night stand with the London sales director. Ill advised; neither of them could wait to bolt for the hotel door the next morning. And six months before that there was the folk guitarist she'd met in that Jazz club on vacation, in New Orleans. But that didn't count; vacation sex.

Both encounters had been empty for her. She felt the urge, sometimes, almost a clinical curiosity, just to check she was still a fully functioning female. But pleasure . . . what pleasure was there in clumsy fumbling and a few thrusts?

None. She had none.

And so there were no boyfriends. Just the one man she thought of too often, although she tried to break the habit. Pierre; brilliant, sparkling Pierre, as golden as champagne. Her mentor in business, sex, and life.

There was the corner, and her offices. House of Massot written discreetly on a small brass plaque. She felt relief at the familiarity of it all. Her life would go on, quite comfortably, with more money, and the settled achievement of her job, of having carved out a little niche in this business all for herself.

'I am glad you came to see me, madame,' said M. Lazard.

'Thank you for making the time to see me, sir,' Judy replied, in her perfect French.

'I think we had better switch to English,' Lazard said. He propped up his half-moon spectacles on the brink of his nose and smiled briskly at her.

Judy bristled; she thought her accent was impeccable.

'And why is that?' she asked.

'You haven't heard?'

Judy sat forward in the walnut-backed chair, mystified. Gregoire Lazard smiled at her. He was tall, and beautifully, very carefully dressed, and he had friendly, twinkling eyes. But they still made her nervous.

'I would have thought you would have heard the rumours,' he said.

Judy shook her head. 'I have spent the last two weeks in London, monsieur.'

'Ah yes, the fashion shows.'

'We persuaded *Vogue* to run a piece on the new collection,' Judy added, pointedly.

'Yes. Congratulations.'

'I wanted to talk to you about my position.' You had to be firm with people, steer the conversation in the direction you thought it should go.

'Oh, Judy. I do not think your position is in any danger.'

Judy stared.

'*Excusez-moi?*'

'English,' he reminded her.

20

In danger? She had come here to be promoted.

'I don't understand what you are talking about, monsieur.'

'Your new boss,' he said. Despite his excellent English, there was a trace of French in the calm tones, even a touch of something underneath it; Slav, maybe, an Eastern European touch. M. Lazard had the slight, rather sexy, hooding of the eyes that made Judy think of Genghis Kahn. Although he was, thankfully, altogether a more serene man. 'And mine,' he added.

Judy exhaled. 'A new boss.'

She could have kicked herself. How could she have missed this? Two weeks in dreary, raining London and she hadn't bothered to read the business press. Her entire attention had been focused on the women's magazines, where Massot had to jostle for space with all the other small designers and the major jewellery houses.

'Somebody bought the company?' she asked, apprehensively. That was a problem. A big one. New brooms loved to consolidate, to fire, to replace. She could easily be swept aside. Even though Lazard said her position wasn't in any danger, how could he possibly know for sure?

'No, nothing like that. It is just that Mme Massot has decided, finally, to have M. Massot legally declared dead.'

Judy froze in her chair, with shock.

'It's been seven years,' Gregoire Lazard continued. He looked at her, then judiciously looked away, perhaps to give her time to compose herself, Judy thought.

She swallowed hard.

'What . . . what does that mean for us, monsieur?'

He shrugged in that particularly Gallic fashion, involving his whole upper body.

'I have no idea. Probably not much. It simply means that Mme Sophie will now control the company and her husband's share of the stock. We expect her to visit headquarters soon, which is why I have asked staff to switch to English. I gather Madame's French is still a little rusty.'

Rusty. After twenty years in France? Judy was shocked at the violent wave of dislike that shuddered through her.

But of course Sophie could afford to have poor French; what did that woman need to do other than order servants about all day?

She could not think of anything to say, so she said, 'I see.'

'I doubt that Madame will enact many changes,' Lazard told her. 'She doesn't seem the type to be much interested in business.'

'You expect her to come here and take an inventory.'

'Precisely.' Lazard inclined his head.

'And then you'll run things much as before?'

'I imagine that is what Mme Massot will prefer, yes.'

'I believe that it's my time to be promoted to Senior Vice-President for Publicity,' Judy said, suddenly and fiercely. She thrust the image of mousy Sophie Massot from her. She had met her once, long ago, at a party to celebrate the launch of a new summer collection. Sophie, slim and dark and only slightly pretty, had stood in the corner clutching her champagne flute, her eyes never leaving Pierre as he mingled and shook hands.

And that, that was what he had preferred to her. To Judy and Judy's fire and passion.

It would make no difference to her that Pierre's widow controlled the stock. She would carry on exactly as though nothing had happened. Judy had come here to ask for a promotion, and so she asked for it.

'Yes, I anticipated that.' Lazard smiled at her. 'But I think we must wait at present for Mme Sophie to define her plans for us. If any.'

Judy's head tilted up, arrogantly.

'Very well,' she said. 'If you'll excuse me, then, M. Lazard, I think I should get back to work. The collections have met some resistance. It's going to be tough, trying to sell them to the press.'

'Of course,' he said. He stood and offered Judy his hand. 'And please call me Gregoire. We have been colleagues for several years now.'

Judy flushed with pleasure. 'Gregoire,' she repeated.

'I may have to bring Mme Massot round to introduce her,' he said, apologetically.

Judy's eyes flashed. She did not want Lazard to say anything open. Her affair was known, but never referred to. And now of all moments she wanted it to stay that way.

'Of course, I'll be delighted to meet Mme Massot,' she said, lightly.

'Good day, Judy.'

'*À tout à l'heure*,' she said, grinning at him, deliberately choosing the informality. Lazard smiled as she left the office. He did everything short of wink at me, she thought. She took the marble stairs down to her own, third-floor office, avoiding the coffin-like Victorian elevator. Her heart was in turmoil. She didn't know what to think.

Sophie Massot. Judy imagined her now, thickened with the passage of time, a plump, boring dowager. She would come round the offices, poke at everything, shake a few hands. Leave M. Lazard – Gregoire – to get on with things. Judy would be forced to endure the meeting, and the sniggering of all the secretaries.

But on the other hand Lazard had asked her to use his first name. A good sign; no, an excellent one. Once Sophie had left, she *would* get that promotion. But I can't stay around for her visits, as she swans in here like the Queen Bee, Judy thought. I'll go home – to New York. Head up the division there. Make my name, maybe put in for a transfer.

But then she thought: No. Why let her hound me out of Paris?

Never. Judy resolved, on the spot, that she would fight. She would never give in to Sophie. That woman had stood between Judy and her only love. Judy hated her, and she would never let that spoiled, pampered woman defeat her again.

She turned on to her own floor. Judy's secretary was already in her office, laying out last night's faxes and this morning's call sheet.

'*Bonjour*, madame,' she said cheerfully.

Judy thought of Pierre, her darling, with his chocolate eyes and his smooth chest lifting above her. The thought caused her physical pain, a stabbing in her side.

'Speak English, Marie,' she said. 'You can speak English?'

'Oh. Yes.'

'Mme Massot is arriving to take over the company,' Judy said calmly. 'And we must all make her as welcome as possible.'

Whatever happened, she would face this like she faced everything; head high and damn them all to hell.

Chapter Four

The bells in Tom Tower tolled nine times. That meant it was five past nine at night. The old clock was exactly one degree west of the Greenwich meridian, and so the clock-maker had decided to set it five minutes slow.

Tom smiled. He loved it. Right now he was in love with the English and all their mad eccentricities. He thought about Polly, the redhead who had just slipped from his room, five minutes ago. She swore like a sailor and left the place reeking of smoke, but on the other hand, in bed . . .

He reclined in the covers over the spot where she had been, breathing in the musky scent of her. He wondered what streams of invective Polly would spew forth if she knew she was the third girl he'd had this week . . .

Ah, college; it was great, wasn't it?

An endless procession of opportunities. His studies weren't going too well, he'd barely scraped through his Mods, and then only because Maman had offered to make a large donation to the Old Library restoration fund. But studying was *way* down on the list of things he'd come to Oxford to do.

Number one was to get laid a lot. So far this was going swimmingly.

Number two was to party a lot. Another check.

Number three was to get a rowing Blue, but he had given up on that one early on. Tom hadn't realised quite what a demanding, incessant drag it was on one's time. They expected you to rise before the sun almost every day, even when it was freezing cold, and to practise until your arms dropped off. That was fine – for the stiff-upper-lipped Englishmen, and their

25

brawny American cousins. Thomas Massot was a civilised Frenchman, however, and he preferred the sun to find him in altogether softer surroundings; silk sheets brought with him from Paris and the willing arms of some chick. Nationality was not important. He was an equal-opportunity employer, like Bill Clinton.

Massot admired Clinton, another foreigner at Oxford. What a taste in women! People laughed at him for it. But of course, the true connoisseur knew that looks, although pleasant, were the least important factor in a woman's sex appeal. An ugly woman who knows what she's doing beats a pretty-but-cold debutante any day, he thought.

Polly, of course, was hot *and* pretty. And gusty and clever. Tom liked her – a lot. She was easily the favourite of his women. For a moment Tom experienced a fleeting pang of guilt. Sex was fun, sure, and he liked his women in a variety pack. But what if Polly found out?

Don't be bourgeois, he told himself; she never will find out. How could it harm her if she never knew about it?

Oh well. It was almost noon. He was going to be late for another tutorial, and Mr Hillard was getting to be tiresome about it, threatening to complain to the Junior Censor. Tom supposed he had better take a shower and go to it.

On his way to Hillard's rooms in Peckwater, Tom stopped at the Porters' lodge. The rows of wooden pigeon-holes stood crammed with post and flyers from all sorts of clubs and societies he had no interest in. The Union, the college beagles; who could be bothered? They meant less time for partying.

There was a letter in his pigeon-hole from his mother. Massot sighed; not another one. He wished Maman would leave him alone. She was forever pestering him to study more, to make some real friends, to stop going down to London in cabs and spending his money in nightclubs. But Thomas was hardly going to travel on public transport, and he had crashed his Porsche too many times on the English roads with their stupid driving on the left.

'You are half English, Tom,' his mother would remind him. Lately they had drifted apart. But the difference between us, Tom thought, is that I welcome it, I know it is natural. And Maman wants to cling to a time when I was five years old, and needed her.

Of course, he still loved her.

He tapped the letter affectionately against his palm. It was written on his mother's signature pale blue Smythson paper, and had that faint scent of violets from the perfume she always wore, the one she had custom-blended on rue Faubourg. For a second, to his surprise, he felt violently homesick for Paris. For some decent food and real coffee. The so-called 'French' cafés round here served greasy, heavy croissants and a vile thick brew you could cut with a knife and fork, and then wrapped in a napkin with a tricolour, and that was supposed to satisfy him? He wouldn't touch it. Pigswill.

He paused, wondering whether to ignore the letter, then shrugged and tore it open.

'Darling Tom,
This is a short note to let you know that I have recently been to see M. Foche . . .

The family lawyer. What could she want with Foche? He quickly scanned the rest of the letter. His eyes widened, and he gasped.

The porter was delivering post to the pigeon-holes around him and glanced at him with concern.

'Are you all right, sir?'

Tom snapped back to himself.

'Oh yes – perfectly – thank you,' he said. He took the letter over to the wastebin in the corner, and methodically ripped it into shreds. His back was rigid with anger.

The porter wisely said nothing. Tom Massot was a good-for-nothing wastrel, just another rich playboy; they had a bunch of those every year. He wondered what the letter said. Maybe one of his girlfriends was up the duff. That would give the little shit something to concentrate on.

27

Massot strode out of the lodge and paced down the warm flagstones of Tom Quad towards his tutorial. He would get that out of the way, and then decide what to do. He thought of Papa, then wrenched his mind away. No! Whatever, whatever happened, he must not cry. Not even have red eyes. This was not child's play, now, this was the business of the House of Massot. He would not have his affairs become the gossip of a bunch of impoverished Britons.

To take his mind off it, he concentrated firmly on Polly and last night. Yes; that worked. That would work for the next hour.

As soon as the tutorial was over, Tom, having grunted his way through a dull analysis of Pope's *Rape of the Lock*, raced back to his rooms, ignoring the cries of his friends who wanted him to come in to lunch at Hall. He locked his door and pulled out his mobile. He hoped his mother was there; not having one of her endless hair appointments or holier-than-thou visits with Father Sabin.

'Sophie.'

'Maman,' he said, switching to French to punish her. They had always spoken English together, but what the hell. He was his father's son. Something she had apparently forgotten. 'You cannot do this.'

She gave a long sigh. His mother was always sighing. Tom raged.

'I have done it, darling. It had to be done.'

'No, no it didn't,' he cried. His heart thudded from the betrayal, from the grief. 'You have no idea if Papa is dead.'

'Of course he's dead. He couldn't be alive; he would never abandon you on purpose.'

He hated her for putting it like that.

'He could still be alive,' he said. 'Maybe he's been hit on the head and lost his memory. He could have amnesia!'

There was a long silence. He could hear her struggling for what to say, and of course it let him hear how ridiculous the idea sounded.

'We both loved Papa,' she said. 'You know, we must give him the gift of mourning him and of celebrating his life. He would want us to do that. You must stop hoping, darling. You should pray for him.'

'Pray!' Thomas groaned. 'Please, Maman. And the House? Now what will happen to the people running it?'

'I take control of it. I'm going into town tomorrow to meet the executives.'

He scowled. 'Maman, that all comes to me when I'm twenty-one.'

'Yes, darling.'

'So you should wait until then.'

'I can't wait another three years. We must take care of your father's affairs, he would have wanted that.'

'No, he wouldn't!' Thomas exploded. 'He appointed all the people who are there now! He chose them! You shouldn't alter Papa's decisions! You should leave that for me. I'm head of House Massot, not you – if he is truly dead.'

'He truly is, sweetheart.'

'You're betraying him,' Thomas said, and was ashamed to find his own voice now thickening with the tears he had been suppressing. 'And you're betraying me.'

'I'm doing all this for you, my dearest.'

'Oh yes, your dearest. But you can't stand to see me take control of my own inheritance!'

'You are eighteen. These next three years you need to be getting your degree. A year ago you were still in school, Tom, be reasonable. You'll have your whole life to run Massot.'

'My father never wanted this for you. He provided for you to stay home, to live very well, Maman.'

'It will be all right, darling.'

'No it won't,' he said, crying. 'Because of you!'

He hung up on her. He wished it was a real phone so he could have slammed the receiver down. Pressing a little red button didn't seem to have the same effect.

Thomas stood up from his bed and caught sight of his reflection in the little age-spotted mirror over the sink. His eyes were bright red and his nose was flushed. He blushed with sheer embarrassment; he looked like the child his mother thought he was. He grabbed one of his monogrammed flannels and washed his face, breathing in deeply until it had returned to normal.

Good. Better, anyway. He was not as young as all that. He picked up his Blackberry and tapped in the name 'Gemma'. She was another of his girls, more pliant than Polly, a little blander, but what he wanted right now. Nothing stressful, a woman who knew her place. He needed to assert his manhood and she would do very well. After Gemma he would go to the bank, check his current account. Take stock of everything he had. Perhaps there would be enough to hire a really good lawyer of his own, not like Foche, that double-crossing old fool. Perhaps he could stop his mother doing this.

If she really loved Papa as he did, she would never have done it. He was ashamed of her.

Oh well; she was not a Massot by birth. He must not expect too much of her. In a few years it would be down to him. *Calme toi*, he told himself. This uncharacteristic action was the only thing his mother had done on her own account since Papa had left. Most likely, other than the dreadful declaration of his death, she would not rock the boat. She knew nothing about anything. She would leave things for him, as was right and proper, and so, perhaps, in time, he might *possibly* forgive her.

But for now he would get himself a woman.

Chapter Five

The car purred silently through the twisting roads of Paris. The traffic wasn't too bad; she would be there in good time. Sophie tried to calm her nerves. She'd felt forced to take this decision – it was in the interests of Tom, and, please God, the worst was over already: the visit to her mother-in-law, and then the letter, and the awful phone call that had followed it.

The loneliness she had been feeling and trying to ignore for so many years was as nothing compared to the loss of her son.

Was that too melodramatic? It did feel like a loss. The cheerful, bright, laughing little boy she had grown up with, altered of course since the night he had lost his father, at the age of eleven, but still at heart her Tom, the light of her life. The only true purpose to her days, to her rising and sleeping. Even back when Pierre had been around, he had not visited her bed often, and the love-making, if you could call it that, had been cold and perfunctory. After Tom's birth it had stopped completely. That was such a relief.

Not that she'd tell anybody – a young wife is supposed to love sex, isn't she? But Sophie hadn't. Pierre wasn't tender, and she wasn't excited; she submitted to it out of duty. Sex was what married people did. But she kept the lights off, so he wouldn't see her biting her lip, the occasional grimace of pain. By common consent, outside the bedroom, they never spoke about it. Pierre didn't complain. And Sophie didn't trouble to ask why not.

Pierre had provided magnificently for them, of course. There was nothing they could ever want. And he would kiss her and squeeze her hand and give her little compliments. Sophie cherished these; she didn't realise she was starving for true affection. But the unbridled love of her baby boy had changed her world, and she had blossomed then, like a daisy uncurling its petals towards the sun.

She had no idea when Tom had started to slide away from her. Eton, maybe. Boarding school. Towards the end of his time there. She agonised again in the back seat of the car, as she had done so many times. Was that a fatal mistake? Sending him away? But Pierre had been so adamant he shouldn't be a mama's boy, and she hadn't wanted that either.

Precisely because he was her only child, her little one, she hadn't wanted to smother him, make him, God forbid, effeminate. And when he started to get a reputation, when she got a call from the school about an affair with a local girl, well. Despite her faith in God, Sophie had secretly sighed in relief. He was a normal boy. Of course she had lectured him sternly. His father would never have done such a thing . . .

Well; she had confessed her relief and gladness and been sternly lectured herself. But now, now she wasn't quite so glad. There were women, countless women, so she had heard in unguarded remarks from his friends. And she believed it. And even though he'd made it into Oxford, he wasn't working, wasn't bothering, was wasting his fine mind.

More hurtfully, he wanted less and less to do with her. It seemed to her that her baby suddenly disliked everything about her.

That call – well. It had been dreadful. Sophie was expecting it, but – dreadful, all the same.

She was doing this for Tom's own good. Sophie snapped open her Chanel purse and took out her spotted cloth handkerchief, a relic from her childhood, a little piece of her English life that she carried with her everywhere. A secret rebellion against Pierre and all his grooming of her as a proper *grande dame*. Of course, not much of a rebellion. She had obeyed him in almost everything . . .

Her marriage came flooding back to her; the years of trying to fit in, the young bride desperate to live up to her millionaire husband's expectations. How her nerves and timidity had kept

32

her silent. The awkwardness at the formal dinner parties; Sophie hadn't even known which fork to use. Pierre's dazzling society friends, aristocrats and moguls, had terrified her. She'd become used to keeping quiet, keeping her head down. Hiding behind Pierre, desperate for the approval he withheld. She wanted to show she was grateful, to prove she could learn – she wanted to be the kind of wife he desired. Quiet and ladylike and modest. In the end, she'd become accustomed to living in his shadow; a beautiful, stylish cipher, and with practice, an excellent hostess. But Tom's birth had changed everything; when Tom arrived, Sophie had come alive.

And now all her baby did was shout and rage at her.

Sophie dabbed the handkerchief to her eyes. She wouldn't think about it any more. Loving your children often meant doing things they didn't like. It was a mother's place to endure the anger and the crying.

Tom had to move on. It was unhealthy to obsess over somebody who was never coming back. And his company, no doubt everything was fine there, but she didn't think she was overstepping her boundaries just to check. It would be a full three years before Tom could take over.

I'm just seeing to this the way I balance my chequebook, Sophie told herself. She still spent on herself, to the cent, only the allowance Pierre had said she should be allotted. And she accounted for every penny. Another childhood habit, as natural to her as brushing her teeth.

This is nothing to be afraid of. This is just a bigger chequebook, she thought. Ah, rue Tricot. There were Pierre's offices. Today was overcast, cooler than it had been, and the grey sky matched the colour of the building. It also matched Sophie's mood. Sombre and serious. She had chosen a suit – Dior haute couture – and kept it deliberately feminine, the required black of mourning, but with ivory buttons, and a matching string of pearls. Massot, of course; Pierre had presented them to her on her twenty-fifth birthday. She also had a touch of scent at her wrist; Chanel No. 19, very light and spring-like. There was no point in her wearing pin-stripes or playing the businesswoman. Sophie did not want to look ridiculous.

As her driver opened the car door and saluted as she walked out, she felt a sudden burst of hope.

Perhaps this would be the last of it. There was the funeral Mass to arrange, of course. She didn't know quite what to do about that. Hold it privately in the château's private chapel. Katherine Massot and Tom would probably both refuse to attend. Katherine despised all priests, and Tom had stopped going to church. She didn't dare push it. She would do things privately for Pierre.

But this was the last awful, public thing. She had confronted Katherine and her son, and now all she had to do was to check on things here and then she could go back to the château and forget all about everything.

Sophie couldn't wait. She just wanted to get back to normal. These confrontations, so unusual for her, left her drained, tense and unhappy.

It was almost summer and she wanted to start work on that herb garden they had planned. All term-time, when Tom wasn't there, Sophie worked on the gardens in the château. It kept her occupied, and it felt useful. You could create things of great beauty that way.

She opened the heavy door with its brass handle and let herself into the offices. Her heart sped up, but Sophie breathed in, trying to slow it. No need to be nervous; why, they're probably all afraid of *you*, the big bad widow who votes all that stock. The portrait of herself was ridiculous, and she smiled.

'Yes? Can I help you?' the receptionist asked, with a touch of challenge.

'Madame,' Sophie said. It slipped out before she had a chance to stop it.

'Excuse me?' the girl demanded, angrily.

'Madame,' Sophie said, apologetically. 'You know – "Can I help you, madame?" We should be polite to our customers, don't you think? Or to anyone who walks in, really. It's just good manners.'

'You have an appointment with somebody?' the girl demanded.

Sophie flushed. She hated arguments. She was no good

at them. But there was nothing for it. She stared the girl in the eye.

Now the girl flushed.

'Why are you staring at me like that? I'll call security,' she threatened.

Sophie did not move. The girl looked at her. She watched her take in the beautifully cut suit, the huge pearls, the Chanel bag, the quiet, unmistakable scent of money. The wheels started moving, slowly.

'Oh,' said the girl, sullenly. 'Of course, you mean, I should say "madame". Do you have an appointment with somebody, madame?'

She repeated this flatly and with resentment.

'With M. Gregoire Lazard,' Sophie said.

The girl flushed again. 'Of course, madame. Please accept my apologies. I will remember what you said.'

'It just makes people feel more welcome,' Sophie said, wanting to excuse herself now she had won the point.

'No doubt,' said the girl, 'madame.'

She hates me, Sophie sighed.

'Name please, madame.'

'Sophie Massot.'

The girl's eyes widened in fear.

'Yes, yes, Mme Massot, at once,' she said, diving to her phone. 'Monsieur, Mme Massot is here.' She listened, then hung up.

'I – he is on the tenth floor, madame,' she said in halting English. 'I am to take you to him.'

'Do the elevators go to the tenth floor?'

The girl nodded.

'I can find the way up there myself.'

'Oh, please, madame,' the girl said, almost crying. 'Do please excuse me and don't mention it to M. Lazard . . . I need the work, the job.'

'I'm not going to say a word,' Sophie said, appalled that she should be frightening anybody. This girl didn't look much older than Tom. 'I only want people to enjoy coming to House Massot, mademoiselle. Please don't concern yourself.'

The girl nodded and bit her lip.

'Everything will be fine!' Sophie said heartily, getting into the elevator. It was very small and dark, lined in red velvet, the old-fashioned sort with the metal grille you needed to pull closed yourself before the thing would start. She shivered and pressed the button for the tenth floor.

Sophie was slightly claustrophobic, and below her, as the elevator cranked and wheezed its way up the stairwell, she could hear the young girl snuffling. Of course, she had been abominably rude, but still . . .

Dulouc, the gardener, would be out there already, with his flask of coffee, raking the moist, crumbly soil that turned over on his trowel like a pat of butter. Ugh, she hated all this. Damn Pierre for getting himself killed, she thought, crossly. She hadn't been here five minutes and already she wanted to go home.

Blessedly, the tomb-like lift juddered to a halt. She pulled open its inner door; an assistant, beautifully dressed in a little navy twinset, of which Sophie approved very much, opened the second door for her.

'I decided to come up by myself,' Sophie said hastily, seeing the older woman's eyes look for the errant receptionist.

'Very good, madame. Welcome to House Massot.' She offered her a brisk handshake. 'My name is Cecile Lisbon, I am assistant to M. Lazard. It is a great honour to have you pay us a visit. I will take you to M. Lazard, if you will follow me.'

Sophie dutifully walked behind her through the offices. They were open-plan, with employees sitting behind their little screens staring at computers or on the telephone. Most of them looked bored, though a few stared at her with open curiosity. It didn't seem to her like the headquarters of a great house of jewellery and fashion; it seemed just like any other office building. When she was a girl, she had visited her father one day in his work at the local paper. The atmosphere reminded her of that. But perhaps all business was the same, and just as dull as Pierre had told her it was.

'In here, madame.' The assistant opened a beautifully carved walnut door, and ushered her in to Lazard's office.

It was tastefully decorated. Sophie had an eye for these things. She took in the soft, royal blue carpet, the cream-coloured walls, the mahogany desk lined with, unexpectedly, navy leather in place of the usual burgundy or forest green. Large bay windows looked over the Parisian streets, where shoppers and tourists and businessmen mingled in the chilly morning. There were no cushions on the window seat. If she worked here, Sophie thought, she would pile up cushions and sit there like a cat, staring into the street and looking for inspiration . . .

But of course that was fanciful, and that was why M. Lazard was the executive and she just a hostess.

'Madame, enchanted,' Lazard said. He came forward from behind the mahogany desk and bowed over her hand, pressing it to his lips in a courtly gesture. Then he pressed his own on top of it. 'I am so tremendously sorry for your loss. M. Massot, or if I may say, Pierre, was a good boss and a good friend. We have all missed him these long years.'

Sophie felt her eyes prickle at the warmth of the greeting. This stranger was kinder to her than her own family.

'Thank you,' she said. 'You know, I do speak French, if you would be more comfortable.'

'Certainly not; I have instructed all the staff to change to English. Please, madame, sit down.'

The chair in front of his desk seemed awfully formal, so Sophie gingerly perched herself on a chaise-longue covered in a gorgeous ice-blue silk.

'I am sure you will not want to be bothered with House Massot's affairs for too long.'

'I hope not.'

'But while you are here, you must read various documents, and you will need to ask questions, to satisfy yourself about the state of affairs. It is hard enough in one's own language at times without having to use a second one. We only employ bilingual staff anyway – we do a large amount of business with London and New York, and, of course, there's De Beers in South Africa to consider. It is good for everybody to brush up their English.'

She relaxed. Well. He wasn't hostile at all, and didn't seem disposed to think her interfering.

'You're very kind.'

'Not at all, madame. You are in charge now, you know.'

He smiled at her and his eyes twinkled. 'So where would you like to start?'

A good question, Sophie thought. She had no idea.

'I've read the company report, but . . .'

'Legal jargon, I know. Impossible to understand. May I suggest something?' he asked, deferentially.

'Of course.'

'Perhaps you would like to meet the department heads, the staff. We could call a meeting, or I could walk you around the place, and you could see everybody working as normal.'

Sophie brightened. 'That sounds perfect.'

'And then, if you have the time, perhaps I could take you out to lunch, and give you an overview of the company, and where we stand. It is important for you to judge our stewardship of Pierre's legacy.'

Sophie smiled. 'Thank you, yes. I should like that very much.' He was very kind and not in the last intimidating, despite being so tall.

'Me too. It's so nice to really talk to you, madame. I wish it could be on a more auspicious occasion.'

'Please call me Sophie,' she said.

Gregoire took her round the building, steering her slight body in his huge one. He was very protective and chivalrous, opening every door, summoning the staff with a snap of his fingers. There were many of them to remember, but that was one thing Sophie felt confident about; painful years of being forcibly turned into the perfect hostess, for Pierre, had trained her, given her an almost perfect recall of names and faces. They were mostly men; Jean-Paul Roubin, wiry, fifties, the head of sales; Richard Roget, a bulldog of a man, acquisitions; Felix Petot, also squat, and a nose flushed from wine, an unlikely head of designers. The head of public relations was Giles Keroualle, in New York today, apparently, but his deputy was an attractive, rather hard-looking woman called Judy Dean. She was the easiest to remember of all the vice-presidents; the only American and the only woman.

'Glad to meet you,' Judy said, shaking Sophie's hand with a firm grip.

Sophie inventoried her; an elegant suit in raspberry wool, rather a bold colour choice. Her hair was a touch too short for real beauty, but she was very striking, no doubt. It was a short-sleeved suit and Sophie couldn't help but note the marvellously toned arms.

She felt slightly inadequate. She was a member of several of Paris's most exclusive health clubs, but hadn't darkened their doors for months. Sophie thought she would feel foolish, taking up free weights and jogging shoes in her late thirties, but this girl obviously did it, and she couldn't be *that* much younger, and she looked fantastic.

'Delighted. Thank you for all the hard work you do for us,' Sophie said.

'Well, thank you for my salary.' The younger woman smiled, to show it was a joke.

'There aren't that many woman working at House Massot,' Sophie remarked.

'No. So many still prefer to stay home,' Judy said coolly.

Sophie paused. Was the younger woman attacking her? But she was smiling, with those very American, brilliantly white teeth.

'I suppose so. But I'm glad you're here; it will be good to have another woman's opinion while I'm looking over the firm.'

'Any way I can assist you, Mme Massot. Just let me know.'

'Judy is one of our rising stars,' Gregoire chimed in.

'I'm sure,' Sophie said. 'Nice to meet you, Judy.'

'Have a nice day,' the younger woman said, turning back to her computer.

'Why *are* there so few women here?' Sophie asked as Gregoire led her down the stairs. She would rather walk than take that tiny elevator; perhaps she would authorise a new, modern one, she thought. Quaintness was nice, but not when it came to lifts.

'They don't apply,' he said. 'Behind the glamour of the showrooms and the fashion shows, the actual business is rather dull. All euros and statistics. Ladies have much better things to do with their time, as I'm sure you know very well, madame. Sophie,' he corrected himself. 'Excuse my old-fashioned manners. It is just the force of habit.'

They reached the ground floor, where the receptionist looked at them nervously, but Sophie smiled, trying to put her at her ease. Gregoire opened the door for her; his car was ready, and he opened the back door so she could slide inside.

'Do you have any objections to La Couronne?'

She recognised the name; that was the new, extremely expensive restaurant that had recently been awarded a coveted third Michelin star for its classic French cooking. A Normandy menu, lots of cream and apples. Sophie found her mouth was watering.

'None.'

'Then we shall go there.' He leaned forward and gave the instructions to the driver. 'I am so looking forward to this. It will be wonderful to have some interesting company.' Lazard looked at her, his blue, slightly slanted eyes dancing. 'I remembered that you were beautiful, of course, but not that you were also intelligent.'

Sophie blushed scarlet. It had been a long time since anybody had paid her a personal compliment, and it had never been about her mind. She looked at Lazard gratefully.

'Thank you,' she said, remembering Pierre's instructions. A lady always receives a compliment gracefully, she doesn't protest it.

'I will try to make this whole thing as painless for you as possible,' Gregoire said. And smiled.

Chapter Six

'Good morning, sir.'

'Good morning, Mrs Percy.'

Hugh strode in to his office and put his briefcase down on his desk, snapping it open and removing a few documents.

'Get me Louis Maitre on the phone, will you.'

'Certainly, sir.' Elizabeth Percy placed a cup of tea, black, no sugar, served in a wafer-thin bone china cup, in front of him, admiring him as she did every morning. She was twenty-eight and very happily married, but there was no harm in looking, was there? Today, like every day, he was beautifully dressed, with that effortless style – she was sure he never gave a thought to it. All his suits were bespoke, of course, and his shoes, and shirts; she thought the only thing he bought retail were his ties. Today, like every day, the tie was perfectly understated, a dark red and navy Paisley. Hugh Montfort's clothes were never allowed to get in the way of his body. Underneath that perfect fit you could still perceive, in the way he walked and held himself, the tight muscles, the sinewy strength of him.

She booked all his appointments, and so she knew his work-out routine; karate five times a week, boxing three, and daily sessions at the gym. He would have been there this morning, kicking a punch-bag, lifting weights. And then back home for breakfast, which he would make himself; scrambled eggs, bacon, toast, and he might be the last man in England to still regularly add a kipper.

The tea she served him now would be the last caffeine he would have today. He would not have wine at lunch, and rarely more than one glass at supper. It was a heathy routine, very much so, but Elizabeth knew Hugh would scoff at any such description. He merely programmed himself so as to maintain the highest energy levels, to help him at work.

He treated his body like he treated everything; as a means to an end.

Hugh tossed the tea back, it was almost scaldingly hot, the way he liked it, and handed his assistant the empty cup and saucer.

'Thank you.'

She removed it silently, and in a few seconds his phone was lit up. He pressed the button.

'M. Maitre, sir,' said his secretary's emotionless voice.

'Put him through, thanks.' She was working out well, Hugh thought with satisfaction. He would never hire another unmarried woman, not to work with him, anyway. He winced at the thought of the last two girls both breaking down and declaring their undying love. How bloody awful, all round, that had been. Of course he had transferred them elsewhere with a rise in pay; but he never wanted to go through such a scene again.

He had no interest in women . . .

'Hugh, *mon brave*.' Maitre's voice pulled him back to the present. 'Congratulations on the Oscars. What a triumph, we have been besieged.' Maitre was his eyes and ears in Paris, and ran Mayberry's small, but always packed, boutique store on rue des Princes.

'Yes; so they tell me.' The new collection was flying off the shelves, so fast it presented a problem; they needed to source more stones, or come up with something new. He couldn't have his stores empty. 'How is the report coming along?'

'It should be with you in a day or so.'

'Give me a preview now. Wait a second.' He put the Frenchman on hold and buzzed Mrs Percy. 'Hold all my calls – nothing must interrupt this.'

'Yes, sir.'

'Tell me everything.' He spoke to Maitre again, and pulled forward a yellow legal pad and his Mont Blanc pen.

'Well, I think the moment may have arrived. *Enfin*.'

Hugh smiled broadly. 'Really.'

That was wonderful news; far better than the Oscar hoopla or the sales of the new collection. He wanted House Massot. The board wanted House Massot. Taking it over would end every problem associated with Mayberry's rapid expansion. He thought covetously of the prime locations, the ancient stores, fusty and ripe for redevelopment, on Bond Street, Fifth Avenue, rue Faubourg Saint-Honoré – they even had a presence in Tokyo, although that store was a giant money-loser. And there were the contracts with the De Beers site holders, the artisans, the designers, the gold mines ... everything.

He had been trying to buy House Massot for the last nine years. Nothing doing. They wouldn't even talk to him. That popinjay Pierre Massot, so in love with his own name and the showgirls of the French Riviera; he couldn't give a damn what was best for his shareholders. And then Gregoire Lazard insisting he must hold to Massot's wishes, even though the man had disappeared off the face of the earth.

Mayberry, under his leadership, had had a clear vision, but not enough money or clout for a hostile bid. Although the balance of power had been shifting, every year, in his favour. And he had never given up.

This was it. This was *the* deal. The one that would make Mayberry into the new Tiffany's. He had sold it that way to Pete Stockton and the Board, and to a man they agreed with him.

'They're in trouble,' Maitre said. 'The latest collection was a disaster.'

'Fashion or jewellery?'

'Fashion. It was practically booed off-stage at the shows. The accessories line, worse. That was received with indifference. Same old same old,' Maitre said, proud of his colloquialism.

'And the jewellery?'

'Continues steady, from what I can discern. But their company accounts are impenetrable. So many intangibles. They gave our auditors headaches.'

'But they verify the figures?'

'They can't contradict them. Not enough information.'

'So their sales are lacklustre.'

'The fashion house must be bleeding money, monsieur. It is a disaster. My wife would never shop there,' Maitre said earnestly.

Montfort smiled; such a French analysis. But he remembered Diane Maitre; a very stylish woman. If she wouldn't shop there, he was inclined to trust her judgement.

'There is something else.'

'Go on.'

'The wife has had Pierre Massot declared dead.'

Hugh exhaled in surprise. 'The wife?'

She had done nothing, said nothing, for as long as he had been following House Massot, even back when Pierre was around. A trophy wife, a cipher of a woman, the kind that is quite content to stay home and give tea parties while her husband cats around with every blonde in France. She'd had two blind eyes to it, from what he had heard. With her enormous château, which had, he believed, a very fine park indeed, perhaps she hadn't cared.

'When did this happen?' He could hardly believe it. Such initiative.

'Just two days ago. A contact in the courthouse called me.'

'And that means . . .'

'She inherits a large sum, but most of it goes to the son. However, he will not take over the stock until his twenty-first birthday. So she votes Massot's thirty per cent, for now, and also takes his place as Chairman of the Board.'

Montfort felt his excitement rise. 'She has no business background?'

'None at all; he married her when she was nineteen. They had a son; that's what she's been doing.'

'This is terrific!' he exclaimed.

Maitre's voice reflected surprise at his emotion. 'I'm glad you are pleased, M. Montfort.'

'Perhaps she will see reason. And if not, we shall go to the shareholders. They were always dazzled by Massot, but his wife . . . they won't care to have their stock reduced by a chairman of the board without a shred of experience.'

'But I cannot imagine M. Lazard will encourage her to interfere. What if she just leaves him alone to get on with it?'

Montfort thought about it. 'Yes; and I suppose she will, if she's half a brain in her head. But we should be able to plant the fear that she will use Massot as her personal playground. Anyway, the best you can say of Lazard is that he's trodden water.'

'He has not been an inspiring leader, monsieur,' Maitre said respectfully. *Unlike you* hung in the air.

'Thirty per cent is a problem, but there's still a seventy per cent float out there.' He grinned. 'Pierre Massot is gone, and now House Massot will be, too.'

'You can do a better job, monsieur.'

Montfort nodded. 'I certainly can.'

'I will send you the report.'

'Excellent. Well done. Goodbye, Maitre,' he said, hanging up. He pressed the buzzer.

'Yes, sir?'

'Mrs Percy. Clear my schedule for next week, would you?'

'Certainly, sir.' She knew better than to ask questions, but he heard the curiosity in her tone.

'I'm going to Paris,' he said. 'Book me in at the Georges V. And Mrs Percy?'

'Yes, sir?'

'You may take the rest of the day off.'

'What?' asked the normally unflappable Elizabeth. 'I mean – excuse me – it's only eight-twenty in the morning.'

'I know. But I shall be working from home today. I need some time to think. Is there anything urgent, meetings that ought not to be rescheduled?'

She quickly checked the screen. 'Just internal ones.'

'Then cancel them.'

'Very good, sir.'

'You do have something to do today?'

Elizabeth Percy smiled. How like Hugh Montfort to imagine that if somebody wasn't working they were at a loose end. Of course she had something to do. She would go home, shower, call Jack at the bank, and they'd go at it like rabbits. Jack could get away for half an hour. And then afterwards maybe she'd go shopping . . .

A day *off*. Montfort never gave her even five minutes off. This was like Christmas.

'Oh yes, thank you, Mr Montfort.'

He appeared in the outer office with his briefcase. 'Well – have fun, then, I suppose.'

'Goodbye, sir,' said his astonished assistant.

What on earth could Louis Maitre have had to say to Mr Montfort? It was as though he'd won the lottery, she thought, as her boss strode out with the same purposeful gait he'd walked in with. She admired the rear view. No, must have been better than the lottery; that was just money, and money would never keep him out of the office.

Oh well. Mustn't look a gift horse in the mouth, and all that. She dialled Barclays in High St. Ken. Maybe she could catch Jack between meetings . . .

Hugh ignored the taxis. It was a fine day, and he preferred to walk. London, for all the choking exhaust fumes and crowds of badly dressed shoppers, was still a marvellous place in late spring. The sky was clear blue, with just a few white clouds scudding briskly across it. He felt a surge of something very rare, not quite happiness, as such, but more satisfaction. Yes; it was finally coming together, and he felt satisfied with himself. It was the same feeling he got when playing chess at the club, when he could look across the board and quite clearly see his checkmate, a mere five or six moves away.

The exercise would help calm him. Whenever he felt excesses of emotion, good or bad, he liked to go for a walk. When he was retired, in what, fifteen years or so, he would get a couple of dogs. He wasn't in Ireland long enough to own dogs there, and you couldn't keep dogs in London, it was too cruel.

No; at present he had no ability to own a dog. Or form any other kind of attachment. Even if he had wished to, he travelled too much.

The thought of Georgiana came back into his mind. For once, he didn't shove it away. Sometimes he needed to think of her, or he would go mad. Work occupied him most of the time, but not always. Today was a beautiful day. He accepted the thought of her, and the pain, quite calmly, and with love.

There was always love.

His wife. Beautiful, although that had been the least interesting thing about her. Everybody had said it was a brilliant match, an old-fashioned, society match; he was the younger son of Baron Montfort, and she was an earl's sister, willowy, white-skinned and graceful; although he wasn't to inherit any estates, nor she, they both had money, enough to live very well indeed. Certainly enough for houses in town and the country, and horses, and enough to put any amount of good-looking, well-bred children through public school. And she was intelligent, too. He had been to Cambridge, and Georgiana had studied at the Sorbonne; just to be different, he had teased her. Theirs was a glittering marriage, the congregation at the tiny country church in Alfriston thick with titles and society photographers. Everybody waited for the fruit of such a dynastic alliance, and speculated on the godparents. A duke, or perhaps even a minor royal?

But nobody had seen it like the two of them. Hugh couldn't care less about dynasties and suitable matches. He didn't care about Georgiana's finishing school or her family's estates in Scotland. All he cared about was her – kind, sexy, funny. So kind; she always saw the good in everybody.

She was his own darling, and he had wanted children with her more than anything in the world. Lots of children. Ahhh . . . a fresh stab, then, at the thought of the baby. Georgie shrieking with joy, racing downstairs waving a plastic stick at him with a couple of blue lines in the little window. And how he'd caught her up and whirled her round and then set her down again gingerly, afraid he might have knocked it loose or something. It was only a little speck . . .

It had ended one night in Dublin as they walked home together after a friend's party. She had stepped out into one of the narrow streets. He heard the motorbike before he saw it;

the old soldier's reflexes still keen, had lunged, reached for her . . . he had caught only her dress. He could still feel the silky fabric brushing ineffectually against him, still see her crumple, and horrified eyes under a helmet. The man sped off. He wasn't looking for a numberplate, he was crouched over her, cradling her. Screaming for help, but knowing, all the same, it was too late. The glassy look in her eyes. And yet so little blood, just a touch at the temple. Georgiana staring up at him, quite mildly, looking amazed . . .

He sat with her in the hospital until the undertaker came. He had gone out to Ireland with a family, and flown back with a coffin.

After that there were no more women. None to speak of. The odd whore, when he felt he couldn't take it. But those girls, even though they were high-class, whatever that meant, disgusted him. Because he was using them, and afterwards, when the hot need had evaporated, he disgusted himself.

Ah; now his mood really was blackening. The image of Pete Stockton, lusting after those shop girls, forced its way into his consciousness. He was like Pete. He, Hugh Montfort. It was an awful thought. He vowed never to do it again, but it was a promise made, and broken, several times now, and he did not trust himself.

Montfort stopped dead in the street and breathed in.

'Watch where yer goin', guv,' somebody snapped at him.

He focused directly on a shop window. Liberty's; the mannequin wearing some outrageous Butler & Wilson costume pieces. At once the thoughts of fat Pete and his own weaknesses were banished. He had thought of Georgiana, and now he could move on. Work had become his life; and now he had been presented with a chance at the ultimate triumph.

Hugh reached his front door and let himself in. As ever, his surroundings instantly soothed him. He had the house set up exactly as he wanted it; rush matting on the floors, dark red wallpaper, William Morris curtains, originals, heavy against his windows. Together with his antique furniture, some of it a gift from his elder brother, taken directly from his childhood home, the whole thing provided a sanctuary. He shut the door on London, and was almost back in the country again.

He hung up his coat and went straight into his study. The laptop was perched incongruously on his ancient mahogany desk, but he didn't reach to turn it on; Montfort needed to think, just to think.

Was there a way of approaching this problem? Something he could do that would secure the deal, without the need for expensive legal counsel and investment bankers?

But there was, of course. The woman. Sophie Massot. It was all down to her now. With her thirty per cent, obtaining a majority stake would be easy.

He smiled. Of course, it would be aggravating, having to go to Paris and charm the smug young widow of such a playboy. He, who had known such happiness in marriage, despised men and women who made a convenience of it. Sophie Massot couldn't wait to get her hands on the château, the riches, the servants, and had never objected to such a charade. She was like so many wives of his acquaintance; little better than a hooker. Just someone with better marketing.

But facts were facts. Mme Massot had the largest shareholding, and was now Chairman of the Board. And it was all to his advantage. Women; he could hardly keep them away from him. Sophie Massot, Montfort thought, would not be a problem. He sat down at his desk, took out a pen, and began to make notes on his proposals.

Chapter Seven

'Come on, babes.'

Polly stood there impatiently, tapping her foot. She was wearing jeans and those ridiculous Wellington boots that swallowed up what was, Tom reflected, really a very well-turned calf. These she had teamed with a boxy T-shirt that covered up all her shape, and under that were probably those greying Marks & Spencer's undergarments she favoured, despite his occasional presents of sexy lingerie; La Perla and Agent Provocateur. She complained the lace was scratchy.

It annoyed him that Polly could be so inelegant, and yet still look good. She had that very pale English skin, milky, and the bright blue eyes that always go so well with red hair. Several of his fellow undergraduates stared longingly at her as they walked past. Tom would have liked to knock their heads off. It was disrespectful; Polly was with *him*.

'I told you, *chérie*, I don't have time today.'

'But you should make some. We don't get weather like this every day, or hadn't you noticed?'

Polly gestured to the sky with one of her aristocratic hands; long, delicate fingers, but the effect was ruined by the fact that she invariably bit her nails. And never applied polish.

'I know.'

The sun was indeed blazing down from a deep blue sky, punctuated only by a few tiny white clouds, scattered across it like daisies.

'Might even turn out to be another hot summer. I fucking *love* global warming,' Polly sighed. She lifted her plastic bag. 'I've got everything. Scotch eggs.'

'Disgusting,' Tom said. But he gazed at her fondly. She was a lot of fun.

'Baguette and pâté,' she added, ignoring him. 'Strawberries. Bar of Dairy Milk. And a bottle of champagne.'

Despite himself he glanced at the champagne; it was an inferior brand.

'That stuff is horrible. All blended. The worst on the market.'

She coloured. 'We don't all own fucking vineyards, Tom. It was cheaper, OK? I get what I can afford.'

He wanted to reassure her.

'I told you, you don't need to pay for anything, Polly; I'll take care of it.'

'It doesn't work like that.' She smiled. 'Look, after the first two glasses you won't give a toss about the quality, trust me.'

'I'd love to go on a picnic with you,' he said, wistfully. Actually, Tom couldn't think of one thing he'd rather do. 'But I've got a meeting this afternoon. I must prepare for it.'

She snorted. 'You, prepare for a tutorial? That's a new one.'

'It's not a tutorial,' Tom explained. He wished he could tell her everything, but he didn't want to expose his mother. 'It's family business, and very important.'

Polly ran her bitten fingers through her lush red hair and sat down on the bed.

'You're no fun,' she said. 'Well, I suppose it'll keep. You can shove this in your fridge. Apparently it'll be nice tomorrow, too.'

'Sounds good,' he said, absently.

She reclined against the pillows, letting her hair spill against them. 'I bet if I wanted a shag you'd have time.'

She grinned, and Tom smiled back at her. 'Make love,' he said.

Polly trailed her fingers across the shapeless T-shirt. The simple motion pressed it to her breasts. Tom tried not to look, but it was difficult. Even though he knew her body so well, it seemed fresh to him every time. Tom sensed his familiar, implacable stirring; the letter from the lawyers became less interesting.

'Mmm,' she said archly. 'Is that what you call it, *chéri*?'

She rolled about over his silk sheets, a tumbling, glorious mess of legs and breasts and . . .

'What's this?'

'What?' Tom asked, wishing she hadn't stopped.

'This,' she said, coldly. She tugged at something that sprang free from the side of his bed. Cheap and padded. He recognised it at once. Gemma's Wonderbra.

'It must be yours,' he said, thinking on his feet.

She stood up, looking daggers at him. Polly was vulgar and low-class, he thought, ruefully, but not unintelligent.

'Go fuck yourself,' she said.

'Polly.' She was grabbing her bag. 'I can explain,' he lied.

'Don't bother. Really.' The blue eyes stared him down. 'I've got no interest. You're slime.'

'Give me another chance –'

'Oh, grow up,' she said, slamming the door.

He thought momentarily about going after her, then dismissed it. It wouldn't work, he knew her. She thought she was so worldly, but a tiny dalliance with another – OK, a few others – and her self-esteem would be shattered. No; Polly Jenkins was not likely to forgive him, and he wouldn't waste his efforts trying to make her.

Tom felt a pang of loss, and tried to dismiss it. Besides, he would have finished with her soon, anyway, he told himself. Maybe not immediately, but surely soon. Polly was never intended to be his wife . . . right? She had none of the qualities he was looking for; well, besides intelligence and sex appeal, he conceded. And good humour. Well, OK, but none of the *important* things Pierre Massot's son must have in a bride. Birth; refinement of dress and manners. Even simple grooming was beyond Polly.

Tom wondered what she would do now. Would she go back to her rooms, or would she go and cry on the shoulder of Mark Allston, the rugby player he had seen her with last Tuesday in the Union bar?

But no; he wouldn't go there . . . They were done. Tom looked at the Wonderbra, dangling pathetically over the chair where Polly had tossed it. He felt a flash of anger. There was no doubt Gemma had left it there deliberately, for Polly to find. He had not thought she would be so devious, with her placid face and mild temper. But women do not 'forget' their brassieres. When Gemma crept out of his bed this morning, she'd made sure she left a calling card . . .

It was cunning, in a sort of animal way, and bold. But he felt no admiration, only anger. He was Thomas Massot and not to be manipulated by some girl from the town. I *don't* feel the loss of Polly, he insisted to himself; only that it's over earlier than I'd planned. Such things should be my decision. I'll finish with Gemma today.

It was a slightly risky policy, because it left him with only Flora, the Scots girl, a dark-headed mathematician and the least interesting of the three. And he had to have a woman, or, more exactly, women. He had needs. One could not ignore them.

But there are always new women, Thomas told himself. It is a simple matter to procure one. A bunch of flowers, a fine restaurant, a couple of smiles, and listening to their chatter without one's eyes glazing over. That was all his technique; all he needed. For now he had Flora. She'd do for a week or so. He planned to be in London a lot, away from Oxford, anyway. There was business to see to. And the added advantage that he would not run into Polly.

Enough! He was annoyed with himself for thinking so much about one bloody girl. He was wasting so much time he might as well have gone on the stupid picnic.

To distract himself from thoughts of Polly, Thomas picked up the letters on his desk and skimmed though them again. He had whittled the candidates down to three; and Messrs. Elgin and Hartford, of Lincoln's Inn, made the best case for his business. He had researched them. They were a small firm, but very old, and of impeccable reputation. That was the clincher. The other firms had made headlines and won big judgments, but he had to consider more than simple victory. There was the reputation of his mother, he thought carefully, and his father's memory, and the good name of House Massot. What was to be done had to be done quietly.

53

Yes; assuming the interview this afternoon was satisfactory, Elgin & Hartford would be getting his retainer.

He was suddenly hungry. Women and food; Tom seemed to need them all the time, these days. He glanced at the plastic bag Polly had left on the floor, then rifled through it. There was indeed a baguette and some coarse pâté, English rather than French, but it would do. And, he thought as he expertly cracked open the champagne, Polly had been right. After a glass or two he wouldn't care. It was inferior, but he could force it down.

But maybe I'd better stop at two, Tom thought. It wouldn't do to arrive at the English lawyers hammered. These were the affairs of House Massot. If he was going to claim his inheritance, he'd have to do it carefully and act like a man.

He poured himself one modest glass, but, as he spread the pâté thickly over the bread, he wished Polly were still there to share it with him.

Chapter Eight

The restaurant was full. It was well designed, and the lobby was perfectly spacious, decorated in clean tones of pale green and white, with carved oak benches and plenty of chairs, but that did not hide the fact that an awful lot of people were waiting to be seated.

'But my reservation was for half an hour ago,' an American man said loudly and angrily, directly in front of them.

Sophie heard the receptionist murmur something calming, but resolute, to the customer. So sorry; other diners were taking longer than expected; nothing to be done; a drink at the bar, perhaps?

'I'm afraid we won't get a table.'

'Don't worry about that,' Gregoire Lazard said easily.

'But all these people have reservations; they are still waiting. We can go somewhere else,' Sophie said. 'I honestly don't mind. I haven't been out to lunch in ages. A bowl of soup in a bistro is fine for me.'

Lazard shook his head. 'A bowl of soup! For Sophie Massot! You are priceless.' He lifted his fingers and crooked them, very slightly. The receptionist noticed, and made another discreet gesture. Within two seconds a waiter was at their side.

'M. Lazard, how nice to see you again,' he said. 'If you will follow me, monsieur, madame, your table is ready.'

'What!' exploded the man behind them. 'If there's a table, that's my goddam table . . .'

'That is a very important personage, M'sieur,' said the receptionist icily, 'and if you cannot contain yourself I will have to ask you to leave.'

The man hesitated as Sophie walked past him, embarrassed. She looked at him apologetically. He shrugged.

'Whatever,' he said.

The waiter led Lazard and Sophie to a table by the window; it had a wonderful view of the boulevard below and the roofs and grey stone walls of Paris. She sat down nervously, looking back in the direction of the irate diner.

'We skipped the queue,' she said.

Gregoire smiled. 'What a wonderfully English thing to be concerned about. But he will not leave. It takes the average person several months just to secure a reservation here. He will not storm out, he hasn't the flair.'

'You have great influence,' Sophie remarked.

He shrugged. 'It is not me, madame, it is your company. The wife of the proprietor gets a discount, and we entertain many of our contacts here.' He scrutinised her face. 'You are still concerned about that monsieur? Allow me.'

Lazard beckoned and another waiter glided to their table. He spoke rapidly to him in French, too fast for Sophie to follow. The man nodded and moved away, and seconds later Sophie saw the angry customer and his frazzled-looking wife escorted to a table.

She smiled lightly. 'Now I'm impressed, Gregoire!'

'You are so considerate; I must be also. I have told them to send over a magnum of champagne from us. Veuve Cliquot Grande Dame, very appropriate,' he said, grinning. Then his face changed. 'Oh – I didn't mean –'

Sophie shook her head. He had meant to compliment her with the *Grande Dame*, great lady, and then realised the champagne was named *Veuve Cliquot* – the widow Cliquot.

'You don't have to tread on eggshells,' she said.

He looked puzzled. 'Excuse me?'

'It's an expression. You don't need to – to dance around the subject, or be afraid to mention my husband. I know I am in mourning, but that is because he has just been declared dead.' Sophie took a sip of water. 'It would have been wrong to put on these clothes before. But I have come to terms with my loss. It has been many years.'

'Yes,' he agreed.

'I believe I am acting as he would have wanted me to. For the sake of our son Thomas. And of course, the company, in which he took great pride; I am just checking all is well with it.' Sophie sighed, thinking of the Massot receptionist, so terrified of her. 'I wish nobody would be afraid of me, Gregoire. Nobody has to mind their tongue or watch they don't bring up Pierre. I am moving on. It's why I'm here.'

He nodded. 'I understand.'

The waiter arrived back with their menus, announced the gratitude of the formerly angry monsieur, and waited for their order. Lazard decided on a steak au poivre. There was a pause, then Sophie realised they were looking at her.

'Oh – give me a few seconds,' she said. It came to her that she had been waiting for Gregoire to choose something on her behalf, the way Pierre had always done. But he had not; he was waiting for her to make her own selection. Sophie wasn't used to that. She decided she liked it.

'The salad niçoise,' she said.

'Of course, madame. Some wine for the table, monsieur?'

Gregoire looked at Sophie; she shook her head.

'Just a bottle of Perrier. It's a business meeting.'

'Very good, sir,' said the waiter, vanishing.

'If you can bear it, I will summarise the position for you,' Gregoire said to her. He was all seriousness, and Sophie willed herself to concentrate and not think about his charming manners, or the way his eyes crinkled when he smiled. 'Naturally, I will provide you with all the reports and documentation when we get back to the office. But for now, an overview?'

'That would be fine.'

He sketched things out for her. House Massot was thriving. The stock price had increased by 9 per cent since the disappearance of Pierre. The jewellery business was magnificent, they boasted some of the world's finest pieces, and their reputation was undimmed. Accessories and fashion continued to be steady – though there had been some slight resistance to the last collection, his excellent PR department was working to overcome it.

57

'Judy Dean,' Sophie said, recalling the hard-looking girl in the raspberry suit.

'She is very efficient.'

'I am sure she is.'

Gregoire Lazard paused. 'Perhaps you would like to get to know her better; as you said, she is the most senior woman at Massot. Apart from yourself, of course.'

'I'm hardly "at Massot",' Sophie said.

He smiled back at her. 'We all work for you, you must get used to it.'

Sophie loved how he did that. He was so respectful, and he treated her without any condescension.

'I would like to get to know her, although I probably shan't stay long in the office.'

Gregoire groaned. 'You're not going to run away to the château, and leave me all alone again, doing boring business all day long?'

She giggled. 'It's not that bad, is it?'

'You have no idea of the tedium.'

'Well,' Sophie said. She paused as the waiter laid their dishes in front of them, and withdrew. 'You seem to have everything under control, Gregoire, so I'm afraid I shan't spend more than a week or so over there once I have read all the papers.'

'The papers?'

'Yes, the papers and reports you said you would give me.'

'Oh, those.' He lifted his eyebrows. 'Of course, you wanted to read them. I had hoped to save you the trouble.'

'I suppose I had better check over everything,' Sophie said apologetically.

'But certainly,' he said, grinning. 'Why should I be the only one to suffer?'

She took a bite of her salad. It was exceptional; the beans were fresh and crisp, the salad dressing used lemon juice instead of vinegar, and they had added some fresh, chopped herbs that made the whole thing smell like summer. She saw that the new potatoes were flecked with tiny specks of truffles, and sighed with pleasure.

Gregoire was poised over his steak, which looked excellent, very tender and bloody. He nodded towards her salad.

'I've always observed that the truly great chefs distinguish themselves in simple meals, rather than complex ones.'

'I feel exactly the same.'

He smiled at her. 'Madame – Sophie, I hope you will not consider me very forward, if I say that it is a real pleasure for me to have you with us. And indeed, I hope that once you have returned to your home – if you truly feel you must – that you will not be a stranger to us.' He paused. 'Well, to own the truth, I want you to not be a stranger to *me*.'

Sophie laughed. 'If I didn't know better, I would say you were flirting with me, Gregoire.'

'Ah! No, madame,' he said, seriously. 'Not that – not flirting.'

She blushed and took refuge in another forkful of salad.

'Excuse me,' Lazard said ruefully. 'I am out of practice – not very good at this. For me it has been too long. Forgive me.'

'Oh,' Sophie said. 'You're doing very well. I mean – I wasn't offended.'

'But I said things too fast. You know already how beautiful you are, and do not need an old fool like me to tell you so. I will just hope we can become friends.'

Sophie's mouth felt dry. It had been so many years since she had been talked to like this. In fact, she wasn't sure she ever had been. Lazard was strong, tall, handsome, and clearly a successful businessman, and yet he seemed to be genuinely fascinated by her. He was sitting there all discomfited – over her. Of all things!

She began to feel herself uncurl a little in the unaccustomed warmth of male appreciation. And there was no guilt. She was a widow, she was a free woman. Not that it would go that far . . .

Although, why not? Why shouldn't it? said a very small voice inside her.

'I believe we are already friends – Gregoire,' she said, smiling shyly.

Chapter Nine

Judy was proud of herself. Everybody had been watching, she knew that much. It was simply too delicious a piece of gossip to pass up. The widow and the mistress; very well, one of the mistresses. But the only one who worked in this company. House Massot was a small, close-knit office. Few people were hired here and fewer fired; many of the secretaries had been working here when Pierre was still around, and had seen him courting her boldly, and the fresh flowers – orchids, and other costly out-of-season blooms – landing on her desk every day.

Life at Massot was not that interesting lately. Nothing much had happened since Hugh Montfort and Mayberry had come sniffing around like wolves, but the last time he had tried had been a few years ago. Damn Montfort; Judy couldn't get a thing noticed right now because his blasted citrines were everywhere. The fashion was for all things spiky and chunky, not for Massot's sedate, important pieces.

She glanced at her secretary, who had been positively bristling with excitement ever since Mme Massot had deigned to show her face. Judy was no fool. She was well aware that as soon as she left the office for lunch – a small chicken salad and a citron pressé – the excited buzz would have swelled round her desk.

She shrugged. She was confident she had carried it off beautifully. Let them gossip.

'Marie, bring me the New York reviews of the last collection.'

'Right away, madame,' her assistant said.

Judy sat proudly behind her desk as Marie brought in the

sheaf of clippings and laid it in front of her. She really didn't need to see them, but she wanted to assert her authority.

'Thank you. And a cup of coffee, please.'

'Yes, madame,' Marie said meekly. She had the guilty countenance of one who knows she has been caught out. Judy didn't really blame her. It would be hard not to gossip, wouldn't it, with the widow so surprising. No; not what she had expected at all. Judy had imagined Sophie with the years thickening her, getting fat and letting herself go once Pierre had disappeared. Of course she would be able to afford the best tailoring, which can slim up to ten pounds off a woman.

But no; she had not expected Sophie Massot to be so elegant. She was, what, a hundred and eighteen, maybe a little less. Petite, at five-five, Judy guessed, once you subtracted the heels. But gorgeous skin, glossy chestnut brown hair, and bright eyes. And simply wonderful style. She looked perfect in black, with that touch of white at her neck, the huge, lustrous pearls. It would be hard to put a value on those pearls. Certainly more than several years of Judy's salary.

Judy silently thanked the gods of fashion that she had decided to go completely jewellery-free for the encounter. Yes, she had those few, good pieces, but she had correctly guessed that nothing she owned could compete with Sophie Massot and her personal collection.

She looked down at the raspberry suit. It was bright; unafraid. She was so glad she had taken the extra time this morning with her hair and make-up. True, Mme Massot was much better-looking than expected. But, Judy thought fiercely, she still cannot compete with me. Not then, and not now.

Let her wear those insane pearls; Judy would compete with her beauty, and let it be all the ornamentation required. She knew all the Frenchwomen in the office had been judging the two of them, and she imagined herself to be the victor.

It is all so much nonsense when women say they dress for men, Judy thought. What do men know about style? Nothing. She wanted the respect of her peers, and in France, for an American, that was quite something to achieve. She was proud of the fact she had made it. Daily she compared herself to the effortless chic of the women around her; her style was far from effortless, but she was sure it could pass muster with any of them.

Her eyes flickered over the press clippings. The best you could say about them was that they were mediocre, but Judy was still quite satisfied. The last collection had been about damage limitation. It had been booed off-stage at one of the shows; she had had to do some fast spinning from keeping that story running everywhere . . .

In a way, we should be grateful for Hugh Montfort and his amazing Oscar-winning protegée, Judy realised; that story had taken up so much ink, the implosion of their fashion brand was relegated to just a few pages.

She sighed. Working for Massot right now was like the *Shawshank Redemption*, trying to tunnel her way out of jail with a spoon. And that was assuming she was able to concentrate . . .

Her phone buzzed.

'Yes, Marie?'

'M. Lazard asks if you have five minutes to see him in his office, madame.'

'Tell him I'll be right up.' Judy depressed the button with triumph. Ah – wonderful. M. Lazard – no, Gregoire, she reminded herself – had managed Sophie Massot, had got her to leave, to trundle on back to Château des Étoiles, and do whatever the very rich did. And since she had managed not to lash out at the woman, at least not *too* obviously, her patience was going to be rewarded.

Senior Vice-President.

Judy smoothed down the fabric of her suit, checked herself in the full-length mirror she had had installed on one wall of her office, so she could always be certain a hem had not fallen nor a button come loose.

The fog in her mind blew away. Sophie Massot was relegated to her proper place. It was Lazard, working him, that was to become her priority. Immediately, Judy had banked the Senior Vice President, and her mind was now on the next goal. Getting Giles Keroualle fired – he was worse than useless – and placing herself in charge of the division.

She rode the elevator up to the executive suite in a wonderful mood.

When she reached Lazard's office, she knocked delicately.

'Gregoire?'

'Come in, Judy,' he called.

She entered.

'I'm so glad – oh. Excuse me.'

Sophie Massot had not left. She was standing there next to Gregoire, smiling foolishly, Judy thought. She thrust her own annoyance down and returned the smile with a brisk one of her own.

'I hope you had a good lunch, madame,' she said to Sophie, through gritted teeth.

'Very nice indeed,' Sophie replied, with a slight blush.

'Judy, Mme Massot is to set up an office here while she goes over our reports and financials.'

'How nice,' Judy said, since she couldn't think of anything else to say. The widow was beaming at her. She struggled to contain her annoyance. Go over the financials, huh? How great, for the mousy *hausfrau* to take an interest. Judy sure felt honoured.

'Yes; we are fortunate to have her with us.'

Judy looked sympathetically at Gregoire. No doubt he wanted her help in getting this well-dressed monkey off their backs. I'll come up with something, she thought.

'I was thinking perhaps you and I could work together,' Sophie said.

'What?' Judy replied sharply. Then she flushed. The comment had taken her completely by surprise. Hastily, she moved to cover. 'I mean – wow. I wasn't expecting that, I mean, you being the owner, and everything,' she blurted.

'You don't need to be afraid of me,' Sophie replied, smiling. Condescending bitch.

'That's good to know, Mme Massot,' Judy said, easily. She had recovered herself now and felt utterly alert. Her palms were damp from the adrenaline.

'But you must call me Sophie, please. And I'll use Judy, if that's OK.'

'It's absolutely fine.'

'It will be nice to work with another woman.'

'Certainly,' Judy said heartily. Does she know? she thought. She must, she must know! Why would she be doing this? The tiny hairs on the backs of her arms and neck were rising. She wondered if Sophie was looking for an excuse to sack her; Judy would hand her no such victory.

'And I believe you are the only native English speaker in the company.'

'That's true, although everybody here is fluent. We take language skills very seriously at House Massot.' Judy couldn't resist.

'I can see that,' Sophie said. The younger woman looked brittle and tense, somehow. Was Sophie being fenced with? But why? No, it must be nerves. 'Well, I'm sure we'll get on famously.'

'No doubt. I look forward to it – Sophie.'

'Excellent,' Gregoire Lazard said. He looked from one to the other with satisfaction. 'I am preparing the rooms opposite mine for Sophie, Judy, and there is another vacant office right next to hers.'

Judy knew it. It was a small, windowless cubicle, half the size of her present office.

'Perfect,' she said furiously.

'If you could ask maintenance to start moving your equipment and files today, you can start in there tomorrow.'

'Of course. And since they will be moving everything, perhaps I should work from home this afternoon.'

Gregoire inclined his head.

'Where do you live, Judy?' Sophie Massot asked.

'On rue des Cloches,' Judy said. She would have given six months' pay to be able to add 'in the apartment Pierre bought me, where we made love every day'. Instead she had to content herself with 'I have lived there for seven years now.'

Judy bit her lip. Unbidden, a sharp image flashed into her mind; Pierre, after a wild lovemaking session here, in this very office, telling her to get into his Corvette; driving her through the city . . .

She'd asked where they were going. He wouldn't say. But when he stopped outside the building, that lovely, eighteenth-century pale grey stone lit up by the fading sun, he'd pointed upwards.

'See that?'

She nodded.

'The penthouse.' And then he'd fished that dangling key out of his pocket. 'All yours, baby.'

It was the greatest present she'd ever had. An actual place of her own. That had been the one moment, the one golden glorious moment, when Judy felt Pierre truly loved her . . .

Gregoire Lazard's eyes lit up with amusement; he looked discreetly down at his desk.

'Rue des Cloches? Oh, how lovely,' Sophie said, warmly. 'I believe that's a very up and coming neighbourhood.'

Yes; I definitely hate her, Judy confirmed.

'Well then, until tomorrow,' she said, smiling brightly. 'Excuse me.'

Back in her office, Judy informed Marie, as calmly as she could, that they would be making the move to the tenth floor.

'*Mais pourquoi, madame*?' Marie asked, dismayed.

She doesn't want to move any more than I do, Judy thought. All her friends are down here, and she too has access to a window.

'Mme Massot has decided she wants to work more closely with me,' Judy said, daring the other woman to say something.

Marie swallowed. 'I see,' she said, reverting to English.

'It is a wonderful opportunity to work closely with the Chairman of the Board,' Judy said cheerfully. 'We must be on our best behaviour, Marie.'

She felt a wave of tiredness sweep over her. PR taught one how to act happy and upbeat at times when you felt the opposite, but this . . . this was going to be exhausting. Smiling and bowing all day long. She hoped to hell Sophie would tire of this charade soon; that woman as an executive? It was like Marie Antoinette playing the shepherdess.

'Marie, have maintenance take care of it. Supervise the

installations. Then you can take the rest of the day off. I am going home now.'

'If someone should need you, madame, how can they reach you?'

'They can't,' Judy said firmly. 'I'll be back in tomorrow.'

'Yes, madame.'

Judy picked up her purse, a plain black Prada with shoulder straps, and walked downstairs and out the front door as fast as she could. She needed some fresh air, to breathe and to collect herself. Hastily she walked towards the centre of town. She would break her own rules about eating between meals and find somewhere to have something sweet. A pastry or two, or a tarte tatin. And a coffee, although she was so jumpy that perhaps it should be decaf.

The day had started out so well; so promisingly. And now . . .

Ah well; she was back to her first rule. Do not think about unprofitable things, things you cannot change. She was Judy Dean, who looked for the advantage in every situation. Every businessperson knows the old chestnut, she told herself as she walked, and felt her heartbeat slow, about the Chinese word for 'crisis' being made up of two characters; the one for 'danger' and the one for 'opportunity'.

She had to find a way to see the opportunity here. Of course it hurt to have the woman that Pierre had preferred to her rub her triumph in her face, but Pierre was long gone. What mattered now was her career. Sophie Massot was, at present, an obstacle. But Judy believed in 'know thine enemy'.

She had always said – kept it in her heart – that she was brighter, more passionate, more alive, than Pierre's wife. And of course, unlike that shadow of a woman, Judy had loved him, most deeply. But maybe now was a chance for revenge. To show the world, and show herself, what Pierre had missed.

Judy would find a way to use the dabbling of the jewel-encrusted wife. And there must be no more veiled displays of hostility, she admonished herself. No; the first thing I must do is get close to her.

Chapter Ten

'I trust everything is in order, monsieur,' said the valet. He shut the door of the closet on Hugh's clothes, which he had quickly and efficiently unpacked. 'Is there anything else I can do for you?'

'Nothing.' Montfort pressed a ten-euro note into the man's hand. 'Thank you.'

'Thank you, sir,' he said, disappearing.

Hugh examined his room with satisfaction. It was lunchtime, so the curtains were drawn back, and he could see rue Saint-Emilion below him, bustling with people and traffic, although of course it was completely silent; the windows shut out all possible noise. He admired the heavy chintzes and ornate furnishings; the Georges V was one of the world's last great hotels, and always made business travel that much less of a penance.

Not that it was a penance today.

He had a meeting with Louis Maitre at three, but he was hungry, and needed to shower and change. After a flight, no matter how brief, Montfort always required a clean shirt. He thought better that way.

He dialled room service and ordered lunch without consulting a menu. A salad, lamb chops with new potatoes, and a blackcurrant sorbet; he recalled they made a particularly good one here. And half a bottle of Krug, as he was in an expansive mood; some mineral water, and coffee, to finish off.

He showered quickly, towelled himself off, and selected a new shirt and suit. The meal was delivered very promptly, and Montfort ate it with relish, although when it came to it he drank only one glass of the wine. Everything was spectacularly delicious, and he made a resolution to come to France more often, merely to eat. A Mercedes had been ordered for him, and was waiting patiently when he stepped out of the heavy gilt doors of the hotel at a quarter to three; and at 3 p.m. precisely, he was walking into the Mayberry showroom on rue des Princes, alive with excitement and the scent of the deal.

Although it was a Wednesday afternoon, Montfort was pleased to note, the place was jammed. Crowds of tourists peered into the brilliantly lit glass cases; Japanese and Americans he could identify instantly, but he thought there were also at least ten Frenchwomen. He could further see that although the store was very full, their carefully designed layout was working. There was no sense of a cattle market.

The hushed, pale grey colour inside the stores, a hue he had chosen himself, was reflected in a calming palette everywhere, from the soft carpeting that deadened the clicks of ladies' heels to the silvery, moth-coloured background of the gem cases, and the walls that looked as though they had been washed in moonlight. The cases were all small, and spaced out; Mayberry jewels, Hugh had decreed, were not to be jumbled together in one huge box. Each range would be separate; displayed to best advantage.

For a few moments he watched the women cooing over the pieces. The brightness of the displays played up his fresh, hip brand; unlike every other jewellery store, you didn't have to guess at the prices here. They were not invisible, or written on tiny paper tags. They were displayed, electronically, on screens beside each piece, along with information on stones and carat weights. The greatest crush was around the 'Molten Sun' collection, his Oscar triumph, but he noticed other lines doing well; 'Bloodlust', the ruby and spinel line, was attracting the attention of the Frenchwomen, and the Japanese ladies were interested in 'Onyx Moon', which, of course, contained no onyx; it was a selection of chokers and brooches in jet, opals and black diamonds.

Perfect; it was fashion, and the dedicated followers were out there, hunting not just for the famous line, but for the next big thing. As he watched, eight more women entered the store; but it was at capacity already, and they murmured to themselves, then left again.

His annoyance mingled with anticipation. Yes, of course customers left, if there was no room for them to see the merchandise. It was a scene most likely repeated in Mayberry stores around the world. He needed space, and prominence. He needed the stores of that dinosaur, House Massot.

'Monsieur.'

He turned; fat little Louis Maitre was standing there, smiling and rubbing his hands.

'Bienvenue,' he said. 'You can see we are doing very well herc, M. Montfort.'

'Indeed.' Hugh nodded towards the back office. 'Shall we go inside? It's a little crowded.'

'Of course. Please follow me.'

Maitre kept his office neat and simple, both traits of which Hugh approved. He pulled up a chair, which was barely comfortable.

'I do not take many meetings,' Maitre apologised.

'That's quite all right.' Hugh waved it away. 'Now what has happened, if anything, at Massot?'

Maitre puffed air out of his lips in a heavy sigh. 'Nothing, monsieur. *Rien*. She goes to the office each weekday. I am informed they have given her an office. But nothing happens; nobody is dismissed, no changes are made. It is as if she were not there.'

Hugh nodded. That was mildly disappointing; ideally the wife would have had some stupid ideas to implement.

'She is seen much in the company of the chief executive, though.'

'Gregoire Lazard?'

'The same. I have people watching the building,' Maitre said shamelessly. 'He takes the madame for many luncheons, and last Tuesday even for a drive in the country he took her. And there is a rumour that she is to invite him to dine with her at her estate.'

Montfort paused. This was new information indeed. He instantly decided it was unwelcome information.

69

'It means one of three things,' he said, thinking aloud. 'First, that she is in fact taking a very close interest in the company and is asking a lot of questions.'

'I doubt it, monsieur. She would hardly start now.'

'Second, that Lazard intends to marry her and control her fortune, and her stake.'

'Or third, that they are in love.'

Hugh's lips curled at the corners. 'M. Maitre, love is never quite that convenient. It is amazing, is it not, that M. Lazard should suddenly fall heavily in love with a housewife?'

'But monsieur.' Maitre was a gossip hound, and eager to show off all the information he had gathered. 'Mme Sophie is more than just a housewife, she is a most attractive lady.'

'I'm sure she was, when Massot married her.'

'No, now. Look –'

He pulled out a sheaf of photos from a drawer of his desk. Montfort was shocked.

'What is this?'

'You said to find out all I could, monsieur,' Maitre said defensively.

'Yes, but; not to have the lady followed,' Hugh replied. He was a little embarrassed. Such things were beneath him; miles beneath him. 'It is my own fault for not being more explicit, but in future, M. Maitre, nobody is to follow Mme Massot, or take paparazzi photos of her.'

'Very well, monsieur,' Maitre said, a touch sulkily. 'I suppose you do not wish to see these, then.'

Hugh laughed. 'As you have them, you may as well hand them over.'

He took the photos and studied them in silence. Maitre had not been wrong in his assessment. Sophie Massot was an amazingly attractive woman. Even in the harsh daylight of these snaps, she looked pulled-together and beautiful in every shot. Not obviously so; her nose was classic, not tiny and even, and her figure was slim, not large-breasted or boasting Jennifer Lopez curves. She was clearly in her late thirties; there were small wrinkles around her eyes and mouth. The euphemism was laugh lines; but she had a serious face, not one that had done much laughing, he thought.

Montfort admired the even, glossy hair, the large eyes, the exquisite dress sense. Black; so she was wearing mourning, which in itself he felt showed some unusual style, these days. But she wore black with such variety and grace it might as well have been a rainbow of colours. On Mme Massot, each outfit was absolutely distinctive. Here was a severe Dior suit, cut 1940s-style, ending just over the knee; next, a dress, with a cropped jacket, the skirt billowing out from under it; the third picture saw her in a Chanel suit; there were no trousers in any of the pictures.

She liked jewellery, he could see that. Many women did, but they had no idea how to wear it. Sophie Massot had that instinct that many rich women lack. She was no Duchess of Windsor, whose collection he thought the ultimate triumph of wealth over taste. Her pieces always complemented, and never overpowered, her clothes; large pearls here, picking out white buttons; ruby studs on the day she went completely black, to punctuate the darkness; a large solitaire diamond, even in a photo you could see it was very fine, and old; that was a Victorian rose-cut.

Montfort immediately adjusted his opinion of the woman. Whatever else he might think of her, she had immense style, and made it look easy. He appreciated the different strands of her dressing; clothes, accessories, and gems came together as beautifully as a piece of music.

'I must meet with her as soon as possible,' he said. 'Is there some way for me to see her without Lazard present?'

'Not if you ask for a meeting. He would never allow it.'

'Then socially,' Montfort said. He wouldn't need long to charm her; he never did. Fifteen minutes at the most. 'Find out her calendar, can you? And get me to an event which she will be attending.' His dark eyes narrowed. 'That is, if you can do it without rummaging through her dustbins.'

'Excuse me, monsieur?'

Montfort sighed. 'Never mind, man, just do it.'

Chapter Eleven

'*Mon Dieu*,' Gregoire Lazard said, softly.

Sophie looked at him. The car had just turned past the pear orchard behind its crumbling stone walls; this was the first view of the house. She was used to it, but of course Gregoire was not. He leaned forward in the back seat to admire it; the plain grey walls, almost honey-coloured in the full light of the sun, the round tower and its pointed cone, the windows glittering like the surface of the lake to their left. It was a hot, even sultry day, with just a whisper of a breeze; the château's grounds showing to excellent advantage, the lawns smooth as a billiard table, the topiary hedges neatly shaved into balls and spikes, the gravel walks lined with lavender.

'You like it?' she asked, trying not to sound too eager. All the time she spent with Gregoire, he was so reserved. Sophie could hardly get him to say, flat out, that he liked or wanted anything, apart from his requests for her company. She decided he was proud, but that was a good thing. He had perfect manners.

But she wanted to please him, to see him enthusiastic for once.

'Like it? Like is not the word,' he said, shaking his head. '*C'est magnifique*. How old is it?'

'It was built in the late seventeenth century. It was the seat of the Barons Rossigny, but they were wiped out in the Revolution. Pierre bought it three years before we were married . . .'

Sophie could have kicked herself. Why did she mention Pierre, why? Was it out of respect for him that Gregoire had not declared himself to her?

'Oh yes,' he said. 'I remember.'

'You must have been here before . . .'

He shook his head. 'We were friends, you understand, but on a business level. He kept his social life separate.'

The car purred on towards the garages, a converted stable-block not far from the main entrance.

'And what is that?'

He was gesturing at the golden stone of the dower house, looking small at this distance, below the lake at the foot of the sloping lawns.

'That is the lodge where my mother-in-law lives.'

'Ah. Mme Katherine.'

Sophie looked at him in surprise. 'You know her?'

'I have only met her briefly, at company functions.' Gregoire added delicately, 'Mme Katherine moves in much different circles.'

Sophie blushed and felt a pang of shame. Gregoire meant, of course, that Katherine had cut him dead. He might be a successful businessman, even Pierre's deputy, but as he had no estates of his own, a man like Gregoire would be nothing more to Katherine than the hired help. And in fact, for him to say that Pierre and he had never mixed outside the office . . .

She wondered with embarrassment if, perhaps, Pierre had treated him the same way. In which case his kindness to her was all the more remarkable. She being the last vestige of a family which had looked down on him . . .

Gregoire had told her he was a Polish immigrant. She hoped fervently his background of poverty had nothing to do with it.

But it most likely had, of course. Her own middle-class origins – Katherine had never let her forget them.

'It is very beautiful,' Gregoire said, 'but perhaps we should go somewhere else. We are near the village of St Aude, I believe they have a pleasant fish restaurant there . . .'

Sophie looked at him with dismay. 'You don't want to see my home?'

He sighed. 'Don't you see? It is because it *is* your home.'

She tensed. Weeks of spending almost every moment in his

company, and still Gregoire, who made her feel so womanly, so alive, had refused to be drawn on his feelings. He complimented her constantly; he sent her flowers; he would interrupt her as she tried to go through Massot papers, interrupt her all the time, with jokes and pleas to take tea with him.

But he was shy, and would not declare his love, or anything except a wish to be her friend. And Sophie could not seem to draw him out.

Was he about to say something at last?

'What do you mean?' she asked gingerly.

He gave a laugh that sounded a little hollow. 'Sophie, you have seen my place.'

'Four times.' He had invited her for three dinners and once, a late breakfast, when he declared he couldn't stand to see her poring over 'those dull figures' for one more minute. 'It's a lovely house,' Sophie added, encouragingly.

Gregoire lived in a brand-new townhouse on boulevard la Reine; a chic brick building with skylights and a courtyard garden, Japanese appliances in the kitchen, and its own cinema room. It certainly cost over a million euros, and he had a collection of twentieth-century sculpture and paintings that was probably worth as much again, Sophie guessed, even though she herself hated modern art.

'It suits me very well. But it is hardly like this. When I see something so beautiful . . .' – and he paused meaningfully, so she couldn't be sure if he meant her or the house – 'it reminds me only that I am not worthy.'

'Oh, don't be ridiculous,' Sophie laughed. She struggled to make Gregoire feel more at ease. 'Do you know the story of my background?'

'No,' he said in a polite way that she knew meant 'yes'.

'Well then,' she said, answering what he hadn't said, 'you know that my father owned a local newspaper in Tunbridge Wells and my mother was a kindergarten teacher.'

Lazard smiled at her. 'You are very kind.'

'But it's the truth,' Sophie said robustly. She felt a frisson of pleasure to have said such a thing openly. Pierre, and more importantly Katherine, had always drummed into her that her dreadfully bourgeois background must never be mentioned. 'Please, Gregoire; relax with me.'

He smiled warmly at her. 'I will try.'

Sophie ordered lunch to be served in the conservatory; it was her favourite room in the house, the least intimidating. They had to walk through the immense stone hallway, past the portraits and the tapestries, and through the Yellow Room, with its silk wallpaper and elegant divans, to get there; but once she had led him through the small wrought-iron door they were surrounded by the scent of growing things, and the odd drowsy butterfly. There was Victorian rattan furniture from the British Raj and giant cushions from Pakistan, in a silken rainbow of colours, were heaped round a glass-topped table. Despite the glass and stifling heat outside it was cool; Sophie had added modern air conditioning, because without it the place would be unusable from late spring until autumn.

'This is delightful!' Gregoire said.

'I'm so glad you like it.'

Bernarde, one of the maids, appeared in her uniform. 'Could you ask cook to send in . . . an *assiette*,' Sophie said, searching for something simple. 'Just some ham and cheese and bread and tapenade. And a fruit salad. What would you like?'

'What is on the menu today?'

Sophie laughed. 'Anything you want, as long as you don't have a hankering for roast peacock or something.'

'Would a cheese soufflé be too much trouble?'

She shook her head, pleased. Perhaps he was going to relax after all. Soufflés took a little while to prepare. 'Lionel's soufflés are outrageously good.'

'And for dessert, monsieur?'

'A poached pear,' he said, decisively. 'And some wine. Anything white.'

'And water. I'll have tea when we're finished.'

'Yes, madame,' said Bernarde. She smiled radiantly at Gregoire, then at her mistress. I suppose it's been a long while since I've had a man to the house, Sophie realised – just one man, unaccompanied by a wife, anyway. She kept a proper distance from her staff, in obedience to Pierre's wishes, but she had always been friendly and pleasant, and paid very well. They were all fond of her, and knew how to make their feelings known.

'I am glad you are going to enjoy your lunch.'

Gregoire brushed his hand across his face, as though to get rid of cobwebs. 'When I am with you, it is difficult not to be happy,' he said.

Sophie blushed.

These past few weeks, she thought, have been the happiest of my life.

The idea shocked her. But it was true; well, always excepting the time she had spent with Thomas, when he was younger. But as a *woman*, aside from motherhood . . . yes. She could not recall having been happier.

What she had dreaded had proved to be sheer joy. House Massot . . . everyone was friendly. Especially Judy Dean; it was lovely, having a friend she could count on. Sophie couldn't quite penetrate the dense language of the reports and files Gregoire gave her, and he was so distracting . . . but then he had warned her – business was boring. He was so open with her, flooding her with paper and information, when really, she reflected guiltily, all she wanted to do was to spend time with him.

Gregoire was not like her so-called friends who came to parties here; dining and dancing twice a month, every month, just as Pierre and Katherine had commanded; twenty of the best families of the arrondissement, faces she knew like the back of her hand, and couldn't really care less about. Sophie was closer, by far, to the servants.

Yes; hers had been a life full of people, but only now was she starting to realise what a lonely one it had been. Gregoire cared about her. Judy was *fun*. She'd had nobody . . .

Well, Fr Sabin, the old priest in the village. He was a good friend. But, of course, he was also a priest. And seventy. Not like . . .

Gregoire was smiling at her. Sophie admired again the pale blue eyes, the blond hair, the rigorous bearing.

'You must have designed this room.'

'I did. How did you guess?'

'The rest of the place looks like a museum.'

'Thank you. At least you can touch things in it, though.'

'I'm glad of that,' he said quietly and deliberately. 'That you can touch things.'

Sophie flushed deeper and felt a faint, almost imperceptible stirring in her belly and breasts. She looked away, confused.

'This room is full of life,' Gregoire said lightly, changing the subject. 'And light. It had to be your work. I imagine it is very pleasant in the winter. I hate the dark.'

'Oh, me too,' Sophie cried. 'That is exactly what I intended it for, so I could be outside yet still inside. When it's too cold I walk around in here, and soak in all the light. It stops me from getting–'

She cut herself short. She didn't want to say 'depressed'.

'I feel exactly the same, all winter long. What is your expression . . . "great minds think alike".'

'That's it,' Sophie said, and they laughed.

'Ah, madame,' he said, catching her hand. 'I do so enjoy spending time with you. It makes it all worth it.'

'Luncheon is served,' said Bernarde, appearing with a tray of heavenly smelling food.

Sophie jumped away from Gregoire as though his touch were electric, but Bernarde smiled knowingly, and Sophie had to rhapsodise over the meal to cover her reaction. Gregoire didn't seem to care; he gave her a long look, and Sophie could still feel her palm, damp where his touch had been, burning against her cool skin.

Chapter Twelve

Judy stepped out of the elevator and put her shoulders back. Another morning in her windowless cell of a room, another morning working next to that simpering idiot Sophie Massot. But she had high hopes it was all coming to an end. Sophie was spending less and less time in her 'office' and more and more time being squired around by Gregoire. The pretence of work was, she hoped, coming to an end, and Judy would have survived – survived again; exactly what she was so good at.

She walked briskly, smiling, to their little corner of the top floor. Marie was already there, awaiting her.

'Good morning, madame.'

'Good morning, Marie. Coffee, please, and today's clippings. And my call sheet.'

'Certainly, madame.'

Judy was pleased to note Marie's expert eyes sweep over her outfit. She could thank Sophie for one thing; she had learned to be even more stylish, even more perfectly chic, since she had arrived. Judy had to raise her game. Mme Massot always looked perfect, always in black without a hair out of place; and little unexpected touches thrown in that lifted her to the heights of elegance, because they were so obviously un-planned. Yesterday's Dior swing coat, for example, inky-black but with that shimmering, palest-pink lining. Judy had just died when she'd seen it. When she was rich, she vowed fiercely, she would have clothes that were just as fine, clothes cut with the precision of a diamond.

For now, she had to struggle and think. Last week, Judy had

even considered writing out a little chart of what, in her carefully constructed but limited wardrobe, went with what. But she had rejected the idea. That would be letting Sophie get too deep into her head.

Today she had gone very simple; a summery dress of pale blue slub silk, a single emerald-cut sapphire suspended from a white gold chain, strappy sandals, and an ivory cashmere cardigan thrown round her shoulders. Her make-up she kept neutral as ever; just some concealer under the eyes, bronzer on her cheekbones, and a dab of Vaseline to make her lips look larger and more moist.

Never at any time did she wear black. She had even retired her black handbags. For now, she would be a butterfly. Judy wanted everyone in the office to see how unafraid of Sophie she was. She would dress beautifully and conspicuously, and aim for the greatest possible contrast . . .'

'Judy!'

She pasted on her most welcoming smile. 'Sophie, hello. Good to see you again!'

'Isn't it a wonderful morning?'

Sophie threw open the doors to the office Gregoire had given her; it was three times the size of Judy's old one, with huge windows overlooking rue Tricot towards the Seine. There was a small silver bowl on her antique walnut desk crammed with low-cut yellow roses; Gregoire had the flowers changed each day.

Judy looked at it enviously, then caught herself. Nothing unproductive, right? So she liked this office? Then make a plan; it could be *her* office, once the widow departed and she got that Senior Vice-Presidency.

'Look at that view!'

'Yes, wonderful,' Judy said, glancing at the plain white walls of her own room.

'It's going to be hot again; but I think the forecast called for a quick shower around lunchtime. Which is perfect, don't you think? Perhaps we shall have a rainbow.'

'Mmm,' Judy agreed sweetly.

'I can't work in weather like this . . .'

'I have to, I'm afraid,' Judy told her. 'But,' she added, taking up Gregoire's line, 'you're right, work is so boring.'

Sophie went to her desk, sat down, and flicked idly through a sheaf of papers.

'More sales reports.'

'He said you wanted to see everything . . .'

'I did.' Sophie sighed. 'But there's so much of it.'

'You see that everything is fine, though, and I suppose that's the important thing,' Judy said. This wasn't strictly true, but Sophie Massot didn't need to know it.

'I wish I could. I feel I'm just thrashing around here.'

'I understand, Sophie,' said Judy, sympathetically. 'You have to check everything out, you can't just trust Gregoire, can you?'

Sophie's dark head lifted. She stared at Judy.

'But of course I trust Gregoire!'

'Yes, of course.' Judy added lightly, 'Up to a point, that is.'

Sophie sat down in her chair, looking dismayed. 'You don't think I trust him, Judy?'

'Coffee, madame,' Marie sang out, arriving back with it. Judy reached for the bone china cup.

'Thank you; place the documents on my desk.' Judy looked at Sophie; she had perceived an opportunity, and wanted to act on it. 'Do you have time to take coffee with me this morning? Or . . . I suppose you're too busy,' she said, deferentially.

Sophie looked pleased. 'No, I'd love to.'

'Another cup for Mme Massot,' Judy told Marie. 'Black, one sugar. Is that right?'

'Perfect.'

Judy waited until Marie had come back with the coffee. 'Hold my calls,' she told her, then she shut the door and gave Sophie her cup.

'I wonder, madame, if I might speak frankly to you.'

Sophie sighed. 'I wish you would. I wish anyone would. And honestly, Judy, how many times do I have to say it? It's *Sophie*.'

'Well . . . of course . . . it's just slightly delicate.' Judy smiled awkwardly. 'You see, M. Lazard – Gregoire – he has been running House Massot since . . . You know.'

'Yes,' Sophie agreed dryly. She knew.

'He works very hard,' Judy said loyally. 'He's in the office all the time. I believe he does his very best for the company, he's dedicated . . .'

Sophie smiled, proud to hear Gregoire described like that.

'He's been a good boss to you, then?'

'The best,' Judy said. She trusted she would soon be able to make those words come true. 'And then, of course, you show up.'

Sophie looked defensive. 'You don't think Gregoire minds?'

'He was very happy to see you,' Judy explained. 'If you want my opinion, I would say he was glad for the chance to show you how he has kept his trust to your family, working the way he has.'

Sophie nodded.

'*But*,' Judy continued. 'You stayed, mada— Sophie. You stayed and you kept going over all the papers, even though he gave you every report . . . you are still here. I think the only way to understand it is that you do not believe what he has told you about the company. You do not trust him to run it, and you do not trust his assurances.'

Sophie looked shocked.

'Of course that is your right, you have a perfect right not to trust anybody,' Judy went on smoothly. 'You're the Chairman of the Board.'

Sophie put down her cup of coffee, stood up and started to pace back and forth in front of the window. What if the American girl were right? What if that was one hundred per cent how Gregoire saw things? No wonder he had not declared himself . . . had not said anything open.

'And this is how he sees it?' she asked Judy.

Judy shrugged; a little slither of cream and palest blue.

'If you were him, how would you interpret it?' she asked. 'Of course, I only know him professionally, as a colleague . . .'

She hardly knew Lazard at all; she had made it her business to stay out of his way until very recently.

'. . . but he's very proud of his work,' she concluded.

Sophie looked despairingly at the reams of paper scattered across her desk. She couldn't make head nor tail of any of it.

'Are things going well at House Massot?'

'Exactly the same as they have been for the last several years,' Judy responded quickly and, she noted with internal amusement, accurately. 'Nothing's happened here. We put out collections . . . we sell them . . . we put out new collections.'

It was a slightly depressing recital, the truth, and as she thought about it, Judy added carelessly, 'Nothing's actually happened since the last Hugh Montfort episode.'

'The last what?' Sophie asked.

Judy could have kicked herself.

'Oh, nothing very interesting,' she said. 'There's a guy named Hugh Montfort who works for an English company called Mayberry.'

'Never heard of them.'

With Sophie's classic styling, this did not surprise Judy. So much the better, as she would not be fascinated by the mere name, like so many others.

'They make cheap jewels. Nothing like House Massot.' Again, the best lie was to tell simply part of the truth. 'Hugh Montfort thought he could expand and take this company over, gobble it up.'

Sophie asked, 'What happened?'

'Your husband couldn't stand the man. Told him what to do with his bid.'

'So this took place years ago.'

'Yes, well; he sniffed around after that, a few times.'

Sophie thought about it. 'He's obviously persistent.'

'Nothing to worry about, Sophie. Gregoire told him where he got off. There's no way he could do us any damage with Gregoire taking care of your family's interests,' Judy said, warmly.

'So, then, apart from this man Montfort, nothing untoward has happened here? Seriously, Judy, I need to know.'

'Absolutely nothing. We're just going along as we always were.'

As far as Judy knew, this was the truth. It was also the problem, something she did not explain to the older woman.

'Then maybe . . . I really don't need to be here,' Sophie said, and Judy fought the urge to close her eyes and exhale . . . yes! She had done it.

'Nobody can tell you that,' Judy said, trying to sound dissuading. 'Nobody can tell you you ought to trust your executives . . . that you have to trust Gregoire. Trust is so personal, don't you think?'

Sophie left the office – for the day, she told Judy – around eleven. It was all Judy could do not to turn cartwheels across the length of the executive floor, past the cubicles and into the water cooler. But she contained herself. Patience; she wasn't quite home yet.

She had Marie call Lazard's secretary for an appointment and, sure enough, he slotted her in right away. Of course. Gregoire Lazard would not have ordinary meetings and lunches, not any more. Everything had ground to a halt so he could look after the widow. Judy spritzed her scent, Hermes 24 Rue Faubourg, into the air in front of her and walked into the cloud, the way all Frenchwomen did. It perfumed her lightly all over, without ever being overpowering. She had no desire to stink like some showgirl.

She walked to Lazard's office, and knocked discreetly on the door.

'Judy, come in.'

'Thank you, Gregoire,' she said, making full use of the permission she had gotten to use his first name. 'May I sit down?'

He waved her to the chaise-longue, which, Judy noted, happened to complement her duck-egg-blue dress perfectly. She sat down, cat-like, on it, smiling and confident of her own good looks.

'I wanted to update you on a conversation I had just now with Mme Massot,' she said evenly.

Lazard stopped giving her that slightly patronising smile and took his seat again. He was now all ears.

'Have there been fireworks in the office?'

'Fireworks? Why on earth would there be fireworks?' Judy asked, smiling firmly at him.

Lazard inclined his head; he seemed to enjoy the tap-dance.

'Two such strong personalities,' he murmured.

Strong personality was not a phrase Judy would have used to describe the widow Massot. Weak as water was more like it.

'Mme Massot and I get on very well.'

'Oh,' he said, and for a second she thought she saw disappointment on his face. 'What was the substance of your conversation, then?'

'Mme Sophie finds the volume of information you have given her to digest rather hard going.'

'I am sorry to hear that.'

'And she asked me about the state of the company. I was able to reassure her that nothing has changed here. And . . . I remarked that perhaps she was taking extra caution, in that she could not trust the assurances of her executives . . .'

Lazard smiled appreciatively.

'Of me, you mean.'

Judy inclined her head.

'And what did she say?'

She noticed Gregoire had actually shifted his body forward; he was literally on the edge of his seat.

'She seemed most disturbed by the implication, and told me she has perfect trust in you. Then she asked me for my assessment of House Massot, and when I reassured her, she took the rest of the day off.'

'I see.'

Gregoire Lazard steepled his fingertips and looked straight at Judy; the sky-blue, slanted eyes were impenetrable, and for a moment she worried. Had she overstepped herself? Misread him?

'Although I do not believe I should be instigating promotions at this time,' Lazard said, 'I have recently been impressed with your work on the London shows.'

They had taken place more than a month ago.

'Thank you,' said Judy.

'And I have decided to increase your salary.'

She smiled coolly; she had gambled and won. 'Thank you,' she repeated.

'You will now receive one hundred and seventy-five thousand euros.'

Judy tensed. One seventy-five? Her current salary was one fifty. She had been looking for a quarter of a million, at least. She wondered whether or not she should challenge Lazard.

'I trust you will consider increasing that soon, Gregoire,' she said.

Lazard's blue eyes held hers, calmly.

'Certainly, Judy, you understand that salary increases as performance increases. If you continue at this level of service, then . . .'

He waved a manicured hand to indicate the infinite possibilities.

Judy nodded. She understood perfectly. She was no longer a PR girl, she was now Gregoire Lazard's eyes and ears in House Massot; and maybe outside it?

'I wonder,' she said delicately, 'if Mme Massot does decide that she will be spending less time in the office . . . I think she should still be updated on our doings here, and, of course, I am quite fond of her. Although it's a little unorthodox, perhaps you might consider my taking some time off, in the workday, to visit her, to continue our . . . friendship?'

'On reflection, perhaps I was a little conservative. Let us say two hundred thousand,' Gregoire Lazard replied.

Judy offered him her hand across the table. 'A pleasure doing business with you, monsieur,' she said.

Chapter Thirteen

It started in such a mundane way. With a holiday.

'Dad.' Sophie screwed up her courage.

'Yeah?'

Mike Roberts didn't turn aside from his copy of the *Mirror*. Not that she'd expected him to. Her dad didn't like her much. Eighteen years of sulking that she wasn't a boy. And Mum only really cared about pleasing Dad.

'I'd like to go to Cannes with Joanna Wilson.'

'Jo Wilson? That girl's a little tart.' Roberts sniffed. 'And where's Cannes?'

'In France. Just for the weekend.' Sophie made her excuse. 'It's cultural . . . and I did get my passport last year, remember?'

'I'm not paying for it. You eat me out of house and home as it is.'

'I've got some money saved up,' Sophie pleaded. 'From my job. Can I go?'

Her father turned and looked at his daughter, all nervous, skinny and timid. She reminded him of his wife in her most aggravating moods. Why couldn't they have had a boy?

'Do whatever you want,' he said, shrugging. 'You're off to college soon, anyway.'

Sophie glowed with pleasure. 'Thanks, Dad.' She looked over at her mother, but Ann was busy with the leg of lamb she was roasting for lunch; as ever, she showed no interest in her daughter's plans.

Sophie crept upstairs to her tiny bedroom and started to pack her small suitcase. Thank God, she thought. Dad hadn't cared enough to stop her. She was going away from here. That was exciting enough by itself, but France!

France was *abroad*. And it was the famous film festival. Joanna promised her there'd be loads of stars and suchlike. Princes from Monaco and rich men. Jo said she was going to find her destiny, and would Sophie like to come?

Well, of course. Jo, after all, was so blonde and golden with her hair she got done at Vidal Sassoon. A little suburban town like Tunbridge Wells was right for Sophie, but it couldn't hold a butterfly like Jo – she was destined for higher things, Sophie reflected.

If Jo was a butterfly, Sophie was a moth; usually with her nose in a book, lost in some trashy romance, concentrating on her studies. She always wore her school uniform, so she never shone out. Even at the weekends, Sophie favoured plain, don't-notice-me clothing. And the boys never did, even though (as Jo patronisingly conceded) Sophie 'could be pretty'.

'You should go for it,' Jo suggested. 'Get really groovy.'

'Like what?'

'Dye your hair platinum-blonde. I could do it for you. Wear short skirts, heels. Get a push-up bra!' Jo tossed her own blonde mane. 'Some blue eyeshadow! Nobody can see how you look under that fringe.'

'Oh, no thanks,' Sophie said meekly. 'My dad would kill me.'

Some girls at school wondered why Jo hung around with Sophie Roberts. Mr Roberts was so boring, just a newspaper man with a middling-sized house. She didn't even have any good-looking brothers.

Well, Sophie knew why; Jo didn't like competition, and Sophie didn't offer her any. Her confidence so dented by her loveless, selfish parents, Sophie was just pathetically glad to have a friend. The motivation didn't matter – not really.

And tonight she felt even more glad about it. She was going to be Jo's lady-in-waiting in France! On a real foreign beach watching real film stars. A glimpse of a life away from her miserable suburban girlhood. It might even be sunny there, you never knew. Abroad was always sunny on TV. Sophie glanced at the rain drumming on the skylight window in her neat, dull little attic bedroom and wished with all her heart that nothing would go wrong; that Dad wouldn't find some spiteful excuse to stop her. Her plan was always the same; head down and stay out of his way.

'I'm bored,' Joanna announced. She lolled against the motel bed with its thin sheets.

'Bored?' Sophie was shocked.

How could Jo be bored? She had dutifully followed her around everywhere. They'd seen all kinds of movie stars and dolly birds, and Johnny Halliday, the famous French singer, had even winked at Jo! Sophie had seen it. They'd drunk wine (Jo had got plastered) and eaten baguettes and splashed in the sea. Actually, Jo spent a lot of time on the beach in that amazing red bikini of hers. Sophie had a swimsuit, but she was too shy to wear it, so she stuck to her shorts and flip-flops.

'We haven't hooked up with anybody.'

'We had a coffee with those French girls,' Sophie pointed out.

'Huh! *Girls*,' Jo said with deep scorn. 'I'm not here for girls. I want to meet a boyfriend. Or a movie director.' She ran her long scarlet nails through her hair, looking at her reflection in the mirror on the wardrobe door. 'I'm here to be *discovered*.'

'Most of the men are a lot older than us.'

'So what, darling? Mature, successful men like young girls. Maybe we could get invited on to a yacht,' said Jo excitedly.

Sophie blushed. The girls on the yachts often sat there with their tops off, showing their boobs to everybody!

'I don't think my dad would like that.'

'Your dad doesn't like anything you do,' Jo said, cruelly but accurately. 'Live a little, Soph! Or at least' – she gave a tinkling laugh – 'watch me do it.' Swinging her long legs off the bed, she wrenched open the wardrobe door, which was sticky. 'Cheap motel,' she said scornfully. 'We should be living in luxury!'

Sophie had to chuckle. 'That's not very likely. You don't really think you're going to meet Prince Charming, do you?'

'If anybody can, it's going to be me,' Jo said confidently. 'Look! I've been saving this one. What do you think?'

She pulled out a see-through white dress and held it up against her body. It clung lovingly to her slight curves, had a dangerously low-cut bodice and a hem that flirted with the tops of her thighs.

Sophie laughed.

'I'm serious!' Jo said. 'It'll look sexy!'

'I think it's a bit much.'

Jo pouted. 'You never want to have any fun. Anyway, have you seen what the other girls are wearing?'

'I only have my pink dress left.' Her pink dress was her favourite. It was a knock-off of one that had been in the magazines, a Jackie Kennedy copy; sitting just on the knee with an elegant boat-neck, Sophie thought it made her look more grown-up.

'Booooring,' Jo said. 'But you wear that and I'll wear the white. We'll go to the Croisette. I heard a rumour yesterday that Pierre Massot is going to be there.'

'Another film star,' Sophie sighed. They were never where Jo thought they were going to be and the two girls just walked around looking for them and getting blisters from their platform heels.

'No – he's a Frog, a jeweller. Owns that famous chain of shops, like Garrard's or something.'

'Oh yes,' said Sophie. She loved jewellery, not that she owned any. But she liked looking in Jo's magazines at what the models and princesses were wearing.

'Anyway, he's gorgeous and filthy rich. And they say he loves pretty girls.' Jo was sliding out of her jeans, reaching for the little scrap of white fabric. 'Just watch me, Soph. It's my night. I can feel it!'

The Croisette beach was packed. It was a warm night, and the light breezes blowing in from the sea were pleasant; so were the scents coming from the local restaurants, all filled to overflowing. Cannes existed for the film festival, and did it magnificently. But Sophie was, if she admitted it to herself, looking forward to going home. She didn't belong here; it was all butterflies, no moths allowed.

'Look!' Jo clutched on to her, teetering on her heels. 'I think that's him, Soph! I recognise him from the papers.'

Sophie looked. She couldn't see much; there was a gaggle of blondes, giggling and mostly wearing nothing but swimsuits, clinging on to a man. He was pointing at a large, gorgeously equipped yacht, and several of the girls ran towards it.

'That's the *Natasha*. That's his boat! It's seventy-five foot, at least.'

'It's very nice.'

'Nice!' scoffed Jo. 'D'you know how much money you need to run one of those things? He has servants. And a big castle near Paris with peacocks in the grounds. He's famous.'

'He's coming this way,' Sophie said, timidly. She had a sudden urge to turn and run. Compared to the tiny scraps of nothing the other girls were wearing, even Joanna's white baby-doll dress looked dowdy. 'Let's go down and paddle in the foam . . .'

'Paddle nothing.'

'Jo – we're going to look a bit silly, don't you think?' Sophie ventured. But her friend ignored her.

'Oooh – isn't he handsome.'

Sophie squinted. Was he? Handsome – in a way, she supposed. Those slim good looks weren't really her thing. But who could quibble? The man was utterly self-confident, moving like one entitled, a Pasha surrounded by a giggling harem. Photographers hovered, snapping his picture – he looked as though he owned the world.

'Oh! Soph, he's heading this way!' Joanna squealed. And he was – he was walking straight towards them. Sophie, in her modest pink dress, her brunette, un-dyed hair falling down on to her shoulders, wanted to cut and run. But that would have looked even more stupid than Jo flinging herself at him. She bit her lip, and hoped he would soon pass on.

He didn't. Pierre had looked out over the crowds of blonde girls in tiny bathing suits, giggling and thrusting their curves forward, and seen her. And he had beckoned.

'Look! He saw me. He wants me to come over,' Joanna said, in a fury of excitement. And then, clutching Sophie, she gasped, 'Don't move! Act natural. He's coming over here. He's coming over here! Say something. Start talking to me!'

'I'm getting cold,' said Sophie, who couldn't think of anything else.

'*Excusez-moi, mesdemoiselles,*' said Pierre Massot, stopping in front of them and bowing slightly. A girl on his arm giggled.

'We're English,' Sophie said, bluntly.

'But of course you are,' he responded admiringly, 'with skin like that.' He turned round and spoke to the crowd of blondes in French; his tones were charming, but dismissive; they pouted, and dispersed.

Joanna smiled up at him triumphantly.

'Mademoiselle,' Pierre said to Sophie, 'would you do me the honour of having dinner with me?'

'What about me?' Joanna cried.

Pierre looked at her, all blonde hair and tumbling legs. 'If you wish to come along too, mademoiselle, I suppose it is all right,' he said.

Sophie blushed. Had she heard right?

Joanna scowled. 'We're busy. Come on, Sophie,' she said angrily, trying to drag her away.

But Sophie, for once, pulled her arm free. She didn't know what made her – but there was something in this man's stare, his eyes, that compelled her. Told her to seize this chance. Just once.

'I'll see you later, Jo,' she said, and to Pierre, she said, 'I suppose I could – just this once.'

'You cow, Sophie Roberts!' Jo hissed. 'Don't bother coming back to the motel.'

Sophie quailed; but Pierre Massot, in his beautifully cut suit, turned his impassive eyes on her former friend.

'Mlle Roberts will not be coming back to your motel at all, mademoiselle. I am looking after her now.' He offered Sophie his arm, and shyly, demurely, she took it.

'Shall we go?' he said. And escorted her off the beach.

She didn't notice the name of the restaurant; only that it was far away from the hustle of Cannes, at Cap D'Antibes. Pierre had taken her there in his personal helicopter; the pilot saluted her as they touched down. She had been so taken aback she could hardly speak.

'What will you have?' Pierre asked, offering her a menu.

Sophie gazed shyly into her crystal glass of champagne.

'Whatever you think best. I don't eat at expensive places very often,' she added artlessly.

'You're extremely beautiful,' he said.

'Thank you.' She blushed.

Massot's dark, calculating eyes swept over her. It was attention, focused like a laser beam directly upon her, and Sophie wasn't used to that.

She liked it.

He probed her delicately, carefully. Sophie answered honestly; she was eighteen; she was hoping to go to college; she wasn't close to her family; she had led a sheltered life.

'And are you religious?'

'Yes – we're Catholics.' Sophie thought she ought to say something. 'We don't believe in, you know. Sex, before marriage.'

He smiled. 'How unusual. And have you had many boyfriends?'

'None at all,' Sophie said honestly. 'They aren't interested because . . . Well, I'm not that pretty.' She self-consciously tucked a strand of brown hair behind her ear.

'Nonsense. You are exquisite,' he said, so matter-of-factly she glowed with pleasure. 'And although you have not had the tools, you have a natural style.' He sipped at his glass. 'No boyfriends . . . you are a blank slate. Tell me, do you enjoy your life?'

'Not that much.' She had stared at him. 'Does anyone?'

'Oh yes.' He smiled. 'I do.'

'Then you're very lucky.'

'I make my own luck,' he said confidently.

Sophie looked at him, admiringly. Of course, now she'd told him they couldn't have sex, he'd never want to see her again. But what a story to tell the girls back home! It was worth annoying Joanna for.

'I would like to show you my house.'

'Do you live near here?'

'Not at all. Just outside of Paris. But we can go in the helicopter.' He regarded her anxious face. 'You can stay the night there – by yourself, of course; and I will send you back to England tomorrow, if you wish, with a first-class ticket.'

'I've got clothes in the motel . . .'

'I will replace them.'

Sophie didn't hesitate. Somehow, it seemed less dangerous to accept than to say no. He simply wasn't the sort of man you said no to.

'Thank you very much,' she said.

Pierre Massot smiled. 'I find you intriguing,' he replied.

'But where are we?' Sophie asked. She walked hastily away from the chopper, its still-whirling blades blowing her dress up around her thighs. 'I don't understand. Where is your house?'

They were standing on a landing pad outside a vast, glorious old château in the middle of a park. It was lit with torches, blazing in the gravel drive; the size of a palace, and just as beautiful.

'Right there.' He smiled.

'That? Isn't that a – a monument? Or a museum?'

'It's a château. Château des Étoiles, to be precise – the castle of the stars. My home.' A thin smile. 'Maybe, one day, yours, too.'

Sophie laughed nervously. 'You're joking.'

'I never joke.' He offered her his arm again. 'I called ahead. My servants have found some clothes in your style, and you will find night things and toiletries in the guest suite, the Orleans suite. There are also fresh clothes for tomorrow, when you may call your parents.'

'My dad's going to kill me,' Sophie whispered.

Massot shook his head. 'I don't think so.'

She looked shyly up at him. Perhaps she'd been wrong. Perhaps Prince Charming *did* exist, after all . . .

And in fact, Pierre had rescued her. Less than two months later she had moved out of her parents' house, been shipped off to France, and married in church like Cinderella, in a huge ball gown personally designed for her at Givenchy Haute Couture, a tiara of pear-shaped diamonds, and antique satin slippers, then taken in a horse and carriage to her very own castle, where in exchange for this fairy tale – and a man who said he loved her – she offered up nothing more exciting than her own virginity.

Pierre was an ideal husband. He gave her everything, and made no excessive demands. And Sophie, although terrified of her new mother-in-law, was an ideal wife; obedient, eager to please, ready to learn, she had let him shape her. There were no fights. The first year it was even pleasant. She still felt as if she had escaped.

After that . . . yes, the bloom had come off, just a little; a very little. Sophie hated the idea of disloyalty; however cold Pierre might have been, however much of a worker, he had been a good husband, given her everything, given her Tom, and Tom was truly, truly everything – her baby, and the love of her life. Sophie believed she had fulfilled her part of the bargain. She had spent almost twenty years becoming the perfect spouse; the last seven of them on her own. She had done everything exactly as Pierre would wish.

That, then, was her last marriage. Sophie thought of Gregoire. Was she really ready for another one?

Sophie wondered later why she had chosen to leave the office; why she hadn't gone straight in to Gregoire, and asked him about what Judy said. Perhaps it was the faintest stirring of suspicion, or intuition. But, as Sophie reflected, she had not wanted to hear that stirring. Not then.

She called her driver from the office and had him wait, then selected a few key reports – at least she thought they were key – and headed to the small, stifling elevator. Lazard's door was shut, and Judy was on the telephone. Most of the workers in their cubicles did not give Sophie a second glance. She rode down the ten floors with an uneasy feeling; was she fleeing something?

It was a mild day, a little overcast. Sophie waited as the

94

driver opened the door for her, then slid herself into the back seat.

'Good morning, madame.' He knew better than to ask why she was leaving so early. 'Where to?'

'Home.'

'Very good, madame.' He pulled expertly into the traffic.

She would go back to the château and just think things through, Sophie told herself. She would . . .

No. The thought of the château suddenly repelled her. It was so huge and so empty. She could sit in the small library with the west-facing windows, the one she had selected out of so many to be her study, but still . . .

'On second thoughts, go to St Aude.'

'Are you visiting Père Sabin, madame?'

'Yes,' Sophie said, and sank back against the buttery leather of the seat.

'My dear – what a pleasant surprise.'

'I hope I'm not intruding, Father.'

'Not at all. I have absolutely nothing to do. Come in, come in.'

Sophie smiled gratefully as the old man beckoned her inside the rectory. She opened the little wrought-iron gate and let herself in, walking down the cobbled path that wound through his tiny garden. Fr Sabin was a great admirer of English country gardens, and had carefully cultivated pansies and hollyhocks and lupins, along with wisteria and ragged dog roses; in the summer, his tiny patch of earth was ablaze with colour and scent.

'I have not seen you in some time,' he remarked mildly. 'Tea?'

'Yes; thank you.' Sophie perched, as she always did, on the edge of one of his ratty armchairs, ripped from the claws of his long-dead, and much-missed, tom-cat Luther – a wicked joke of the old priest's, to call his cat that – and stained with tea and coffee and the occasional splash of pastis. Sophie was always trying to buy Fr Sabin new furniture, and he invariably accepted her donations with pleasure and promptly spent them on the poor.

The priest busied himself in the kitchen; she could hear the swish of his soutane as he bent down to the fridge for milk. He was old fashioned, and still dressed in a black robe and biretta. Sophie shuddered to think of the chaos in the tiny room as he fussed with the electric kettle, but she forbore to offer any help. Fr Sabin was proud of his independence; he wouldn't let her come and clean up his place, pay for a maid, or even make the tea.

'I'm sorry,' she said. 'I have been busy, in Paris.'

'Just a moment.'

Sophie stared out of the window at a heavy foxglove, a fat bumble-bee burrowing inside one of its bells. She could feel herself calming down.

'Here we are,' Fr Sabin said, reappearing triumphantly with a chipped mug full of black tea, a Tetley's teabag still inside it.

'Perfect,' Sophie lied brightly, as she fished the tea bag out and discreetly dropped it into a wastebin. Fr Sabin prided himself on his tea-making skills, even getting the Tetley's sent over once a month from a nun friend of his in Cardiff.

'You have been to Pierre's company,' the priest said. It wasn't a question.

'Yes; I wanted to check that all was well. It's Tom's inheritance, you know,' Sophie said, a bit defensively. Though why? She had no need to defend herself against one of her oldest and kindest friends. 'And I think Pierre would have wanted me to make sure all was in order.'

'No, you don't.'

Sophie started. 'Don't what?'

'No, you don't think that,' Fr Sabin said patiently. His green eyes were rheumy and bloodshot with age, but the mind behind them was still perfectly agile. 'Your husband would never have wanted you to be involved with his business, Sophie; never.'

She put down the tea, shocked. His words echoed Katherine's, and Tom's. And maybe because he was the one saying them, she understood that they were true; they both knew they were true.

'Pierre had decided ideas about his wife; you getting involved with the company is the last thing he would have wanted.'

Her face fell. Now, she thought, I know why I feel so guilty all the time.

'Then you think I am doing the wrong thing, Father,' she said, miserably.

'Certainly not. You're not stupid, girl, whatever Mme Katherine has been saying to you lately.'

'But you said that Pierre—'

'Your husband was a fool. May he rest in peace,' the priest said, crossing himself. 'A fool, and –' he checked himself. '*De mortuis nil nisi bonum*. What he wanted is irrelevant. He is dead; and you have the responsibility now. I only say, my dear, that you should not delude yourself. You are doing this because you should; for Tom. But also, you are doing it because you want to.'

'Because I . . .' Sophie's voice trailed off. Because she *wanted* to?

Duty, honour, preservation, motherly love . . . all of those she could accept as motivations. But not that . . .

Sophie was so used to doing what she was asked to – being compliant, true to Pierre, the only way she knew how, which was to follow all he had asked her to do.

Except, her friend and confessor was now telling her, for this. Taking control of House Massot; Pierre would absolutely have hated it.

'You think I am acting selfishly?'

'I think you would have done it for your son's interests, but I also believe you wanted to do this; Sophie. For yourself.' The old man gestured to her rapidly cooling chipped mug. 'Drink up, dear.'

She took an obedient sip.

'That is a good thing, you know, my child. You are allowed to want things. And you are allowed to do things.'

Sophie thought of Gregoire.

'It's possible I may not spend much more time there, anyway. I trust the executives who run things . . .'

'You're not telling me something,' he remarked. 'A man?'

97

Sophie blushed furiously. 'Father!'

'Ah hah.' He cackled. 'I thought so.'

'That's not a sin,' she said anxiously.

'Why should it be? You are a widow; you have a death certificate. Of course, I think it's a grave error.'

Sophie took a fortifying slug of the tea. This was not like Fr Sabin; not at all. Usually they discussed nothing more interesting than village politics.

'The man is obviously somebody you have met at work.'

'How do you know that?' Sophie cried.

'My dear young woman' – she was hardly that – 'you haven't *been* anywhere else.'

'Oh.'

'And you are very rich, my dear, and also his superior – what is the English word? His boss.'

'He has money of his own. He is a rich man.'

'The rich never seem to object to more money,' Fr Sabin pointed out. 'Of course, it is up to you, my dear. But . . . some people like to think of you as incapable.'

Sophie's mind flickered to Katherine . . . to Pierre . . . for a second, to Tom.

'Don't prove them right,' the old man said.

She went back to the château and ordered tea; non-stewed, this time, Lapsang Souchong, and scones with warm strawberry jam. Lionel made it each year from the tiny wild berries that grew on the fringes of her oak wood, and it was heavenly. Sophie was eating with great pleasure when the call came through.

Mme Delon, her social secretary, came in with the telephone.

'Excuse me, madame; a M. Lazard to speak with you.'

'Thank you, Celine.'

'Sophie.' Gregoire's voice, warm and comforting. She could feel the yearning start, yearning to be held, complimented, loved . . . maybe she should take it slow, like Father had said . . . maybe she should be suspicious . . .

'I hope you are feeling well? Judy told me you left the office early.'

'I'm fine, Gregoire.'

'Listen,' he said, the words tumbling out as though in a rush. 'Judy was very upset. She came to see me. She thinks she said too much to you.'

'Judy needn't worry.'

'You must know that what she said is nonsense,' Gregoire went on. 'I don't feel you mistrust me . . . don't let that keep you from us. I *want* you to be happy, Sophie . . . I want you to stay at House Massot until you are quite comfortable with the job I'm doing. Or longer! Stay forever, as far as I am concerned.'

Sophie leaned back on the gold brocade of the sofa, feeling almost dizzy with relief. See! She thought triumphantly. He is asking me to stay . . . no emotional blackmail . . . Father is wrong about him . . .

'No, Gregoire,' she said. 'There's no need for me to stay there any more. I'm sure you're doing a perfectly fine job. Judy tells me you are, and she's a bright woman. And I looked up the stock price – I see it's risen, like you said. Nine per cent.' She glanced at the reports she'd brought with her, stacked neatly on top of a desk. 'I trust you,' she said, and felt the weight lift off her shoulders as she said it.

'You trust me,' Gregoire said. He sounded overjoyed, almost weepy. 'You trust me,' he repeated. 'Sophie – that means so much.'

'You're welcome.' She was pleased at his emotion, maybe just a little surprised.

'I wonder if I could come over and visit you. Nothing to do with the office. I should just like to see you,' he said.

Sophie's face lit up. She was right! Gregoire *was* holding back because she worked with him. Now he'd come to her, and tell her the truth – he loved her.

'Please do,' she said, trying to keep it light.

'I shall be there as soon as I can. I can't wait,' Lazard told her.

Sophie hung up, hugging herself. Neither can I, she thought. Neither can I!

Chapter Fourteen

The Palace d'Epée, a sixteenth-century Italianate building nestled inconspicuously on rue de la République, was alight. The gates that protected its fine old courtyard from passing traffic had been thrown open; huge torches flamed along the lawns, illuminating the uniformed flunkies who were directing limousines to the paved parking lot in the back. Normally the palace was a rather uninspired museum of Roman Gaul and France under the Merovingians, but tonight, Hugh thought, it had reacquired a touch of its pre-revolutionary lustre. His own limousine was in a long queue to get to the front, where a security guard, immaculately polite yet well armed, would check his details. There were policemen and secret service agents everywhere; his soldier's eye picked them out easily enough.

Hugh supposed it was hardly surprising. *Le tout Paris* would be here tonight. He knew of three ambassadors who were attending, including the American one. It was a benefit for literacy programmes, hosted by the wife of the President of France; attendance was practically compulsory. Louis Maitre had had to pull strings to get him in, this late, but he'd managed it.

Hugh made a note; the man deserved a bonus. He was a little attack dog, worrying away at Hugh's problems like a terrier.

Ah; they were there at last.

'Name?'

'Hugh Montfort.'

The man scanned his list. 'The Honourable Hugh Montfort?'

'Yes,' Hugh said.

'Your driver may pull up, monsieur. You are seated at table twenty-three.'

'Has my friend Sophie Massot arrived?' Hugh asked pleasantly. 'I forgot which table she is at.'

'Oh, yes, monsieur; Mme Massot was one of the first to arrive,' the man said, in a slightly more friendly tone. 'She is a great benefactress to our work. She is seated at . . . table five tonight, monsieur.'

'Thank you,' Hugh said. 'Drive on.'

He smiled. This was going to be easy.

The ballroom, cleared of display cases, had been transformed. The party designer had outdone herself on the commission; rather than strain to link the decor to literacy, somehow, she had gone for classically elegant; a string quartet in black tie, the walls draped with billowing white chiffon, myriads of candles in cut-crystal holders, everything soothing and creamy, a snowy paradise without the cold and wet. A waitress came by and offered him a glass of champagne, which he took; Perrier-Jouet, he noticed; non-vintage, but still good.

He made his way swiftly through the tables until he could see number five, still a few metres away from him. He scanned the crowd, his sharp eyes running over hundreds of rich, beautifully dressed French ladies. Where was she . . . where was she . . .

Ah; there. Standing by the pillar, talking to an older woman in a plain red sheath. Sophie Massot was pristine, he thought, in a floor-length, tailored black dress, silk over satin, with a shawl of black lace – almost certainly antique. Heels of some sort; you couldn't see them, but Hugh could tell from the way her body was poised. And her earrings; they were quite breathtaking; briolette diamonds that tumbled like raindrops, throwing out light everywhere, and swinging with every slight movement of her head. They showed, to beautiful advantage, her long neck and the slim curves of her face, and softened the severe lines of her hair, her chestnut locks pulled up into a formal chignon.

Montfort approved immensely; she was very dignified. But still, stylishness was one thing, and business sense quite another. This was the wife who had allowed her husband to cat around France, quite openly, all those years. He reminded himself of that, and was a little ashamed of his shallowness in changing his opinion of her just because of the way she looked.

He sipped his champagne reflectively and looked around the room for Gregoire Lazard. There was no sign of him. Hugh was patient; he might be in the loo, or fetching Sophie a drink – any number of things. He toyed with his champagne and waited a full ten minutes; but Mme Massot appeared to be on her own. Eventually the lady in red drifted off, and Sophie headed towards her table, a look of boredom crossing her face, which he noted she quickly banished.

Well; it's no surprise she has social graces, he reminded himself; what else has she had to do all these years?

This was the moment. Never one to require an opportunity to present itself twice, Hugh walked boldly towards her.

'Excuse me – Mme Massot?'

She turned towards him, her head lifting automatically at the English voice. It made the briolettes dance and sparkle in the candleight. She has grey eyes, he thought; unusual; very pretty.

'Yes?' she said.

Hugh bowed slightly. 'I don't believe we've been introduced,' he said. 'But I wonder if I might have a few moments of your time, madame. My name is Hugh Montfort.'

She reacted with a little start, then calmed herself. Oh well, he thought, it would have been asking too much to hope she'd never heard of me.

'Certainly, Mr Montfort,' she said, coolly. 'How may I help you?'

And a pretty voice, he acknowledged; Southern England modulated by years and years across the Channel.

'I have a proposition to put to you, Mme Massot, and would rather do it when you are not surrounded by advisers,' Hugh said. He gave her the dry smile that had women panting after

102

him on three continents. 'You're in charge, and I would like to talk to you directly.'

'Mr Montfort,' Sophie said, her voice now pure ice. 'This is a social occasion, sir. I trust you are not planning to bring up business.'

Hugh stiffened. For all he regarded himself as un-snobby, he had an innate sense of his place in the world. Sophie was beneath him in class, for all her elegance and style, yet she had just rebuked him on etiquette.

And she was right. It stung.

For once he had no comeback. He simply could not continue; she had as good as accused him of behaving in an ungentle-manly manner.

'You are perfectly right, madame,' he said – damnation, was he actually about to blush? Hugh could not recall having felt more discomfited. It was the last thing in the world he had expected her to say to him. 'This is not the time. Please excuse me.' And he bowed again and began to walk away.

'Just one minute,' Sophie said, halting him in his tracks. 'Permit me to save you some trouble, Mr Montfort. The answer is no; and it will remain no.'

'You have not seen the figures, Mme Massot.'

'The chief executive of my company is M. Gregoire Lazard,' she said. 'I believe you know him.'

'He is not a man with your shareholders' best interests at heart, madame,' Hugh said firmly.

She was not to be swayed. 'If you have a proposal to put to him, please do call any time during business hours. I am sure he will see you.' The grey eyes and dark lashes, he did not think she used any mascara, they were so naturally dark, swept over him disdainfully. 'Our number,' Sophie said, 'is in the phone book. Good evening, sir.'

And she swept away from him in a marvellous silken rustle, leaving Hugh standing there, frustrated and furious, and yet, despite himself, somewhat admiring. He had to admit, it was a stylish insult. *Our number is in the phone book.* Yes; excellent. She didn't sound brainless, but on the other hand, the alternatives were worse, he reminded himself.

He went and found his own table, where he was, necessarily, sitting with a bunch of strangers. they all knew each other, and after perfunctory introductions, left him to his thoughts.

I hope I'm not such an amateur as to be swayed by a pretty face and good conversation, Montfort told himself, sternly. If Sophie Lazard were not as stupid as he'd thought, she must then be a very calculating woman, and incredibly selfish. She had permitted a charade of a marriage, and now she was prepared to deny her shareholders, and her son, value for their stock, for what? To indulge a lover? Pathetic; and he was pleased to feel his resolve harden again.

'And what brings you to Paris, M. Montfort?' asked one of his companions at the table with a smile. Her husband was an investment banker, and he noticed now that she was wearing Mayberry earrings; beads of lapis interspersed with iolite and sapphires and flashing white zircons; from last season's 'Icicles' collection.

Hugh returned her smile and made sure he spoke loudly enough for her husband to overhear.

'I'm in Paris to take over House Massot,' he said.

When he got back to the hotel the first thing he did was call L.A. Hugh was often grateful for the time difference; if he had ideas in the middle of the night, it didn't matter – he could still get Pete Stockton on the phone.

'He's playing golf, sir,' said Maisie, Pete's assistant. She had a little-girl breathy voice that annoyed him, but he was trying to get used to it.

'Put me through please,' Hugh said, tiredly.

Pete was less likely to go somewhere without his wallet than without his cellphone. He could hear Maisie sighing in disapproval, but ignored it. It was Monday afternoon; more work, less play would suit his chairman better.

'Hugh, old bean,' Pete said resentfully. 'Is it important?'

Pete fondly believed he had the Brit lingo down pat, and Hugh never had the time to disabuse him.

'Sorry to interrupt your game,' Montfort lied. 'I'm in Paris; and I'm about to launch a full takeover bid for Massot.'

'Something's happened, then? Excuse me, Peter,' he said to his companion. The resentful tones had vanished, as Hugh had expected. The call was about money, Pete's favourite participation sport; golf could not compete.

Hugh brought him up to date.

'They're treading water,' he concluded. 'The shareholders will hate the idea of the widow and the CEO.'

'And even with the family holding there's enough of a float out there?'

'It will be difficult,' Hugh conceded. The mother had stock of her own, too. 'But they do not have fifty-one per cent even if they all vote the same way. We need to convince the shareholders.'

'You're confident.' It was a statement, rather than a question.

'They have no sentiment about the name; they care about their portfolios. Yes, I'm absolutely confident. I want authorisation to proceed with a bid; assemble the financing, legal, everything.'

'I got my Blackberry with me.' Of course you do, Montfort thought. 'I'll have it faxed to you within twenty minutes.'

The only good thing he could say about Pete, Hugh reflected, was that where his own money was concerned, he knew how to move fast. Montfort had convinced the board completely that buying House Massot would lift them to the level of Tiffany's. Pete Stockton now wanted this deal almost as much as he did.

'Thank you,' he said. 'I'm much obliged.'

Hugh hung up and went into the marble-clad retreat of his sumptuous bathroom to brush his teeth. By the time he had finished, an envelope had been slid discreetly under his door. It contained the signed authorisation from Pete Stockton.

Montfort smiled and put it beside his bed. He slept well, as he always did before a fight.

Chapter Fifteen

Sophie couldn't concentrate. She thanked God, for once, for Katherine. Her mother-in-law's rigorous social training came in useful at a moment like this, when she had to smile and dance, and avoid offending anyone, even though her thoughts were otherwise engaged.

How dare he?

She could hardly believe it. How dare he! Her husband's long-time enemy, to come up to her at a charity ball, and try to take advantage of her? Just because Gregoire had to work tonight. Hugh Montfort must have planned it; have known she was going to be alone. He must think me as dumb as a rock, Sophie told herself. What, that I wouldn't know about him? That I would sign over Tom's thirty per cent to some takeover shark?

It occurred to her that in fact she wouldn't have known about Hugh Montfort, if it hadn't been for Judy Dean; and she felt a rush of gratitude at the thought.

Gregoire had never mentioned him. But most likely he didn't want her to be bothered.

Sophie fought to keep her composure.

'Sophie, you are not eating?'

Richard de Belfont, Baron de Fosin, her neighbour, bent over her solicitously. Sophie regarded her plate; duck with a bitter apple sauce.

'Oh yes; delicious,' she said faintly, forcing down a forkful.

'Sophie never eats, Richard,' said Margot, his wife, with a thin smile. 'How else do you think she stays so slim?'

'Margot, you're too sweet,' Sophie said automatically. Her

eyes scanned the table; six of Pierre's favourite people, favourites in that they were all titled or very rich indeed; and to her right, a politician, a junior minister in the culture department, the 'spare man'. He'd been ogling her hopefully all evening, but she could barely respond to his energetic compliments and polite conversation about the château.

Oh hell, I wish Gregoire were here, she thought.

Of course he couldn't be with her every moment. He had come out to the country, or had invited her out to lunch, every day since she'd left the firm; ever since the day she'd decided not to come in any more, and Gregoire had driven straight out to the country, kissed her hand, and told her that he loved her.

Sophie toyed with her duck and her glass of champagne. Yes, she would think about Gregoire, that was the way to go. He had taken her in his arms and kissed her, in a very practised way; and although she'd been stiff, and resisting, he hadn't minded. He told her he knew she was Catholic, and he would wait . . .

But I was expecting to melt, she thought. Oh well; perhaps it was just lack of practice. It had been seven years, after all . . .

This train of thought was not completely satisfactory, but she forced herself to consider Gregoire's kindness, his willingness not to push, to go at her pace. And he'd called and sent flowers every day and come as often as possible; of course there would occasionally be nights when he had to work.

In fact, before this evening, she reflected guiltily, she'd almost been looking forward to it. Just a little. Well, before he declared himself she'd been longing for him to say something, and now that he didn't leave her alone, she wanted a break; I'm just perverse, Sophie thought.

But she'd certainly changed her mind when Hugh Montfort appeared. She wanted Gregoire then. He would have told him where to go.

When Sophie thought it was safe, she discreetly looked over to Montfort's table. He was seated so she could only see the back of him, but he appeared unfazed by her rebukes. He was deep in animated conversation with the other benefactors.

She'd thought that at the very least he would have stormed out.

As soon as it was safe, Sophie excused herself and made her way to the cloakroom. The assistant handed her her coat with a smile of approbation; it was an old-fashioned, gorgeous silk brocade from China, mostly silver-grey, with pearl details. But Sophie had little time to enjoy the flattery. She summoned her driver, and waited impatiently for him to come round.

From time to time she glanced back nervously into the hall. Had Montfort seen her leave? She was sure he must have done. But he hadn't followed her. She rehearsed two or three put-downs, just in case he did.

He's not what I would have expected, Sophie thought. Except for his class; the name Hugh Montfort spoke volumes. But she had pictured him as an indolent, weak-chinned public school boy, looking to glom on to the success of Pierre and Gregoire, and sulky when he was refused.

Montfort had been nothing of the kind. He was her own age, maybe just a touch older; well dressed, without too much care taken about it, which she never liked in men. Tall, like Gregoire, but stronger. Indeed, he made her shiver, although the evening was balmy. He was very muscular, and tense when he moved; predatory, in more than the corporate sense of the word. Sophie longed for the comfort of Gregoire right now.

As soon as she had slid into the back of her limo, she reached for the phone and called his direct line at the office. Nobody was there. She gave the driver his home address.

The car pulled along the gravel drive into the neon stream of night-time Parisian traffic. Sophie was almost the first to leave, but she didn't care. She had put in an appearance; that was sufficient, as representative of the House. And now she had something a little more fun to do.

Well, there was a tinge of fun to it, she admitted. Of course she was madly in love with Gregoire, and being courted was very exciting, but still . . .

Truth to tell, she had found the time away from the office just *slightly* dull. Looking back on it, even studying reports hadn't been so bad. And there was Judy Dean to talk to.

Judy had come down to the château for a visit, but it wasn't quite the same. Sophie had actually enjoyed working. It wasn't true work, not like Judy's – she knew that – but it had been fun to try, at least, to wrap her mind round something more important than planting schemes and estate management.

And now she had some important information – now she could help Gregoire! Their enemy was on the prowl again. Of course, Gregoire would know how to defeat him. She wondered, a touch anxiously, if he'd be offended, if she asked for updates?

Ah; here they were boulevard de la Reine, with its modern townhouses, all in a row. Gregoire's was the third, and she could see the light was still on. A car was parked outside, a little Renault, so she had the driver wait in the next space, and climbed out, carefully lifting her coat and dress so that mud didn't splash on the hem. She had a good dry-cleaner, but one couldn't ask for miracles.

Sophie rang Gregoire's bell. She heard light footsteps running down the stairs, and the door opened.

'Yes?' said a young woman.

Sophie blinked. The girl was no more than nineteen, with dyed blonde hair cut just below her chin in a long bob. She had a pretty face and undistinguished brown eyes, and was wearing jeans and what looked like a man's shirt, thin red stripes on white.

'Sorry; I must have picked the wrong house,' Sophie said, in confusion. The development was expensive, but the houses were identical.

But then she heard heavier footsteps, which she recognised; they were his. Gregoire came running downstairs, smiling at her. He was wearing a white shirt, a tie, and trousers, and smelled of aftershave. He kissed her hand, gallantly.

'*Chérie*!' he said. 'Welcome; it's so good to see you.'

Sophie stared uncertainly at the young woman.

'Excuse me,' Gregoire said. 'This is Lise, my new assistant. Lise – this is the lady I've been telling you about – Mme Massot, who owns the company.

'Delighted to meet you, madame,' Lise said. 'It's a great honour.'

Sophie shook hands, feeling stupid.

'We decided to come back here and work, as there was such a quantity of it; it's late, and I thought I should at least buy Lise a pizza,' Gregoire said. Sophie glanced into his sitting room; there was indeed a pizza box open on his expensive green glass coffee-table. She smiled.

'I didn't think you were a pizza kind of guy.'

'From time to time,' he said. 'Come in, come in.'

The young girl stood aside as Sophie moved into the hallway.

'Wow, what a dress,' she said.

'Thank you,' Sophie replied, a little awkwardly. She looked at Gregoire, who immediately came to her rescue. 'Lise, since Mme Massot is here, I'll knock off for the night. You can finish typing everything up at home.'

'Uh, yes, monsieur,' said the girl.

'Just make sure you're in early – seven-thirty,' Gregoire said easily.

'Yes, monsieur. Goodnight, madame. Nice to meet you.'

'And you,' Sophie said, glad when the door had shut behind her. 'I'm sorry, sweetheart; I didn't think you'd still be working at this hour.'

'We were almost done.' Gregoire clasped her hand. 'I'm so glad you're here; you're so much more interesting than dull work on diamond suppliers. Allow me,' and he shrugged off her silver coat. 'It is a fabulous dress, darling. Did you manage to survive the evening without me?'

'Funny you should ask,' Sophie said, sitting down on one of his woven-leather chairs. She felt on more familiar ground now; jealousy of a secretary, what could be more stupid? 'I met someone unexpected.'

'And who was that?' Lazard moved into the kitchen. 'Tea? Coffee? A *digestif*?'

'Something decaffeinated, if you have it. Camomile would be lovely. Anyway, it was Hugh Montfort.'

Sophie watched Gregoire as he busied himself in his sleek chrome kitchen; his back stiffened.

'Are you sure?' he asked.

'Perfectly; he introduced himself to me.'

'And made an offer for the company, no doubt,' Gregoire said, laughing.

'Yes, he did.'

He spun on his heels, staring. 'What?'

'He said he had a proposition for me. But I told him the answer was no,' Sophie reassured him. 'I told him to talk to you.'

Lazard poured boiling water into an earthenware tea pot. 'What did he say to that?'

'He informed me that you "did not have the interests of our shareholders at heart",' Sophie said, 'pompous ass.'

Gregoire, she could see, took this badly. His hands were trembling as he set out cups and saucers.

'He's an oaf,' Lazard spat. 'An interfering fool.'

'Don't worry,' Sophie said. 'I didn't believe him for a second.'

Gregoire took a deep breath, then two, then came back beside her and set down the cup.

'Sugar?' he said.

She shook her head, and he caught her hand and kissed it again; more passionately, this time. It made Sophie wriggle just a little.

'Gregoire . . .' she said, faintly. 'I'm sorry, I just . . . I need more time . . . it's been so long.'

That sounded like an excuse. Even to her. Sophie flashed on Pierre, and her squirming distaste whenever he came to her bed, peeled back the covers, and lay down next to her, where she stayed still and fearful, gritting her teeth and hoping he'd soon be done.

Gregoire smiled softly, then reached up and traced a smooth fingertip against the line of her neck.

'Don't worry, darling, I know you are religious.' He stood up, to Sophie's relief. 'I think it's charming,' he said. 'A beautiful woman is not always so virtuous.'

She looked down. She wasn't some kind of saint, if that's what he thought.

'Stay there a moment, my darling,' he said, and disappeared into his bedroom. Sophie sipped her tea and tried to calm herself. She had to get used to a man's touch, that was all it was. No need to be afraid. He was hardly going to jump on her right now . . .

Gregoire reappeared and crossed the room towards her. Then, taking her hand again, he knelt at her feet. Sophie stared as he produced a little red box.

'It isn't Massot,' he murmured. 'I hope you don't mind . . . I want to have fresh memories, just for us. It's Cartier.'

He flicked open the box. It was a huge, very fine diamond, oval cut and set in platinum; expensive but boring. No, classic, Sophie instantly corrected herself.

'It's beautiful,' she exclaimed dutifully.

'I hope before long to change your name, as well as your jewels,' Gregoire said. 'I was going to wait, but why should we wait? Sophie – you know I love you; will you marry me?'

She said yes, of course; she couldn't think of any other answer that was reasonable. Gregoire loved her, she loved him . . . she must do. He was willing to wait for her; he had money of his own. And she was so tired of being lonely.

He triumphantly slipped the ring on to her left hand, next to her other engagement ring and wedding band. It didn't fit, but he assured her it was the work of a day to have it corrected.

'And we must be married as soon as possible. You'll tell Tom. Perhaps we can arrange the ceremony at the château, by next week.'

Sophie laughed. 'Next week? Don't be silly.'

'You forget, I have to wait to make love to you until we're married. You can't blame me for being eager.' Gregoire came and perched himself next to her on the couch. 'But seriously, darling; we love each other, delay is foolish.'

'A wedding is a happy day – there's no need to rush it.' Planning a nice wedding would give her something to do. 'And besides, I must break the news to Tom, gradually. He's had a lot to cope with lately.'

'He'll be fine,' Gregoire said, a touch impatiently. 'He must learn that you have a right to move on.'

Sophie stared. 'We're not getting married next week, Gregoire! Be reasonable. I haven't even been in mourning six months. Besides, the Church will make you wait at least six months, and to go to marriage classes . . . although Fr Sabin will do that for me . . .'

'Six months!' Lazard exploded. 'But he's been dead seven years. I don't *have* six months . . .'

Then he caught hold of himself, and shook his head.

'Look at me; I am being so stupid. It's only that I have been planning this, and already the time without you seems too long to me.'

They were soft words, but Sophie shrank back a little; the fire in Gregoire's blue eyes had surprised her; she'd never seen him angry like that.

He perceived the look. 'Ah, *chérie*, now I have frightened you, and at such a happy moment.'

'It's all right. You're just enthusiastic.'

'Exactly,' he said. 'You know when something has been building up . . . and when you make the leap, you want it to happen as soon as possible.'

'I understand,' Sophie said. She stood up. 'I'll let Fr Sabin know tomorrow, anyway.'

'Yes,' Gregoire said eagerly. 'Maybe he can get us a dispensation or something. Make it faster. In return for a donation . . .'

He caught her look and held up his hands. 'OK, OK. I'll wait as long as I have to, and just hope it won't be too long.'

Sophie handed him back the ring, that was too small and waited as he fetched her coat and helped her into it. She told herself it was fine, and in fact it was flattering, if Gregoire was on fire to marry her.

Her eyes swept over his place; not her own taste, but definitely expensive. Gregoire was a proud man, she excused him; she looked at the portraits of himself, opening a Massot store, in a group of businessmen, even shaking hands with a former Prime Minister of France . . .

A chill crept over her heart; she looked a little closer. Gregoire was clasping M. Jospin's hand in his, and smiling. He was dressed in a charcoal grey suit, a navy tie . . .

. . . and a white shirt, with thin red stripes.

She'd seen it before. Very recently.

It was the shirt Lise had been wearing.

'Are you OK, my love?' Gregoire said tenderly, draping the coat across her shoulders.

Sophie wrenched her eyes away, and used Katherine Massot's techniques of composure for the second time that evening.

'I'm fine – all the excitement, you know, darling,' she said. 'See you tomorrow,' and kissed him on the cheek.

He opened the door, and Sophie, her heart thumping, was thrilled to see her driver, still there, waiting patiently for her, his headlights dimmed.

He got out to open the back door for her, and Sophie climbed in. 'Home,' she said, instantly.

'Certainly, madame. I trust you had a pleasant evening?'

Sophie made no reply. She was looking at Gregoire Lazard as he stood on the steps. He seemed to have sensed that something was wrong. He was staring at the tinted windows of her car, as though he could see through them; and although, at first, she thought it must be fanciful, Sophie felt a sudden, frightening wave of malice.

But then her car moved off, and he turned and went into the house; and she was able to breathe out.

Chapter Sixteen

'You do understand, Mr Massot, that your position is a delicate one,' Leonard Elgin said.

Tom scowled; he hadn't come all the way to London to have his grandmother teach him to suck eggs.

'Of course it's delicate; that's what I've been trying to explain to you,' he said impatiently.

They had pulled out all the stops for him. The ancient chambers in Lincoln's Inn were quietly, decorously abuzz with news of their new client. Tom had been ushered into the largest meeting room, and ensconced in one of the leather-backed chairs under a fine Edwardian portrait of a judge. Both senior partners, Messrs Leonard Elgin and Crispin Hartford, were present. Tom could see they were trying to contain their eagerness.

'The matter will certainly require the most discreet handling,' Hartford agreed. Like his partner, he was a man in his fifties, with a decorous, quiet air Tom approved of; precisely what he wanted after his mother's behaviour.

'So what are my options?' Tom asked.

'Under the terms of the will, Mme Massot is in an unassailable position. She inherits five million euros, and is guardian, until your majority, of your estate; which comprises the château and all other holdings, including thirty per cent of House Massot stock.'

'So we challenge the will.'

'We can do that, certainly. It won't work,' Mr Elgin said. 'You do realise that, sir?'

'Then what would be the point?' Tom demanded, annoyed.

'To gain an injunction preventing Mme Massot from acting until the case is heard. We can file a number of motions,' Mr Hartford said encouragingly. 'And if we are fortunate, we may be able to delay her. After all, you are only three years away from total control.'

'Ah.' Tom looked at them with a touch more respect. 'Drown her in paperwork; yes, I like that.'

'And we could possibly challenge the declaration of death . . . if you have any evidence your father is still alive.'

He looked away. 'I wish I did.'

'Of course you do realise, Mr Massot, that you have some stock of your own. Five per cent; a gift when you were born.'

Tom nodded. 'I can't do very much with that, gentlemen.'

'And your grandmother,' Mr Elgin went on, slyly, 'the will mentions that she has ten per cent.'

'Fifteen per cent of the stock is substantial,' Mr Hartford murmured, discreetly. 'If you received enough shareholder votes, Mr Massot . . .'

Tom leaned forward. Brilliant! Why hadn't he thought of that? Grandmother! She had dignity, she valued his father . . . she wouldn't stand for what Maman was doing, any more than he would.

'Yes? What?' he demanded.

'You could demand a seat on the board. And naturally, the other board members would be aware that in a few years you will control everything.'

'Forty-five per cent, including the stock of the elder Mme Massot.'

'One doubts they would be all that keen to oppose your wishes.'

'Mme Massot could find her plans blocked.'

Tom stood up. The two older men regarded him with dismay.

'I hope we haven't been too precipitate, sir?' asked Leonard Elgin. 'There are other ways, quieter methods . . .'

'Where's the retainer agreement?' Tom demanded. It was handed to him; he removed the platinum, custom-made Mont Blanc pen his mother had given him last Christmas from his jacket pocket and signed with a flourish.

The lawyers looked at each other with suitably muted triumph.

'Coutts will transfer the two hundred thousand to your corporate account later this morning,' Tom pronounced. He had made his decision; this was the right firm; now he simply wanted to get out of here. I am a man of action, he thought; Maman will think better than to trifle with me.

'Thank you, Mr Massot.' Mr Elgin offered him a firm handshake across the table. 'We are delighted.'

'It's a great honour to be working with you, sir,' said Mr Hartford.

Tom shook hands coolly; such respect was no more than his due.

'Of course,' he said. 'Good day, gentlemen.'

He took the train back to Oxford, first class; Tom had found that English taxi drivers are an inexhaustible source of conversation, especially when a man wants to think. He was going to have to give them up; his first action in the last few days that would have pleased his mother.

The English countryside rushed quietly past him. It was, he had to acknowledge, very beautiful, if one liked that sort of thing; gentle meadows, copses of trees, fat white sheep, mellow and contented in the hot summer. But nothing, certainly nothing to France, he thought with pride; nothing to the elegance of formal grey stone, graceful buildings in symmetry, the manicured lawns and schematic walks of his father's park; villages where the houses were planned, not jumbled together. London was cluttered, Paris, refined; he wanted to go home.

The simplest way would be to leave. Oxford was no prison. He could send movers, clear his rooms; take lodgings anywhere, there were some fine luxury places to rent on the Left Bank. But, although loath to do anything that Sophie wanted, he was not *quite* ready to throw away his degree. Oxford was still pre-eminent among the world's great universities, and although he wouldn't confess it now, Tom had been proud to make it in. He planned a safer out. He would go to the Senior Censor and request rustication. One year away. That would be enough to stop Maman messing with his inheritance; and then he could return to the girls and the parties . . .

Polly would still be there in a year. Tom flinched at the thought. True, he was busy – he was heartbroken – but yet, but yet; he still thought about her. Could he win her back? If he returned in triumph, sole controller of his father's vast holdings, a celebrated *homme d'affaires*. More than just an heir. Tom had a strong suspicion that being an heir would mean nothing to a girl like Polly. What was it the English called it? Trust fund brat. A man needed to show himself a man to get rid of such a label, and Thomas Massot was ready to do it. Nobody complained about the Rothschild boys, or the Rockefellers. It was so old fashioned to consider twenty-one the age of majority, anyway. Legally it was eighteen, had been for years . . .

The train pulled into the station at Oxford. Tom was glad. His plans were made, and now all he wanted was to set them in motion.

At the end of this bitter fight, he would have put things right. The world was becoming clearer to him. He needed to save his mother from herself, be his father's son. And win Polly back. She was different from other girls – intelligent, beautiful, daring. There were, indeed, better groomed and more delicate girls out there, and he had certainly enjoyed his stint as a playboy.

But now he'd lost her, Tom was starting to think there was only one girl for him.

'But I don't understand *why* you have to leave,' Flora said. Her plump bottom lip was quivering, and her eyes were brimming, threatening to spill into tears at any moment.

Tom looked at her, uncomfortably. It was so undignified, this display. What had he seen in her? That she was pretty?

'I told you, dearest; family business,' he said lamely. 'Mind if I smoke?'

'I'd rather you didn't . . .' Flora's voice trailed off. Tom was already reaching for his packet of Gauloises. 'Of course if you need to . . .'

She doesn't have the energy to fight, he thought. Polly

would have slapped the carton out of his hands, but Flora just moped. He sighed; the thought of Polly had spoiled the pleasure. He put the carton back. Anyway, a cigarette would just delay his getting out of here, which was the most pressing problem.

'That's all right,' he said, wearily. He looked at the girl; slightly heavy, in rather a sexy way, with big lips and breasts to match, dark hair, a sprinkling of freckles and that incredible accent. He had wonderful English, but Scots and Welsh threw him; as did Yorkshire, or thick Birmingham; how could the British cram so many voices into such a small island?

'I'll miss you terribly,' she said meekly. Tom wondered if it were true. For all her great shape and sensuous mouth, Flora McAllister was rather a dull girl, studious, with a placid temperament. She only got really excited when discussing her subject, and who the hell was interested in mathematics?

'We're great friends, and I'm sure we'll meet again,' Tom said carefully. He was trying to give her a coded dismissal. After that towering row with Gemma, who also got weepy, he had no desire to repeat the scene. Sex with Flora was mechanical, relief of his urges and frustrations; it had been a penance to lie there afterwards, when her body seemed doughy instead of curvy, holding her while she slept, mouth open and snoring lightly. Yes; it was good he could get away from this.

'D'you think we'll still be able to date? I could come to France on the ferry about once a month. You could pick me up at Calais,' Flora said hopefully.

'Darling,' Tom pressed her plump hand to his mouth gallantly, 'if we're realistic, it'll be impossible – you have your studies, and you mustn't disrupt them . . .'

Flora looked concerned; he knew she was after a First, maybe more. A Fellowship of All Souls had been mentioned.

'And I'll be too busy. Nothing but the utmost concern for my family could keep me from you,' he lied. 'Perhaps when we've both achieved our goals, we can get together again, and if our hearts are free . . .'

He left it hanging there, and to his great relief Flora nodded.

'Och, I suppose it's best,' she said thickly. Her accent always got worse when she was emotional, which was thankfully rare. 'But I'll miss you, Tom. You were different,' she said.

He glanced at her with surprise and warmth as he reached for his shirt. Different! Damn right he was different. He liked cow-like Flora a little better now she had said that.

'I'll see you at supper, *chérie*,' he said, kissing her on the cheek and making good his escape. As he strode back to his rooms, top button rakishly undone so everybody would know what he had been doing, Tom made a note to himself. Flora was a good girl, he thought, a little complacently. He would call the Massot showroom in Bond Street and have them send her a gift. Something plain, but valuable; a brooch, perhaps. He remembered a fine spray of gold with antique seed pearls and pink sapphires, his mother had pointed it out to him last year. He would send her that, with a note; 'A token of my esteem. Until we meet again. Thomas.'

Yes; that would do very well. He smiled smugly. That was stylish, and it was incumbent on him to develop style, the style that becomes a man of property and business. Parting from Flora had been mercifully easy. He hoped the college would be as accommodating.

'I have letters here from your tutors.'

Mr Butters was the Senior Censor of Christ Church, and Tom wondered if he had ever disliked anybody quite so much. Why, the academic was pacing up and down in front of him like a general in front of an unruly subaltern. What were academic salaries in England these days? He would be surprised if the man made eighty thousand euros a year. And he was dictating to *him*, Thomas Massot, heir to many millions, and future controller of one of Europe's great fortunes?

He said nothing.

'They report that your work has been most unsatisfactory.'

'My last essay got a Beta plus,' Tom responded, with a touch of defiance all his struggles couldn't suppress.

'Indeed; but Mr Hillard tells me you have a fine mind, the type that ought not to be satisfied with Betas of any sort.'

Tom was amazed. Hillard had said that?

'That's very kind of him.'

'On the contrary, young man,' Mr Butters said, staring at him with those piercing hazel eyes, 'he is quite disgusted with you. Ignorance is forgivable; laziness is not. You have no hope, no hope at all of a First if you carry on in this manner. You do understand that?'

Tom regarded Butters's threadbare waistcoat and ill-fitting trousers, and the red pinching mark his spectacles made on the bridge of his nose. He felt uncomfortable with this line of questioning, and told himself it was both impertinent and irrelevant.

University tutors seemed to forget they were not schoolmasters. They were two adults together, were they not? He hadn't come here to be hectored.

Butters was waiting for an answer.

'I have been under a great deal of pressure, monsieur.'

'*I* am not French,' said Butters dryly, 'and as you are reading English, I think we had better stick to that.'

I hate him, Tom thought. He said, 'Of course, sir.'

'What pressure, precisely, have you been under?' Butters asked, folding his arms.

'My father . . . my father has recently been declared dead,' Tom said, hanging his head and hoping for sympathy.

'Yes; I had heard. But that event took place just a few weeks ago, whereas the inattention and sloppiness began halfway through your first term.'

Tom stiffened. He had imagined mention of his father's death would put an end to the interrogation. They were nightmares, the Christ Church faculty, but nonetheless had a reputation for great compassion and elasticity whenever an undergraduate had a real problem, family or otherwise.

He thought fast.

'Monsieur – *Mr* Butters. I know I have not been doing as well as I should. The pleasures of independence rather distracted me.' He saw this small measure of truth had not gone down badly. 'And I had resolved to, as you say, pull my socks up.'

To Tom's aggravation he saw the Censor swallow a smile at his colloquialism, delivered with that permanent trace of a French accent he neither could get rid of, nor wanted to.

'But the news of my father's death, that he is declared dead, that has shaken me. I find I cannot concentrate, I can think of nothing else.' To his horror, Tom found he was becoming emotional. His voice shook; he struggled. 'I will certainly fail my degree, or you will send me away, if I have to continue to try to study at present; but if I can take a sabbatical, you can rusticate me . . .'

Butters had noted that the boy's eyes were reddened. Tom angrily dashed his sleeve across them, and then tried, pathetically, to cover the gesture with a cough.

The older man softened. 'If we rusticate you, Mr Massot, do I have your word that when you return here you will do your best to vindicate the trust the admissions officers placed in you?'

This was an unexpected question. Tom did not want to give his word. Giving his word was a serious matter. But there was nothing for it other than to say 'Yes.'

'Good,' the Senior Censor continued. 'Every year, many more students apply to the House than we can take in. We select from the best, and disappoint the others, sometimes crushingly. There were at least fifteen qualified applicants for your place, Mr Massot.'

Tom sulked; he couldn't help it if others were too stupid to qualify.

'We shall see you promptly at the start of next Michelmas but one,' Mr Butters said. He shook Tom's hand briskly. 'Good day.'

After that, it was the work of a few hours. He called a firm in London and a storage facility in the Banbury road, and arranged for his possessions to be moved. There was nothing he could not leave behind; Tom kept nothing too personal here. He rang the Massot store in Bond Street, and asked about the brooch; it had been sold, but the salesman, who was enjoyably deferential, recommended another, a flower with leaves of gold, petals of mother-of-pearl, and a fine garnet in the centre. Tom agreed, and made the arrangements. It would be sent to Flora McAllister at once. He felt virtuous; that was a kind way to leave her.

Flora had not been devious like Gemma, or unforgiving like Polly; she deserved it. Still, I won't be sorry to be rid of the lot of them, Tom thought.

He left notes for some of his drinking buddies; none could particularly be called friends, except possibly Simon Lancaster – a brilliant but reserved historian, and, like him, heir to a lot of money. Tom and Simon had been close since they had discovered this; although Simon seemed to regard it as an unwanted burden. He could not have been more unlike Tom if he'd tried, and yet the two were firm friends. Simon admired Massot's rakish success with women and complete disregard of academic work; Tom said and did things he would not have dreamed of himself. And Tom, although he would never have admitted it, liked Simon's steadiness of purpose and quiet, methodical achievement.

He walked quickly over to the bar to find him. It was six, and Simon invariably went to the bar at that hour, drank two gin and tonics, and then returned to his rooms to study. Tom would say a temporary goodbye; he would have Simon over to Paris as a guest, he thought; show him some real living. He could shake that English reserve out of him.

He ran along Tom Quad, then cut down towards the bar. It was crowded as usual; the subsidised alcohol, one of Oxford's greatest pleasures, was as enduringly popular as ever.

Tom scanned the room. A few acquaintances beckoned him over, shouting drunkenly, but he grinned and shook his head. A few weeks back he'd have been here first and got drunk with the best of them; today it seemed somehow beneath him. I'm growing up, he thought, proudly. Simon was not here – he'd have to go and call on him in his rooms, otherwise he would have to phone him. He had no intention of delaying; he wanted to get out of this little English backwater right now, and be on the Eurostar to Paris before midnight.

Then he saw her. Polly. She was standing there, her red hair tossed back, laughing with those gorgeous white teeth. She was wearing one of her usual scruffy outfits; a Metallica T-shirt, low-cut jeans, Doc Marten boots, cheap Indian-style bangles jangling on her left wrist. She was, he realised, quite staggeringly beautiful. And she looked so happy. Tom stared, mesmerised, as Polly turned her face away from him. He saw she was standing next to Mark Allston; and she kissed him on the cheek.

Rage overtook him. Rage so intense, so thick, he could feel it clogging his throat. He couldn't speak.

'Oh-ho,' said one of his drinking buddies, nudging another man in their crowd.

They're amused, Tom thought; they all think this is *funny*. Thoughts rushed in on him, making him dizzy. Allston's brawny arm around Polly's waist now; his hands, pinning her to the bed like Tom's had done; his fingers over her soft, warm body; Mark kissing her; Mark . . .

Tom shoved his way through the crowd, sending drinks spilling, ignoring angry shouts of protest. He marched up to Mark Allston.

'Get your hands off her!' he shouted. 'She's mine!'

Allston looked down at him and chuckled. 'It's the Frog Prince,' he said, at which the crowd around him exploded with laughter. Tom did not care for them, or their opinion; he despised them all; peasants.

Polly looked miserable. 'Mark –'

Mark Allston looked down at Tom. He was six feet tall and thick, with shoulders like Atlas.

'Or what? You'll make me?'

'That's right.' Tom stared at the arm which had tightened possessively round Polly's small waist.

'You and whose army, mate,' Allston said dismissively. He turned back to the bar.

Tom reached out and pulled Allston sharply, viciously, to face him; the Englishman considered him a moment, then shook his head.

'Just fuck off, will you,' he said. 'I only fight people my own size.'

Massot coloured. He was five ten, but Allston had at least fifty pounds on him.

'Time for a new rule, *cochon*,' he said, and pulled his hand back, ready to strike – but Polly stepped forward and caught it.

'Stop it, Tom,' she hissed.

'Stay out of it,' he said.

'I will not. I can be with whomever I want. You're just making a fool of yourself.'

He turned to look at her. 'And what are you doing? Standing here, draped over this – this monkey?'

Allston said, 'That's it', and started to roll up his sleeves.

'Don't,' Polly said to him. 'Look, Tom, you cheated on me, OK?'

His heart ached. 'You're mine,' he said. He couldn't believe how much it hurt.

'I'm not yours. Or his. I make my own decisions,' Polly said, and started to cry. Allston stared at her.

'You with me, Poll?' he asked.

She came to herself, threaded her arm through his. 'Yeah. I'm with you.'

'Now get the fuck out of here, Massot, or I'll take you out myself,' Allston said to him, with menace. 'And stay away from her.'

Tom ignored him. He looked at Polly; she turned away, and he saw her fingers stroking Allston's arm, reassuringly. She had done that to him, before, and he'd liked it.

'Polly –'

'Just go, Tom,' she said.

And he did; out through the bar, and the crowd of sniggering students, some of them his drinking buddies, laughing at him. His eyes were blinded by tears; he angrily blinked them back, and of course there was no going to see Simon now. He collected his tags then stormed out of the front gate, under Tom Tower, ignoring the insolent porter who never tipped his cap, and walked quickly, stiffly up to Cornmarket, where there was a taxi rank.

'The station,' he said.

Come; compose yourself, Tom thought. This weakness is inappropriate. He'd been wrong about Polly being the one. She was nothing, an easy lay; he'd forget her. He wrenched his mind elsewhere. There was a train leaving at a quarter to seven; assuming no delays on the broken-down British railway

125

system, perhaps the worst in Europe, he would get to London, and then on the last Eurostar out, tonight.

There was only one question, Tom told himself as he began to calm down. Would he book himself into a hotel? Or go straight to see Grandmère?

But no; a hotel would be wiser. It would be hard enough to avoid detection during the day; at night, the sound of a car trundling up the château's gravel drive would be unmistakable. He had no wish to alert Sophie – not yet. When the confrontation came, it would have to be on his terms.

Chapter Seventeen

Sophie woke to the sun streaming through the windows of her bedroom. Their bedroom; it had been Pierre's and hers for many years, and he had thought it the finest in the château. At first she had found it overwhelming; the green silk wallpaper, the priceless antique furniture, Louis XIV and earlier; there were pieces from the 1500s in this room, and their magnificent canopy bed, draped in deep gold silks and carved with oak leaves and vines, he had told her, was from the reign of François 1.

She had grown to love the room; it was incredibly rich, but so, so beautiful. Usually waking in her bed, the whole expanse of it hers, was a glorious moment. Sophie would lie still for a few minutes, soaking in the light from the easterly windows, and plan the day; with baby Tom, and later, in her garden.

Today she felt nothing but unease. She groped for the reason, and as she stirred into full consciousness, it came back to her.

Gregoire. And last night.

The girl; the shirt; his impatient anger.

There was an ancient bell-pull to her left, which still worked. She tugged on the worn red rope, and within a couple of minutes Bernarde had appeared.

'Good morning, madame. Your usual breakfast, madame?'

Rather surprisingly, given her anxiety, Sophie felt hungry. She ordered crispy bacon, scrambled eggs, Lapsang Souchong, and a bowl of strawberries; apart from the strawberries, a proper English breakfast, the kind she had not had for years.

'Certainly, madame.' Bernarde smiled her approval; the staff were always trying to mother her. 'And M. Lazard has already called for you four times, madame; but I told him you were not yet risen.'

'Yes; thank you, Bernarde. If he calls again you can take a message.' Sophie nodded to herself. 'And ask Richard to have the car ready in an hour. I will need him most of the day.'

'Yes, madame,' Bernarde said. Her eyes betrayed concern; but Sophie was not inclined to be forthcoming, and she withdrew.

She ate well, knowing now why she was hungry; she had work to do, and there was much of it to get through. Perhaps the shirt was not conclusive – somebody who wanted to could make excuses, all kinds of excuses; that maybe Lise owned a similar shirt, maybe she'd spilled something on what she'd come to his house in, and needed to change. However, Sophie knew better. She had seen it with her own eyes. It was too convenient, his hiring a new assistant. No; they were lovers, and she felt dirtied, even though he had never slept with her.

Added to which, there was the hurry – his insane rushing her to the altar. She had not liked that. It made her feel uneasy, even before she suspected him. Sophie finished her food and rang for a servant to clear it away, then went into her bathroom. She ignored the antique tub and its marble surround and headed for the modern, American shower she'd had installed last year, despite Tom's protests. Its powerful jets blasted and scrubbed her, and she stepped out feeling invigorated.

Her closet, a vast thing, formerly a small study, had two or three outfits laid out for her perusal. Sophie glanced at them all, but rejected the choices. She wanted something altogether different today; something businesslike.

There was a black, wasp-waisted Richard Tyler suit with jet buttons, extremely fitted, tapering off exactly at the knee. Sophie chose that, with a sage-green shirt underneath, Woolford tights, five dernier, barely there for the Parisian heat; and a pair of plain court shoes by Stephane Kelian. She made up quickly, just some foundation and a little blusher; Sophie had long learned not to overpower the beauty of her skin.

Then there was a spritz of her custom-blended perfume, and jewellery; Sophie picked fast, the way she always did; a cuff of hammered eighteen-carat gold studded with green tourmaline cabochons, to pick out the slight flash of colour in her shirt.

She checked herself in the mirror. Very good. Unaccountably, Sophie felt a burst of pleasure and excitement. Now why should that be? She ought, by rights, to be miserable . . .

The answer danced behind her consciousness. She wasn't ready to acknowledge it at first: relief. Of course, there was relief. It suddenly seemed as clear and luminous as the sunshine through her lead-panelled windows – she had not loved Gregoire. Sophie was lonely, and flattered, and she had enjoyed, even revelled in his company; those pleasant, easy manners, the deference, the well-aimed compliments to her mind, as well as her body. But love; no. It was why she had shrunk from his touch. She knew that this morning perfectly well, as though somebody had sat down next to her and patiently explained it in words of one syllable.

But the excitement she felt, she wasn't sure exactly . . .

It will come to me, Sophie thought. She turned away from the mirror, satisfied; chose the day's bag, a Kate Spade number in crocodile skin with a bamboo handle, slipped her purse, compact and lip gloss into it, and headed for the sweeping marble stairs, her heels echoing on them as she hurried, almost ran, down to the car.

'Are we headed for the office, madame?' her driver asked.

Sophie shook her head. 'Rue Faubourg, Richard. Take me to the Massot showroom.'

There was, she supposed, nothing actually *wrong* with it. The carpets and drapery were clean; the long display cases were not dusty; there was an adequate supply of staff – more than adequate, indeed, for the four customers who were wandering, looking bored, down the length of the cases, guessing at the prices out loud, and clearly not about to buy anything. The staff had reached the same conclusion, apparently, since nobody was offering to help them; there were four women and two men, and they were all standing around looking bored.

The place has the atmosphere of a library, Sophie thought. There was the Massot logo, a gold eagle holding a diamond in one claw, painted on a beige background on the walls and stamped into the matching colour of the carpet. It was an uninspired pattern. Today was Thursday; she would have hoped for more of a crowd.

It occurred to Sophie that if the best first impression was merely 'nothing wrong' then, of course, everything was wrong.

She walked in through the doorway and headed for one of the cases. The display ran the length of the showroom, one case on each wall; pieces were grouped by type. The first case was of rings. That made sense; rings were always the greatest sellers, followed by earrings.

'Can I help you, madame?'

Sophie looked up. A young woman had sauntered over, and was giving her a perfunctory smile. At least she offered to assist me, Sophie thought. But she was not about to give her any prizes; Sophie Massot knew perfectly well that her manner of dress exuded money. In any shop she entered, the assistants rushed to serve her.

'I'm just looking, at present,' she said.

'But of course, madame,' said the girl, distantly. As she walked away, Sophie examined her. She was wearing a plain white blouse and navy skirt, tights and pumps; but the top button on her blouse was frayed, and there was a dusty smudge on the waistband of the skirt. The display case hid her legs, or Sophie would have looked for ladders in her tights.

Angered, she glanced down at the merchandise, and softened a little. Yes, the pieces were very fine, still. This side of the case was obviously the cheaper rings; smaller stones, less ornamentation. Nevertheless, each piece was beautiful. Massot used good stones, nothing worse than very slightly included diamonds, and each coloured gem had to be translucent. Sophie admired the stock. Their cutters still used the more expensive methods; old mine-cut and rose-cut diamonds; and there were unusual designs on the shanks, engravings of leaves, and serpents.

Not that you could pick much of it out. The beige velvet of

the background did not show off the stones; there was no light on them to make them sparkle, and too many pieces, too close. To someone less interested than she, Sophie knew, they would all blend into one; a pretty, glittering blur, but nothing remarkable; no single jewel would stay with you.

She moved on round the room, methodically examining each case. Bracelets; earrings; brooches; necklaces; even a few tiaras. House Massot did not go in for anything else. There were no anklets, no toe rings, nothing indecorous. But the stock there was glorious, things she would have worn with delight – but everywhere shown to least advantage.

Sophie lifted her head from the last case, containing a set of very beautiful fire opal and orange zircon necklaces, bold and imaginative pieces all jumbled together, and dull against the beige. She would have chosen a dark green damask to set off so much fire. She looked around the showroom. The four window-shoppers had left, and it was now completely empty.

Sophie regarded the small knot of staff evenly. They were now chatting with each other, ignoring her. Sophie noted sloppiness of dress in each of them: the men had ties loose, or not even present; one of the women had on too much make-up, and another had straggly hair . . .

The door to rue Faubourg opened and a young woman came in. She was wearing a Burberry coat, and Sophie could see a flash of neat tights – no ladders – and smart blue leather heels. She walked straight into the back, and re-emerged a second later. Sophie watched as she marched up to the other staff and said something sharp in a low tone, nodding towards Sophie. The first girl responded – rudely, from her manner – and then the young woman, smoothing down her dress, hurried out from behind the counter to Sophie.

She was a brunette, and younger than the rest; Sophie judged her age to be no more than twenty-three. She was wearing an inexpensive but serviceable blue dress, a modest sheath, with a crisp plain cardigan, and basic make-up; Sophie caught a hint of Chanel No. 5.

'Pardon me, madame,' said the girl with a bright smile, 'but are you being assisted?'

131

Sophie shook her head. 'It is a little late for you to be coming into work, isn't it?'

She could see the question had thrown the young woman, but after a second's pause she responded politely, 'Yes, madame; I do apologise. There was an accident on the metro and our train was delayed. Madame is right, of course; the staff should be present when customers are here.'

Sophie smiled warmly. Her manner, as well as her dress, was a million miles from that of her colleagues.

'I was looking for a pair of earrings,' she said. 'What do you recommend?'

The girl stepped back slightly and looked earnestly at Sophie, studying her face for a brief second.

'You have an oval face and a pale complexion, madame. Most stones will look good against your skin; you can certainly wear longer earrings, and for evening I would recommend them. We have some beautiful things I believe would suit you; but not everything we carry will complement you so well; some of the bolder choices that mix primary colours would not suit your style, I believe.'

'Why don't you show me,' Sophie said, neutrally.

The girl led her back to the earrings case, opened it up, and selected five or six pieces, all choices Sophie might have made herself; cornflower-blue sapphires, teardrops of pure gold, dangling lines of cabochon emeralds and peridot, angular shapes in mother-of-pearl. She displayed them reverently, described the stones and the workmanship.

'Very lovely, but I don't think these are for me,' Sophie said.

'If budget is a problem, madame, I can suggest some different pairs; not made with the same gems, but they would look equally lovely against your neck.'

'I'm not in the mood to shop today,' Sophie said.

The girl's politeness did not vary for an instant. 'Very good, madame; I hope you will return soon and permit me to show you some more pieces. It has been a pleasure to serve you.'

Sophie glanced at the girl's colleagues. They were lounging against the wall, watching her with expressions that ranged from amusement to contempt.

132

'Thank you, mademoiselle; you have been most helpful,' she said to her. 'Tell me, have you worked at House Massot long?'

'No, madame; just these six months.'

'You seem to have a great appreciation for jewellery – what is your name?'

'Claudette, madame; yes – I love it,' she said passionately. 'It is a most beautiful art form, and one in danger of being forgotten – amongst all the flashy things.'

Sophie sighed with pleasure. At least, then, she would have somewhere to start with.

'Claudette,' she said, 'I am promoting you to manager of this store. I am Sophie Massot, Chairman of the Board of House Massot.'

Claudette's eyes widened, but she was too shocked to say anything.

'What is your current salary?'

'Eighteen thousand euros, madame,' Claudette whispered.

'That's all?' No wonder we cannot attract serious staff, Sophie thought. 'Well, as of now, it is forty thousand euros.'

Claudette swallowed hard.

'Your first task as manager will be to let go the other staff.'

'All of them?'

'All of them,' Sophie said implacably. 'Do you not see how they are dressed, mademoiselle? House Massot sells pieces aimed at very rich women. They are used to being served by people who take pride in both their work and their appearance. When one is selling fine gems, the two things go together, don't you think?'

Claudette nodded.

'But, madame, who will run the place?'

'You're in charge,' Sophie said. 'Don't you have any ideas?'

'Actually, I do. There are some staff in the other stores who think as you do, madame. Maybe too many staff . . . you could take the best ones and dismiss the rest, and you would still have enough in each showroom, I think, for the current volume of customers . . .'

The store was empty; nobody had entered in the last quarter of an hour.

'Delicately put,' Sophie said with a smile. 'There will be changes coming, Claudette; plenty of them.'

The girl glanced back at the others, who were now openly staring at them, expressions hostile.

'But what shall I say is the reason for their dismissal?'

'You could always try the truth,' Sophie said. 'Inappropriate dress, inattentiveness to customers, socialising on company time. You can handle it, can't you?'

Claudette looked at the group again, and gave a small, resolute toss of her head.

'Oh yes, madame,' she said. 'Certainly.'

Richard dropped Sophie off at rue Tricot an hour later. She had anticipated Claudette and visited all the Massot stores herself; besides, although she had confidence in the girl, Sophie was in no mood to trust anyone.

It was not that surprising to find it the same story every-where. Exceptional jewels displayed, and served, with a sloppiness of presentation, and a lack of enthusiasm, that was simply breathtaking. They were either empty of customers, or contained the barest trickle. Sophie wondered how they stayed profitable. Presumably the prices were so high that a very few sales could keep the stores afloat.

But a 9 per cent rise in the stock . . .

Ideas came to her so thick and fast that she felt almost overcome. Sophie's throat rose with tears of embarrassment. She was bitterly ashamed of herself. There were such basic questions, questions she had not thought to ask before. She had been blinded by Gregoire's smile and dancing eyes. As she arrived at the offices, she resolved instantly to put a stop to it all. But there was fear, too; of him, and his reaction, and of what she might find, once she started to dig.

The vast majority of their family wealth, Tom's money, was bound up in this company's stock. It was his inheritance. And more than money, it was a name. She knew what it would mean to her son to see House Massot destroyed. Hugh

Montfort, the threat from outside, was still there; but before she could think of a defence, there was the danger from within.

Last time she had arrived here, Sophie saw now, it had been a charade. An expensive, shameful charade. A dreadful calm descended over her. For that, she had nobody to blame; neither Gregoire Lazard nor lazy shop assistants; for that, she could blame only herself.

Well; she had promised Claudette that things were going to change. No time like the present. She told Richard to park the car, and walked into her husband's offices.

Chapter Eighteen

'Nothing but a diamond can scratch or cut a diamond,' the children chorused. 'Because a diamond is the hardest thing known.'

Vladek was silent; he sat in his thin, rag-like clothes and stared at the book.

'Vladek, I don't hear you.' The teacher, Mr Kovec, was angry. 'You don't join the class. Do you understand?'

The boy lifted his head and stared back, impassively.

'I understand perfectly, sir.'

'Then you are insolent.' Kovec couldn't stand Vladek. Skinnier than most of these little brutes, he had those dark, brooding eyes that disturbed the older man. Most of the orphans were easy to manage; they cowered in fear, or fawned, in the hope of an extra scrap of food or clothing. They never answered back and knew their betters. In time they would grow up and be given jobs by the state – the boys, at least; the girls would try desperately to marry, or fall into begging and prostitution. And the orphanage was so poorly heated, at least a handful did not survive each winter.

Kovec, a Pole who had taught in this place for fourteen years, had initially felt some guilt. And then, to relieve himself of the guilt, he discovered anger – which was much easier to handle. And vodka. Now there was a bully's casual cruelty in everything he did. Once a bright man with a future in Warsaw, he had crossed a Party apparatchik and been exiled to this hell-hole. Unable to take it out on anybody else, he made sure he shared his misery with the children.

Vladek most of all. First, someone had dared to give this

little Russian bastard a good Polish name. Second, Vladek was strange. He could not be cowed. He seemed to live in a world of his own. There was a hard shell about him that no amount of physical pain could crack.

But Kovec liked to try.

'Get up here,' he snarled. 'Put out your palm.'

Some of the children winced. One little girl whimpered – Kovec glared at her, and she subsided. A few of the larger boys jeered. Like any prison, there was a hierarchy in here, and the rules were strictly enforced. Yet Vladek refused to go along with them. He kept to himself, and the playground thugs, unsettled by his large eyes and fixed stare, left him alone.

Kovec reached behind him and took out the larger of his two rulers. He hit it menacingly hard, on the desk.

Vladek slipped out from his chair and came up to the front of the room. He didn't say a word; he merely extended his little palm.

Kovec felt a momentary pang of shame. But he ignored it. He slammed the ruler down, hard, on the boy's open hand. A white pressure mark appeared on the palm, to be replaced by a red welt. Viciously, Kovec hit him twice more.

He was about to tell Vladek to extend his other palm, but then his eyes met the boy's.

Vladek was staring at him. The hate was to be expected. But there was something else in those eyes. Something so cold, so terrible, that Kovec physically flinched. The evil eye – that was something they still believed in, in the East, when the fires sunk low in the evenings.

'You may return to your seat,' Kovec blustered, to cover himself. 'I hope you've learned your lesson, Vladek.'

The boy sat down again, but did not reply.

'Tell me about diamonds,' his teacher said.

'Nothing but a diamond can scratch or cut a diamond, because a diamond is the hardest thing known.'

'Yes. And what else do you know?'

Mother Russia was not very good at providing warmth, or food, or medicine. But knowledge – she offered that, and lots of it, to her children. And Kovec had an inkling that the boy Vladek was highly intelligent.

'They are made of carbon; coal, under great pressure. They are cut from rough. They are very beautiful.' The seven-year-old was solemn. Kovec glanced at his hand; it was swollen from the beating, yet the child acted as if nothing had happened; his young voice did not quiver or shake. 'Rich people own them.'

'Yes.'

'And when I am grown I will have many diamonds,' Vladek said.

The class erupted with laughter and derision.

'Get something straight, boy. You're a penniless orphan, a bastard. Your parents didn't want you. Same as all the children in here. You need to get your head out of the clouds and understand reality. You'll be a working man – if you're lucky.' Kovec turned his head and spat into the waste-paper basket. 'Most likely you'll wind up a drunk or a beggar. With that attitude of yours.'

The boy gave him a contemptuous smile. Kovec pretended not to see it. He would beat Vladek another time. For now, he just wanted to move on.

The kid was a creep.

Chapter Nineteen

'Gregoire,' Judy said.

He did not look up from his desk, which annoyed her. Judy thought she'd spoken pleasantly enough. She cleared her throat.

'Gregoire – excuse me.'

'Yes? What is it?' he asked irritably.

Instantly she was enraged. How dare he act irritated? He was the one at fault, here. She bit her lip to stop from snapping at him. Dealing with obnoxious people was one of Judy's key strengths. I will not let him overthrow my composure, she thought.

She pressed her hands to the side of her new suit. Chanel; real Chanel, yellow tweed, two inches off the knee and fitted to her slender body like a calfskin glove. It had cost more than she wanted to think about, but it was a celebration of her new pay cheque.

Judy had felt that she could afford it, and she'd bought it. It was a fabulous feeling, to be wearing something as fine as anything Pierre's placid widow would have hanging in her expensive closets.

'I'm so sorry to bother you,' she lied, 'but there seems to have been a slight problem.' She gave him her most winsome smile. 'My new raise – the two hundred thousand you promised me – it hasn't come through.'

'What?' Lazard demanded. He was staring into space, tapping a pencil smartly against the side of his desk. The sound was most irritating.

'My money isn't there,' Judy repeated, more directly. 'My last pay cheque – there was no difference.'

'These things take time,' Lazard said distantly.

Judy smiled briskly; she was not about to be put off.

'Not if they come from the chief executive,' she said. 'You only need to say the word.'

He dragged his eyes to her, as though reluctantly; the prettiness of the suit, and aptness of the matching enamel daisy earrings, apparently lost on him.

'Later, madame,' he said.

'I understand your busy schedule,' Judy said, doggedly. 'So I've taken the trouble to prepare this for you.' She presented him with a neatly typed company memo, authorising her raise in salary – two hundred thousand euros to VP Judy Dean, effective immediately. There was even a little dotted line. 'If you'll just sign there,' she said. She offered him, uncapped and ready to go, her own pen.

'*Sliuha*!' Lazard exploded.

Judy drew back. Her French was good, but that wasn't French. It wasn't welcome, either.

'You think to crowd me – you women!'

The fair eyebrows knitted above his pale blue eyes. There was threat in them, and Judy shrank back. She had good instincts, and snatched up the memo before he could destroy it.

'I'm sorry,' she said quicky. 'It doesn't matter – I'll come back another time.'

She retreated at once, thinking, with a queasy feeling in her stomach, of her groaning credit cards. The repayments alone were going to be difficult; if he did not come through she would have to call the bank . . .

But he would come through. Calm yourself, Judy thought. He wants you to get close to Sophie . . . he wants you for that . . .

She had been overwhelmed the last few days. Giles Keroualle, with his elegant, disdainful air, had returned from New York – without good news on the collections – and demanded updates on all her work. And she had had the trouble, although welcome, of moving from the top-floor windowless cubicle back to her own office.

There had been no time to call Sophie. And Lazard was no longer right next to her. Maybe that was the trouble; out of sight, out of mind . . .

Judy returned to her desk. Even the admiring looks of the secretaries, all Marie's friends, at her chic flash of yellow and white did not console her. Gregoire's rage was unexpected, and had left her shaky. Angry, but also fearful. Her connection with him had been all her hope of breaking out of this rut. She couldn't afford to upset him.

A nasty idea occurred to her. What if Sophie Massot left, Gregoire lost his connection with her, she returned down here, and it was as if the last month had never happened? She would be back, writing press releases, keeping her head down . . . but this time with more debts, and no hope of promotion.

It hadn't just been the suit. Judy had upgraded her life to the woman of consequence she'd felt she had become. There was a gorgeous, fast little car – a Porsche Boxster in Lagoon Green. And she had purchased an investment piece, a pendant shaped like a peacock feather; twenty-two-carat gold, sapphires, rubies, emeralds and lapis. Something she had seen in the rue Faubourg store over five years ago, and had always coveted; but she had passed it by because she could not afford it . . .

Now it was hanging in her leather-lined jewellery case; but apparently she still could not afford it.

Judy thought of the repayments on her present salary, and paled. Maybe she should return it. Say she'd changed her mind . . .

Tears came to her eyes and she flushed with shame. Return it? They would all know the real reason why, those snobby bitches in the showroom. No; she could not bear the shame. She would have to find a way, somehow.

Sucking up to Gregoire Lazard, she understood with a sinking heart, was still her first, best hope.

But somehow she no longer felt confident he was her ally. He seemed totally preoccupied.

Once again, Judy Dean was on her own.

It was just before lunchtime when she looked up from the papers on her desk; the latest slew of magazine clippings, few of them good.

Marie was standing in the corridor, giggling with Françoise Delmain, M. Keroualle's assistant. She had hushed her voice, and the two of them kept glancing back towards Judy's office. They were whispering animatedly.

Judy put her head down again, a dull glow on her cheeks, as she considered her options. Goddam Marie. She had shut the door to Lazard's office, but what if Marie had been listening in? Or what if it was too loud anyway, and her secretary had overheard?

Confront them? No; that would make it so much worse. Judy imagined being exposed to whispers and giggles wherever she went. Anger at Lazard bubbled up in her. He had humiliated her, exposed her to this . . .

Judy stood up. Marie wears a plain brown dress and carries a cheap bag, she reminded herself. Let them giggle away, I'm the most senior woman in this company. Marie doesn't have enough ambition to fill an egg-cup. She'll never be anything, and I'm going to make it.

She put on her brightest, happiest smile and walked out into the corridor.

'It's a great morning, isn't it, ladies?' she said sweetly to Marie and Françoise. They had returned to French, and Judy's French was accentless, whereas their English sounded Gallic. She enjoyed this small demonstration of skill, especially while they were laughing at her. 'Marie – can you cover my calls? I think I may step out to lunch. I'm in the mood for a croque monsieur.'

This was a joke, and they all knew it; one did not maintain a figure like Judy's on ham and melted cheese.

'Of course, madame,' said Marie humbly. It didn't fool Judy for a second. Instantly she assumed her carpeting upstairs, had indeed been overheard. High spots of colour returned to her cheeks, but she smiled as though nothing had happened.

'Excuse me, madame,' said Françoise pertly. 'But don't you think you should wait, given what has happened?'

Judy squared her shoulders, feeling the silk lining of her beautiful suit move against her toned skin.

'And what, exactly, has happened, Françoise?' she asked ominously, daring the other woman to be open.

'Why, madame.' Françoise rounded her heavily lacquered eyes with exaggerated innocence. 'Have you not heard? Mme Sophie has returned to the office.'

Work was impossible, of course. Judy, after a request for coffee, which they saw as the feeble grab for composure it was, retreated to her office. She felt light-headed, dizzy; as though she could hardly breathe. She was not safe. It was not over. Pierre's wife had changed her mind. She would be here permanently, interfering with Judy.

I'll never get that money, not if she stays, Judy thought, bitterly. It was too much of a jump. Mme Massot would query the expenditure . . .

She thought of Pierre, with a momentary flash of hatred.

How dare you go, she thought. How dare you go and leave me with her? And then a few seconds later, she felt the old, almost forgotten wail, a keen in the depths of her soul; why her? Why would you choose her, and not me? I loved you, loved, loved you . . .

There was a knock on her door.

'Your coffee, madame.'

Judy forced herself to smile; though it felt like a rictus grin.

'Thank you, Marie,' she said, switching back to English. 'That smells heavenly.'

'Shall I prepare to have our things moved again?'

'Has Mme Massot instructed us to move?' Judy asked calmly, and then when Marie shook her head, she added, 'So we will wait for her.'

'Yes, madame,' Marie said, her plump body tense with the deliciousness of renewed scandal.

'Find out if Mme Massot is available, would you?' Judy asked brightly. She would take the only course of action open to her; she would meet this head-on. 'I want to introduce her to M. Keroualle, now he is returned. She'll want to know every member of this department.'

'Yes, madame,' Marie said. She stared at Judy, slightly puzzled, which Judy took as a great triumph. No; she would rip out her newly manicured nails before she would cry in front of any of them.

A second later Marie buzzed through on Judy's phone.

'Mme Massot cannot be found at present, madame – she is in with M. Lazard.'

Judy heard only the excitement in her assistant's tone.

'Come in here a second, Marie.'

When she appeared, the older woman was fidgeting; almost bursting with secrets she wanted to spill. Judy didn't need prompting. She made herself smile conspiratorially.

'Something is happening up there?'

'Oh – Hélène Facteur told me, madame – there is shouting.'

'Shouting?'

'From M. Lazard's office,' said Marie, dropping her voice to a whisper.

Judy hadn't expected that. She shivered with excitement herself. And fear; something was happening – whatever it was, she sensed at once that it would mean a fresh chance for her.

'Who is doing the shouting?' she whispered back.

'Madame and Monsieur,' Marie said. 'It is very loud,' she added.

Judy leaned back. 'Very exciting, but keep it to yourself, Marie. We mustn't gossip.'

'Of course not, madame,' said Marie, as complacent as Judy about the hypocrisy. She withdrew, and Judy spun her chair to face her window. Her heart was thumping in her chest. What could it mean?

And more importantly, how could she use it?

Well, fortune favours the brave. Her daddy had always said that, back in Oklahoma, and Judy had believed it – enough to travel to New York City, and then to take a job in Paris; trust in that motto, she thought, was why she was wearing Chanel right now, instead of worn-out duds in some worn-out farm town.

She stood up. She was going upstairs.

A few moments later, the elevator doors opened and Judy strode out. The employees in their cubicles all had their heads down, and were tapping at keyboards or shuffling papers; an attempt not to be noticed. But they were worker bees. Judy was not.

She heard the rage long before she got to Lazard's office. Sophie, despite Marie's report, was not shouting. Judy could hear her tones, low and clear. Gregoire was doing the shouting; and he was very loud indeed.

Judy thought, I will knock on the door, and attempt to make peace. They will both be grateful . . .

But as she got to within a few steps of Gregoire's door, it was wrenched open. Judy halted, shrank back. Sophie was standing by the window, rigid and pale; Judy noted her knuckles were white as she gripped the top of Gregoire's chair. Gregoire himself stormed out, his fair skin flushed with anger, his eyes blazing.

He turned round towards Sophie, and said, in rapid-fire French, 'You will be hearing from my lawyers.'

Sophie Massot inclined her head very slightly, then her grey eyes were trained on Judy, who had flinched away from the towering anger of her boss.

'Judy, good to see you,' Sophie said coolly. 'Come in, please.'

Lazard looked at Judy, as though noticing her for the first time, then looked back to Sophie, and cackled. '*Sliuha*,' he said. 'Very good – the two friends.'

'I am quite prepared to call security,' Sophie told him calmly. 'Leave now, monsieur; your services are no longer required.'

'We'll see,' Lazard responded. But he turned on his heel, stiffly, and marched to the stairway.

The worker pool watched him go in total silence.

'Come in to . . . *my* office, please, Judy, and shut the door,' Sophie Massot said calmly.

Judy shivered a little; had Sophie found out? But there was

145

nothing for it except to do as she was told. She lifted her chin, and walked boldly into the room, closing the door firmly behind her.

As soon as the door shut, Sophie Massot said, in a newly shaky voice, 'Dear Judy, I'm so glad you're here.'

Then she burst into tears.

Judy rushed towards her. She felt a mixture of emotions, not all of them pleasant. So Sophie had fired Gregoire – good; and trusted her – better; and yet, as much as she loathed the woman, it was hard not to feel sympathy for somebody who was actually crying.

'Sophie – don't cry. Look, here's a handkerchief.' She unclipped her bag and drew forth one of her neat little squares, crisp white Irish cotton.

'Thank you,' Sophie sobbed.

Stop the goddam crying, Judy thought fiercely. I don't need to feel anything for *you*. She reminded herself it was a knee-jerk reaction. Judy steeled her heart against further compassion. This woman was the reason, she believed, that Pierre had never married her, had always had to leave her every night; the reason Judy got little gifts of holidays, instead of his arms around her; the reason she spent Christmas by herself.

'I've been so stupid,' Sophie said, gulping for air.

Judy wasn't about to disagree.

'Sit down,' she said, pulling Gregoire's chair out, solicitously.

'Thank you.' Sophie dabbed at her eyes, struggling for, and achieving, a measure of control. She waved Judy to the Eames chair in front of the desk. 'You too.'

Judy sat, obediently. 'Do you want to talk about it?'

Sophie looked at her; reddened eyes, but with a directness that made the younger woman uncomfortable.

'Do you think I did wrong to fire Gregoire? You seemed devoted to him.'

Judy paused. The baseball fan in her immediately tagged this a 'fast ball', but Judy was ready for every pitch.

'I believed he worked very hard . . . I told you he was always in the office,' she said humbly. 'And that's true, but of course,

I don't know what he did there. I just handle PR.' She gave an expressive shrug. 'From where I was sitting he seemed devoted to the company. Was I wrong? I trusted him.'

Sophie nodded. 'So did I; I've been a fool.'

Judy decided to gamble, again. She put her cropped head down, humbly, and summoned up a thickness in her throat.

'But I've been working here for years. I should have seen it,' she said. 'You'll want my resignation. I'll bring it up to your desk right away.'

'Resignation? Oh, no – there's no call for that – that's not what I meant,' Sophie said, quickly. 'You were loyal – I admire loyalty.'

'Has he been embezzling money?' Judy asked. She did not have to fake interest in that.

Sophie sighed. 'Nothing so dramatic. I made a few calls from my car before I got here today – calls I ought to have made months ago.' Judy saw the other woman flush with embarrassment. 'First, I rang my broker. Well, Pierre's broker,' she added with a little self-deprecating laugh. 'I never did much stock trading . . .'

Judy was almost relieved to find the black hatred bubble up in her again as Sophie spoke. The mention of the little things they shared together, husband and wife, hurt as much as the platinum wedding band on Sophie's left hand. Stockbrokers; physicians; even a fax machine. She had an immediate flashback of the time she had seen a fax she'd sent to Pierre at the château, printed off, in Sophie's in-tray; the computer lettering on the top saying *Monsieur et Madame Massot*. The pain, then, had been as keen as a knife. Now, it was just a dull ache. She hated Sophie for that, too; without Pierre, her heart had hardened.

'It's true that the company stock has risen nine per cent. But what I did not understand was that the *sector* has risen over twenty-five per cent. It's not a gain; it's a substantial loss. My son's inheritance has suffered.'

Judy tried to look sympathetic. Poor young Massot heir, now only worth thirty million when it could have been fifty. That'll break your heart every time, she thought.

Sophie was making it easy.

'My second call was to our Human Resources department. Do you have any idea how much Gregoire, and the other directors, were paying themselves?'

Fascinated, Judy shook her head.

'He took home a million a year,' she said. 'So did each of the others, who sat there and presided over the decline of the House. And I asked about perks.'

Judy had a sick feeling in her stomach. A million euros. Every year.

'What perks?' she whispered.

'Cars and drivers, twenty-four hours a day, all year long; rides on private jets; art – at company expense; maids; a cook – for each of them; vacations for "research".'

Sophie smiled bitterly. 'Do you know of a large jewellery market in Mauritius, Judy?'

Judy shook her head, not trusting herself to speak.

'Nor do I. Why, the perks alone for each one of them came to a great deal more than your annual salary. Almost double it, in fact.'

Judy breathed in, raggedly.

'Are you all right?' Sophie asked, with concern.

'I'm fine,' Judy managed, although her heart was thumping. 'Fine . . .'

She felt light-headed with sheer fury. So Lazard, and the useless shower of board directors who never showed their faces, never attended a show . . . they had gotten millions – perks worth double her salary . . .

Judy had worked, doggedly, for years; fifteen long years at this company; and what she had to show for it was a flat, a modest savings account, and a few good jewels; nothing. That was what her life was worth, apparently; nothing. It cost a lot of money to look this good. Judy's salary went on memberships to the best gyms, chic outfits, the nicest bags, the must-have make-up; things that changed every season, cost the earth, and wound up fit only for donation to a charity shop.

Style was costly.

She thought of her longing for the Senior Vice-Presidency and a raise to two hundred, maybe two fifty . . .

How Gregoire Lazard must have laughed. Chump change, for a chump. And then he hadn't even authorised it. Couldn't be bothered to put down one stroke of the pen she had offered him.

'Don't worry, Judy,' Sophie said earnestly to her. 'We are going to start afresh – change things round here. I know you – I trust you. I've already reviewed your personnel records.'

Judy experienced a fresh thrill of dislike. The thought of Sophie Massot combing through her files, checking up to see if she'd been a good girl. It was insupportable. She consoled herself with the fact that Personnel would never have dared to include the most important detail: the love of Pierre Massot.

And it had been love, she told herself defiantly; even if she had shared him, shared the sex of him, it had been love, a certain species of love. Passion. Something Mme Massot, she could instantly tell, knew nothing at all about . . .

Gregoire; the directors; Sophic; Judy hated them all. She had been grubbing away for so many years, for nothing, while they lazed around with everything. It was indeed time for a change. It was time for Judy Dean to get something for herself, for once; a real slice of the action. She wasn't in this for Sophie, or Gregoire, or any of them; not now. Judy was in it for herself.

She smiled brightly. 'I'm glad,' she said. 'I think there are ways I can help.'

Chapter Twenty

'It's great to meet you.'

Edgar Lowell shook Hugh's hand with a firm grip. He nodded politely.

'And my partners, Karl Epstein and Willoughby Strachan.'

'How do you do,' Montfort replied.

He was standing in the conference room of Lowell Epstein, one of America's newest investment banks. Despite this fact, and the secondary fact that they operated out of Boston, instead of the centre of the world, New York, the room radiated confidence. It had cost a lot of money to bring antique oak panelling to the walls of these offices, located on the sixty-second floor of a brand new skyscraper; the carpet was overlaid with an Aubusson rug, there was a Turner hanging in the corridor outside, the secretaries all wore Donna Karan, everywhere he turned was the quiet, reassuring hush of money, and lots of it.

'Where's the head of your M & A department?' Montfort asked, once they had waved him to a seat. Mergers and Acquisitions, the lifeblood of big Wall Street deals. House Massot would be both.

'That's Jake Feingold.'

'Great guy.'

'He'll be along in just a moment.'

'We wanted to take a few minutes to get to know you ourselves,' Lowell concluded.

Montfort smiled thinly; he had not come here for chit-chat.

'It's amazing to meet the Boy Wonder,' Karl Epstein said. 'That's what they call you, yes?'

'The press can say foolish things,' Montfort agreed calmly.

He hated that epithet. But it was better than the first, the Axe Man. The business press gossip columns had christened him that when he'd first arrived at Mayberry, and had immediately laid off over 30 per cent of the workforce. The company was insanely over-manned then, and he had not regretted it. Neither had he regretted closing ten money-sucking stores.

In time, of course, with greater success, they had expanded. He had created three times as many jobs as he had cut. That was natural market economics.

It had not stopped him being hated.

Even with the success, the new jobs, the publicity for British design, few outside his company regarded Hugh Montfort with any affection. He knew it, and did not care. The soubriquet 'Boy Wonder' conveyed it exactly; a calculated mixture of admiration and contempt.

'You know, apart from the financials, we think this is a perfect deal,' Edgar Lowell said. He was fifty, perhaps; a Boston Brahmin, pale-skinned and weak-chinned, no trace of the regional accent. 'Massot is over, but perhaps you can make something of it. I used to buy Massot jewels for my wife.'

'And Mayberry ones for your girlfriend,' Strachan cackled. He was fleshy, and Montfort had heard tales of dissipation; a paler version of Pete, then.

'I am only interested in expanding our brand. This deal is about logistics and supply; Massot has them, we need them,' Montfort said coolly.

'I'm sure we can structure something of interest to the shareholders,' Karl Epstein said. He was bookish, and the man Montfort preferred to deal with.

'It needs to be more than of interest; it needs to be unmissable. There is only fifty-five per cent floating out there. I need everyone. Every institution, fund manager, individual holder. I need them all.'

Hugh Montfort held the eyes of all three of them.

'There is no room for mistakes,' he said. 'If your bank wants this business, you will be exposed; the press will be watching. The consequences of failure will be as bad for you as for us.'

Willoughby Strachan felt himself begin to sweat. The limey was threatening them. It was a powerful threat, too. As a new bank, hoping to attract M & A business, they simply could not afford to fail in public. But the rewards of masterminding such a high-profile takeover . . .

He thought of his personal stockholdings.

Strachan was driven by the two gods of the market; fear and greed. The Englishman with the hard jaw and uncompromising manner apparently knew this.

They were being played; and yet he could not, they would not, say no.

'There won't be any failures, Mr Montfort,' he said, resenting him. 'Let me call our deal team in.'

Hugh Montfort sat back against the burgundy leather of his chair.

'What a good idea,' he said.

The meetings took all day, and when he was finished, he went back to the hotel. The Boston Hotel was the finest in the city, and provided, amongst the many amenities of his splendid rooms, a comprehensive guidebook; entertainment choices in one of the oldest cities in America. He could have attended the theatre, concerts, a fine Museum of the Revolutionary War, had he chosen to have his face rubbed in it. Or sports; Boston had prominent teams in basketball and baseball. His taxi's radio had announced the presence of the New York Yankees at Boston Stadium, and the callers were full of excitement and bile; it was the oldest rivalry in American sports.

It might have tempted him under other circumstances. Hugh took frequent trips to the States on business, and he had, from long stays in hotels, begun to watch baseball; it seemed preferable to the news, which was depressing, and mostly, to him, irrelevant. He was rather surprised to find he loved the game. It was far faster than cricket, and very strategic; the pitcher and batter engaged, if it was a close contest, in a sort of mental chess.

Hugh had begun to follow the sport from a distance. Boston boasted the most passionate fans in the country; even though they kept losing, they just loved the team all the more. The Yankees, on the other hand, kept winning; and both teams hated each other. This year's Boston Red Sox were unusually strong. It would be an excellent game, and the concierge could have managed a box, given enough money.

But he knew perfectly well he would not be watching a floodlit baseball diamond tonight.

Tonight he was going to have a woman.

Hugh inventoried his feelings, as he always did. Excitement; need; disgust. His conscience putting up its usual feeble struggle. You shouldn't do it . . . you're no better than Pete . . . this is beneath you . . . you'll hate yourself tomorrow . . .

His body replying in kind, to every such objection. Yes – so what?

Hugh grit his teeth and headed into the bathroom. He would shower and change, sometimes that diminished the urge.

Not tonight, though. He enjoyed the sensations, but the temptation was too urgent. He was ashamed of himself, but made excuses; you fought it for so long . . . for weeks . . . you can't help yourself . . . nobody's perfect.

He swathed himself in the voluminous white bathrobe they provided and removed his address book. The number for Boston was listed, like the rest of them, under a single name – Karen.

He summoned her from memory. Karen; she was the brunette, the former Miss Wisconsin. Five-eight, about a hundred thirty-five pounds, her breasts were real, although he thought she might have had them lifted. She was thirty-four – he never saw a girl under thirty – and lived in a luxurious condo on Columbus Avenue; a full service, doorman building, the kind that comes with its own pool and health spa. Karen told him she owned the condo herself, which meant she was relatively affluent; that she'd be getting out of the life shortly.

All these things reduced his guilt. The women he picked were never too young, nor too poor; Montfort hated to think of the girls as vulnerable.

But of course it was all a joke. They did it because they needed to. Possibly this girl had debts; gambled, most likely, did cocaine. He picked the ones who at least didn't seem to be hurt, but it was the same as adding diet gin to your tonic. Well and good, but in the end, just window dressing.

His pulse quickened as her telephone started to ring. Maybe she wouldn't be there, and the need would be ignored, this time, because he had no choice.

'Hello?'

She was there. Hugh sighed inwardly.

'Karen? This is Hugh Montfort.'

'Baby.' He could hear the smile in her voice, and no wonder. He never asked what the girls charged; he left an envelope with a thousand dollars on the bed once he was finished.

'Are you free this evening?'

Memories started to crowd him now; the hollow in her long neck, the scent of her expensive shampoo; her white, straight teeth, eyes brightened by drops; the carefully toned body.

'Nothing I can't get out of,' she said.

'I'd like to drop by now.'

'Fine by me, sugar.' Karen purred into the phone; he remembered her as like a cat, sleek and sinewy. 'You sound tense. Maybe we should start with a massage. I have all these different oils . . .'

Montfort stood up. 'I'll be there in ten minutes.'

'You can't stay?'

Hugh looked over his shoulder at the girl, lying naked and unembarrassed in the middle of her satin sheets, her eyes, a kind of muddy green, flickering appreciatively over the taut muscles of his body, the scar along his back. She didn't ask about the scar, being sensitised to Hugh, which was half, more than half of what made a good hooker. But he knew it turned her on; when she was bucking underneath him, her fingernails always went there, scratching, tracing the line.

'I'm sorry, I can't.' He continued to button his shirt.

'That's a pity.' She stretched luxuriantly, arching her back;

displaying herself for him. 'I could give you another hour, two even. No charge.'

He shook his head. 'Sorry.'

'Don't look so depressed, sweetie,' she said, with a slight touch of annoyance. 'Nobody died.'

Montfort wondered if that was true. Afterwards, he felt as though something had died. Pride, perhaps, or hope. Just a little, every time; death by inches.

Karen's condo had floor-to-ceiling windows with a fabulous view of downtown Boston; the skyscrapers jabbing upwards, silhouetted by neon against the night sky; many windows still ablaze; like all American cities, it didn't sleep.

He dressed quickly, but still neatly. Montfort had a soldier's habit about that. His bed was always perfectly made, his shoes always gleamed.

'Don't be such a stranger the next time,' the girl said. 'You're always so long between visits.'

She used a kind of diction that made him imagine this was rote; her customary send off. He reached into his jacket pocket and removed the envelope, laying it gently on the bed beside her.

She received it with a gracious nod of the head. 'Thanks much, hon.'

'Thank you,' he said, politely. 'Have a good evening, Karen. See you next time.'

'Hey – it was fun.' She lay there and looked up at him, and a slight gleam entered her eyes. 'I get a lot, and you're one of the best.'

'Thanks,' he muttered.

'We could try some other stuff next time you're here. Dress-up, maybe. Or toys . . . you ever used props? I got friends, too. Girls, boys . . .' she shrugged. 'I guess just girls, for you . . .'

Hugh shook his head, mutely. He felt the embarrassment as hot over his body as the need for her had been hour before.

'You're great, baby. Imagine if you loosened up.' She sighed. 'You're so vanilla.'

'I have to go,' he said, and let himself out, as fast as he could manage it.

155

As he stood waiting for the elevator, he thought he heard her laughing, back in the apartment; yes, she was definitely laughing. But it didn't sound amused, it sounded bitter. They were sometimes like that, particularly when the sex had been especially athletic, or passionate. Because no matter what happened in bed, he was up and dressing seconds after he had finished. It offended some of the girls; too brutally honest, perhaps, about the transaction.

Karen had revenged herself nicely, though, if that had been her intent. Talk of sex toys and other girls – *boys* – dressing up . . .

Because it was just sex, wasn't it? Any kind of friction or titillation, she didn't care; and she didn't see why he should care. He found every such suggestion disgusting, and felt completely cheapened by it. They were the same motions, the same sensations, as with Georgie, but that had been so precious to him. There was nothing in common except the relief.

The elevator came and he climbed into it, pressing the button for the lobby. He wished he wouldn't have to think of Georgie at times like this. But he always did. This time seemed worse than usual.

He wouldn't use this girl again, but it made no difference. There was that vile sense of having betrayed her, somehow; yet he had never cheated on her, never wanted to, not even for a minute.

I'm sorry, he said to her, quietly. Forgive me.

She would always have forgiven him, of course. He wasn't sure that he could forgive himself.

It was a balmy night, and he decided to walk back to his hotel instead of taking a cab; to breathe and think, and work through the disgust. He was tempted to promise himself he would never do it again; but that resolution was so shallow, this time he didn't even bother to make it.

Somehow that was the most depressing thing of all.

The street lights beckoned him on. WALK/DON'T WALK . . . everything spelled out. He wished life were that easy. Oh well, at least, if his pattern were to continue, he would not need a woman again for at least two months. Karen had been unusual,

156

for him to succumb quite so soon after the last girl. He wondered what the trigger had been; the deal, the stress? Montfort doubted it. He lived for work.

He instructed his subconscious to bring him the answer, and on the corner of Main and Elm it did. He had been restless, charged, since the night of the benefit gala; since his meeting with Sophie Massot.

He took another shower as soon as he got back to the hotel; washed the smell of her off him, the sweat and heavy perfume she used; Poison by Dior, very appropriate. He was able to smile slightly at the thought. There was no point regretting something he had done and would do again.

Hugh was relieved to find himself ravenously hungry. Karen had been supple and enthusiastic, and the physical act of sex for him was as strenuous as a workout. He rang room service and ordered a steak and fries with mineral water and a decaffeinated espresso; the mini-bar was generously stocked, and he selected a rye on the rocks; something he would never have considered touching at home, but this was America.

The meal came in short order. It was very good, the steak crisped on the outside and meltingly tender when he cut into it, the fries were thin-cut, hot, and delicious with salt and pepper. He polished off everything and was enjoying the coffee when the phone rang. He sighed; it was late, and he had wanted to get to sleep. This could only be Pete.

'Yes?' he said.

It wasn't Pete. It was Louis Maitre, and he sounded incoherent with excitement.

'Monsieur! I am glad I tracked you down at last. Monsieur, there is news.'

Montfort forgot everything else. 'Yes? Tell me.'

'The widow Massot has gone mad,' Maitre said.

'Slow down, Maitre,' Hugh said carefully, 'and tell me exactly what has happened.'

The flight back to London took an eternity. Montfort could not sleep, and the distractions of films, indifferent meals, and champagne had no power for him. He took out a notebook from his briefcase and began to jot his thoughts down on paper.

Sophie Massot was 'on the rampage', Maitre had said – an image that made him smile, despite the blackness of his mood. That woman in the dress of raven silk, with the briolette diamonds, as cold and proper as a dowager queen – he could not see her 'rampaging' for anything or anybody.

And yet the facts were there. A few phone calls had confirmed them. House Massot stores in London, Paris, New York and Tokyo, closed – shutting their doors to visitors. Nothing but their lacklustre brand of fashion and accessories was trading. Staff had been fired across the globe – not made redundant, but dismissed for cause. The predictable lawsuits had been filed; the company had hired a London lawyer, Brocket, Sterns, to take care of those cases.

Montfort knew Brocket, Sterns; they were sharks, ruthless, the kind of firm he might have selected himself, in the circumstances.

The Chief Executive, the indolent Gregoire Lazard, had been escorted from the Paris offices by security guards. He too had filed a multimillion euro lawsuit. Meanwhile, at Sophie's request, Brocket, Sterns was apparently investigating compensation and expenses for the rest of the Board of Directors.

Maitre's network of informants told him House Massot's bankers were nervous. Their stock had dropped a full 3 per cent and continued to slide. Meanwhile, shareholders and analysts were demanding information, but the PR department had not released so much as a statement.

'She is *completement folle*,' Maitre triumphed. 'Your task will now be easy, monsieur.'

Montfort had asked when the next shareholders' meeting was.

'Six months, monsieur. By then the collapse will be complete.'

I wonder, Hugh thought.

He had good instincts for any kind of threat, and they were prickling now. Montfort didn't like it. Any of it.

He glanced out of the window; the thick clouds below him

meant it was dull over the Atlantic, but up here, above them all, it was as clear and sunny as ever. Usually his mind worked best on planes; no phone calls, no distractions.

But today he was frustrated. No matter how he turned events over in his mind, he could not make sense of it.

A stewardess passed him.

'Excuse me.'

'Yes, sir?' she said, smiling warmly at the gorgeous Englishman.

'How long until we land?'

'With the tailwinds, approximately four and half hours, sir.'

'Thanks,' Hugh said. His fingers drummed impatiently on his arm-rest.

'Can I bring you something? A drink . . . champagne . . . coffee?'

'I'm fine.' He smiled impersonally. 'Thank you.'

'I could fetch you a portable video unit if none of our selections appeal,' she said, unwilling to move away from him quite so soon. Some girls married people they met on flights. Look at Lisa Halaby, she'd met the King of Jordan and become a queen. This guy was so sexy, with that clenched jaw and that strong body. I could relax him some, she thought wickedly.

'Do you have a copy of the *Financial Times*?'

'Yes, sir. I'll bring it to you.'

All business, she thought with a sigh. What a pity.

Against his wishes, Montfort was tired when they touched down. The temptation was to go straight to the office, possibly stopping by the Massot showroom in Bond Street, but he did not want to make any moves when he was exhausted. He had the driver deliver him home, took a long bath, and went straight to bed.

When he awoke, he considered everything again. It was 2 p.m., so he made himself a Gruyère omelet and a large pot of coffee, flicked through the papers, and headed for the office. First, though, he stopped to see the Massot store for himself. Montfort believed that one should always check a site, if possible. You could find things out that weren't immediately apparent on paper, sometimes.

It looked horrible; in the middle of the opulent prosperity and conspicuous consumption of London's main shopping artery, there it was; the venerable storefront covered in plywood; all the windows completely sealed.

There was, however, a small notice fixed to the front door. He bent closer. In neat black lettering it said simply: *Closed for refurbishment. Open 14 July.*

14 July; Bastille Day.

Montfort felt a wave of unease, and then a pressing sense of urgency. If his suspicions were correct, he had to call the investment bank, and the board. And he would need a financial PR firm – experts. There was no time to lose; no time at all.

And he must get back to Paris. At once.

Chapter Twenty-One

'Monsieur Thomas Massot,' the butler said.

'Thomas.' His grandmother stood in a slither of silk and held out her rail-thin arms to him. 'It's so wonderful to see you.'

'And you, Grandmother,' he replied. He took a deep breath, drinking it all in. Relief flooded him – to be speaking French again, to be announced properly, as a man of stature; everything in the dower house exactly as he recalled it; his grandmother, elegant as ever, ladylike in every particular . . .

It was as though the last few months had never happened. The house was a sanctuary for him.

'Do sit down,' Katherine Massot said. 'Let us have some refreshments. Tea?'

He shook his head. 'Too English.'

She smiled at that. 'Of course, darling. Then coffee and petits fours.'

As he had got older, Tom had lost his childhood sweet tooth, but he would not have dreamed of contradicting her. His grandmother was still formal, and despite her words, possessed a detachment, a distance when she spoke to him; but today he was inclined to see this as a virtue. She had not changed one degree. His father had always approved of Grandmother, always been proud. If only Maman would imitate her – then there would be no need for what he was about to do.

'That sounds delicious. Thank you,' he said.

'Come closer to me.' The old lady patted the chaise-longue beside her with one wizened hand, and Tom rose obediently and sat beside her.

She was wearing a fine gown of chocolate brown silk

trimmed with cream lace, and a Massot bracelet, thick moonstones set in twenty-four-carat gold; and there were gleaming pearl buttons on her ears, clips, naturally; his grandmother's generation had not been fond of piercing. She smelt of *Violette de Parme*, exactly as she always did. Katherine had used the same scent since he was a child. It was blended especially for her on Faubourg St Sainte-Germain, and now the memories, rosy ones, rushed in on him. Tom squeezed her forearm.

'Dear Grandmother,' he said, with feeling. 'You're not going to scold me for leaving Oxford?'

The old lady tilted her head subtly.

'Oxford is your mother's concern, my dear,' she said coolly.

Tom sensed the disapproval. He felt supported.

'Your destiny is with Papa's estate, here. Not in some English town among dusty books,' Katherine pronounced.

'And with Papa's company,' Tom said, carefully.

Katherine sighed. 'I do not know if there will be much of the company left, Thomas. You will need to content yourself with the château. Of course, there is plenty here to occupy a young man; the grounds need supervision, and the lake must be restocked every year. And the staff managed . . .' she shook her head slightly. 'I *had* hoped, of course, to see you working with Papa, at House Massot, if he would return; and carrying on his legacy if not.' She shrugged. 'But as it is . . .'

One of the maids materialised with the coffee and petits fours and served them. Tom helped himself to a tiny macaroon. Even though his appetite had entirely deserted him, he was concerned not to upset his grandmother.

'But what do you mean?' he asked when the woman had gone. 'Surely Maman can't have done that much damage. It has only been a couple of months.'

'You have not heard?'

Katherine's old eyes stared out of her tall, lead-paned windows, gazing up the park towards the château. 'Perhaps I ought not to say anything,' she murmured, not looking at him. 'It is delicate; a mother and her son . . .'

Tom swallowed; his mouth was dry.

'Grandmother; if something is wrong, I beg you will tell me now. It is my company, after all.' Resentment burned in his cheeks. 'Or it ought to be.'

'Well, that is true.' His grandmother turned her eyes back to him, then gazed at her lap. 'It seems your mother has dismissed the men Papa hired. She has involved the company in legal struggles. She has closed the jewellery stores – not just in France but across the world.'

Tom paled. 'You are joking.'

'I wish I were, my dear.'

He removed his hand from his grandmother's arm, sprang to his feet, and began to pace around the room. Katherine watched him intently.

'And what is the cause? What explanation has she given for such behaviour?'

'None,' Katherine said, crisply. 'She tells the press nothing. House Massot is plunged into rumour and speculation. It is the talk of Paris.'

Tom felt nausea rise in his throat. It was even worse than he had suspected. He was glad he had moved so swiftly, though perhaps not swiftly enough.

'Grandmother, I have to ask you a favour,' he said, gravely.

'There is something else, my darling.'

He stared. There could not be more?

'I fear that this *precipitate* action by your mother may have stemmed from something . . . well, unfortunate.'

Tom knew the old lady well enough to understand that the matter must be truly awful. For Katherine, these were strong terms indeed.

'Go on,' he said with a calmness he did not feel.

'There were rumours . . . more than rumours, I'm afraid, of a – how shall I put it – a liaison.'

He stared at her. 'What?'

'A liaison between your mother and the chief executive of the company. A man your father chose and employed himself.'

'But . . . but . . .' Tom knew he was spluttering, but he could not help it. 'That's disgusting. It cannot be true. She would never . . .'

'Your mother is convinced your father is dead,' Katherine said mildly. 'You must remember that. I am sure she convinced the executive of it, also. After all, she had that piece of paper.'

Tom had gone cold with shock. He made a feeble effort to collect himself.

'I am afraid it is quite true,' said Katherine, relentlessly. 'The servants gossip, you know. She had him as a guest to the château many times ... went to his house ... was quite devoted, from what I understand.'

'She brought a lover into my father's house?' Tom repeated. The betrayal and pain were overwhelming.

'While still dressed in her mourning weeds!' Katherine exclaimed. Then shook herself, deliberately. 'Oh my darling, forgive me; I must not criticise your maman in front of you.'

'I think we are past that stage, Grandmother,' Tom said flatly. 'And so, now there is, what? A lovers' quarrel?'

'One can only presume so.'

'And she dismisses him.' He brooded on it for a while. The man – he was disposed to loathe him, but how much more to hate his mother. This man saw only a death certificate. Meanwhile, his mother had been twice a traitor; taking a lover, and then dismissing from his post the man his father had selected to run Massot while Tom came of age.

'It is almost as if she wants rid of every trace of my father,' he said aloud.

'You must try to forgive her,' Katherine said, without conviction. 'But my Pierre – how this hurts, Thomas. And there is nothing we can do about it.'

He spun on his heels on the Manchu dynasty silk rug and faced her.

'Ah no, that is where you are wrong,' Tom said. 'If you will help me, Grandmother, I think we shall be able to act.'

He persuaded her to take a walk with him in the grounds of the dower house; there was a fine walled garden, mostly laid to lawn, with gravel walks lined with rose bushes, lavender, and other formal plantings. The day was very hot for May, but Tom offered his arm, and promised they would walk slowly. He did not want the servants eavesdropping on family business.

'Ah, yes . . . my shares.' Katherine had insisted on bringing her fan, an antique made of ivory, exquisitely carved with a filigree pattern; she swayed it quickly back and forth against the languor of the heat. 'I hadn't considered them for years. Finance is incredibly boring.'

Her white eyelashes flickered, almost as if she were batting them at him. 'My Pierre took care of that sort of thing.'

'But there are rather a lot. I have half that amount myself, that I can use now. If, Grandmother, if you would trust me with your shares . . .'

Tom felt nervous; his entire plan depended on this. At Lincoln's Inn it had seemed the natural and proper outcome; now it came to the point, he felt he was asking for a great deal.

'You want me to give you my shares? But of course, if you need the money. All I have is yours.'

He started. 'No – not give them to me. Assign me your votes, make me your proxy. With fifteen per cent of shareholder votes I would receive an automatic seat on the Board of Directors. Even Maman could not remove me.'

Katherine turned her snowy head. The rheumy eyes regarded him appraisingly.

'Well, well,' she said softly. 'Perhaps, after all, there is something of your father in you.'

Tom squared his shoulders. 'More than something, Grandmother,' he said proudly.

'I will summon M. Foche and draw up the papers today.'

'Make sure he knows it is secret; he is not to go running to Maman,' Tom said bitterly. 'Foche is the one who gave her those papers, and let her declare Papa dead.'

'Your mother was determined; Foche had no choice. It is foolish to blame him; he is nothing but a functionary,' Katherine said with contempt. 'And what will you do with a seat on the board?'

'I was thinking of lawsuits. But there are some already; enough to delay her plans.'

'The law is a start.'

'And although I will not gain control of the shares until my twenty-first birthday, on the Board I can force Maman to resign.'

Katherine smiled. 'How, pray, will you do that?'

'I will show her how damaging her actions are; and if she will not resign, then I will go to the shareholders and ask them to pass a vote of no confidence. She would not be able to stay then. The stock would plunge.'

The old lady's arm tightened on his arm.

'Yes, that might work,' she said, quietly. 'You are, of course, very young.'

'Young does not mean stupid,' he said.

'I know, my dear. It is convincing other people that will be hard. But not, of course, impossible.' The fan stilled, she concentrated; he was amazed at how roused she was, how far from her usual topor.

'I know Pierre would have wanted this,' she said, with complete certainty. 'And I will see to it his will is not overcome. You are his son.'

'His heir,' Tom said righteously. 'Me – not Maman.'

'I prefer to say his steward.' Katherine looked sharply at the young man. 'Or have you also given up on him?'

'Never,' Tom vowed. His voice trembled a little. 'Never. Till I see his body.'

Katherine nodded, satisfied, and walked on. She wore custom-made pointed buckle shoes, very old fashioned, and they crunched on the gravel. His grandmother was so light that he thought a slight breeze might have knocked her over. Yet when she spoke, her voice was like iron.

'Our task is to ensure you appear credible,' she said. 'From now on, you must be a man, Thomas; nothing you say, nothing you do, must distract from it.'

They had turned past a wall of gloriously flowering clematis and were back at the house.

'You are staying at a hotel?'

'Yes,' he replied, surprised at the question.

'Take an apartment; something magnificent,' she said. 'I will pay for it. You are not a guest in Paris, not a tourist. Call me this afternoon when you have found somewhere; I will speak to Foche.'

She smiled radiantly at him.

'And after that,' she said sweetly, 'you and I will go out to dinner.'

'Somewhere very public.'

'Exactly.' Katherine nodded. 'You are learning, my dear.'

'I trust it meets your approval, monsieur?'

The lettings agent nodded and rubbed his hands eagerly. 'It is one of our finest properties . . . a jewel. Of course, you would know about that.' He laughed at his own joke, but the boy, the Massot heir, did not speak. 'We have others if this is not to your taste,' he added hastily. 'Several others . . . perhaps something more modern?'

Tom turned his gaze to the little man. 'It will do, monsieur. I gather my grandmother has already advanced you the necessary monies?'

He wanted to get this over with. He found the agent's giggling and joking impertinent.

'Oh yes; that is all arranged.'

'Then have you some papers for me to sign?'

The man practically fell over himself in eagerness. 'No, no, monsieur. With you that is not necessary. We are well acquainted with House Massot. It's all yours.'

'Excellent.'

'Perhaps a drink to celebrate, then.' He withdrew a bottle of champagne. Tom glanced at it; Moët, non-vintage and non-imaginative. 'Compliments of the agency, monsieur – shall I open it?'

Tom said 'No, thank you,' very distantly and dismissively.

The man's face fell; he finally got the message.

'Very good, monsieur – I shall leave my card. If there's anything further I can do for you, anything at all . . .'

'Thank you. Good day,' Tom said, instantly.

Discomfited, the agent put down the champagne, which had been hanging rather limply in his hand, on a side table, and fished out a card, which he placed next to it. Then he gave one last obsequious smile and let himself out of the front door.

Tom looked around the place with resignation. As he had said, it would do. It was a luxurious apartment, nineteenth-

167

century, four bedrooms and two salons, somewhat baroque; fully furnished with real, though unremarkable antiques; the correct address on the left bank, and a glorious view of the Seine. It was rented at twenty thousand euros per month, and would be an acceptable temporary headquarters.

But the soullessness of the place depressed him. It was not a Massot property; nothing like Château des Étoiles. He was here because his mother had forced him to be; forced him out of his home, out of his inheritance.

Grandmother . . . well. She had been a surprise. There was a hidden steel to her ancient frame, and it almost made him feel sorry for Maman. But she had brought this on herself, and, he promised himself virtuously, he would give her every opportunity to retreat with grace.

He tried to force himself into a more cheerful mood. He was back in France, there was that to be thankful for. And maybe he could set things aright. Hush up his mother's scandals, and take his place at the helm of House Massot. Perhaps there would not be any struggles after he showed his hand.

He strode to his rented windows and looked down over the traffic to the river glittering red and gold in the sunset. Perhaps things would all work out for the best . . .

But somehow he doubted it.

Chapter Twenty-Two

At first Sophie was shocked at what she found. It was more, much more, than a little corporate thievery; Gregoire Lazard and the directors with their hands in the till. There had been waste, inactivity, rot, in almost every area of House Massot. The same staff, free from the threat of being fired, had been on the payroll for years; and without Pierre there, with Lazard uninterested, the decline had been steady and constant.

Every year since his death, revenues had dropped, market share slid, the share price stagnant. The more she uncovered, the more Sophie understood it was only because the analysts were not paying attention that their shares had dropped through the floor.

The banks had been asked for more and more capital. They were now pressing for a repayment of their loans. It was debt that had already been restructured, more than once. Sophie was not technically minded, but she learned fast. Her intelligence was keen, although her personality was mild, and the more she bent her mind to it, the more incompetence she uncovered. Letters, reports, sales charts, banking summaries, the dry, precise figures, so unemotional on paper, told a shocking story; a great company crumbling into dust.

If the truth be told, it was on the brink of destruction.

The first thing she did was to find herself some competent advisers. Judy Dean was a true support. She gave Sophie lists of executives she thought should be replaced. They were long lists; Sophie fired them all. M. Giles Keroualle, Judy's boss in PR, was the first to go.

She hired independent lawyers and accountants and began

a lightning-quick review. Every meeting confirmed it: House Massot was on the verge of ruin.

Sophie reflected that if she thought about this too much, she would be terrified. And she did not have time to be terrified. She had a company to rescue, for herself, and for her son.

There were still assets, still things House Mossot had to offer. A brilliant, and underpaid, team of jewellery designers; stores in the best locations; pipelines to De Beers' sight holders; contracts with independent suppliers of the best gems in the world. And, of course, a handful of people she could trust.

Apart from the last, it was these assets that Hugh Montfort wanted. It made House Massot a takeover target. There was a shareholders' meeting in three months, and Sophie knew exactly what would happen; word of the disaster behind the serene grey façade of their offices would leak out. The share price would plunge. Hugh Montfort would make a bargain basement offer, acquire Massot for a song, be the big hero, she reflected bitterly; and her son's inheritance would be decimated, while her husband's life's work would be lost for ever.

She was not about to let that happen. Sophie was determined. She would save the company, fight off Montfort, restore House Massot to glory, and leave Tom what Pierre had intended for him.

The place to start, as ever, was with people she could trust.

The last report was delivered to Sophie on a Monday morning. By the time she closed the slim blue file, she had already determined what to do.

She picked up the phone and called down to reception.

'Good morning, madame.'

'Celine,' Sophie said, glancing at the personnel list in front of her, 'could you come up to my office a moment?'

There was a quick intake of breath – the girl was frightened. But she said, 'Certainly, madame,' meekly. The receptionist's manners had greatly improved, ever since that first day, and Sophie had been kind to her, always smiling at her and wishing her a good morning. Even before she'd fired Gregoire, Sophie had seen gratitude, real gratitude, in the girl's eyes.

The knock on the door came promptly, less than a minute later.

'Come in,' Sophie said.

Celine Bousset, the receptionist, entered Sophie's office timidly and stood in front of her, her eyes lowered. She was wearing a smart, simple shift dress in dusky pink with a matching cardigan, neat pearl studs, and flat shoes. Sophie noted the hair in a formal pleat, the rose-pink nails, her groomed eyebrows. She had mentioned to Celine once that dress was as important as manner when you sat on reception, and since then, the girl had striven to dress well, on her limited budget.

Sophie appreciated it. Celine was making an effort. It was more than you could say for half the vice-presidents in this company.

'Please sit down,' she said.

The girl sat, opened her mouth, then thought better of it.

'Don't worry.' Sophie smiled at her. 'I'm not going to fire you.'

She breathed out, a ragged sigh of relief. Sophie thought there were even tears prickling in her eyes. She recalled Celine's panic on the first day, when she'd thought she was going to get fired; how she'd plead that she needed the money.

'I have a lot of work to do here, Celine.' Sophie glanced out of her window, Gregoire's old window, to the fine view of rue Tricot, basking in the summer heat. 'And not a lot of time.'

'Are . . . are we all going to lose our jobs, madame?' the girl stammered.

'Why do you say that?'

'Some of the girls say the company is going to be closed down,' Celine replied, nervously. 'And we are all to be dismissed.'

Sophie stiffened. 'The girls are wrong. Anybody who wants to work hard will still have a position here. But I do not want you to be the receptionist any more.'

'I hope I have not offended you again, madame.'

'It's not that. I need an assistant. Somebody I can trust. Somebody who is not linked to the previous management.'

'Me?'

'You fit that description, don't you?'

Celine's hazel eyes rounded. '*Certainement*, madame, I am not linked to management. I am not linked to anybody,' she said artlessly. 'I only answer the phone.'

Sophie grinned. 'Good. Then you are hired. The salary is twenty-two thousand euros.'

The young girl's face creased in delight. 'Oh, madame! Thank you. I know computers . . . I can type . . .'

'You'll need to come in very early. We start work at eight sharp. And you will not leave until six.'

'No problem, madame. Oh thank you, thank you, madame.'

'Your first job is to find me a new receptionist.'

'I know just the girl,' Celine said, confidently.

'Then as soon as she is installed, you will come up here.'

There was another knock on the door, and Judy Dean opened it.

'Sophie, hi,' she said. 'I've arranged the meeting with the designers, as you asked. They'll be here today at eleven. And all the PR staff.'

'Excellent.'

Sophie smiled at her friend. Then she noticed little Celine Bousset was also staring at Judy, with an expression she did not approve of; it was cold, a little contemptuous. She had a moment of unease. She hoped Celine was not one of those girls who hated to work for other women.

'Mlle Judy Dean is the new Senior Vice-President in charge of our publicity, Celine,' Sophie said coolly. 'She now runs one of the most important divisions in our company.'

'Yes, madame,' Celine said, her eyes snapping back to Sophie's at once.

'If Mlle Dean wants to be put through to me, or to see me, her calls take priority. And I expect you to render her every assistance. Is that clear?'

Judy smiled tightly.

'Perfectly clear, madame,' Celine said meekly. 'I will always be ready to assist you, Mlle Dean,' she said to Judy.

The American girl nodded; Sophie felt satisfied.

'Then I will see you shortly, Celine. You may go,' she said.

The girl got up and quickly excused herself from the room.

'Do you have a moment now?' Judy asked.

Sophie smiled at her. 'You heard what I told my new assistant.'

'Thanks.' Judy came in and sat down in front of her. 'Mind if I ask you some questions?'

Sophie leaned back in her seat. 'Go right ahead.'

Judy smiled. She looked strained, though, Sophie thought. Despite her promotion, and the salary increase that had accompanied it, Judy had a brittle quality to her; tiredness around the eyes that the best make-up couldn't conceal, and a taut, tense way of holding herself that made her seem uneasy, out of place.

Her clothes were pitch-perfect, but Sophie thought they too contributed to the impression the younger woman gave. Judy Dean always looked as though she'd marched straight off the pages of *Elle*, but that was the problem; it was as if she was trying too hard.

Everything about Judy was always of the moment. She would carry the latest bag, wear the hot shoes of the month, and the result was that she looked as if she'd been dressed by a stylist. There was so much effort in it, Sophie thought.

Today Judy was wearing a BCBG Max Azria dress in silk georgette, purple with little cap sleeves; it had a lilac lining, and a pink trim. Very summery and flirty, but Judy had carefully teamed it with lilac pumps and a sweet little bag, this summer's pale blue from Coach, and she wore a large, heart-shaped amethyst drop down the vee of the neckline. Her earrings were dangling bezel set blue topaz, a stone cheap enough for Judy to wear it in a decent size; she had rose blusher, white pencil to brighten up her eyes; everything co-ordinated. Judy looked like a model on a photoshoot. It was identikit dressing, far too matchy-matchy.

When Sophie looked at her she wondered if the girl ever relaxed.

I'll bet her underwear is matched and is a shade of either pale lilac or blush pink, Sophie thought.

'I'm wondering what's going on,' Judy said brightly.

Sophie blushed a little at her train of thought. 'What do you mean?'

'Well, you had me call Herr and Frau Brandt.'

Their designers. Sophie nodded.

'And we've issued no press statements for the last month, but now you've summoned the whole department.' Judy tried to smile, but it didn't reach her eyes. 'I'd like to get a jump on whatever you're going to announce.'

'I'm sorry, I'm kind of flying by the seat of my pants,' Sophie said, trying out an Americanism on Judy.

'You sure are,' she said. 'You don't mind if I offer some constructive criticism?'

'That's what I'm paying you for,' Sophie said, easily. 'Nobody has to be afraid to speak their mind around me.'

Judy tried, and failed, not to stiffen. 'Then I gotta tell you, you need to come clean. We fired all those guys, and that's good, but you've been holed up with the lawyers, the stores are closed, designers are getting commissions . . . I can't stave off the press for ever. And the rest of the staff need to know what's up. Morale is non-existent.'

Sophie said gently, 'But you've been talking to them, Judy. Reassuring them?'

Judy started slightly. 'Me? Oh, sure. Of course.'

'Then all you need do is wait til eleven.' Sophie sighed. 'It'd take me too long to repeat everything; I'm just going to get a run-down from the staff, and then tell them my plans. After that your team can start talking to the press. You can write the press releases once we've had the meeting.'

Judy nodded. She felt humiliated, again, but wasn't about to show it. Not to Sophie Massot, of all women. If Sophie didn't want to share, that was fine with Judy. She could not care less.

Judy knew perfectly well there was no way of saving this company. It was worse than she had ever suspected.

'I can hardly wait,' she said, smiling. And it was true. She wanted to watch Sophie fall flat on her face. What kind of a rabbit did she think she could pull out of the hat? The trophy wife, who hadn't trained in business a day in her life?

'Then I'll see you at eleven.' Sophie smiled back, but Judy took the comment for what it was; a dismissal. She rose carefully.

'See you then,' Judy said.

Judy closed the door behind her. Fine, let Sophie keep her pathetic little secrets. She would indeed enjoy the 11 a.m. meeting. Sophie would finally spill whatever plans she had for the company, if you could call them that. Brilliant, so far – closing down the jewellery stores, the only part of Massot actually making money; sending the stock through the floor. Judy was thankful she'd sold hers years ago, or her net worth might have plunged.

She smoothed down the chiffon of her dress as she headed back to her office.

'*Bonjour*, madame,' said Marie respectfully.

Judy nodded. '*Bonjour*.'

Since the day Gregoire got fired, everything had been different. There were no more looks and whispers. Judy was sure the rumours still went on, but they went on out of her earshot. Everybody knew she had the ear of Mme Sophie, and when blood had started flowing, Judy was there, directing it. Françoise, Monsieur Keroualle's own assistant, had been reassigned to the typing pool!

Nobody else wanted that. Judy was now deferred to and respected. And feared. Marie, when pressed, had reluctantly told Judy her new nickname was 'Mme La Guillotine'. But far from being furious, Judy had laughed.

She could hardly help it. The release of tension was necessary. Judy's emotions were see-sawing all over the place; day to day, she had no idea how she kept herself together. It was a constant battle, and she thanked God she was in PR, and knew how to lie for a living.

Of course she had to see Sophie. See that wedding ring every day. Watch Sophie take ownership here, in Pierre's place; Pierre, Judy's love, the man who had never cared two straws for Sophie. That was bitter, and time did not make it any better. Every day that Sophie Massot came here, impeccably, quietly elegant, asserting her rights, was another day that part of Judy died.

On the other hand, she knew, she had never had such an opportunity. The stupid, spoiled bitch *liked* her. Of all the people in the world, Sophie was giving Judy the chance to have revenge on those who had scorned her, muttered about her, laughed at her, kept her down. It was through Sophie she had finally got rid of Giles; was running the division, at last. Through Sophie that she got the money Gregoire had cheated her of. The fact she no longer had to run the gauntlet of stares was wonderful. Judy was feared; and she triumphed, savagely, in her new power.

But even the triumph had a bitter edge. Judy had longed to head up the division for so long, and now that she did, she couldn't care less about it. What joy was there in being head of PR when Sophie had the whole company? What pleasure was there in being Senior Vice-President if Pierre's wife was Chairman?

She hated Sophie for it. Achieving her dreams, and finding them ashes.

Judy didn't know, yet, exactly what she was going to do. But she knew what she wanted. Money – real money, a slice of what everybody else was getting. Power; not just being the head of some stupid division, reporting to Sophie. She would not rest until Sophie Massot respected her as an equal. No, Judy thought, as a superior. She was not about to put herself on the level of some placid fool of a woman who had married for money; a woman who'd had Pierre next to her all those years, and never let him touch her heart.

Lastly, of course, she wanted revenge. She had suffered humiliation for too long to turn the other cheek. Enough of all that; nobody would pity Judy Dean any more.

Sophie was about to reveal her plans. And then Judy would decide what to do with them.

She thought she already had a pretty good idea. There was one person who would, most definitely, be in the market for that sort of information.

Hugh Montfort.

Chapter Twenty-Three

Heinrich Brandt sat next to his wife, Gertrud, and tried not to look as nervous as he felt.

The room was carpeted with a thick weave, navy, and its walls were painted in soothing Wedgwood blue. On the long table were vases of cream and pink roses, a cheerful splash of colour, and heavily scented; and in front of the old couple, and all the executives sat around them, were glasses of fresh citron pressé with crushed ice. Everything had been done to make the atmosphere pleasant. But it did not help him much.

Herr Brandt did not want to be here. He lived quietly with Gertrud in a small village near Wengen, in Switzerland; one without too many skiing runs. It escaped the worst of the tourists in the winter and was sheer delight in the summer. His luxurious house was very comfortably appointed, purchased with the fees from twenty years of designing jewels for House Massot; he hated to leave it. The Brandts' concessions to the modern world included a studio for sketching new designs; a workshop attached to the house; and a fax machine. If he had to communicate with Paris, that was the way he preferred to do it.

But the skinny, hard-looking American girl in the rich clothes had rung them and insisted. And Gertrud told Heinrich not to say no. They should have saved more, but their eldest daughter had got married and needed an apartment in Geneva, while Hans, their son, had got it into his head that he wanted to take an MBA at Harvard.

This cost money. A lot of money.

Heinrich knew only that House Massot was in big trouble,

177

and there was a possibility his cheques would stop coming. He fretted about it. He was presently sixty-five. What other house would take on a designer from a firm that was about to go bust? Harvard was off, and the Geneva flat would need remortgaging. He thanked God he owned his chalet free and clear.

This had to be bad news. Heinrich glanced out of rheumy eyes at his wife. Her sharp gaze was scanning the room, taking it all in, as he had. For all the convivial arrangements – there was a sideboard laden with coffee, warm croissants, fruit, and charcuterie – nobody seemed relaxed. The men and the American woman were sitting there, as tense as he was. Perhaps they, too, were anxious about money. But then again, who was not?

He understood that changes had come since the widow of the founder took over. Heinrich disliked all change, especially when it affected him. His wrinkled hands gripped the tall glass of citron pressé and he took a nervous sip. It was delicious, but he would have preferred a shot of schnapps.

The door opened and a woman came in. Everybody stood; this must be the widow, he thought. She was a beautiful woman, dark-haired and elegant; Gertrud twenty years ago had never looked that good. She was wearing a fitted black suit which showed off a slim, yet delightfully curved body; a shirt of ivory satin, and two thick rows of pearls, which he noted at once were over fourteen millimetres apiece, lustrous and quite magnificent.

His baleful glare softened just a touch. On her right hand she was wearing a simple solitaire, a ruby ring, emerald-cut in four carats, translucent and extremely fine. It was one of his wife's pieces; they had made it perhaps twelve years ago. He remembered the stone. They had both agreed it would be criminal to ruin such fine material by crowding it with any other accents. Not even the clearest diamonds could enhance such a ruby.

He supposed if he were to be ruined, it would at least be by a woman of taste.

'Please don't get up,' she said, and they all sank to their

chairs again. 'This shouldn't take long. I am going to outline our plans for House Massot, and then Mlle Dean will begin to form her strategy, as to how best to release them to the media.'

She turned and looked straight at Heinrich.

'Herr and Frau Brandt, it is a great honour to have you here.'

'You did not give us much of a choice, Fräulein,' Gertrud said, but Heinrich nudged her in the ribs.

'Thank you for the *Fräulein*, but I haven't deserved that for two decades,' the widow said, smiling most disarmingly. 'And I am so sorry to have inconvenienced you. But you and Frau Brandt are the heart of House Massot and of everything we plan to rebuild.'

There was a short, stunned silence.

'Then you did not bring us here to dismiss us?' Gertrud rasped.

'Dismiss you?' She shook her dark head. '*Gnädige Frau*, why on earth would I want to do that? You are the most precious asset this company possesses.'

Gertrud hesitated; Heinrich could see her trying, and failing, to repress her plain-talking nature.

'I have read that the company is about to fail. We thought surely you will wish to replace us with younger – modern – designers. Ones that string citrines and canary diamonds on chicken wire. And such things,' she said, with contempt.

Sophie Massot smiled. 'No, indeed. House Massot does not make trash.'

Judy Dean said, 'It is trash that sells.'

'To Mayberry customers,' Sophie responded. 'Not to ours.'

Judy smiled thinly. 'If I may, Sophie, it has been very hard to get *Elle* and *In Style* to cover our collections. Even our jewellery collections.'

The older woman inclined her head. 'Of course; we do not sell to *Elle* readers. Nor should we be trying to.'

She leaned forward, placing her hands on the table, holding the gaze of everybody in the room.

'While my husband has been gone' – Judy stiffened, but Sophie did not see it – 'House Massot has lost its soul. We have diversified, with no success. The fashion division is an embarrassment.'

There were murmurs of agreement.

'Our jewellery has lost ground to Tiffany, to Cartier, and especially to Mayberry. But it is different from all those houses. We are more individual than either Tiffany's or Cartier's. Our pieces are designed by Heinrich and Gertrud, made by skilled artisans. They are one-off – they are bespoke. And at the same time, the prices reflect this.' Sophie glanced at Judy. 'I'm afraid we've been advertising where there are no customers. We are haute couture, and whatever we may do in the future, at present we need our core customers back.'

She paused.

'They will not return the way House Massot is now. Shabby stores filled with underpaid attendants who do not love jewellery and who take no pride in either their work or appearance. Pieces crowded together, their beauty unable to breathe. And our *marque* devalued by the travesty of a fashion division that nobody wears and nobody buys.'

'But change will take years,' said one of the executives combatively.

Sophie shook her head. 'We do not have years, monsieur.'

'To re-form the fashion division? Find new designers . . . spend on advertising . . .'

'I am closing the fashion division, effective immediately,' Sophie said flatly.

The man blinked. 'You can't.'

'I can. And as of nine o'clock this morning, I have.'

Judy spluttered, 'But – but those are assets. All the stock. The collections. We could sell them, find a buyer . . .'

'And have them go out with the name Massot? It will devalue the jewellery.'

'But that's ridiculous!' Judy protested, forgetting herself. She thought of all the pleading, all the jockeying, the work she had done over that stupid label. The endless calls to New York, the bribes to journalists at the fashion shows in Milan and Paris, even London – no show had been too minor for her, when she was grubbing for notice.

And for what? Sophie was scrapping it.

'Judy,' Sophie said, 'let me ask you. Would you wear it?'

Judy swallowed hard. She was forced to reply, 'No.'

'No more would I. I went to Maison de Lis yesterday to have my hair done.' Maison de Lis was one of the most expensive, and chicest salons in Paris; Judy saved up to go there once a year for her signature cut, which she then had trimmed at cheaper places. She nodded.

'It was very crowded,' Sophie continued, relentlessly. 'I saw Prada, I saw Versace, I saw Richard Tyler, I saw Chloe . . . I never saw one Massot piece. Not even a bag.'

'The banks won't let you eliminate those assets,' another man said.

'They have no choice. They lent money to the company, not to a division. And the loans are not due for three months.'

'I am already taking calls from our bankers,' he insisted, anxiously.

'Then you may reassure them their loans will be repaid on time,' Sophie said calmly.

'And how do you plan to reclaim our customer base? What you see as our customer base?' Judy asked.

Sophie said, 'If you'll just look at the screen, ladies and gentlemen.'

She dimmed the lights in the room and took up the button that controlled the projector. Judy heard a soft click and the screen filled with an image.

Judy stared. She heard the slight intakes of breath all around her.

'This is what I've been doing for the last few weeks,' Sophie said. 'The store designers and I worked in secret; you will excuse me, but I didn't want our plans to leak out prematurely.

'It's quite beautiful, madame,' a man said, and there was a small ripple of applause in the darkness.

Jealousy surged in Judy's chest, thick jealousy, and rage. She felt quite light-headed. She was thankful the room was dark; in her lap, her fingers twisted, the knuckles clenched.

She was gazing at a picture of a House Massot showroom. That was what it had to be, but the interior was unrecognisable.

Out had gone the long cases, the beige carpet, the dull lighting. Instead the walls were dressed in a silky, delicate shade of palest pink; the display stands were painted in grass green, and the floors were covered in boards of polished oak. There was natural, recessed lighting in the ceiling; the display cases, instead of lining the walls, were grouped in five or six individual stands around the room. The dull wheat-coloured linings had been replaced with inky-blue velvet, and individual pieces glittered against them; even from the photograph's distance, you could make out a necklace here, a ring-case there. Marble plinths were covered in cascading showers of fresh roses, pale greens, pinks, and blues, were everywhere. The effect was supremely feminine, floral and expensive.

It took Judy's breath away. She instantly wanted to go shopping.

Sophie pressed the button again. A man and a woman stood in the frame, impeccably dressed. The woman was wearing a classic Chanel suit in pink tweed; the man a sober, dark suit, which Judy assumed was bespoke.

'And these are our customers,' Judy said.

Sophie laughed. 'Actually, these are our shop assistants. The young woman is Mlle Claudette Chiron, the new manager of our flagship store on rue Faubourg. The young man with her is M. Edouard Peguy, a former history of art student at the Sorbonne. He now manages our store on rue des Princes.'

'They look pretty rich to be shop assistants,' a man said.

'That's the point; those are the new uniforms. The men's are made in Savile Row, in England; the women's are by Chanel.'

Judy raised her eyebrows. 'We are dressing our *shop assistants* in Chanel?'

'The customer of House Massot is receiving nothing but the best; in service; in atmosphere.' Sophie flicked on the lights and nodded at the Brandts. 'And of course, in gems.'

It took me years of slaving to afford my one Chanel suit, Judy thought. And she goes and dresses *shop assistants* in it.

She could never wear her yellow Chanel again. Not in this office. She stared at Sophie, her heart thudding with jealous loathing, so hard that she thought the older woman must sense it.

But Sophie was ignoring her. She was smiling that aggravating, calm smile of hers, nodding at the Brandts.

'*Gnädige Frau, mein Herr,*' she said politely. 'It is the genius of your designs that will now be in the spotlight. They have always been our strength, but lately that strength has been hidden. I propose to double your salary and grant you stock options, and ask, in exchange, that you select at least ten further young designers that we will put on the payroll, and then train them to your own exacting standards.'

The old man stood up, and Judy could see his eyes were red. She groaned inwardly. He wasn't about to cry, was he?

'It is not necessary to pay us more money, Mme Massot,' he said with dignity. 'You are one who cares about our life's work. You will show the world what we have made.'

'You are an artist, *mein Herr*. I will certainly try. But even artists deserve to be paid for their labour. Indeed you must accept it,' Sophie smiled gently, 'because I promise you, I intend to make a great deal of money from the genius of you and your wife.'

Spontaneous, and prolonged, applause broke out around the table as the old man sat down again. Judy groaned inwardly. They were clapping Heinrich Brandt, but Sophie Massot, too. Judy did not deceive herself. Sophie's plans were imaginative and daring.

She would have loved to have thought of them herself. Meanwhile, Sophie, the housewife, was standing here, lapping up the plaudits of her colleagues.

She heard herself ask bitterly, 'Sophie, how much will all this cost?'

The applause was forced to die down. Judy went on doggedly, 'Even with a discount, and fewer staff, your "uniforms" will cost a hundred thousand. The write-offs of the fashion division . . . the interior design . . . it can't have come cheap.'

She had scored a point. Concern registered around the table.

'Yes, it has cost a lot of money. With the write-offs, and overtime that got the stores ready, I estimate around nine million euros.'

There was murmuring then; discontent. It pleased Judy

intensely. Sophie did not seem to care, but that must be a mask!

'And there will be more costs to come,' Sophie went on, cool as you like. 'This new direction must be publicised. But not in the traditional manner. You can brief your contacts in the press, Judy, and bring me releases – I must approve them all. But that will not be the main way we are going to announce our rebirth.'

'Then what will be?' a male executive asked her.

Sophie smiled. 'We're going to throw a party,' she said. She smiled at the old couple. 'And Herr and Frau Brandt, I will need your help.'

Chapter Twenty-Four

Judy locked the front door of her apartment and stepped out into rue des Cloches. It was another glorious day; two small white clouds were all that marked the serene blue of the sky. It was cool enough at present, but that was only because it was seven in the morning. Later it would get hot; maybe too hot.

Judy always dressed carefully, but today she had taken particular pains. It was not enough to be chic and businesslike. Today she also wanted to be pretty.

Today, she was going to see Hugh Montfort.

It was an odd thing, she thought, as she walked carefully down the street, smiling at the young man on his bike who whistled at her; the baker, opening up, who shot her a wolfish grin. Once she had decided to fight, she had actually relaxed. The tension and stress of the last few months, the proximity of Pierre's widow, it all melted away. Judy understood, this morning, the terrible cost of being out of control. She had felt trapped, like a bird that flies into a building, and can see no way out again.

Perhaps, too, it was more than the arrival of Sophie. That dreadful fact had brought things to a head. But as she reflected on it this morning, her L K Bennett heels clicking down the cobbles, Judy thought the claustrophobia had lasted much longer than that.

Ever since her lover had disappeared, in fact.

She had stayed at Massot, where they paid her salary, and endured the stares and whispers for so long they had become white noise, something in the background. But all that meant was she had been living under constant, never-ending strain.

185

It was not enough for the vultures that Judy's heart was broken.

She had lost Pierre, first, and most dreadfully. But just when the keen pain had settled into a dull ache, then the rumours started; gossip, right in front of her, in pretended ignorance of her love affair. The tales of Pierre's other women. How there were, while he had been seeing her, at least eight others; and hookers, and one-night stands on top. Pierre, they told her, was a goat. He would stick it in any girl willing to take it, Françoise had told her, with muted triumph.

That had shattered her; those weeks.

Only gradually was Judy able to talk herself out of the black fog. She would never know the full truth. But Pierre had been tender, he had been sweet; he had helped her career; he had bought her the apartment, given it to her, free and clear.

Their love meant something; Judy clung on to that through all the years ahead, until Sophie Massot showed up, tore the scabs from her wounds, and set her heart bleeding, again.

At first Judy had not been able to see her way. But Sophie Massot had now given her the opportunity, and she would not need asking twice.

She saw the little café on the corner of rue Tabac. Jacques, the owner, was outside, serving a customer; he saw Judy and waved cheerfully.

She smiled, and waved back. It occurred to her, depressingly, that these relationships, with waiters, people who served her every day, were the closest she came to friendships.

Judy Dean had trusted nobody for years.

She shrugged her lilac silk cardigan round her shoulders. She would not think of anything depressing today. Today, she was going to change her life, and bring the Massot nightmare to an end.

Judy was ready to move on.

'*Bonjour, mademoiselle,*' said Jacques, flatteringly. '*Très belle aujourd'hui.*'

He kissed his fingertips, extravagantly.

'*Merci.*' Judy took her seat at an outside table for two. She did not have to be ashamed of sitting alone, she thought; a pretty woman never did.

Today, she knew, she was pretty. She had chosen an Emporio Armani shirt dress in dusty pink, the cutest lilac heels, a small Dooney & Bourke shoulder bag, lilac leather with a purple trim, and then the DKNY silk cardigan. The only thing French she was wearing were her Massot diamond studs; small, but fine yellow diamonds; one of the nicest pieces she owned, sparkling and summery, an early gift from Pierre.

It pleased her to wear something of his today.

Her make-up was light. Judy had used nothing more than foundation, a sheer Chanel blush, tinted lip gloss and a touch of mascara. She had slept well last night, and her skin was still glowing from this morning's run and her Eve Lom cleansing cream, and she'd chosen Ralph Lauren's *Romance* because it was rose-based, and matched her sunny mood.

Jacques brought her usual breakfast. Sweet, milky coffee – so good – and a warm, buttery croissant, flaky and delicious. Judy refused cheeses and meats. Not this morning; it was all she could do to manage the croissant. She was nervous, in a delightful way. This might be the last day she would have to dance attendance on Sophie.

And then, finally, she was going to take back control. She would bring House Massot crashing down, and all her tormentors with it.

'Good morning, Judy.' Sophie Massot gave her a businesslike smile that annoyed Judy intensely. One staff meeting and the housewife thought she was a Harvard MBA.

'Hi,' Judy responded.

'You look very pretty this morning,' Sophie said.

'So do you,' Judy lied. She thought Sophie looked tired; the black dress and jacket she had chosen today just showed up the pallor in her face, and there were no pearls to soften her complexion. 'You know, I think we shouldn't bother with a press release.'

'Oh?' Sophie leaned back in her chair, one groomed eyebrow raised enquiringly.

'Yes,' Judy said confidently. 'You see, your strategy is all about luxury, haute couture. I think a press release would trvialise it.'

'You may have a point there.'

'I can give the press background briefings instead.'

'Sounds good.'

Of course it does. A press release Sophie would see; it would have to be positive. Unlike the poison Judy was pouring into the fascinated ears of her press contacts; off-the-record tidbits about costs and waste, about the insane whims of a spoiled woman, somebody who had dismissed, to date, about three hundred Frenchmen from their jobs, men with families to support . . .

'Tell me what you think of this,' Sophie said.

She slid a heavy envelope across the mahogany desk. Despite herself, Judy was curious.

'What is it?'

'A sample invitation. They are being hand-delivered right now, across Paris, to four hundred of the most aristocratic ladies in the city. Old money, and the best families.'

Judy flushed. Was her department working behind her back?

'Who gave you that list of names?' she asked casually.

Sophie shrugged. 'Oh – they are just out of my address book, you know.'

'Of course,' Judy acknowledged, hating her.

'Contacts of Pierre's,' Sophie said, making it worse.

Judy broke open the envelope, which was sealed with red wax, bearing the logo of House Massot, the eagle and diamond. A stiff cream card, with embossed black letters, requesting the pleasure of the company of Baron and Baronne de Chantilly. Inside the envelope there was also a small package wrapped in pale green tissue paper, shot through with tiny eagles in gold. It was addressed, with a tiny hand-written label, in beautiful calligraphy, to Mme la Baronne.

'Our new wrapping paper,' Sophie said. She sounded childishly excited, Judy thought. 'You like it?'

'Very nice.'

'Open it up.'

Judy obediently peeled off the label and unwrapped the tissue paper. A glittering object fell out; it was a brooch, a beautiful piece shaped like a leaf, the rich, almost orange colour of twenty-four carat gold; effortlessly chic and simple. Judy admired the workmanship; it was impossible not to. There was a bale on the reverse, discreetly hidden, so it could be turned into a pendant.

She could think of hundreds of ways to wear the design. Conventionally, or round the hat; holding a Hermès scarf in place; funky, in the band of a hat, or on a belt. It was a gorgeous and very practical piece of jewellery.

'And . . . you have sent every one of these ladies a twenty-four-carat brooch?' Judy asked, disbelievingly.

Sophie nodded proudly. 'Of course, not everybody has got a leaf. The Brandts created twenty different moulds; each piece is a limited edition of twenty. Every design is nature-themed. We have bees, lilies, roses, moons, suns, fish . . .'

Judy made herself say, 'Everything classic.'

'Absolutely. I think the swan is my favourite.'

'That's quite an invitation,' Judy said. Her mouth felt dry. 'How much did it cost?'

Sophie winced. 'You don't want to know.'

Oh, but I do, Judy thought.

'I suppose you must have your secrets,' she said lightly. 'But Sophie . . . all this stuff has to be costing a bomb.'

'We must spend money to make money.' Sophie Massot's eyes were determined. 'The company was falling apart.'

And I think you just pushed it over the edge, Judy mused.

'I wonder . . . I have a crunching migraine today.'

'Oh, I'm sorry.'

'Would you mind if I took a few hours off?'

'Go ahead.' Sophie nodded. 'We'll need you rested.'

'Thank you.' Judy's hand hovered over the leaf. 'May I borrow this? It might be useful for PR.'

'You can have it,' Sophie said. 'It's only a sample. We sent Baronne de Chantilly a stallion. She keeps a large stable of horses.'

'Well,' said Judy, before she could stop herself. 'Isn't that just lovely,' and she turned and walked out of Sophie's office.

There's something wrong with that girl, Sophie thought. Maybe she was working her too hard. But it couldn't be helped, not at the moment. The future of the House hung in the balance.

After the party... that's when she would give Judy a vacation.

Clutching the brooch in her hand, Judy raced from the office. She saw the new girl on reception, a mousy brunette, and told her to direct all calls to Marie. And then, as she emerged into the blazing sunlight of rue Tricot, she was free.

Judy pulled her sunglasses from her bag and belted her cardigan casually around her waist. Her reflection, attractive and slim, stared encouragingly back at her from the window of the pharmacy opposite the office; and the approving glances of the women passing her warmed her like the sunshine on her skin.

She headed to the Left Bank and hailed a taxi.

'L'hotel Crillon,' she said. 'Vite!'

It was still only eight-thirty. Sophie had arrived early. With any luck, her quarry would still be there.

Hugh Montfort glanced over his agenda. Mrs Percy had faxed it to him promptly at seven. She had offered to come to Paris, but he didn't think it necessary, at least, not yet. The office in London had to be manned. And anyway, he could summon her and have her here in a few hours if it came to it.

His first meeting was due to start in twenty minutes. The M & A team, over from Boston, were putting the finishing touches to their offer. Montfort had to review the financial PR one last time, and after that, House Massot would be in play.

It was going well. He had a splendid appetite, and had ordered a large, French breakfast; pastries, coffee, some delicious cured ham, tiny cheeses; it felt rather indulgent to be packing these away at breakfast, but he enjoyed every bite. The hotel had a good gym, and a large pool; he had enjoyed a fifty-length swim at daybreak, then towelled off and completed a punitive circuit on the rowing machine, following that up with weights. His muscles were now pleasantly warm, the

190

endorphins from his workout mingling with the pleasure of the coffee and food; and perhaps the anticipation of battle.

There were still some variables: his lack of knowledge of quite what Sophie Massot was planning. Louis Maitre had hit a brick wall; it had to happen some time. But he thought, on reflection, that he may have been overly concerned. House Massot's share price was in free-fall, and she had barely three months. What could she possibly do in that time?

His main concern now was speed. He had to make his offer before the shrinking share price attracted bigger, badder buyers than Mayberry. Fortunoff's, Tiffany, or one of the big American chains, perhaps.

He pushed the breakfast tray aside and looked out of his window. A beautiful day; clear skies, plain sailing. Hugh breathed in, deeply. He had the scent of his elusive quarry, and the chase was almost over.

He reminded himself to enjoy it. He would choose not to think too much about the emptiness that almost certainly waited for him on the other side of victory.

The phone rang.

'Hugh Montfort.'

'Good morning, sir,' said the receptionist in impeccable English. 'I have a young lady here waiting to see you. Her name is Miss Judy Dean.'

Judy Dean? He didn't remember any women on Lowell Epstein's team.

'Ask her what company she's from,' he said, warily.

'Very good, sir.' There was a brief pause. 'She says she works at House Massot.'

Well, well, Montfort thought.

'Ask her to come up,' he said. 'And tell the meeting in conference room two I've been delayed. They can start without me.'

'Certainly, sir.'

He waited a minute or so, then the knock on his door came, and it was with a most enjoyable curiosity that he said, 'Come in.'

* * *

191

Judy forced her heart to slow down. She had removed her sunglasses in the elevator, checked her appearance for a final time. There was no point being nervous; she was playing a grown-up game, right now.

Montfort would be incredibly grateful. She had to make sure that gratitude translated itself into dollars.

She opened the door. His suite was every bit as sumptuous as she had expected. I want to be rich, Judy thought. I want to be able to stay in places like this, and go first class, and wear important jewels. People made it, all the time. This guy had. Why not her?

He was standing silhouetted against his large window, but he took a step forward, hand outstretched.

'How do you do. I'm Hugh Montfort.'

'Judy Dean,' she said, her voice trembling just a touch.

Oh, forget it, she thought. He was just *so* attractive. Her eyes took him in, and in a split second, had inventoried him – the urbane, confident face, dark eyes and hair, the supremely muscular body; Judy, the fitness fanatic, could imagine what it was like perfectly. He was that rare creature, she thought, the strong man who would also be fast. She'd read up on Montfort. He had been in the British Army, and decorated for valour in the Falklands. The well-cut suit and crisp shirt and tie did nothing, absolutely nothing to hide what was underneath it: an unreconstructed male; a killer.

She couldn't help herself. Feelings she thought had died when Pierre vanished tumbled in on Judy. She blushed with confusion as warm, trawling tendrils of longing curled in her belly, in her breasts and groin. She looked down, then took his hand.

He had a firm, dry grip; but she could sense he was holding his hand loosely, that if he wanted to, he could crush hers.

Judy was dry-mouthed. She felt guilty for the first time that day. Hugh Montfort was so much more attractive, even, than Pierre had ever been to her. Pierre was dominant . . . ruthless, yes; a big businessman. But Montfort – Montfort now, versus Pierre then – he would have made mincemeat of her lover.

Pull yourself together, she thought, sharply.

'Have a seat, Miss Dean.' He showed her into the sitting room of his suite, and Judy sat carefully in one of the armchairs. Her fingers curled around the gold leaf brooch, gripping it tightly.

'Are you here in some official capacity?'

Judy shook her head, mutely. She noted, with a thrill of sheer pleasure, that Hugh Montfort also liked what he saw. His eyes were trickling over her body, running slowly, assessingly up her long legs, her firm, well-turned calves; his gaze lingered for a second on her breasts – not long enough for discourtesy, but long enough for her to see – then it stopped at her neckline, on her collarbone, before breaking evenly to hold her eyes.

Judy felt weak with lust. She ran her tongue over her lips.

'Unofficial,' she managed. 'Very unofficial.'

He spread his hands, leaned back in his chair. 'I'm all ears.'

The girl was aroused. That much was obvious. Hugh was used to women flirting with him and sighing after him, but this girl sitting in front of him was so turned on he could practically smell it. She was blushing; her pupils were dilated a little. She was somewhat hard-bodied for his taste, but undeniably attractive, and Montfort found her interestingly responsive.

Her desire was quite naked. He did not like short hair or long nails, but her desire for him was powerful; it stirred his body, and he had to remind himself of his policy. No women, except hookers. That was humiliating and soul-killing enough. He would never love again, and the strain of a sham relationship was something he could do without.

He would enjoy throwing this girl casually over his bed and giving her what she so clearly wanted. But afterwards . . .

No.

'I have information on House Massot,' Judy said, boldly. 'You can use it in your take-over bid. Expenditures . . . huge costs incurred. The shareholders will go nuts. Once they learn of this, they're bound to support you.'

'And in exchange for this, Miss Dean, you want . . .?'

There was a slight coolness to his tone which she resented, and Judy lifted her chin defiantly.

193

'One million euros.'

'One million euros,' Montfort repeated. 'What if I think what you have to say isn't worth that much?'

'You will,' Judy said confidently.

'And what will you do with that money?'

Judy decided she wanted Montfort. She didn't need to think about it too much. She wanted him, ached for him. They were in a hotel room. The way he'd looked at her . . .

She rested her hand languidly on her collarbone and deliberately undid one button of her dress.

'I think that's my business, Mr Montfort,' she said, and extended her leg, flashing him more than a glimpse of thigh; displaying the very tip of a garter belt.

His eyes glinted.

'You are not happy at House Massot, I take it.'

'It's a joke of a company,' Judy said. 'I'd be happy to come and work for you.'

She imagined that glorious possibility; a new Pierre; better, more manly; and unmarried. A jolting crowd of sexual images tumbled into her mind. It would be like it was when Pierre first summoned her. Sex in his office. Sex in her office. His touch in the elevator. All day long, aware of her own thighs, her womanhood. Not like now, when she was so cold, so dry. Hugh Montfort would wake her up again.

'Not for Sophie Massot?' he asked.

Judy said with sudden vigour, 'I hate that goddamned bitch.'

Montfort looked at the slim beige file in her hands; at the exquisite gold leaf brooch she was clutching. He knew she had something; the final piece in his puzzle. He wanted to know it rather badly. The same way he wanted to shove that teasing little dress the rest of the way up her thighs, and take her, immediately, perhaps more than once.

He stood up.

'Thank you for your time, Miss Dean,' he said with cold courtesy. 'But I am not interested.'

Judy just sat there. 'What?'

Her thigh was exposed; flushing, with anger this time, she quickly hid it.

'That's your cue to leave,' Hugh Montfort said.

Judy stood up; her cheeks were bright red.

'But you need this to win.'

'No,' Hugh said. 'I don't. I rather respect Mme Massot. And I intend to beat her in a manner that is entirely above-board.'

'Well,' Judy responded sharply. 'You saw me, Mr Montfort. So you're not as pure as all that.'

He grinned; inclined his head. 'Touché.'

Judy moved towards him where he stood by the door. Her body was still on fire, and she was sure his was, too.

She stood just a little too close to him; so as to let him see the swell of her cleavage under the button she'd left undone.

'Are you sure you won't change your mind?' she murmured.

He smiled. 'Quite sure. And allow me.'

Montfort reached over and did up the button on her shirt. Then he opened the door to his suite.

'Off you go, Miss Dean,' he said. 'Don't make me call security.'

Judy started. Then the rage and humiliation started to build in her, making her sweat, making her dizzy. Her throat was too thick to speak, even to curse him. She gathered up her file, and stormed out of his suite.

Montfort closed the heavy door behind her, and, as she marched off towards the elevators, she heard him. Chuckling to himself.

Chapter Twenty-Five

Hugh looked at the journalist with distaste. They were sitting in a conference room at the Crillon, and she was the sixth interview he'd given today. A necessary evil; Mayberry's bid had been announced, and his financial PR firm insisted on using him, personally, to appeal to the shareholders.

'You're a star,' Missy Kaufman, the wiry American girl, had told him. 'The business pages are so boring. Editors will kill for a chance to spice it up with someone like you. An English gent, a widower, a war hero –'

Hugh held up his hand. 'Nothing about my wife. Or my past.'

'But it's so romantic, Hugh –'

He eyed her coldly. 'I said nothing.' His tone was final. 'That is to be a condition of giving the interviews. If my business background will help get press, you can use that.'

Missy sighed. 'Can I at least use the Oscars?'

'Certainly,' he said, thankful the danger had passed.

But the day had been wearing, nonetheless. Journalist after journalist asking the same questions. This girl, thank God, was the last. Amanda Fife from the *Financial Times*. She was plump, but hard-looking, and persistent.

'This is all about the stock price, as far as we're concerned.'

'Yes, but wouldn't you agree that families can't just treat companies they have a stake in like their private playgrounds?'

'Of course.'

'Her husband may have founded the firm, but Sophie Massot has no business background.' Amanda's lip curled. 'She's been a stay-at-home wife and party hostess.'

'You'd need to ask her about that.'

'Since she took over, the stock price has lost a third of its value. And continues to sink.'

'That's why we hope shareholders will vote to accept Mayberry's bid.'

'Do you think that just because she controls a large stake she should be able to do what she likes with the company?'

'Of course not.'

'And she's fired hundreds of staff around the world. Closed one entire division without even looking for a buyer. What do you think of that?'

He thought it was a very good idea; inspired, in fact.

'I think shareholders will have the chance to voice their anger shortly, by voting for Mayberry.'

'Of course, you know all about that sort of thing. When you started at Mayberry you had no qualms about firing hundreds of people yourself.'

'Of course I had qualms; but it had to be done.' Hugh couldn't take another minute. 'And I'm afraid that's all I have time for, Miss Fife.'

He stood and offered her his hand.

'It's Ms Fife,' she said, waspishly.

'Ms Fife,' he agreed.

She smiled at him. 'Don't worry. We have to be tough in interviews. But it'll be a positive piece.'

'I'm glad to hear it.'

'The shareholders can't wait to dump Sophie Massot, from what I'm hearing. Spoiled bitch,' she said with contempt. 'People have their savings in that company. But she's too rich to care.'

'We don't know that.'

'Sure we do. When you sit on your ass for ten years, then come in and destroy something, that's all we need to know. Well, she'll be out in three months.' The girl nodded at him. 'Good to meet you,' she said, and, mercifully, walked out.

He waited five minutes, enough for her to clear the lobby, and then left the hotel himself. The day was strangely cool, foggy and with a chill in the air, freak weather blowing into the heat of the Parisian summer; Hugh did not mind the cold snap. He wanted to walk and to clear his head.

Was Sophie Massot a spoiled bitch?

On paper, everything confirmed it. And yet, he nonetheless thought not. There was that one, surprising encounter at the library benefit.

He had remembered her, often, in fact. The unsurpassed elegance of her raven silk ballgown and teardrop briolettes; she was breathtaking. And attractive in the most dangerous way, more than superficially. Her face was pretty enough, considered conventionally, but nothing out of the ordinary. Sophie Massot's charm was in her elegance, her style, and more than that, her personal dignity.

Women made Hugh Montfort edgy, pleased, aroused, in turn; they did not often make him feel small. But Sophie had sharply corrected his arrogance. He admired her for it.

He walked through the drizzle, grey skies matching the grey stones of the city. It had been a snapshot of a woman, nothing more. And yet; she interested him.

Sophie Massot was a puzzle. Nothing about her bearing fit the facts.

He had reached the Left Bank, and realised he was heading for rue Faubourg, and the Massot showroom. Hugh had been given a brief note. The showrooms were redesigned, and foot traffic appeared to be slightly up, but nothing to cause them any alarm. A non-event, then.

He still wanted to see it for himself.

There was a doorman outside, in a navy uniform and old-fashioned cap, who sprang to open the door.

'Good morning, sir.'

'Good morning.' Hugh nodded. If that was the first change, he approved of it. He noticed everything; the man's immaculate, wrinkle-free uniform, his pleasant manners; the gleaming brass trim on the new glass doors, and the heavy, reassuring heft of them as they opened – soundproofing, he thought; and was proven right, because as the door closed behind him, it swallowed up whole the sounds of the street, the hum of people and traffic.

He took everything in with a quick glance, and was immediately impressed.

Montfort had been to some Massot stores last year. This was unrecognisable. The interior of the showroom was full of flowers in fragrant cascades of pastels; not flowers, no, just roses. He admired the blond woods, the new cases, the deep blue velvet, the lighting, the assistants; it was all very rich, very feminine.

'Good morning, sir.'

A young woman in a pink Chanel suit had materialised by his side. She wasn't pretty, but she was, he noted, extremely well put together. There was a small brooch of gold – pure gold – a bar, with her name on it in raised letters; CLAUDETTE CHIRON. Montfort felt a thrill of appreciation. Assistants in Chanel, and their nameplates a piece of jewellery; twenty-four carat.

'Can I offer you any assistance this morning?'

'I think I'll just look,' Montfort said. There were ten other people in the showroom; four of them browsing, the rest being helped with purchases. He could see tissue paper and ribbons. A dowager who had just finished paying walked towards him, and he realised the carrier bag was made of pale pink satin, stamped with the Massot logo in gold.

'Very good, sir. Do please summon me if you have any questions.'

Mlle Chiron smiled at him and melted away.

Questions? He had hundreds. Who was responsible for this magnificent look? He might want to hire them. More importantly, for his bid; how much did this cost?

He walked over to one of the cases; this was a grouping of necklaces. Not like his own firm, there were no ranges; each piece was bespoke. There were also no prices.

Was this madness? The free-spending caprice of a spoiled bitch, as the journalist had charged? Sophie Massot indulging a talent for interior design with other people's money?

He bent to examine the pieces in the case.

They had been grouped stylistically. This case was full of bold colours and styles, while the one a few feet from him gleamed with the discreet tones of silver and moonlight; opals, platinum, pearls and zircons.

These pieces were more modern. Hugh eyed them with the appreciation of a connoisseur. They reminded him a little of Jean Schlumberger designs, the great twentieth-century master; bright green tsavorites threaded with violet tanzanite; yellow sapphires and emeralds; coral branches linked with diamonds and iolites, a necklace redolent of the ocean floor. There was flair, but it was never obvious; the colours contrasted, rather than clashed. He coveted each one. It was bitter that Montfort had no woman to hang them on. The yellow sapphires and emeralds, he thought at once, would have done very well for Georgie; they were vernal, like daffodils, showily beautiful, but with a certain irreverence that guaranteed good taste.

He moved on to a different part of the room. Brooches. The Cinderella of modern jewellery; so few houses made decent brooches any more. The younger set just did not wear them.

Massot apparently did not care about the younger set.

A quick glance estimated that there were more brooches in this room than any other kind of piece. And what brooches: animals, flowers, bars, geometric shapes; something to suit every taste, though not, he saw, every wallet. Montfort admired the creativity – aquamarine, peridot and diamonds in an art deco style; a surreal Humpty Dumpty in ivory and yellow beryl; pink topaz, seed pearls and garnets on a rose; moonstones with amethyst accents; a Star of David in cat's eye and ruby, very unusual; a brilliant-cut green tourmaline, set with chrysoberyl and turqoise cabochons in black gold.

He felt quite privileged, even uplifted, to see work of this quality on sale. Surely gems like this belonged in museums.

There was a classic peacock feather aigrette brooch in the centre of the display. Montfort nodded to himself; a student of jewellery had made this one. He knew he should keep his presence here secret, under the radar. But he could not help himself. He lifted his eyes, searching for the girl who had greeted him.

She was standing behind the counter and noticed him at once. She came out to him promptly, her kitten heels clicking delicately on the wood floor.

'What can you tell me about this brooch?' Montfort asked, pointing to it.

'You have an excellent eye, monsieur. That is the tribute of one of our designers to Tiffany's feather brooch, containing the Brunswick diamond, which was exhibited in America in 1876.'

'The Centennial Exhibition in Philadelphia.'

She smiled. 'You know your history, monsieur.'

'But that is not a yellow diamond,' Montfort commented, nodding at the gloriously sparkling gem set in the centre of the feather.

'No, monsieur.' The girl waited, as it was clear Montfort wanted to guess.

'It doesn't have the depth of a yellow sapphire. Not quite beryl tint, either. I think it must be a very fine citrine with an unusual lemon cast.'

Claudette inclined her head. 'Monsieur is absolutely correct. The small stones outlining the surrounding diamonds are yellow sapphires, however.'

Hugh sighed with pleasure. 'Magnificent.'

'Are you interested in purchasing the piece?'

'I am,' he said. He had no idea why, except that it was outstandingly lovely, and he intended to have it.

'This piece is ninety-five thousand euros.'

'Expensive,' he commented.

'Yes, monsieur. But unique.' Claudette smiled. 'There are over six hundred stones in the piece, exactly like the original. Unlike the original, though, the artist has used colours other than yellow; sapphires, emeralds, rubies, imperial topaz, and peridot as well as the white diamonds that form most of the piece. This, I think, ensures it is a tribute, rather than a copy.'

Hugh nodded.

'If the style appeals, monsieur, I can show you some other,

smaller examples that may suit your taste that are under fifteen thousand.'

'No; this is the one. Wrap it up for me, please.'

'Certainly, monsieur.'

Her face showed no surprise that he was making such a costly purchase. She removed the brooch delicately from the case, and carried it to the counter, where a second well-dressed assistant, a man this time, wrapped it expertly in gossamer-soft tissue paper and royal blue ribbon, placing it in a rose-coloured jewellery case. It nestled, glittering, against the satin, and Hugh thought with satisfaction that it might be the most beautiful thing he owned.

He wrote out a cheque, which Mlle Chiron took without examining it.

'Thank you very much, M. Montfort,' she said.

His head lifted. She had not looked at his handwriting, which must mean she recognised him. It suddenly struck him that his romantic impulse was foolish. The press would love that story. Hostile bidder seduced by Massot's new look.

'Mademoiselle –' he began.

'It is all right, monsieur,' she said quietly. 'At House Massot we maintain complete confidentiality about the purchases of our clients. All our clients. Without exception.'

'Thank you, Mlle Chiron.' Hugh paused. 'For what it is worth – I have been most impressed today.'

She bowed her head slightly.

'Monsieur is most kind, but perhaps he should direct his compliments to the party responsible.'

'Who is?'

'Mme Massot, of course,' she said.

He went to lunch at a small café tucked down a side street. It didn't have much of an awning, and the menu in the window was only in French. Hugh correctly deduced he would get an outstanding meal there. He ordered wine, a half-carafe of rough house red, earthy and delicious, and then duck confit with fried courgettes and an apple flan. Everything was exceptional; the meat meltingly tender, yet crispy, the vegetables deliciously fresh, the flan light, buttery and not too sweet. The place was crowded, but Hugh didn't care. The food lifted him out of himself, and besides, he wanted to be alone.

Mlle Chiron had arranged to have the aigrette delivered to his hotel, with instructions it be placed in the safe. Montfort was not afraid of being mugged; men had tried twice before, once in the West End and once in a rough part of Los Angeles, and both had left with broken bones and smashed noses. But he knew he was distracted, and didn't want to worry about leaving it somewhere.

Everything was going well. The press, the shareholder response. All the pieces seemed to be falling into place. Whatever the hard, sexy American's information, he did not think he would need it.

All I have to do is wait for the shareholder meeting, Hugh thought; and Massot will be mine.

It would be his greatest triumph as a Mayberry executive. His brand lifted to world domination . . .

And after that . . . then what?

He chose not to face that question. Hugh took a final sip of the excellent house wine, then summoned a waiter and asked for coffee and his bill. The man hurried back with some black filter, also good; freshly made and fragrant, not stewed in a pot for hours like so many restaurant coffees these days. The bill was ludicrously small; Hugh tipped fifty per cent.

He walked out to the street, avoiding the waiter's effusive thanks. A taxi was passing, slowing because of the narrowness of the road, and Montfort hailed it.

'Bonjour,' he said. 'Rue Tricot, s'il vous plait.'

He trusted his instincts, and they told him to go and see Sophie Massot.

Sophie picked up her phone. Her new secretary was buzzing her. Celine had proven to be incredibly grateful, and hard-working, and had kept her head down. Sophie was delighted with her; there had been no repeat of her stand-offishness to Judy Dean.

'Yes, Celine?'

'Madame.' The girl's voice was nervous. 'Madame, there is a

203

person to see you. But I don't know if you will wish to see him.'

'An appointment?' Had she forgotten a meeting with Herr Brandt? Or one of their gemologists?

'No, madame. It is – it is M. Hugh Montfort.'

Sophie jumped in her chair. 'Hold on a second, Celine.'

Montfort? What should she do? It was arrogance, incredible arrogance, for him to turn up at her office and assume she would see him. Maybe she ought to tell Celine to get security and have him thrown out.

No, that wouldn't do. She would have to see him. He might use it in the press, otherwise. More of those vicious stories that Judy couldn't seem to stop.

There was a tray on her desk. Responses to the party invitations. So far they had had only one refusal, from the Duchesse de Nevers, and she had asked if her daughter might go instead. Sophie considered stacking them away somewhere. The party was, after all, her secret weapon.

But again, no. That did not fit the style of Massot she was working on.

'Show him up,' Sophie said.

While she waited she stood and went to the mirror; antique and full-length, a fine nineteenth-century piece Sophie had brought in from the château. Making a good impression had always been a priority, because Pierre wanted it. But it was now the heart of her business, too.

She still looked well, she thought. Today's suit was Roberto Cavalli, a fitted jacket over a pleated A-line skirt, and underneath it, a silky Prada blouse in gunmetal grey; at her neck a Massot pendant, a piece in the Hungarian revival style – cornflower blue sapphires and pink, mis-shapen conch pearls set in filigree gold. It was ornate, with an Islamic influence, so Sophie wore only plain gold studs as earrings, and no other jewellery than her wedding band.

For the first time, she wore her hair loose. It looked sexy, and she rather liked it. Sophie felt a little more daring; she'd dropped the court shoes and was experimenting with heels; they changed her walk, and she was feeling younger, more confident. She was going to have to handle this by herself.

There was no Gregoire Lazard to look to for help.

'Come in,' she said when he knocked.

Montfort entered and bowed slightly.

'I ought to have called first,' he said. 'You are good to see me on short notice.'

'Have a seat.' Sophie took hers, determined not to lose time on pleasantries.

She took him in. Hugh Montfort was just as she remembered him; confident, good-looking – insanely good-looking, in fact. But not in a smooth, conventional way. His face was weather-beaten and looked tired; he was too muscular, and he moved in a precise, controlled way that many people would find unsettling. Including herself.

And yet she acknowledged he was very handsome. If you were into the rugged type. Sophie never had been. Square jaws and thick arms reminded her of her father, and he had been a bully; never hit her, true, but that's not the only way to scare people.

Pierre Massot and Gregoire Lazard were very different. Tall but slight, precise dressers, even-featured – soothing, even.

Hugh Montfort did not sooth her. He registered as dangerous. Sophie felt the tug of attraction in her body, but tried to ignore it.

She had got involved with only one other man after Pierre, and it had been nothing but disaster. Saving Massot was a duty. More than that, it had become her life.

An attraction – even a strong attraction – to the man who wanted to destroy it . . . no, she thought again, that won't do.

'Mrs Massot—'

'Madame. My husband was French, and I honour his memory,' Sophie said firmly. She tried to make sure this was true.

'Mme Massot.' He inclined his head. 'I visited your show-rooms in rue Faubourg today.'

Sophie said nothing. Let him make the running.

'May I say that your refurbishment is outstanding. The design is excellent, the lighting, the display – all superb.'

'I am glad you were pleased,' she responded coolly.

'I became a customer of House Massot.'

Sophie's eyes sparked a little interest at that. 'And what did you buy?'

'A peacock feather aigrette, after the first piece Tiffany designed.'

She nodded. 'I know that brooch. It is a very beautiful piece; you have good taste. But then again, all our pieces are beautiful,' she added, with some firmness.

'So they are. But, Mme Massot, they are bespoke, and the prices are outrageous. You cannot make money in the haute couture market. May I give you my opinion?'

'You never seem to hesitate on that point.'

He grinned. 'Perhaps not. Then let me say, fashion houses – jewellery houses too – make most of their money, almost all of it, in selling lesser-priced pieces to the masses. The individual stuff is just a loss leader. Chanel makes its money in scent . . .'

'House Massot does not sell to the masses, Mr Montfort. And nor do I intend to. Our jewellery will remain bespoke. And we will be profitable. There is nothing to limit us as to perfumes, however, in the future. For now, I intend to restructure the company and focus on our core market. This will mean more value to the shareholders than your low-ball offer.'

Hugh sat back, surprised. She wasn't right – of course not – but the short speech displayed at least a basic understanding of business.

He thought, as she sat there, bolt upright, in her black and pearl grey, with that stunning, just-right pendant – full of her own dignity, and bristling with hostility – that she was maybe the most attractive woman he had ever seen.

A flush of anger and guilt ran through him at his own betrayal. Georgie – Georgie was the most attractive. He would love Georgie till he died. There was no space for anyone else.

'You have no time for that. You only have a couple of months.' His tones were clipped. 'Not enough time to convince your shareholders. After years of mismanagement.'

'We'll see,' she said, mysteriously.

This annoyed Hugh. He ploughed on. 'I understand you

want to keep your husband's empire alive. And I find the Massot rebranding quite convincing. So I am here to make you a new offer.'

'I'm listening,' Sophie said.

'If you will back Mayberry's offer for the stock, we will now no longer dissolve Massot. Our plan was simply to occupy your stores and use your supply pipelines. However, after what I have seen, I am now prepared to guarantee Massot's survival, for five years at least, as a division of Mayberry jewels – our high-end division. Massot will have a corner in every Mayberry store selling a few select pieces. We would continue to employ your talented designers. And I can find a position for you, yourself, in terms of design and decor of our worldwide stores. Thus your family would still be involved with House Massot.'

Montfort sat back.

'Well,' Sophie said. 'Let me make you a counter-offer, Mr Montfort.'

He spread his hands. 'I don't think I can do any better, Mme Massot . . .'

'I will buy Mayberry,' Sophie said. 'I'm sure I can get financing for such a bid after our successful relaunch. I will turn Mayberry into our young adult brand, because I feel the company is greatly overvalued. It's a fad, and fads change. Mayberry may, however, provide us with a good network for future lower-end cheaper jewellery, or any ready-to-wear mass lines we may produce under a name other than Massot. Or our perfumes, perhaps.' She smiled briskly. 'You should take me up on it now. After you fail at the stockholders' meeting, your reputation, and your company's share price, will suffer. Market psychology, you see.'

Hugh laughed. 'You are very bold, madame. I admire your spirit.'

'Thank you.'

He stood. 'Thank you for your time.'

Sophie nodded; the exquisite pendant at her neck glinted against her warm skin. He noticed the faint crinkles around her eyes and he loved that. She was no green girl, with no ideas of her own, no experience of life. To him she was the picture of elegance and bravery.

He paused. 'I would want you to believe that I came here today because I was impressed. Because I admire what you are trying to do. In fact, once we have taken over this company, I can do what I like with it, including keeping the Massot brand active, as I just described. But I wanted to offer you something, you personally.'

'And I thank you for the kind thought.' Sophie, at last, gave him a very small smile. 'But I think you will find we can take care of ourselves.'

She opened her drawer and took out an envelope; an invitation to the party, with the name left blank. There were thirty of those, just in case, for extras, or employees who wanted to attend.

Sophie removed the top from her Mont Blanc pen and carefully wrote in Montfort's name. He saw she had it correct; The Hon. Hugh Montfort, and written in a delicate, cursive hand.

'What is this?' he asked.

'If you are free, we are having a little party on Friday evening. In the rue Faubourg showroom.' Sophie smiled. 'I think it may surprise you.'

He took the envelope. 'Of course I'll come,' he said. 'And thank you for seeing me.'

Sophie offered her hand. 'I'll have Celine show you out.' Enough was enough, she thought. She could make magnanimous gestures, too; but Hugh Montfort was her enemy, her son's enemy, her husband's enemy. Sophie was not about to let a passing fancy blind her to that.

Gregoire Lazard was the last time.

Chapter Twenty-Six

Tom bowed half-heartedly.

'And this is Celeste de Fortuny, and her sister Margot.'

Two more moon-faced girls with weak chins. He sighed inwardly.

'They are the daughters of the Marquis de Fortuny, you know, darling,' his grandmother persisted.

'I know the Marquis,' Tom acknowledged. They had met several times at Maman's interminable dinner parties at the château. De Fortuny was a dullard with a face flushed from too much testing of the product of his own vineyeards, and his daughters looked scarcely more interesting.

'And here is Louise Tatin.'

'Enchanted,' Tom said, kissing her hand. Louise was a slight improvement. She had red hair and reminded him of Flora.

'And her young man, Georges, the younger son of M. Grecques, the Minister of Finance.'

'How d'you do,' Tom managed. So the slightly pretty one was taken, no surprise there. God. How much more of this? Grandmother's parties, and salons, and introductions, were wearing him out. Tonight was the worst; fifty of her closest friends and their children for dinner in the rented apartment, Paris's most costly caterers, no expense spared. The adults had mostly left after the sumptuous dinner. Even Tom had enjoyed the dinner; it was a rush to finally sit at the head of his own, long table, grandmother presiding at the second one. The caterers had brought it in, laid it with the finest linens, crystal glasses and silverware, punctuated it with vases crammed with lilies and orchids, and beeswax candles, and then served a meal of utter magnificence. If he was honest, he had enjoyed all those dukes and barons as his guests; he had revelled in the free flow of vintage champagne, the caviar and other *amuse-gueles*, the nettle sorbets, the Normandy cheeses, the truffled butter, the succulent roast geese. It was all extremely French, extremely *haut*; a mark of respect to his father. Grandmother wore an impeccable Givenchy gown of moss-green satin and dripped with Massot emeralds and diamonds. The one concession to England had been at his own request: Charbonnel & Walker chocolates. One simply could not get better, neither in Paris nor in any Brussels confectioner, and Tom would rather have the best than be a purist.

French was, of course, usually best. But sometimes the British did some things well. Such as chocolates. And women.

The adults had left, and now Grandmother was pressing the acquaintance of a string of bland society girls on him. Even imagining them without their clothes did not help much.

'It's a wonderful party,' Louise Tatin said.

Tom bowed again. 'I hope you enjoy yourself. Delighted to meet you, Georges. Would you excuse me a moment?'

He evaded Katherine's waspish stare and fled to another corner of the room. What was the point? The names went in one ear and out of the other. He had been seen in society – made the point; a Massot was back, a true Massot, to take control. Grandmother had invited select gossip columnists; come tomorrow this would be all over the papers. Then he had to find some executives, charm some bankers; it would be a two-way vote between himself and Mayberry, and Tom wanted to get to work.

Right now he would settle for a drink.

A plump waitress was hovering near the trust-fund brat of some property developer. Tom nodded sharply at her, and she plodded over to him, bearing a merciful flute of ice-cold vintage Pol Roget. He picked it up, resisting the temptation to slug it back in one go and get another. That was impossible here. Too many moon-faced witnesses.

'So, M. Massot.' A girl sidled up to him. She was a modelly type, the kind *Vogue* hires because they have an 'interesting' face; small-featured and far too thin, with a cultivated air of *ennui*. Tom thought with longing of Polly; her laughter, her ample breasts. But that made him miserable, so he took a fortifying sip of champagne and tried to remember her name.

'Call me Tom, please . . .' what was it '. . . Henriette.'

'Minette,' she said, her face clouding.

'That's what I said. Minette.' He smiled at her.

'So . . . I am looking forward to your mother's party,' Minette said. 'Will you be there?'

Tom desperately tried to pull her details from the files of recent introductions stored in his memory. Minette . . . yes, there it was – Minette Roux, daughter of a banker and his Italian principessa of a wife.

'What party is that?'

'Oh, you know. On Friday. The one at House Massot, at the showroom. To celebrate the reopening.' The girl smiled; she had bad teeth, probably owing to acid from self-induced vomiting to keep her weight down. Polly always relished her food.

'I have not seen my mother since I returned to Paris last week. But I intend to. I doubt I shall come to this party.'

Tom thought that was as diplomatic as he could manage. He would have to remove Maman, but he was a good son, he thought self-righteously. He would not allow *le tout Paris* to make them into mortal enemies. Once Maman had been restored to her proper place, they would be back to normal. Or almost; he could never forget his mother had declared Papa dead.

'But it is the great triumph of House Massot. At least, that's what all the rumours say.'

'They are just rumours. The House will triumph again, of course – after I have taken over.'

The girl's pinched face clouded in confusion. 'You are not throwing this party, monsieur?'

'My mother and I have a minor disagreement,' Tom said with dignity. 'And please call me Tom.' He wanted to change the subject. 'I like that brooch,' he said.

On a dress of ochre velvet that hung too loose about her

211

scrawny frame, the girl had placed a very elegant twenty-four-carat brooch; a delicately carved crab, holding a luminous fire opal between its claws. The rich russet colours complemented the shade of her gown; it was, at least, an attractive pairing.

Her eyes bugged. 'But it's Massot,' she said. 'Your mother sent it to me. Well, she sent one to everybody who was invited. Not a crab, like mine. But a brooch, anyway. A different one for everybody.'

Tom paused. 'Let me get this straight, Minette,' he said. 'My mother sent an original Massot piece to everybody she invited to this party?'

'That's right.' The girl smiled her bad teeth at him. 'And do you know, Tom, everybody's just *delighted . . .*'

He felt sick. So – his dear maman was turning House Massot jewels into cheap promotional freebies? Tom was sure Papa would be turning over in his grave – no, not that; he would be furious. When he came home.

'I expect they are very pleased to receive a House Massot piece for nothing,' he answered coldly. 'Whether the shareholders will enjoy this recklessness is another matter.'

'So . . . you won't be coming?'

She really was as thick as pigswill. 'Excuse me,' he said stiffly, and walked away.

Katherine was holding court on a chaise-longue at one end of the salon. A crowd of young people had gathered around her, and she was talking animatedly, waving her splendid filigree ivory fan. Her eyes lit up as Tom approached, clutching his champagne flute as though it were a life-saver.

'Ah; there you are, darling. I thought we had lost you for ever.'

'My apologies, Grandmother. I was talking with Minette Roux.'

'A very charming young woman,' his grandmother pronounced.

'Tom, Mme Katherine was just telling us stories of your father,' Margot de Fortuny said. 'All about his first *atelier* on rue d'Agusseau. And his first piece, the eagle brooch. Holding the diamond.'

Tom softened. 'That is magnificent. Still the greatest piece House Massot ever made.'

That brooch was now the logo of the House; his father, Maman had told him, repurchased it at incredible cost from the private collection of an Infanta of Spain, and it was now housed under a glass case in Papa's old sitting room, in the château.

'Oh, I love all House Massot's jewellery,' said Louise Tatin, sycophantically.

'And I.' Julie Hebèrge, a young baronne, smiled at him. 'The brooch your mother sent me when she invited me to her party – is quite charming, I assure you. A spider, made from solid gold with the tiniest eyes of jet . . .'

Tom nodded. 'Have you heard about this party, Grand-mother?'

Katherine looked at him calmly. 'Of course I have, darling. All Paris has heard of it.'

'I see.' She had not seen fit to inform him.

'I was going to mention it to you tonight; to ask your advice on what I should wear.' Katherine smiled at the crowd of courtiers. 'Tom advises an old lady on her *toilette* so I do not make a fool of myself.'

There was a chorus of dissent.

'What you will wear? But we are not going, surely?' Tom asked, shocked out of discretion.

Katherine fixed him with a watery eye. 'But of course we are going, my dear,' she said softly. 'It is your party. For it is your company. That is what your father intended.'

He was finally alone at one in the morning. Hélène Duloc, a curvy brunette daughter of some publishing magnate, had practically offered herself to him as a bed partner, but for once Tom was not interested. His mind was too busy. He needed to be by himself, and besides, she was half drunk, and he preferred them sober. Nice tits, though; maybe he would call her tomorrow.

After his grandmother had been picked up by her chauffeur, and the last guests had made their farewells, the catering company had most efficiently packed everything away; they had twenty people on the job, and within fifteen minutes his apartment was as pristine as when they had first arrived.

It was a great relief. Of course, at the château he would not have had to worry. He could simply have removed to the library, one of the drawing rooms, his father's smoking room, or the kitchens; anywhere, really, and waited for the servants to clear the stuff away in the morning. In the apartment, however, Tom did not have the luxury of that space.

He walked into his spotless kitchen and reached for the coffee-maker; they had thoughtfully laid out some decaffeinated blends. Tom selected a Jamaican Blue Mountain, and poured in a little cream. He chose a couple of moist macaroon cookies; the sweetness, and richness of the coffee, was soothing.

He felt a touch uneasy. More than a touch. What was Grandmother planning? To see Maman at this party for the first time? They must quarrel. It might ruin the party, but it would also damage the reputation of the House, and, more importantly, of his family. Surely Katherine could not want that. Yet he was sure, for all her correct words, that his grandmother had little time for Maman.

Tom could not be so harsh. Yes, she had behaved appallingly, but it was all new. Some kind of mid-life crisis. Since Papa had gone away, his mother had been the picture of ladylike elegance, keeping her state in the castle, throwing the right parties, and doing nothing improper. He thought all those years of good behaviour had to count for something. She must be corrected. But it must be done with respect.

He perceived a malice in Katherine's bloodshot old eyes that disturbed him.

On the other hand, she was right. He could not be shut out of that party. *He*, and not Mother, was going to control House Massot. In three years he would get all his shares, including the large block she voted.

To stay away would be to concede defeat. To legitimise her takeover of the company.

So; he would go, then. But he would not create a scene. He would need to speak to Grandmother about that.

Tom took his Limoges cup over to the window; even at this hour, cars were streaming past, lighting up the soft night with harsh neon lights. Paris was a modern city, full of bustle, full of money. It was in this city that his father had raised himself from a poor apprentice jeweller, eking out a living repairing watches and resizing rings, to the founder of a great empire, a great marque. Papa had wanted Tom to carry it on, as his heir and only child, and his mother, who had never had to strive a day in her life, was dismantling it.

He was dreading the party. There must be some kind of confrontation. He loved his mother, but right now he disliked her heartily for making him go through all this.

It sounded like an insane extravagance. Sending Massot jewels free to hundreds of people. This on top of outrageously costly renovations, and closing the fashion division. Well, the shareholders would have had enough. He would let Maman enjoy her last hurrah, and then there would be the shareholders' meeting, and it would all be over.

He would have to grow up fast. To rebuild Papa's empire, first. And then try to rebuild his family.

Chapter Twenty-Seven

'The Body of Christ,' Fr Sabin said.

'Amen,' Sophie responded.

She extended her tongue; the altar boy held the paten beneath her chin, and the old priest reverently laid the Host upon it. Sophie stood and made her way back to her pew. Holy Communion was over; she knelt down again and tried to pray.

It was hard, today. Sophie stared at the smooth wood, its knotted surface worn glossy and soft from hundreds of years of parishioners, kneeling and sitting. The dark pews were a little small for twenty-first-century bodies, but nobody complained; they were beautiful, as the tiny church was.

Sophie fixed her gaze on the bronze statue of the Sainte Vierge above the altar and tried to concentrate, to give thanks for the Sacrament. But the Virgin was holding her son; clutching him to her as though she would never let him go.

The image of motherhood filled her eyes with tears, and she had to turn away. Tom was here. In Paris – with that interfering old witch! With Katherine. But no, she mustn't call her an old witch – that was not Christian charity. Sophie struggled, and turned her gaze to the stained-glass windows, they had a nice, safe picture of St Genevieve . . .

'Let us pray,' Fr Sabin said.

Sophie breathed out, relieved, and got to her feet. Father finished the last prayers, asked them to bow their heads, and gave them God's blessing. As soon as he had pronounced the final 'Amen' of the dismissal, Sophie quietly slipped from her pew, genuflected, and hurried from the church.

She emerged into the dazzling sunlight blinking back tears,

and looked around for her driver. Where was he? She didn't want anybody to see her crying. The family breach at the château was all over the village, and this would only make it worse . . .

Sophie couldn't see Richard. There wasn't a parking spot to be had anywhere in the street. She supposed he was circling the village. Inside the church the sounds of the last hymn were dying away. Sophie started to walk hastily in the other direction. She had to get away; she could call Richard on the mobile, have him pick her up outside Café Marianne. The walk would distract her long enough to regain some composure.

'Sophie.' Fr Sabin, old and out of breath, had rushed out to catch her, soutane flapping, one bony hand on his hat. 'Sophie, where are you going?'

'Excuse me – excuse me, Father. I can't stay.'

'But you must, indeed. Go round to the rectory. The door's open.'

'Not this Sunday –'

'Certainly this Sunday. This is about young Thomas, *ma chère*?'

'I –'

She couldn't manage it. The lump in her throat resurfaced, too thick to be swallowed, and a fat tear trickled down her cheek.

'Just go,' hissed the old priest. A fat lady trundled from the vestibule, eyes narrowing as she saw Sophie crying. She moved animatedly towards her, but Fr Sabin intercepted her with an expert grace.

'Mme Estelle – how nice to see you again. Where is monsieur this morning? Sick? I am sorry to hear it . . .'

Sophie fled through the priest's garden to the safety of the house.

'Where is your driver?' Fr Sabin said, handing over her mug of stewed Tetley.

'He's parked up the street. I called him. He'll wait.'

'Sophie,' the priest scolded. 'It is very bad that you have him work on the Sabbath. You must stop it immediately. You can drive your own car, for once.'

'I never learned.' She hadn't got round to it, as a teenager; and then Pierre found her, and there were always drivers. Sophie had broached it once, but he wouldn't hear of it. Mme Pierre Massot did not drive; she was driven. 'Anyway,' she went on, since the priest had opened his mouth again, no doubt to tell her to walk, 'Richard is Jewish, Father; he takes Saturday off.'

'Oh. Humph. Very well, then. I keep an eye on these things, you know.'

'I know.'

'How is your tea?'

'Delicious,' Sophie lied.

Fr Sabin took a sip of his own coffee. It smelled wonderful. Sophie looked at it wistfully.

'I heard about your son's return,' he said.

She was jerked back to her sorrow. 'From whom?' Sophie demanded. 'Who could know that?'

'Everybody, my dear,' said the priest, as though it were a foolish question. 'You know St Aude.'

Sophie bit her lip. Well, of course everybody knew. Why not? She was starting to understand just how sheltered, how controlled, her life at the château had been under Pierre. It was a big world, and she needed to get up to speed. She was not the obedient little woman – not any more.

'I think he hates me,' Sophie said. 'My – my baby.'

'Of course he does not hate you.'

'I finally found out on Friday. From my secretary,' Sophie said, humiliated. 'Celine came to see me and asked if I knew. She was so nervous, telling me. But she didn't want me to look foolish any more.' She swallowed. 'They've been giving parties – Tom and Katherine. And going to dinners, the theatre, always with our friends – people I thought were my friends. It's been in the papers, even. I just don't read the gossip columns.'

She fished a handkerchief out of her black quilted Chanel purse and blew her nose loudly.

'Have you spoken to him?'

'I don't know where he is.' Sophie shook her head.

'And Mme Katherine?'

'She is not at the Dower House; not when I call. Her butler will not admit me. She does not take my calls.'

'She deliberately refuses to talk to you?'

'That, and she seems to be mostly in Paris. Thick as thieves with my child.'

'He is also her grandson.'

'She has no right to come between us!' Sophie said, with a fresh burst of tears. 'What is she doing? She's always hated me, always! Tom should be in Oxford, studying for his examinations. He's thrown everything away!'

'You can't be sure. Perhaps he has come to some arrangement with them.'

'Not likely.' Sophie thought of the parties, the womanising, the drunkenness, the tutors' warnings. 'He never bothered with his college.'

'You could call and ask.'

'I won't ask strangers for news about my own son!' Sophie burst out.

Fr Sabin took a calm sip of his coffee.

'Excuse me – excuse me,' Sophie said, wretchedly.

He waved it away.

'And did the young woman tell you anything else?'

'Yes.' Sophie put down her mug of tea. 'She said they are planning to come to my party. The relaunch of our brand. Both of them, although they weren't invited.'

'You can hardly shut them out.'

'Exactly. The press will be there, Father. I have no time, you see, to turn the company around before the meeting; but I have to make sure the shareholders believe I *can* turn it around.'

'So this party is highly important, for your work?'

'It's everything.' Sophie dabbed at her eyes.

'And you fear your son and Mme Katherine are out to ruin it?'

'That, and . . .' Sophie shivered. 'They have access to a significant block of stock. I checked with our lawyers. Fifteen per cent, if you combine it.'

'But you have more . . .' the old man scrunched up his face. 'Business bores me, Sophie, I'm afraid. I am more concerned with your son. With your whole family. It seems to me, my dear, that if you reconcile with your son, the danger in your business will also go away.'

'There is still Katherine.' She wanted to add 'that bitch', but he was a priest. 'I'll never convince her.'

'Mme Katherine has . . .' he chose his words '. . . a highly developed sense of propriety. With your son and you in harmony, she would not dare to vote against you, because it would cause talk.'

'You might be right.'

'And do not be too hard on her, Sophie. We must love our enemies.'

Sophie gritted her teeth. It was easier said than done.

'Besides, you have only lost a husband. She has lost a son. You are a mother – you must feel for that. You will not stop loving Tom when you are eighty.'

'I suppose,' Sophie said, softening marginally.

'Without Pierre, Tom is her only blood. It is true he is your son, and only her grandson, but he is Pierre's boy. Consider that she may feel he is all she has left.'

Sophie tried. She really did. But all that would come out was, 'She is a spider.'

Fr Sabin smiled. 'You know, you're changing. I see it in you, ever since you went to the office. You're more independent – more confident. Happier underneath, even with the stress.'

Sophie was surprised. 'Thank you.'

'You're finding out that you have a brain, and you are enjoying using it.'

'There may be something to that, Father.'

'You can handle this situation. Now, more tea?' Fr Sabin looked at her rapidly cooling and almost full mug. 'Didn't you enjoy it?'

'Oh – it was lovely. But no, thank you.' She looked at his cup of rich, creamy coffee. 'Maybe some coffee, for a change?'

'Oh no. Too much caffeine is bad for you.' Fr Sabin went

triumphantly into the kitchen. 'I got some *decaffeinated* Tetley. From Cardiff. I'll make you a cup of that.'

Sophie went home an hour later. The priest had turned the conversation to other topics; her garden, the village's new mayor, the August fête for the Feast of the Assumption. But Sophie's mind had never left Tom.

Of course he was right. He usually was. She had been afraid to reach out, since Tom was so obviously here to plot against her – coming in behind her back, and going to Katherine.

But that was stupid. Tom was her baby. He was throwing a tantrum, that was all. She would only be playing into Katherine's hands if she let it escalate. She had to find out where he was living and speak to him, right away.

Sophie ignored the tray of cold cuts that cook had left out for her in her garden room, and reached for the phone. Celine would know – she would be able to find out. She was a good girl, and Sophie was very glad she'd promoted her.

But there was no answer. Celine must be out, enjoying the summer weekend with a boyfriend somewhere.

Sophie tapped the phone against her chin. Who else? Who else might know?

Of course. Judy Dean. She dialled her cell phone.

'Sophie?'

'Hi, Judy. Is this a good time?'

There was a pause. 'Of course. For you, any time.'

'Oh – thank you. I hate to bother you on Sunday.' Sophie, blushing and stumbling, explained. What Celine had said, and did Judy know, had she heard . . . did she have any ideas . . .

'Of course I've heard,' Judy said innocently. 'The whole of Paris knows Tom is around. You mean you didn't?'

'I didn't,' Sophie admitted, utterly humiliated.

'I wonder,' Judy said in her sing-song voice. 'I can make a few phone calls for you. And then I could drop by the château, if you like. That is, if you want company.'

Sophie exhaled. 'Oh yes, please. Thanks so much, Judy.'

* * *

Judy brought her new car sharply, crisply to a halt in front of the main entrance; the Porsche's wheels crunched on the gravel. She stepped out, careful to close her knees together, as she had seen Sophie do.

Pierre's widow was waiting eagerly for her on the steps in front of the large, arched wooden front door; she wore a long dress of black silk and a matching jacket; Judy could not tell the designer. No jewellery today, just her wedding ring, and her chestnut hair loose around her shoulders.

Sophie looked horribly elegant, even without ornamentation. Judy felt the adrenaline course through her, again. By contrast, she had gone the whole hog. She wore her grass-coloured Dolce & Gabanna suit with a crisp white tank, her new peacock feather Massot pendant – small, but so gorgeous – Pierre's canary diamond studs, and fawn-coloured driving gloves, calfskin, from Hermès. Judy had on her dark glasses and carried a sea-green leather bag from Dooney & Bourke.

Bloody Sophie. Trust her to make Judy feel overdressed.

She didn't know why she had wanted to come out here. Only that she could never resist. It was like worrying a tooth. Though it caused her pain every time, Judy could not leave it alone. There was that curiosity, that horrible curiosity of the mistress that had never left her. What was his family house like? How had he lived? What was his bedroom like? His bathroom? Their child's quarters?

Well, she had seen the château now – all through it. Sophie had given her the grand tour. And her answers. Pierre and his family had lived sumptuously. While she, for years, had struggled to make the rates on her little apartment.

Judy had thought the apartment was quite the gift – proof of Pierre's devotion – until she saw this place. And realised it was nothing. Perhaps he saw it as merely a convenience. More discreet than a hotel room . . .

Walking through the grey stone house, with its elegant rooms and its formal parks, and antiques that would grace the Louvre, Judy had felt her thoughts go into such turmoil she hardly knew what she was feeling.

Sorrow; loss; rage at Pierre, and at Sophie; glad, ferocious triumph, that the wife had no idea she was hosting the mistress. That secret, at least, she still possessed. This may have belonged to Sophie. But Pierre's heart had not – had it?

Would it have amused him, seeing the two of them there? Wife and mistress? Or infuriated him?

Judy wasn't sure, and didn't care. She hated Pierre for choosing Sophie and staying with Sophie. And she hated him for dying, and leaving her.

She smiled and waved at Pierre's wife. 'Hi!' she said.

'Hi.' Sophie kissed her. 'You look fabulous today. Dressed up for something special?'

She *does* think I'm overdressed, Judy thought with loathing. 'Just summer,' she said lightly.

Her tone sounded brittle; Judy told herself to be careful. She was on edge; it had been a bad couple of days. She felt so tense she was almost cracking up. It was that English bastard, Montfort. Judy had been overcome, immediately overcome. Offered herself to him; and instead of taking her, he'd thrown her out, and laughed at her.

She hated him. Hated Mayberry. Hated Massot. Hated all of them.

Her first impulse had been to quit. But she needed money. Where the hell would she go? And so here she was, today, sucking what pleasure she could from the fact that Sophie Massot was unhappy. A breach with her boy; Pierre's boy. And his mother. Trouble in paradise, Judy thought snidely, and although it sounded petty, she really didn't care.

'Did you discover anything?' Sophie asked, eagerly.

'Oh, certainly. He's staying at a rental in the Apartments Dauphin on the Rive Gauche.'

He had rented a place? But Château des Étoiles was his home!

'And the phone number?'

'That I couldn't get you. But I know people. Firms . . . private detectives. They could find it out.'

'Is that legal?'

'Probably not. Depends how badly you want to know,'

Judy said brutally, and covered it with a smile. 'Don't ask, don't tell.'

'I see.' Sophie's pretty face fell.

'I'm sure it's just a teenage whim,' Judy said. 'Whatever the problem is. What *is* the problem, Sophie? If you feel like talking about it, of course.'

'Oh – certainly.' Sophie looked back at the forbidding height of the château. 'It's Sunday, it's everybody's day off – I only have an *assiette* to offer you.'

'I saw a nice restaurant in the village.' Judy opened the side door to her green Porsche. 'Hop in. We'll do a girly lunch, set the world to rights. What do you say?'

That could only be *Fruits de la Mer*, the seafood place Lazard had wanted to go to. Sophie winced at the memory, but nodded. 'Why not,' she said.

Eating out was the last thing in the world she wanted to do, but Judy had come all the way out here. Sophie could hardly say no.

The restaurant was fairly large, for such a small village, and had a touch of arrogance about it; the proprietor, M. Foucault, served the best fish dishes within a twenty-mile radius of Paris; he was booked all season, and his prices reflected his fame. He did, however, keep a few tables empty for villagers and possible celebrities; Sophie Massot qualified on both counts, and, bowing, Henri Foucault showed her and Judy to seats by the bay window.

The tables were country oak, the decor uncompromisingly old fashioned: candles on every table, though not lit for lunch, prints of fishing, hardwood floors, sweet peas, gloriously fragrant, and roses in small vases.

He asked if they wanted something to drink. Sophie opted for Perrier; Judy asked if she could have champagne.

Sophie said of course, and ordered a split herself. She felt she had to, just to be sociable.

Judy smiled; so many white teeth, Sophie thought. Judy Dean was so buff, so fit. Just looking at her made Sophie feel old and exhausted.

'Let's order,' Judy said. 'I'm famished.'

Sophie had no appetite. She chose a small rocket and endive salad and a dressed crab; Judy picked more extravagantly. She started with a dozen oysters, which Pierre had considered an aphrodisiac; it amused her to eat these in front of the frigid wife. Next she chose a risotto of fennel and rock shrimp, and finally ordered a raspberry sorbet served with coulis.

She knew how to play her hand. She made small talk, complimenting Sophie on the remodelling, lying about how well Sophie's changes were being received. Her hostess just kept her face turned away, as though she couldn't bear to think about it.

'Please. Judy.' Sophie finally turned to face her, and Judy saw with a quick thrill of interest that her eyes were red. 'No business – it's the weekend. We get enough of that Monday to Friday.'

'Of course. Would you like to discuss Tom? It must be very painful for you –'

'No – thank you, but no.' Sophie's back was rigid with tension; Judy knew the pose all too well.

'I understand.' Judy smiled. 'Coming on top of the business with Gregoire,' she added, lowering her voice sympathetically.

The barb hit home. Sophie breathed in sharply, as if in pain. 'You don't think – you don't suppose Tom heard about that?'

'I don't see how he could have avoided it,' Judy said, her malice a bright flame in the pit of her stomach. 'The press printed the rumours – after all, Gregoire's lawsuit – it is for sexual harassment, as well as unfair dismissal.'

'Oh God,' Sophie groaned. She felt dizzy, and reached for her champagne. It was cold, a necessary prop. She drank and let the alcohol take the edge off her anxiety.

'Shall we get some more? I'd love another glass,' Judy said brightly. She wanted Sophie tight, and indiscreet. Knowing her secrets gave Judy power. If she had to stay at Massot – for now – she would do it from a position of control.

'Whatever you like,' Sophie said, weakly, and Judy ordered a bottle of Veuve Cliquot.

'Let's talk about something else.'

'Sure,' Judy said, filling up Sophie's glass. She took a sip of her own champagne; delicious, like the oysters. She decided she was enjoying herself immensely. 'Like what?'

'Anything. I don't know. You.'

Sophie turned her grey eyes on her companion. 'Tell me about yourself, Judy. We're all business. Apart from those days when we were discussing – you know –'

'Gregoire Lazard,' Judy said loudly.

Sophie flinched. 'Yes. Apart from then – we really only talk about the office. I'd like to know about you.'

'Why's that?' Judy slipped another oyster into her mouth, swallowed, and dabbed the juice away with her napkin. Mmm, it was good. 'I'm not very interesting.'

'But of course you are.' Sophie made an effort. 'An American in Paris, the only woman executive at Massot – you're fascinating.'

'I came over here young. Met Pierre,' Judy knew it was dangerous to be talking like this. But sitting in this restaurant, in Pierre's own village – discussing it with Pierre's wife – gave her a sick feeling of triumph. And besides, she still loved discussing him, even after all these years. Even with Sophie. It thrilled her just to hear his name spoken. 'Pierre hired me right away. Gave me my chance, you might say. And I stayed with House Massot ever since.'

'What was my husband like to work for?'

Judy gazed at her evenly. 'He was a lot of fun,' she said, softly. 'A lot of fun.'

'You sound like you miss him.'

To her horror, Judy felt her own eyes prickle. No. She would not cry. 'I do,' she agreed. 'He was one in a million.'

'Everybody says that – how unusual he was.'

'Well, you would know.'

Sophie sighed. 'I never saw that side of him. I think he must have left it in the office.'

Judy teetered. She wanted to know, of course – wanted to know everything. And yet she thought she might hate to hear the answer.

'Was it', she heard herself say, 'a *very* happy marriage?'

Sophie looked into her champagne flute for a few seconds.

226

But she trusted Judy; and anyway, she couldn't wear the mask for ever; she was tired of wearing it.

'Not as much as you might suppose,' she said.

Judy felt relief flood her soul. She was weak with it. Then it was true, Pierre hadn't loved Sophie, he *had* loved her, not Sophie, he was Judy's . . .

'I married too young.' Sophie was still talking. 'I didn't feel the same about Pierre as he felt about me. We had our differences, but he always said his family was everything to him – me and Tom. He said he would die before he gave the two of us up.' She looked at Judy shyly. 'Now I wonder if I felt the same.'

Her words were like iced water, drenching all the warm hope that had been there a second ago. *My family is everything.* Pierre had said that to Judy, also, once. And she had tried to ignore it.

Judy tried to say something, but the words would not come out. She was saved by the waiter, bringing their main course.

'Well,' she managed when he had gone. 'I'm sure that your family troubles will be over by next week. After the party, we only have three months till the shareholders' vote. And then you can relax.'

'Yes.' Sophie shook herself, shook away the memories that clung to her like cobwebs. 'I will have saved my husband's company. It's what he wanted. And it's for our son.'

She smiled bravely at Judy.

'I can't bring him back. But I can save his company. House Massot feels like more than business, Judy. It feels like our legacy – that saving it is saving the Massot family.'

Judy calmed herself; all the jealousy, all the anger. She nodded at Sophie, her eyes bright.

'Oh, sure,' she said.

And she knew what she had to do.

Chapter Twenty-Eight

There was no way he could not go, of course. For one thing, he had accepted, and Hugh was old fashioned; his word was his bond.

For another, it promised to be the most important event of his business career. Sophie Massot's party would eclipse even the Oscars in that respect.

He looked at himself in the mirror. Montfort's black tie was always the same; he merely checked, briefly, to see everything was as it should be; no creases in his jacket; his tie angled correctly.

He picked up the small package sitting on his dressing table and weighed it in his hand. It had taken Hugh a little while to select the perfect gift. It had been a difficult case. He invariably brought his hostess a present, and it was usually jewellery; one of the more tasteful pieces in the Mayberry line.

Obviously, he could not give Sophie Mayberry jewels. And even without their battle over a fifty-million-dollar company, he would never have offered her a Mayberry piece anyway. Sophie's background was solidly middle class, but her bearing, her intelligence, her grace, all made him think of her as more noble than many stuffy duchesses or contessas. Montfort would have found an antique for Sophie; something not necessarily of huge value, but definitely lovely.

As it was, he could not offer jewellery. Wine or chocolates would have been completely out of place; a painting or piece of art, too ostentatious.

He had chosen, therefore, with extreme care.

His telephone rang.

'Yes?'

'Your car is ready, monsieur.'

'I'll be right down,' Montfort said.

He put on his coat, picked up his gift, and left his suite. His limousine was purring right at the entrance to the hotel. It was a clear night, some stars visible even through the lights of the city. The cold snap had passed, and the air was refreshingly cool, not chilly; a perfect night for a party.

His driver shut the car door behind him and Montfort settled into his seat.

'*Maison Massot, rue Faubourg Saint-Honoré,*' he said.

The car slipped into the fast-flowing traffic, and Hugh felt something odd. Anticipation. That was it.

Excitement was to be expected, perhaps. Sophie appeared to be under the delusion that one party would rescue her ailing company and win back the hearts of her shareholders. He would be there himself – he would see that it wasn't true.

Tonight was the last gasp of his old adversary, Pierre Massot.

But something told him that he wasn't being quite honest with himself. His excitement was more than the satisfaction that House Massot would soon be his; that he would have achieved his goal for Mayberry.

He was looking forward to more than that. He was looking forward to seeing Sophie Massot again.

Tom sat with his grandmother in the car, his heart thumping.

He wondered if she felt the same. Katherine was stiff backed, and hadn't spoken a word to him for the last twenty minutes. She had arrived with her driver to pick him up, quickly perused his dress, accepted compliments on her own, and they had set off for rue Faubourg.

He wanted to say something. Other than to praise Grand-mother's gown once again. She had certainly pulled out all the stops. Tom didn't think he'd ever seen Katherine Massot in such fine estate. She was so dressed up, it was almost as if she wanted to look *good*, rather than maintain her normal elegance. Her *coiffeur* had constructed an elaborate up-do, winding her fine white hair into a gleaming knot, spraying it with something that gave it an unnatural sheen, and then securing it with three splendid combs crusted with pave diamonds; her face was powdered, her cheeks had an extremely careful rouge to them, just enough for a rosy cheek, not overdone and clownish. Katherine's gown was of pale grey silk fringed with silver lace, and around her neck she wore an enormous choker of seed pearls and diamonds, as thick as a collar; it concealed all the crepey skin of her old age, and a boned bodice and skirt gave her a figure she had not possessed in nature for many years.

His grandmother had neglected no detail. Tom had to admit she looked magnificent. A dowager queen of France would have found it hard to outglow Katherine Massot tonight. Her feet were clad snugly in pointed slippers made from antique Chinese silver brocade, shot through with gold thread worked into birds and dragons; her bony hands were concealed in pure white calfskin gloves from Hermès, and her whole body was wrapped in a hooded cloak of gunmetal cashmere, perfectly soft and luxurious. When she removed the gloves, the long sleeves of her ball gown ended in silver lace which would cover the backs of her hands. As for her fingers, which could not be completely hidden away, Katherine had chosen gems that would distract any eye: on her left hand, a flower worked in flawless marquis diamonds; on her right, the Tiger's Eye ruby, a Massot signature – a huge oval Burmese, pigeon's-blood red, perfectly translucent, a fourteen-carat stone set between two three-carat light green sapphires.

Her bag was a beautiful pouch of silver satin with a white gold handle, secured to her slender wrist by a silken thread; and she was tapping her ubiquitous ivory fan against her knee, thoughtlessly.

Tom was glad to see the fan. It provided the only familiarity in his grandmother's appearance. Katherine's magnificence tonight was unmistakably scored with malice. He had mentioned to her that he hoped they would not embarrass Maman, and that Papa wouldn't have chosen any scandal, and Katherine had said 'Of course', coldly and superbly; that was the sum total of his conversation on the subject.

He shifted in the back of the car, his mind ticking. They were approaching rue Faubourg, for which he thanked God. Tom was sure tonight was going to be miserable, and he wanted to get it over with.

His mother had been trying to reach him. She had somehow got hold of the unlisted telephone number at the flat, and had left him five messages; entreaty in her voice, which plucked at his heartstrings. He wasn't quite ready to talk to her; Tom screened out the calls.

But although it felt disloyal to Grandmother, who had offered him her help when he needed it, perhaps he would take the opportunity tonight. Draw his mother aside into some corner, talk to her, become friends again. If Maman had betrayed Papa, declaring him dead, refusing to wait a few years . . . even devaluing the stock . . . he still had to give her the benefit of the doubt.

Tom missed his mother. The more time he spent with Katherine, the more he missed those things he had previously dismissed; latterly, even despised – Sophie's warmth, her calmness, her demonstrative love of him. She was gentle, and her son had mistaken it for stupidity.

Surely Maman had not *meant* to betray his father. Surely she was just misguided. She had maintained her mourning, shown him the proper respect. And that story of a lover, well. That was Grandmother's story. Tom didn't know his mother's side of it. Perhaps he had been wrong in not waiting to find out.

Yes; as the car slowed to a crawl in the party traffic, Tom made up his mind. Maman was just misguided. They could be reconciled. Anyway – maybe she was doing a little better at House Massot than he'd given her credit for.

Tom didn't believe Sophie had had a total personality transplant. She would still have respected Papa. Mistakes could be forgiven.

Tom's mood lifted. Perhaps tonight wouldn't be so bad after all.

Judy's taxi had stopped moving. She resisted the temptation to bark at the driver. This was Paris traffic; you had to be Zen about it, or say goodbye to your blood pressure. She didn't

231

want to arrive flustered, either; this party was important, and Judy wanted to appear at her best.

Judy had hand-picked the press for the evening, and she was to be there, to see they reported it for what it was; a disgraceful waste of shareholders' money.

Judy would paint a vivid picture. Extravagance; selfishness; recklessness. Little old ladies with their pension funds ruined by Massot's plunging share price. Far from reversing that course, she was sure tonight would confirm it. The opulence of the details Judy had seen took her breath away.

She would not even need to do much planting. The spending would speak for itself.

The taxi was moving again. Judy snuggled into her pashmina; she was warm, but her hatred was cold inside her, hard as any jewel.

She wore a contemporary dress. There would be plenty of ball gowns here tonight; Louis XIV opulence, nothing Judy could compete with. She had gone carefully for contrast, instead. Judy was no stuffy dowager in diamonds. She would shine as what she was; modern, fresh, American. The anti-Sophie, perhaps.

Her outfit was a one-piece in scarlet; it was silk, embroidered with tens of thousands of sequins, heavy, made to fit her perfectly, in the *atelier*; it was long and had a fishtail and a fitted bodice, a tank-style neckline that showed off her graceful arms and strong, polished shoulders. Judy had spent ten thousand euros on the dress. She did not regret one cent.

She carried no jewels, of course; the dress was all glitter, and required none. And Judy did not choose to compete in that area. One day; when she could out-dazzle the lot of them. Not tonight. She was absolutely bare of ornamentation. Even her ear lobes were free of studs.

She had a small, solid metal red sequin Judith Leiber bag, and cherry Manolos; perfect matches to the dress. That, and her fire-red lipstick, was all the accompaniment Judy required. She had a simple black Joseph coat over the top, and she was certain that when she took it off, there would be gasps.

Sophie had told her that Hugh Montfort was going to be

there; just mentioned it in passing. That made it all the more vital for her to shine. Judy was confident. She looked stunning. She would let that bastard know just what he'd missed.

'Good evening, sir. May I see your invitation?'

A courteous man in one of the Massot uniforms, a bespoke suit, smiled briskly at Hugh. He had been speaking French.

'Here,' Hugh said in English, handing it over. A little test.

The man examined it quickly. 'Very good, sir, thank you very much,' he replied in excellent English. 'Enjoy your evening.'

Hugh was impressed. The pavement was swarming with invitees; plenty of middle-aged ladies in furs, despite the heat; a number of cloaks; gentlemen in cashmere coats. Everybody looked very grand indeed, and despite the crush, the Massot employees were handling it beautifully; drawing this banker to one side, that countess to another; invitations were getting checked, and invitees ushered in, without any pushing, or unseemly bottlenecks.

He glanced to his right and saw, a discreet distance away behind a velvet rope, the section for gatecrashers. There were a number of them – well-dressed types, but without that opulence which distinguished the real guests – enterprising members of the press, perhaps. Massot security men in dark coats, their biceps like steel, stood arms folded and implacable to any excuses; and there was a patrol car of the *gendarmerie* parked close by, just in case any frustrations got violent.

Hugh slipped his own invitation back into his jacket pocket. He was about to walk inside, when he was distracted by a vignette too fascinating to ignore.

A silver Rolls-Royce, a vintage model, pulled up in its turn in front of the red carpet. The chauffeur got out and opened the back door, head bowed; a very old lady and a teenage boy disembarked together.

The glittering crowd around Hugh drew back a little; he heard the discreet murmurs, the familiar sounds of well-bred gossip. Everybody was staring at the couple. Montfort himself took a step aside, and observed them.

There was a brief pause. The seated Massot staffer, in her pink Chanel suit, swallowed dryly, and asked, with great nervousness, to see the lady's invitation.

She drew herself up. Hugh admired her; she was splendid. *'Je suis Katherine Massot,'* she said, coldly, *'et j'entrerai.'*

The crowd stared. The woman was utterly magnificent, shimmering in silver and lace, huge jewels on her hands, a sparkling collar at her neck; beside her, the young man – Hugh guessed he might have been twenty – stood, also haughty, but silent, and possibly, Hugh thought, a little embarrassed. He wondered if this was it – a scene, and the party already ruined, and he had not even got inside. Behind the velvet rope, the reporters and other predators were fascinated, snapping pictures – scenting blood on the red carpet.

The door to the Massot showroom opened wide, and with a swish of silk, Sophie Massot came out.

Hugh's jaw dropped. And so, he noted, did Katherine's, and the boy's. The mother-in-law glared disdainfully; the boy looked shocked and hurt, his face a picture of dismay.

'Katherine! Tom!' Sophie said, clearly and distinctly. She leaned forward and kissed them both on the cheek; both were still as stone. 'How lovely to see you! This is such a nice surprise. Please do come in,' and she stood aside, ushering them into the room.

Katherine Massot paused, but there was nothing for it; she nodded icily at her daughter-in-law and swept inside, and her grandson followed her, without another glance at his mother.

For a second Hugh thought he saw a flash of pain on that pretty face; but Sophie rearranged her features, and went back inside, once again the picture of serenity.

The crowd closed ranks, murmured again, this time in tones of approval; the reporters sank back, annoyed. The crisis had passed.

Hugh made his way inside. He wanted to observe the mother and the son. They were major stockholders. And he also wanted to see Sophie again, in that incredible dress. Montfort hadn't thought she could get any more attractive, but he had been wrong. Sophie had ditched the black; she was not in mourning. Her gown was pink – and what a dress, he'd never seen anything like it. As he entered the Massot showrooms to the low hum of appreciative conversation, the gentle strings of a quartet, and the chink of champagne glasses, Hugh Montfort was already looking for her.

Judy moved inside and made straight for the cloakroom, where she was able to ditch the plain Joseph coat; she shrugged it lightly from her shoulders, using the tight muscles of her upper back. And she was rewarded.

Just as she had foreseen, the gasps came. Judy stood out. She was admired. Even the old women standing around her, in their clichéd ball gowns and overdone rocks, even the cream of Paris; they were admiring Judy Dean, the mechanic's daughter from Ohio.

Triumph and satisfaction mixed with her rage. It was a heady sweep of emotions, and Judy's eyes gleamed as she made her way back into the main room. A waitress passed and offered her a flute of champagne. There was a choice, she was told; rosé, brut, or demi-sec.

Judy accepted a glass of rosé. It was very good; she thought Perrier-Jouet, certainly vintage. The pale colour, pink grapefruit, complemented her gown. Judy was chic, absolutely chic, in this room full of full skirts and lace shawls; her sequinned shift stood out a mile.

Her sharp eyes scanned the room. She had the facts within ten seconds. Certainly the party was a success on the face of it – everybody had accepted, and they were all here; *le tout Paris*, everyone of a certain social stratum and astronomical wealth. Most of the ladies present were wearing their free brooches prominently. But of course, Judy had anticipated this. Yes, everybody was here – but what did it matter?

She had been right. Reckless, reckless spending – the evidence was all around her.

The vintage champagne was just the beginning. The insanity of dressing assistants in Chanel had been exceeded, utterly. Waiters were circulating with the kind of foodstuffs restaurant writers dream of eating; caviar, naturally, mounds of it, but also entire trays of the finest Provence truffles, sliced and delicately fried; *petits crottins*, little cheeses studded with wild herbes; miniature mousses scented with lavender honey; bitter chocolate soufflés in porcelain pots as small as egg-cups; fried flowers of courgette; olive tapenade; a sorbet of elderflower; lemon and strawberry ice-creams; tender medallions of beef in coarse pepper . . .

Sophie had hired for the night, at impossible expense, one of three chefs in France to have four Michelin stars at his restaurant, and the food was sublime.

The showroom was glorious, much of which Judy had already seen. Sophie had kept it, apart from the circulating waiters, exactly as it was during business hours; the only ornamentation were the tall fountains of pastel roses, whose fragrance mingled with perfume and the delicious smells of the food. Sophie wanted to show her guests a House Massot showroom, just as it was.

But there was one key difference tonight – one which, Judy thought triumphantly, would finally convince any observer that Sophie Massot was an irresponsible rich playgirl, not to be trusted with running a public company.

There were no cases over the jewels. The glass had been removed – removed everywhere. Necklaces, rings, bracelets, earrings – priceless, absolutely priceless gems, over nine million euros of retail value in this flagship store – were left open to the air; to the eyes, and fingers, of any party guest who wanted to touch.

And not just touch. They were picking them up, trying them on; dandling strings of emeralds between their fingers. The dowagers playing with Massot stock as if it was a pile of toys.

Judy smiled. No doubt some of these old bitches were slipping the odd diamond ring into a pocket or an evening bag. With this crowd, who would ever catch them? It was madness!

She glanced around, checking the room for her tame reporters. There they were – conveniently standing together in a knot – Pauline Vente from *Paris Match*, Bernard Frimes from *Le Figaro*, and Jeanne Anse from *Vogue*. Judy could see from

236

the raised eyebrows, the excited huddle, that they were just as shocked as she was.

She beamed; her plotting was falling into place. Savaging Sophie was going to be child's play.

Judy took a large sip of her chilled champagne, and strode expectantly towards them. Of course, she had to be subtle . . .

'*Chérie*,' the women greeted her. Judy exchanged air kisses and shook hands solemnly with Bernard, as she always did.

'What a party!' Pauline said. There was a catty tone to her words; music to Judy's ears.

'Isn't it?' she said. 'Very expensive, of course, but I'm sure it's all worth it.'

Her tone was deliberately evasive; the reporters circled.

'How much, exactly, Judy?'

'Why are the jewels unprotected?'

'This clientele is very old. I haven't seen anyone here at the fashion shows. Perhaps one or two . . .'

'Who authorised the free brooches?'

'Is that real Chanel that assistant is wearing?'

'Great decor. How much was it?'

'I heard Lionel Teron was catering tonight.'

'My dears, my dears.' Judy held up one manicured hand and looked pained. 'You can't ask *me* to comment. You know my loyalty is to Sophie.'

'It's a fabulous dress, darling,' said Bernard, to soften her up. 'But tell me – why are the widow Massot – the *elder* widow Massot – and the heir here?'

'Where?' Judy asked.

He gestured, and Judy's head snapped around. My God, she thought, it is true – they are here – they have come. Katherine Massot, resplendent in silver, looking almost pretty – and a tall, louche young man next to her – handsome – sullen. They were talking together, animatedly.

The young heir, Thomas, suddenly turned his head and looked in their direction. His gaze fell on Judy without seeing her. He was staring into the middle distance, talking to Katherine.

Judy gasped. The boy – the man, he was a man now – was

the picture of Pierre. Maybe about the chin there was that touch of Sophie, he had her slight cleft, but for the rest of it, it was Pierre – dear God, it was him . . .

She felt the room go dark. She swayed dangerously on her Manolos.

'Judy,' said Jeanne sharply. 'Are you all right?'

'Are you drunk?' asked Bernard, naughtily.

'No – I'm fine, fine,' Judy managed. She steadied herself. 'I'm just fine. It's the heat.'

The others exchanged looks. The party was air-conditioned.

'I expect it's a great shock to see those two here,' Jeanne said, with a sly grin. 'Rumours are that Mme Katherine is none too pleased with Mme Sophie. And nor is the heir. Any truth to it, Judy?'

Judy shook her head. 'You know I can't tell you that.'

'Ah-ha!' said Pauline, triumphantly.

'I'm sure Thomas and Katherine Massot fully support Sophie. We'll see at the shareholders' meeting.'

'We will indeed,' said Bernard. 'A family feud! How delicious.'

'And Hugh Montfort,' Pauline Vente chimed in. The woman hadn't aged well; she was a crow in black velvet and unimpressive diamonds. What a lack of style, Judy thought, to wear your diamonds to a party like this if they aren't much to write home about. Pauline's two-carat ring might as well be a chip in here, so dwarfed was it by everybody else.

But Pauline, the least chic woman employed by the bible of chic, did not care. Her job was to report on gossip. And her eyes were sparkling brighter than Sophie Massot's briolettes.

Judy followed her eyes. Yes, there he was; Montfort. Just as handsome as before, but it had no further effect on her. He was sipping champagne and watching the room. Gauging his competition.

Montfort had nothing to worry about with Sophie. But plenty to worry about with her.

'Why is he here?' Pauline asked. 'He's the opposition. Is Sophie playing games with her shareholders' money?'

Judy tried to look shocked. 'What a suggestion, Pauline!'

'This whole party is a risky, pompous gesture.'

'I can see it now,' Jeanne said. 'Sophie Massot. The new Marie Antoinette!'

'Let them eat caviar,' Bernard agreed.

'Oh, you mustn't write anything of the sort,' said Judy, unconvincingly. She glanced back at Thomas Massot; then at Hugh. She had to excuse herself. Her work here was done; the journalists were ready to eat Sophie alive.

'You must be kind,' Judy said. 'Sophie means well,' she added, damningly. 'Enjoy yourselves.'

She squared her shoulders and moved off towards Montfort. Not that he mattered; he did not. But Judy had to let him know she was not scared of him.

The crowd parted as she moved through it; her lean, muscular body red and predatory in its glittering, sequinned sheath. Judy flattered herself that there was that in her eyes which forbade too much argument.

A few of the men present, old barons and counts and other social lions, bankers and ministers in their fifties, looked at her approvingly as she passed. Judy saw the flickers of appreciation, the corresponding anger flashing in the eyes of their wives, and she fed off it; adrenaline crackled through her, she pulled back her shoulders, better displaying her still-high *embonpoint*; Judy did fifty push-ups a day, and if she couldn't firm the fatty tissue of her breasts, she kept the muscles just above them so tight and hard that they still faced north.

She felt alive when these men looked at her. It salvaged her pride. The mirror told her she was still attractive; now these men, the cream of Paris, pre-Revolutionary money, told her the same.

Montfort be damned. Judy lifted her head. She would go to him, defy him to his face. Then let him find Sophie, wherever she was, and the two of them could fence little barbs at each other all night long.

A brilliant idea, a flash of inspiration occurred to her. She would find Thomas Massot. And with his help, she would destroy them both.

Tom moved to a corner. His grandmother had excused herself to go to the bathroom; he was alone. Thank God.

He drained his champagne flute and beckoned a passing waiter.

'You were drinking rosé, Monsieur? I only have demi-sec. Allow me to fetch—'

'It's fine,' Tom said, cutting him off. 'I'll take this.'

Alcohol. It was all alcohol.

He felt weak and depressed. The shock, the dreadful, shaming shock. Just as he had planned to speak to Maman and put an end to all this, as he had been convincing himself of her respect for his father . . .

Sophie had greeted him and Grandmother. And she was not in mourning. There was not a stitch of black anywhere on her body. Not even anything sombre, purple or navy. Instead, she was wearing pink.

And not just any pink. His mother had been wearing a glorious, certainly antique, empire-waisted dress of the palest rose-pink, decorated with white seed pearls, so it glittered and shone, opalescent against her fair skin. Her hair was secured into a chignon with ivory combs set with diamonds, and she wore pink diamond earrings – true pinks, one of the most valuable diamond colours on the planet – pear shapes, four carats apiece, worth millions, and a necklace, quite exquisite if not so valuable, of naturally pink conch pearls threaded with pale green peridot. The centrepiece, a rare large peridot, round-faceted and ten carats, sat just above her cleavage. Drawing attention to it. His mother, in an eighteenth-century gown that actually showed her cleavage; and this in front of the best, the noblest couples in Paris.

Tom had actually struggled for breath, so embarrassed, so furious, was he. Maman debasing not only his father's legacy, but also his name.

He had nodded to her stiffly, and walked away, with his grandmother.

Tom took a slug of his fresh champagne flute. As soon as Grandmother returned he was getting out of here. They'd come; they'd made their point. Now they should leave, and allow his mother to debase herself without a family audience.

So much for keeping it quiet. He had no compunction about that, not any more. He would call a press conference first thing tomorrow morning, and announce to the world that he and Katherine would vote their stock against his mother.

Montfort watched her.

There she was. She did not see him; her attention was taken up by some dowager in a pale blue ball gown. The old lady was examining a ring; it had some kind of green stone, and she was slipping it on and off a wizened finger.

Sophie, a vision in rose, was talking to her with polite attention. Her manners were as beautiful as her gown.

Damnation, but she was beautiful. And sexy – so incredibly sexy. He wondered what the slender figure looked like, under that gown. Still in her thirties, and it showed; the woman seemed younger and more vibrant every time he saw her. She stirred his blood, profoundly.

Hugh wanted her.

He could not shake the idea that she was the most attractive woman he had ever known. Not the most conventionally pretty, true; but there was something about her, her courage, her bearing, that attracted Montfort with amazing intensity.

He struggled with himself. The guilt was ever-present. He tried to summon the vision of his Georgie, his dear Georgie. And she was there, she never went away, but the idea did not work the way it usually did.

Normally when he thought of Georgie the woman before him would lose all her power, become plain and dull, and put him in no danger.

Not this time. The old woman said something, and Sophie laughed; he watched her, and his guilt withered. Something sparked inside him, something strong. Hugh felt a rush of gladness; at that moment, he didn't care about Massot, or the deal, or anything related to business.

His soul, which had been so long dead in its own personal winter, started to crack open; just slightly, but perceptibly. Like the pale green shoots of snowdrops thrusting up, through snow and ice, into the weak light of a January day.

Hugh's breath quickened; he felt engaged, immensely glad. He took a step towards her. He had no idea what he was going to say. Something. It almost didn't matter.

'Well, good evening.'

Reluctantly, he turned around.

The American girl was there. Standing in front of him. Judy – that was her name – Judy Dean. She was wearing a scarlet dress, a glittering, flashing column of red sequins; it was a perfect choice for her, Montfort thought; it matched the bright rage she took no care to conceal.

She was younger and harder than Sophie in every way. Her personality, but her body, too. Attractive arms, tanned and gleaming with body oil, came out of the dress that showed off every curve of her trim body.

But Judy was less attractive now than she had been to him before. The athletic look appealed to a certain type of man; Hugh, however, was not that type.

'Good evening,' he replied, without interest.

That seemed to fan the flames.

'I'm surprised you dare to show your face,' Judy said.

Montfort looked at her. Her entire outfit was calculated; no jewellery, so on paper she knew the elements of style; the highest heels, the right bag. But she was trying too hard. Everything was a challenge with this girl, he thought with a flash of insight.

He pitied her.

'I might say the same about you,' he responded wearily.

Judy tossed her head. 'Like you're so lily-white.'

'Nobody is that. Now, if you'll excuse me, I must—'

'Judy,' Sophie said. 'How nice to see you.'

They both spun around. Sophie had wandered through the crowd; Judy hadn't noticed her, and she flushed, an unattractive red; Montfort also felt discomfited.

'*Chérie.*' Judy moved forward smoothly and kissed Sophie on both cheeks. 'You look stunning,' she said, dutifully.

'And so do you. What a dress,' Sophie replied.

Judy smiled, but her heart ached. How, how did Sophie do it? The black had gone, and that gown, that perfectly soft and feminine gown – if Sophie could have seen Judy's choice in advance, and deliberately picked the one outfit to overshadow it . . .

She couldn't help herself. She glanced at Montfort, and saw her own judgement echoed in his eyes. He was gazing at Sophie with an admiration even Judy could not ignore.

She felt faint with envy. And hurt. Why did she always, always come second?

'The party's going very well, don't you think?'

Sophie was looking at Judy, but talking to them both. Hugh Montfort looked dazzled, and Judy felt it happening, all over again. The man who had refused her advances drooling over Sophie – older, soft-bodied Sophie, with the tiny wrinkles around her eyes and mouth.

It was Pierre again. Sophie was preferred. Sophie was the choice.

'Very well,' Judy said, softly. 'I must circulate. Promotion. Have a pleasant evening, Mr Montfort. Buy some Massot jewels.'

She raised her champagne flute and pivoted on her heel, walking away from the two of them, as fast as she could manage on three-and-a-half-inch heels.

Sophie looked after Judy, approvingly.

'She's a hard worker,' she said. 'You should see the files she showed me. Ten years of press clippings, and she didn't have much to work with. Our fashion line was a disaster.'

'Unlike your jewellery?'

'The jewellery was fine,' Sophie said. She couldn't quite look Montfort in the eye. The look he was giving her disturbed her. She felt that treacherous attraction in the pit of her stomach; she tried to ignore it. 'It was the presentation that was the problem.'

'This presentation is perfect,' Montfort said.

'Why, thank you.' Sophie tried for humour, but the look on his face stopped her cold. She took refuge in a sip of champagne.

'But as I said, it is too expensive. And too late.'

'I think not,' Sophie said. 'Have you listened to the guests?'

'I have just arrived.'

'Then you haven't heard them talking. House Massot, from tomorrow morning, will be a going concern again.'

'You're drinking white champagne,' Montfort said. He wanted desperately to shift the conversation from business. 'Rosé would have matched your dress.'

Sophie laughed. 'But I prefer demi-sec,' she said, lifting her glass. 'Sweet champagne – I suppose you think that's frightfully bourgeois.'

'I think a person should drink what the hell they like.' Montfort smiled, and she smiled back, an artless grin, the first moment of real fellow-feeling they had had; it thrilled him.

'It's only bourgeois to care about what other people think?' Sophie asked.

'Something like that.'

'Oh, hell,' she said, suddenly, and Montfort turned to see three guests bearing down upon them. He recognised one of them – Bernard Frimes, from *Le Figaro*; he had given him an interview about Massot last week.

So this was the press, then. Montfort watched as Sophie stepped back, and the wall came down between them again.

He watched carefully.

'How cosy,' one of the women said. 'A little tête-à-tête?'

Sophie smiled briskly. 'I'm just showing Mr Montfort how House Massot's new collection is thriving.'

'It's a fabulous party. How much is it costing your shareholders?' said the other woman, tartly.

'Judy Dean is our PR director.'

'Judy only gives us the party line,' Bernard Frimes said. 'And we want the truth.'

'The truth is that our relaunch is incredibly successful,' Sophie said. 'Look around you.'

'My dear.' The thin, older woman in black placed a spindly hand on Sophie's delicate cap sleeve. Montfort stiffened; he wanted to brush it off. 'It's true that it's a wonderful party, and if it were *your own* money, nobody would quibble.'

'All we see,' Frimes said with a saccharine smirk, 'is your guests playing around with millions of euros' worth of valuables.'

'Very risky.'

'Highly imprudent.'

Hugh bristled with frustration. He wanted to jump in and defend Sophie. In fact, he wanted to put one arm round her waist and shepherd her away from this pack of mongrels. Take her somewhere else. Such as his hotel room.

But Hugh had shareholders too. He was supposed to be fighting her. Hugh ought to be enjoying this savaging; instead, he regarded the journalists with barely concealed contempt.

Frimes turned to Montfort. 'You're bidding for this company, monsieur. Have you a comment on this reckless spending?'

Hugh stared him down. 'My bid has been announced. I was invited to this party, and I came.'

'This supports your pitch to your shareholders . . . this . . . *fiasco*?'

Montfort looked at Sophie.

'My admiration for the jewels of House Massot is a matter of public record. Our bid is on the table. And other than that, as a guest, it would be highly inappropriate for me to make any comment tonight.'

'A very English attitude,' Frimes sneered. 'But what would your own stockholders say to that, Mr Montfort?'

Hugh, the business automaton, looked at Sophie, and decided he really didn't give a damn. For the first time in years, Hugh was starting to feel there was more to life than money. Sophie in that dress was utterly distracting.

'Ladies; monsieur.' Sophie smiled at the vultures with an effortless grace that renewed his admiration of her. 'I'm about to give a speech, and after that, you may ask all the questions you want. Excuse me, please.'

She nodded gracefully to them and stepped aside, through the crowd, towards a dais where a microphone, wreathed in flowers, had been set up.

The reporters looked at Hugh; but his face was granite. They knew they would get nothing there, so they melted away, looking for Judy Dean.

Sophie stepped up, lifting her skirts with her hands; they were delicate, but a little weatherbeaten. Montfort thought of her spending time in a garden, bent over and covered in dirt; it was an appealing picture.

She moved towards the microphone, and he saw, out of the corner of his eye, the reporters swarm around the American girl. Her face was alight. She was, he knew, briefing them against Sophie. Subtly; but that's what she was doing.

He made a decision. Whatever else happened, he would disabuse Madame Massot about her protegée. Sophie played a straight bat; she deserved at least that much from him.

'Ladies and gentlemen.' Sophie's soft tones rang out over the room, and there was instant silence.

Hugh watched the crowd: Tom Massot and the mother-in-law in the corner, staring up coldly – there was trouble there; the reporters, eyes gleaming; Judy Dean, with a rigid air of triumph; the guests, appreciative and warm, many of them with priceless pieces dangling from their hands.

'Thank you all very much indeed for giving us the pleasure of your company this evening. Tonight marks the relaunch of House Massot, which my late husband founded.'

Montfort watched the younger Massot struggle with himself.

'Pierre made this one of the great houses of France, one that would export the classic French tradition of excellence in bespoke jewellery all over the world. Tonight I honour him, and his vision. I hope that some of you may choose to purchase some of the pieces laid out for your perusal; and whether you do or not, may I wish you all a very pleasant evening.'

There was an immediate, warm, round of applause. Sophie lifted her head; the diamonds in her ears, pink as the first blush of dawn, glittered beautifully in the spotlight.

'Do any of you have any questions?' she asked. She looked directly at the three reporters, standing next to Judy Dean.

She's fearless, Montfort thought; absolutely fearless.

'Yes.' The black-clad old witch was not impressed by Sophie's courage or her poise. 'Can you explain to my readers why your guests are being allowed to handle all these *incredibly* expensive jewels, without any security inside the party?'

'Certainly.' Sophie smiled back softly. 'You see,' she said, 'we are all ladies and gentlemen here.'

There was a gasp, and then a murmur, and another spontaneous, and prolonged, round of applause. The crow-like woman glanced around her, taken aback, then pulled out a notepad and began to scribble.

'Anything else?' Sophie asked.

There was silence from the press, and she said, 'Please enjoy yourselves,' and stepped delicately down into the crowd. They swallowed her up, and Montfort could not see her any more.

As he watched, the first grand lady, in a ball gown of yellow satin, made her way to the counter. She was holding a large necklace of pink stones. Hugh thought he recognised it; it was a magnificent piece, tourmaline set with alexandrite, that rare stone that changes colour in the light, and costs more than a fine diamond.

He didn't think that necklace would go for much shy of three quarters of a million euros.

A Chanel-clad assistant, without any fanfare, spoke quietly to the lady and was wrapping it up; tissue paper and pink satin, tying up the ribbons, as a gentleman followed, carrying a bracelet, a cuff of hammered gold, set with cabochon rubies, a baroque piece; and then another lady, holding something too small for Montfort to make out. And as Hugh watched, he gained a perverse satisfaction from seeing the rush to the counters, these people, members of the most exclusive set in Paris, actually queuing up – they were too well bred to jostle – to purchase gems; pieces that started at around fifteen thousand euros.

Every assistant in the place was occupied; it was a storm – a very monied, very polite, but insistent, storm. Montfort recognised it from its less exalted parallels with his own collections. The dowagers did not shove each other out of the way, but the choice of pieces was shrinking, and with polite insistence they were manoeuvring to get to the open cases, to select a Massot piece from this evening; not to be left out.

Hugh did not think there would be any buyer's remorse in the morning, either. He had fetched his own *aigrette* from the safe several times, just to look at it; the intricate workmanship and sheer beauty of it had never failed to please him. The expense, in retrospect, seemed quite immaterial.

He glanced out over the crowd. Sophie Massot was out of sight. She was at the centre of a knot of guests; all of them, he felt sure, must be congratulating her.

Montfort handed his empty champagne glass to a waiter and threaded his way towards her. Sophie saw him arriving; she murmured polite excuses to her admirers, and came over to him, smiling proudly, her pink diamonds sparkling.

'Well?' she said.

'Impressive. I don't think it will change the result of the vote, but I concede you may have made it interesting.'

'From you, high praise indeed,' she said.

Montfort wanted to kiss her, quite badly. He contented himself with a slight bow.

'I must be going.'

'To adjust your bid, perhaps,' she said, boldly.

He smiled. 'Certainly not. I have a piece of advice for you, however.'

'I'm listening.'

'Don't trust Judy Dean.'

Sophie's eyes widened; the slight flirtation in them, which she could hardly help, vanished.

'But what do you mean?'

'Exactly what I say.'

'If you have something to accuse her of, you had best tell me now, don't you think?'

Sophie's eyes flickered uneasily towards Judy, deep in conversation with the reporters.

Montfort shook his head. He had warned Sophie; he could not be so ungentlemanly as to lay out the particulars for her.

'Judy is my friend,' Sophie said, firmly.

Montfort nodded impassively. 'Thank you again for the invitation, Mme Massot,' he said politely.

He made his way quietly to the cloakroom and left. Sophie's grey eyes followed him all the way out.

'Amazing.'

'Perfect.'

'Indeed; it is remarkable.' Pauline Vente smiled thinly at her colleagues. Each was now wishing the others away; as it was, they would have to share the scoop. 'What a turnaround,' Pauline said. 'Look – they are going to buy up every piece in the room.'

'It is the new Parisian success story,' Jeanne pronounced. 'The *dernier cri* in couture gems.'

'Judy,' Bernard asked excitedly, 'tell me. Are all the pieces individual? All of them?'

Judy was forced to nod.

'Then once they are gone, they are gone? Just think – it is like buying an artwork.'

'An excellent comparison,' Pauline agreed.

'There will be a storm for Massot pieces. Not just in Paris, I think.'

'With this workmanship they are bound to rise in value.'

'Look, there is the Principessa di Savoia. She's buying . . . what is that?'

'Earrings. Sapphire droplets, I think.'

'Where she leads all Milan follows.'

'I have to get out of here,' Pauline said, with triumph. 'My deadline is tonight.' She would scoop the other two, and they glared at her.

'So . . . you really think this will make a difference?' Judy asked desperately. 'I mean, it's just one party. You think other people will react like this?'

'With this heat? It's certain.' Jeanne's eyes narrowed. 'You do *want* Mme Sophie to succeed?'

'Of course. You don't know how relieved I am. With all the expense . . .' Judy let her voice trail away, but nobody was taking the bait.

'Well spent, every cent of it.'

'I'm glad to hear it,' Judy said. She was too angry to continue; she could not let them see her disappointment. 'I must mingle – excuse me.'

She slipped away from them, looking for the one person who still had the power to turn this evening around.

Katherine Massot had left before Sophie gave her speech. She announced, with imperial disdain, that she had seen enough; she had delivered stern comments to several of her friends, and she had told Thomas that her driver would return her to the dower house.

Tom had meant to go with her, but he had missed his chance. One of the dull girls from his own party had buttonholed him, and his grandmother, never known for her patience, had swept from the room in a swish of silver silk, the doormen practically bowing as she left.

Tom had cursed, but all was not lost. He still had his mobile; a limo service had been summoned. They were late; party traffic, maybe. He checked his Rolex. If they weren't here in ten minutes, he would start walking.

Guests were buying; masses of them. They were buying, and then they were leaving, clutching their purchases in his mother's newly designed rose-satin bags. The party was thinning out, and he had no desire to be stuck here with Maman. The conversation that would ensue would not be pleasant. He'd had a couple of drinks, and he was angry; a sober corner of his brain warned against more public humiliation.

Tom might do something dreadful. He might yell; in front of all the nobles and socialites. Worse, he might cry.

Forget waiting; he would leave immediately. It was too risky, to stay here, with his mother in that low-cut gown . . .

'Excuse me.'

Tom looked up. A woman was standing in front of him. She was attractive and polished, in her mid-thirties; a real hardbody, wearing a slinky, shimmering sheath dress in crimson sequins. She had a slim figure, and she spoke English, with an American accent.

'Yes?' he said.

'You must be Thomas Massot?' She extended one hand, and Tom shook it. 'I'm Judy Dean. I had the honour of working for your father.'

'How did you know it was me?' he asked, stupidly.

The girl smiled; she had perfectly straight, white, American teeth. She looked healthy and vigorous, a million miles away from the dusty old ladies and broken-down men in their penguin suits.

'Looked in the mirror lately?' she asked. 'You're a perfect likeness of him. What are you, twenty-three? Twenty-four?'

Tom smiled stupidly; she was bold, she reminded him of Polly.

'Eighteen,' he said, flattered by the question.

Judy sighed. 'Too young for me. Alas.' She winked at him.

Tom was enchanted. And through his drunkenness, his masculine pride was piqued.

'Certainly not,' he said, enunciating his words carefully, not wanting to slur them. 'A man is a man. And anyway, you can't be more than twenty-eight.'

Such outrageous flattery. The American girl was thirty-five if she was a day, but Tom didn't care; she was a *good-looking* thirty-five. He had a practised eye for women, and knew that Judy had the kind of body that would wear well. Her weight-lifting would keep the years at bay, she was naturally lean, and she had high cheekbones – even at fifty, she would still be striking.

This assessment flashed through his head as the compliment hit its mark; Judy, embarking on her deliberate seduction, was surprised and flattered.

She blushed; the slight vulnerability made her all the more appealing to Tom. He looked round once more at the thinning room.

'Would you like to get out of here?' he asked. 'My car's late, but I'm sure we can find a taxi. Maybe there's a decent café round here . . .'

He wanted to sober up; cool night air and a decent pot of coffee would be a start.

Judy nodded. 'If you hit the side-streets there are some excellent places. I know one not far from here where they do wonderful espresso and pâtisseries.'

Tom said carefully, 'That sounds perfect', and offered her his arm.

Sophie stayed late. When the last guest had gone, and the clean-up crew had started their work, she went over the evening with her staff. There had been nothing but compliments, although Claudette remarked, with delicate tact, that Mme Katherine had not seemed wholly pleased. Sophie waited as they tallied up the night's sales; two hundred and seventy-three pieces purchased, practically one per couple, gross receipts in euros, almost twenty-six million. Several of the most important necklaces and bracelets had been among the purchases.

The success was almost immaterial, though, compared to the reaction of the press. They would write the story up – with breathless approval – sales would soar, the stock price would rise. Sophie exhaled; she was vindicated.

She thanked the staff, sent them home, and got into her waiting car. Richard knew better than to engage her in conversation; the traffic had cleared up, and Sophie was soon out of the city, heading for St Aude and the château, alone with her thoughts.

For the first time in months her thoughts drifted back to her husband. She thought of Pierre; how close she had come to losing his legacy. But, she thought, with any luck, she had saved it.

It was a clear night; the stars were brilliant in the inky velvet of the sky as the neon haze of Paris receded into the distance. Sophie watched her home, the château, as it loomed into view; grey and forbidding against the moon, but nevertheless, sternly beautiful. What a life, what a gift her marriage had been. For all its flaws, she was beyond material worries. Pierre had not really asked so much of her, after all.

Tonight, she felt with weary satisfaction, she had repaid her debt. In saving all he had worked for, protecting the inheritance of their son. She settled back against the soft leather of the car seat as the tires crunched on the gravel drive.

Sophie felt free. Once this shareholder business was concluded, she would get to work. Real work, expanding, growing House Massot. She would hand it over to Tom, when the time came, in better shape than she'd found it. Better even than Pierre had left it.

The thought gave her a strange satisfaction. Tonight had been a triumph, and she took great joy in it. She would not duck it. Sophie obviously enjoyed business; she was naturally good at it. Even with all the drama, her self-esteem had risen from her time at Massot.

'Here we are, madame.'

Richard pulled in, and came around to let her out of the car. The butler, Junot, was opening the front door; in her bathroom her warmed towels and cashmere robe would be laid out; the silk sheets on her bed would be turned down; cook would have the milk warming, in case she wanted a hot chocolate.

'Thank you, Richard. That will be all, tonight.'

'Very good, madame.'

He got back into the car and drove off.

'Good evening, madame,' Junot said. 'Would you like anything from the kitchen, madame?'

Sophie ordered a glass of milk and some fruit and cheese; she hadn't eaten at the party, she'd been too busy mingling.

She thought about her son as she climbed the ornate marble stairs to her room. Tom had not spoken one word to her; had not so much as kissed her on the cheek. Katherine's sumptuous dress and icy stare flashed back to her, and Sophie felt the press of anger, of chill resentment in her heart; at least Tom would have seen for himself she was not mismanaging his affairs.

And now the party was over, and the threat of public scandal had passed, she would reach out to him. Sophie would not surrender her baby boy to Katherine's bejewelled claws. If necessary she would go to his apartment and wait there for him to arrive. When all was said and done he was still a teenager, hormonal and sulky; it was the order of the day.

She reached her room and ran her bath. When her snack arrived she dismissed all the servants. The brie was delicious, the ripe pear and lightly sugared raspberries too. Sophie ate slowly, enjoying herself, and began her night-time ritual.

But she could not put the thought of him aside for ever. Hugh Montfort was there, constantly there, at the back of her mind. As she slid into the warm water, she pictured him, and her last image, before she fell asleep, was of his dark eyes, looking intently at her.

Chapter Twenty-Nine

Judy knew the perfect spot. She led Tom, who was weaving slightly, away from the city's main arteries, the nightclub crowds, and the traffic. There was an all-night bistro just off quai des Augustins; it catered mostly to locals, and the food was, consequently, superb.

The decor was rough, and Tom might have thought twice about it under other circumstances. A young toff in black tie was too tempting a target. He could take care of himself, all right, but he was drunk, and there had been a few fights at Oxford, incidents enough to prove to him that without co-ordination he was liable to receive more damage than he could inflict.

But his companion had attitude; attitude that was proof against everything. Tom watched in admiration as she entered the dive, shrugged off her designer coat to reveal her cherry-red column of sequins, and was subjected to a hail of wolf-whistles; whereupon all she did was laugh and blow a few kisses, and the tradesmen and workers on their night shifts were eating out of her hands.

Tom thought her quite splendid. The fog of alcohol was slowly lifting, the chill night breeze and exercise having made the first dent, but she still looked stunning; sexy and self-possessed, lean like a tigress. How different, how very different from the vapid society girls at the party at his flat. He loved women like this, women that made a man come alive; *interesting* women.

She kissed the proprietor on both his rough cheeks and cracked a joke with him, and he showed them to a booth in the back, deep in shadow and away from prying eyes. The man also produced, with a flourish, a candle in a bottle, and lit it. He laughed, he thought it was amusing; but Tom was grateful. Candlelight made even the toughest atmosphere more romantic. The café had grimy white walls and a breeze-block ceiling, but it was warm, it was dark, and the pretty girl was smiling at him; Tom felt a pleasant glow of contentment.

'And what will you two lovebirds have?' the owner asked.

'Coffee,' Tom pronounced. He smiled at the characterisation; this man at least didn't think he was too young. He imagined Judy's body, sinuous and writhing; he would like half an hour to prove to her he wasn't a boy. 'Lots of coffee. And some aspirins.'

'I'll have a cognac,' Judy said. 'And Perrier; and apart from that, Gaston, bring us whatever you recommend.'

The man grinned. 'Hungry?'

Tom shook his head; Judy nodded hers.

'Fine. Leave it to me,' he said.

The coffee arrived first; served in bowls, as it was closer to breakfast than supper, with fresh milk. Tom added two heaped spoons of brown sugar, and gulped down three aspirins; he almost instantly began to feel better. Judy, meanwhile, sipped her drink, alternating with gulps of Perrier, served in a thick glass with a rough wedge of lime and lots of crushed ice.

'You come here a lot?' Tom said. It was banal, but he had to say something. There were plenty more questions, but he would not start on the seductions till the caffeine and aspirin had kicked in.

'About twice a week. I run, every morning.' Judy sighed with pleasure. 'Five-thirty to six-fifteen, round here, sometimes. It blows away the cobwebs.'

'You look great on it.'

'Thank you.' She smiled confidently; Tom liked her all the more for not being diffident. He hated coyness; Judy was anything but.

'After I shower and dress, I find a café, somewhere with great food, and I eat a huge breakfast.'

'You like to eat?'

'In Paris, who wouldn't?'

Tom thought of the rail-thin girl with the bad teeth. Judy showed the difference between skinny and slim. He beamed at her; every time she opened her mouth she said something he approved of.

'French food – the real stuff, not the muck they serve to the tourists – is one of the great pleasures of life. You wouldn't believe the stuff they serve in Ohio, where I'm from.' Judy made a face. 'When I go back to visit my family we go to diners. Ugh.'

'I can imagine. I've studied in England.'

'I heard you were at Oxford?'

'That's right.' He took the pot and poured himself a second bowl of coffee, black this time. The drugs were working their magic; his headache was receding, his speech was clearing up.

'Try this,' the owner said. He laid down two dishes; before Judy, a dish of sizzling pork chops cooked with peppers and tomatoes, rubbed with sage and onion, accompanied by a couple of thin slices of fried Camembert. It smelled so good Tom even regained an appetite. In front of Tom, on a chipped white plate, he laid savouries and sweets – some pastries, apricot and white chocolate, tiny macaroons, which were handmade and so delicate he wondered how the thick callused fingers had produced them, toasted croutons with anchovies, stuffed mushrooms, and some crumbly cheese straws.

'My God,' Tom said, wolfing down three pastries. 'These are spectacular.'

'The place is always full, day or night.'

'But they find a spot for you.'

Judy inclined her head. 'I'm a good tipper.'

'It's not that, mademoiselle; beauty has privileges in France,' Tom said, gallantly.

'You flatter me, M. Massot.'

'I hope you will call me Tom.'

'Then please call me Judy.'

She smiled at him, and he blossomed in the warmth of her approval. She looked wonderful in the gentle glow of the candlelight, which made her sequins glitter and sparkle, eating her pork chops and fried cheese with relish.

'How long have you worked for my father?'

'I've been working for Pierre for fifteen years now,' Judy said.

Tom noted her use of the present tense.

'I won't accept he's dead,' July said quietly, 'until I see a body.'

He nodded and ate an anchovy savoury, so that she would not see his eyes redden almost automatically. She was so loyal, and she was merely an employee. If only his own mother had half her devotion.

'That's how I feel,' he said. 'And so now you work for Maman?'

'I do,' Judy replied non-committally.

He could not contain his curiosity. 'How is she, as a boss?'

Judy carved off a small sliver of fried cheese. 'I'm afraid I will offend you.'

'Try me,' he said, darkly.

'I don't like it. She treats the company like her toy. Changes . . . many changes. Spiralling costs.' Judy shrugged those strong shoulders. 'The party tonight was a success, but still . . .' she looked directly at him. 'To be honest, Tom, if Pierre did not come back I always assumed I'd be working for you.'

'And you should be.'

'Tell me.' Judy went fishing. He was hooked, now, this handsome boy; she felt powerful, and she was enjoying it. 'What does the dowager Mme Massot think of this situation?'

'She disapproves. It is not what my father wanted.'

Judy sighed. 'And meanwhile, that limey bastard Montfort is sniffing around.'

'Yes,' Tom replied glumly. He was sure he could save Massot from his mother; not so sure he could save it from Hugh Montfort.

'He was there, you know.'

'Tonight?' Tom stiffened. 'I didn't see him.'

'Oh no, he was there. Which is typical of your mother, I'm

afraid.' Judy drank deeply of her iced Perrier. 'It's all a game to her.'

'Well, I'm going to put a stop to it,' Tom said, with great bravado. 'First thing in the morning. I will call a press conference. Announce to the world my father's wishes, and that Grandmother and I will vote our stock against Maman.'

'But how would that stop Hugh Montfort?' The pretty girl in front of him zoomed in, with unerring accuracy, on his major problem. 'Won't the shareholders just see a family quarrel? They'll throw their hands in the air and go with Mayberry.'

'I'll figure something out,' Tom said, with more confidence than he felt.

'You know, I wouldn't call that press conference,' Judy said softly. She drained the last of her cognac and set the glass down, twirling the stem between her strong fingers.

'You wouldn't?'

She shook her head. 'If you are serious about taking over, Tom, there may be another way.'

He looked at her. She was so quiet, and sure, and sexy; he wanted to believe her, with everything he had.

'And it would get rid of Montfort too?'

'If you are prepared to suffer a little compromise, yes it would,' Judy said.

The plan had come to her while she was sipping the cognac; it was due in part to the alcohol, loosening her up, presenting her with imaginative possibilities Judy Dean would normally be blind to. But it was perfect. It was obvious, once she'd come up with it, it would work; it would screw Sophie and Hugh Montfort, both, equally.

She would finally be revenged.

'Yes . . . it would,' she repeated, and smiled.

Tom looked at her gleaming eyes, and saw the excitement. He wanted her, more than anything. It had been weeks since he'd had any woman. And this American was not just any woman.

He thought triumphantly of Polly. If only she could see him right now. Judy Dean was not a placid pudding like Flora or a simple roll in the hay like Gemma. Judy was a woman worth courting. In her mid-thirties, sophisticated, with all the guts of Polly, but all the polish his ex-girlfriend lacked. She would not cling to some stupid English rugby player. She was independent, free, and clever.

'I would like to discuss it with you,' he said. 'But I would also like to see you again. Not to talk business; just to see you.'

'You're right.' Judy turned and signalled for the waiter, and Tom threw down two hundred-euro notes.

'Come again any time, monsieur,' he said; 'but wait here till I get a taxi. It's a rough neighbourhood.'

Tom agreed with him; he was sober now, and wanted to get Judy back to his flat, and out of that dress.

When the cab arrived he helped her into it, and gave the driver his address on the rive Gauche.

Judy widened her eyes. 'But why there?'

'It's my apartment,' Tom said, kissing her hand. He was already anticipating his lovemaking. She thought he was a boy, so he would need to be rough; teach her otherwise.

'And why would we be going there?' Judy drew back from him. 'I've only just met you, Tom. You don't take me for one of your easy college girls, do you?'

Tom's lust withered and died. He sat back from her; frustrated, but still glad. So she had refused him. All to the good; she was a worthy woman. He resolved to court her, properly. She sat there on the ripped and stained leather of the cab seat, stiff and haughty, with the perfect amount of *froideur*.

'I'm sorry,' he said.

'Rue des Cloches,' Judy told the driver. He swung around, and she unsnapped her glittering metal bag, the crystals glinting under the neon streetlights. 'Here's my card,' she said. 'If you want to see me again, you can call me.'

'You can be sure I will.'

Judy turned her head away; he admired the firm lines of her long neck under the close-cropped hair. 'We'll see,' she said maddeningly.

Tom dropped her off; she did not so much as give him a chaste kiss on the cheek before he waited, watching her enter her apartment building. But that was fine; just fine. As the car headed back to the Left Bank he was quite sober, but light-headed with pleasure.

Who would have thought it? Some good had come of that wretched party, after all.

Chapter Thirty

'You like the purple?' Claudia held up a swatch. 'Or the beige?'

'I don't give a shit,' Pete Stockton grunted.

Mayberry's Chairman was sitting in his vast mock-Tudor mansion in Bel Air, listening to his wife. He thought he'd rather have been almost anywhere else. Ugh! He wasn't cut out for the family thing. Why did she have to bother him?

Claudia made a face. 'Pete! Enough with the potty mouth. Paulie will be back from camp soon, do you want him to hear his father talking like that?'

Pete glanced at his wife with dislike. By now she should know he didn't give a damn about interior decor. Every goddam season Claudia had to draft in some new high-priced faggot, the latest 'it' designer, to redo the Malibu mansion. His furniture changed around so often he could never find anything.

'I guess the beige,' he said.

It was the right choice; she beamed at him. 'You know, honey, *I* thought the beige. Purple is a little out there. Donna said we should think about *toile de jouy*, but I can't stand that stuff. It's so year two thousand. It's over, you know? And any kind of print gets so dated. Ellie Krebs did her place in Shabby Chic. Shabby Chic! That's insane, nobody's done Shabby Chic since the mid-nineties . . .'

Claudia was well away. She let loose a stream of babble, seeming not to care when Pete flopped into his couch, the big leather sectional he wouldn't let her change, and grabbed the remote. There was a baseball game on, the Dodgers losing to the Red Sox, and it suited him fine. Pete didn't give a shit about sports, either, but eventually Claudia would get the message and go away.

He had to stick around to welcome Paulie back from camp. He'd eat supper here, their cook had some kind of roast beef thing going, and then he'd take a ride to one of the girls – Pete was in the mood for Lily today, blonde and stupid and pliant enough as long as he kept the presents coming.

Mostly he let his mistresses slide at the weekends – it was too much trouble to make up excuses – but today he needed it. Claudia's bleating was too much to take. Pete worked hard and he needed to unwind.

The House Massot deal was the perfect excuse. Even Claudia knew about it – there had been so many urgent phone calls and demanding memos from that self-righteous prick Montfort. If Pete said he had 'work', Claudia would buy it. Sometimes he suspected she knew about his little diversions and *she* didn't give a shit.

Well, that was fine. Pete liked his life how it was. He had no reason to disturb things. As long as Claudia didn't embarrass him by getting herself a bit on the side – everybody knew it was different for men. But he didn't think there was much danger of that. Claudia hated sex with him, so how horny could she be?

She got excited about shopping. Home decor. And, of course, jewels.

She'd stopped talking now and had moved back into the kitchen to yell at the cook. The House Massot diamond earrings he'd given her, three round bezel-set canaries that dangled from her lobes, flashed in the California sunlight; Claudia loved them, never took them off even for day time.

Pete liked giving her jewels. A man's wife was a reliable indicator of his worth, as much as his house or the car he drove. In a town like L.A., where everybody went by limo, a wife was actually a more convenient status symbol. He didn't know much about jewels; but even Pete could see that House Massot was altogether classier than Mayberry. He dined out on the success of his firm, but owning House Massot – that would be another step up.

Stockton thought about Hugh Montfort. He couldn't stand the prick. Yeah, sure, it had been a smart hire. Montfort had made them all a hell of a lot of money. But at what price? His holier-than-thou attitude had bugged Pete from the start. And people gave *him* the credit, all the credit, even though Pete was the Chairman of the Board. Hadn't *Pete* been the one to hire the guy? As far as he was concerned, Montfort could take that snooty British attitude of his and stuff it. He was just the help. No fancy suit and soldier-boy body would ever be able to hide that.

Not for the first time, he wished he could lose Montfort. The limey got in the way of Stockton's reputation. Once the Massot deal was done, he'd like to look for another CEO. Hugh Montfort wasn't the only guy in the world who knew how to run a jewellery chain. He could poach from Tiffany or Louis Vuitton. Even Gucci.

It would have to wait, though, until Massot was in the bag. Things were looking good; Sophie Massot had fallen flat on her face, just as you'd expect from a broad, and they only had a short while to go . . .

'Honey . . .'

'What the fuck. Can't you see I'm watching the game?'

Claudia smiled serenely and extended the phone. 'Call from Europe. It's that nice Hugh Montfort. You should have him over for dinner. He's quite the gentleman.'

Pete wanted to respond, 'Fuck Hugh Montfort', but it might be audible down the line. He hated it when Claudia got all moony over that pasty-faced Brit.

He snatched the receiver. 'Yeah?'

'Afternoon, Pete. Sorry to trouble you at home.'

'It's the weekend, Montfort. This better be important.'

'I can certainly call back tomorrow, if you'd rather.'

Rather. Of course he wouldn't rather. The Englishman had called his bluff. This deal was worth about forty-eight million dollars, and he wanted to know every detail.

'That's OK,' he was forced to grunt.

'There might be a problem.'

Stockton flicked off the television and sat bolt upright.

'What the fuck does that mean? A problem?'

'Pete!'

He covered the receiver. 'Cut it out, honey. I'm busy.'

'I don't believe it will be serious, but Mme Massot threw her party, and it was a success; she sold several million euros' worth of jewels, and I have reason to believe there will be good press coverage.'

Stockton saw the difficulty at once. 'How good?' he barked.

'I anticipate very good.'

'Good enough to change the stockholders' minds?'

'Well, that's the question.'

'And what's the fucking answer, Montfort?' Pete barked. His heart was thumping; his fat palms were sweaty, thinking of all the money he might lose. And yet there was a distinct pleasure in being able to yell at his CEO.

'Don't talk to me like that, Pete,' said Montfort in a bored tone.

Pete swallowed his rage and dislike. 'You're right, you're right, I'm sorry.' The limey would not be bullied; he'd have no hesitation in hanging up on his boss, they both knew it. 'We Yanks haven't learned to be as suave and cool as you Brits.'

'On the contrary, I believe most Americans are extremely courteous,' said Montfort, coldly. I hate the son of a bitch, Pete thought. 'At any rate, the answer is, I believe, no. There isn't much time to go before the stockholders' meeting, and the stories will run for about a week. I expect the Massot stock price to rise, perhaps up to three points, on anticipation of possible other bids. We will organise a counter-offensive, and perhaps we might, at the last minute, raise our bid by about four per cent.'

'Four per cent! That means that fucking – I mean that *blasted* party will cost us millions.'

'We were buying Massot at a spectacular discount, anyway. It's better to be secure of our bid.'

Pete made a great effort and heaved his bulky body from the leather couch. His body was slow, but his mind was fast.

'There aren't that many shareholders around,' he grunted.

'Thirty per cent voted by the wife. Another fifteen is in the family . . .'

'My information is that they will not vote with her. They plan an independent pitch to the shareholders.'

'Any danger there?'

'None. The son is eighteen, the grandmother's age uncertain, but shareholders won't like either of them as a candidate to replace Mme Massot.'

'And so we basically will need the support of almost all the other shareholders. All the fifty-five per cent that's floating.'

Montfort didn't say anything; they both knew this. Pete was thinking aloud.

'What can we count on?' he asked.

'At least thirty-five per cent, in the hands of trust funds, pensions, other institutional investors. They won't be swayed by press; I've had their commitments for some months.'

'Good. Good.' Fucking Montfort, Pete could not deny he was competent. More than competent. 'But we still need the rest. There's a full twenty per cent in petty shareholders, private hands?'

'I'm afraid so.'

Forget Lily, or any of the other girls. Forget his plump son coming home from camp. Pete wanted nothing more than to get out of this sweatsuit and get into his office. It was a dangerous situation. He needed to think.

His only consolation was that the Englishman had, for once, fucked up.

'This is a freaking disaster,' he yelled. 'Two weeks from deal time and you let that French bitch throw some freaking *party* and—'

He was listening to a dial tone. Montfort had, indeed, hung up on him. Fuck! He threw the phone across the room.

'Is everything OK, honey?'

His wife was hovering. Like him, Claudia had a finely tuned antenna for money. She had been spending their future Massot cash in her head for the better part of a year.

'I gotta go to work,' he grunted.

'But you'll miss Paulie.'

'Give him a kiss from me. It's an emergency, OK?'

'Sure thing, honey.' His wife knew when not to press it. She had no intention of rocking the boat.

Stockton considered things for a moment. This was kinda shocking. Everybody knew Hugh Montfort was the hardest-assed businessman in jewellery. He was freakin' famous. How could he have screwed up like this? How could he let some playbody's trophy wife – well, widow – put one over on him? Was he banging her, or something?

It wasn't possible the girl was good at the job. She hadn't even gone to college. Child bride and kept woman. What would she know about it?

What the fuck. He, Pete, had to sort out the mess.

His first call would be to the Crillon, leaving a grovelling message of apology for Hugh Montfort. Otherwise, he knew he'd have a resignation letter on his desk first thing in the morning. Montfort was not the type to threaten; he'd just walk. No, Pete would have to eat humble pie. Again.

The thought made him furious, and he struggled with himself. It wasn't good for his blood pressure. He kept a flask of twenty-year-old malt whisky locked in his desk drawer; time for a medicinal glassful, Pete thought.

Fucking Hugh Montfort. Fucking Sophie Massot.

'Claudia, call my driver,' he barked.

Chapter Thirty-One

She woke at dawn; it was not quite six. Sophie lay against her soft, down-feather pillows, and watched the dawn through her lead-paned windows; pale peach light streaking against the blue, the promise of more fair weather.

She slipped out of bed, her bare feet cold against the flagstone floor, and padded across the room to look out over her grounds. The château's manicured park stretched out below her; the lake was a dark circle, its waters not yet sparkling in the sun. Behind it, beneath the slope of the lower lawn, was her mother-in-law's residence; the elegant Georgian lines of the Dower House.

Sophie wondered how Katherine had slept. Not well, she thought; not well.

It would be hard to forgive the old woman. She had never thought her antipathy to her son's bride, her rejection of his choice as unworthy, would go so far; to try to drive a wedge between Sophie and her baby.

Nevertheless, they were family; and neighbours. There would have to be a reconciliation, whether Sophie wanted one or not.

She watched the sun rise over her grounds. When would she get a chance to enjoy them again? Sophie wanted Tom to be here; wanted to picnic with him by the lake, discuss new planting schemes in the pear orchard with him. He would have to meet M. Lindeur, the estate manager. In three years it would all be his; their vast estate, and the duties that went with its upkeep.

Perhaps very soon. Very soon it would all be over.

She turned from the window and went to take her bath. Her thoughts ran over the party last night; Sophie felt an extremely pleasant calmness. She had done all she could. Either the press coverage would persuade the shareholders to give her vision a chance, or it would not. Either way, it was now out of her hands.

Bernarde had chosen a good outfit. Sophie was now out of mourning, and she was experimenting. Her outfit was playful, but had a business edge; she couldn't help wonder how Hugh Montfort might rate it. There was a *Comme des Garcons* silk dress, just above the knee, olive with jade buttons, a dark green scarf by Joseph Tricot, dangling pearl and garnet earrings and a hammered gold cuff bracelet; plus a Prada crocodile skin tote and daring high-heeled pumps.

Her clothes reflected her growing confidence.

Sophie added a peridot and citrine necklace to lighten it up a touch, applied a spritz of rosewater, and called for her driver.

Something was niggling in the back of her mind. Despite her satisfaction and the warm promise of the day, and a reconciliation with Tom, there was still something amiss.

Hugh Montfort. No – she wouldn't think about him now. Not yet. Maybe once the bid was played out.

But it had to do with Hugh, all the same . . .

Her telephone rang.

'*Richard vous attends, madame.*'

'*Merci. Je viens.*'

Sophie shut her bedroom door and walked down the sweeping marble stairs; Junot was already at the door, holding it open for her; the Rolls-Royce was purring on the gravel drive outside.

She wished her butler a good morning and slid gracefully into the back of the car. It would come back to her, Sophie thought.

And as Richard pulled noisily out of the drive, stones crunching beneath the tires, it did.

Judy Dean. Montfort had warned her about Judy Dean.

*   *   *

Celine Bousset was prepared for anything.

She was having a wonderful morning. First René, her boyfriend of three years, had dropped a hint that he might finally be ready to marry her. She'd been ecstatic, of course; and then when he'd left for work, had suddenly started to wonder if, in fact, she wanted to marry *him*.

The thought had lasted all through her careful breakfast of black coffee and a very small croissant; Celine was watching her figure. She wasn't far off thirty, and she'd heard too many horror stories about one's metabolism screeching to a halt and suddenly landing you with thirty pounds before you knew where you were. Beauty and slimness were almost synonymous, as far as Celine was concerned; she wanted to keep herself attractive for as long as possible, in that effortless way Sophie Massot managed it.

It was also sunny. And the party had been a success. There were still four invitations left over, kept as last-minute spares, but nobody had needed them; that meant four beautiful brooches. There were a tulip, a comet, a hare, and an ox; Celine was hoping to drop a hint, maybe Sophie would give her the hare.

She'd set the stage. Her boss, whom she adored, was endlessly generous and kind, if a little naïve, but it didn't hurt to be ready. Celine had tidied Sophie's office with extra care, chosen specially gorgeous flowers – creamy, scented orange blossom and pale green roses – picked a very smart outfit of her own, a crisp navy skirt suit with a white cotton shirt by Emporio Armani, and finally, as a crowning touch, had picked up some of that flavoured American coffee Mme Massot was fond of – cinnamon – and decanted it from its white paper holder into a bone china cup; it was still piping hot when Sophie had arrived at the office; Celine had timed it perfectly.

The little buzzer on her phone went off.

'Yes, madame?'

'Could you come in here a moment, Celine? Ask the switchboard to take all my calls for a few minutes.'

'Certainly, madame,' Celine said brightly. She thought she would ask for the hare, although the comet was very pretty too, with pavé diamonds along its tail to make it sparkle. The hare was simply gold, but she preferred its design; there was a fluidity to the running animal that Celine thought the picture of grace. Even with her raise, she could never afford a brooch like that. The most she could hope for in the way of jewellery would be the no doubt tiny ring René would present her with. If she let him, that is.

She knocked on the door. Sophie was sitting in her chair, looking thoughtful. She was wearing shades of olive and forest green that set off her colouring wonderfully. So elegant, Celine thought. Her husband really must have been some kind of fool . . .

'Close the door behind you; sit down, please.'

Celine winced. Sophie did not sound as if she were in the ideal mood Celine had been hoping for. The delicious cinnamon coffee was cooling rapidly, untouched, before her.

'I want you to discuss something with me, something confidential.'

'Very well, madame,' said Celine, warily. 'And what is that?'

'You hear company gossip, don't you?'

'I never pay any attention to it, madame,' Celine lied earnestly.

'It's OK.' Sophie smiled, held up one hand. 'You're not in any trouble – anything you say is going to be just between us. Well, at least,' she corrected herself, 'I won't say where I heard it.'

'*Bien*.' Celine smiled, flattered. She liked Sophie; it would be wonderful if Mme Massot would take her into her confidence. Better Celine than –

'Judy Dean. It's about Judy Dean.'

Desastre. Celine said a quick prayer she wouldn't have to discuss the scandal in public.

'What's the matter? I said you are in no trouble.'

And what if Madame got angry?

'But Judy Dean is your most particular friend, madame. You told me – remember?'

'I know I did. But you can forget that, now. I've heard something, from . . .' her boss hesitated '. . . from a person I trust. Is there something about Judy I ought to know, Celine?'

271

Celine stared. 'You are serious, Mme Massot?'

'Perfectly.'

'You mean you did not know?'

'About what?' Sophie asked impatiently. 'Spit it out. If there's something to tell, tell me now, please.'

Celine hesitated. Really? She didn't know? How could Celine break it to her? She was a good woman – a nice woman. Celine was overcome with pity. Whoever would have believed this savvy businesswoman could be that naïve?

'I thought you knew, and did not care, madame. In France – some people don't. Rich people.'

Sophie stared at her, waiting.

'It is M. Massot,' Celine muttered. 'Everybody knows. I thought . . . you had to know. But some here say you did not.'

'Pierre?' Sophie blinked. 'What about him? He's been dead for seven years.'

'But Mme Judy has been here longer than that, madame.'

Sophie gasped. She was amazed; and Celine stared back at her, equally amazed. How could Madame be surprised? With M. Pierre such a whoremonger, legendary, really.

But the Englishwoman *was* surprised. Celine watched the emotions running over her aristocratic features in quick succession. Understanding; shock; calculation; and lastly, humiliation. Her breathing had quickened, like a struggling fish on dry land.

Tiens! Poor Sophie.

'Are you all right, madame?' Celine asked, alarmed.

Sophie took a deep breath. 'I'm fine – fine. It's just a shock.' Celine watched her struggle with the information. 'Judy slept with my husband? How often? Was it after a Christmas party, or . . .?'

'Oh, madame.'

Celine was squirming.

'Tell me the worst. Tell me everything.'

'You must understand I wasn't here when this took place. I was only a teenager. But it's what I heard.'

'Very well.'

'Mme Judy was the lover of M. Massot for many years,

almost as soon as she came here to Paris. He promoted her and he bought her her apartment. That was his gift to her. No mortgage or anything,' Celine said, with a note of envy. But she caught herself. 'When he left, nobody dared do anything to her in case he returned.'

'And was he going to . . . to divorce me and marry her?'

'Oh! No, madame,' said Celine, eyes wide. 'No, indeed. Many people here laugh at her, madame. Because she is only one of his girls, after all. She thinks she is special, but who knows how many there were. I don't know if he bought flats for all of them, but there was jewellery, and you know a good necklace can cost *more* than an apartment . . .'

'All of them?' Sophie said faintly. 'You mean there were others?'

Celine stared. Was it possible? 'You truly did not know, madame?'

Sophie couldn't respond.

Celine bit the bullet; if the wife had really been that blind, it was better to get it over with. There was no reason Sophie Massot should be the only woman in France who didn't know of Pierre's habits.

'Madame, I am sorry,' she said gently, and with a certain air of maturity. 'You have always been kind to me. Everybody thinks, maybe you don't know about Judy. But nobody imagined you did not know about the rest. Monsieur Massot, while he was alive, he was one of the most notorious *amants*, I don't know the word. A . . . libertine. He had many, many women. Girlfriends. Everybody knows it. Girls that last a month, two months. Girls in different places. Sometimes prostitutes, very expensive . . .' – she cleared her throat – 'Forgive me, madame. But mostly just ordinary girls, I think. He picks them up, gives them gifts and money. It was happening before you even marry him.'

Sophie felt ill. Her head was swimming, and she was just trying to hold it together. The worst thing was to see the pity in her young secretary's eyes. Celine wanted to hug her – that was obvious; she, the great chatelaine, the millionaire widow, was the object of empathy.

And where Celine pitied, Sophie had no doubt, others held her in contempt.

Sophie was angry at herself. It was an open secret? Everybody knew but her. She imagined all those dutiful years of parties, all that socialising. Were they talking behind her back? Laughing at her? Did *Katherine* know?

She struggled to appear calm.

'And it didn't stop? Once we were married?'

Celine shook her head. 'Not from the stories the older women here tell me. But as I say, I wasn't there.'

'Then how do you know it's true?'

'I don't, madame,' the girl said simply, 'but everybody else says it. I could get one of the older women up to talk to you, if you would prefer.'

But Sophie believed Celine, every humiliating word. But then again, she had trusted Gregoire. And Judy.

And Pierre, she reminded herself.

No more; even if it cost her further anguish and shame, she wanted it proved.

'Yes,' she said. 'Who do you recommend . . . wait . . . let me call Human Resources. I will select somebody myself.'

Celine sat there, feeling sorry for her, as she dialled Human Resources, and asked for the names of some women who had been with the company over ten years, and who worked in Publicity.

'They are sending me Françoise Delmain and Marie Pousse,' Sophie said.

'They would know, madame.'

'Show them in when they get here. Hold all my calls.'

'Yes, madame.'

'And Celine – *merci*.'

'*C'est rien*,' Celine said, sympathetically. She let herself out. She would bring up the brooches some other time.

Judy immediately knew something was wrong.

Marie disappeared without saying a word to her, and then, barely five minutes later, her phone buzzed.

'Judy Dean.'

It was Sophie.

'Come up to my office immediately,' Sophie said. Then she hung up.

Judy replaced the receiver carefully. Then she stood up, removed the photo of her mother from her desk and calmly put it in her bag. She also walked out to the coat-rack at the end of the floor – head up, head up, Judy – and unhooked her Burberry mackintosh from its peg.

There was nothing else to take. Judy was not one of those women who cluttered her desk space with stuffed animals and a plastic mascot, or who tacked up posters of handsome films stars or snapshots of Hawaii.

On some level she had always been expecting this day. From the moment Pierre left. It had been seven long years of danger, and she was ready at any moment to make a dignified exit.

Sophie knew.

There was no other explanation for it. Sophie knew about Judy and Pierre. Judy was surprised by her own reaction. She went through the motions, as she had rehearsed them in her head. Slowly, refusing to rush, she put on her coat in front of the typing pool, she arranged her bag comfortably, and she smiled to herself. But inside, she was far from calm.

It didn't matter; not any more. Not now she had the boy. Judy felt no fear, only an odd, wild elation; even a relief. She would be able to confront Sophie, indeed she would have to. Finally, she would be able to say everything she'd ever wanted to, from the first moment, all those years ago, when Judy had realised that because of this little mouse of a limey, Pierre – great, spectacular Pierre, as she'd thought of him – would never be hers.

She walked over to the elevators and pressed the button. The door pinged, and a manicured hand drew the ancient folding iron grille aside – Françoise, with Marie close behind her, stepped out. Françoise stared at Judy with naked triumph; Marie, however, blushed, and looked slightly sorry, under the veneer of her pink-faced excitement.

'*Au revoir, Marie,*' Judy said.

'*Il faut dire "adieu",*' Françoise sneered.

'*Pas du tout,*' Judy corrected her. '*Je reviens.*'

Marie started to say something, but her gloating friend dragged her away. Judy pulled the grille and pressed the button for the top floor; she could hear the breathless gossiping starting, a low hum, as the creaking machinery began to haul her upwards.

Oh yes, there was no doubt about it. Sophie knew. The little chit of a girl, Celine Bousset, was sitting bolt upright in front of her office, a look of defiance on her unimpressive face. Judy wanted to ask her if she had been the one to tell, but decided against it. She would not waste time; would not be caught bandying words with secretaries while security was summoned to haul her from Pierre's company.

There was only one woman worth speaking to.

Judy opened the door to Sophie's office, without bothering to knock; she closed it behind her, and then stood in the middle of the room, facing her.

Sophie Massot looked her over, taking in the coat and handbag.

'Sit down,' she said.

Judy stayed where she was; she tilted out her chin.

'I think not,' she said. 'Let's make it short, shall we? I've got things to do.'

'And that's all you've got to say? No apology? No excuse?'

Judy laughed. 'Apology? For what?'

'For sleeping with somebody else's husband, for a start,' Sophie said coldly. 'Of course, I now know you were nothing special, just one in a long line of girls. I daresay he had you on a schedule. Did you have to co-ordinate dates with the other women?'

Judy's face flamed; the barb struck home.

'At least none of us co-ordinated with you,' she said.

'I'm disappointed, Judy.' Sophie thought she was such a cool cucumber; Judy loathed her. 'I would have thought you would have too much spirit, too much individuality to be part of such a production line. Being in a harem is so terribly dull.'

Judy fought back.

'Maybe there were others –'

276

'Apparently there's no maybe about it.'

'At the time, I didn't know.' Her lip curled. 'I was as in the dark as you, Sophie – well, almost.'

'You certainly knew there was a wife and child.'

'Don't come over all virtuous with me,' Judy snapped. 'Please. You married him when you knew next to nothing about him. Oh, I'm sure it was his sparkling personality that attracted you. Nothing to do with the huge castle and millions of francs.'

'Pierre had a family.'

'I *loved* him,' Judy said, drawing herself up. She spoke proudly, looking Sophie full in the face. 'That's what you don't seem to get. I loved him. We had passion. And I wasn't just another girl. I was with him for years. He gave me my flat . . .'

'Very bourgeois; I'd have expected Pierre to stump up with something a little more elegant. But I daresay he wanted you somewhere nobody of quality would recognise him.'

'He was with me three times each week.'

'And you probably got drunk by yourself every Christmas. Oh, I know the type. It's such a cliché, Judy.'

'You can say all the clever things you want.' Judy stared at her. 'Oh yes; you have style, Sophie, I'll admit that. Plenty of style. But not an ounce of warm-blooded love, or passion. Your marriage was nothing but duty. You told me so yourself.'

She forced herself to stand firm. 'Pierre came to me for love.'

'He came to you for sex. You, and the others. Hookers too, I'm told. I daresay buying you a flat and having you in the office simply worked out cheaper.'

Judy burned. She would not allow this woman to have it all her own way.

'I'm no hooker,' she retorted. 'Maybe you should look in the mirror, Sophie. The difference between me and you is that I loved Pierre. You already told me you didn't. But you stayed married to him. We had sex – yes, great sex – and he gave me companionship. And I loved him. With all my heart. You can't say the same. You're the one who married without love and stayed married without love. Who's got integrity here? Me? Or you? You say he only wanted me for sex; I say he only wanted you for a child.'

Sophie recoiled; there was too much truth in Judy's barb. Her whole marriage had been a lie, all the years of her married life, just a fantasy; a hollow fantasy, where the only real love was Tom.

'Get out,' she said, wearily. 'You're a snake; you don't value yourself, and that's why you don't value others.'

Judy smiled; she had landed a good blow there. Little miss perfect could feel things, then. Like Judy; she could feel pain, too.

'My husband may have chosen me to bear his son,' Sophie said, as Judy picked up her handbag, 'but that's something, Judy Dean. That's family; the love I gave my baby, the love he gave me back. I'm sure you tried your damnedest to make that go away, to make Pierre pick you over us. But he never would, would he?'

'Goodbye, Sophie,' Judy said.

'He chose me,' Sophie said, calmly. 'In the end, he chose me. Always remember that, Judy. Pierre could have been with you; but he didn't want to. It's as simple as that.'

Tears prickled in Judy's eyes; Sophie's words ripped the scars on her heart, made the wound fresh and new again.

Sophie didn't love Pierre; his betrayal of her would never hurt as much as his rejection of Judy. The widow was right, and they both knew it.

'You couldn't split my family,' Sophie said, with terrible clarity. 'And now, goodbye.'

But instead of crumpling, instead of fleeing in tears, Judy paused, turned back, and said, with a terrible little smile, 'Really? We'll see.'

Then she turned smartly on her heel and walked out.

Sophie sat there for a couple of seconds, then snapped out of it. She wasn't going to let Miss Dean play head games with her; not any more. She rang the front desk and security and informed them that Judy Dean had been fired, and was not to be allowed back in the building after she had left it, not even to fetch personal belongings. Next she called Personnel, dictated the letter of dismissal, and instructed them to pack up anything Judy had left behind her and courier it, with the letter, round to her apartment.

Then she called Françoise Delmain again.

'You used to work for M. Keroualle, before Miss Dean had me dismiss him?'

'Yes, madame. For eight years.'

'Then you know how to distribute a press release?'

'Yes, madame.'

'Very well. Send this out immediately to our list of magazines: "Ms Judy Dean, former Senior Vice-President and Director of Publicity at House Massot, has been dismissed. Her replacement has not yet been announced."'

'Certainly, madame,' said Françoise triumphantly.

Sophie passed a hand across her forehead. Her temples were beginning to throb with stress, and she felt sick. She had no doubt that Marie and Françoise would have spread the news of the confrontation; it would be all over the company by now. By the end of the day, boyfriends would know; the gossip columnists would be all over it. Bitchy little pieces wondering how long Sophie had known. Recaps of her husband's apparently legendary career as a philanderer.

How stupid, how blind and passive she would seem. Or worse, like Celine had assumed; as one of those gold-digging trophy wives for whom not caring about adultery is the only sophisticated attitude.

Sophie was a private woman. The thought made her ill. She wanted to talk to Fr Sabin. Or even just to go home, and be alone.

That was not an option.

'We will need to find somebody to fill Judy's slot,' she said firmly. 'Françoise, email me the names of contacts at the top three publicity agencies in Paris. For now we will outsource.'

'At once, Mme Massot,' said Françoise, respectfully.

Sophie made up her mind. She would have somebody blue-chip and respectable hired before lunchtime; for the next few weeks it hardly mattered who. And after briefing them, she would have to track down Tom.

This was Paris. Rumour and gossip moved faster than lightning. He would read about this in tomorrow morning's papers; reporters might track him down, hound him for a quote . . .

Sophie had to tell him.

She stood up from her chair, edgy, and paced around the room.

But wait, wait. Don't do anything rash.

Tom worshipped his father, still. And Pierre was dead. It had hurt him enough when Sophie had to declare that legally. Could she now wound him again by destroying Pierre's memory?

Yes, the gossip columnists would run with the story. But it would be a blind item, a sneering little number without the real names of the participants. After all, they couldn't prove anything, and Pierre, when alive, had been highly litigious. The papers would all assume Sophie would be the same way.

She had money, and power. No; they would not name names.

So then, why should she?

Sophie knew now, and it was bitter, and dreadful, what a humiliating lie her marriage had been. But their son didn't need to share that pain.

I will not tell him, she thought. I will never speak of it to anyone. My husband is dead. Let them gossip; let them say it to my face, if they dare.

Nobody would. After all, nobody had ever said anything to her; not for fifteen years.

Sophie blinked back the tears in her eyes, and took a moment to compose herself. Then she returned to her chair, and clicked on to her email. There would be press reaction from the party last night; she needed to hire somebody to deal with it, and as soon as possible.

Chapter Thirty-Two

The feeling had lasted all morning.

It was there when Tom woke up, alone in the comfortable sterility of his rented bed; it was there as he processed the humiliations of last night; as he dressed, and made coffee, and called the limo service.

The behaviour of his mother – bizarre and humbling as it was – seemed to fade a little, seemed less fresh, when he thought about the American girl.

Beautiful; and spirited. She fascinated him, sexually; he wanted to prove himself with her. He was more than just a boy.

And, apparently, she had a plan as well. Something better than just voting 15 per cent against Maman and hoping for the best.

He would go to see his grandmother; it was a duty visit, it had to be paid. Tom did not forget that Katherine controlled two thirds of their stake. She had been right about Maman's attitude, but he regretted that. Tom was not looking forward to sitting there as the old lady gloated.

But it was his mother's fault. She had given Katherine that right.

When he thought of that pink, low-cut gown . . .

The telephone rang. Tom walked over to the stand in front of his windows, overlooking the Seine; he watched the sun glitter over the water, the boats laden with tourists ploughing through it, as he picked up the receiver.

'*Ici, Thomas,*' he said.

'Tom, it's Judy.'

He grinned, stupidly. 'Oh. Good morning.'

'Can I come round?'

He glanced at his watch. 'I really want to see you, but I have to take a ride out to St Aude. I must visit my grandmother at the château. After that, if we could do lunch? I'll pick the place this time.'

'If you could just defer that for an hour. Is that possible?'

'It's something important?' he asked, catching the urgency in her tone.

'Yes. You know the idea we were discussing last night? I'd like to explain it to you. It will concern your grandmother too, after all. When you visit her, you can tell her all about it.'

He didn't need much persuading. 'That's fine,' he said, trying not to sound too excited. 'Come round.'

He gave her the address, cancelled his car, and put on a fresh pot of coffee.

Judy looked beautiful.

That was the first thing that registered. Tom noticed it with relief; ungallant of him, perhaps, but still. It would have been a blow for her beauty to evaporate with the harsh light of day.

He needn't have worried. She was, on close inspection, still as firm and lithe as she had been under the moon, clad in a scarlet sheath. Today Judy wore another bold dress, a yellow cotton shift with embroidery in green thread; it was sleeveless, and showed off her tanned, muscular arms and slim runner's calves. She was wearing dangling earrings of iolite and white zircon; they moved and flashed, they were sexy, and youthful – nothing like a Massot piece.

Judy kissed him on the cheek.

'You like them?' She touched one long fingernail to her ears. 'They're Mayberry.'

'Come in.' He showed her inside, proudly; he took pleasure as her eyes rounded at the luxury, the space, the high ceilings. 'Of course, this is a rental,' he said. 'Nothing to the château.'

'But that's your mother's.'

'Only for another couple of years. After that the whole estate will be mine. The stock, too.' He felt proud as he said it. 'Coffee?'

'Please.'

'I don't know if you should be wearing Mayberry earrings. They're the enemy.' Tom thought of his mother. 'The enemy without, at least.'

'Ah,' Judy said. 'Well, that's what I want to talk to you about.'

He served her coffee at the little table for two set under the window; plenty of cream and sugar. There was nothing to eat, but that didn't matter. She was talking, in that fast, confident way the Americans have; sketching a plan that was immediately obvious, brilliant in its simplicity.

'And Mayberry would go for this?' Tom asked. He didn't trouble to play it cool, not now. Not with what she was saying.

'Of course. You'll never be in such a good position to dictate terms.' Judy leaned forward, her enthusiasm showing in her posture, in the gleam in her eyes, the tense set of her shoulders. 'They've spent money on this deal. And their reputation. If they lose, Mayberry's own stock will fall.'

'Then my mother's party helped us.'

Judy nodded. 'Her own success last night will strangle her. You see, it cannot be denied that from a purely commercial point of view, it was a masterstroke.'

'I thought it was tacky.'

'Yes,' Judy tried not to show her impatience. 'But those many sales; the reporters present will run stories. So will others. I assure you, today there will be a run on Massot showrooms. Not just in Paris, but across France, in Rome, and in London. By next week the buzz will be in New York and Tokyo. Fashion loves a story like this; the revival of haute couture, jewels considered as works of art. Sexier than a painting, and more portable.'

'And Massot stock will rise.'

'And shareholders may very well reject Mayberry's offer. Even some of their institutional investors may pull out. A deal like this can fall apart very quickly.'

'I see.' Tom drained his coffee; he was starting to get jittery. The next one should be decaffeinated. Was it that, or was it the prospect of real power, at last?

'Mayberry will not want to lose in the vote.'

'And with the stock they already have, *plus yours and Katherine Massot's . . .*'

'They could just take over.'

'No need for a vote. Majority control transfers.'

'And what would they do to obtain our votes?'

Judy leaned back and spread her hands. 'Almost anything, M. Massot.'

He smiled at her. 'You know it's Tom. You don't need to speak so respectfully to me.'

'Well, as the future chief executive of House Massot, you deserve a little respect.' She winked at him, and Tom was enchanted.

'Then we ask that Hugh Montfort be dismissed.'

'Indeed.' Judy looked solemn. 'That will satisfy your father's honour. He always hated Montfort.'

'And require that I be named Chief Executive – now, not merely in three years.'

Judy said, 'Of course, they will want to name a few of their own people to management spots.'

'But as long as I am head of the company.'

'You would be.' Only nominally, but she didn't say that. 'And of course you don't actually sell them your stock. You will keep the forty-five per cent in the family. It will always give you protection; in three years you will control it all.'

'And my mother?'

Judy sighed delicately. 'She loves you, I'm sure she'll come round. You can announce the deal carefully. Go to see her, after it's done, of course. I would advise distance from her until it's finalised.'

'Of course.'

'I have something else I must tell you, too. I resigned from House Massot today.'

'You did?'

'I took the view that I could no longer go on working for

Sophie. Not after meeting you. What she is doing is against the wishes of your father, and my first loyalty must be to his heir.' She gazed at him soulfully. 'I hope that doesn't offend you, Tom.'

'Offend me?' He caught her hands in his; for all her years, her slim, feminine hands were dwarfed inside his. He liked the look of them in there. 'Nothing you could ever do could offend me. I think you're marvellous.'

Judy blushed. 'You're just being kind.'

'I'm not,' Tom said urgently. 'I assure you.'

'Well?' She looked at him expectantly. 'Do you approve?'

'Very much; and not just of the plan.'

Judy touched her finger to his lips. 'You mustn't tease me, monsieur.'

'I think you know that I'm quite serious. I want to take you out to lunch. And then to dinner.' And then to bed, but he didn't say so.

She stood up, in a single, powerful movement, pushing the Sèvres porcelain cup away from her.

'First let us go and see Mme Katherine,' she said. 'It all depends on her.'

Tom called ahead, from the limo, to alert the servants; one didn't turn up at the dower house with an unannounced guest. His grandmother was a stickler for form, and he feared Judy might be kept waiting in the hallway; or worse, refused entrance altogether.

He waited on the phone until Tatin, Katherine's ancient butler, announced that Madame had said any guest of Monsieur's would be most welcome. Tom breathed out in relief. There would be no scenes.

At least, he hoped not.

Everything Tom relished about Judy – her ferocity, her spirit, her independence, even her fitness – his grandmother would disapprove of. He had no doubt about that. He hoped she would have the sense to be self-deprecating, modest, and admiring; to pay Katherine her due, and after giving homage, to say very little.

'Perhaps, once we get there, I should do the talking,' he said, eventually. 'Grandmother is very traditional.'

'Oh, I understand completely.' Judy turned her head away from the sun-dappled woods leading up to the estate; they would soon be pulling into the driveway of the château itself. She smiled reassuringly at Tom. 'You must tell her everything; it's a family decision. I have nothing to do with it.'

'It's your plan.'

'An idea; the merest suggestion. Just something I think Pierre would have wanted.'

He nodded. 'I know my father would agree. But as he isn't here, you'll have to let me be the one to thank you.'

'I'd like that,' Judy said, softly.

'*M. Thomas Massot et Mme Judy Dean*,' Faubert, her butler, pronounced solemnly.

Judy smiled politely; she squared her shoulders. Now was a moment to stand strong, she reminded herself. She would not be overawed by the sumptuousness of the dower house; in many ways, it was superior to Sophie's château. The Chinese silk wallpaper and Sun King furniture simply illuminated the Georgian grandeur of the house, the dignity of its grey stone lines, the perfect beauty of its lawns and carved yew hedges.

And the house was nothing if not a reflection of its owner.

Judy was ushered into the presence of the magnificent Katherine Massot. The boy, Tom, was nervous; she too, but she would have died before showing it.

Katherine had looked oddly attractive yesterday night, as though, by careful artifice, she had peeled off twenty years. She had crafted something out of the ruins of her former beauty. Today, that spell had been broken; Mme Massot was once again an old woman, and instead of beauty, her weapon was elegance, and steely, unassailable dignity.

She was sitting in her parlour, and did not rise to receive them. She wore a dress, peach silk with a lace trim, and a sedate string of lustrous pearls; her white hair was pinned up in a chignon with an old-fashioned lace cap atop it, and her face was carefully powdered and made up.

Tom led the way. He brought Judy over to his grandmother, and, switching back to French, said, 'It is wonderful to see you this morning. You look beautiful.' Then he kissed her on both cheeks, and turned to Judy. 'Grandmother, may I present my friend, Miss Dean?'

Katherine extended a bony claw; Judy fought the urge to curtsey.

'It's a great honour to meet you, madame,' she said, reverently.

'I take it this is more than a social call, Tom? Since you are doing me the honour of introducing me to Miss Dean?'

'It is,' Tom said.

The old lady waved them both to sit down; Judy perched on the edge of the couch. It was, she thought, authentic Louise Quatorze, and might be worth more than her entire apartment.

'I will call for coffee,' Katherine said.

'Thank you, but I dare not. I've already had too much today.'

'Miss Dean?'

'I'm fine, thank you, madame.'

'Then we will move on to sherry. It's gone eleven.' The old lady nodded to her butler, who disappeared. 'And so, Tom, you have something to say to me?'

'It was Judy's idea, Grandmother,' Tom said, warmly, 'and I think it will solve our present dilemma . . .'

Judy sat, her eyes downcast, as the boy explained the plan. She had to admit, he was quick; there was no fumbling, no unnecessary language. He laid it out in simple strokes, faster than she had done, and then he waited.

She dared to raise her eyes. The old woman was lost in thought. The butler reappeared, offering them all small crystal glasses of sherry. Judy accepted; it seemed the thing to do, and she could always count on a little alcohol to mask her nerves.

She usually despised sherry, but this was, in fact, delicious. It did not surprise Judy that Pierre's mother would have the best.

'I think it is an excellent idea,' Katherine said at last.

Both her guests felt their heart rate reduce; Judy congratulated herself with another sip of the clear golden nectar.

'You know how to contact the correct person at Mayberry, madame?'

'I do, madame. His name is Pete Stockton, and he is the Chairman of their Board.'

Judy was slightly annoyed that neither servant nor mistress called her 'mademoiselle', but she would overlook it. Katherine Massot's 10 per cent was key to her revenge; at least, to half of it. She looked slyly under her lashes at the boy, as beautiful as Pierre, but in the prime of his vigour.

He, too, was the key to everything . . .

'Tom,' his grandmother said. 'Why don't you go for a walk in the rose garden? Miss Dean and I are going to get a little better acquainted.'

Tom looked at Judy. She shrugged, minutely; Katherine Massot was not a woman to be gainsaid.

'Certainly,' Tom said. 'I'll return in a few minutes.'

He smiled encouragingly at Judy, and left the parlour by the side door. The old lady turned to Tatin.

'You may go,' she said, 'and see to it that we are not disturbed.'

'Very good, madame.' He bowed and withdrew, closing the doors behind him.

Judy squared her shoulders; the old woman sat there, like a spider, controlling; she tried to meet that watery gaze.

'Your plan is an ingenious one, my dear,' Katherine said. 'It will provide my grandson with a great deal of money. And control.'

'That is what his father would have wanted,' Judy replied.

Katherine sighed delicately. 'Ah yes; his father. You were his father's mistress, of course.'

Judy started. 'What?'

'You heard what I said, madame.' Katherine's eyes hardened. 'Pray do not play games with me. I knew Pierre. I knew where he went, and with whom he spent his time. Sophie may have ignored his lovers; I, however, did not.'

Judy hesitated, but there was too much certainty in the mother's tone.

'I loved Pierre,' she said, with a touch of defiance.

'Many people loved Pierre. Many women. You were one of several, Miss Dean.'

'Excuse me, madame,' Judy said, gathering her strength. 'But I am aware of that.'

'Now,' Katherine replied. 'You were not, at the time.'

How does she know all this? Judy wondered.

The old lady's eyes were curious. 'You must have hated Sophie very much?'

Judy felt the old, stabbing pain in her heart. 'She did not deserve him,' she said flatly.

Katherine cackled. 'Ah; there, we can agree. So many women; some of them at least *interesting* . . . for him to choose that pudding of a girl . . .'

'Why did he not divorce her?'

Katherine moved her hand; her silk gown rustled. 'No need. She never did anything wrong. And she provided him with an heir. And yet, I believe,' she added thoughtfully, 'that if he should return, he might. He might divorce her. Now. For what she has done with his company, admitting the suits of other men.'

Judy's eyes widened. 'You don't think he's still alive?'

'Oh, I'm quite sure he is.'

'You have some proof? Some new fact?'

Katherine sighed. 'I have a connection with Pierre; a connection with him no other woman will ever have.' Her eyes flared. 'None of you has known him as I have. If he were dead, I should know it.'

The old woman is delusional, Judy decided.

'You have never taken another lover,' Katherine said. 'But now you wish to commence some affair with Thomas. Yes?'

Judy's mouth opened.

'You may as well tell the truth. I shall find out sooner, rather than later, I assure you.'

'Tom looks a great deal like his father.'

'But he has none of his spirit,' Katherine said. 'His disposition he has inherited from his mother, almost entire. Except perhaps a little stubborness; and even that may be hers, too, if recent events are anything to go by.'

'I do like him,' Judy said.

'You don't love him. Yet you are prepared to annexe him. Is it not so?'

'You don't understand me, madame.'

'Oh, I think I do,' Katherine said. 'I think I do. Tom will be very rich. And of course, he is Sophie's boy, as well as Pierre's.'

Judy opened her mouth to respond, but couldn't think of the right thing to say.

'You realise that once you begin with Tom, it will be finally over between you and Pierre?'

Judy stared. Over between her and Pierre? The man was dead. It had been over for almost a decade.

'I understand that, madame,' she said.

'Then I will not stand in your way. But if you want some advice, move swiftly. Sophie will be trying to reconnect with Thomas, as soon as she can.'

Judy was dumbfounded, but said carefully, 'Thank you, Mme Massot.'

The old woman smiled. 'You may call me Katherine, Judy.'

The parlour door opened again and Tom walked through it; silhouetted against the warm noonday sun and azure sky, he was so like Pierre that Judy's breath caught in her throat.

He looked at the two of them warily. 'Everything go well, Grandmother?'

'Oh, very well,' Katherine said sweetly. 'Judy and I are going to be great friends.'

Tom looked relieved. 'Shall we all have some lunch, perhaps?'

Katherine shook her powdered head. 'I am tired, *chéri*; it's time for my nap. And anyway, I think you should be calling . . . M. Stockton, is it?'

Judy nodded.

'You have no time to lose,' Katherine pronounced. 'Goodbye, my dear.'

Judy stood as Tom kissed his grandmother on the cheek. She shook hands with the woman, clasping her bony fingers in her own vigorous ones, and then the butler was bowing them out, and they emerged from the elegant gloom of the dower house into the blazing sunshine of August, with the hired limo purring patiently on the gravel semicircle of her drive.

'She's right, you know,' Judy told him. 'Let's head back to the city. You call Pete, and once that's done we'll know if they'll go for it. Then we can get some lunch.'

'And after lunch?' Tom gave her a long look.

Judy let her lips part; her tongue flicked out and moistened them.

'Well, baby, I guess we'll find *something* to do,' she teased.

Chapter Thirty-Three

The heat was unbearable in L.A. Even his state-of-the-art air-conditioning didn't seem to make much difference. As soon as Pete stepped out of the car, or the office, or his home, he was engulfed in a thick blanket of muggy, sticky heat you could part with a knife. Six coats of Sure didn't stop the tell-tale wet patches appearing under his arms; he wore dark colours, but even so, he had to change his shirts up to four times a day.

Anyway you cut it, August was a pain in the ass.

He was glad to be in the air. First-class was always a pleasure. And he was headed for Europe, where the weather was bearable.

And of course, his task was pleasant.

It had taken barely fifteen minutes after that wonderful call came in to persuade the other board members. A couple of them bitched about Montfort's performance, but nobody could really argue against the deal; it was just too perfect, too much money.

What would it hurt to give the kid some stupid title? They'd work out an iron-clad contract that gave him no rights – full consultation, no action. Stockton wasn't sure exactly who he'd put in charge. But it wouldn't be Tom Massot. And it wouldn't be Hugh Montfort, either.

He loved the kid, right now. The kid could have any title he wanted. Pete would set him up with a fancy office, an expense account and a Tootsie Roll of a secretary. Tom Massot was better than Santa Claus; he'd given Pete Massot, and all its millions, and he'd managed to take Montfort away at the same time.

'Champagne, sir?' The stewardess was hovering over him; she was in her late thirties, competent-looking and heavy-set. Not like in the good old days, when pleasing businessmen was more important than courses in air safety and disarming terrorists, and all the air hostesses were bleached-blonde dolly birds in their twenties.

But he wouldn't let anything ruin his good mood today.

'Sure,' Pete said. 'Why the hell not.'

Hugh had had a busy morning. Two days since the party, and it had been as he had feared; the press were slavering over House Massot's must-have original pieces; they had compared Herr and Frau Brandt to the great masters, describing their work as a mixture of Paulding Farnham and Richard Bapst. He had visited the Massot showrooms on rue Faubourg and New Bond Street, both of them humming with activity; there was buzz; the stock was up; the Bourse analysts were tapping away at their reports.

It had taken a lot of press spin just to stand still. Montfort's line was 'too little, too late' – one good party, even one good collection, could not wipe away eight years of mismanagement . . .

He had also spent hours on the phone to his institutional backers; pension fund managers concerned they were missing a trick. Hugh believed all would still be well, but he was grateful the vote was not far away.

He hung up on the latest fund manager with relief. It was noon; early for lunch, but he wanted to get out of the hotel, away from the business press, and give himself a chance to think.

Montfort told Mrs Percy that he would be back at two. Normally he abhorred long lunches; but it might be as well to be unavailable for as long as possible. Allow some of the fuss to blow over, and the investors to regain their senses. There was a feeding frenzy, but he thought it would soon die down. The more he seemed unconcerned, the better. Mrs Percy, his highly efficient London secretary, had flown out that morning to assist him over the next few days.

'And will you have your mobile with you, sir?'

'No. You know I can't stand the wretched things.' Hugh pulled his mobile out of his briefcase and handed it to her. 'In fact, you take it, Mrs Percy. That way I can't be tempted to answer.'

'Certainly, sir.'

Mrs Percy gave him the crisp smile he so approved of, and Hugh left his suite.

It was good to get out of the hotel. He hated air-conditioning; hated anything artificial. His soldier's body was used to extremes of heat and cold. He had only been persuaded to install central heating in the castle in Ireland because otherwise the pipes would freeze; and his mother would complain, when she stayed, that she was never warm enough. Hugh would have preferred to make do with a roaring fire and a goose-down blanket. He liked the heat of summer and the cold of winter; it reminded him of the seasons, and made him feel alive. It seemed a terrible modern affectation to insist on its being sixteen degrees Celsius, whatever the actual weather outside. Montfort preferred to eat fruits in season, instead of strawberries in December and plums in March; artifical hot-housed ones always tasted watery; and he took pleasure in the world the way it really was.

Step outside in Paris in August and you would feel the power of summer. Tourists sweated, heat reflected so strongly off the pavements that if you walked barefoot, you would burn. Montfort relished it; he turned his face towards the sun, closing his eyes, and letting the heat permeate his skin.

He would find a really good restaurant and have a wonderful meal. It was ideal not to have his phone with him; no tiresome journalists could call and interrupt, and he couldn't call anybody, even if he wanted to.

And he did want to – very much. Although it would be suicidally stupid, he wanted to call Sophie Massot.

There were any number of pretexts; he could thank her for inviting him to the party. Or he could ask her again to vote him her stock. She would say no, but at least it was a legitimate reason to call . . .

He didn't care in the least about the deal; Montfort wished it were done. Would she still see him, afterwards?

The feeling simply would not go away. It would not evaporate. He thought about Sophie constantly. She hovered in the back of his mind. He didn't think it was just another passing fancy; he wanted to take her out, to get to know her.

His need for hookers, for the urgent relief of sex, had dwindled lately. There were girls in Paris, skilled, well off, discreet, but he had not felt tempted. His thoughts were on Sophie. Which was insanity, of course; of all the women in the world, to fall for his target . . .

'Sir!'

Hugh looked behind him, startled. Mrs Percy was running towards him, out of the hotel. He was immediately annoyed; no phone call could be that important. But he stood and waited for her as she stumbled towards him, trying to run in her heels.

'Yes?'

'I'm very sorry, sir,' Mrs Percy panted. 'But it's urgent. It's Mr Stockton, sir.'

'I'll call him back, after lunch.' Sod Stockton; Hugh hadn't liked his manners lately.

'But he's not on the phone. He's here. In your suite.'

'He flew to Paris?' Hugh asked. Stockton hadn't said anything about that. What the hell was he playing at?

'Yes, sir; and he's waiting for you. I'm awfully sorry, but he demanded I fetch you right away.' Mrs Percy lowered her voice, as though Pete Stockton could hear them through double-glazing and the roar of the traffic. 'He watched you walk away from your window; he can probably see us right now. I couldn't put him off till after lunch, I'm terribly—'

'Not to worry, Mrs Percy; you did the right thing.' Hugh nodded reassuringly at her. 'Quite right to come and fetch me. Are you very out of breath?'

She leaned over, nodded, gasping; Hugh offered her his arm.

'We'll walk back together,' he said. 'No rush.'

'But Mr Stockton—'

'He can wait,' Hugh said firmly.

* * *

Pete Stockton was waiting in Hugh's hotel suite when he got back. He was sitting in one of the chairs, his body uncomfortably squashed into its elegant lines; he made no attempt to get up as Montfort and his secretary entered the room.

'I just managed to catch him, sir,' Mrs Percy said brightly. 'Can I get you anything for your meeting? Some tea or coffee, or mineral water?'

'No. This is gonna be short.'

'Very good, sir; I'll wait through here.'

Pete waved a fat hand at her. 'Stay here, honey. This affects you, too.'

Elizabeth Percy blinked; she didn't like being called 'honey', unless it was by Jack; certainly not by a fat sleazeball like Pete Stockton who, rumour had it, was a world-class sexual harasser. And what could he possibly have to tell Hugh that would involve her?

She looked uncertainly at her boss; Montfort made the smallest of hand gestures, to tell her to relax.

'I was just about to go for lunch, Peter,' said Hugh. 'Care to join me?'

A distasteful task, but it had to be done. He could hardly refuse to invite the Chairman.

'I don't think that would be such a great idea.' Pete Stockton took a metal cigar case out of his shirt pocket, theatrically withdrew a Monte Cristo, bit the top off it, and lit it up.

'Are we celebrating something?' Perhaps he had news on some more stockholder commitments.

'*We're* not. I am.' Stockton drew in a mouthful of fragrant smoke and let it drift out of his nostrils.

'How shall I put this,' he said with evident relish. 'Let me see . . . Hugh, you're fired.'

'What?' gasped Mrs Percy.

Pete turned to her. 'You're his assistant, sugar? Great. I want you to go to your laptop and change all the passwords. Zip up all his letters and files and send them straight to me. Make sure he's denied access to any and all Mayberry data, starting immediately.'

Hugh tried to take it in. 'May I ask why I'm being fired?' he said.

'Sure,' Pete said expansively. 'You're being terminated for cause. Lousy performance with the Massot deal.'

'We're still going to make that deal.'

'We certainly are, but you're not gonna be a part of it. You failed to prepare for this party – look at the stock price, for Christ's sake. And you failed to investigate all the avenues.'

'What the hell does that mean?' Montfort snapped.

Stockton smiled smugly. 'You'll find out – once Mayberry owns House Massot. Now you're fucking fired, so get your shit together and get the hell out of the hotel. Mayberry is paying this bill. Same goes for you, sweetheart. Get back to London, you can take that underwater train. Pack up his office. Make sure he takes nothing, I mean not even a goddam Biro. He walks away with anything, you're out on your pretty ass.'

Elizabeth Percy said, 'Screw you, fatso. I quit.'

Hugh turned to her in surprise, then started laughing. 'Priceless,' he said.

Stockton's piggish eyes narrowed; he'd expected Hugh to plead, not laugh. Everybody knew Mayberry was the limey's life; gave him a sense of purpose. And who did the bim think she was?

'I expect you want to know the full story, Montfort,' he sneered.

'Not at all; I couldn't be less interested.' Hugh offered his arm to Elizabeth again. 'Mrs Percy, I believe we were going to lunch?'

Pete Stockton stared at them, furious, as they walked out the door and down the corridor. He was so angry to be cheated of his moment of glory that he found his face had gone all red. Then a column of ash dropped on to his fresh-pressed pants.

'Fuck!' he said.

Laughter drifted back to him from the corridor. Well, they could both go to hell. It was an act, he thought, calming down. Any way you cut it, Hugh Montfort had just been unceremoniously canned right before closing the biggest deal of his career. He'd made enough enemies at Tiffany and Cartier and

Garrard's . . . he was done, that arrogant fuck; done like a Thanksgiving turkey!

That thought made him feel a little better. Montfort and his girlfriend could stiff-upper-lip-it all they wanted. He knew they were wrecked inside.

He was hungry; he'd order some food himself, a burger and fries, not any of that French shit that always made his stomach so upset. And then he'd take a car down to the Massot showroom; see what he was about to take over. Maybe pick out a piece for Claudia. That should stop her bitching for a day or two.

Hugh flagged down a taxi and gave it directions to place de la Madeleine.

'Where are we going?' Mrs Percy, her bravado evaporated, looked a little shell-shocked.

'I think we deserve a splendid lunch,' Hugh told her. 'Something really French. Lucas Carton is acknowledged to be one of the great restaurants in the city. I have known M. Senderens, the sommelier, for years.'

'That sounds wonderful, sir.'

His secretary was white and shaky. Hugh was almost glad; concentrating on her meant he didn't have to think overly hard about his own position.

'You don't have to call me "sir", any more, Mrs Percy. Remember?'

'Oh; yes.' She tried to smile. 'Then you should call me Elizabeth.'

'Elizabeth.' He tried to reassure her. 'You mustn't worry about what just happened in there.'

'Well, it was my decision.' Elizabeth wrung her fingers in her lap. They had just bought a flat with a horrendous mortgage, and they needed every penny of her salary and her bonuses. 'I just don't know what I'm going to tell Jack . . .'

'That's Mr Percy?'

She nodded mutely. Montfort had never taken a close interest in her personal life.

'I have plenty of friends who will be very glad to employ an assistant of your exceptional worth,' Montfort said. 'And for the moment – what were you making a year with me?'

'Thirty-six thousand,' Elizabeth whispered. Montfort had been incredibly generous. Where would she find somebody else to match him?

'Then I shall give you two years' salary. Possibly as a nominal payment. I'll talk to my accountant as to the best way to avoid gift tax.'

She stared at him. 'But that's seventy-two thousand pounds, Mr Montfort.'

'If you're to be Elizabeth, I may as well be Hugh.' He took her hand in his. 'It's quite all right; I am a rich man, and what you did in there was very brave. And gave me far more than seventy-two thousand pounds' worth of pleasure,' he added, thinking of Stockton's pudgy face.

The taxi drew up; Montfort paid and led Elizabeth into the restaurant. They were seated immediately, and she tried to relax; the sumptuous surroundings and quiet hum of monied diners made her slightly uneasy.

'It's just good food.'

She smiled; he was a real old-fashioned gentlemen, Hugh Montfort, trying to put her at her ease.

'So what's good here?' she asked.

'I can confidently say, everything,' Hugh said. 'Shall we start with some appetisers?'

He ordered a couple of glasses of champagne, Perrier-Jouet Belle Epoque, and smoked oysters for himself.

'Oh, pick for me,' Elizabeth said. Her French was shaky, and the menu seemed frighteningly complex.

'Very well.' Hugh ordered her a salad of Breton lobster and white beans with cream and dill, followed by lamb *brochettes* in a thyme sauce; for himself, he chose roasted perch with watercress purée, and accompanied them with half-bottles of exceptional red and white wines; Elizabeth didn't understand the wine waiter's rapid-fire French, but she knew delicious wine when she sipped it.

The food was, indeed, outstanding; she chewed slowly, savouring each bite. Who would have thought lamb could taste like this? It melted on her tongue; the flavour had five or six layers, and she ate with Hugh in companionable silence for a few minutes.

It took a glass of champagne and another of Château d'Yquem before she got the courage to ask, 'Why did he do that?'

Montfort shook his head. 'He has always disliked me; but apart from that I see no reason for it.'

'Was it Mrs Massot's party?' Elizabeth pressed timidly.

'That's an excuse.' Hugh gazed down at his meal. 'No, something's happening that gave him the courage to dismiss me.'

'But why? It's insane. Without you there wouldn't even be a Mayberry.'

He smiled thinly. 'I believe I have made some difference to the company's shareholders, yes.'

'What are you going to do?' Elizabeth Percy was pink-cheeked with outrage. 'You have to sue them, sir – I mean, Hugh.'

'I shall do no such thing.' Hugh shrugged. 'There's no need; I have every confidence that the business press will represent my service to the company for what it was. Lawsuits are expensive and long-winded, as well as terminally dull.'

'Then you'll go to somebody else. To Cartier. Or Tiffany's.'

Montfort shook his head. 'Fifteen years at Mayberry haven't made me too many friends.'

Elizabeth said fiercely, 'Start your own business, then. You can do it better than any of them.'

He sliced deliberately into his fish. It was very good, the watercress adding just the right touch of bitterness; calibrated to his mood, perhaps.

The thought made him smile.

'I don't think so,' he said. 'Not yet, anyway. It's almost always a mistake to make major decisions on the spur of the moment.'

Elizabeth fretted. 'But you need to work, Mr – Hugh. You need to have something to occupy you. You've always been like that. Otherwise you'll . . .'

She realised she was getting too close to the truth for comfort, and her voice trailed off.

'I'll think too much about my wife?' he asked gently.

She blushed. 'I'm sorry, I shouldn't have mentioned it.'

'It's quite all right. I'm just surprised you knew.' Montfort looked closer at Mrs Percy, as though seeing her for the first time. 'Did other staff talk about that? In the London office?'

'About you and Mrs Montfort?' Elizabeth nodded. 'Lots of them. Most of the staff around the world, actually. I used to get emails . . .'

Now Hugh was shocked. '*Emails?* From staff, asking about Georgiana?'

'I deleted them all,' Elizabeth said defensively.

'But why would anybody care?' Now he was angry. 'My grief . . . I didn't talk about it; it is entirely private.'

'You have to understand, you were famous at Mayberry,' Elizabeth explained. 'What you did . . . it determined our pay, our Christmas bonuses, even our stock options . . . people were always talking about you, asking about your love life.' She smiled disarmingly. 'Most of those emails came from women, you see.'

'Oh.' He had the good grace to smile. 'I see.'

'I wouldn't discuss you.'

'I'm sure you didn't.'

'But your previous secretaries . . .' Elizabeth said delicately.

Hugh winced. Of course, Rosa Vasquez and Charlotte Hurst; both had eventually broken down and sobbed their love for him into his chest or shoulder, ruining a couple of perfectly good suits.

'They talked about me?'

'They talked of little else. Your . . . dwelling on Mrs Montfort.' The words used had been 'obsession' and 'morbid', but she forbore to spell that out. 'You know, sir, Hugh, at first everybody dreaded you. The firings – the redundancies.'

'I realised that.'

'But later, as they got to know you – and that you apparently cared about the stockholders, and the staff – they liked you.

They cared about you. It's not all that surprising that they gossiped.'

'And the conclusion?'

'That without your work you would fall apart.'

Hugh took a sip of wine and reflected. People were not as unperceptive as he had assumed. It was, he knew, a perfectly justified view of his character.

Mayberry, and its revival, and then its move to world dominance, had been his life. He enjoyed the game; it was chess against multiple partners, against the markets, the established houses, the press, the suppliers. Winning had been everything.

And now, when he was close to the deal that would have constituted final victory – pouf – with the gloating words of a fat slob, it had all evaporated.

'Maybe that was true, once.' He admitted it. 'But no longer. That's not what my wife would have wanted.'

'And what about you?'

Hugh thought of Sophie.

'It seems to me there are other things worth living for. Things that, on balance, are even more important than big deals.' He grinned. 'You know what I'm realising, Elizabeth?'

She shook her head.

'That Mayberry was just a job. And no job is worth getting bothered about.'

Elizabeth Percy gaped. 'Are you *sure* you're feeling all right?'

'Never better.' He spooned up a little more purée. He was free; entirely free. All of a sudden Montfort felt a great rush of gratitude. 'It's a beautiful summer day in Paris, and I can do whatever I like. You've finished, Elizabeth. Can I tempt you with some pudding? They make a vanilla cake with bitter almond cream that's absolutely sensational.'

'Thank you. I'd like that,' said Elizabeth. She still wasn't sure about Hugh. Maybe it would hit him later. He'd just been fired, and yet he was sitting here smiling like it was his birthday.

'And then I'll drive you to the airport and send you home. First-class.'

'That's very kind,' Elizabeth said.

He was gorgeous; so gorgeous. She couldn't blame the other girls. She would miss working for him, but . . .

Elizabeth glanced down at her wedding ring and thought of her lovely dependable Jack, and felt more than a bit disloyal.

Yes; maybe it was all for the best.

Chapter Thirty-Four

'Here, here, madame.'

Sophie looked up to see Celine, smiling and laying another article on her desk. 'The agency just sent this over.'

She scanned it quickly, and nodded. 'Very good.'

The latest piece was from *Women's Wear Daily* in New York; the latest glowing review of the new haute couture collection; the pieces in the Fifth Avenue store were racing out the door.

'There are new stories every day.'

Sophie nodded. She'd hired Burton-Marseller, the PR giant, to handle her press for now; they were expensive, but they were also doing an outstanding job. The afterglow from the party was constantly fanned into fresh flames, and they'd told her the good coverage would last until the stockholders' meeting.

'That's wonderful, Celine.'

In truth it felt a bit flat. She'd been busy, but even the chaos of the last few days – ordering more stock as fast as the Brandts and their apprentices could turn them out, managing the press, talking to analysts – even that could not banish the shock of Judy from her mind.

Well, not Judy – Pierre.

Judy didn't matter. She was just a bitter ex-mistress. Sophie was determined to forget her, and simply to resolve never to trust anybody so easily again. That was her own fault; she hadn't learned from Gregoire.

But her husband . . .

That was humiliation, real humiliation; it had been with her every time she closed her eyes to sleep, and every moment she woke up. She imagined that every woman in the Massot offices was discussing it; she imagined it was the talk of all Paris.

And she, Sophie, had been blind; hadn't suspected . . .

Hadn't cared?

When Pierre had to 'work late' she'd never murmured. Never questioned. And now she had to ask herself why.

She had promised, at the altar, to love Pierre. Had she ever kept that promise? If she examined her conscience, Sophie wondered. She recoiled from the tag of gold-digger; and it hadn't been overt avarice, that was true. But still, Judy's words had stung. Maybe Sophie wasn't looking just for money, but she had wanted to escape. Very much . . .

Was it love, with Pierre? Or just gratitude?

Had he ever loved her? For some men, sex and love don't mix. They can be quite separate; so she was told. Was it that way with her husband?

'Celine.' She looked up. 'Did you try my son's numbers again?'

Her assistant nodded. 'I'm very sorry, madame.'

They were all set to answer; his cell phone, his apartment, his private line at the château; Sophie was tried of leaving messages.

'It's not your fault,' she said. 'Please call me a taxi; and take my messages. I'm going out for the rest of the day.'

She didn't know whether to laugh or cry. It was so inherently ridiculous, what she was doing, that she should smile about it, but Sophie felt her mother's love reduced to this, skulking in a bistro just off the Left Bank, watching the entrance to the building where her Thomas had rented a place; rented somewhere just so he would not need to live in their home. And that thought made her throat thicken, and set her eyes prickling with tears.

But it had to be done. If Tom wouldn't speak to her, wouldn't take her calls, she would have to see him. In person. And if that meant waiting here all day for him to show up, so be it.

She had some camouflage. She had a novel, an old copy of *Persuasion*; it was a story she loved, but couldn't concentrate on. Sophie just sipped her indifferent coffee and toyed with her salad; this was a tourist restaurant, with menus and prices in English, and the food was appropriately sub-par.

But they wouldn't bother her. She could spin it out all day. She would have a salad, then soup, then a soufflé, coffee, petits-fours; then herbal tea, and cakes; and so on to supper, if necessary. She had already done the important thing; found the maitre d' and tipped him a hundred-euro note, saying she wanted to be left alone to think.

'Something else for you, Miss?'

The waitress was a German, Sophie thought; benefits of the EU.

'I'll take an ice cream . . . strawberry is fine . . .' she paused; that was him, that was Tom! Walking down the street. 'On second thoughts, nothing.' Sophie hastily snapped open her Coach handbag and pulled out a fifty-euro note. 'For the bill.'

She jumped to her feet and rushed out of the door, leaving its little bell clanging behind her.

Crazy broad, the waitress thought. But what the hell, it was a twenty-euro tip. She crammed the fifty in her pocket and headed back to the kitchen.

Sophie ran; he was walking slowly, head down, lost in thought. Her heart pounded; she felt ridiculously nervous. Passers-by were staring; she couldn't have cared less.

'Tom,' she said. 'Tom, stop. It's me.'

He looked up, startled, and his mouth opened; he just stood there. He made no move towards her.

'This has to stop,' Sophie said, and to her horror her self-control deserted her, and she started to cry, right there in the street; great sobs, tears rolling from her eyes.

'For God's sake!' He swore. 'What are you doing?'

'Tom,' Sophie said, miserably. 'You're my boy . . . you have to talk to me.'

He flushed. 'Come inside. Stop making a spectacle of yourself, Maman!'

Hastily, he fished out his keys and fumbled with the lock, letting the heavy white door swing open; he glared at the small crowd that was forming, and gave his mother a gentle push to get her inside.

As soon as the door shut she turned to him. 'Darling, I—'

'We have a doorman,' Tom said, low and urgent. 'Please, Maman, for heaven's sake. Just follow me to the lifts, OK? You can talk in my apartment.'

She nodded, blinded by tears, and followed him. This wasn't going anything like she had wished. Tom hadn't looked guilty, or moved; he seemed only concerned with getting her out of public view.

He was still estranged from her. The pain was acute. Sophie swayed; she thought she might pass out.

'Here.' Tom took his mother's arm, and led her into the elevator, firmly waving away offers of help from the concerned doorman behind the desk.

The lift took them up smoothly and Tom let her in to his place; it was as sterile and soulless as she had imagined; millions of miles from his set of rooms at the château, with their wonderful view of the pear orchards and the stables.

'Sit down,' he said coldly. 'Do you want a handkerchief?'

'I have one.' Sophie fished a neat square of cotton from her handbag and blew her nose.

'Are you feeling faint? Do you need something sweet? Hot tea, perhaps?'

The words were solicitous, but the tone was not. Sophie dabbed at her eyes. She didn't know where to start.

'I'm fine. Look, darling, I know you're upset about Daddy—'

'I believe you have no idea how I feel about my father,' Tom replied flatly. 'You have declared him dead with no proof –'

'Not this again.'

'You defy his wishes and try to usurp my inheritance; making the family an object of ridicule. I only had three years to go.'

'I didn't have three years . . .'

'What, Maman? You think that somehow you were qualified to come in and take over the company, but I wasn't? You don't have any business experience; you didn't even go to university.'

Sophie flushed deeply.

'I was studying at Oxford. What made you think that you would be my superior?'

'Well,' she said, carefully, wounded. 'You weren't exactly studying very hard, sweetheart. I didn't think you were mature enough . . .'

'If anybody's showed immaturity it's you.' Tom struggled to control himself; he ticked off the points on his fingers. 'You delcare him dead; you defy his wishes; you denigrate me; you embarrass the family; while you're still in mourning you start an affair – no, don't say anything, I know it all.'

'I didn't sleep with him!'

Tom winced. '*Please*. As if I want to know. But you romanced him while wearing black for Papa. And then, then,' he said, 'as soon as six months ticks off the clock, off goes the black. I suppose my father isn't worth a year's respect? He gave you *everything*.'

'Tom—'

'I'm not finished.' He looked at her and his eyes were flint. 'You then crown it all by debasing House Massot with that little *party*. You give our jewels away for free and you show up, in front of all Paris, in pink – pink! Like Father didn't matter. And you are wearing a dress that's practically indecent.'

'Indecent?'

'Designed to show off your cleavage. Maman, you're *thirty-nine*,' he said with withering distaste.

'It most certainly was not indecent. It was empire-waisted –'

'Well, you embarrassed *me*. Again. As though you hadn't learned from the disaster of your last lover. You laid us open to all of it.'

Sophie struggled with herself and regained a little control.

'Tom, I love you,' she said. 'I did all this for you. You have to believe that.'

He sighed. 'I wish I could, Maman, I really do. But I think this was some kind of mid-life crisis on your part.' Tom sat down in a chair opposite her and looked at her gravely.

'I want you to come home. Back to the château. Your rooms are waiting.'

308

'I don't think that's the best idea right now,' he said.

'But *why* isn't it, Tom?' The tears were threatening again. 'We can work this out.'

'I don't think we can. Whatever you may believe, I am an adult, Mother. I am going to look after my interests and Papa's interests where House Massot is concerned.'

'There's another three years –'

'No, there isn't. It will shortly be no longer your concern.'

Sophie blinked. 'What do you mean?'

Tom shook his head. 'It doesn't matter. Look, of course I love you. I'll always love you,' he said. 'But at the moment I'm afraid I don't like you very much.'

She recoiled; a stab of agony surged right through her, worse than any heartache Sophie had ever known. The dizziness returned, and she swayed on the chair.

Tom noticed; he was concerned, and came over to her.

'Maman,' he said, urgently. 'We can put this behind us. Just leave the company alone. Leave it today. Sign over the stock you vote to me, now. You know it's all coming to me anyway. Just go back to the castle, and I'll come back and be with you. I can introduce my girlfriend—'

'You have a girlfriend?'

He hesitated.

'You won't like her at first,' Tom admitted. 'But once we've explained everything, I know you'll come round. You want us to be a family again, and so do I. You just need to stop standing in the way of what Papa wanted.'

He pressed her hand and stood up.

'House Massot was my father's. And now it's mine. As soon as you see that, this can all be over.'

Sophie looked at her tall, strong son. He was so like his father, his shoulders square against the blazing sunlight streaming into the room; stubborn and proud, half-man, half-boy. She was sure he believed he was ready, but she knew otherwise.

It was the worst thing about being a parent. Having to deny and refuse somebody you loved so much more than yourself.

She would die for Tom without a second thought. But love

for him meant not letting him destroy everything he had in the world.

'I can't do that, Tom.'

'You mean you won't.'

'I can't; I won't; you're not ready.'

'We'll see about that,' Tom said. 'I'm sorry it has to be this way, Maman.'

Sophie stood up. 'So you won't come home?'

'Later,' he said. 'I told you, I intend to assert my rights to the company.'

She knew Tom couldn't do anything; he didn't have enough stock. But perhaps this wasn't the moment to point that out. Sophie went over, kissed him on the cheek; Tom awkwardly patted her on the back.

'Then I'll see you in a month. After the stockholders' meeting,' she said bravely.

Tom walked to the door and opened it. 'Can you see yourself out, or should I come with you to get a taxi?'

'I'm fine. I'll walk.' Sophie set her lips tight. She didn't want to say too much; didn't want to start crying again.

'Goodbye, Maman,' Tom said. And as she walked over to the lift, he shut the door firmly behind her.

Chapter Thirty-Five

They were coming in faster now. They always did. Summer was over, and autumn was curling dreadfully, inevitably down towards winter; the deep, long dark of winter in Northern Russia, where the cold was so desperate it ran down into your bones, and the beautiful blanket of snow wrapped the frozen earth up, hard as death. No wonder people drank.

It was a prosperous business, selling vodka and beer to miners and party officials, on the outskirts of Minsk. The tavern had a supply of alcohol, a blazing fire, tables for cards; it wasn't hard to fill, even in the long summer evenings. But when winter came around, the place was packed. Men didn't want to go home to their fat wives in the dark. They chose to drink a little, gamble, look at the blaze, laugh, talk about women. Leer at women, if any were ever brave enough to show their faces. Mostly it was just the whores, and Pyotr discouraged them inside his bar; he didn't want any trouble for the party bureaucrats. They could drum up their trade outside the door.

Vladek despised those women, too. Young and desperate . . . and selling their bodies. Why should those sluts pollute the bar? If they were poor, then they could work. They could make something of themselves, the way he, Vladek, had done.

His real name wasn't Vladek. But he had decided to call himself that. Vladek meant 'ruler'. He had learned that in the orphanage, along with many other facts taught by Mr Kovec, and others; the history of the glorious Communist Revolution, with geography, with tales of capitalist aggression. And while the other kids sat there, sullen, thinking of nothing but the hunger that gnawed at their bellies, Vladek had sucked it in.

He would better himself, for such was his destiny.

Vladek swept the floors for the eighteenth time that afternoon. He smiled, nodded at the patrons as they swaggered in, blowing on their hands and calling at Pyotr to pour them a shot – or six. Blowsy, rolling drunks, they were all peasants. Like the other kids at the orphanage; mining or chopping wood, manual labour, that was their destiny.

He had noble blood in his veins, though; things were going to be different for him.

'Vladek! Get over here.'

Pyotr bellowed at him. 'The latrine has blocked up again. Sort it out before the first shift clocks off.'

'Sure, Pyotr,' Vladek said. The boy gritted his teeth; shovelling stinking human refuse, that was what Pyotr thought he was good for!

But he didn't show his disgust. There would be no complaints. Whatever Pyotr wanted done, he did. It was why Pyotr hadn't thrown him on to the street that first night, when he ran away from the hated iron gates of the orphanage, struggled ten miles into the settlement, in his thin, darned pants, terrified he might faint from cold. Because had he done so, of course, he would have died.

Every spring, when the snows melted, they found bodies in this town; men who got drunk and passed out in the forest. Nobody could survive a Siberian winter night without warmth. The drifts and flakes gently, lethally covered the bodies, and they never bothered anyone again.

But Vladek was strong. And determined. He could still remember the light over the door, shining out at him like a beacon of salvation. How he'd snuck in behind a group of welders from the factory, run to the coat rack and hidden himself, giddy with the warmth of the furs. But he hadn't slept, although he longed to. He had grabbed a broom and gone around sweeping up. That night, luckily for him, Pyotr had indulged in his own product. While he lay passed out on the counter, Vladek had diligently cleaned up, stacking the chairs on the tables, locking the tempting box that held the piles of roubles, notes and coins.

The bar had never looked so clean. When Pyotr woke, groaning, he thumped the hell out of Vladek; assumed he was a thief. But Vladek twisted away, his nose broken and bloody, refusing to run, refusing to leave; he managed to show Pyotr how he'd kept all the cash locked up. He offered to clean the place, and managed it, and to let Pyotr have fun with the customers.

The barman was suspicious. He didn't need another set of wages. But Vladek held up his hands; not a rouble, he only asked for the scraps of food the customers left, and permission to sleep on the cloakroom floor and wash in the bathroom.

Pyotr agreed; and Vladek had a job. The potatoes and fish he scarfed down nightly were hot and welcome, there was sometimes even fruit; a half-withered apple smuggled in from town. He didn't drink the alcohol, though; Vladek hated to be out of control. He despised Pyotr, who even after one year had never offered to pay the boy, or let him sleep in his house. He despised the drunken miners putting off going home to their nagging wives. He especially despised the Party commissars, lording it over everybody, but winding up just as vodka-sodden as the rest at closing time. They were the only men there with a chance to get out of this hell-hole, and what did they do? Stay, and work at being big fish in a small pond. But really, Srebrinka was so small it was more like a puddle.

Vladek hated Communism anyway. Equality and fraternity? He saw only misery; instead of the peasantry being oppressed, now everybody was. He was sure that noble blood ran through his veins. He would be the heir, the long-lost, forgotten heir, of some fine White Russian family. While he ate leftover scraps and hugged the ashes of the fire for warmth, when he splashed freezing water from the tap under his armpits in the morning, it burned him; he should be riding among these people in a sleigh drawn by dogs, tossing coins to them while they scrabbled before him in the dirt.

He did not dream of getting a Party job, of becoming a foreman, or of taking over the bar. Those were the destinies patrons predicted for him if they were in an expansive, drunken mood; if they noticed him. Vladek scorned them for their tiny

313

horizons. He wanted to be ensconced in a palace, eating on silver platters, served by fawning staff. That was his ambition.

It could not be satisfied here. One day . . . he would find his family. For Vladek knew his blood was his destiny. He would have a coat of arms. He would have an inheritance, squirrelled away in Switzerland perhaps, to protect it from the apparatchiks . . .

'Get on with it! Slacker!' Pyotr screeched. 'Those latrines won't clean themselves!'

Vladek blushed with rage and ducked into the back. More men were coming in now. He didn't want people to see him doing this. He struggled with a filthy pole to unblock the stinking clogs, and then wiped it down with a rag. He threw everything out, washed his hands in water, and then poured turpentine on them, to sterilise them.

It stung, but Vladek did not care. He hated to be *dirty*. More than anything. Despite his limited means, he was meticulously neat and clean. He washed his clothes in melted snow, he trimmed his hair and nails with a knife, and bathed daily in the icy tap water of the men's latrine. And he kept his tiny area of the coat cupboard perfectly organised; his saved roubles, the occasional tip, the objects that men lost which he'd claimed and might use some day; he even had a working pocket-watch, and a fur hat . . .

He emerged from the bathroom.

'They want vodka. Pour easy,' Pyotr growled. 'That big one there, he's with the Party. Came in from the city to inspect.'

Vladek obediently looked over, and there, sitting on a bench, already half-soused, nasal hair sprouting and food stains on his shirt, was his father.

Vladek stared. His heart thud-thudded. But it was incredible. There was no mistaking it. Vladek's own nose had been exactly that way before Pyotr broke it. The man had the beady eyes and long lashes, and the sharp, angular chin. There was a beard, which disguised it for a few seconds, but he *was* Vladek. To the life.

His initial reaction was joy; but that lasted barely a couple of seconds. Almost at once, he became disgusted. Why was the man so drunk? It was only five o'clock. And slovenly? He was a Party man, but he was dirty, boorish. He was fat, without discipline. And he had a braying, unpleasant voice . . .

'Where the hell's my drink?' the man screeched. He looked right at Vladek. 'You! Get over here!'

The boy hurried over.

'Vagabond,' his father said. 'Whoreson!'

Vladek poured, quietly. And listened.

'Speaking of whores,' one of his companions, a skinny fellow with a moustache said. 'Did you see the selection outside the door there?'

'Ugly bitches,' the Party man said. He belched.

'I liked the redhead. Good legs. I might try her later,' said another.

'That's Katya.' The moustached man leered. 'I've had all of them. She's OK.'

'You should watch yourself.' Vladek's father grabbed his glass, vodka sloshing around the inside of it. 'Some of them have the pox or crabs. Your dick'll fall off.'

The other men laughed. Vladek stumbled back behind the bar and grabbed his broom again. He swept around their table, eavesdropping.

'Or worse,' his father said. 'They'll trick you and get knocked up. And expect you to pay for the bastard.'

Vladek felt his earlobes throbbing. He dropped his head to hide the redness in his cheeks, the blood burning on the tips of his ears.

'It happened to me,' the man said, self-importantly. 'Years ago. The whore tried to pin it on me! Me, a family man.' He snorted in disgust. 'I have real children. And a wife. What did she think, I was going to feed a hooker's brat too?'

'Did she get rid of it?' the skinny man asked.

Vladek's father shrugged. 'Who cares? If she knew what was good for her. I told her she could do that or dump it in an orphanage. Nothing to do with me. A whore's kid, better off dead anyway. Besides,' he added, gulping down his drink in one shot, smacking his lips, 'I gave her some money. Told her to get out of town. Or else. You can't be soft with these sluts, they go to your wife. Mess up your real family.' He banged his glass at Vladek. 'More!' he yelled. 'You, don't you see I'm empty?'

Vladek turned, gave him a brilliant smile. 'Right away, sir,' he said. He brought the bottle over and poured freely, for the whole table.

'That's more like it,' his father grunted. He tossed him a coin; Vladek caught it expertly and put it in his pocket. Checking that Pyotr wasn't looking, Vladek put the bottle down in front of his father.

'Compliments of the house,' he said.

As they roared approval, not looking at him, Vladek snuck away. His bright eyes swept the bar, gauging the temperature outside, the patrons' thirst, his boss's level of intoxication. A rush swept through his body; it was as though his skin were tingling. Vladek had, he instantly realised, been preparing for this day for a long time. Now it was here, and he would risk everything. And he was immediately, fiercely glad.

It was odd, he thought later, when there was time for reflection, how he hadn't wondered what he was going to do. It all seemed so obvious. He ducked behind the bar, and under the guise of cleaning up, quietly opened the cash box. There were a few notes on the top; he left those, and took the rest – all the other paper money and a few coins. Then he went to the coat cupboard; he ignored his little store of objects, except the pocket-watch. He stole one of Pyotr's furs and a pair of gloves, and stashed them by the door. Then he took a copy of the newspaper from somebody's pocket; it would have the times of the local trains inside.

Nobody noticed Vladek scurrying about, even carrying a fur coat. He always hung the coats up and brushed off the snow. Nobody cared; they all just wanted their drink. And tonight he was more than usually attentive. Neither Pyotr, nor his father, Ivan – that was what they called him, Ivan Nikoleivich – was permitted to have an empty glass for even a second.

When the fire burned low in the grate and the ashes were starting to glow, most had left; even the men at his father's table had thinned out. The pig was still drinking though, almost snorting the vodka; it would miss his mouth at times and drizzle down his cheeks like drool. Vladek noted it with an almost clinical hatred. The man had no control. He shamed himself. Really, Vladek thought, he would be doing him a favour.

'I'm going home,' Pyotr slurred to him. 'Lock up and don't steal anything.' He stumbled out of the front door, as Vladek knew he would.

Now there was nothing for it but to wait. Vladek took the vodka bottle back to his father's table. They had all left, except the skinny man and the fellow with the moustache, Alexis.

'Please, sirs,' he said, grinning encouragingly. 'Have a couple more. For the road.'

His father farted loudly; the other two pretended not to hear it.

'Nah,' he said. 'Got to drive to town. I have a car,' he boasted. 'I could make the Politburo.'

The skinny man wavered and crashed head-first on to the table.

'But sir,' Vladek said. 'I'll drive you, if you like. It would be an honour. And then you could enjoy yourself.' He proffered the vodka again.

His father yawned. 'Take me now,' he said. 'I'm tired. I have a family to get back to.' His eyes blurred with drunken tears. 'My boys,' he said, nauseatingly. 'I do everything for them . . .'

'You're a hero, Ivan,' said Alexis, sycophantically grinning.

'Help me up!' his father barked at Vladek.

'Right away,' Vladek said. He gently heaved the man to his feet. His father swayed, backwards, forwards, and stumbled, but Vladek was there. His arms darted out and caught him before he hit the sawdust on the floor.

'You want a hand?' Alexis asked. He was weaving too, Valdek saw with satisfaction.

'That's OK. You get home to your wife,' he said.

'I'm getting a whore,' Alexis said. He cackled. Vladek considered doing something about him, but decided, no; he didn't want additional distractions.

Slowly, he dragged his father into his coat. It was a well-made fur, better than Pyotr's, waiting by the door. As Ivan mumbled curses at him, Valdek put on the stolen coat and slipped the money and watch into his pocket. He put the gloves on, too. They were necessary; as soon as he opened the door, the cold hit him in the face like a punch. Alexis would not get lucky tonight; the whores were long gone.

'Which is your car?' Vladek said, like he didn't know. It was the sturdy little Moskovich, standard black, with only one dent on the fender. A working car for a rich Party man.

'Tha' . . .' said Ivan. He drunkenly fumbled in his pocket for the keys. Vladek was there before him; he fished them out between a thumb and forefinger, and dragged the man to the vehicle. He unlocked it, and shoved Ivan into the front seat; then turned the key in the ignition.

The Moskovich spluttered and choked a little, and then the engine spurted into life.

Vladek felt powerful. He pressed his foot on the gas, and the car sped off down the road, bumping over the potholes, going towards the city. In the seat next to him, his father's head lolled back, and he started to snore.

Vladek enjoyed the drive. It was more than the strangeness of the big machine, headlights on, eating up the road; it was the knowledge that he was now a criminal, running away, running to his destiny. If they caught him, it would be the Gulag. But that was of no concern; they wouldn't catch him. The police out here were slugs like Ivan. They didn't care about anything other than warmth and women and booze. By the time they even started to look for him, he would be long gone. In America, perhaps, or London. Living the good life.

OK, he could see Vladivostock now; the lights of the city sparkled below him, at the foot of the hill, like diamonds scattered on black velvet. He drove a little further; it would maybe snow, and he had to be within easy walking distance, in case the car failed once he was done. When he'd found the right spot, Vladek pulled over by the side of the road. He let the car idle, went around to the passenger side and dragged his drunken father out, on to the snow.

The man's eyes flickered as the cold air hit his face. It was truly freezing now. Vladek reached down and scooped up some snow in his gloved hands. He then rubbed it on his father's cheeks, and Ivan woke up, completely, angrily. He stared drunkenly at Vladek.

'What the fuck are you doing?' he said.

'I'm about to murder you,' Vladek replied, coldly.

Ivan shook his head. 'Don't be . . .'

He looked at Vladek's eyes. 'No!' he shouted. He swung a heavy fist towards the boy, who yawned and sidestepped it, then aimed a sharp, vicious kick to Ivan's groin.

Agonising pain flared through him. He groaned and fell to one knee, throwing up under a tree. A little flurry of snow drifted from the lower branch on to his head. Vladek noted that the man had a bald patch. This infuriated him; he didn't want to go bald. He kicked Ivan again, harder.

'Oh God!' the man swore. 'No! Why?'

'You don't recognise me,' Vladek said. 'Yet I am the mirror of you. I am your son. The son of the whore, the son you wanted aborted.'

'I didn't!' Ivan said. He moaned again, then twisted his head, looked at Vladek. Even through the pain and fear, there was curiosity. Vladek hated him. Where had that emotion been when his mother was pregnant?

'I gave her money,' Ivan said. 'Son . . . son . . . be reasonable, I had a family.'

'I was your family, too.' Vladek's voice cracked with rage.

'You can forgive,' the man said. 'We can start over . . . don't hurt me, son.' He shuddered. 'I'm so cold,' he said, pathetically.

'Yeah. It was cold in the orphanage, too. Lots of days,' Valdek said. The fury and hatred rose in him. He reached forward, while his father moaned and begged, and circled his neck with his hands. Then he choked him, squeezing violently, while Ivan kicked and jerked. His legs landed on Vladek a couple of times, but he ignored the pain. He stared at his father until his terrified eyes rolled back in his head.

Vladek let go, checked for a pulse. There was none. He took the money from his father's wallet, then kicked some snow on top of him. Later tonight the white blanket would come down. It would not melt; there would be more and more snow.

Maybe they would find Ivan in the spring. Maybe not. He really didn't care either way. He got back in the car, whose engine was still running, and closed the door. Then he drove carefully down the hill, towards the city.

Chapter Thirty-Six

Sophie didn't want to go back to the office; but there was no real alternative. Richard was waiting there with her car. If she caught a taxi out to St Aude – and the taxis could always be persuaded into the country for the right amount of money – she would need to call, and make up some excuse as to why she hadn't used Richard; then call him and ask him to drive to the château without her.

Of course it was inevitable that the servants would gossip. But Sophie wanted to keep it as private as she could; this pain was all her own; she would not drag her son into it any more than she had to.

This might as well be a normal day at work. She tried to comfort herself as she walked back through the baking Parisian streets, heading towards rue Tricot, breathing in deeply so her nose would lose that tell-tale redness. It could have been worse. Tom had agreed he loved her – that much she could be thankful for. She knew horror stories of women, scions of French society, who through some quarrel or other had become estranged from their children; they were still alive, somewhere in the world, but dead to their mothers.

Sophie would rather die than let that happen to her and Tom. OK, so it hurt. 'I don't like you very much.' That hurt, bitterly. But she had to see the positives in this situation, or she would go mad. Tom said he loved her – and he had heard her say it to him. Tom said he would come back home once the shareholders' meeting was over. That much Sophie had. She would cling to that.

The rest, the other, dreadful things – the accusation of

betrayal of Pierre – she could overlook; but her own boy had practically called her a slut, indulging a mid-life crisis and selfishly usurping his property . . .

No. No; that line of thinking would start her crying again. Sophie didn't want any questions from Celine. There was quite enough rumour at House Massot as it was.

She contemplated changing route, walking to rue Faubourg. Popping in to the Massot showroom to watch the brisk business Claudette told her they were doing, had done every day since her party; to remind herself that whatever Tom imagined, she, Sophie, had an innate feel for the business. She loved jewels, believed in them as art, as dreams you could hold in the palm your hand; and the stock price reflected her ability.

But that was weakness. Sophie had to get back to the office, to call more small stockholders, give more interviews, get her plan out there. The AGM was only weeks away; there was no time, not a second, to rest on her laurels.

Work had one other thing to recommend it, she thought, as the sun beat down on the back of her neck; she adjusted her Hermès scarf to keep her pale skin from burning. It was a wonderful distraction. It would take her mind off Tom, and all the sacrifices she had to make to do what was best for him; in his interests, though against his will.

Here it was . . . rue Tricot. Sophie sighed, pulled herself upright; she would call Lizzie at Burton-Marseller and see if she couldn't get herself another couple of interviews this afternoon. Every small shareholder counted; they all had to believe in her . . .

She walked into the lobby and smiled at the new receptionist, a pudgy, neatly dressed girl called Thérèse; the girl was wearing a cream twinset with neat Massot pearl earrings – Sophie had issued them with her hiring slip; of course the first face anybody saw must be wearing Massot. All the girls had the earrings, and the security guards on night shift wore plain gold Massot cufflinks in their shirts.

'Good afternoon,' she said.

'Good afternoon, madame.' Thérèse smiled easily at her;

Sophie was pleased the staff no longer trembled just because she bore Pierre's name. 'How are you?'

'Very well.' Sophie headed for the ancient lift.

'Excuse me, madame, but you have a visitor. He said he didn't have an appointment.'

Sophie turned round; there, sitting on the couch, looking sun-tanned and incredibly handsome, was Hugh Montfort.

She blinked; but it really was him.

Sophie sighed. 'Really, Mr Montfort. Another surprise visit? Shouldn't you be working on Mayberry's offer for this company? If you're still trying to persuade me to sell, you're wasting your time. I have no intention of giving away my son's inheritance to a bunch of cowboys hawking blue topaz and vermeil.'

Montfort chuckled. 'Blue topaz and vermeil; ouch, that's cruel.'

'I'm glad you're amused.' Sophie turned away. 'I really don't have time for this.'

'I'm not here as a representative of Mayberry.' Montfort glanced at the receptionist. 'I really would prefer to speak to you privately; but if you aren't prepared to see me, I shall, of course, withdraw.'

Sophie hesitated; he was too polite to simply dismiss.

'Very well. I can give you ten minutes,' she said, and pressed the button for the elevator.

Sophie asked Celine for some coffee, then closed the door to her office.

'May I sit down?'

Hugh kept his tone neutral. He was taking a risk. A real risk, not a business one. He was about to gamble with his heart, and if Sophie was going to shoot him down, he preferred to be as little exposed as possible.

'Please.' She waved him to a seat and sat behind the desk. 'You do realise that your coming to see me will be everywhere in the next ten minutes. It's hardly appropriate behaviour for somebody determined to mount a hostile bid.'

'It would be, if I were such a person.'

Again, Hugh delighted in the freedom of it.

'I don't understand.'

'I told you I was not here as a representative of Mayberry. I was fired this morning.'

'What?'

He loved that look of confusion on her face.

'I was fired.'

'Is this some kind of a joke, Mr Montfort? Because it's in very poor taste.'

'No joke, I assure you. I was fired. I have called my broker and had him liquidate my entire holding of Mayberry stock. All intercourse between that company and myself is now at an end.' Hugh shrugged. 'So you see, I'm not here on some nefarious purpose.'

'But why?' Sophie asked. 'What possible reason . . .?'

'The excuse was your party, in fact. That I should have prevented it.'

'And how could you?'

'That, they didn't say.' Hugh inclined his head towards her. 'The party was a wonderful idea, as was your identification of your core customers; had it been a little further from the date of the AGM I think it would have caused me real problems. As it was, I did not anticipate any.'

'You think you would still have got the votes?'

'I would have. I must tell you, I think they still will. Although Mayberry's own stock, my broker informs me, dropped a point on the rumour I'd been dismissed.'

He watched her bristle. She was a fighter; he loved that animal courage.

'Then thank God they fired you,' Sophie cried.

'Why, thank you.'

'Excuse me.' Sophie stood up, agitated. 'I don't mean to be discourteous, Mr Montfort, but if our revival wouldn't have been enough, perhaps your firing will. I can use it – I can run stories about the chaos at Mayberry – persuade the smallholders that, long-term, their shares will suffer –'

'Of course, you must try everything.' Hugh tried to let her down gently.

'What do you mean by that?'

'I mean that I believe they have already mopped up enough votes for a majority stake.'

'But that's impossible. They'd need almost the entire independent float.'

'Yes. So perhaps I'm wrong. I hope so.' He smiled at Sophie. 'For your sake, Mme Massot.'

'So you came here to let me know that you'd been sacked? So I could use it?' Sophie stopped pacing, sat down again. 'Thank you. I'm most grateful.'

'No.' He shook his head.

She stared. 'There's more?'

'Not about the company.'

'Then what?'

Hugh sighed. 'I suppose it's inevitable that you seem surprised. I would like to ask you out.'

Sophie gazed at him.

'Out,' Hugh repeated. 'You know, lunch, dinner. A date. We could do something, if you prefer; go to the theatre, or a concert. But I prefer a simple meal, at least to start off with.'

'But why are you asking me out?'

'Why does a man usually ask a woman out?' Hugh smiled again; now he'd said it, he was absolutely at ease. 'Well. Sophie, I should very much like to get to know you better.'

Sophie looked at Hugh, and blushed. This moment had been something hovering on the edge of her fantasies; she'd tried not to think about it. And now it was here, Sophie felt frightened.

Just a little.

'I don't know if it's such a great idea.' She thought of Gregoire, of her frigidity. 'I don't think I'd be very good company.'

'I wish you would allow me to be the judge of that.'

'Relationships with men are not my strong suit, apparently,' she said. And then wanted to kick herself. Apparently? Would he ask her what that meant?

But Montfort held off.

'If I might make an observation, Mme Massot –'

'As you've asked me out, it had better be Sophie.'

'Sophie.' He smiled. 'A beautiful name; and it suits you. English and French – I suppose you've become a little of both.'

'I suppose so.' She smiled back; it was impossible not to bask in the warmth of his attractiveness.

'Anyway, I was going to observe that all I am asking for is the pleasure of your company at dinner. We could enjoy a meal, and if you still feel uncomfortable, I won't pursue it.' He gave a sudden, wolfish grin. 'At least, not indefinitely. I will confess to planning a little persistence.'

'Just a meal?' Sophie asked suspiciously.

'That's all; just a meal. I realise this is a stressful time for you. I am aware of some of the pressures you have been under lately, from people in whom your trust has been misplaced. You are still trying to fight the Mayberry bid. I understand that you may be feeling overwhelmed.'

She couldn't help it; she gave a bitter little laugh, very unlike herself.

'Excuse me,' Sophie said. 'But you don't know how true that is.'

'I know some of it. It used to be my business to know.'

'Do you have children?' she asked.

Montfort shook his head. 'I lost my wife and child long ago.'

'Oh. I'm sorry. I didn't know there was a child.'

'Unborn,' he said. 'But real to me.'

Her throat thickened, and she had to turn her head away; she thought of Tom's cold face.

'I was hoping', he said, 'that a good dinner with me might reduce some of those pressures. But I will understand if you feel unable to, right now. In which case I shall return with the request once the Mayberry bid is decided.'

'No, it's all right.' Sophie smiled weakly at him. 'I think I'm tired of sitting here, calculating what people will think.'

'I'm pleased,' he said softly; Sophie looked down. 'Can I pick you up from this office?'

'Better not.' She could imagine the stories. 'Do you know where my house is?'

'The Château des Étoiles? Very well. It's quite magnificent.'

326

'I would rather not meet there, either. At least, not yet.'

'I understand.'

'There's a little restaurant in St Aude, the village. The last time I went there it was with Judy Dean, but I can't let that spoil it for me.'

'*Fruits de la Mer*; I've heard of it.'

'I'll book a table for eight.'

'I'll be waiting.' Montfort stood, smiled at her, and walked out.

There was a knock on the door; it was Celine with Sophie's coffee.

'Thank you.'

'You're welcome, madame.' Celine could not contain her curiosity. 'What was that about?'

'Just business,' Sophie lied airily. She took a sip; it was cinnamon-scented; her favourite. Her mood had lifted. All of a sudden, things didn't seem quite so black, or so desperate.

She smiled warmly at her secretary.

'Madame, I was wondering,' Celine began.

Sophie sighed. What next?

'About the invitations to your party, madame. There are some left over . . .'

'I don't think that's a problem.'

'Oh! No, madame. I was just wondering if.' Celine's courage failed her. 'If I might . . .'

Sophie smiled; light dawned. 'You would like one of the brooches?'

'If it's all right, madame. They are very beautiful, and I could never afford . . .'

'Take them all.' Sophie pulled open her desk drawer and fished out the last four envelopes. 'You can wear one and use the others for Christmas gifts.'

Celine stared. 'Oh, thank you, madame! Thank you so much! I don't know how to thank you!'

'Well, you can start by getting me Burton-Marseller on the phone,' Sophie said, grinning. 'Right away.'

'Of course.' Celine fled back outside her office, clutching her prizes, and within thirty seconds Sophie's phone was lit up.

She took the call, glancing at the clock on the wall. Three-thirty. Time for one radio interview. Then she would have Richard drive her home.

The rigours of the day had exhausted her. Thank God for coffee, she thought. All Sophie really wanted to do was to get back to the château, take a long, luxuriant bath, and dress for dinner.

Something stirred inside her when she thought of Montfort, and however her son might disapprove, Sophie was determined to be beautiful.

'Well, you kept your word,' Sophie said. 'You were waiting.'

Montfort stood up as she approached the table.

'Half an hour,' he said. 'And worth every second of it.'

She blushed. 'You're very kind.'

He pulled out her chair, and Sophie sat down. She was wearing a red velvet dress, cut with perfect simplicity, with little cap sleeves and a fluted hemline, and a delicate necklace of moonstone and garnet, and small plain pearl studs in her ears. Her hair hung loose and gleaming around her shoulders. Her body, revealed even under the modest lines of her gown, was slim, but not hard, soft and feminine, which he preferred to the hardness of women's bodies today; either from excessive running, or from surgery. Sophie Massot had nothing of that, nothing artificial.

Montfort drank in the beauty of her face, without staring. Her grey eyes were luminous, the handful of freckles, the fine lines around eyes and mouth, these were also attractive; hers was not a face that had experienced a great deal of fun, or pleasure. It was very serious, and yet quite innocent. She was expectant, he decided. Waiting; still waiting for something,

He calmly summoned up a vision of his Georgie; the only woman he had ever loved. She was still smiling, still beautiful to him; but the pain was fading.

He said to Sophie: 'I think you are the most beautiful woman I have ever seen in my life.'

Her head lifted, and she blushed deeply.

'Come on, Hugh, don't say things like that,' Sophie murmured.

'It's perfectly true.'

'I know something about you,' Sophie replied, with a touch of spirit. 'You're not the only person who can do research. There are photographs of you in magazines with girlfriends; models – even film stars. Women in their mid-twenties with retroussé noses. Famous beauties. So it's hardly the truth. I appreciate compliments, but you don't need to lie.' She smiled. 'Although I admit I took my time choosing the dress.'

He smiled back. It was amazing, the ease of it; he liked her, immensely.

'Is that what you think?' Hugh asked.

'It's what everybody thinks. The press – everybody.'

'Then everybody's wrong. Those women were not my girlfriends. I went on some dates, certainly.' He shrugged. 'None of them worked. And as for the legendary attractiveness of these women, although I wouldn't deny they were pretty–'

'What a concession.' I'm teasing him, Sophie thought, amazed at how relaxed she was.

'Some of them very pretty. Even beautiful. But none of them had that spark that raises a woman to what you are now.'

A waiter appeared, and Hugh ordered a bottle of Chablis.

'Beauty is not wholly on the inside, whatever the platitude may say. But it does take more than even features and a certain level of proportion in the figure. A pretty woman without a spark of grace is a cipher. And one possessing that spark, though in photographs she may be outshone by a model, in real life will always be the one who attracts an intelligent man.'

Sophie paused. 'I think that's the loveliest thing anybody's ever said to me.'

Hugh grinned. 'It's funny; I never thought it through until seeing you. But it's absolutely true. I wouldn't trade one meal with you for a year in the company of fifty models.'

'And this is your first glass of wine?' Sophie asked.

They smiled at each other, like children sharing a secret, and Sophie started to feel very strange, almost spellbound; something was gradually stealing up on her. She thought that maybe it was hope.

They probed each other over the food; Sophie ordered *moules marinière*, a speciality of the house. They were delicious, faintly scented with garlic and parsley, in a white wine broth she mopped up with crusty bread; Hugh, who didn't care what he ate, chose a plain Dover sole with lemon and butter. It was excellent, and his salad was crisp and full of summer herbs.

It was easy to talk. Sophie felt as though she'd known Montfort for ever. He instinctively understood her. He didn't belittle her, or say flowery things, he listened gravely, and made her feel that what she had to say mattered.

He seemed interested in Tom, and when her love overwhelmed her, and she started to cry, there was no awkwardness; he merely said, 'I'm sorry', and waited for her to calm herself.

'It's because he loves his father.' Sophie dabbed the tears away. 'I know that. Whatever Pierre was, he was Tom's father. But I'm the one who's always been there. Even when Pierre was alive, he was out – always out.' She thought briefly of Judy. 'I never wondered why, and maybe that was wrong. I was at home playing with our baby.' Her shoulders drooped again. 'And yet it seems that he prefers his father to me . . . it's almost as if I didn't count.'

'I doubt that.' Hugh took a slow sip of his wine. 'Tom doesn't love his father; he hardly knew his father. Rather, he loves the *idea* of his father, which without the man there to contradict it, is a stupidly rosy picture.'

He put his large hand over her small one, and Sophie didn't pull away.

'It's not a unique situation. Divorced women all over the world go through it. The children, when they grow up, realise the falsehood of the image. Tom has nothing more sinister than a longing for two parents.'

'But what he said about me . . .'

'He's still young enough to feel repulsion at the idea of his mother as a sexual creature. He'll grow out of that, too.'

Sophie flushed. 'My gown wasn't sexual . . .'

'Indeed it was.' Montfort winked at her. 'Although perfectly modest. But Tom is not quite done with his adolescence. He's still at the stage where he would prefer you in a burka.'

Sophie laughed weakly. 'I suppose so. You're very good at making me feel better, Hugh.'

'I hope I am,' he responded seriously.

'And you.' She turned those shining grey eyes to him. 'Why haven't you remarried? Are you . . .'

Sophie's voice trailed off.

'Am I what?'

'I'm sorry.' She twirled the stem of her wineglass. 'I was about to say something impertinent.'

'Please go on.' He gazed at her. 'I mean it; I want to hear what you have to say.'

'Then I was going to ask if you, too, have been holding on to a fantasy image.'

'You mean about Georgiana?'

'Yes.'

'She was no fantasy.' He sighed. 'If only you could have known her.'

'That's not what I meant. I was asking if you have not connected with any other woman because of your wife . . .'

'Yes.'

'Then the fantasy part is that to you, on some level, Georgiana is still alive.'

Hugh stared.

'I'm sorry.' Sophie drew back. 'I knew I shouldn't have said that. Now I've offended you.'

'No – you haven't.' He paused. 'You mean, I suppose, that I have been feeling as though another woman would be a betrayal; something that would only be true if my wife were still living.'

Sophie nodded.

'You're right.' He sighed. 'My God; you're perfectly right. I didn't realise it. But I loved her so much, and so deeply, I didn't want her to be gone.'

'I don't think she is gone,' Sophie said.

'Ah yes; you're religious.'

'You?'

Hugh shook his head. 'I've seen too much horror. And banality, and cynicism; which sometimes seem worse than horror. That doesn't seem to fit in with a God.'

'Well, I won't try to convert you. Don't worry.'

'Feel free to try,' he said, lightly. 'If anybody could make me believe, I think it might be you. You make me imagine that things are possible; things I had not hoped for.'

Sophie looked down.

'We hardly know each other,' she murmured.

'But it doesn't feel like that, does it?'

'No.'

'I want to see you again,' he said. 'Soon. Will you see me?'

Sophie lifted her head and smiled.

'Of course,' she said. 'You know I will.'

Hugh took her hand in his and smiled gently at her. It was the strangest thing, he thought; he was happy.

They lingered over dessert and coffee; Hugh chose some stewed rhubarb, and Sophie toyed with her homemade lemon ice cream. He called for the bill, finally. Neither of them wanted the meal to end.

'I should ring for Richard.'

'Your driver?'

'Yes; he's parked a few streets away.'

'You could cancel him; let me walk you home. It can't be two miles to the château.'

Sophie thought of the servants, and what Tom would say. 'Better not.'

'Of course.' He was terrified of pushing her; the night had been perfect. Peter Stockton, Mayberry, his exploded career, all seemed trivial; completely insignificant. Seeing this woman again was all Hugh cared about.

'Dinner tomorrow?' he asked. 'There are a thousand out-of-the-way places in Paris where nobody will ever find you.'

'Yes. Just call and let me know where.' Sophie frowned. 'I hate having to hide,' she said.

'It won't be long. Your meeting will take place soon.'

'I can't wait. I'm sick of it all.'

'Shall we walk to the car?' Hugh offered her his arm. He

wanted to prolong every second. She was standing right next to him, and he was already missing her.

'Thank you.' Sophie smiled at him, her gentle smile, radiant and kind; it danced behind her eyes, and seemed to come up from her very soul. 'I'd like that.'

Hugh leaned forward and kissed her.

There was no question in his mind. He had to do it. She was so gorgeous, and hot, and sweet – and Hugh had wanted her for so long. Her mouth, her lips were inches from his. Hugh did not think about it. He took her in his arms, and kissed her, hard. And Sophie melted against him – didn't struggle. Just for that moment, she abandoned herself.

It was that moment that told him he had fallen in love.

Chapter Thirty-Seven

Katherine tensed; every cell in her aging body felt vital and alive. Her hands tightened on the receiver.

'Are you sure?' she said. Then she added, 'Very good', and hung up.

For a moment she sat there, revelling in it. The stupidity of the girl. To bring him here, to Pierre's own home, to Pierre's village. As though Katherine would not find out.

Sophie had never been right for him; that much, she was sure of.

Now, at last, the boy would know it too.

She grasped the arm-rest of her eighteenth-century chair and, carefully, hauled herself up. Faubert materialised from nowhere.

'May I assist you in some way, madame?'

'Yes,' Katherine said. 'Call my driver. I am going to visit my grandson.'

Judy exchanged smiles with Katherine as the old lady swept into the drawing room. They were the thin, unpleasant grimaces of women who would never trust each other. But this was a strategic alliance, and Judy thought of herself as a careful player. Katherine Massot was fond of the grand gesture – Sophie's party had demonstrated that – and she instinctively knew this was something important. She moved behind Tom, possessively stroking his shoulder.

'It's so good to see you, Katherine,' Judy said. 'But do tell me – is this family business? I really wouldn't want to intrude.'

The old woman arched her neck, a ghost of coquettishness in the motion.

'I – I really don't know,' she said uncertainly. 'It seems to bear both on the family and on the business. You're advising us on the matter of Tom's company, Judy... perhaps you ought to stay . . .'

What an actress, Judy thought.

'If you think so,' she said lightly.

'What's the matter, Grandmother? You look upset,' Tom said. He had an ugly sense of foreboding. His grandmother normally never stirred from the dower house before noon.

'I don't think there's anything for it but to say it, darling; your mother has formed an alliance with Hugh Montfort.'

'Nonsense,' Tom said, flatly.

Judy's eyes widened. The shock of it rushed through the pit of her stomach. So . . . She was right? Montfort, too – Montfort, who'd rejected her, loved Sophie?

'My father hated Hugh Montfort. Mother would never do that.'

While Tom blustered, Judy tried to collect her emotions. If Sophie was dating Hugh, she really *hadn't* loved Pierre.

'It's quite true. They dined in the village last night.'

'In St Aude?'

'It was a romantic engagement,' Katherine added relentlessly. 'They were holding hands. Courting.'

Tom didn't want to believe her. He felt sick.

'Who told you such a thing?'

'The proprietor of the restaurant. And my friend Mme de Gres, who happened to be there that night with her daughter.'

Katherine's reedy voice spoke with total certainty.

'Tom, if she would bring him to your father's village, and parade him before your father's friends, how long before she moves him into his house? Into *my son's* house?' she added for good measure. She walked across the room to him. 'You are his heir, his protector.' Katherine placed her hand on his arm. 'You must *do* something . . .'

Judy watched in fascination as Tom shrugged her hand off. The disbelief in his face had shifted to rage. He was like Sophie in that, she thought detachedly; Pierre would never let his emotions show . . .

'Oh, I will do something.' His young voice, was so angry, so hurt. 'Watch me.'

Katherine sank on to a chair in the corner of the apartment as her grandson picked up the phone.

'Room 612,' he snapped when it was answered. 'Stockton? This is Tom Massot. I agree to your terms. Fax the contract to me at the apartment. Yes, right away. I want to be installed in that office this afternoon. Can you do it that fast? Good.'

Judy exchanged a glance with Katherine; the old lady never flinched, but her eyes were glittering with excitement. She almost shuddered; one wouldn't want to be on the wrong side of that woman.

Tom was punching more buttons.

'Bernarde? This is M. Massot. I will be taking possession of the château today, Barnarde. Mme Massot will be moving out. Have all the staff start packing her personal effects immediately.' There was a pause; he reddened. 'Do as I say, damn your eyes, if you want to keep your position! Do you understand me? Very well. The moving vans will arrive at six p.m. Be sure that none of Mme Massot's things remain behind; not so much as a locket.'

He slammed the receiver down.

'Judy, can you arrange the removal vans?'

'But . . .' She thought it behoved her to say something. 'Honey, didn't you say she'd been to see you? That she was trying to reconcile?'

'She's dating my father's rival,' Tom said flatly. 'A man he hated. If she wanted to reconcile with me, that was not the way to go about it.'

He took a deep breath and walked to the window of the apartment, staring down at the Seine, obviously trying to stay calm.

'Take care of this for me, Judy. I am going to the office to see my mother.'

'Shall I come too, darling?' Katherine asked.

Tom shook his head. 'If you would arrange the end of this lease. I shall be taking possession of the château, tonight.' His young face was with hard with anger. 'It's mine. And this is going to end. Right now.'

Sophie sat in her office, humming to herself. The calls had slowed now; instead of giving interviews, she was reading the delicious results. The press coverage was overwhelming. The weekly magazines were just being published; next it would be the monthlies. Her party would get two months of exposure. And sales – sales were through the roof . . .

She was miles away from the timid widow who had walked into this building. She had had the courage to battle her demons, inside and out. And she'd rescued this firm.

Sophie was proud of herself.

Independence. It was new; but it suited her.

But she couldn't deceive herself. It wasn't just the sense of the threat lifting that was making her happy.

It was Hugh Montfort.

These feelings – they were amazing.

Her whole world felt new; like coffee on the terrace overlooking the lake – a life suddenly, surprisingly, full of possibility. It was the start of something strange, but wonderful. She had started to sing in the shower; started to wear heels, to shorten her hemlines.

Of course, it was early days yet – very early.

But today, Sophie was happy.

There was a knock on the door.

'Yes, Celine?'

Her secretary entered, full of excitement. 'Excuse me, Mme Massot, but you have a visitor! It's M. Thomas.'

Sophie jumped to her feet, overjoyed. Tom! Coming to see her? Could it be true? A wild hope rushed through her. If he wanted to talk, maybe she could try again on the Judy front. Persuade him to dump her.

'Sweetheart – come in, come in,' she said. Tom entered, but did not sit down; Sophie saw he was upset. 'Celine, could you give us some privacy, please? And hold all my calls.'

'Of course, madame.'

Celine shut the door.

'Is it true?'

'Is what true? Tom – calm down. Sit down.'

'That you are dating Hugh Montfort. Papa's enemy. And that you brought him to our village.' Tom's eyes narrowed. 'Without informing me.'

Sophie sighed.

'I didn't want you to find out like this –'

'I see.'

'We haven't even –'

'All right, that's enough,' Tom said. 'Please spare me the couple talk.'

'I understand you're angry, Tom.' She was surprised to find herself so calm. 'But I'm an adult, and this is my business.'

'An adult. Yes, and as I have repeatedly told you, so am I.' He held up one hand, and his mother was almost amused; so imperious, but still, technically, a teenager. 'And I've made some decisions. Since you pointedly refuse to respect Papa's wishes.'

'Your father has nothing to do with my seeing Hugh.'

'He would have hated it,' Tom replied flatly.

Sophie said nothing. This was true, of course. And since Judy's little bombshell, nothing she cared about.

'First, you're fired. The company has been sold. I'm here as a courtesy to allow you to get out of my office before the press arrive. Second, I am taking possession of Château des Étoiles. I will not have Hugh Montfort entertained there as a guest. Your lover is not welcome in Papa's house – in *my* house.'

Sophie blinked. 'What?'

'You heard me, Maman.' Tom's youthful features were implacable. 'The staff are packing away your things. The removal vans are heading there now. You may tell me where you want them sent.'

'The château is yours,' she said numbly. On that point, Pierre's will was clear. 'You're throwing me out?'

'I take it you will not give Montfort up?'

Sophie shook her head. 'I won't be blackmailed, Tom. Things are complicated.'

'I believe they're perfectly simple. Where should I send your dresses?'

She looked away, bitterly hurt. Unwilling to let her son see her cry.

'Give them to charity, for all I care. I want no part of them.'

'And you must leave the office.'

'Don't be foolish,' Sophie snapped, losing patience. 'You don't have the stock to vote me from the Board and you don't have the votes. And nor does Mayberry. Not since the party . . .'

'That's where you're wrong,' Tom said, and she hated the tone of triumph in his voice. 'We've done a deal.'

'A deal?'

'With Mayberry. Grandmother gave me voting rights over her stock, too. When we sold to Mayberry, they had enough for control. I'm to be installed as Chairman and CEO.'

Sophie felt all the joy woosh out of her. Her stomach turned over.

'Tell me that's not the true,' she said weakly.

'It's quite true.' Tom set his jaw mulishly. 'I told you I was going to take my inheritance. You could have stopped this at any time.'

'Tom,' Sophie said. She felt panic rising, rushing at her throat. 'They're tricking you – they're all tricking you. Don't you see that?'

'I've already signed the papers. You're a minority shareholder now, Maman. And you've been removed.' Tom marched to the window. 'I think you should leave.'

'I will.' Sophie picked up her handbag. She wanted to say something. To tell Tom she loved him. To explain. To warn him . . .

But it all seemed too late; and his back, hostile and set against her, told her not to try it.

Sophie's eyes watered. She wasn't even sure if Tom loved her, not any more. He had expelled her from her home, from her business. And he'd done it for Pierre . . . for that cheating, betraying, controlling bastard . . .

She had never realised it before. All those nights she had cried for Pierre, prayed for his safe return, refused not to give up on him. He had gone, leaving her and her son in a prison of his own making.

'I love you, Tom,' she said quietly. Then she walked out of the office and shut the door behind her.

She had never hated her husband. Until that moment.

Chapter Thirty-Eight

He never forgot the first moment he saw her.

She was standing there in the market square, and she was wearing red. Amid all the grey, drab clothes of the merchants and the workers, she stood out, brilliant and unafraid. She walked with the confidence of a rich woman, and the peasants scuttling along under the shadow of the medieval buildings drew aside as she passed, for she was obviously important.

Vladek stared. He swallowed the last of the pastry he had expertly stolen from a baker's shop two miles away, and saved for his lunch. It had been good, with cheese and real meat; he could feel the protein landing, solid and comforting, in his empty stomach. But the pleasures of eating faded instantly when she strutted by.

He catalogued everything that was great about her. The soft red wool of her clothes, like something from the West. The neat, high-heeled black shoes. A quick glance at her calves told him she wore real American nylons. Her hair, dyed black, he thought, was carefully swept up into a pillbox hat. She had a neat little handbag, black leather with a golden clasp. It was quilted. It must have been imported, he thought. No way that came from Russia.

But she was walking away from him, that fine, rounded bottom mincing towards the edge of the square.

Vladek thought she was the most elegant female he had ever seen. Nothing like the fat farmers' daughters or the gaudily painted whores with their bruised skin that he encountered around Talinn every day. Not even like a Party member's wife, well fed and nicely dressed. No, she had style, true distinction; she was a Monarch butterfly in a room full of moths.

She looked . . . rich.

He stirred. He wanted her. But not just physically; Vladek felt a sting of white-hot desire. He instantly needed to do more than screw her. He wanted to possess her. She was the kind of woman who was destined for him.

It bothered him that he was in the shabby clothes of a petty thief. But he had kept himself neat, as always. And he still had confidence, and pride.

He strode up to her, and caught her by the arm.

'Excuse me, madame,' he said.

She wrenched her arm away, trying to stride on ahead. 'Leave me alone,' she snapped. 'I don't give to beggars.'

She was icy cold. His admiration deepened. He said, firmly, 'Look at me.'

His tone demanded assent; she turned around, reluctantly, and glanced down at him. Vladek held her eyes.

'You are the most beautiful woman I have ever seen,' he said, matter-of-factly.

She did a double take; then arched those plucked brows.

'I'm a married woman.' She gave an artificial laugh. 'And you're just a boy.'

Vladek noted that she was not shoving him away, nor calling for help.

'Your husband does not please you,' he said. He could tell this in the way she walked. 'And I am not a boy.' He reached out with one calloused fingertip and stroked her down the side of the cheek, a soft gesture of claiming, as though she were a thoroughbred mare that belonged to him.

She drew back; but not before they had both felt her move, just a tiny bit, under the unexpected caress.

'You're young enough. And I'm not so very beautiful,' she said.

Vladek answered with scorn, 'Your husband is a fool who does not know his woman. You are a jewel.'

She had stopped pretending to walk away; she smiled a bitter little smile.

'What kind of a jewel?' she asked.

'A diamond,' he said at once. 'Very fair, and very cold. But with light around the heart.' He moved closer to her, invading her space, thrusting his face near hers; he could see the liner she used around her lipstick.

'Where is your husband now?' he asked.

'At work.' She was staring at him, as though trying to come to a decision. 'He's a banker.'

'That's good,' Valdek said softly. 'Take me to your house.'

It wasn't a request, and she waited only for a second. Then she said, 'This way', and gestured down one of the crooked, beautiful medieval streets that led away from the square.

'What's your name?' he asked her.

They were lying together, pooled and exhausted, in the warm linen sheets on her oak bed. He had a hand draped over her thigh; she had been soft and golden, as he knew she would be, receptive, and malleable.

Vladek felt he was home. It didn't concern him that this was another man's house; he had taken ownership of the female, and he would take ownership of the rest.

'Natasha,' she said. 'Natasha Ilyeva Garin.'

He nodded. He did not like the name. She would have to change it for him.

'And you?'

He smiled. What did it matter? He would not give her the name 'Vladek'. Maybe they were looking for Vladek, and anyway, he had no family. He would be whatever he chose to call himself. 'Yuri,' he said, smoothly. He kissed her hand, then stood up, unashamed of his nakedness, his skinny body. He walked into her bathroom and shut the door.

It was wonderful; American style, with a Western shower, hot water on demand, clean white tiles and soft towels. He stood for a long time under the warm droplets, washing himself from top to toe with the French lavender soap she had in a little dish. Then he shaved, carefully, and washed his hair. It felt glorious, and he took the husband's plush bathrobe and wrapped it around himself.

'What are you doing?' she cried, when he emerged. 'He'll know you were in there!'

He shrugged. 'A man who is so blind as not to see you will not notice anything.'

She smiled.

'You will tell him the robe needed washing,' he said.

'Where do you live, Yuri?' Natasha asked. She rolled around on the bed, arranged her body to display herself to him. 'When can I see you again?'

He chuckled. Her need was so transparent.

'I am a thief,' he said. 'I live everywhere and nowhere. I have nothing. I steal what I need.' He moved on the bed, ignoring her shocked face, touching her above the knee. 'Does that scare you?' he asked, enjoying the reaction. 'Do you want to call for help?'

She tossed her head. Really, she was magnificent.

'No,' she said, thick-voiced. 'It wouldn't do me any good, would it?'

'None whatsoever,' he said. He pulled her to him, hard, and kissed her deeply.

After that it was easy.

Natasha was his opportunity. He felt himself in love; yet there was always that element of separation. She was his desire, but also, he could use her; if there was a conflict, it did not concern him.

He knew that as much as he loved her, he loved himself far more.

She provided for his needs, and he for hers; he was insatiable, every day, often more than once, he would take her, and work her body until she ached. And, added to the pleasure this gave him, there were practical considerations. Natasha spent money on him, rather than herself; he rented a small apartment, close to her house; he bought woollen, American suits; he ate well; he owned several pairs of shoes. And as he groomed himself, he became ever more attractive to her, until she forgot that she was paying for every rouble of it.

He saw her husband once; a small mole of a man, spectacles

344

perched on his greying head, scurrying to the bank in the centre of town. Estonian bankers could act as a conduit to Swiss lenders, and he worked for members of the Party; communist wealth secreted away in the West. Hence all the money; it was from the estates of White Russians, he thought, of princes and counts. Well, so be it. Vladek – or Yuri, as he currently thought of himself – believed in the survival of the fittest.

He considered killing the banker. But it was too dangerous. The man was not a fat buffoon like Ivan whom he could dump under the snow. He would be missed; people would talk. A shame, since Yuri hated the thought of that slug pawing at his woman, his property. He wanted to live in the townhouse, openly. He wanted to spend that money without it coming from Natasha. Why should the banker have a right to it? He was a thief, too; except he did it via telegram and Swiss franc.

After a few months, he sensed danger. People in the square – not talking openly, but he sensed the glances, the whispers when he and Natasha walked by. That was enough; Yuri prided himself on his escape skills. He had no need to be warned twice. Besides, it was already time to move on. Not from Natasha, he felt generous towards her; she was still his woman, and swore she loved him. No; he would take her with him, even though the supple curves of her body were starting to lose some of their charms. The tiniest lines around her eyes were minutely deepening; the tone of her skin fading, just a little; but he noticed it all. Yet she pleased him, and he determined to keep her. But it was time to leave Talinn. It had served its purpose. He was no longer a street rat, an urchin with scuffed shoes and ragged hair. He was now well dressed, bathed and clad; he was on the way to the man he would become, he had taken the first steps to his great destiny.

Estonia – all the lands of the Soviets – had nothing for him now. It was time for London, for Washington or for Rome. Great men did not live here. Perhaps Moscow . . . but even Moscow was cold and dark; not enough of a theatre for him.

Yuri never doubted himself. And so insistent was he on escape, that Natasha did not doubt him either. After one conversation, she passionately committed herself. She would flee with him, north, over the wastes, into Finland. He warned her that she risked torture and death if caught. She answered that she did not care, that life without him would be the cruellest torture.

It was a good answer. He set their plans in motion.

Chapter Thirty-Nine

'Baby,' Judy said. She moved behind Tom, her long fingers digging expertly into his back, kneading and pushing at the muscles around his spine. He was so tense. But she knew what she was doing, and despite himself, he sighed with pleasure.

Judy. Efficient as always.

'You have to relax. I know you love your mom,' she cooed. 'But this is all a part of growing up. Becoming a man.' She used her most reasonable tone. 'Later on, she'll thank you for cutting the apron strings. No matter what she thinks right now, I'm telling you, hon. No woman wants to raise a mamma's boy . . .'

That was the wrong thing to say. He tensed again, and moved away from the bed.

'I'm not a pawn of my mother,' Tom said flatly. 'And I'm not a pawn of my girlfriend, either.'

His eyes looked so like Pierre's when he got angry. Judy felt weird; instinctively she gathered her legs back into her body. She dropped her gaze, not liking it.

'I will protect my family,' Tom said, self-importantly. He looked at Judy, who had lowered her head, and softened his tone. 'I know you mean well, *chérie*,' he added.

'I do.' She lifted her head again, defiantly. 'I love you. I want only the best for you.'

'And I appreciate that,' he replied, with a touch of Pierre's arrogance. Judy flushed with annoyance; why didn't he say he loved her, too? 'I have arranged for you to have your job back,' he said.

Ah! Anger forgotten, she jumped off the bed, beaming. 'Really?'

She was truly beautiful, Tom thought, when she smiled. It wasn't often; there was a solemn core to Judy Dean, despite her soft words and hot body. It fascinated him. When she smiled like this, though, she showed some vulnerability; it was as though something shattered in her. Tom wasn't sure he liked it.

'You got me my job back? You're a doll!'

'And at a responsible salary,' he said, ignoring the Americanism. 'Half a million euros per annum.'

Judy sucked in her breath. She felt a little light-headed. She would not have to trade in her car or her jewellery, after all. She was rescued. She was safe.

It had worked.

'That's fine, darling,' she said, lightly, trying not to sound too excited.

Half a million today, a million tomorrow. Why not? Anything was possible.

'Providing, of course,' Tom said lying, lazily, on the bed. 'that you perform sufficiently well.'

There was a heavy emphasis laid on the word 'perform', and Judy gave him a brittle smile.

'Baby, you know I will,' she said.

Tom smiled and pulled her to him. Judy arched her back, displaying her buff, strong muscles for him.

Both of them ignored their unease.

Tom was trying not to worry about his mother; he could lose himself in Judy's taut, tight body. And Judy was trying to shake off that slightly dirty feeling. Tom's remark didn't help, nor did how much he looked like Pierre; what had attracted her, now repelled her. As soon as Tom was more than theory, she had recoiled from him.

And what did he mean by 'perform'? She was *good* at PR! She deserved half a million, and not because she was some-body's girlfriend . . . Pierre's, or now Tom's . . .

But that led her back in a circle. Judy could not afford those thoughts. Yes, Pierre had lied to her. Judy was not his only other woman. He had demeaned her, why should she care? And so what if Tom was his son? *She* was not related to Tom, and she owed Pierre less than nothing . . .

But her feelings . . .

No. Judy physically shook her head as she moved on top of Tom. She wouldn't go there. She had set her course, against smug Sophie and that bastard Hugh Montfort, and even against the memory of Pierre. In the end, she would triumph. She would be mistress of Château des Étoiles. She'd win, and they'd all choke. And serve them right, too.

Judy bucked against Tom. She gritted her teeth and arched her neck in an approximation of passion – that way, she didn't have to look at him. Instead, she took in the elegance of her surroundings.

She'd made it to the château!

Sophie had been chatelaine here; and soon she, Judy, would replace her. It was a revenge she'd waited years for.

Worth a few sacrifices!

'Have another cup of tea,' Fr Sabin pressed her.

'Thank you, *mon Père*, but no,' Sophie said, delicately trying to get rid of her Tetley's bag without him noticing.

'A biscuit, then?' he asked. 'Garibaldi? Rich Tea? McVities?'

She shook her head, suppressing a smile. The old priest was so determined to make her feel at home, but for him, Britain was still stuck in 1981.

'What is the trouble this time, then, my dear?' he asked.

Sophie sighed. She didn't really know where to start. She felt somewhat foolish.

'Perhaps I can help,' Fr Sabin said. 'You are distressed because your son and Mme Katherine have sold Pierre's company; and because you want to start a romance with M. Montfort. You fear this will further estrange your son from you. Is it not so, Sophie?'

She was shocked; but when she looked up, Fr Sabin's eyes were calm, and there was an analytical glint to them. She forebore to ask him how he knew. He'd reminded her before; this was a small village, and she *had* taken Hugh to Fruits de la Mer . . .

'Yes. I know I can't give Tom a veto power over my love life.'

Her old friend nodded.

'*Merci, mon Père,*' Sophie said, pressing his withered hand. 'But that's not the only problem. I worry about Tom. He's so young . . . and stupid.'

'Tom Massot is not stupid.'

She blinked.

'He is stubborn and full of pride, but he is not stupid. Both his parents are intelligent, and so is he. You may rely on that, Sophie.'

'If he comes to his senses, it'll be too late,' she said. 'His inheritance is gone for ever.'

Fr Sabin shrugged; 'Material things,' he said.

'With respect, Father, you are a priest. To most people, material things matter.'

The old man said: 'Then they are short-sighted. But Tom is the head of the company now, is he not?'

'It's window-dressing.'

'I do not understand the term.'

'Ceremonial,' Sophie said. 'He will have no power . . . no influence . . . he'll see.' She paused. 'And I have another worry.'

'What?'

'He's being ensnared,' she said, and anger balled like a fist in her stomach. 'By a wicked, an immoral, woman. An American . . . An older woman. Who cares nothing for him and who is motivated only by hatred of me.'

'We are not meant to judge, Sophie,' said the priest.

'I know this to be true about her. Because she told me so!'

'She told you she did not love Tom?'

'She implied it,' Sophie said, hotly. 'And . . . she's evil.'

'*People* are never evil,' said Fr Sabin. 'Although they may do evil things.'

'Oh, Father, spare me the psychology!' Sophie cried, agonised. She twisted her hands in her lap. 'I'm sorry,' she said, miserably. Now she was shouting at an old man. 'But you don't know her! She . . .' Sophie flushed. She couldn't quite believe how humiliating it was to have to talk about this to another person. 'She was, for many years, my husband's mistress; make that one of his mistresses. But he favoured her

350

above the others, he bought her a flat in the city.' Sophie glanced at her nails, to avoid having to look at her friend. 'Her name's Judy Dean, and she worked at Massot. When I arrived, Judy befriended me, but she hates me – she was trying to ruin me. She had something to do with this deal, I know it. And she *told* me she despises me. Next thing I know . . . she's got her hands on my son.'

Sophie risked a glance. The story had hit home; Fr Sabin's rheumy eyes were grave.

'You tell me this woman has had intercourse with both father and son.'

'Yes,' Sophie said. She pushed up out of the tatty armchair, and went to look out of the window. She didn't want Fr Sabin to see the fear and rage that were pulsing through her, and, she was sure, would be written on her face. 'Judy's a bitch,' she said, coldly.

'That's enough!' the priest said sharply. 'You forget yourself. She is a person made in the image of God, Sophie. You will mention that remark in your next confession.'

Sophie shuddered, trying to control herself.

'You can't understand how a mother feels. It's as if she has her talons around my heart. And she's squeezing. Sometimes I think I can't breathe.'

Sophie swayed on her feet and burst into tears.

'Come, sit down, sit down,' Fr Sabin said. He guided her back to the chair, and Sophie allowed herself to be led. 'Sophie, you must not regress.'

'I don't understand.' She grabbed her Chanel bag, fished around for a handkerchief.

'Ever since you made the decision to have Pierre declared dead, you have been a changed woman,' the priest said. 'It was slow at first, but the more you ran that company, the more you became determined, energised – I do not want to see you become a frightened little mouse again, dear girl. You must be strong. You must protect your son and yourself.'

'How?'

'No, I will not do the work for you. You know what to do. You tell me.'

Sophie blew her nose loudly. She was beyond embarrassment at this point. Why play the elegant madame? He knew her as she was.

'You're right.'

'Usually, yes,' the priest said. 'Although I did not know about Pierre. And I am sorry. Marital fidelity is vital.'

'That's because you can never think ill of anybody,' Sophie said. 'Which is why you're a priest, and I . . . wouldn't make a very good nun.' She thought of Hugh, and she blushed.

'Tell me a plan of action. I want to see the new Sophie.'

'Very well.' He was right. 'I'll call Tom in the office.'

'Good.'

'And talk to him about Judy.'

'And what will you say?'

Sophie paused. 'I can't tell him,' she said. 'About his father, I mean. Tom loves Pierre. I don't want him to know what kind of a man his father was. It would destroy him. Tom still worships him. He believes he's alive. What kind of a mother would I be, to ruin his love?'

'But there are other things you can say.'

'Yes. I'll tell him Judy befriended me, in the matter of the company, and betrayed me. I'll tell him she told me she hated me, the day she got sacked.'

'That's reasonable,' the priest said.

'And then I'll tell him about Hugh. That I'm going to see where this leads.'

'You will risk that?'

'I love Tom,' Sophie answered, firmly. 'But I'm his mother, not his daughter.'

'Bravo,' the priest replied.

'I'm a widow. I am free to marry. I believe that . . . something might come of it.'

She didn't tell him it was a little more than that. She felt she was in love. But Sophie had only just started to date Hugh, and she had looked foolish enough for one day.

'And then?'

Sophie shrugged. 'Isn't that everything? I'll find a place to live, I suppose.'

'You will need to start some kind of business,' Fr Sabin said. He smiled at her with his wonky teeth. 'You enjoy that, Sophie, and you are good at it. I would not recommend another stint as a housewife.'

Tom Massot stretched behind his desk and tried to enjoy it. This was victory, he thought, staring out of the window. So why was he so restless?

Paris was quite brilliant today; the city had a permanent magic, but this morning, with the first chill of autumn hovering under the crisp sunlight of the day, there was an extra freshness which was welcome after the muggy days of August. In the street outside, his connoisseur's eye picked out the French women in their chic little outfits, relishing the change of weather; there was a lot of nutmeg and chocolate, leather gloves, rich russet sweaters; the bark-and-berry palette of the season, punctuated with the odd flash of dark green and occasionally gold. The men, meanwhile, moved with purpose; refreshed after the languor of summer, wanting to get down to business.

An ideal time to be a chief executive, then.

He spun on the chair his mother had occupied and examined the office. It had been redecorated according to Tom's wishes; that much, at least, they had done, he thought . . . the feminine flowers and soft throws had gone, and he had selected dark woods and scarlet leather, the preferred choice, as he remembered, of his father in the billiard room back home. It was something he had held on to as the memories of Papa faded. He was fiercely proud to have the office as he imagined Pierre would have wished it. And like his father, Tom cared about image; it mattered very much to him that he put his stamp on the place. He had certain articles spread out in front of him. MASSOT IN CHARGE, said one. THE SON RISING, said another. Of course, those were not the only articles that had appeared. The PR people – Judy – tried to keep some of the others from him. He'd angrily told her he wanted to see everything. And she'd argued with him!

'Judy, in the office I am your superior,' Tom had shouted.

He was tempted to add, 'and out of the office, too', but held back. Surely she would already feel the social gulf between them, and he didn't want to rub it in.

'But, honey.' Judy had lowered her voice, but she was looking at him sharply with those bold eyes. They stirred him, and he felt a touch less angry. Tom preferred challenging women; such as Judy, or . . . Polly . . .

Whatever. Polly was the past. Judy was far more stylish, anyway.

'But, honey – it's only going to upset you.'

'I'm not a racehorse, Judy. I don't need soothing and I don't need managing.' Tom's dark eyes swept over her. 'Sometimes, I think you imagine I'm stupid. I'm not; I'm young. Don't make the mistake of confusing the two.'

Judy swallowed. 'I'm sorry,' she said. 'Of course we will send you all the press.'

And she had.

Tom could see her reservations had good cause. He wanted to think the carping was envy, bitterness from petty little journalists who hated wealth and power, who would drag him back to the Bastille if they ever had the chance. After all, there was certainly a carping note to these stories; HEIR TODAY, GONE TOMORROW? That was the *Financial Times*. He supposed it was mildly amusing, if you were a sour British prig angry that Hugh Montfort had failed to capture a glory of France.

But other stories had the same message. He was a figurehead only; the important decisions would be taken in L.A., by Pete Stockton. House Massot would crumple. And the one he most shuddered at . . . that the brand would be diluted, the jewels mass-produced. His family name would be prostituted, and he would sit in a nice office with a pretty secretary, and be powerless.

Tom noted that the phone had been silent. Despite his assurances, Stockton had not been in touch. His dissatisfaction increased, and he rose from his desk and walked to the window.

Very well, Tom thought; I will do something about it. I must prove to Mayberry the value of House Massot, exactly as it is; as Father wanted it. If the fat slug Stockton will not come to me, I will go to him. The thought made him feel a little better. A plan gave him a sense of control, and he comforted himself against the notion that was starting to take a hold of him; that, despite what he'd said to Judy, if he wasn't stupid, he had at least *been* stupid . . .

Hey, Tom thought. Chief Executives all over the world report to Boards. I'm no different from Howard Stringer at Sony or Meg Whitman at Ebay . . .

The phone rang; he jumped a little, then felt foolish. Howard Stringer probably did not jump when the phone rang. He pressed the red light.

'Yes?' Tom said, snappishly. He wanted to sound as though he'd been in the middle of reading a report on the latest De Beers site allocations. 'What is it, Celine?'

'Excuse me, monsieur.' Celine was presently now working for Tom. He hadn't wanted the inconvenience of recruiting a new assistant. 'But I have a woman on the line for you . . .'

'From where?'

A beat. 'Monsieur, it's your mother.'

Tom flushed. A nasty mixture of guilt and loneliness.

'Put her through,' he said. There was a click. 'Hello?'

'Tom.' It was her. And she sounded odd. He'd expected a lot of emotion, but his mother sounded calm.

'Darling, we need to talk.'

'Not about House Massot, Maman, what's done is done.'

'No, nothing to do with business, darling. It's about Judy Dean.'

'Mother . . .' Tom was firm. 'I know you disapprove, and I know she's a little older, but I must make my own decisions in love.'

She was dating his father's hated rival. How did she have the balls to nag him about Judy?

'Then make it an informed decision. She's a wicked person, Tom.' Sophie hesitated. 'I can't tell you why. I suppose it would be useless to ask you to trust me.'

'You clearly don't trust *me*, if you won't tell me your mystical reason,' Tom said sarcastically.

355

'OK. While I was at House Massot, she befriended me – but lied to me. Judy promoted the cause of Gregoire Lazard, and she told me she was loyal to me. While all the time she was running to you and Katherine, to broker a take-over. Just be aware of that, Tom, Judy told me lies – and supported the romance with Gregoire – while it lasted.'

'I doubt you needed much encouragement there, Maman.' Tom's tone turned sharp.

'She's a snake, Tom. Sucked up to me and lied to me. Think about it. Would Papa approve of her?'

Ouch. That arrow found its mark, and he was silent.

'I tell you what,' he said eventually. 'I'll give up Judy Dean if you promise never to see Hugh Montfort again.'

As soon as the words came out of Tom's mouth, he held his breath. He'd surprised himself. But of course it was true. He would pay any price to rescue his father's name from this dishonour, and his mother from this predatory vulture. Compared to that, Judy was meaningless to him.

On the end of the phone there was a little sigh; and with it, all his hope evaporated.

'I can't make bargains like that, Tom.'

'Then don't lecture me,' he said bitterly. 'And Maman – don't think to call me again until you sever your relationship with this man.'

There was a long pause.

'Do . . . do you still love me, Tom?'

His mother's voice was painful, wavering. Tom couldn't help it; the sound of her unhappiness immediately brought tears to his eyes. But all the pain was her fault. Why couldn't things have stayed as they were!

She'd ruined their lives.

'I'll always love you,' he said thickly. 'But I'm ashamed of you.'

He hung up, and walked quickly to the window, so that if his secretary came in she wouldn't see him crying.

Chapter Forty

Judy personally supervised the firing of Françoise Delmain. Françoise had gloated when Judy was sacked; it was good to return the favour.

'You can't fire me,' Françoise had insisted, colour high in her cheeks. 'For what? It's unfair dismissal. I'll sue.'

'For the inappropriate comments you made to another employee upon their dismissal. Me,' Judy said. She smiled thinly. 'By all means bring a suit, Françoise. We will defend it vigorously. And as you know, House Massot has deep pockets.' She extended her hand, to let the new cocktail ring Tom had given her glitter in the sunlight streaming in from her window. It was a fine, translucent oval ruby, surrounded with pear-shaped emeralds; the reds and greens glinted beautifully together like a scarlet rose in its petals. 'Besides,' she added with a sweet smile, 'don't you think you've made quite enough enemies?'

Françoise looked at her nervously, then dropped her head, admitting defeat.

'I'll collect my severance on the way out,' she said.

'There is no severance. You're being fired for cause. There's no reference, either.' Judy smirked. 'I hope you aren't behind on your mortgage, Françoise.'

'You bitch!' Françoise exploded. She wrenched the door open, banging it on its hinges. 'I'd quit anyway,' she yelled.

'Oh yes. Sure you would!' Judy laughed.

Françoise's eyes, that had sneered at her the day Sophie called down to Judy's office, blazed with loathing. She raised her voice. 'Maybe I would. Nobody wants to work for a woman who first sleeps with the father, then the son!'

Judy gasped; her entire neck and head flushed with blood.

'Ha! You're as red as a Breton lobster!' Françoise cried. 'You thought people didn't know!'

'You're insane,' Judy said. 'Delusional.' She depressed a button. 'Security? Get up here immediately – and throw Françoise Delmain into the street. Right now!'

'I'm going, you little tramp!' Françoise tossed her head, delighted that she had managed, at least, to land one blow. 'And maybe I'll call *Paris-Match*. I'm sure the gossip hounds will pay handsomely for this story!'

Red alert. Judy summoned all her powers. She forced herself to be calm and leaned forward, saying quietly, viciously; 'I wouldn't do that if I were you.'

'And why not?'

'Because I'd hope to live a long and happy life. Quietly.' Judy held her gaze, with a threatening look. 'Put it this way; I'd hope that *nobody* spreads such a rumour to any paper or magazine. Because if it gets out, I will blame you. And so will Tom Massot. And that would be –' she whispered – 'unhealthy.'

Françoise's defiance crumpled like a popped balloon. 'I understand,' she said. 'I – I will go quietly.'

'Get out,' July said with contempt. The elevator opened, and two burly security guards appeared. Judy nodded at Françoise, and they flanked her.

'Take her out through the front,' Judy ordered. 'So everyone can see she's history.'

Françoise tried to look defiantly back at her; but it didn't work. She was afraid, and her eyes filled with tears. Crocodile tears, Judy thought. She watched the delicious sight of her enemy being frogmarched away through the staring crowd of Massot employees, many of whom had worked with her for years, gossiped about Judy with her.

Judy saw the fear in their eyes, saw them turn away from the weeping Françoise. Excellent. That would show them who was boss.

She clenched her fists, her palms moist from the adrenaline. It was, just like the cliché had it, a fucking jungle out here. If you weren't tough they'd eat you alive.

Judy wouldn't listen to that father-and-son stuff. She'd stay strong.

Focus on the future.

'Get me some coffee!' she snapped at her new secretary.

'Certainly, madame.'

'And get me Tom Massot on the phone. Now.'

That snarky comment about Pierre had upset her. Judy wanted to speak to Tom, right now. They *did* have a relationship. They were in *love*.

I'm not a goddamned trophy! she thought.

There was a click, and then Tom's voice. She braced herself; he'd been a little distant lately.

'*Chérie*' – that was a good start – 'it's good to hear from you.'

Judy smiled.

'Are you free for lunch?'

'For you, always.'

'I'm glad. I've got something important to ask you.'

Judy's head swam. She could hardly stop the grin from breaking out all over her face. Tom would ask her to marry him. It was like the years of heartbreak hadn't happened. She would be Judy Massot! Well, Sophie, she thought – the Queen is dead, long live the Queen!

The grandeur of it all floored her. Judy was faint with triumph.

'That's wonderful, darling,' she said lightly.

'Why don't you come up here?' Tom asked.

'I'll be right there. Love you.' Judy hung up, and walked out of her office. 'Forget the coffee, Christine,' Judy sang as she stepped into the elevator. After all, she had more important things to think about!

Tom didn't think it through. He didn't want to. Thought was dangerous right now. Tom needed to act, to get back a sense of self-control. He felt like a man tossed at sea, clutching on to a rock while the waves crashed around him; groping blindly for anything he could do to help himself.

Judy walked through the door. Tom gave her a brisk smile. She was a fine-looking girl, and as sexy today as ever. His practised eye flickered across her. There wasn't an ounce of fat on her thighs, no softness at all – until you reached the breasts.

Judy noticed his assessment and sat down, leisurely stretching her legs; angling her toe to give him a glimpse of her firm calves. Tom's heartbeat slowed a touch. Judy was good, he'd have to give her that; quite the corporate executive, but feminine with it. Never once had she behaved or dressed in an unladylike manner.

Not like Polly.

But he wouldn't dwell on Polly. *Judy* was the polished companion a man like him deserved. Stop, Tom told himself, before you think yourself into knots.

'You know I've moved into the château.'

'It is your house, sweetheart,' Judy said mildly. She strained to keep the excitement out of her voice.

'I want you to move in with me.'

'Oh, Tom,' Judy sighed. It was a moment of sheer bliss. He was going to propose. It was all real!

'Yes . . . I want you to move in with me. We make a great team, Judy.'

There was a fractional pause.

'Move in with you!' Judy said, trying to infuse her tone with joy. 'Sure I will. That is . . . I wouldn't do that for anyone else, you know.'

What the hell?

Move in with him? She was bitterly disappointed. But it was early days, she guessed.

I better take it, Judy thought. For now.

She stood up, the super-heels throwing her body into all the right angles, and walked towards her boyfriend, giving him a little bit of a strut, a bit of sass. It was that calculated, confident sexiness she knew Tom loved.

'But you're the boss,' she purred, drawing her nail tips lightly through his hair. 'You make your own rules.'

Tom grinned. He pushed a button on his phone.

'Celine, hold all my calls. And no admittance to anyone.'

360

'Yes, Monsieur,' she said.

He pulled Judy down, into his lap; her eyes were gleaming, her lips parted.

'Nice outfit,' he said. 'Let's mess it up.'

'I hope you are finding the room is satisfactory, madame,' said the porter.

'Perfectly. Thank you.' Sophie pressed a ten-euro note into his hand, but the man still hovered.

'And is madame planning a long stay?'

She looked at him dully; his venal eyes were sparkling with curiosity. No doubt he'd be on the phone to the tabloids the second he got out of her room.

If this was being a celebrity, you could keep it.

'That will be everything,' she said coldly, 'thank you.'

He took the unsubtle hint and retired, shutting the door behind him.

Sophie exhaled and glanced around the suite she'd been staying in since the eviction. It was certainly luxurious. There was a vast bedroom, his and hers bathrooms decked out in ivory and brass, a balcony overlooking the Seine, Persian rugs and an unhealthily large display of flowers.

She couldn't wait to get out of there.

Tom hated her. Hugh had left and had been out of reach, dealing with business on his estate in Ireland. Katherine's malicious tongue infected all of Parisian society. And Judy was bringing her poison into the heart of Sophie's family.

Right now, Sophie didn't give a damn if she never saw Paris again.

She picked up the phone and dialled. Her heart was in her mouth. Please, God; let him be there . . .

He was.

'Montfort.'

'It's me.'

She could hear his lazy smile through the phone line.

'So it is. And I was starting to feel forgotten.'

Sophie couldn't flirt.

'Where are you, Hugh?

He caught her tone. 'You're upset. What is it? What's happened?'

She swallowed, hard. 'Tom found out about us.'

'I see.'

'It was stupid of me to bring you to the village.'

'It certainly was not,' Hugh said, firmly. 'I only wish you had told him right away. What did he say?'

She gave a miserable laugh. 'Well, let's see. He evicted me from the château. He and Katherine sold their stock to Mayberry. They have fired me. And Tom personally came to chuck me out of the office.'

There was a long silence.

'Where are you staying?'

'In the Victrix.'

'A hotel?' Hugh was appalled. 'Come to Ireland, darling. Come and stay with me.'

A fat tear rolled down her cheek.

'No pressure, I promise you. I have plenty of spare bedrooms.'

'I'll think about it.'

'Would you like me to come to you? I might be able to get a late flight from Shannon.'

'No, that's OK.' Hearing Hugh's voice had made her feel better. There was, after all, somebody out there who cared for her – other than the old priest. 'I need to be by myself, at least tonight.'

'Very well,' he said reluctantly. 'But call me first thing in the morning. Either way. Or I'm coming to get you.'

'I will.'

'Goodnight,' he said, and after a moment, 'I miss you terribly.'

'Goodnight,' Sophie said, blushing.

She hung up and gazed out of the window at the sun sinking below the grey stone rooftops of the city of light. The conversation had calmed her. This was the end of something, yes, but not her life; not her story.

Sophie dialled room service and ordered an excellent meal; coq au vin, half a bottle of Burgundy, a tarte tatin, coffee and a bowl of fresh fruit. When it arrived, she ate slowly, savouring every mouthful; and she thought things through.

It was her instinct to stay. To go and see Tom, demand a hearing. Demand he see sense. But she knew that was not the right thing to do.

Sophie loved her son. But it was time for him to grow up. He had chosen to do it the hard way.

So be it, then. She would let him make his own mistakes.

Maybe it was tough love; but if she caved, if she dumped Hugh, bargained with him, pretended his actions with the firm had no consequences – then Tom would become the ultimate spoiled brat.

I've been way too easygoing, Sophie thought. Tom wanted all this. Now he's got it. It was time to let him figure things out for himself.

She would get a good night's sleep, then take a limo to the airport in the morning. She'd go to see Hugh. Sophie had never been to Ireland; this would be a holiday. And a chance to figure out if her feelings had any substance. True love, this time? Or infatuation?

She would find out. And whatever the answer might be, Sophie would start a new life.

'We're just starting our descent into Shannon,' said the captain's voice on the tannoy. 'If you'll fasten your seatbelts, return your seats to their upright position . . .'

Sophie was only too glad to oblige. Even first-class, she hated flying. The stewardess smiled obsequiously as she collected the glass flute of indifferent champagne that Sophie had nursed throughout the short journey; she'd been fascinated by Sophie's jewels, and was sure she was some kind of European royalty. Or maybe a film star, someone she just didn't recognise. Who wore diamond studs like that? They were almost the size of pebbles . . .

Sophie gazed uneasily out of the window as the plane came into land. On the one hand, the earth seemed horribly far below her; on the other, she was foolishly glad not to be over water. She'd rather die in a fireball than drown in the sea. She shook her head; stupid, morbid thoughts. It was childish to have a fear of flying, wasn't it? What would Hugh say? He'd been a soldier, faced gunpowder and lead; he'd probably have no patience for the small phobias of a pampered widow like her.

She felt a bit stupid, in fact wholly inadequate. One thing you could say for the château; even if at times it had been the proverbial gilded cage, at least it was a cage she *knew*. It seemed as though every part of her old life had evaporated along with Pierre's company. A year ago she'd been a placid married woman, living in luxury on the dividends of millions of shares. Now she was a widow, with no home, no income, no relationship with her son.

That's right, Sophie chided herself; nothing but a paltry few million euros and a world-class wardrobe of priceless jewels!

She had to stop the self-pity. It was stupid. She had done her best, and she knew in her heart she would do the same again in similar circumstances.

And perhaps she wasn't being completely honest.

The plane banked, and she instinctively grasped the armrests of her seat. The ground was rushing towards them now, green and beautiful, the houses like the tiny wooden ones in Tom's old playset.

'Don't you worry, miss; it's a very safe way to travel,' the stewardess said.

Sophie smiled thinly. 'I'm sure,' she managed.

Crazy. All modern people flew. But under the fear, there was a little flame of excitement – almost of relief. She might have hated flying, but that hadn't stopped her. She had hated confronting Tom, but that hadn't stopped her, either. Courage wasn't about not being afraid, in the end; it was about acting, no matter how you felt.

And Sophie was on this plane.

The plane grunted and shuddered as the wheels dropped down. Sophie smiled. She was here, and she was going to meet Hugh.

Maybe it was mad. Maybe there'd be reporters right there at the airport. But she almost didn't care. Let the reporters say what they liked. Things couldn't be any worse than they were with Tom right now, could they? Sophie had nothing to hide; she was a free woman, and she liked Hugh Montfort. A lot.

And now she was in Ireland. At his request. About to stay in his house, and figure out if they could mean anything to each other.

The plane jolted. She pressed her head back against the soft cloth of her luxurious seat, but when she glanced outside, they had landed. A wave of joy and anticipation washed through her.

Hugh was here. In a few moments, she'd see him again. It had been months, and Sophie found she couldn't wait. She felt so light, she could float.

She was free – free of so many things. And Sophie had the strangest notion. She would step off this plane and into a whole new life.

He remembered it clearly, even years afterwards.

Hugh had been sitting in a study in the East Tower. It was one of the smaller living spaces in the castle, but one of his favourites; a snug, ancient little room, with curving walls, a fireplace, and a lead-paned window that looked west, to the wood. He had had a local craftsman install thick oak book-shelves, and he had filled them with leather-bound volumes mixed with pulp novels from the fifties and sixties. He especially enjoyed re-reading one of his first edition Bond novels, with a glass of Scotch, while the sun set over the forest and red light bathed the grey stone walls.

His study had not seen much use these last few years. It had been all business all the time. Now he was back here, though, the place was starting to seem like home.

But if his body was at rest, Hugh's mind travelled. It winged across the Irish sea, banked at the Channel, and turned to Paris.

Sophie.

She was like a fever that wouldn't quit. He tried to shake the feeling that if this didn't work, nothing would; that if the new glimmer of hope, the possibility of personal happiness, was taken from him, that his life was over.

He liked her; he respected her.

And he wanted her.

Those long, tapering legs, her tiny waist, shapely breasts – he was driving himself nuts imagining her naked. It was desire, though, not lust. Hugh was torn with curiosity. All that femininity, and a loveless marriage. She had poured it into her son. He could tell – practised with women, as he was – how she'd been in Pierre's bed; nervous, cold, almost certainly a virgin, and one that had never warmed to sex.

He wanted, badly, to try. Not try, in fact; do. There was no doubt in Montfort's mind that in his arms, Sophie would be different. Utterly, spectacularly different. He didn't think she'd ever been turned on, not really; never wanted to let go. If he could make her his, he would teach her, in the full flower of her womanhood, what that was like. And sex was so much better, so infinitely better, when you knew that after you'd come you wouldn't be full of disgust, of self-loathing.

Hugh had wanted the hookers; sure. But he'd hated himself for the physical need, the mechanical, ugly nature of it. And he'd wanted Georgie. That had been different; a good thing, one that made him feel alive.

Wanting Sophie, wanting to feel the taste of her lips, her belly, her hair in his hands, that was the same way. He wanted her to be his. To be with her. For ever. The problem was going to be talking her into it.

They'd only gone on one date. The damned business with her son meant he hadn't seen her since. And now, after the call earlier that evening, Hugh wasn't sure he'd see her again.

He set his tumbler of whisky aside, distracted; laid down his novel. Damn it, he wouldn't just accept it. He'd swim back to bloody Paris if necessary. Whatever it took to win her. To get his ring on her finger, and her body into his bed –

And then the phone rang.

'Montfort.'

'It's me.'

So it was; and he felt as though he were suspended in glass, waiting for her to give him a decision.

'I'm glad to hear from you. Are you coming?'

'I'd like to. There's a flight that lands at Shannon at ten tomorrow.'

A rush of gladness swept through him. 'Just in time for lunch. I can have cook make you something. Or would you prefer to go to the village pub?'

'The pub. Much rather,' Sophie answered, and laughed. 'I haven't eaten in a pub for years.'

'I hope you can stay a good long time,' he said, seriously.

'Let's take things as they come.'

Yes; let's, Hugh thought. He was immensely cheered. 'I'll be there to pick you up. Do you have a lot of luggage?'

'One suitcase; I'm going to get some new clothes.'

'You really are starting over. Well, make sure you include some wellies and a mack. We'll be doing a lot of walking.'

'It sounds blissful,' Sophie said. And he thrilled to hear the smile in her voice.

'I aim to please. See you tomorrow.'

'Goobye, Hugh.'

Energised, he hung up and bolted from the study, half running down the wide stone staircase that led to the entrance hall. Mrs O'Connor, his head housekeeper, was in the kitchen, talking to Miss Miers, his cook, sixty-eight years old and the best in County Cork.

'Mrs O'Connor.'

'Yes, sir?'

A motherly, comfortable woman, she was completely unflappable. Hugh smothered his excitement; he didn't want to appear like an overeager schoolboy.

'Can you get the Oak Room ready? I'll be having a guest to stay for a while; a lady.'

'Very good, sir.'

Mrs O'Connor rather superbly turned to Miss Miers and went back to getting lead shot out of pheasants. Hugh hovered a bit.

'I'm sorry, Mrs O'Connor, but do we have any women's things ready?'

'Such as what, Mr Montfort?'

'You know.' He felt awkward. 'Shampoos . . . soaps . . . bath oils . . .'

'Plenty. And before you ask, night things, dressing gowns, slippers as well.'

Hugh stared. 'But Mrs O'Connor, I haven't had any women to stay here for over eight years.'

'That's right,' the housekeeper said, and finally cracked a smile. 'But we always hoped you might, one day.'

'Meet the right girl and come to your senses,' added Hannah Miers with a loud sniff.

'Ah. Right. Well, I'll leave you to it,' said Hugh, and absolutely felt himself blush as he headed back upstairs.

Emily O'Connor turned to her friend and heaved a huge sigh of relief.

'Well, finally,' she said.

'It won't work, you know,' Hannah replied. 'Your man's a great brooding lump of a thing. Never saw anything like him.' She pursed her lips disapprovingly. 'Handsome lad like that, rotting away by himself.'

'You never know. Give the girl a chance. All it takes is the right one,' Emily said, ever the optimist. And the two women smiled at each other, hopefully, like teenagers sharing a secret.

It was strange that Hugh didn't feel awkward. It seemed like the most natural thing in the world, as though Sophie were coming to him for the hundredth time, not the first. As if she'd been away for a week or so, and Hugh was just here to pick her up.

He leaned forward and broke into a wide grin. There was Sophie, coming out of customs, pulling her suitcase. God, she was sexy, he thought.

'I'll get that,' Hugh said, springing forward. She blushed, and looked at him; she was so beautiful today. She didn't look like a woman grieving. For Tom or anyone else.

Hugh grabbed the case.

'Shall we get in the car?' he asked, because she didn't speak.

'Oh – yes,' Sophie said.

For a second, though, he didn't walk. Hugh wanted, badly, to kiss her; but he didn't believe in public displays of affection. So he squeezed her hand, and looked her full in the face. It was like drinking a large glass of water after a long, gruelling run; he felt the life flood back into him.

Sophie was looking up into his eyes; although he knew her to be a mature and confident woman, in this moment there was still a nervousness, a vulnerability about her. Hugh suddenly realised that it was his reaction. He hadn't kissed her, and now she was afraid his feelings for her had evaporated already.

Sophie was too used to French manners, Hugh thought; he'd have to remind her what side of the Channel she really came from. He traced one rough finger against the softness of her palm.

'Let's go home,' he said.

'Sounds good.'

He walked her to the car, threw the case in the trunk, and held the passenger seat open for her. When Sophie slid inside, he waited, then turned to face her.

She looked at him, eyes darting all over his face. Hugh heard her breath quicken.

'What?' Sophie said.

'Just this.'

He bent his head towards her and kissed her. Lightly, on the lips; but with a slight tease, brushing her skin, almost claiming her mouth, but then pulling back.

Sophie responded, instantly. Her mouth parted softly, and when he drew back, he could see that the blood had flushed into her cheeks, that her pupils were dilated, her pulse raised.

Oh, she'd be passionate. Hugh knew it. And he sensed that she did, too.

'We'll be there in less than an hour.' Hugh turned his eyes to the road, deliberately breaking the spell. He smoothly put the car in gear. As she pretended to look out of the window, he felt her disappointment.

Hugh always loved the ride out to the countryside, but today it was different; and infinitely better. Sophie loved the wild fields, the thick woods and soft bogs that lined their route; it was like seeing Ireland again with a newcomer's eyes. His eyesight seemed to have become keener, all his senses sharper. He noticed the gleam of a stream in the forest, relished the wind in his face, blowing the strands of her hair loose from its elegant chignon. He wanted to kiss Sophie, he wanted to make love to her. But he also felt hungry. And hopeful, and if Mayberry or Massot came into his mind, it was to wonder that he had ever considered them worthy of a moment of his precious life.

Seeing his home for the first time with Sophie was like waking from hibernation; the blood sang in his veins, and his eyes, he knew, were alight with pleasure. He enjoyed everything, even noticing the beautiful handling of his racing green Aston Martin as it took the sharp corners coming into Kilcarrick.

Hugh felt invincible, as though nothing could ever go wrong again.

'I hope you aren't expecting too much,' he said.

She turned those gorgeous grey eyes on him. 'What do you mean?'

'Well, Kilcarrick Castle isn't like Château des Étoiles. It's small – it's not a family seat. When I bought it, it was a ruin. Took me eight years to restore, and I'm not quite finished.'

Sophie smiled wickedly. 'You mean it's just your jobbing castle?'

He chuckled. 'Exactly.'

'Do you have hot water?'

'Yes; and electricity and lots of fires.'

'That's what I wanted to hear.' She sighed with contentment.

'This is Kilcarrick,' he said, spinning the car left and parking. There was a space just off the market square, by the Victorian stone Celtic Cross that dominated it. 'We'll have lunch before we go to the castle, shall we? Just the two of us.'

'Why, do you have other guests?'

'Of course not.' Hugh chuckled. 'I'm a miserable old sod, ask anybody; I never socialise. But there are staff. Have to be – it's a big place, and I've abandoned it for far too long.'

'I see.' Sophie got out and looked around her. 'Wow. It's a beautiful village.'

'Isn't it.' He loved Kilcarrick; it typified the mixture of gorgeous old houses with grey slate roofs, cobbled streets and chic little Internet cafés that characterised Ireland these days. 'The Celtic tiger's been roaring for years, but the traditional side of the country's still there.'

'Do you drink in this pub, too?' Sophie asked, turning in through the front door.

It was called the Black Lamb and had an inviting little garden and pink dogroses round the door.

'Often.' Hugh looked straight ahead.

'How are ya, Hugh?' the barman called out. He was a strong man, and his eyes flickered over Sophie with interest.

'Great, Jack. Yourself?'

'Can't complain.'

'I'm sorry.' Hugh steered her to a little corner table near the back window; Sophie looked at the horse-brasses and the low-hanging black beams on the ceiling. 'Village pub; you'll be the news of the day. You know how gossip is.'

'Well, we're used to that.'

Jack sent over a lad with a couple of menus. Hugh recommended the shepherd's pie; Sophie opted for it, and he had a rabbit stew. They both ordered cider.

'Gosh, I haven't had cider in . . . for ever.' Sophie held it up to the light, admiringly. 'There are things you miss in Paris.'

'I don't think the great Katherine would approve, do you?' He was surprised that he felt bold enough to tease her about what she was leaving behind, but on the other hand, sod it; Hugh was comfortable with Sophie, and he needed to see if she felt the same way.

'No. Well – sod her,' Sophie said with vigour.

Hugh laughed. 'Is this the same Sophie Massot I left in St Aude?'

Sophie shrugged. 'I thought about things, that night. Before I called you back.'

'Tell me.'

'And I decided that I have to get on with my own life. And let Tom get on with his. Not abandon him, you understand. But let him make his own mistakes, let him go. Perhaps that's the best thing I can do for him right now.'

Hugh paused. 'I'm impressed.'

'Why?'

'You've spent your entire adult life pleasing other people. It takes guts to decide to please yourself.'

Sophie smiled. 'Thank you, Hugh.'

'Especially, I would imagine, when you love your child.'

The waiter came over with their food; Sophie took a forkful of shepherd's pie.

'Delicious.'

'Nothing fancy, after French cooking.'

'So much the better,' she said. 'You know – it's amazing. I've just lost my house, my son's estranged from me, and I've been thrown out of the only career I've ever had.' She laughed. 'And I actually feel – just tremendously happy.'

'I'm glad.'

'I feel so free. As if I got out of jail. Not having to deal with the press – or think about Katherine, that evil old witch. And I know that I'll eventually reconcile with Tom.'

'You've left, now. Often that's what it takes to truly miss someone.' Hugh took a long pull at his cider, which was crisp, chilled and excellent. 'I confess, I thought you'd be a pool of tears.'

She thought about it.

'Somewhere along the way, I became confident. I think it was running House Massot. After I fired Gregoire Lazard. I had been settling into my old ways . . . being a little woman, relying on the big strong man. When I found out he was cheating on me – tricking me – I had no more excuses.'

Hugh nodded.

'It was all down to me. And the strange thing was, not only could I handle it, but I was also bloody good at it.'

'You certainly were,' he said, admiringly.

'If it hadn't been for Katherine poisoning my son, right now, his inheritance would be secure.'

They ate for a minute or so in companionable silence.

'I know that Tom will come back to me. When he understands things a bit better than he does now. He's been pampered and babied all his life. In fact, if I'm honest, much of this was my own fault.'

'You can't blame yourself.'

'Can't I? I believe I can – I must. I was the parent at home with Tom. I was the wife who did everything Pierre asked me to. It's almost as if, when he married me at nineteen, I froze myself in aspic – preserved myself as exactly that nervous teenager. Why didn't I challenge Pierre? Why did I raise Tom according to *his* methods? He wasn't even there. I should have gone to court, got hold of House Massot long before last year.'

'Sophie,' Hugh shook his head, 'you're rewriting history. You've changed – you can't judge your past actions by the person you are today.'

She seemed unconvinced.

'Well,' she said, and her beautiful eyes stared into the crackling fire. 'Never again, Hugh. I'm going to do what I think is right, and I won't be asking anybody's approval. Not Katherine, not the memory of Pierre, not even Tom. I'm capable. The debacle with Massot has taught me that, at least.'

'Which is valuable.' Hugh forked up a piece of the braised rabbit; it was sensational, melting into the herbs and broth. Sophie's speech had given him an idea. But this was not the time for it.

Right now was not about business.

As if she'd read his thoughts, Sophie changed the subject.

'It's a wonderful pub. Do you drink here often?'

'About once a week.' He added, 'And it used to be daily.'

'When your wife died.'

'That's right,' he said, unembarrassed. 'That was my first stage of grief. Anything to get unconscious. They threw me out a couple of times. But I've made up for it since.'

Well, this was new, he registered; he was discussing this with another person – with a woman – and it didn't feel awkward, not even slightly.

Sophie said wistfully, 'That's true love.'

'Oh yes,' Hugh agreed.

'I think you're lucky to have had it,' she said, 'because I never did.'

They finished the meal, Sophie appearing to savour every bite. And as he looked at her relaxing, Hugh surrendered. It was definite; he was in love.

Afterwards, he drove her home. Outside Kilcarrick, the road forked to the left, and Hugh spun the wheel slightly to turn into the castle's two-mile-long drive. It wound through the wood, and the thick trees closed over them, the autumn sunlight streaming through the leaves.

The trees gave way to an open wildflower meadow, and Sophie started, then clapped her hands.

'What's that for?' Hugh asked, amused.

She sighed with pleasure. 'Oh, it's so beautiful!'

His castle loomed in front of them, and Hugh was overjoyed to see it. Despite his years of neglect, his only occasional visits, when Mayberry allowed him a paltry week off for Christmas, it still seemed warm, almost gleaming. The grey stone glowed softly in the setting autumn sun; the huge oaks with their golden leaves that were dotted around his small park were beautiful; the castle was small, rugged, hunkered into the landscape and doggedly prepared to repel all comers. In the past, men had died trying to take her. Today, the most protection he'd need would be against the odd impudent journalist.

'It's rough,' he said. 'But hard and reliable. I like the place. Still, it's nothing like the château.'

'You've never been to the château.'

'True. But I've seen pictures. It's a baroque masterpiece, smooth and ornate. This is much less ornamented; and much less luxurious.'

Sophie laughed. 'Maybe castles are like dogs,' she said. 'Adapting to their owners?'

He grinned back. 'Maybe.'

Hugh parked the car on the gravel, and stepped out; Sophie waited for him to come and open her door. Her hand was light in his as he helped her out of the car and took her case.

The door opened and Mrs O'Connor came out to greet them. Hugh made the introduction, Sophie smiled at her kindly.

'Nice to meet you, madam.'

Sophie shook her hand. 'I've heard a lot about you, Mrs O'Connor.'

'And I you, ma'am.' They were both lying, Hugh thought, and he liked them all the more for it; it showed such innate good manners to try to put others at their ease.

'Is everything ready, Mrs O'C?' he asked.

'It is, Mr Montfort; just as you asked. And there's a nice fire in the drawing room and the sitting room. Shall I show Mrs Massot to her room?'

Hugh nodded. 'And then I'll take her round the place, and perhaps we'll have some tea, if that can be arranged.'

'Of course it can, sir. Come this way, madam,' Mrs O'Connor said, and she scooped up Sophie's case and ushered her forward busily. Sophie raised a brow, but Hugh winked at her; he wanted her to feel comfortable, and uncrowded. He preferred a woman show her to her room.

He walked inside the hall; his old Wellingtons were still there, stashed in the boot room, and on the grey stone walls, the pictures of his ancestors hung over a vase of some slightly faded chrysanthemums, but that was because Mrs O'Connor was thrifty. It was familiar and welcoming. Hugh made his way to the drawing room; it had a fine view of the copse of oak trees down by the stream that bisected his grounds – a good fishing spot, with trout in the deeper places. There was indeed a fire blazing against the slight chill outside, and he settled in his old burgundy leather armchair and waited.

Sophie came down ten minutes later, after Roberts, his ancient butler, had brought out the tea. She was wearing a beautiful dress of raspberry silk with three-quarter sleeves, adorned with a whimsical Massot brooch; a strawberry, glittering in clusters of ruby and pink tourmaline, with grass-green leaves of tsavorite garnet. He loved it. Her feet were now encased in supple black leather heels, Christian Louboutin, he thought, and she had a plain gold bracelet around her left wrist. Her beautiful hair was loose around her shoulders, and she had freshened her make-up with a tiny hint of bronzer on the cheeks; she looked warm, like the fire.

'That looks wonderful.' She indicated the tea tray.

'Doesn't it? I think they pushed the boat out. But then, I did call ahead.'

'Shall I pour?'

He nodded. 'Black, no sugar.'

Sophie added a little milk to her cup and one spoonful of sugar. Hugh watched every gesture, drinking it in, the curve of her wrist, the gold glinting on it, the graceful arch of her back.

'I wasn't hungry, but I am now,' she said.

The tray was groaning. There was the traditional tiered platter of small pastries, a substantial plate of fruit cake, some hot, crumbly home-made scones with rich golden clotted cream, jam from the wild strawberries on the estate, and thin-cut sandwiches; slices of roast beef and horseradish, smoked salmon on brown bread, and Mrs O'Connor's favourite chicken with rocket and mustard.

Hugh took a scone; Sophie took several sandwiches, handed him his tea, and then unapologetically demolished them. He loved her for it; this was incredible – she had no awkwardness, none at all. She seemed as natural in his home as the ivy curling around the battlements, and she made him comfortable . . .

Well, perhaps that was the wrong word. The line of her neck, the gentle swell of her breasts under the dress, the trim waist, the cool eyes – he found her homely, but breathtakingly excitable. He cast around for something to say. This was really very unusual. It was always women who were nervous near him, and not the other way around.

'Lapsang – my favourite,' she said.

'Almost the only tea worth drinking. But Sophie, I forgot; I was to give you the tour before tea.'

'It's better like this. I need the caffeine.' She smiled up at him with those luminous eyes. 'And besides, you don't want my stomach rumbling. Your hall might echo, or something.'

'Right.'

'Besides, we've got plenty of time,' she said, wryly. 'It's not as though either of us has an office to go to, any more.'

He nodded. She was just so beautiful, and her eyes were laughing, and her mouth was slightly open. There was a tiny crumb on one corner of it, like a beauty spot. He reached out to brush it away with his thumb.

She tensed, instantly – but not with fear, not with rejection – Hugh felt the softness of her face under his calloused hands, the thud, thud of her heart – and he leaned forward and kissed her.

Hugh brushed his lips lightly over hers. Sophie sat there, unmoving at first, then offered her mouth to him, just slightly, a little gift – he put his hand behind her head, before he knew what he was doing, and seized her, pulled her to him, sharply; her mouth parted, and his tongue trailed across the top of her lips, teasing . . .

She moaned; he slipped his arm lower, around her slim waist, sending the tray of pastries crashing to the stone floor; they slid off the chairs, he was lying next to her, on the flagstone floor, on the edge of his Moroccan carpet. Everything was alight in his mind, the fire, her dress, the warm blood he felt pulsing between his hands, her belly and breasts as she arched into him . . .

'No,' she said. 'No . . .' and pushed him back, panting. Flushed. 'I'm sorry –'

'It's OK,' Hugh said.

Damn it. He wanted her. He was aroused beyond measure and horribly frustrated. But he cursed himself. The woman had only just stepped through his front door, he had servants in the kitchen, and he was practically ripping her clothes off?

'It was too soon. I'm sorry. We have plenty of time.' With a Herculean effort, he pulled away from her and took her hands in his; they trembled, and he felt the dampness of the adrenaline on her palms. 'You're not going to run away, now, are you?'

Sophie was blushing, he saw the mottling on her skin; yes! Hugh thought, with fierce exultation. She's frustrated. She wants this too.

'Of course not,' Sophie said. 'I just – got carried away.' She smiled, embarrassed. 'Technically, it's only our second date.'

'Right.' He winked at her, and she laughed.

Chapter Forty-One

It didn't matter how hard he tried, Tom couldn't shake the feeling something was wrong.

You would never know it, of course, from the way his grandmother acted; their return to Château des Étoiles had been picture perfect. Katherine, insisting that Tom's return should be as his father would have wanted it, engineered a grand pageant. The staff were all lined up outside the front steps, forming a long line towards the house. As Tom stepped out of the limo, offering his hand to Judy, they had each greeted them as they passed by with 'sir' and 'madame', the women giving little bob curtsies, the men inclining their heads. It was as though he were royalty.

Tom couldn't get the scene out of his mind. As he gazed out of his bedroom towards the lake – *his* bedroom, once his mother's and father's room – the unpleasant memory returned. Instead of feeling grand, he had felt foolish. Behind the obsequious words, Tom knew, there was contempt, pity – loathing, even – in the case of his mother's former driver. He hadn't told Grandmother. Katherine would have insisted on having the man dismissed at once, and Tom had no interest in further scandal.

And Grandmother had positively glowed. Possessed with inexhaustible energy and what Tom felt was inappropriate joy, she'd shown him around his childhood home; the portraits of both his parents still hung in the entrance hall, but beyond that, it was transformed; all traces of his mother's presence removed with lightning speed. The clothes and shoes in her dressing room, vanished; his own suits hung there now. Her modern books gone from the library; her gardening gloves from the rear lobby. Katherine had even put new plants in the conservatory. His mother's occasional private bedroom, the one she hadn't shared with Papa, had been assigned to Judy, with the comfortable styling of a guest chamber.

Grandmother had made it clear that regardless of their relationship, she, and not Judy, was the chatelaine.

And Tom found that was the one aspect of his homecoming he felt comfortable with. Grandmother had wasted no time; the week after they moved in, she threw a little soirée, with a hundred and fifty people Tom had not been seen since the affair in his Paris apartment. Celeste and Margot de Fortuny, and their father, the Marquis; Georges Tatin, without his pregnant wife; many other forgettable types; all swilling the best champagne from his cellars and practically kissing his ring. There were some hand-picked gossip columnists, known for their obsequiousness to the rich and famous, and the party got the write-up it deserved; much was made of Tom's new independence, the mastery of the estate and company, and pleasant remarks were made on Katherine's impressive gown of severe gun-metal satin and her stupendous necklace of brilliants.

Judy, of course, hadn't been able to compete. Surely few women could, indeed; but Tom admitted to himself, as he watched a heron rise from the sparkling waters of the lake, victoriously carting off a perch – Mother knew better than to use koi – Judy had not been in any sense disastrous. She was subdued, and didn't say much more than 'good evening', and 'I'm sure Tom is delighted to see you'. There was no attempt to present herself as the hostess. And her dress was – well, suitable; navy velvet, with a sapphire pendant he had presented her with.

In fact, he'd been giving her a lot of jewellery lately. It saved having to talk.

Because something felt wrong. Like that dress. Certainly presentable, but uninspired. And Judy's whole presence in this house. Tom sensed that she held herself very carefully. Was that what he wanted in a girlfriend?

She was . . . uneasy.

Perhaps with good cause. This was the first time he'd really given himself permission to think things through. Tom hated to admit he'd made a mistake, but it was becoming clearer that he had to do something. Judy Dean was intelligent, and charismatic, and interesting. But she wasn't inspiring any feeling in him. And as good as she was in bed, he felt a little exhausted; the hardness of her body, at first so sexy, now was slightly repellent. He wanted softness in a woman. Judy's steel core reminded him, in unpleasant ways, of his grandmother . . .

It's a joke, Tom thought. I'm meant to be the big man around here, but I still think of my mother. And Grandmother is chivvying me along like a hen being hurried back into the coop at night. And I'm stuck here in the countryside with a woman that I don't really want, presiding at my family table.

He was due downstairs for dinner shortly. Judy had told cook she wanted roast pheasant with chestnut sauce and candied walnuts, one of his favourite dishes. There would be mashed potatoes, peas, and a glass of good claret. All very pleasant – but how much more pleasant, Tom thought, if he didn't have to eat it with Judy.

Right now she was at the office. Thank God; he would be better able to think without her here.

Well. His grounds did look inviting, bathed in the warm light of sunset. Tom decided to go for a walk; he wanted to clear his head.

'You're looking around, my dear.' Katherine reached across to Judy and patted her on the knee. 'You mustn't *stare*, you know; it's not done to look impressed.'

'I wasn't –'

But it was no good. The rheumy blue eyes were still sharp with that cynical gaze. Judy knew she'd been caught out. She flushed; how she loathed Pierre's mother! Oh, it had been a convenient alliance, but the bitch never passed up an opportunity to show that she was still queen bee.

'It is a very beautiful house,' she muttered.

'All true estates have a dower house.' Katherine smoothed her long skirt, vintage Chanel tweed, paired with the matching jacket tailored to her still-slim form; she wore a cream silk shirt by Givenchy and a necklace of pearls the size of marbles, their lustre soft against the wrinkles of her skin. 'This is, I believe, one of the better ones in France,' she added complacently. 'And my dear Pierre had a great hand in choosing the décor,' she added.

She gestured at the antique Chinese wallpaper, the curtains of pale orange dress silk fringed with cloth-of-gold, the cream-and-cornflower tones of the priceless Persian rug that underlay her Louis XIV chairs and Chippendale sideboard.

'He always had such great taste,' Judy forced herself to say.

Katherine looked at her. '*Has*, Judy, *has*.'

'Let's hope so.' She took refuge in her coffee. Bitch! Why did Katherine always twist the knife, talking about Pierre? And throwing parties, to show that Judy was not the hostess. It was as though she was trying to rub in the nasty feeling that Judy couldn't smother for too much longer – that this little adventure was Pierre, part two.

Judy was in the house with Tom – but not his wife. She was at the parties – but not the hostess. She got gifts of jewels – but no engagement ring . . .

Judy perceived quite clearly what Katherine was saying, in her roundabout, spidery way; I'm family – you're not.

Katherine smiled thinly at her, to show she knew what Judy was thinking. Very well, I'll grasp the nettle, Judy told herself.

'And do you get used to it – all this luxury?' she asked. She lifted her head, brazenly drinking in the antiques, the architecture, the liveried servants; the butler hovering nearby with the silver Georgian coffee-pot, and Katherine speaking as though he weren't even there. Two could play that game.

'But of course.' Katherine arched one silver eyebrow, disapprovingly. 'If one comes from a good family, one hardly needs to "get used" to it.'

Judy was unbowed. In fact, she felt a stirring of her old self . . . something that she had shoved relentlessly underground, when the affair with Tom started. She was sick of playing the good girl. How far had it got her, anyway?

She regarded Katherine with loathing, and decided to stir the pot a little.

'And are you?' she asked. 'From a good family, I mean?'

Katherine made a motion that, were she younger, might have been interpreted as tossing her head.

'Being an American, I wouldn't expect you to understand,' she said, 'but the House of Massot is a very old French family . . .'

'All families are old,' Judy said, unfazed. 'Adam and Eve, right?'

Katherine stiffened.

'I see it now,' she said, with a dangerous silkiness to her voice. 'You're so like poor Sophie, my dear . . . common girls from common backgrounds . . . it doesn't do to have people from your class coming into society. It's unkind, really. You have no idea how to behave, and you do rather *linger* past your usefulness.'

'And you?' Judy adopted a similarly light tone; she found she was actually enjoying the fencing. Maybe Katherine was banking that Tom was sick of her . . . but Judy had a suspicion Tom was sick of Katherine. After all, his grandmother couldn't satisfy him in bed.

There was, as she considered that point, that sick feeling . . . the words of Françoise, about Pierre . . . father and son . . . but Judy wouldn't go there. She told herself she loved Tom. And if she played her cards right, one day this house could be hers. She would sit in Katherine's gilt chair, and the servants would fawn over her. 'And you, Katherine? What's your background? You aren't a Massot by birth, are you?'

Katherine Massot stared at the American girl, sitting there as cool and impudent as you please, with her jewels – gifts from Tom – glittering inappropriately at her wrists and lobes; she was overwhelmed by them. A typical, brash New World slut, she decided.

'I'm afraid our conversation has left me a little fatigued,' she declared. 'Would you mind very much if we terminated our little tea party?'

Judy stood up. This was typical of Katherine, who'd summoned her imperiously to tea out of the office. Katherine wanted to draw her into the web; she would try and truss her, and suck the juice out of her, the way she'd done with Sophie.

But I'm no Sophie, Judy thought. I'm not weak. I'm not trusting.

I'm a match for her.

'Of course not, dear Katherine,' she said brightly. 'I do hope you feel recovered by dinner. It's Tom's favourite. He does love to indulge.'

She invested the last word with as much meaning as she could, and pirouetted on her heels. It was a pleasant evening, and she'd walk back up to the château – that always made her feel better.

The butler bowed and scraped, but nonetheless physically hustled her – in a very discreet way – towards the door. Judy pretended not to notice, but rage boiled inside her. Ignoring him, she marched smartly out of the front porch and down the weathered grey steps of the dower house, her shoes crunching on the gravel of the drive, until she hit the tarmac. It was three quarters of a mile back to the château – a short walk, and a welcome one; Judy wanted to work on her demeanour. Tom must not see her angry. No way.

The château, with its ornate towers and grey stone crenellated walls, was lovely – so breathtakingly lovely. There was nothing Judy had ever seen to match it, no billionaire's penthouse on Fifth, no modern luxury pad in Miami. No, this was old, old money – the oldest – the kind that even Wall Street couldn't give you. Judy glanced down at Tom's latest gift, a ring of canary and white diamonds, a perfectly formed daisy. World-class jewels, and a château, and an estate. It was a fairytale – the Massot fairytale. She had clung to Pierre, had always hoped that what he'd given to that mouse Sophie he might give to her.

It had never happened, but now Judy had another chance. Forget those dirty feelings when she slept with Tom. Judy kept her eyes on the château. Focus; that was what it was all about. Keeping her eyes on the prize . . .

The house soothed her, and she started to cast her eyes around the grounds. Screw Katherine, look at the lake. Look at the woods, blazing with autumn leaves; the orchards, the stables . . . Judy felt her depression lift. An almost savage desire overcame her. She wanted this place. She wanted to be more than a guest, more than a footnote in the saga of the Massots. Always the worker bee, never the queen. It made her sick. It had to change.

She started; there was a familiar voice. Tom's. What was he doing? It was coming from the stone bench under the weeping willow, a little way off the path. Instinctively, Judy froze. She didn't want to be seen; she didn't want to explain where she'd been: her little joust with Katherine should stay secret. But who was he talking to? They had no visitors, not today . . .

She moved away from the path, very quietly; Tom's back was to her, and now she saw; he was on his mobile phone. Judy hesitated. If he saw her . . .

But she wanted to know who it was. Information was her currency. And although the sharp points of her heels were sinking into the manicured lawn, she crept behind a broad spreading yew tree, a little way from him. And listened.

'Yeah, well.' That was Tom, but not the voice she knew. It wasn't so dignified. It was rougher, edged with longing, and the accent was gone – he sounded so *English*. 'I feel the same way,' he said, gruffly. 'And your exams . . . you got the results?'

There was a pause. 'Really. Congratulations,' he said. 'I didn't have you figured for a nerd.' Another pause. And then he laughed.

Judy shivered. She had never heard Tom this way – not so young and pompous; relaxed, even light-hearted. Not with her.

'And that's definite, is it, Poll?' he asked, teasingly this time. 'You're missing out, you know. There's no good coffee that side of the Channel.'

The wave of nausea that rushed up over Judy took her by surprise, and she actually thought she might throw up. She swayed dangerously against the tree, feeling ill, the blood rushing to her head. Tom was still talking, and laughing, thank

God, and he didn't turn round. Judy scooped up her shoes, and ran – ran on her padded feet, ran, getting grass stains and daisy petals crushed into her Woolford's, ran up the hill, away from him, towards the pear orchard. That way she could walk back to the house without being seen . . .

Judy ran. Years of training, and her body obeyed her. She was fast, her muscles taut, even without sneakers. She wished she could keep running for ever. At least her speed was there for her – at least she could control that . . .

After some time, she became aware that she was crying. That would not do. She slowed, stopped beside the dead trunk of a fallen apple tree.

Judy knew exactly who was on the other end of that phone. Conversations she'd had with Tom had pried it out of him; his seeming insouciance didn't fool her. The girl had mattered to him. Very much. A young girl, much younger than Judy.

Polly was her name. Poll, for short. And Tom was laughing and joking with her.

Judy slipped her heels on and headed left, towards the kitchen garden entrance to the house. There were some servants there once she got inside, but she ignored them; she coughed a little, as though to explain her red eyes, and ran up the first marble staircase in the great hall, to her private room.

Judy thought of Katherine. And Sophie. The Massot women, proved right again. Of herself, unceremoniously dumped. She could cling on here – she was confident enough in her own sexual ability to know that – but she was now on borrowed time. How would Tom do it, she wondered? A clean break? A shame-faced phone call? A letter – perhaps containing some kiss-off jewellery?

Certainly she would lose her job. And her new car – everything that she prized.

Judy's heart thudded in her ribcage. Well, it wasn't going to happen again. She was not about to be dumped by the son after being sidelined by the father. Screw the Massot girls. Screw the Massot men.

That thought stuck. She paused; went into her bathroom. First, she carefully washed her face, and made up; pinks, to go with her Chloe dress for dinner.

Then she went to the medicine cabinet, that beautiful ornamental thing, an age-spotted mirrored door surrounded by ivory; she took out her contraceptive pills, and methodically flushed every last one of them down the lavatory.

Judy smiled to herself. As a tactic, it was as old as the hills.

But then so was love. And so was revenge.

The French had some marvellous inheritance laws, she now recalled; it was illegal to shut a child out of the will.

Marriage or no marriage, Judy could control this family for ever. And she was determined to do it.

Chapter Forty-Two

Sophie had never had so much fun.

That first evening, she wrote a letter to Tom.

My darling boy,

I'm staying with Hugh Montfort at his place in Ireland for the time being. He had no personal enmity with your father; and I hope one day you'll give him a chance.

I want you to understand that I feel no anger towards you. I believe Granny and you have made a mistake, but you must sort that out for yourself. I will always love you. One day you'll understand that loving a child doesn't always mean conforming to their wishes.

You can call me on my mobile any time. I hope to see you soon. And don't trust Judy. I know for a fact she doesn't love you.

Love,

Maman.

She posted it herself the next day, in the village. And then, with some difficulty, she made herself forget about Tom.

After the first day or two, it wasn't hard. Ireland was gorgeous, and Hugh showed her the time of her life. They rode out over his fields, they hiked through the woods, he insisted that she tried to fish; and even though it was wet and cold, and she felt stupid wearing one of his old cricket jumpers, Sophie managed to catch a tiny trout; it gave her the thrill of a lifetime when she unhooked it and let it slip back into the stream. They went to fairs, and bought local food and crafts. She became a jumble sale expert, and enjoyed the Harvest Festival.

388

While Hugh worked out in his gym, two hours every day, Sophie took some time and just enjoyed a book.

Every sunrise, she felt a little more life flood back into her limbs.

As much as she loved the place, she loved the man more. Hugh was nothing like Pierre, nothing. His dominance, what she had thought of as dominance, now seemed like petty psychological bullshit. Sophie was ashamed she'd ever fallen for it. Pierre had been faithless, controlling, weak. Hugh was a real man. He had fought for his country. He'd taken his shirt off once, in front of her, when he slipped on a stone and fell in the stream; Sophie had seen the scars.

She'd seen the finely muscled chest and strong arms, too, and the dark smattering of hair. And she'd wanted to see the rest of it.

Hugh. He was a friend, a protector, a confidant. Sure. But he was also her man. Sophie longed for him, physically, in a way she had never experienced. Not with Pierre, and certainly not with Gregoire. With them she'd only wanted to seem desirable.

Hugh was more than a mirror. He was so stunning, so confident, manly, utterly gorgeous. He'd kissed her like he owned her. That first night. And Sophie was afraid to kiss him again, because of what might happen. Now she knew him better, she also knew herself. Once she started to kiss him, she'd never stop.

'It's getting cold,' Hugh said.

'I don't mind.' Sophie hugged herself. 'I feel perfectly warm.'

It was true. They were trudging through some crunchy bracken, following a forest path that led back to the castle from the village. It was undeniably beautiful; ash, yew, pine, and oak . . . a mixed forest, golden in the full fire of autumn. Yet she had hardly seen any of it. They'd gone to lunch in the village, at the pub; Hugh had ordered pork chops and roast parsnip, and Sophie had some *moules à la marinière*, and a glass of wine; she couldn't recall a meal she'd enjoyed more. And Hugh suggested they walk home.

A slow, long, beautiful walk. Sophie felt quite dazed with

love. It was amazing; it was everything she'd imagined and never received. The desire, enough to make her faint, and yet the familiarity; the sense that he'd always been there, and please God, would never leave.

It was like being drunk, without the hangover.

Truly, in love.

In fact, she knew that better than she knew almost anything, right now.

'Hugh.' Sophie stopped, by a patch of bracken. 'Can I talk to you for a minute?'

She tried to keep the tone light; but Montfort wasn't fooled for a moment. He stopped dead, and took her hand.

'Of course,' he said, gently; reassuringly. 'What's up?'

'It's about us.'

'Is it because you haven't heard from Tom? I can talk to him, if you like –'

'No, not Tom.' The thought of Hugh calling the château almost made her laugh. 'And I don't think that would be such a great idea.'

'I'll have to get to know him eventually.'

'It's, you know. Something else.' Sophie blushed and felt stupid. 'It's my religion.'

'Your what?'

'Religion.' She stared at her feet. 'I can't sleep with you.'

Hugh stopped and raised a brow.

'Well, that's a bit of a facer. Have you taken a vow of chastity? Joined a nunnery?'

Sophie squirmed. 'You know what I mean. I just – it's been a month –'

'I've been counting the days. I assure you.'

His black eyes swept, assessingly, over her body; Sophie flushed as though the tight jeans and sweater were transparent.

'I just don't want you to think I'm teasing you. Or . . . leading you on.'

'No sex before marriage.'

She nodded.

He turned away. 'I understand. Come on, Sophie – let's get back, before you get a chill.'

Hugh walked on through the forest. And her stomach turned over. That's it, then, Sophie thought. That's the end. He wanted me the first day. But he's not going to wait for ever.

It's finished, she thought. And she picked up her boots and trudged on, determined that she wouldn't let Hugh see her cry.

Hugh had never thought of himself as a good actor. He could keep his own counsel, in business, and in war; that was about all, though. At present, all he wanted to do was to get away from Sophie. Long enough that she wouldn't be able to guess.

When they got back to the castle, he pecked her distantly on the cheek and asked to be excused.

'I have to run an errand in Cork; bloody insurance. Do you think you'll be all right by yourself for a while?'

Her face was glum, but she struggled to smile.

'Don't mind me,' she said. 'I'm in the middle of a Jilly Cooper reading marathon. I wanted some time to finish *Octavia*.'

'See you later, then; tell Mrs O'Connor what you want for dinner – all right?'

'OK,' she muttered, turning to go up the stairs.

Hugh exhaled. He'd made it. He rushed out to his garage, retrieved the Aston Martin. He thought it would take two hours. He had been mulling this over since the middle of last week, when she'd been laughing with him after dinner, and he had determined this moment would come. He'd made several calls, and prepared; now he fished out his mobile and rang Paul.

'I'm thinking this evening.'

The restaurateur clicked his tongue. 'What time?'

'Early – six. I have to turn this around before she gets herself a sandwich at home. D'you think you can pull it off?'

'No problem. In fact, I only need an hour. Forty-five minutes, even.'

Hugh was taken aback. 'So fast?'

'For you, I've been practising,' the chef said.

'You have my gratitude,' Hugh answered, and snapped the

phone shut. He was touched by the good wishes of these people he knew only slightly; his housekeeper, his cook, the owner of his favourite village restaurant. For the first time that day, he felt a sliver of nerves penetrate his happiness. He trusted that none of them would be disappointed.

He could make it to Cork in twenty minutes flat, if he ignored the speed limit. Hugh pressed his foot on the accelerator, and the car took off down the road like a hare flying across the fields.

The sun had just set when he returned to the castle, and the blue sky of twilight was still streaked with gold. Hugh hurried inside and was met by Mrs O'Connor.

'Has Mrs Massot eaten?' he asked.

'She's still in her room, sir. She did ask for a salad half an hour ago –'

Hugh's shoulders slumped. Damn it.

'– but I told her cook was still in Kilcarrick, finishing the shopping.'

'Well done!' said Hugh, who could have kissed her. 'Would you go and get her, and ask her if she'd like to come out for dinner with me? Tell her it's nothing special, she shouldn't bother to change.'

'Yes, sir.' The older woman hovered. 'And best of luck to you,' she added.

Hugh grinned and gave her a solemn wink. 'Thanks, Mrs O'Connor.'

'Where are we going?' Sophie asked. She still felt gloomy; Hugh had asked her to take care of her own dinner arrangements for the first time since she'd arrived in Ireland.

She felt like a deflated balloon. It couldn't be long, surely, before Hugh made some excuse and asked her to leave. He was masculine – very modern, not sheltered like her. He wouldn't be the kind of man who was prepared to wait.

Sophie thought this might be her last night here. Why make it hard on Hugh. It would much easier if she left than if he had to try to get her out. She'd had a fantastic, glorious month with him. She didn't want it to end on a sour note.

'It's just a little local place. Called the Blind Pike.'

Despite herself, she smiled. 'Great name for a pub.'

'It's not, it's actually an excellent bistro. Only place with a Michelin star for a hundred miles, in any direction. Paul Begala is the chef, he's a great cook. All local produce, everything seasonal, very traditional dishes. His mutton stew has to be tasted to be believed. And he does a lobster thermidor that just melts against the tongue. All his fish is fantastic, in fact.'

Sophie was hungry. 'That sounds delicious. I must say, I've eaten more with you than I ever did in my entire life.'

That came out sounding rather personal; she blushed and wished she hadn't mentioned it.

'Ah, well. That's the exercise. You're walking, riding all the time here. Frankly, I think you could do with fattening up a little.'

He glanced ahead. 'Here we are.'

'Did you make reservations? I suppose if it's got a Michelin star, it must be very crowded.'

'Usually is,' Hugh agreed mildly. He parked, and went round to help her out of the car. A quick glance inside confirmed Paul hadn't let him down.

'Thank you.' Sophie closed the door. 'What beautiful music.'

'That's his daughter, Brona. She plays with the London Symphony Orchestra. She's back here on holiday.' Now the moment had arrived, Hugh's nerves had returned. 'Come on in.'

The door swung open, and Begala, a thin man with sparkling eyes and a broad smile, was standing there.

'Ah, Hugh, it's yourself. And Mrs Massot. Nice to see you here, ma'am. If you'll follow me, your table's ready.'

Sophie smiled and walked in through the oak porch. And gasped.

The small restaurant floor was completely empty, apart from a single table for two set in the centre of the room. An antique silver candlestick was placed on a white cloth of delicate Irish linen; it was mirrored by hundreds of small candles placed all over the room. The walls had been hung with green silk, and huge vases of flowers were everywhere, along with arrangements of berries and twigs; the scent of roses, all colours, rioting against the dark green backdrop, was everywhere. Wearing a dress of red velvet, Brona, sitting unobtrusively in a corner, was plucking a lilting melody from her fine golden harp; a silver ice bucket filled with crushed ice held a magnum of Krug.

'Hugh.' Her heart jumped into her mouth. 'What's going on?'

Begala smiled, and melted discreetly away.

'Supper,' Hugh said, grinning. 'Why don't you sit down. You're shivering . . . are you cold?'

Sophie shook her head. 'Nervous,' she whispered.

'Strangely enough, me too. Let's have some champagne.'

He pulled back her chair, poured her a glass, then, changing his mind, took her trembling hand in his and sank to one knee.

'Sophie, the more I know you, the more I love you,' Hugh said, simply. 'I admired you before I ever met you; I was struck the first time I saw you; and now I miss you if you even leave the room.'

A tear rolled down Sophie's cheek. But she smiled.

'My darling.' Hugh kissed her hand. 'Will you marry me?'

'Yes,' she whispered. 'Oh, yes – oh, thank God! I love you, Hugh. I love you so much.' And he got up and gathered her in his arms and kissed the life out of her.

'Thank goodness for that,' Hugh said when he finally let her go. 'I was going to wait – have an excellent meal, you know, lull you into a false sense of security with tons of champagne – but then I realised I'd be far too jumpy to eat more than two mouthfuls unless I found out right away.'

Sophie laughed; for the first time in ages, she felt utterly light and free. 'I agree. I couldn't have managed a mouthful. And I'm *starving*.'

'Ah.' Hugh slapped his forehead. 'The ring – the bloody ring! I drove like the devil to Cork to get it, and I was so overwhelmed I forgot to even get it out.' He fished the small leather box from his pocket and opened it. 'I hope you like it.'

Sophie looked down. The ring took her breath away. It was

a beautiful emerald-cut canary diamond, a rich buttery yellow, flanked by two icy clear white trillions, set in twenty-four carat gold.

'Yellow diamonds suit you, I think,' Hugh said. 'Because wherever you go, you bring sunlight.'

She was dumbstruck.

'If you don't like it . . .'

'No – no, I think it's the most stunning ring I've ever seen.' Sophie held out her left hand and he slipped it on to her finger, feeling as though he was claiming, for himself, the only prize that would ever matter. 'It's beautiful. It's unusual. It will always remind me of you.' She kissed him on the lips. 'And it sparkles.'

Hugh had an arm around her; they were lying comfortably together on a red damask Queen Anne chaise-longue, one of his favourites, in his bedroom, watching the glowing embers of the fire. 'I can't believe I'm engaged.'

'Regretting it already?' Sophie smiled up at him. God, she was beautiful, he thought; so full of life and warmth. And still stylish, even after a long walk, and a bath, and dinner; she was in a tailored silk skirt, navy with gold embroidery. It looked somewhat like sari silk, he thought; gorgeous, and unexpected, and had twinned it with a soft cadet-blue silk shirt, and a large string of pale gold pearls. Sophie was one of those women for whom style was never contrived. It was as instinctual with her as breathing, and her appearance complemented her solemn inner grace.

'Never.' He paused. 'I surprised myself, and yet – it doesn't seem shocking. It seems like a perfect fit. We've only known each other a short while . . .'

'On paper.' Sophie shrugged. 'But I feel so used to you.'

'Used to me?'

'You know what I mean,' she insisted.

'So what happens, now?'

'First, we have to tell Tom.' A shadow passed across her beautiful face, but Hugh could see that she was still determined; he had no doubts about that now. She was solidly his. 'And then we'll go to my priest, Fr Sabin. He'll instruct you, and do the wedding. They usually make you wait six months.' She glanced at him. 'Maybe I can speed things up . . .'

Hugh kissed her gently on the lips, forcing himself to keep it light, although every muscle in his body wanted to reach out and take her to himself.

'I think I can wait six months,' he said, but he shifted his body slightly, so it wasn't pressing against her, all the same. The curve of her back was intriguing to him; better to avoid temptation. 'It seems as if I've been waiting many years. Since the day Georgie died.'

'You'll have to tell her family.'

'I'm sure they'll be delighted.' Indeed, it was ironic that Hugh had drifted out of touch with them because of their tiresome good wishes, and urgings that he find somebody else. There could never have been anybody else.

Except there was. Thank God.

'What are you laughing at?' Sophie asked him. 'You're always grinning.'

'I'm not; I'm just happy,' he said simply.

It was true. If he paused to consider how he was feeling, the joy was always there. It wasn't big and splashy, not the sort of thing to make him want to jump up and down. But it was still omnipresent; quiet but deep, a lake, not a waterfall.

'So then we get married. And maybe have some children?'

'It's a little late for that. Unfortunately.'

'You think so? Anything can happen. You're not too old to have children.'

'It's very unlikely,' Sophie said, and this time the cloud hovered a little longer.

Hugh was perturbed. 'Good God, you can't think I'd blame you if it didn't happen, darling. It would just be a lovely extra bonus. A lifetime with you would be more than enough for me. Frankly,' and he heard his own voice roughen a little, despite himself, 'I thought I should never be happy again.'

Sophie turned round to stare at him.

'You were depressed?'

'Nothing like that. Not depressed – but not happy, either. I had moments of excitement, of professional triumph; the best you could call it was a certain satisfaction.' He thought that put it very well; and, indeed, he had worked plenty of eighteen-hour days at Mayberry just to get that satisfaction.

Hugh reached out and took her hand. 'And that's changed, now.'

Sophie hesitated, as if she weren't quite sure whether or not to say something.

'Go on.' Hugh read her mind. 'Look, darling, now is the time to thrash things out. Once we're married you can't run away. That's what Catholics believe, right?'

'No divorce.' She smiled broadly. 'Which is fine by me. You're the one who should worry.'

They kissed again, gently.

'It wasn't that,' Sophie said, after a long moment. 'It was the business. You know, what we might do after the wedding.'

'Don't you ever get angry – thinking of Peter Stockton? Because when I think of Judy Dean, and him' – And Katherine, she stopped short of saying – 'I find myself getting furious. They tricked my son. And I know that Stockton will ruin the company . . .'

'Yes; there's no doubt about that, unfortunately.' Hugh decided not to sugar-coat it. 'There were multiple times, even within Mayberry, which makes mass-market jewels, that I had to stop him trashing the quality of the product. I wanted Mayberry to be another Tiffany. Lines of avant-garde jewels. Stockton would always argue for the cheaper stones with poorer quality, or that we should downgrade the gold – ten carat, for example, instead of fourteen . . .'

'Ten-carat gold? Women's fingers would stain. That's not really gold at all.'

'Of course not. But his instinct is always to save money. He has no conception of quality or of branding.'

Sophie sighed. 'I pity the shareholders, not just Tom.'

'They made their choice when they sold to him.'

'Well, mostly they sold to you.'

Hugh inclined his head. 'True. But it's no good crying about it, Sophie. That's business. And no matter how glorious the product – in Massot's case, sheer beauty – it's still, in the end, just business.'

'I don't think so,' Sophie said. 'Consider this. Massot was built up in one generation . . .'

'Two, if you count Pierre's uncle. Wasn't he a jeweller?'

'A jeweller and a watchmaker, but having one small *atelier* on the West Bank in the sixties is hardly an empire. Nothing happened until Pierre built Massot up.'

'Yes. The man sounds like a first-class weasel, but he knew his jewels,' Hugh conceded. 'And he had an impressively ruthless business style. I admit that.'

'And if he built up House Massot in one generation . . .' Sophie slipped off the chaise, and started to walk around the room. She was magnificent to watch, and he enjoyed it; the silk pooling around her long, slender frame, her eyes alight with enthusiasm, her hands gesticulating. 'Then why can't somebody else do it? Why can't somebody else do the same? Why not *us*?'

'Start a jewellery business?'

'House Montfort. Why not? The letter M seems to be in vogue in gems these days.' She was joking, but, he saw clearly, she was also quite serious. Sophie came back to him and grasped his hands. 'Look, Hugh.' She spoke urgently. 'You're a wonderful businessman. With an incredible record. You could get a loan. I'm sure investors would fall over themselves to lend you money. And my party, my redecoration – it got some press; I could design the showrooms for you.'

Hugh chuckled.

'You think it's a stupid idea?'

'Certainly not. I'm only laughing because I had planned on suggesting it to you.'

She beamed. 'You mean you want to? Start a company with me?'

'I certainly do.' He pulled her close and kissed her. 'A company. A marriage. A life. The works.'

Chapter Forty-Three

Judy had a plan. And it was a simple one.

Show Tom Massot a good time.

Show him *such* a good time that he'd forget his little student. Judy was inventive, in and out of bed; surprising him half-naked in his office, in the back of the stretch limo, skinny-dipping in the lake; and then cramming his nights with the finest Paris had to offer. The best new restaurants, the hottest exhibitions, the finest shows . . . she'd have dragged him to Disneyland Paris if she thought it'd do her any good. As it was, there had been that day trip shopping in Rome, and the private jet that took them to dinner in Gibraltar . . .

And it was working. Judy gave him such a dizzying array of outings, sex, food, even her own clothes . . . every day, she was a new woman. Like goddam Madonna. Age should not wither her infinite variety; not if Judy could help it. She was rising at six, before him, each day, and exercising like a maniac.

If there had been a repeat of the disastrous Polly phone call, Judy hadn't heard it. And even Katherine was less of a thorn in her side, because Tom and Judy were never at the château. Let her dine alone in the dower house, the old witch, and leave Judy be. She could have her ancient butler for company.

But . . . it sure was exhausting.

For a moment Judy felt an overpowering sense of weariness. Maybe if she took just *one* night off . . .

She dialled Tom's mobile.

'*Ici Thomas*,' he said. It struck Judy, briefly, that she felt no thrill of happiness on hearing his voice. Not like Pierre.

'Honey, I'm so sorry. Got to cancel on our date tonight.'

'Why, what's up?'

He didn't sound too upset. Judy wasn't sure if that was a good thing for her or a bad one.

'A combination of factors; work, and I think I'm just feeling a little burnt out. You know? I was thinking of going for a drink with some of the girls' – that was a joke, they all hated her – 'maybe getting a massage. Do you mind terribly?'

'Not at all. You have fun. I'll see you later.'

'What are you going to do tonight?'

There was that reedy note in her voice; damn it, she hated to sound whiny.

'I don't know.' Tom spoke carelessly. 'Maybe read a book. Call some mates from college. I've been losing touch with my old friends, it'll be good to catch up.'

Judy's stomach churned. She wished she hadn't asked.

'I think that's a great idea!' she said merrily. 'Just make sure you get enough rest. You're gonna need all your energy later.'

He chuckled. 'You're insatiable.'

'Always,' she said.

He hung up. Judy listened to the click and the dial tone, then slowly replaced the receiver. She looked round her office. There was work to be done, but she had no appetite for any of it. Judy felt sick. She closed the blinds on her door and curled miserably across her couch.

Tom put the phone down and was surprised at the extent of the relief he felt.

Judy was sexy, no doubt about that. And he'd been enjoying himself. But he was totally exhausted, and besides, he felt a bit guilty.

There was no future with Judy. He knew that now. All his energies had to be focused on House Massot.

That wasn't going so well right now.

Judy; well, he ought to break up with her. But she had given him the perfect excuse not to. It was never the right time, and the way things were going, the right time wouldn't arrive for months. Every day, some new pleasure; every night, that smooth, firm body slipping in between his sheets . . .

Tom felt guilty even thinking about it.

Well; he wasn't *technically* cheating. It wasn't as if he was back together with Polly. Not yet.

Tom just wanted to be, more than anything.

This is another opportunity, Tom thought. I must stop being a coward.

Ugly word, but accurate. Yes; he had been a coward. It was always so easy to say 'tomorrow'.

Well, no putting it off any more. He would wait for Judy to come home tonight and break the news, as gently as he knew how. There was somebody else . . . or should he just say things weren't working out?

I'm growing up, Tom thought, as he walked out of the front door, past his scowling butler. When Grandmother wasn't around, all the staff made faces at him. And who could blame him? Tom had not treated Maman well. Maybe she had made a mistake, maybe she had lowered herself in dating that pig, Lazard, but . . .

It was strange. Tom had imagined that all his problems would cease the day he ran Father's company. And yet, now he had everything he had wanted, even coveted – the company, the château, the girl – it seemed very empty. He'd rather be in a punt, on the Cherwell, or rolling around laughing at Polly, in her scruffy jeans and unfeminine sweatshirt. With Judy, he never laughed.

Or playing cards with Maman, who always lost.

She'd lost in the big game of cards, too.

Tom walked over to his eighteenth-century desk and retrieved his mother's letter from the secret drawer where he kept it stashed.

He missed her so much. It hurt so horribly. If he were honest, he was starting not to care she was staying with Montfort. Tom still wanted to see her, to wrap her up in a bear hug.

Those words – about always loving him.

For weeks now, they had kept him strong. Massot was a bloody disaster, let's face it, and Tom had no idea how to fix things. And Judy was exhausting. Katherine was back to her usual cold self . . .

Tom scanned the letter for the millionth time. He reread the line about Judy. Maybe Sophie did know something about her.

Well – that was one barrier between them that he *could* dismantle.

And Tom was going to do it. Tonight.

He would walk out to the orchard and see if any of the plums were ripe. When he was younger, Tom had loved going out there with Maman, hunting through the trees for those tell-tale signs of purple, pulling down the branches and trying to bat off the ones that were out of reach; stuffing the sun-drenched sweetness in his mouth, laughing while Maman tickled him . . .

No menopausal romances were going to change any of that.

The trees calmed him. The plums were still streaked with green, but he admired their beauty; it was late afternoon and a gloriously sunny day. Tom made a decision. He sat on a mossy stump, fished out his mobile, and called his mother.

'Hello?'

'Mum, it's me.' Tom realised he was using the Anglicism she preferred.

'Oh darling – darling Tom. It's so wonderful to hear from you. I love you, angel.'

'And I love you.' Tom was embarrassed to find he had a lump in his throat. 'We mustn't let this come between us, Mum. I – I'm sorry I threw you out of the house.'

'It's all right, darling. I understand you thought you were protecting Daddy.'

He didn't want to talk about that.

'Hugh never felt any personal enmity with your father. I promise. Will you give him a chance?'

'I'm going to break up with Judy,' Tom said. He wanted to change the subject.

'Oh, thank God.' Sophie heaved an audible sigh of relief. 'She wasn't right for you.'

'I agree. You see, I can see reason.' Already he felt a lot happier. 'It's always been you and me, Mum. I shouldn't have lost sight of that.'

'I can understand why you did.' His mother started to cry. 'Darling, I just want to see you. Shall I come back to Paris?'

'That'd be great,' Tom said, cheered. He didn't want to see Montfort, especially not in his own house. Plus, he didn't think he could spare any time away from House Massot and its sales meltdown.

'Then I'll be there tomorrow.' There was a hesitation. 'Tom – I've got some news. Do you think you can take it calmly?'

He laughed, despite himself. 'Oh Mum – this is going to be bad, isn't it?'

'I'm sure you'll think so at first. But promise me not to fly off the handle.'

Tom could hardly refuse. 'OK.'

'I've spent over a month here with Hugh. We – we're in love, darling. Last night he proposed to me.'

'And you accepted.'

'Yes.'

'And you were going to tell me – when?'

'I wanted you to call me. If you hadn't, in a day or so.'

The happiness of a few moments earlier seeped away from him. Tom thought of his father, and felt a black pit of despair come up from nowhere and engulf him. A chill wind blew through the plum orchard, and he shivered.

'I can't accept him, Mum.'

'I understand that. But you will.'

'Maybe you shouldn't come – right now.'

'Oh Tom!'

There was the disappointment in her voice. He struggled with himself.

'Look – I don't want you to see this bloke, much less marry him. I still think Papa might be alive.'

'Darling –'

'We won't get into that now. But I do know one thing. Even if you do marry him, I'll still love you. You'll always be my mum. And we'll see each other some time soon. Just – just not now.' A tear rolled down Tom's cheek, and he brushed it off, angrily, glad he was alone. 'That good enough?' he asked, gruffly. No way did he want his mother to hear his voice crack.

'Yes.' She was teary, too. 'Yes, sweetheart – my darling. That's fine, for now. I love you, Tom.'

'Me too, Mum,' Tom said, hanging up. Then he put his head in his hands, and surrendered to his private grief.

Judy sighed with relief. It had been a long and brutal day, and she was thankful to be turning into the long drive of the château. The last golden leaves of the oaks were tumbling to the ground; the real cold of winter was setting in, and she was looking forward to a hot bath and a blazing fire in the drawing room.

Tom had been being extra-polite lately. She was starting to feel hopeful on that front. All the humiliation would be worth it if she could come out of this as Mme Tom Massot.

Judy indulged in a pleasant little day-dream as the tyres of her Porsche crunched on the gravel of the château's drive. Yes. That was perfect. It was the way she'd finally be revenged on the lot of them. She'd marry the son, take over the business – Tom was supremely easy to do it to. Once the honeymoon period was over, she could do it, no problem.

Let that old bitch Katherine gnash her teeth; she'd be dead soon, anyway.

No more humiliation. No more being the loser in love.

Judy was sick of second place.

I'm going to do it, she told herself. I'm going to make him propose. It's going to happen tonight.

Judy walked up to the steps of the porch, and the large walnut door swung open; that butler, whose name she could not recall, bowed to her.

'Good evening, madam,' he said in perfect English.

She nodded back, coolly. Yes. This was the life.

'M. Massot is waiting for you in the drawing room, madam. He asked if you would join him for a cocktail.'

How charming. Judy deigned to turn and smile at the butler.

'Why thank you,' she said, sweetly.

She normally didn't speak to the staff. After all, she was hardly on their level. But Judy made an exception for the bearers of good news.

She crossed the marble floor of the hallway, pausing to fluff out her new hairdo; fifty euros for a wash and blow-dry at Jean Phillippe's, Paris's latest hot hair salon, and worth every cent. After a horrid day at the office, Judy always stopped by. She wanted to look absolutely fresh for Tom, at her best, every night. No exceptions.

The rear-view mirror had offered reassurance on the way home; her lips in that sexy fire-engine red, matching nails, a bold scarlet dress, and black Manolos, with a chunky gold bracelet from one of the Mayberry collections. Her dark hair curled at the nape of her neck. Judy gave herself a little shake, and pushed down on the brass handle.

Ah . . . perfect.

It was the scene of her dreams. There was indeed a blazing fire crackling and hissing in the eighteenth-century hearth; the curtains, antique orange silk fringed with gold thread, were drawn against the cold; and the shadows of the furniture danced round the walls lined with books.

Tom was standing by the polished mahogany table. It was set with cut-glass decanters and tumblers, a silver bucket of ice with tongs, and slices of lemon and lime.

He looked frighteningly like Pierre. And yet, not. Too young, too green. Judy was never satisfied with Tom; he couldn't rouse her like Pierre had done. Oh, he looked the same, but the fire was never there; the dominance; the total control . . . as the young girl, the hero-worshipping mistress, Judy had looked up to Pierre Massot, and he'd been able to bend her however he wanted. Now, with Tom, she was the one doing the manipulating . . . she was in charge . . .

It wasn't sexy. It wasn't love. It was like sickly sweet methadone, instead of heroin. And Tom could never get her high . . .

But he was still Tom *Massot*. The riches were his. The castle was his. The jewels. The *name* . . .

The last vestiges of tension drained from her body. She flashed him a come-on smile.

'Hey, Tom,' she drawled. 'A drink would be perfect. It's like you read my mind, baby.' Judy strutted across the room

405

towards him. 'It's been a rough day. I can't stand those bastards.' She shook her head to display her fluffy hair to best advantage; the salon made it look like a Timotei commercial.

'I'm sorry to hear that.' He sounded a little nervous, and a jolt of electricity shot through her. Was he about to pop the question? 'What will you have?'

'No alcohol; I'll just take some juice.' She stuck out the tip of her tongue and licked her lips.

He silently poured out a tumblerful of the fresh orange juice; it came from the château's own orangery and it was utterly perfect. Judy took the tumbler gratefully, and chinked it against his glass of whisky.

'A toast,' she announced, 'to—'

'Judy. Wait.' Tom glanced at the door. 'Is that closed?'

'Absolutely.' She winked. 'We're private here. Why, did you want to christen the room? I think we've had sex most everywhere else . . .'

Tom swallowed. 'Yes – and it was wonderful. I – I've got something to say to you, though.'

Oh shit. It's going to happen.

Judy couldn't stop the smile, although she tried to.

'Go on, Tom,' she said. 'Go on, honey.'

'Judy – you're a wonderful person,' Tom said. 'And we've had a lot of fun together. And – I'm fond of you.' The last wasn't strictly true any more, but it was a white lie. 'But this relationship isn't going anywhere. I think for both our sakes that we should break up. You'll need to move out, so if you want I can have the staff pack your cases.' He ploughed on. 'It just wouldn't be fair to waste your time.'

Judy was staring at him with a rage he had not thought possible.

'I'm sorry,' he finished lamely.

She threw the juice in his face. It splashed all over Tom's suit, ruining it; his eyes stung.

'You fucking bastard,' Judy said. 'Just like your father.'

'Leave my father out of this,' he said coldly.

Judy laughed; high-pitched and manic.

'So that's it?' she demanded. 'That's what I get? Six months of being screwed by an inferior little prick, then thank you and goodbye? Packed out of the house, with nothing to show for it?'

'Not all love affairs end in marriage. You knew that.'

At least he hadn't assumed she meant a pay-off. But fuck him, Judy thought, infuriated.

'I knew I trusted you. I knew you asked me to move here. I thought that meant something.'

'It meant I wanted your company.'

'Oh, sure.' She laughed bitterly. 'You wanted a convenience. A girl to hand. And now you think you don't need me, I'm out. On the trash heap.'

'Let's be adult about this, Judy.'

'Adult? You're a whiny little brat. You sold Massot for nothing. You're not your father, Tom. You're a pale fucking imitation. No fire in the belly. No guts.'

That stung.

'Again, I will ask you not to mention my father,' Tom said flatly. 'You hardly knew him. You are not qualified to comment, Judy. You're not a member of this family.'

That last one had her screaming. Judy heard her own voice, wild and high. But she didn't care. All she saw was Tom – looking like Pierre – casting her out, dumping her, demeaning her.

You're not a member of this family.

'I am,' she screeched. 'I am a member of your *precious* little family! And I always will be! There's nothing you can do about it – nothing at all!'

She saw the look of horror and disgust on his face as the implication sank in. And she loathed him for it.

'That's right, you piece of shit,' Judy said. 'I'm pregnant. I'm carrying your goddam *baby*.'

Chapter Forty-Four

I have to shake this off!

Tom told himself that almost a thousand times an hour, but it did no good. He'd got up in the morning, and the nightmare was still there.

His baby. Judy's baby.

Tethered for life to an older woman his mother hated and he couldn't stand.

He had no idea what to do.

Or what the hell he'd tell Sophie.

So, he'd try to put it off. Taking over Massot had been an utter disaster. Tom's ideas for reviving sales had been disastrous. Nobody liked his cost-cutting in the sales room; there were mass resignations of key staff; he had no idea how to recruit; negative press was flooding in and the Brandts, the design leaders, had quit. His testing of replacements wasn't going too well. And the accountants wanted a lot of answers . . .

He knew he was in over his head. The shiny corner office was one thing. Knowing how to use it was another.

'Celine!' he shouted. 'Could you bring me another cup of coffee?'

His secretary popped her head round the door and raised her eyebrows.

'Another, monsieur?'

'Believe me. The jitters can't get any worse.'

'I'll make a decaf,' she said, rolling her eyes.

Mayberry stock was sinking. And the meltdown at Massot was a huge part of it. Tom pushed a hand through his hair, sweating. The stress was unbelievable. It was only nine-thirty and already he wanted a drink.

His door opened.

'That was quick,' Tom said.

But it wasn't Celine. And he knew instantly that this shitty day was about to get much, much worse.

'Hi, kid,' said Pete Stockton.

Stockton was as blunt as he was unpleasant. He stank of sweat, a stench that was only partially disguised by the sickly sweet smoke from his Cuban cigar.

'You don't look so pleased to see me.'

'Hi, Pete.' Tom sounded calmer than he felt. 'Don't call me kid.'

'Oooh.' The pudgy slob rolled his eyes. 'Big talk from a guy that's about to get canned.'

'What?'

'Canned. Fired. Sacked. *Au revoir,*' Stockton gloated. 'Ain't that how they say it in Frog?'

'You can't fire me, Pete. We have an agreement –'

'Had. An agreement. Now I've got your shares I really don't need you. And to be frank, nor does anyone else. Specially not my shareholders. I'm taking this job away from you and giving it to a real expert. Continuity, that's what they want.'

'Giving it to whom, exactly?'

Pete Stockton grinned. 'Your mom's old pal. Gregoire Lazard. I'm reinstating him and giving him your office. Poetic justice, since it was a Massot who canned him. Don't you think so?'

Tom flushed with anger. 'You can't. I have it in writing. I become Chairman and Chief . . .'

'Yada yada yada.' Stockton described a circle in the air with his Monte Cristo. 'Need to read your contracts a little better, kid. Said I'd make you Chairman. Didn't say for how long. Got to fire you; stock's down almost seven per cent. To be honest, though, would have done it even if the stock went up.'

'Why?' spluttered Tom.

'Don't like you. Privileged little brat, never had to work for it. Snooty Eurotrash. You and Montfort and your hoity-toity mom. That uptight old maid nearly got me fired.

409

Refusing to sell. I tell you,' Stockton chuckled, his chins wobbling, 'she wouldn't have made a rookie mistake like you. Guess that's what you get for selling Mommie dearest down the river!'

Tom didn't hesitate. His fist lashed out and caught Stockton in the temple.

'Ahhhh – FUCK YOU! I'll fucking sue! I'll – aaaaahhhhhh!'

Tom's left foot had swept up neatly and kicked him in the balls. Stockton squealed and toppled over, clutching at the table.

Celine had been listening outside the door. She opened it, and stared at Tom, wide-eyed.

'Call the police! Call the goddamned police!' Stockton shrieked.

'Why, monsieur?' said Celine quickly. 'Then they'll arrest you, for I saw you assault M. Massot, completely unprovoked.'

'Bless you, Celine.'

'And I quit. I don't want to work for a man like that,' she said, then held the door open for Tom as he followed her out.

'You didn't have to quit for me,' Tom said gratefully.

She looked at him coolly.

'I didn't. I heard what he said about Mme Massot. She was an amazing woman to work for.' Celine looked at him with disapproval. 'You were wrong to dismiss her, monsieur. She was brilliant.'

Tom sighed.

'Mme Sophie inspired everybody here. If you want to understand why people quit, that is the reason. She was the difference. She was good with the staff. She understood jewels. She understood beauty.'

'And I didn't.'

'No, you didn't.' Celine was firm. 'But you might have been able to learn.'

Stockton's moans rose up from behind the closed door.

'He's crying,' Tom observed.

'Like all bullies, he is a coward.' Celine sniffed. 'I'm going home.'

'Can I drive you somewhere?'

'I have a car. Tell me, M. Massot, did Madame explain to you about Judy Dean?'

Tom froze. 'She told me she didn't approve.'

'Nothing more?'

'Is there something more?'

Celine considered a long moment.

'*Non,*' she said finally. 'It is not my place. But take my advice, monsieur. Call your mother. There is much, I think, you have to learn from her. And not just about diamonds.'

Chapter Forty-Five

'Nothing will change his mind, darling.' Hugh put an arm around her shoulders – there wasn't much else he could do. 'Nothing but time. I'll speak to him, but I think he needs a little distance.'

'Yes.' Sophie stared, dry-eyed, at the Alps, rising beautifully above them. She hadn't actually cried since Monday. That was something.

'And don't forget that it wasn't like last time. He said he loved you.'

She nodded. 'That is true. But it's so frustrating – my own son thinks I'm betraying Pierre. Not the other way round.'

'Then just tell him the truth.'

'You know I can't.'

Hugh was silent. He agreed; Sophie could not expose the father's mendacity and contempt for marriage to the son. The boy loved a dream, and the Sophie he knew would never take that away from him. It was that strength of character that proved to Hugh how right, how perfectly and utterly right he was to love her.

'In which case, our plan is the right one. Your old priest, he's fairly canny.'

'You would say that.' He was gladdened to note a very small smile. 'Because you just want to get me into bed . . .'

Hugh, never religious, thought some God-talk had been called for. After all, as much as he loved her, Hugh was the obstacle between Sophie and her Tom. He couldn't help that, and watching Sophie cry was impossible.

Hugh had been surprised, pleasantly so, at his meeting with

Fr Sabin. The priest, wearing a splendidly ratty nightgown, had ushered them in to his overcrowded, messy little cottage. He had pumped Hugh's hand, patted Sophie lightly on the back and then forced a large brandy on her. He wasn't maudlin, and didn't offer platitudes. Instead, Fr Sabin suggested applying to his bishop to waive the six months.

'I have, after all, been your spiritual director for the last sixteen years,' he said, adding dryly, 'and for the most part, you haven't given me concern.'

Fr Sabin had then fixed Hugh with a warning eye. Hugh felt a bit guilty; it was as if the chap could see into his bedroom. He coughed.

'I can instruct you on marriage, tomorrow, myself. The primary requirement for you, M. Montfort, is that you agree to bring the children up Catholic.'

'If we have any,' he'd been surprised to hear himself say, 'why not?'

Hugh didn't believe. But he wanted to. It would be nice, in the end, to have hope. To think he might see Georgie again, and his baby . . .

And if there *were* children, by some miracle, Hugh wanted them to have hope, too.

'But the wedding – Tom won't come,' Sophie said miserably.

'My dear child, Thomas won't attend in any case. As your priest, I advise you to make the commitment before God, and continue on with your lives. It's while he thinks he can stop this marriage that Thomas will be most opposed. After you're wed, he'll have to live with it. In my judgement, marrying sooner, rather than later, is your best chance to reconcile with your son.'

Sophie nodded, and stopped crying. Hugh took her back to the hotel. The priest had been shrewd. Perhaps faith in God wasn't just for the credulous and the cowardly.

Hugh was pleased it was going to be a church wedding; but mostly, he was just glad that Sophie was going to be his.

'This is it.' Sophie's voice pulled him from his thoughts. 'Wengen.' She clutched at him. 'Oh, Hugh. It's so exciting.'

And, he realised, it was.

'Come in, come in, please.' Heinrich Brandt bowed and smiled, and Gertrud clucked around them, taking Sophie's fur coat and hanging it in their cloakroom. 'You are very welcome. Coffee? Schnapps?'

'Coffee would be terrific,' Hugh said. It had been a long day, and he wanted to be sharp.

'It is so good to see you again, Frau Massot,' Heinrich said. His old eyes sparkled, and Hugh thought he meant it. 'You are most welcome in our home. Do you like it?'

Sophie glanced around; it was a luxurious modern chalet, furnished, rather incongruously, with every kind of modern gadget. There was a Japanese-style waterfall in one corner of the sitting room, a huge gas fire with the effect of true flames, and a flat screen modern TV on one wall.

'It looks very comfortable,' she said, truthfully.

'Ach, we're getting old. We need to be warm, these days; we need soft edges, and baths that are easy to get out of. You helped us afford this. And later, we can get a nurse to come, whenever we wish.' Heinrich pumped Sophie's hand again, enthusiastically. 'You helped us afford all this, Frau Massot. It's a wonderful deal for us. And the pieces for the party, they helped, no?'

'We saw pictures,' Gertrud chimed in. 'Of the new stores.' She clapped her hands, like a child. 'Beautiful . . . finally, the pieces, the jewels, are displayed as they deserve. And people notice. *Vielen, vielen Dank*—'

'But I am forgetting my manners.' Herr Brandt bowed to Hugh. 'Herr Montfort, you are welcome here, also. If Mme Massot trusts you . . .'

He didn't sound wildly enthusiastic.

'Thank you, sir. May I sit down?'

Hugh was waved to a seat; Sophie sat with him on a low-slung leather couch, which he found uncomfortable. On the other hand, Frau Brandt's coffee was delicious; strong, and with a hint of cardamom. The Brandts nestled together opposite them, across a table of smoked glass; Hugh saw them clutching each other's withered hands, and hoped that he and Sophie

414

would wind up like that; other than the décor, perhaps, it was an engaging picture.

'We have come to make you a business proposal,' he said.

'I feared as much.'

Sophie and Hugh exchanged glances.

'The answer is no, Herr Montfort.'

'I see. May I ask why?'

The old man shook his head. 'I have taken to reading the papers, sir, in the last couple of years. I have read of you, and your firm. And I have seen pictures of some of the . . . *pieces,*' he added disdainfully. 'You will excuse me, but Gertrud and I do not wish to be involved in selling – forgive me – such ugliness. There are many women in the world today who do not even know what a parure is, who will wear tin alloys that masquerade as gold . . .'

'Some of those necklaces were made of *chicken wire,*' Gertrud added, appalled. 'Really, Mr Montfort – how could you sell such things?'

Hugh was slightly taken aback. They made it sound as if he'd been selling drugs.

'I wanted to make money,' he said flatly. 'And I divorced my job from my personal taste in jewellery, such as it is. Mayberry reflected my wish to make money for my shareholders, some of them pensioners relying on dividend income.'

They seemed unconvinced. But he was relaxing; this was, after all, a meeting, and meetings were what he was good at.

'My personal taste and yours may differ,' he said. 'My home, for example, uses more antiques . . .'

Gertrud giggled, a little shamefacedly.

'We used to have more antiques, but now we want comfort,' she said. 'But never does it hurt our jewels, Mr Montfort.'

'And my own taste there is entirely the same as yours. In fact, I believe that you are the pre-eminent artists working in stones and precious metals today.'

'We are,' Heinrich said simply. 'There is no question.'

Hugh bowed slightly. 'When I wanted to buy House Massot I visited the showrooms that Sophie had redesigned. I knew of the quality of your designs, of course, but once I saw them

415

properly displayed, I was entranced. I bought a piece myself, even though I took a significant risk that my doing so would make it into the business press, and hurt my bid. And even though' – his eyes slid towards Sophie – 'I had no woman in my life to give it to.'

Their eyes lit up with interest.

'Which piece?' Heinrich asked.

'An aigrette, a homage to the Tiffany piece.'

'I remember,' he said. 'That was quite lovely.'

'I thought so. I paid almost a hundred thousand euros for it.'

'And you have never regretted the purchase,' he said, proudly.

Hugh smiled. 'Indeed, I never have. And it is that level of beauty – or something approximating it – which I wish to sell.'

'We are to start a company,' Sophie said, 'which will make multiple pieces, lines of jewellery, using the more inexpensive but natural stones, and which will sell only classic designs. There will not be any white or rose gold used, or any platinum or titanium; we will make purely traditional pieces. Of course, they will not be as perfect as the aigrette. But I want to bring fine, classic jewels to those who cannot afford the prices of House Massot.'

'We are preparing our financing,' Hugh added. 'And we wish you to be the chief designers; to design the signature collections and to train the younger designers who we will hire, at your direction.'

They glanced at each other.

'Mr Montfort, we are getting old.'

'Mme Massot, you have provided for us so well, to live in our old age . . . we are looking forward to our retirement . . .'

'But aren't you still employed at House Massot?'

'You are joking, no?' Heinrich's old faced creased further in disgust. 'We resigned, madame. As soon as we heard you were forced out.'

'And not only us. Mlle Claudette Chiron, and Edouard Peguy, they also resigned. Mr Stockton cut salaries for the staff –'

'They are moving Mayberry collections in with House Massot.'

'They are trying to sack many of the expensive Massot designers. Lillian Brooks, they fire her . . .'

'If you wish, you could hire Mrs Brooks, if you work for us. We would only give you a budget. The design, the materials, everything would be sourced through you.'

'I love jewellery,' Sophie said passionately. 'When it's truly beautiful. And it's a dying art. If you work for us now – for a year, maybe two – you can train the next generation, you can ensure that your work will survive.'

'And meanwhile, we will see to it that you get the credit you deserve. For too long, you have toiled in anonymity. Our first collection would be entitled "The Brandt Designs".' Hugh was extemporising, but he saw the excitement on their faces. He ploughed on. 'I will arrange a private exhibition at an exclusive London gallery. And we will invite the world's press.'

'Like your party to relaunch House Massot?' Gertrud asked Sophie, timidly.

Sophie smiled. 'Bigger, far bigger. That was only a practice run.'

'Give me two years,' Hugh asked them. 'And I will give you two million dollars, US, plus five per cent of the profit of the company.' He gestured at the room. 'If you like this, you could buy more of them. Or hire some servants, perhaps. Be waited on hand and foot.'

'Servants!' Heinrich spluttered. But Montfort saw the idea appealed to him.

'Why not? You have laboured all your lives and for an inadequate reward. You are comfortable now, certainly. But why not work just a little longer and go out in a blaze of glory? Why not become truly rich? And all the while, allowing ordinary women to wear truly fine jewels. We will not be another Tiffany; we will make unique, elegant gems that do not look as though they rolled from a production line.'

'I . . .' Heinrich licked his lips. 'Will you excuse us?'

Sophie nodded. He rose, slowly, from his couch, holding out a hand to Gertrud; the two of them shuffled into the open-plan kitchen.

Hugh held his breath. It was odd; while he was waiting to

find out if Sophie could love him, the jewellery business had held no fascination, but now that she was his, it was consuming him.

Was it healthy? Perhaps not; he had first been drawn by the need to obliterate his grief. Now Montfort wanted revenge. He kept replaying Pete Stockton's gloating as he barked that Hugh was fired. He read the *Wall Street Journal* and the *Financial Times*, and he watched the steady drip-drip-drip of articles chronicling the decline of Mayberry. Bad press. Nasty blind items. Shareholder flight. The stock, slowly but inexorably declining. The almost visible loss of confidence.

It angered him. So many years of hard, brutally hard work. All those long flights to Tokyo, all those months courting De Beers in South Africa. Montfort had built Mayberry. He had revived a dull, profitless little brand and made its shareholders rich. It had taken careful strategy, ruthless acquisition, trimming the fat and laying workers off. And in the process it had revolutionised an industry.

Now, something so trivial as a personal jealousy would destroy it. Pete Stockton was about to drive two formerly profitable houses into the ground.

Montfort wanted to punish the man. He wanted to avenge Sophie, and Tom, for her sake. And he was also tired of being number two. In fact, these days he was slightly ashamed that he had ever worked for any company in which he did not have a majority stake.

He wanted his own house. And the Brandts were key.

They came back into the sitting room. He was relieved to see they were smiling.

'Six per cent, Mme Massot, and you have a deal.'

Sophie glanced at Hugh. He nodded.

'Deal,' he said. 'Let's go to work.'

Chapter Forty-Six

'Beautiful,' he said. He bent and kissed the hand of his bride. 'Don't you think so, Natasha?'

Natasha struggled with the cruel question. He smiled at her; he enjoyed watching her squirm. There were tears in her eyes, and she was biting down on her lip as she forced a smile.

'Yes, Pyotr,' she half whispered. 'I do.'

Good. She was still obedient. He intended to test her. So far she had not strayed. She called him by his new name, Pyotr; it amused him to slip from one identity to another as he left his old life behind. She had led him to her relatives, and stuck to the story he'd fed her; Natasha had wanted to escape, and Pyotr had selflessly offered to help her; he had sacrificed all his own wealth on the altar of her desire.

Of course, her relatives in Espoo had welcomed Pytor with open arms. Especially the grandmother, Katerina. Natasha was her favourite granddaughter, and she cooed and billed over Pyotr.

He was a saviour.

He was a hero.

And he was the favoured suitor for Natasha's niece, Aud.

Natasha's brother, Sven, had married a French girl from Nîmes, come back to Finland, and prospered. After the war, the French nation was desperate to pick up the pieces of their shattered lives, and one way to do it was to return, after rations and austerity, to glorious cooking. Marianne had relatives in the restaurant trade, and Sven made a fine living shipping Finnish delicacies – fresh fish, smoked meats, fermented honey. The entire family bought a large suburban house with a plot of garden. They owned a colour television and an American car. Sven supported his grandmother, his ageing father, Alfred, and one plump, plain daughter.

He had called her 'Aud' after the great foundress of Iceland, Aud the deep-minded. Alas, the name was no more appropriate than Helen of Troy would have been. Aud was simple and boring. She helped her father in his store, showed no desire to attend college, and seemed to have no ambitions other than to get an extra helping of pudding every night.

Sven tried to love his daughter. He had no idea why she had not turned out like Marianne, his stylish wife, or his long-lost sister Natasha, the passionate one who had eloped to Estonia with a rich banker so many years ago; both of them women who had been prepared to enter whole new worlds for love, to cast off the familiar and leap into the darkness. Aud just stood around, gaining weight and owlishly squinting at the television. She showed no interest in dressing up, or flirting with boys. For all her docility, Aud had an instinctive grasp of one thing; she was not attractive, and she would never be attractive. She gave up men as a bad job and dedicated herself to helping her father.

All Sven wanted was for his only child to show some spark of life. Often, he felt like shaking her. Sometimes, he felt like shaking his wife. He was nothing like this. Where could Aud's bad genes have come from?

And then came the night his life, and Aud's, changed for ever.

It was cold; pitch-black, the way October nights in Espoo often are. He woke, frightened, clutching his warm woollen blankets to his chest. A nightmare? No; he realised there was a thunderous banging on the door.

The police. Someone was dead. His store had been burned down. Heart pounding, he pushed his wife away from him as she reached out to clutch at his nightshirt, tugged on his boots and raced down the stairs. Aud had crept out of her bedroom; she watched from the landing as Sven wrenched open the door.

'Sven, let us in.' It was a plaintive cry. 'I'm so cold. So cold . . .'

He stared. But the sight that met his eyes did not alter. There were two figures shaking with cold on his doorstep, their lips blue in the light of the street-lamps. One of them was a skinny, pale young man in a soaking wet fur coat, his eyes dark and wild. The second of them was his sister.

'My God!' he said. 'My God, Tasha! You're alive – you're here!'

Her teeth chattered. Sven pulled her to him in a bear hug, then almost recoiled. Her body was freezing, and there were crystals of ice in her hair.

'Aud!' he roared. 'Marianne! Get down here. Aud, lay the fire. And then draw a bath. Marianne, get some roast elk and my bottle of whisky. Hurry!'

As he hugged Natasha, the pale young man slipped quietly inside the house and shut the door. He looked up at Aud and said, in perfect Finnish, 'Make that bath barely lukewarm, or we will get chilblains. The fire must wait until we have thawed.'

Sven's mouth opened, then closed again. The man looked like a drowned ferret, his skin was pale with the chill, and his eyes horribly red from lack of sleep. But he spoke with such confidence he could have been the Mayor condescending to pay Sven a visit.

'Who are you?' he muttered.

Tasha looked nervously at the stranger, who held her gaze coolly. He answered staring into her eyes, not even looking at Sven. It was not until a year later that Sven would recall that moment as odd.

'My name is Pyotr Vladekvich,' he said.

There had never been such a night in his household. His father and grandmother had never thought to see Tasha again. They were overwhelmed with joy, weeping and hugging Natasha, blessing Pyotr and the gods that had driven him to make such a desperate attempt. As she recounted the tale of their escape to her family, Pyotr announced that he would take the first bath. Sven was sure the water must have hurt, with the man close to hypothermia, but no sound came from the room. He brought fresh clothes for his guest – his own best suit and shirt

– and announced that he would shop to buy him a wardrobe tomorrow.

The man emerged, looking four sizes too small for Sven's clothes, yet somehow neat and defying laughter. He said a quiet word to Tasha, and she instantly tore herself from her father and grandmother and followed him to the bathroom. Marianne selected a warm nightgown and robe for her, and fleece-lined slippers, then busied herself in the kitchen, delighted to see her husband so happy. Despite their good fortune, Sven always missed his sister, and then there was a cloud over their daughter's prospects. He had not smiled much lately. Here, in the world's far north, winter was a serious business, and it was hard to find nuggets of joy in the long darkness. But tonight, with their guests in warm clothing, there would be a fire, and wine, and whisky from Scotland, rare roast meat, and warm baked potatoes . . .

The family settled around the fire. Marianne served them on their laps. Tasha told the story, her teeth still now, sipping gratefully at the whisky, one eye on the blazing fire as though it were the most beautiful thing she had ever seen. How her husband had started to drink, then to beat her, and finally had threatened murder. How Pyotr, a merchant from the market square, had challenged him when he hit her. How the banker had threatened to call for the secret police. Escape had been their only option, and without papers there was only one way; to buy an old-fashioned sleigh, take what supplies they could and a pack of dogs, and set out on the long, wretched journey across the frozen wastes to Finland.

North from Estonia on the train, with stolen money, bargaining and arguing in small, no-account towns for dried fish and meat, furs and rosehips, dried for their vitamin C. A gun battle when a local red army captain asked the wrong questions. Risking imprisonment and torture, and even death in the snow; and lastly, making the attempt, days and nights lashing at the huskies, gnawing on tough, half-frozen food, cutting the carcass of one dead dog to feed to the pack, the brutal cold that they thought would kill them, overnight, huddling with the remaining animals under the fur coat; and at last, though they'd thought they must die, reaching Finland – and freedom.

Selling the dogs, for a pittance; their kopecks and roubles no good here. Hiking and scavenging their way to Espoo, praying – as Natasha said with tears – that somebody could tell them of Sven, and his family. And now she and her young saviour, who had risked his own life to bring her to freedom were here – it was a dream –

Katerina and Alfred were sobbing, Sven was wiping his eyes, Marianne clapping her hands. But Aud said nothing. She had shrunk back into the background after laying the fire.

Pyotr, Sven recalled, was gazing at her; gazing at her as though he had never seen anything more beautiful. And as Sven watched in amazement, his daughter had lowered her eyes, shyly, then glanced back up in Pyotr's direction. And then she did something she very rarely did, indeed never other than at mealtimes.

She smiled.

Even in the midst of his joy at Tasha's safe return, and his fascination with the harrowing tale of her flight across the Steppes, Sven had not been able to stop the mundane hope that flared instantly in his heart. It was a straw – how could a man like Pyotr, a death-defying Russian adventurer, ever be interested in his lumpen pudding of a daughter?

'So, Tasha, Pyotr,' he asked. 'The two of you – are you now to marry, are you in love?'

Pyotr answered immediately, again, his gaze steady on Sven's sister.

'No,' he said. 'Natasha and I are only friends. I did my duty by her as a Christian. She is still wed in the eyes of God, and besides, there is the wide difference in our ages. We will remain friends. Indeed, Natasha tells me it is her dearest wish to see me happily married.' He smiled at Tasha. 'Is that not so, my dear?'

She hesitated only a second before responding. 'It is, Pyotr . . . my dearest wish.'

My God, Sven thought. How ill she looks . . . how grey . . . As though she were still cold.

'Here, Tasha,' he said. 'Have some more meat – you need iron.'

Tasha shook her head. 'I – I'm not hungry,' she said. A moment before she had been ravenous. Perhaps her stomach had shrunk from her ordeal, and now she was full, Sven thought. 'I'm tired,' she said. 'So tired. . . . In fact, I think I'll go to bed . . .'

'Of course, my dear.' Marianne clucked over her like a chicken. 'You shall take our bed, Sven and I will sleep on the couch until something better can be found.' She glanced at Pyotr. 'My dear Pyotr, I don't know quite where we can put you . . .'

'There's a couch in my room, Mama.' Aud spoke up, startling her mother. 'Mr Vladekvich can sleep there.'

'Thank you.' Pyotr lifted his eyes to hers, and with astonishment, Sven thought he saw interest there. 'That's very kind of you, Aud.'

Maybe more. Maybe . . . desire.

Oh please, dear Lord, he prayed. Let it be so, and I will never cheat my taxes again. Or gamble, or drink vodka in the mornings. Grant me this one wish. Let my daughter marry!

'Yes,' Natasha said. She smiled brightly, but there was a false note in her voice. Sven wondered what was wrong with his sister. Alas, ever since her return from behind the Iron Curtain she had been acting strangely. Going for long walks in the cold, or spending entire days shut upstairs in her room; Alfred had moved into Katerina's room when the old woman died in the spring. Sven was afraid Tasha's brain was addled.

'She looks very pretty,' she said, in her flat monotone.

'Indeed she does. You are a princess, Aud, my darling,' Sven cried. He clapped Pyotr on the back. 'And you, my boy – you are a lucky dog, to be stealing away my daughter.'

'I know.' Pyotr smiled back. 'I can never repay you for this gift, Sven.'

There was a lump in his throat and his eyes misted over. It was the other way round – completely, Sven thought, guiltily. It was he who owed Pyotr, for the incredible, unexpected joy of seeing his daughter like this. About to be married. And transformed by joy and love.

Secretly, her father admitted to himself that 'princess' and 'beautiful' were overdoing it. But Aud had changed. In the winter that Pyotr had moved in, she had bloomed under his interest. She had lost her appetite, and gained an interest in dresses and make-up. She had struggled to join conversations, and talked with wild enthusiasm about travelling the world. Sometimes her lack of knowledge made Sven wince, like when she spoke of how Russia had joined the Nazis in the war. But Pyotr never made fun of her, even if his own sister could not resist the odd cruel remark.

He made excuses for Tasha. She had been through a lot. And she had brought him Pyotr, pale and skinny and without a cent to his name; but he had been as good as Prince Charming to Sven.

Aud had lost weight. Aud was lively, talkative, and full of laughter. It was as though a stone had rolled from Sven's back. He caught some local boys whistling after her once, in the spring, as she stepped out in a new dress Marianne had imported from France. He scolded them, but he had exulted in his heart. His daughter wasn't made magically bright, or beautiful, but she was normal.

Normal was all he had ever asked for.

And his longed-for son-in-law had more than this to recommend him. In exchange for food and board, he had offered his services to Sven's business. It was transformed in a mere matter of months. Over the winter, Pyotr burned up the telephone lines. He contacted fresh customers, arranged discounts on shipping, even bought up the business of Guthmund Ejilsson, long a thorn in Sven's side. New accounts and orders appeared overnight. Pyotr was a ruthless, even callous negotiator, and Sven stepped back to allow him to play hardball. It was a wise decision. Money had flooded in, and he was about to buy a nice house in a new neighbourhood, closer to Helsinki. Espoo wasn't big enough for Sven now.

He paid Pyotr, of course, but apart from new suits and shoes, Pyotr had saved every penny. He wanted a place of his own, he told Sven. He wanted to be able to support a family. This, with a loving glance at Aud, who gazed adoringly back.

When the engagement was announced, Sven had proudly presented Pyotr with a dowry. Ten thousand American dollars. It was a huge sum of money, enough to keep his daughter in style. Aud had clapped and squealed, and Pyotr had shaken his hand, warmly, and told him that this would be the foundation of everything he was to become. He said he was destined for great things. And Sven believed him.

He looked at his daughter, now, dressed in that long, white dress, a medium size – she wasn't even fat – with a short white veil and a diamante tiara in her hair, and he smiled. He did not think he'd ever see her looking so beautiful ever again.

And he was right.

They were married at St Stephen's chapel, the Lutheran parish he occasionally attended, with family and a few friends from the business. Aud clutched a small bouquet of red roses – imported from European hothouses, but she deserved the best – and Pyotr wore a dark suit. He had asked Natasha to be matron of honour. She was very striking in her red sheath, dark hair piled on top of her head, but Sven thought she looked old and drawn; there was that manic air about her. To contrast with Aud, she carried a bouquet of white roses; Sven saw that Tasha clutched them hard around the thorny stems, and tiny droplets of blood studded her pale hands. When Pyotr kissed Aud at the minister's invitation, he thought Tasha swayed on her feet. Was she thinking of her own husband? Was it relief her niece had finally got herself a man?

The unpleasant thought occurred to him that perhaps Tasha was jealous. But surely not. She had never said a word. And besides, just as Pyotr had pointed out, he was far too young for Natasha. If she were to remarry, it would need to be someone her own age.

Sven found comfort in that reflection.

It was barely a week later that Pyotr said at the dinner table that he had an announcement.

'It's time for us to be off. Aud and I are going to live in France. Every family needs its independence. I'm sure you're desperate to be rid of us anyway.'

This provoked a storm of protest. Marianne cried, Alfred mumbled something about staying together, and Sven shook his head and tried to sound convincing.

In fact, he thought it would be an excellent idea if Pyotr and Aud went to France. Pyotr's financial skills could be put to better use at the import end of the business. And to tell the truth, Sven was sick of living in a house with five adults. He wanted a little peace and quiet in his prosperous middle years. If Pyotr wanted to move to France, preferably the sunny south, Sven and Marianne could come and visit their grandchildren during Finland's brutal winter.

'Aud's a French citizen through you, Marianne, and as her husband I have now obtained a passport.' Pyotr reached into his pocket and produced the slim, leather-clad document.

'That was fast,' Marianne said.

Indeed. Sven was not surprised. Pyotr was the type to make plans and act swiftly on them.

'We leave tomorrow.'

Marianne set up a wail, but Pyotr did not respond. Aud awkwardly patted her mother on the back.

'Long goodbyes are worse,' she said. 'I'll call you, Mother – I'll call you as soon as we dock.'

'We sail at dawn,' Pyotr said. 'No need to accompany us to the harbour.' His voice was strangely remote; even cold, Sven remembered later. 'I hate scenes.'

'It's better for me to call you,' Aud said again. 'Looking to the future, not the past.' She gazed adoringly at her husband. 'Pyotr and I want to go somewhere warm, buy a house and start working on your grandchildren.'

Sven was glad to see this last comment provoked smiles from his wife and father. Aud hugged everybody tearfully, and he brought out a bottle of champagne.

'But I'll drive you to the port,' he said. 'You'll have cases. And the taxis are unreliable.'

'We're not taking anything except a change of clothes. I

believe in travelling light. The less baggage the better.' Pyotr glanced at Natasha, who had sat silently at the foot of the table, staring at her hands. 'And Natasha has already agreed to drive us. She's up early in the mornings anyway.'

'Well, that's good of you,' Sven said. He smiled at his sister. Perhaps she had got over whatever was bugging her. 'And then you will come back to us.'

'Yes, darling,' his father croaked. 'At least I will still have my little Tasha.'

Tasha nodded but said nothing. Yes, Sven thought, it was better that the young couple should leave. He wanted his sister back, the adventurous, passionate girl he used to know. And he wanted his daughter to embrace her own future.

When Sven woke up the next morning, they were gone. Their furniture and possessions were left neatly in their old rooms. He waited for Natasha to return and to tell him all about the departure.

She did not return. Aud did not call. Anxious, they contacted the police and the immigration authorities. They were told that Pyotr and Aud Vladekvich had docked at Calais a week after leaving Finland, but that was the last Sven heard of his daughter.

He never saw any of them again.

'We'll park here.' Pyotr nodded and Natasha pulled over. It was a darkened alleyway, back from the lamp-lit street and at least half a mile from the docks.

'What?' Aud glanced about her. 'That's silly, darling. We can get a lot closer.'

'I prefer to walk; stretch our legs.' Natasha said nothing, she simply opened the door and got out.

Aud gazed at her aunt with annoyance. She wished Daddy had driven them here. Natasha was always giving her mean looks or making snide remarks. She crowded Aud when she wanted to be alone with Pyotr.

'It's raining,' she pointed out. But Pyotr said nothing, so, obediently, she got out of the car. Perhaps it was sentimental –

perhaps he wanted to take his time saying goodbye to Finland. Even so, it was cold.

'Do you have your passport? It would be just like you to have forgotten it,' Natasha said, with a sharp contempt that shocked her niece.

Stung, she retorted, 'I've got it right here.' Aud pulled it from her breast pocket.

'I'll take that,' Natasha responded. She moved in and tugged the document free from the younger girl.

'What are you doing?' Aud demanded.

Her aunt turned away. 'You won't be using it,' she answered. 'I will.'

'You're crazy,' Aud cried. 'Darling, tell her to shut up!'

But her husband had approached her, and there was a strange look on his face. Not adoration, not affection. He looked . . . Indifferent. Even a little bored.

'You can't seriously have imagined that somebody like you could hold my interest, Aud,' Pyotr said. 'You've been useful, but that time is at an end.'

'Wh – what?'

'You heard me. Kneel down,' he said.

'What? Why?' she shouted. Aud suddenly felt terribly afraid. She wanted her father.

'Because I'm going to kill you,' Pyotr said.

She believed him.

'No!' she screamed.

Pyotr bent swiftly and took up a large stone that was lying by the side of the road. Aud tried to run, but Natasha grabbed her and held her back. Wildly struggling, Aud stared at her, pleading for her life.

'Why are you doing this?' she screamed. 'You're my aunt!'

Natasha looked at her with loathing.

'How dare you touch him?' she hissed. 'Can't you see he's mine!'

'No!' Aud sobbed. 'You're supposed to love me!'

Natasha thrust the girl forwards and Pyotr brought the rock down, in an efficient little arc, against her temple. A spot of

429

blood oozed from the wound, and she crumpled to the ground, silent.

Natasha bent down and stripped the coat off Aud's motionless form.

'What do you know of love?' she said.

Then she stood up and smiled brilliantly at Pyotr.

'Follow me.' He started walking.

'Anywhere, my darling,' she said brightly. She trotted along behind him, like a dog at its master's heels.

Chapter Forty-Seven

Judy smiled carefully at Christine.

'I'm just going to the bathroom,' she said. 'I'll be right back.'

'Certainly, mademois—'

Judy didn't get to hear her assistant finish the thought. She raced to the executive bathroom on their floor as fast as her pale peach Jimmy Choos would carry her. She only just made it. Shoving her way into the first open stall, she sank to her knees and retched violently.

A second later and she'd have been puking on the bathroom floor.

Judy heaved until there was nothing left to bring up. It had been like this four days out of seven, every morning. And when she didn't vomit, she sure felt like it.

Judy was under the kind of stress she'd never dreamed possible. Now he'd been fired, she was fair game at the company; all her colleagues insulted her.

There was a new regime in town. And it wasn't one that offered her any protection.

For the first time in eight years, Judy had no cover at Massot. And she was learning just how much they all hated her. Even her new assistant was openly scornful.

That bastard Gregoire was installed back in his old office – Tom's office; and he delighted in putting her down. Gregoire made crude remarks daily, as though he saw her as little more than a high-class hooker.

And Tom was endlessly distant. The best Judy could say for herself was that she was still at the château. He couldn't bring himself to evict the mother of his baby.

And she clung to that, she clung on to it like grim death.

He wasn't going to win.

Nor was Sophie, nor was Katherine.

She was Judy Dean from Iowa, and she was no goddam quitter. Judy was part of the Massot story; part of this big chess game. And she was utterly determined to win.

Sitting at his desk, Gregoire Lazard cursed. His secretary had just presented him with another express despatch from his lawyers; Tom Massot had filed another deposition in his suit.

The brat was not giving up.

Lazard hated the Massots. All of them. Why wouldn't they just *go away*? He thought of Sophie, how close he'd come . . . So close. And now he was back here again, trying again. Lazard clenched the paper in his hand. *Pierre Massot, you have got away with this for too long . . .*

There was a crack, and his boss burst through the door. Lazard sighed in disgust. He wished the American would go away, too.

'Goddamnit!' Stockton roared. 'Have you seen the goddam ticker lately, Lazard?'

Lazard spun on his swivel chair. He despised his new boss and today he simply couldn't be bothered to hide it.

'Don't blame me for that,' he snapped. 'Mayberry's your company. I only look after Massot. And I've only just got here.'

'Quit making excuses,' Stockton snarled. 'I brought you in to stop the rot. Instead, we're sinking like the *Titanic* in a cement overcoat.'

Lazard said softly, 'I can't do anything until you can control the story. All I hear about is Montfort Jewels.'

'I told you not to mention that bastard!' Stockton screeched. Little flecks of spittle dewed his lips; he was revolting, Lazard thought. 'You're up to your old tricks again. Treading fucking water while the competition chews you up. Sitting collecting a pay cheque. Why d'you think we targeted Massot in the first place? Because you suck.'

Lazard was tired. And bored; bored with the whole company,

with that oaf Stockton, with the Massots. He wished he could send them all to hell. But he needed the money . . .

'Then you're going to look pretty stupid for hiring me back,' he hissed, surprised at his own venom. 'And remember, you're the one who put it on the front pages. Your hand round my shoulders, that Judy announcing me as your personal choice. Remember?'

Stockton did remember, only too well.

'This is all your fault,' Lazard said, calmly. 'You're the genius who fired Hugh Montfort . . .'

'You'd better thank your stars I did. He'd never have hired you. He held you in the same contempt I do . . .'

'Oh really,' sneered Gregoire. 'The contempt Wall Street has for you is far greater, I'd say. Without Montfort you've been exposed as the talentless bully which, monsieur, everybody always thought you were.'

'You snivelling little rat,' Stockton cursed. 'I'll have you fired, you worthless piece of shit.'

'I do not think you will.' Lazard laughed. 'You fool, don't you realise I'll just go to the press? Tell them about this little ego trip you're pulling, how you only keep Judy on because she's dating the Massot boy? You've got bosses too. The board can fire you, and we both know that at this point you're skating on the thinnest ice around.'

'Fuck you,' Stockton glowered. But then he chewed his lip, because it was true. 'If they fire me, you go as well,' he pointed out. 'Nobody's going to stick with a hiree of mine who can't deliver. You better hustle, you frog-eating loser. Because if I go, you go.'

They glared at each other with mutual hatred.

Mayberry's takeover of Massot had been a total disaster. The markets reacted poorly to the loss of Hugh Montfort, but then word had leaked of the mass resignation of the key showroom staff; the defection of the chief designers, who weren't under contract; and the lawsuits filed in London, Paris and New York on behalf of Tom Massot, demanding reinstatement as Chief Executive and millions of euros in compensation. Stockton had expected that at least they would be dismissed, but the

Massot boy was fighting pretty hard. Motion after motion headed his way, from Elgin and Hartford of Lincoln's Inn, Louis Foche of the rue Faubourg, and Roberts, Estrada and Jones of Fifth Avenue, New York. Massot had apparently got wind of many of their cost-cutting drives and he objected to them all. Mayberry was being sued under every possible mode of international corporate laws.

Aggravated, Stockton had offered to settle. But the spoilt brat informed him he wanted nothing except Pete's own resignation and Gregoire's along with it. 'Or you can both be sacked,' the note had informed him, 'which I would find preferable.'

The press were loving it, of course. Any excuse to rake up the near-mythical story of the Massots again. Their spectacular wealth, the jewels, the château. And of Pierre Massot's inexplicable disappearance.

And all of that was *before* Montfort Jewels launched.

Damn, Stockton thought, how he loathed Hugh Montfort. Detested him with every atom of his being. Just when he'd finally manage to kill off that arrogant prick of a limey, the asshole rears his ugly head like Glenn Close in *Fatal Attraction*. Starting from scratch, he announces to the whole world that he's starting a jewellery company, and that it's everything Mayberry/Massot 'should have been'. His exact words. And just to emphasise the point, he produces those croaky old Brandts, Claudette Chiron and her gang from the showrooms, and – best of all – Sophie Massot, to whom he's freaking *engaged*.

The press went ape-shit.

Stockton couldn't stop it. His overpaid mouthpiece Judy Dean certainly couldn't stop it, she was another waste of space. Everybody ran rivalry articles. Everybody ran speculation about Montfort poaching the 'best' Massot had to offer. And everybody featured pictures of the jewellery, along with the address of the website.

That was the last straw. Here he was, trying to battle overhead costs and staff problems, trying to design a way to show Mayberry crap in a Massot space, and Hugh had simply done an end-run around the whole logistical nightmare. He sold his shitty brooches and rings on-line. Not a dime in rent, not a cent in salary. It was pure profit.

And, so the press delighted in telling him every few days, Hugh Montfort was raking it in. If he'd been publicly traded, his stock would be reaching for the stars right now. Meanwhile, Pete's was in the toilet.

He'd lost money. This year's bonus was down the can. Pete's stock options had declined, and there were option calls on some investments he'd punted on. He might even have to sell the summer place in the Hamptons. Claudia bitched at him down the telephone – every night.

One day he'd have his revenge on Gregoire Lazard.

'If I go, you go,' Pete repeated sourly.

'Yeah, yeah,' Lazard said rudely. He turned away and flipped through the papers. There were more glowing reviews of the first Montfort Collection out today. *Vogue* had hit the stands, and it approved. Big time.

'We have to stop all this good press they're getting. We have to make the Tom Massot lawsuits go away.' Stockton chewed his lip some more, toying with the ulcer that had developed there. 'How can we make these people seem like the tawdry little fucks they really are?'

Lazard paused. Then he shot up out of his seat as though somebody had lit a firecracker up his ass.

Stockton cursed. 'Don't jump like that,' he said, clutching at his heart. 'I don't like shocks.'

Lazard ignored him. 'We use Judy. Judy Dean.'

Stockton rolled his eyes. 'Give me a break. She's bullshit. PR Director? She hasn't been able to do a thing for us. The novelty value of using Massot's girlfriend wore off a while ago. In fact, I been meaning to fire her. One more half-mill salary we can take back.'

'No, you don't understand.' Lazard smiled thinly. 'We use *her* to draw fire away from *us*. You want tawdry? I have a scandal so huge that nobody will pay attention to our restructuring any more. And the Massot woman, at least, will retire from the spotlight. She's a timid little mouse,' he shrugged.

'She's nothing. There's no way they'll take the heat. It will destroy mother and son.'

'I suppose you'll get round to telling me what the *fuck* you're talking about.'

'Judy Dean isn't just the girlfriend of Tom Massot,' Lazard said. 'She was also the mistress of Pierre Massot. Or should I say, one of them.' His lip curled with disdain. 'But she stuck around longer than most. Pierre bought her an apartment in rue des Cloches. Promoted her. He was the only reason Judy kept her job. Now the kid looks like his father, she's banging him too.' He smiled nastily.

'Let me get this straight. She screwed the father *and* the son?'

Lazard nodded.

Stockton grinned broadly. 'Fucking beautiful. Did the wife know?'

'By the end, she did. It was all over the company. It's why Sophie fired her.'

'And the kid?'

Lazard shrugged. 'The kid's a selfish little prick who threw a tantrum over Mama taking his slot. I don't know if they're even talking.'

Stockton chuckled. 'Wonder how she feels about her possible daughter-in-law? Or does the son ask what the dad was like in bed?' He smirked. 'The press will have a field day. I can't wait to see these hoity-toity aristos dropped in the shit. House Massot? More like the Addams Family.'

'We can do better than that. Let's play it smart.'

'Go on.'

'Call the Massot kid. He's so concerned about his precious family name, tell him we'll publish this whole affair unless he withdraws all lawsuits and signs off on a statement of support for us and the direction of the company. A real kiss-up statement. I'll write it myself.'

'I like it.'

'And then we call the wife. And Montfort. Tell them to wind up their little rhinestone business unless she wants her boy's name dragged through the mud.'

436

Stockton's eyes sparkled. 'Not bad, you devious little fucker.'

'And as soon as that's done, we spill the beans on Judy's affair anyway,' Lazard said, exultantly. He thought of Sophie's expression – that proud bitch, she'd had him fired. He would enjoy humiliating her. He'd make sure to turn the knife, too.

'We'll call a press conference. Announce that's why we're firing Judy Dean. Go into detail. Have employees available to give background interviews on the record.'

'Perfect. Let's do it.' Stockton nodded at Lazard. The little toad might just turn out to be a good hiring decision after all. 'Call Tom Massot right away. Let's see these stuck-up bastards dancing to our tune for once.'

Lazard kissed the tips of his fingers. 'My pleasure.'

Tom glanced again at two articles he had put to one side. The first was a *New York Times* profile of Montfort Jewels. They had a large photograph of two of the pieces from the first collection. A mermaid brooch, gold with inlaid mother-of-pearl on the tail, minute diamonds scattered through the hair, and jet eyes; and a choker, an intriguing piece of very fine strands of gold shaped like a series of spiders' webs, with an onyx spider sitting in the hollow of the throat.

It was quite unique. He understood at once that this was some of the finest work the Brandts had ever produced. No wonder the markets were going crazy.

His mother's new company was a unique success. Despite his troubles, he was proud; he admitted that. He was proud of her.

Hugh Montfort. Tom still loathed him – so he told himself. But it sounded a little less convincing each time. As the press sniffed around, printing lots of ugly innuendo about Maman from that pig Gregoire Lazard, Hugh and Sophie said nothing. Absolutely nothing.

It dignified them; it was a gentlemanly response. Just like Camilla Parker-Bowles, his mother said nothing. Which left the muck-rakers with nowhere to go.

But once Tom filed his lawsuit, Sophie and Hugh put out a short statement:

Sophie Massot and Hugh Montfort support Thomas Massot in his lawsuit against the Chairman and Chief Executive of Mayberry. As former executives of the companies involved, we note with dismay the plummeting sales and declining stock price that have accompanied the new management's regime. Fine jewellery is not fast food.

Style. Tom knew something about Montfort's manner of speaking; he knew that note had been written by him.

It was brilliant. It was savage. All the papers ran it.

Tom could almost see Stockton gnashing his teeth.

Tom was tempted to pick up the phone. But in the end, events took over. There were too many flights to New York and London to meet with the lawyers.

For the first time in his pampered life, Tom Massot was working hard.

And the strange thing was, he enjoyed it.

Tom saw clearly now. He'd been a fool; gulled by the promise of a fancy-sounding title into surrendering complete control. And he'd done it because – well, because he was a sexist. And childish.

Tom wanted Maman to stay exactly what she was – a mother; to stay home, to garden, to give parties. He'd wanted her to wait, so Papa could – one day – come walking back down the drive.

Tom passed a hand across his forehead. Yes. He'd brought on this disaster. And why?

Because in his head it was still that warm summer's evening, when Papa had come to kiss him goodbye.

He'd waited for Papa to come back.

And in his heart, Tom knew he was still waiting.

Sophie had changed all that – blown away the idea that things could be restored to how they were. Which was why Tom fought her so hard. His mother had never worked, never dated. Why should she start now?

Tom was slowly coming to understand her motivations. She'd done it for him, and herself, too. And he'd been wrong to blame her.

In a short time, she'd successfully relaunched the brand, hired competent staff, and almost fought off a hostile takeover –

Hostile. It sure was. He knew that now. And he, Tom Massot, together with his grandmother, had handed victory to them.

He tried not to blame Judy and Katherine. What could they know? It had been his job to see that the deal was sound. He was at fault, nobody else. Judy had no shares, and his grandmother was an old woman.

But how wrong she had been.

Tom picked up the phone and dialled the dower house. Faubert, Katherine's ancient butler, answered.

'Salut,' he said.

'This is M. Massot. Is Mme Massot at home?'

'She is, monsieur.'

'You may expect me in a few minutes.'

'Very good, monsieur.'

He'd go and have tea with Grandmother. Why not? There was nobody else left to talk to.

'Tom, my dear.' Katherine walked towards him with stately deliberation; he feared she had a poor hip and might find walking painful. She was elegant as ever, in a long gown of moss-green silk, a string of pearls and a flawless Indian emerald on her left hand. The familiar scent of powder and her custom-blended rose perfume enveloped him. 'How good to see you. Tea? Cakes?'

'Some coffee would be fine.' He wanted nothing, but Katherine would feel cheated if she couldn't make a fuss of him.

She signalled to Faubert, who withdrew.

'I have not seen you much lately,' Katherine chided him. 'You must not leave an old woman on her own. You are my only support, you know.'

'But what of all your friends from Paris?'

He knew his grandmother had calls and visitors every day of

439

the week. For all her age, she was an important social Lion of Paris; she sat like a queen and received fawning tributes.

'They are not true friends.' Katherine snapped open a small ivory fan lying on a mahogany side-table next to her couch, and started to fan herself. 'I have no true friends, you know.'

'Who knows what a true friend is, these days.' Tom thought of Polly. He hadn't spoken to her since that day under the willow tree.

'How are you, darling?'

'Well.' He hesitated, not sure how much to burden her with. 'You know, Grandmother, things aren't good at the firm.'

'Pierre's company will survive,' Katherine said complacently. 'You worry too much.'

'It will survive – perhaps.'

The watery blue eyes turned on him. 'What do you mean, darling?'

'We made a bad deal, Grandmother. When we sold our shares. They've fired me, and they are doing a dreadful job. Our shares have declined in value.' He paused. 'Quite steeply.'

A momentary flicker of concern. 'We are still wealthy, of course?'

Tom nodded. 'Right now, yes.'

'This house is your father's.'

'Mine,' he corrected her.

'Darling.' Annoyance flashed across her features, and Tom made out the ashes of a ruined beauty there. 'I thought we were agreed that your father is still alive. I won't have talk to the contrary in my house.'

Tom mirrored her annoyance. Had Katherine even noticed he said he'd been fired? All she seemed to care about was the value of her trust fund.

'Technically, it is my house,' Tom repeated. 'I don't know, Grandmother. I am starting to think that Maman was right. As she was right in what she did with House Massot.' He sighed. 'Certainly she made less of a hash of things than me.'

'Your mother knows nothing.' Katherine snapped. 'She is the one who gave up on Pierre. And now she has poisoned you . . .'

440

'Please, Grandmother,' he protested. 'I haven't spoken to Maman for over a month. This is my own conclusion. You can't read the balance sheet without seeing the same thing.'

'Business!' Katherine frowned. 'Your mother is a housewife. She knows nothing of business. That is Pierre's sphere. She made a fool of herself.'

'On the contrary.' Tom was rather angry now. His grandmother had no cause to sound so . . . *spiteful*, there was no other word for it. 'Mother has started a new business, and it is doing very well indeed. Rather better than House Massot. She has an instinctive flair for jewellery.'

'Pierre would hate that.'

'My father is not here.'

'And is she still shacked up with that man?' Katherine demanded.

Tom hesitated. He didn't like the idea of Hugh with his mother. Perhaps he never would. It was disconcerting to think of one's parents as romantic. But the venom with which Katherine Massot was talking called for some defence.

'Grandmother,' he said calmly, 'I'll trouble you not to use that tone when you speak of Maman. She is a legal widow, and she is engaged to Montfort. We've had our differences, but we are all still a family, aren't we?'

There was a little pause.

'Of course we are, darling.'

Her tone was placid. But Tom was uneasy. He was noticing subtleties he'd missed, before. Tension in her voice. Her eyes sliding away from him.

'And speaking of family,' Katherine said brightly, 'when are we to welcome the new Mme Massot?'

'What do you mean?' he said.

'Why, Judy, of course, darling.' Katherine smiled. 'Your choice is certainly courageous. She's so much older than you, so children may be a problem. And she isn't well regarded in Paris; no family, no status. A "working girl", I believe the term is.'

'That's a term for a prostitute.'

441

'Really?' his grandmother drawled. 'Some other expression, perhaps.'

'A career girl.'

'And yet, her career doesn't seem to be doing all that well. In fact, from what my friends are saying, darling, she appears in the newspapers and on the radio saying nasty things about you. They say she supports you being fired . . .'

'She's employed to do Massot's PR.' He looked at Katherine, sharply. 'I thought you didn't know I'd been fired.'

Another minute pause.

'Of course I knew, darling, I said how shocked I was. You must *listen*, Tom.' Her eyes slid away again. 'But perhaps it's all for the best . . . I do think that maybe you weren't the best person to run the company either . . .'

He blinked. 'What do you mean?'

Faubert arrived with the silver coffe-pot; Tom leaned back in the seat and allowed himself to be served. His eyes did not leave his grandmother's face. He was processing information, much of it unpleasant.

'Thank you,' he murmured to the servant. Faubert looked mildly surprised; Katherine, disapproving.

'You don't thank someone for doing their job,' she snapped.

Tom was ashamed of her ill manners. He looked at Faubert, apologetically.

'You're so like your mother,' Katherine said, angrily. Then she gave a little shimmy, and seemed to pull herself back together.

'And Judy – we were on the subject of Judy, weren't we? She is very different from Sophie, I think. Do the two of them get on?'

There was an exaggerated innocence to this comment.

I need to get out of here, Tom thought. I have to get away – to think.

'I won't be marrying Judy, Grandmother,' he said, flatly.

Katherine smiled; and for the first time since Tom had come, he thought it was genuine.

'I think that is a wise decision, Thomas,' she said, silkily. 'No doubt Miss Dean has been interesting – and perhaps *entertaining* . . . but surely not suitable . . .'

He stood. 'Thank you for the coffee, Grandmother. I must be off.'

'Darling.' Katherine sat still; Tom went to her, bent down, and kissed her on the cheek; he could see the rouge carefully painted on her paper-thin skin. 'Come again soon. You mustn't be a stranger,' she chided. 'We're family.'

'Yes.' Tom straightened up. 'We all need to remember that. I'm going to England for a few days, to visit Maman.'

Katherine sat bolt upright. 'With Hugh Montfort. Your father's enemy.'

'Mother says he wasn't Papa's enemy. If she's to marry him, I think I owe him at least a chance to explain.'

'You owe him nothing.' Katherine pursed her lips together in disgust. 'I can't believe it, Tom.'

He stood firm. 'I am determined to be reconciled with my mother. I will meet Montfort and ask him these things myself.'

'So.' Katherine glared at him; he saw fury in her eyes. And something else.

Dislike.

Tom was shocked. But a veil had slipped, and he knew what that look meant.

'You join your mother in betraying Pierre,' Katherine snapped. 'I always knew in the end that was how it would be.'

'You forget yourself,' Tom said coldly. 'I understand that Papa is your son, Grandmother. But he is also my father. And there is nobody in the world that loves him more than I. Nobody is betraying him.'

Katherine turned her head away.

'Please leave my house,' she said.

'I will.' Tom bowed stiffly to her. 'And I shall expect you for dinner shortly, when Maman comes back to visit. I can't allow my family to break up like this. You must see Maman, Grandmother, if you are to continue to live on the estate. This is my mother's home too.'

Katherine's pale blue eyes narrowed. 'This is Pierre's, not yours. What I do and where I go are up to him.'

'There's something I think you'd better get used to, Grandmother,' Tom replied coolly. 'My father is not here. I'm in charge now. If you doubt that, I suggest you ask your attorneys.'

He turned and walked to the door. 'I wish you a pleasant afternoon, Grandmother,' he said, and walked out.

Chapter Forty-Eight

'Excuse me, sir.'

'Yes, Mrs Percy,' Hugh said, not without a touch of weariness. It was one of the distinct pleasures of starting his own company to be able to hire Elizabeth Percy again. Hugh was paying her salary anyway, as he remarked, and it would be better if she did some work for it.

But some days hers was the last voice he wanted to hear. Montfort Jewels was a success, and that success came at a cost.

Hugh was working so hard he occasionally lost track of the date. Meeting suppliers, flying across the globe, interviewing staff, obtaining distribution, and talking to analysts; his days started at six and ended at seven, and there was usually no time for lunch.

Sophie's calendar was almost as severe. They had no show-rooms yet, but she was designing the look of the shops; Sophie handled marketing, from the websites to the press campaign. She also hired the front-line staff, and talked to the designers. When they met for dinner, there was mutual exhaustion.

But there was also excitement; and more importantly, there was love.

They were to be married in three days. And right now, Hugh simply wanted to leave the office.

'It's seven, Mrs Percy,' he said warningly. Couldn't the woman manage his call sheet? Ah, stop it, Montfort, he told himself; you're getting tetchy.

'Yes, sir.' Elizabeth's eyes danced; she remembered when all Montfort wanted to do was to stay in the office. 'But it's important. There's somebody to see you, sir.'

'Does he have an appointment?'

'Well, not exactly –'

'Then tell him to make one,' Hugh said shortly. 'I'm going home.'

'Sir, it's Tom Massot.'

Hugh paused. 'Is that a joke, Mrs Percy?'

'Absolutely not, sir. Shall I show him in?'

'Yes,' Hugh said. 'Of course. And then you can leave. I'll lock the office.'

'Very good, sir,' said the unflappable Elizabeth. Hugh got up from behind his desk; if there was about to be an ugly scene, he didn't want his secretary witnessing it. Fortunately, the other staff had gone home.

There was an unfamiliar churning in his stomach.

Sophie loved this boy. Hugh wouldn't feel about her as he did, were that not true. And Tom hated him.

Montfort was used to dismissing the opinion of others. He made his own way, and the rest of the world be damned. But in this case, he didn't have that luxury.

He hoped the boy wouldn't try to hit him –

The door opened; Elizabeth Percy, cool and reserved, said 'Mr Thomas Massot, Mr Montfort.'

'Thank you,' he said, and to Tom; 'Please sit down. Or shall we go somewhere else?'

The Massot boy looked awkward; Hugh did not offer his hand. Perhaps he would refuse to shake it.

'This is fine.'

'I'm glad to meet you,' Hugh began. 'I'm glad you came.'

The boy shrugged. He was young and handsome, Montfort saw, but there was little of Sophie in his face. Dark eyes and hair, and a wiry frame; he carried himself as one who has lost some confidence, but perhaps that was a part of growing up.

'I had to. You are marrying my mother.'

'I love her,' Hugh said quietly. 'Very much. I cherish her, and I hope you will at least give me the opportunity to prove my worth to you.'

'In your business, you were an enemy of my father's,' Massot responded.

Hugh noted the tone; it was fairly neutral.

'I wouldn't put it that way. That implies a personal element to a matter of commerce. In the time that I wanted to acquire House Massot, when your father ran the firm, we never spoke. I didn't know him. I felt no personal enmity towards him.' Hugh struggled to keep his words to the exact truth. 'Look, Tom, if I may –'

The lad nodded.

'I'm quite sure that your father was not happy with my attempts to take over his company. He said as much. But there was nothing personal in it. We did not even know each other. House Massot was a good fit with my company, and I wanted it.' He sighed. 'I hope you can accept that.'

Massot nodded. 'I can see why you wanted to acquire it.'

'All I can tell you is that I never allowed personal feelings to influence me in business. I've heard myself described as a robot.' Hugh smiled slightly. 'Fair enough, until I met your mother.'

'You said "allowed",' Tom pointed out.

'Ah. You caught that. Yes, I admit I am now partly, even substantially, motivated by my personal wishes.'

The boy stiffened. 'In what regard?'

'In that I wish to effect the complete ruination of Mr Peter Stockton.'

Tom grinned. 'Ah. Some common ground,' he said.

Hugh was relieved, but didn't let it show on his face.

'And M. Gregoire Lazard. The first for my own sake, the second for your mother's.' He paused. 'And yours. Sophie believes that both of them combined to cheat you of your inheritance, and that you were seduced by bad advice.'

To his amazement, at that comment the boy's eyes reddened, and he turned away smartly, covering himself with a cough.

'You could say that.' Tom took a step forward and offered Hugh his hand; Montfort shook it, delighted.

'If you hurt my mother, I'll kill you,' Tom said.

Hugh nodded. The idea of this slip of a lad killing him, a battle-hardened soldier, was amusing, but he admired Tom's guts.

'You know our wedding is due to take place very soon.'

'Why do you think I've come?'

Hugh marvelled. Maybe there was something to the idea of a God, after all. His prayers, if you could call them that – all his private, quiet hopes – had been realised. Tom was here, the boy was being reasonable; and there was nothing, now, to cloud Sophie's happiness.

'To see your mother, I hope. Shall we go?'

Tom gave him a wary smile, but it was more than enough for Hugh.

'After you,' he said.

They stepped out of the taxi at Seacourt Place. Hugh and Sophie had moved into his townhouse, temporarily; London was the perfect transportation hub, and it seemed more convenient to be there than New York. Hugh hadn't permitted Sophie to stay in Paris. Not while Tom was daily ridiculed in the national press.

'This is a gentleman's house,' Tom Massot remarked.

'Thank you.' Montfort smiled inwardly at the arrogance of youth; his splendid Georgian house had been in the Montfort family for two hundred years; he was the son of a peer, and who knew where the Massots came from? They were the ultimate in nouveau riche, and sticking 'House' in front of the surname did not change that. But who cared. Today he was simply glad to see the prodigal son in front of him without a horsewhip.

He rang the bell.

'My mother may cry.'

Hugh thought that was a likely assessment. 'She's a woman,' he said. 'Goes with the territory.'

Massot glanced back at him, amused.

'Coming,' his mother's voice sang from the hall. Tom was struck by the joy, by the liveliness of her tone. Judy never sounded like that; with her, it was always forced.

The door wrenched open. Sophie saw Tom, and screamed.

'Lovely to see you, too, Maman,' he said.

Sophie flung herself on her son, her arms snaking around his neck. She covered his neck with kisses.

448

'Tom! My baby. Tom – Tom –'

'I think I'll just go and have a shower,' Hugh said loudly. Sophie paid no attention; he hadn't expected her to. But he managed to close the door behind his half-smothered future stepson, squeeze past his fiancée, and make his way up the stairs.

As he was lathering himself up in a cloud of Floris soap, Hugh heard Sophie's laughter floating up even over the noise of the water. And he thought it was the most pleasant thing he'd ever heard.

They ate dinner at home. Hugh called, and the Ritz sent it over; a compliment paid only to the most special of clients. There was gently cooked foie gras with truffles, a roast grouse with chestnuts and buttered parsnips, and an espresso mousse with white chocolate liqueur sauce. He provided other staples himself; the Jamaican Blue Mountain Coffee, the vintage Krug, some Charbonnel and Walker chocolates. Hugh was gratified to see both his guests attacking the food with an excellent appetite. The conversation was light – small talk about the château and its gardens, about Katherine and the staff – but the emotions were heavy; Sophie's eyes never left her son's face. She was alight with joy and contentment, and Hugh knew the final piece of the puzzle had now been replaced.

'Where exactly is the wedding?' Tom asked.

Hugh glanced at Sophie. Tom had been sent the sole invitation, which had gone both to his office and to the château; clearly he had not even opened it.

'At the Jesuit church in Farm Street. Fr Sabin is coming over especially to marry us.'

'And how many guests?'

'Counting you and the priest, two,' Hugh said.

He blinked. 'No guests?'

'None. We wanted this to be as low-key as possible.'

Tom nodded. He began to look at Hugh with a new respect.

'We haven't told anyone, and the date hasn't been published in the church bulletin. We're hoping to avoid the press.'

'You have no family?' Tom asked Hugh.

'We're not that close – and I think they'll understand. My people have never been fond of circuses. There's an old saying in England that a gentleman should be mentioned in the press only three times; when he's born, when he marries and when he dies.'

Tom laughed. 'I like it.'

'I haven't been able to manage that,' Hugh told him. 'But I'm working on it.'

'The press are evil,' Tom said, with sudden venom. 'If you knew what I've lost because of them . . .'

'Darling –' Sophie interrupted.

'I'm sorry.' Tom made an obvious effort; he glanced away, took a large sip of champagne, and a forkful of grouse. 'This is splendid. One would almost think the English could cook.'

'Is something wrong, Tom?' Sophie was not to be put off. But her boy smiled firmly at her.

'No, nothing,' he said. 'And no more unpleasant subjects. We will concentrate on the wedding. Where are you to honeymoon?'

'No honeymoon,' Hugh said. 'The new firm is too busy; we'll take a long weekend at my place in Ireland and be back at work on Tuesday morning.'

It was a cold, grey November morning. And Sophie thought it was the happiest day of her life.

She had removed to a hotel for the night, not wanting Hugh to see her in her wedding dress. That was bad luck; and as a wife, she had had enough of that. Tom could hardly dress her; she was totally by herself.

She had bathed and spritzed on a little scent. Then she dried herself, slipped into her Rigby & Peller lingerie, delicate cream silk and lace, and walked to the drawing room of her suite.

The dress was there. Sophie walked across to it, stroked it gently. Yes; still gorgeous, still perfect. She was not a vain woman; but there could be no doubt that today, she was going to be beautiful.

But that was the least of it. She would be happy. She would

finally be able to experience true love. And her son would be there.

There had been wealth and ease in Sophie's life, but not love; not much love. Apart from Tom, there had only been distance, disapproval, and deceit.

Today that would all change. Today, in the middle of her life, her real life was about to start.

Quickly, she stepped into the dress; her practised hand found the hooks and eyes at the back. She applied a light touch of make-up, and put the tiara in her hair.

It was her only piece of jewellery. She would never wear a Massot gem again; let Tom give them all to his future bride. But this was special. It was a delicate coronet of ice-blue aquamarines and diamonds, and it had been worn by Lady Georgiana Montfort, Hugh's first wife, on her wedding day.

Sophie touched it softly. She whispered a little prayer for Georgie. And for herself. But she was sure everything would be fine. Hugh giving her the tiara was perfect; he had made his peace with the memory of his first true love. Sophie hoped that their marriage would be as blessed as Georgie's had been.

She would have taken six months with Hugh over seven years with Pierre, any day. But now, God willing, she didn't have to choose.

She was forty. But she was still vital, still beautiful. Sophie's life had been a long wait, she felt, for this moment.

She was to be a bride, a mother, an accomplished career woman. She wanted that; success in her own right, at last; not as somebody's wife.

And it was about to start. All of it.

She picked up the telephone and dialled reception.

'This is Sophie Massot.' It was the last time she would ever have to say that. Thank God! 'Please have a taxi waiting for me in reception.'

This was a very discreet hotel; if a bride walked through the lobby in a cloud of pewter silk and silver thread, by herself, at seven o'clock in the morning, nobody would say a word.

* * *

The church at Farm Street was Gothic and quite spectacular. Sophie had attended Mass here now for ten weeks; she had felt instantly at home. There was incense, there were priests in old-fashioned vestments, there was Gregorian chant. Even Hugh had not objected to coming with her; he had sat quietly in the pews with his eyes closed.

Sophie paid the taxi with a fifty-pound note from her tiny satin purse, edged with seed pearls, and told the driver to keep the change. The heavy wooden doors of the church were ajar. She walked inside and saw them: Hugh, standing at the end of the aisle; Tom, looking wonderful in morning dress, his best man; old Fr Sabin, stooping but smiling, waiting for her. And she heard the organ, swelling – one soloist, singing, in a voice clear as glass, the ancient Latin hymn:

> *Veni, Creator Spiritus,*
> *mentes tuorum visita,*
> *imple superna gratia,*
> *quae tu creasti, pectoral . . .*

Sophie's eyes prickled with tears, but she was smiling. She walked down the aisle, processing down the empty church with a dancer's grace. She saw the love light up Hugh's gaze, the amazement, all her beauty reflected there; she kissed Tom on the cheek; he squeezed her hand, and she saw that he was not unhappy. And her entire being flamed with a delight she had never thought she would know.

Fr Sabin smiled at her as fondly as though she were his natural daughter; in a way her own father had never looked at her.

'Dearly beloved . . .'

They went out for a post-wedding breakfast, which Hugh insisted was traditional. Sophie wanted to change, but he would hear none of it.

'They can't ruin the wedding now,' he said. 'And there's no need to hide. Let's have a little fun.'

They went for breakfast at the Victrix, the ancient hotel off

Mayfair. Hugh explained to his new stepson that this hotel made the best breakfasts in England; nowhere else cooked his kipper exactly the way he liked it. The staff greeted them with surprise and delight, and led them into a small, ivy-clad courtyard garden; the rain had ceased and the sun was now shining brightly, with an unseasonal determination. The wooden chairs were covered with soft cushions, and the tables were eighteenth-century oak. Sophie recognised a few of the other diners from endless Parisian parties, and Hugh introduced her to some of his friends; aristocrats, businessmen, and two Cabinet ministers breakfasting with the leader of the Opposition.

'Are they plotting a coup?' Tom was intrigued.

'If so, this is a good place for it.' Hugh shrugged. 'It's one of the most discreet hotels in the country.'

Nevertheless, Sophie noticed, the diners were carefully glancing their way; trying to be unobtrusive, but mostly failing. Hugh would nod and smile at them, and raise his champagne flute; some looked sharply in the other direction, others waved back.

'This isn't the sort of place that tolerates the press,' he said, 'but I'll warrant this story will hit the wires in less than twenty minutes. Shall we order? I'm famished.'

They were served by unobtrusive waiters who didn't bat an eye at the wedding gown or morning dress; buck's fizz, bacon, tomatoes, toast, a kipper for Hugh, boiled eggs and mushrooms; Tom chose scrambled eggs with smoked salmon and a large, fragrant pot of coffee, which he conceded was delicious; and Fr Sabin was coaxed into eating some delicate eggs Benedict seasoned with pepper and chives. It was a merry meal, and Sophie's happiness swelled; she felt the weight lift off her, as though she had been walking through life with dumbbells strapped to her ankles, and they had now been removed.

At the end of the breakfast she signalled the waiter.

'May we have the bill, please?'

'There is no bill, Mrs Montfort,' he said. 'The chef offers his congratulations, sir, madam.'

Hugh smiled. 'Very kind. Thank you.'

Sophie thrilled. She'd just been called Montfort, and she loved it. Getting Pierre's name off her was like bathing away a layer of dirt; she revelled in it. But her eyes went to Tom, to see his reaction. Would he wince? Would it hurt?

He was frowning and staring off into the distance; she observed that he hadn't noticed or cared. He was anxious, and it didn't seem to be about the wedding . . .

Sophie turned to Fr Sabin.

'Dear Father,' she said. 'Would you like to come home with us? Stay for lunch, or overnight?'

'Good Lord, no,' he said. 'I have Benediction at four. I shall get on the undersea train. It's a marvel, you know.' He glanced at his watch. 'In fact, as it's nearly nine-thirty, I should be going.'

'We'll drop you off,' Sophie said. She felt guilty for being relieved, but she wanted a few moments alone with her son.

Sophie poked her head into Hugh's kitchen, where Tom was fiddling around with the coffee-maker.

'Darling. Are you busy?'

He shook his head.

'Then go for a walk with me.'

Tom looked doubtful. 'What about Hugh?'

'He can fend by himself for a bit.'

'It's his wedding day,' he protested, but unconvincingly. He wanted to speak to Maman, and there hadn't been an appropriate moment yet.

'We aren't taking time off; we have our entire lives for that.' Sophie walked inside the room; she had changed into an elegant, but everyday, Catherine Walker suit in dark green wool, and a soft cream blouse. No jewels but her engagement and wedding rings and, Tom admitted, she didn't need them. He was proud of his mother's élan. 'Hugh!' she shouted. 'Tom and I are going out.'

'All right, darling, see you later.' His voice floated down from the study. 'I'll go to the office.'

Sophie ushered Tom out of the front door; it was mild and sunny now, and they strolled towards Hyde Park, in silence at first.

'I suppose I must call your grandmother.' Sophie glanced at her son. 'I'll do it when we get back. Has that been upsetting you, darling?'

'No.' He was surprised he was so transparent, but also relieved; now he would not have to fence around the subject with her.

'Then what is it?'

'My girlfriend – my ex-girlfriend. Judy Dean.'

'Your *ex*-girlfriend.' Sophie heaved a sigh of relief. 'So you've broken up?' she asked, trying to keep her tone flat.

'Yes.' Tom chewed his lip. 'Maman, when we talked before, you told me that Judy had done something wrong ... And that is why you so objected to her?'

Sophie nodded.

'What was it she did?'

She shrugged. 'It's not important, Tom.'

'It is. It's very important. You must tell me.'

'I can't say. I have my reasons.'

'And I have mine,' he said, with a touch of anger. 'It matters – for our family, it matters.'

Sophie stopped and leaned against a white-painted railing. 'What's happened, Tom? Tell me.'

He groaned, and passed a hand through his mop of dark hair. 'I've been very foolish – very stupid,' he said. 'Mother – she's pregnant.'

Sophie gasped and swayed on her feet. The busy London street wavered before her eyes; her son's strong arms came up under her elbows.

'Maman! Maman! Are you OK?'

'I'm fine – fine,' she whispered. She clutched at him until the world stopped spinning. Oh, my God, Sophie thought. Oh, dear God –

'I shouldn't have told you,' Tom said, gloomily. 'On your wedding day.'

'No.' Sophie controlled herself. 'I had to know.'

'I broke up with her and she told me.' Tom sounded so miserable. 'I didn't know what to do, so I put her in the east wing of the château. And I came here – to see Hugh. I couldn't handle this by myself.'

'Well, if it brought you to speak to him, the cloud has a silver lining.' Sophie tried to process every thought that was running, racing through her head. 'I won't deny that she's not the first daughter-in-law I would have chosen –'

'Daughter-in-law!'

'You will reconcile. And marry, of course,' Sophie said. 'You liked her well enough to go out with her –'

Go out. Such an effective euphemism.

'So I'm sure you can recapture whatever . . . the two of you . . . once had. You have a baby now. And the baby will need its father.'

'I can be its father if we're not married.'

'Of course you can,' Sophie agreed. 'But it won't be as good – not as good, not as perfect, for the child. It depends on the kind of sacrifices you are prepared to make for your flesh and blood, Tom.'

'The child,' he muttered.

'Your child. Your baby,' his mother said gently. 'And my grandchild.' There were tears in her eyes, but she smiled. 'It's part of you, and I love it already, Tom. Babies are the best thing in the world. Judy being pregnant is *wonderful* news.'

'You're mad,' he said. He glanced at her eyes, bright with tears; she was smiling and crying at the same time. 'Too much emotion in one day, it's turned your head, Maman.'

'No,' Sophie said, intently. 'It really is wonderful, angel. Whatever's in the past can stay in the past. I can make peace with Judy. Let her know she's accepted into the family . . .'

'I haven't agreed to marry her yet.'

'And nobody can force you.' Sophie started walking again. 'If you truly think life with her would be intolerable, then don't do it. But if you think you could learn to love her, you ought to. Yes, you could be a visiting father. But children do better in a home with two parents who love them; and children need their dad.' She paused. 'You, of all people, know that.'

Tom nodded. That hit him, hard.

Maman was right . . . she was more than affectionate, she was wise. He suddenly cared. Judy's pregnancy was more than an unpleasant fact; it was his baby, his little baby . . .

He could sacrifice for that. He had admired Judy . . . and he could get that feeling back . . .

There was pain, though. He didn't love her. And at once, as he contemplated marrying her, he stopped dancing around the thought of Polly.

I love Polly. I always have, he thought, and I pushed her away. I fucked that up, like I fucked up House Massot, like I fucked up with Maman . . .

Tom felt very young. And not in a particularly good way. He said this.

'And now I'm to be a father. I don't know if I'm ready for it.'

'Nobody ever is,' Sophie said. 'Trust me on that one.'

'So. What was the quarrel you had with Judy?' he repeated. 'You can understand that I need to know.'

Sophie hesitated; 'Well – that she felt I was usurping your place in the office,' she lied. 'She didn't think it was right that I look over, being just a wife. She was jealous because she was a professional woman, and I'd just inherited the corner office.' Like all the best lies, that one had an element of the truth to it.

'I can get over it. And I'm sure she will, too.' She allowed herself to feel one moment more of anger; at how Judy would triumph . . . grabbing the son where she'd failed with the father . . . and Sophie would be forced to help her . . .

But I won't let Judy dictate my actions, she decided; I don't want to give her that power. The child was *Tom*'s baby. She would love it as she would love any child he might have.

In the end, Judy would learn; a baby changes everything. And if she loved it, she would stop mentioning its grandfather. It'd be weird. Sophie almost laughed; when had her family not been weird?

'That's everything?' He looked sceptical.

'That's enough, don't you think?' Sophie deflected the question. 'Tom, you should go home tonight. Talk to Judy. Decide what the two of you are going to do. Even if you don't get married, you'll want joint custody, and you should offer her complete financial support, her own apartments in the château . . .'

Tom thought of Polly; and his baby.

457

'I'll propose,' he said, heavily. 'I want my baby to know *his* father.'

'Talk it through with her first.' Sophie kissed him on the cheek. 'And I will go home and tell your grandmother my good news.'

'Good luck with *that*.' Tom grinned.

'It has to be done. And we must remember her attitude is only from loyalty to her son. You'll understand that love – soon.'

'I'll get a taxi. I'll go straight back home.'

'I think that's best; call me when you two have discussed things.'

Tom hugged his mother. 'I love you, Maman.'

'I love you too,' Sophie said, and her heart soared with happiness. Never mind Katherine, never mind Judy Dean. She had her child back; with Tom and Hugh, Sophie felt she could take on anything.

Chapter Forty-Nine

Judy savoured the moment. It was finally happening. A Massot was offering her the world. His hand – his name. Her gaze on Tom was feverish, bitter, and triumphant.

'Judy, please.' He was pleading with her, the little bastard – begging. I *despise* him, she thought; he's not Pierre, he's nothing. 'We're going to have a child . . .'

'*I'm* going to have a child.' She shrugged. 'Or maybe an abortion. I haven't decided yet.'

'My God, you can't,' he said.

'I can do whatever I like.' She withdrew a packet of Gauloises from her Donna Karan jacket, enjoying his consternation, and lit up, daring Tom to say a word. It was a new habit, forced on her from stress at work. Now, Judy watched with relish as he shrank back, dismayed.

'That's not good for the baby,' he muttered.

'That's none of your concern.' She turned away. 'You weren't so bloody solicitous last time I saw you. Before you ran off to *Maman*.'

Tom struggled with his anger and fear. Now he was here, he absolutely loathed her. She was threatening to kill their child. And this was the woman he was meant to marry?

'I just needed a little time to think. Judy – be reasonable.' He couldn't stand to beg her, yet he must. 'Isn't this what you wanted – didn't you tell me, I'd led you on?' Each word ripped at him. 'So – I can offer you everything. Marriage, the name, the house.' He weakly attempted levity. 'All the jewels you can wear.'

'And what does your precious mother think of that?'

Tom gritted his teeth and ignored the insult. 'She spoke warmly of her grandchild. She tells me there is nothing that cannot be patched up – you and I, her and you – she wanted me to propose. For the child's sake, we can make a family.' He paused. 'Judy, she said the past was in the past.'

Judy laughed, wildly. Tom wondered if she were a little drunk.

'If you don't want to marry me, I can still look after you. You can move into the château permanently; I will assign you an entire wing and set up a trust fund. You could live off that income. We will share custody of our baby and at least we could live in the same house . . .'

'And parties.' Judy flashed him a lazy, contemptuous smile. 'Would I be the hostess? What's the precedence at Château des Étoiles? You're the young king . . . and if I don't want to wed you? I won't stand behind that old bitch Katherine. Or Sophie Massot.'

'Don't speak of my grandmother in that way, Judy; and it's Sophie Montfort now.'

'So it is.' She tossed her head. 'And I could be the new Madame Massot.'

'If you want to,' Tom said, clearly hoping the answer was no.

'You know, Tom, your grandmother has been a bitch to me. She's certainly been a bitch to Sophie. Something you don't choose to notice, I suppose.'

He recoiled.

'So I'll call her whatever the hell I please. And if you want to stop me from aborting your brat, you're not exactly in any position to lay down the law. Are you?' Judy was laughing. 'It seems that for once, in this fucked-up family, *I* hold all the cards.'

Tom walked to the window and stared out of the lead-paned glass, looking down on the kitchen garden; two of his cooks were out there gathering herbs for dinner. He did not want Judy to see the hatred that was brightly written on his face.

'Yes,' he said heavily. 'It does seem that way.'

'Well, I'll tell you what,' Judy said, twisting the knife. 'I'm

460

not sure I want to have your child. At any price. I can't stand you, and I can't stand your family. If I *do* go through with it, I'm going to want independence. You'll be buying me an estate – in my own name, and you'll pay all the taxes. I'm going to need staff . . .' She dragged one manicured finger across the back of a Louis XIV chair, rustling its velvet cushion. 'You can keep me in the manner to which I'm *going* to be accustomed, if you want me to keep your baby.'

'Blackmail,' Tom responded flatly.

She smiled condescendingly. 'Tom, darling, that's such an ugly word – after all we've meant to each other.'

'I'll pay your price,' he said. He didn't turn round to look at her.

'Oh, I know you will,' Judy said coolly. 'But I haven't decided if that's what I want to do. I'm not that maternal a person.'

There was a rustle; the sound of her crocodile-skin bag slithering off the chaise-longue.

'I'm leaving,' she said. 'I'm going to my flat; I'll call you when I'm ready.'

There was the sound of the door closing. Tom stayed motionless, listening to the clack-clack of her Manolo spikes on the sweeping marble staircase.

He thought of how the day had started, watching his mother marry Hugh Montfort, watching the mutual love in their eyes; the profound happiness that had radiated from his mother, visible in every gesture, every glance.

And here he was, begging to be allowed to spend the rest of his days subsidising some nasty American bitch.

He felt sick. And tired. He wanted to just lie down on the bed and go to sleep, and wake up back in his old life. Back at Oxford; back dating Polly; back before any of this had ever started.

But his life was going to go on. And he was all out of options.

Judy drove. It was fortunate that the journey back to the city was second nature to her now, because her mind was churning, like her belly. She was sick with excitement, and malice; she hardly saw the road.

Why hadn't she thought of it before?

There was no way she could ever *marry* the Massot boy. None. He was too like Pierre, and too different – a cheap mock-up, a cardboard cut-out. He revolted her. The thought of him inside her sickened her now. There was no dominance, no magic; just a cocky boy, easy to manipulate.

Easy to defraud.

She ignored the repellent memories that crowded her and made her skin crawl; sucking up to him, seducing him, just to keep his interest – that of a man she couldn't stand. In the beginning, Tom had just looked like Pierre. Later on, she could not forget he was Sophie's son – the child of the woman she hated – the evidence, walking and talking, that Pierre had never chosen *her* . . .

It had been a mania – a sickness – not to lose twice, not to let Katherine join Sophie in triumphing over her . . .

And this was the perfect answer. A pregnancy, one he'd do anything to have her keep. She pressed her foot on the gas. She finally saw her way clear.

No more Massots. If she could not have Pierre, the love of her life – Pierre, her god, her king – she would have no other . . .

But for fifteen years of longing, fifteen years of pain . . . for her lost career, and her broken heart . . .

They would pay. They would pay, and go on paying. She would bleed them dry. Screw Montfort, screw all of them. It would be House Dean, why not? Great dynasties started somewhere.

She slowed as she hit traffic. Coming into Paris, where drivers regard red lights as merely polite suggestions, you have to be careful. Judy's breathing steadied. Her mind, however, was clear, perfectly focused; sharp with hate.

She would take the Massots, mother and son, for whatever she could. And then wash her hands of the lot of them.

Judy reached rue des Cloches. The towering, elegant eighteenth-century façades that loomed over her, so familiar, seemed small, claustrophobic; she longed to get out, of Paris, maybe of France. But with her having been in the country for so long, it was a part of her. She also desired to destroy the Massots, to supersede them, on their own territory . . .

She parked on the street, and fished her key from her Versace handbag; it had been a while since she'd been here. The plants would be dead. She tried to remember if she'd cleaned out the fridge, or if there were any foul-smelling foodstuffs rotting there . . .

Housekeeping. It had been a while. Of course, with her new salary Judy could have bought a townhouse; someplace far nicer. But she would never give this place up. It would be her pied-à-terre for ever. It was her connection with Pierre; the solid, enduring proof that he had loved her, that whatever Sophie and Katherine said, Judy wasn't just another girl . . .

Pierre bought her this apartment; and when she looked at its cool grey walls, Judy chose to see love.

She nodded to the attendant in reception, whose head did not lift from *Paris-Match*, and climbed into the ancient elevator, the twin of the creaky Victorian beauty in the office. It stopped at the top floor, and Judy got out. She had a two-bedroom penthouse, and her own roof terrace; she had cherished her glass of wine there in the evenings, watching the sun sink over Paris's lovely roofscape, dreaming of Pierre, dreaming of a great future . . .

She slung her overnight bag over her shoulder and turned the key in the lock. She braced herself for the stink of decomposition, and pushed the door open, dropping her bag in the lobby.

Judy's eyes flickered to the living-room couch.

And she screamed. And screamed, and screamed.

Pierre Massot was sitting there.

He looked at her. And he smiled.

Chapter Fifty

'This is perfect,' Natasha said. She looked around the tiny, cramped apartment. It was the basement of an apartment building in the fourteenth arrondissement. Almost windowless, it had one tiny slit, three feet by six inches, that rose above the pavement; you could watch the heels of people walking past. But it was central, and dry; there was a tiny shower cubicle, with hot water, and a lavatory that worked; a steel-framed double bed, a refrigerator and a heat lamp.

And most of all, it was cheap. Pyotr had hired it for a few hundred dollars, no questions asked, for a year. He had given his full name to the landlord. Natasha, of course, was listed as Aud Vladekvich, citizen of France. She had thrilled to hear him call her 'my wife'.

'It's a dump. We're not staying here.'

She knew better than to argue.

Pyotr tossed her a few francs. 'Go to the market and buy something to eat. Make sure you talk to the stall owners. Tell them you have just moved to the neighbourhood, from Finland. Tell them the building we are living in. Complain about the apartment.'

'But why?'

Natasha twined her manicured fingers nervously through the hair at the nape of her neck. Pyotr had been strange, lately. Going places in the middle of the night. Away for hours, every day. Not speaking to her. Yet then he would come back, push her down on the bed, and make intense, dizzying love to her. Pyotr scared her, thrilled her, and confused her; he was like a drug, and she was hooked.

'Don't ask questions,' he said. 'Just do it.'

And then he walked out.

It was a warm, pleasant spring day. The breeze was attractively cool, the city sparkling in the sun; the long, formal façades of the university in the Latin Quarter pleased his sense of beauty. Pyotr strode along the streets, his eyes taking it all in. It belonged to him, he thought; it was his destiny.

There were no more thoughts of London or New York. Those places were vulgar; beneath him. Pyotr saw Paris, and desired it intensely, desired France like a lover. Here the women were unfailingly chic, the food excellent, the public spaces unsurpassed. It was worthy of him.

He changed direction. He would walk to the place Vendôme, his favourite spot in the city. The glorious open square, a vast column in its centre upon which perched a statue of Napoleon, pleased him. Napoleon was an interesting man; Pyotr had no desire to risk his skin in battle, but otherwise . . .

It was a new world; there were easier ways to build empires.

But first, he had to erase the past . . .

He turned aside before reaching the square. Vendôme was the great centre of the Parisian jewellery trade, and in the little side streets and cobbled alleys that surrounded it were satellites of the industry; gem merchants, hiding behind tiny, unmarked store fronts; leather goods salesmen; and watchmakers.

And there were also jewellers. Small-timers, those who could not afford the high rents and luxury addresses of place Vendôme itself. Pyotr had been exploring the area for two months, very discreetly. He had worn caps, and glasses; he had gone early in the morning, late at night. He knew how to blend in. Already, his French was perfect.

Ah, here it was, the store of his target; shabby, run-down, with peeling paint on the doors and dirty windows facing the street. The stencilled name on the wooden sign said *Giles Massot*.

He pushed open the door. The little bell tinkled, and as he waited, glancing around at the almost bare shelves, the sawdust on the floor, the dust that lay thickly on the tops of the cabinets, he was rewarded; the terribly slow, dragging sound of old

465

footsteps coming down the wooden stairs in the back of the store.

It was the old man. He stumbled a little on the last step, and Pyotr rushed forward; he was in time, and Giles Massot clutched at his strong, wiry arms.

'*Merci, merci, mon brave.*' The old fool smiled toothily at him. 'You're a good boy, Pierre. And I'm getting old . . .'

You certainly are. Pyotr lifted him up, returning the smile with a warmth he did not feel. He despised weakness in others more than anything. This man was a senile fool, and he was dirty. There was no pride in this house, or this shop.

'Thanks, my dear uncle,' he said. 'I'm glad to see you so well. Where is Aunt Mathilde?'

'Preparing our breakfast.' Giles nodded proudly. 'Why, you are just in time. She is laying out the patisseries now. You must come, you must join us.'

'It would be my pleasure,' Pierre said truthfully.

It was time. Why put it off? There was an optimum moment for action, and the moment was now.

'Mme Minette came to visit her yesterday.'

'Oh?' he asked with interest. Minette, the baker's wife, was the biggest gossip in the quarter. When not boasting of her grandchildren who had emigrated to Quebec, she was tattling about her neighbours.

'You did say she would be a good friend for Mathilde . . .'

'She's full of lively conversation; my aunt needs the company, don't you think, Uncle Giles?'

'But of course, of course. You are a clever lad.'

Indeed, he had encouraged the friendship. It was important that the whole place be intimately familiar with the return of the Massots' long-lost 'nephew'.

'Mathilde told her all about you and your dear maman . . . we can't wait to meet her.' Giles beamed. 'It is so good to have Jean-Paul's boy here, after all these years. When we had no children of our own . . .'

He followed Giles up the stairs into the tiny apartment that sat over the shop. It was old, and rather beautiful, in a faded way; the seventeenth-century structure of the house used mature, thick oak; oak that muffled small and reedy noises.

Pyotr closed the door carefully behind him. The wife was clucking around in their tiny kitchen; he heard the whistle of a kettle starting as the water hissed over the stove top. Perfect. He crossed to the window; the street was empty – the delivery men had gone on their rounds, but it was not yet time for work.

Mathilde walked into the apartment and smiled; she peered at him over her glasses.

'Pierre!' she croaked. 'What a joy to see—'

Pyotr stepped forward smartly and punched her in the temple. It was a precise blow, and the old woman crumpled to the ground, noiselessly.

For a second Giles Massot hesitated. He could not take it in. His mind scrambled to put the pieces together. Then he gazed at his fallen wife and looked back at Pyotr with horror.

'Who are you?' he screeched. And then, 'Why?'

Pyotr shrugged. Really, what a pointless question. As Giles Massot feebly swung at him, he shoved the old man to the floor. He screamed, so Pyotr kicked him in the groin, which winded him. The noise became a dull moan. Pyotr went to the bedroom and fetched a pillow; then he put it firmly over Giles's working mouth, and held it there for some minutes.

Eventually the man stopped moving.

He went downstairs. There were some old grey sacks in the back of the store, moth-eaten but serviceable. He bundled each corpse into a sack, and positioned them into balls; once rigor set in, an awkward position might be noticed.

The old man's car keys hung on a rusty nail by the kitchen sink. Pyotr calmly turned off the kettle. Then he slung the first sack over his shoulder, went down to the alley by the side of the house, and opened the door of the Renault. The woman fit into the trunk; the man he placed on the back seat. He reversed carefully into rue Lunette. Then he drove back to the dingy basement. The best thing about that building was the underground parking lot. He had selected it with his usual caution, and that painstaking preparation was about to

467

pay off. Nobody would see him unload these two. And nobody would see him leave.

'But who are they?' Natasha asked, almost pleading.

She stared in fascination as Pyotr laid each body out on the bed; the man looked distressed, his face livid with blood, his eyes red; the woman simply frozen and slack-jawed. She knew he had killed them. She did not care. She gazed at Pyotr, feeling her passion mount. He trusted her enough to show her what he had done. She was his partner. His woman.

Natasha thought of Aud, briefly, and with hatred. Her fingers tightened on Pyotr's sleeve. No woman would ever be to him what she would be. He shared this with her, and only her.

'How can you ask that?' Pyotr said, grinning. 'That's your brother- and sister-in-law.'

She stared at him, not daring to ask more.

'Step back.' He produced a small can of petrol from the back of the car, doused the two bodies with it, and sprinkled the bed and the heat-lamp. 'Move towards the door. We don't want any of this on your pretty dress.'

She obeyed him.

'Walk out on to the pavement. Cross the street, and wait for me by the Café d'Argent. Go.'

A minute later, hovering on one foot, she saw him; Pyotr, walking fast, and intently, and smiling. Natasha glanced towards the window slit; smoke, black and thick, was pouring up from it.

'Turn around,' he said, not looking at her. 'Walk down the street. Keep going until you get to the metro station. Then get in and ride to the Tuilleries. There's a restaurant there, Il Greco. A table is booked under the name Pierre Massot.'

Natasha stared at him, nervously.

'If the maitre d' should ask, your name is Katherine Massot,' he said. 'And you're my mother.'

She opened her mouth to ask a question. But he had gone, vanished down a side street. She hesitated, but then heard

468

shouts; people had noticed the fire. A woman yelled, and the acrid scent of smoke hit her nostrils . . .

She put her head down and walked in the direction he had commanded her.

'Please, Pyotr –'

'Pierre,' he replied sharply. 'Get used to it . . . Maman.'

'Pierre.' Natasha felt sick. 'Please, darling, tell me something . . . what is happening?'

He nodded.

'I know you are intelligent, Katherine,' he said. She winced as he used that name, but her eyes did not leave him. 'So I will tell you this only once.'

'I understand . . . Pierre.'

He smiled coldly. 'Good. It was necessary that we should fashion a new life for ourselves here. For obvious reasons, this includes a new identity.'

She nodded.

'Pyotr and Aud Vladekvitch, if anybody ever traces them to Paris, were burnt to a crisp in an illegal basement apartment.'

'I see.'

'I have been paying visits to my aunt and uncle, Giles and Mathilde Massot. They own a jeweller's shop near place Vendome.'

She nodded, intently.

'It is a small place, and poorly run, but they have some stock; some money, which they store in the house; and no close living relatives.' A shrug. 'Except us. I am the son of Giles's brother, Jean-Paul Massot, who moved to Morocco years ago and disappeared. You are his wife. He died of malaria before he could write to Giles about us.'

He's brilliant, Natasha thought. But the story jolted her.

'How can I play your mother – *Pierre* – when we are lovers? People will notice . . .'

She laid her hand on his arm. Angrily, he brushed it away.

'Listen.' It was a hiss; she recoiled. 'Katherine . . . you and I will not be lovers. You cannot be my wife. You are too old. I want another kind of woman to bear my heirs.'

'What?' she asked. Tears prickled in her eyes. 'What are you saying?'

His eyes held hers, with that unearthly calm.

'You were the first woman I singled out,' he said. 'And you have been loyal. I prize loyalty above other qualities. Beauty is never enough; it's only a start. Katherine, any other female I would have cast aside.'

Through her tears, she shuddered. She thought of her niece, screaming. She knew what that meant.

'I have a destiny,' he said. 'And you can be at my side. I will found a dynasty, and I offer you a position other women cannot have.' He shrugged again. 'I have appetites. I will satisfy them. There will be many, many girls.'

She flinched; his words stabbed at her chest.

'But they will not mean anything to me. I am offering you a place in my house, for ever; as my mother, as grandmother to my children. I will be rich; I will have the kind of wealth your husband never dreamed of. And you will be a great lady, and you will stay close to me.'

'Yes,' she said, weeping. 'Never leave me, my darling . . .'

'My wife, the mother of my heir, must be young, and virginal,' he said. 'Pure . . .' He gave a cruel smile. 'Which you, my dear, are not.'

'But I love you,' she said, in a small voice.

'I know. And this way, you can share your life with me.' He gazed at her, the dark eyes fathomless. 'But you will be, from this moment, my mother. Even when we are alone. Always. With no breaks. That is careless; that's how lesser minds get caught. You must think of yourself as Katherine Massot. Mother of Pierre Massot, and sharer in his fortunes.'

She brushed her hand in front of her streaming eyes.

'I will see how much you love me,' he said. 'You can leave here, and my life, as Natasha, or you can remain as Katherine. This one time, I will permit you a choice.'

She fought down the lump in her throat, dabbed away her tears; and when she raised her head she managed a haughty toss of her head.

'I am Katherine Massot.'

He took the bottle of Chablis from its ice bucket and poured her a glass.

'We will eat a fine meal here, Maman,' he said. 'And then we will go to the store my uncle left to me, while he took my aunt to visit her relatives in America.' Pierre raised his glass in a toast. 'We have work to do.'

Chapter Fifty-One

'Good evening,' Pierre said.

Judy swayed, clutching at the door handle. She thought she might faint. Every cell in her body flooded with fear and adrenaline.

There was a rustling of chain, and M. Kelo, the old man in the apartment down the hall, opened his door. He peered at Judy.

'What is the matter?' he asked peevishly. 'What is going on?'

That snapped her out of it. Judy wrenched her gaze from Pierre, and turned round.

'Noth – nothing,' she stammered. 'I saw a spider . . . I'm afraid of them . . .'

'You should grow up,' he said, annoyed, and slammed the door.

She stepped gingerly into her apartment and closed her own door behind her.

'I am not a ghost,' Pierre said, calmly.

Judy flushed. In one wild instant, the thought had crossed her mind.

'Are you OK?'

He nodded.

'How did you get in here?'

'You did not think I would buy you a property and not retain a key.'

Her heart slowing a little, she stared, drinking him in. His body was thin beyond its usual leanness; he looked emaciated, and she saw dark welts on his skin.

'I must get you to a hospital,' she said.

'No. No hospital.' He shook his head. 'I will recover here, with you. I anticipate it will take a week for me to be restored to health. You will supply me with everything I need.' His tone held an unmistakable threat. 'And you will, of course, be discreet.'

'What happened? Where have you been?'

'Your drinks cabinet was locked.'

'It's new.' She heard her own voice, apologetic, eager to please. It was the Judy she had always been with him. 'I'll open it . . .'

'Do you still have the Château Lafitte '68?'

Thank God, she thought. She had retained it; Pierre had remarked on it once . . . and she hadn't wanted to let it go. Wild gladness replaced the terror. He was truly back! And he was here! With her!

'It was your favourite.' She fumbled in a drawer, found the tiny silver key. Words tumbled out of her as she nervously retrieved the bottle, and uncorked it. 'So I kept it. Pierre, my darling, I waited for you to come home . . .'

He accepted a glass, breathed in its fragrance, and drank deeply.

'Good,' he said.

It was a single word. Yet Judy sensed in it some long, intense yearning. Whatever had happened, it had been very dark . . .

'I am hungry. Get me some food. Filet mignon.'

'Of course, darling . . .'

Judy scrambled for the phone. She quickly selected the best restaurant close by that she could count on; the Chève Rouge, they did a lot of corporate business for Massot. She ordered a meal, six courses, with elegant dishes that cooked fast; crème caramel, the beef, a salad of beets and oranges, petits-fours, chocolates and coffee, and demanded that it arrive within twenty minutes. After their grovelling assurances she hung up, and turned back to Pierre.

'Where have you been, my sweetheart?' Judy asked timidly. She wanted to touch him, to hold him, but she was shy – scared of the man in front of her.

He gazed off into the distance.

'I went home,' he said.

In the end, it had been a memory, long buried, that had summoned him.

His father, falling to the earth, in the snow. The ground, exposed beneath him. The strange colour, unremarkable at that time; a yellow-brown, weathered, rough and glinting . . .

And vanity; a weakness. Not pride, of course. Pierre Massot was full of pride, and he thought it justified. Every day since those first moments in Giles Massot's old shop, since the first telephone call he had made to De Beers, he had earned the right to pride. His brilliant acumen, his total ruthlessness, had made his peers jealous and his enemies afraid; he had ruined careers at a stroke, beggared suppliers, driven the competition into bankruptcy, and the women . . . how he had charmed the women. Within six months, they flocked to place Vendôme; and later, to rue Faubourg.

The meteoric rise of House Massot was unexpected, by all save himself. And Katherine.

He had enjoyed the natural rewards. The fine house, first, and then the château; what pleasure to drive out the French nobles whose seat it had been for four hundred years. The women, beginning immediately; drugs, once; he had not relished the loss of control. There were the fastest cars, the bespoke suits, the servants. He had enjoyed setting Katherine up, grand beyond measure, richer than any French duchess, or Italian principessa; living a sterile life, watching him, eating with him, unable to touch him. There was a savagery to her devotion that he found amusing. And in his way, he had compensated her.

Until the day he found Sophie Roberts, on the beach.

He instantly knew he must have her; she radiated innocence and purity. She was, of course, naïve, gullible, overly religious; stupid qualities, but ones that suited her for the task he would assign her. It helped that she came from parents who couldn't be bothered with her, and longed to get out; it helped that she was pathetically grateful, and wedded to a bourgeois idea of marriage, and fidelity. As with Aud, he had enjoyed Katherine's reaction when he made the introduction; but unlike Aud, Sophie possessed ample beauty, and innate style and grace.

Had he written his requirements on a piece of paper and magicked them into existence, he could have done no better.

Of course. Success was his destiny.

And soon enough, she was pregnant. Pierre found her laboured tension in bed unpalatable; there was too much good-girl, no passion; unlike his mistresses, she did not adore him, or cling to him. When she gave birth to a son, he left her bed for good.

The boy interested him only academically. An heir was a necessity. It was pleasing to see that he resembled his father. Pierre occasionally played with him, and took pleasure in the physical resemblance. At work, he had discovered the most amusing of his many girls, Judy Dean; a young American, unlike his wife. Ambitious, pushy, in awe of his business achievements, she was erotic and adventurous, and made his days at the office more fun; he bought her an apartment, and kept a key. Some of the other women fell by the wayside. He kept only one or two, besides Judy, for a connoisseur must always have variety.

And then, it seemed, his life was settled. The riches, the wife, the 'mother', the status, the son, the favoured mistress; all was in place. There was the odd pathetic attempt at a takeover, of which Mayberry Jewels was the most tiresome, but nothing serious.

And Pierre Massot began to get bored.

That was his weakness.

He desired excitement. Sluts were too easy, drugs beneath him. He wanted to be applauded, not for his new identity, but for his old. And he had promoted a man within the company who did not deserve it.

Gregoire Lazard.

Lazard was a mediocre manager at best. Pierre had summoned him to his office to fire him, and to do it cruelly, leaving the man abjectly humiliated and unemployable. There were no second chances at House Massot.

But as soon as he saw him, he changed his mind. And for one reason.

A glance could tell; Gregoire Lazard was not French.

He was Russian.

He knew instantly. There was the pallid skin that years of French sun could not totally alter; there were the slightly slanted eyes, with the hooded lids; there was a hard way of carrying himself that the man had not been able to shed.

And on a whim, as Gregoire introduced himself in fluent French, Pierre shook his hand, and said *'Priviet, kak dela?'*

The man blinked. He made a good recovery.

'U menya vsyo harasho. Menya zavout Grigoriy.'

Pierre nodded; he had asked the man's name, and he had surrendered; in Russian.

'Menya zavout Pyotr,' Pierre had replied. And then switched back to French. Oh yes, he was French, of course; but he had spent his childhood in Morocco, and then some teenage years in the Soviet Union.

'I do not talk about it,' he said.

Gregoire bowed. 'Of course.' But his eyes were alight with curiosity.

He was promoted, and soon became Pierre's deputy. Pierre enjoyed the freedom to speak Russian with the man, to drink vodka, and taste caviar; he knew that Gregoire, in his sneaky little way, had tried to discover more. But the trail was cold; he had covered his tracks too well.

And Gregoire did not dig too deeply. Pierre gave him a first-class seat on the gravy train. He took a perverse pleasure in the man's suspicions; he *wanted* someone to believe he had come from the dark, cold land to the East, and carved himself an empire in the City of Light. Gregoire was a useful hatchet man, a dogsbody, and lapdog; he jumped to Pierre's commands, and the younger man ensured they were often shaming; Gregoire, as favourite, like Katherine, like all his satellites, must know who was boss.

Over time he came to trust Gregoire completely. From disdain, rather than admiration, he knew he was safe with this puppet. And he chose to tease him, speaking Russian ever more frequently, dropping in references that only a true Russian would know.

And then, at last, Gregoire came to him.

'It's a new find,' he said. 'Siberia. Diamonds. Hundreds of square miles.'

Pierre blinked. 'What?' He scoured the news daily, and the wires had had nothing. 'Is this a joke?'

'No joke. They found kimberlite in the northern forests.'

'And the government has taken it?'

This was Russia now, not the Soviet Union, but would the new capitalism survive a find of this magnitude? Diamonds were one of the great sources of wealth. An entire nation, South Africa, had been built on the stones.

More than anything in the world, Pierre wanted his own diamonds. He was bound to De Beers, as a lackey, like any other site holder. He paid their prices and he did so without comment. Their way or the highway.

The loss of control disgusted him. The monopoly of another disgusted him. He imagined what it might be like to have his own mines, and the thought was intoxicating. To think that he, Pierre Massot, who had come from . . . that wasn't important, he told himself. He deserved it, though. He deserved them. He *had* to have them, and then the circle would be complete. His journey would be over.

'They don't know.'

Pierre stopped pacing his office. He turned and looked slowly at Gregoire Lazard. Dull-witted fool he might be, but Lazard had all his attention.

'Then how do *you* know?'

'I still have contacts.' Lazard had boasted that his friends, gangsters all, had purchased his ticket to the West when Russia was still under Communism's grip, and *Perestroika* was just a theory. 'Some *moujiks* found a stone in the soil, washed from a riverbed. They sold it in a mining town for a handful of American dollars. It was a piece of rough.'

Pierre licked his lips.

'Did anybody cut the stone?'

'It wound its way to the Giaperellis in Milan.' Pierre nodded; he knew them well, Angelo and Gepetto; they were shady, but brilliant, and they agreed to cut rough without knowing its provenance, and had made a fortune laundering conflict diamonds.

'It was orange,' Lazard said. 'A brilliant, true orange, eight-carat oval. I hear it looked like a fine spessartite garnet.'

Pierre's eyes sparkled. Spessartite was perhaps his favourite stone; tangerine to blood-orange, it combined the warmth of fire with the coolness of a diamond, passion in control. He never gave spessartite to any of his women. It was his own stone, and he wore a museum-quality round set in deep twenty-four-carat gold in place of a signet ring.

But how much better than spessartite would be a real orange diamond. What the kimberlite must be, that was pushing great hunks of rough on to the surface of rivers.

He felt a lust for acquisition that momentarily surprised him. Yet why should it? He was rich, true, but not in the league he wanted to be in. He dominated Paris, yet he was not the richest man in France, let alone the world. In that playground of the Rothschilds and the Gettys, he had still not earned admission . . .

The man who owned diamonds would be different.

He would no longer be a merchant or a jeweller. He would be an owner. He would be De Beers.

'Who owns the land?'

'It is in private hands. The Kamazhak family have much of it. And they do not want diamonds . . .'

The Kamazhaks were devils; some of the cruellest of the Russian mafia, they robbed, shot, and bribed at will. They ran drugs into the decadent West, and they regarded themselves as rulers of a vast tract of Siberia.

'They would sell the unpopulated areas for ready cash, and supplies of weapons and trucks. Perhaps we could send somebody there, to do a deal.' Gregoire looked hopeful. 'You're running the firm . . . Perhaps I could go.'

Surprised at his transparency, Pierre laughed disdainfully, and launched into rapid-fire Russian.

478

'I don't think so, Gosha! Little Grigoriy Mikhailevitch, finding himself the lord of miles of Siberian diamonds!'

'But they need somebody that speaks their language. And knows their culture.'

'I assure you that I qualify on both accounts,' Pierre sneered. 'Do you think I am going to trust you with buying land with my money, in my name? You would never return.'

'You don't trust me, Pyotr,' Gregoire sulked. 'You prefer your pretty mistress downstairs, you talk to her of business . . .'

His eyebrow lifted. 'Only for my own pleasure. She's far more amusing than you, of course, but she's a woman. A female . . . Do not be concerned; you brought me this information, and you will be rewarded.' He went to his desk. 'I want a report. No copies. Everything you know. Names and numbers of your contacts. I will go to Siberia. It will be secret, of course. Nobody must know where I have gone.' He smiled thinly. 'I will not even tell my wife. I should be back in a month.' He patted Gregoire Lazard on the back. 'And in the meantime, you will be in charge. Acting Chief Executive, with the use of my office, and all my privileges. And a salary of ten million francs a year.'

Lazard's catlike eyes widened. 'Ten million francs!'

'You understand what that buys, Grigoriy. It is not your management expertise.' Pierre's lip curled again. 'It is your information, your loyalty, and your secrecy.' His voice threatened softly. 'You should not fail me in any area.'

'I will not. I will get you the information, Pierre . . . Pyotr. Today. And when will you be leaving?'

Pierre raised a brow, as though it were a stupid question.

'Tomorrow,' he said. 'When it is time to act – you act.'

He only remembered, much later, how Gregoire Lazard's smile had deepened.

'Oh yes,' Lazard had said quietly. 'I agree with you.'

'Home? But this is your home,' Judy said.

Her voice snapped him from his memories. 'I will tell you later. First, I want to know what has happened here. With my firm, and my family.'

Judy blinked. He did not know.

Pierre was here, and he didn't know. Any of it. How could she tell him? *How could she tell him she had slept with his son?*

She prevaricated. 'But my dear, it's been so long . . .'

'Summarise,' he said, coldly.

Judy sat down, and, very carefully, began.

'Your wife betrayed you . . . Gregoire stole . . . Gregoire and Sophie were lovers . . . I tried to stop it . . . she came to the office . . . the stock started falling . . .'

He listened impassively as she recited the tale.

'And my mother?' he asked. 'My son?'

Judy made a split-second decision. 'He was a fool,' she said, contemptuously. 'And weak. He sold your company – he and Katherine – and they set him up as a puppet. But then Mayberry fired him.'

'Mayberry.' It came back to him. 'Hugh Montfort . . .'

'Pete Stockton,' she corrected him, and filled him in.

'So.' And now anger, indeed rage, was written bright across his face, and Judy shrank from it. 'My wife – my *wife* is a whore . . .'

Judy was glad to see it; how often had she longed for him to hate Sophie, to despise her the way she did . . .

The bell rang. She reluctantly took her gaze from Pierre and went to the door. The food had arrived; Judy took the tray from the compliant waiter, and shut the door in his face. There was no question of payment. Her credit was more than good.

Pierre closed his eyes; she saw purple bruising around the lids. He breathed in, deeply.

'I will eat,' he said.

Judy served him at table. It was the oddest meal of her life. Pierre ate slowly, almost agonisingly so; he was clearly half starved, but he would not rush even a single bite.

He had perfect control. It killed her.

'This is acceptable,' he said, at one point. 'You will have them deliver breakfasts, lunches and suppers here. With wines, and fresh juices and coffee.'

'Yes – of course. Whatever you say, darling.'

'They will leave the meals in the hallway. You will pay with your card.'

She nodded.

'And of course, you will quit work. There must be a reason that you are staying in the apartment, and ordering food.' He made a gesture. 'Depression, perhaps.'

'I'll be glad to quit.' Judy wanted to shout for joy. 'I hate Pete, and I hate Gregoire even worse –'

Pierre stared at her. 'Lazard? I thought you said Sophie dismissed him.'

'Oh yes, but Pete Stockton rehired him – to show "continuity".' Judy withdrew a cigarette and lit up; her fingers were trembling, so she walked to her balcony. 'It didn't work. The stock is tanking. Nothing helped, not firing your son, not ousting Sophie.'

'And Gregoire is there now?'

'At work. Every day.'

'I've changed my mind,' Pierre pronounced. 'You will return to the office. Now. You will find the personnel files. Get me every detail on Lazard. His address. His car.' He pushed back his chair and stood up. 'Call here as soon as you have it. Be fast.'

'I – yes, I'm going . . .'

Judy hesitated. Pierre would be alone – there was a TV set here. He would watch the news. He would learn about her and Tom – if he didn't already know . . .

'I must tell you something,' she said.

'It's not important. This is.'

'No – it does matter.' Tears clouded her eyes. She was a professional spinner, yet Judy had no idea how to manage this information. 'You have to understand that I thought you were dead, my darling . . .'

Pierre turned round. And his eyes on her now were chips of ice.

'You have betrayed me, Judy?' he asked flatly. 'Is that what you are to tell me?'

'I missed you,' she blurted. 'So much . . . so long . . . every day . . . and he looks so like you – I – I went out with Tom . . .'

Pierre's eyebrows lifted.

'It's over now!' she wept, almost hysterical. 'It's over! It was never serious . . .'

'You slept with my son?'

His tone was dry, analytical. She nodded, terribly ashamed.

'Can you ever forgive me?'

'For what?' he shrugged. 'I see the child inherited some of my taste.' A thin smile.

Judy felt sick.

'Come, come, we have never been bourgeois,' Pierre said. 'Why would I care?'

He saw her expression, and added gently, 'You are mine, not his; you will always be mine.'

'OK.' Judy sobbed. 'OK . . .'

'Now go,' Pierre told her. 'I am trusting you with something important. It matters to me very much.'

She did not argue. The worst was over. She shut the door, and went to the street to fetch her car.

Tom watched from the window as Judy's car sped down the drive, and wondered idly where she was going. He thought about calling his mother, but it was late; she would be with her new husband; their first night married . . .

He winced; he might have made a fragile truce with Montfort, but he still did not wish to think about that. There was Katherine, but he was still angry with her; and Grandmother had never been affectionate, not in the way he needed at the moment.

Then there was Polly. But he couldn't call her now. Not right now.

His head was racing. So many thoughts. A surfeit of unpleasant emotion. He hated the mother of his child, that was what it came down to. And she was right, total bitch that she was; he could do nothing about it. She would beggar him, and he'd pay her, just to keep his baby alive.

He walked out of Judy's suite and crossed the main stairway on the first floor; the ornate mouldings and gilt leaf on the ceilings oppressed him . . .

Mother had often complained of it; and he knew why now. It was a ridiculous house for one person. It made him feel small and lonely.

He walked to the great polished banister that curved down to the lobby. The east marble staircase was four storeys high. He wondered what Polly would do if she were here . . . probably whoop and slide all the way down, screaming . . .

That was what the château needed! A bit of life, a bit of light!

Tom walked into his own suite, thinking hard. He had calmed down now. He entered the bathroom. It was sumptuous; but all he wanted was a hot bath. To wash the smell of Judy, her carefully perfumed skin, away from him.

He tossed some Floris bath essence into the steaming water. He wished he had some Radox, which Polly always used, but this would do. He luxuriated in the basic physical pleasure of warm water, and wondered how he would handle this.

It was all his own fault.

He decided; he would give Judy whatever she wanted. But if she demanded marriage, after tonight, it would be under duress. He would marry her only civilly, not in a church . . . and divorce her as soon as the child was born. At that time, he would give her an estate, but take the baby. What was money worth, if it couldn't buy him justice? He would hire armies of the best lawyers in Europe. Or he would bribe her with still more cash. Whatever it took.

And then he'd marry Polly. If she'd have him. Which wasn't at all certain . . .

Another thought came to him.

Bribes. Money. Wasn't that what all these bastards wanted?

In the end it was only money that they cared about.

He had a weak case, maybe a non-existent one, as far as House Massot went. The only reason it hadn't been dismissed was the brilliance, and relentless, highly paid persistence of his army of lawyers . . .

What if there were an easier way? What if he just *bribed* the fat slug of an American and his French lickspittle lackey? After all, why slave for Mayberry if you can retire with a private income? Stockton might control the shares, but Tom could buy and sell that toad ten times over . . .

Brilliant, he thought; and so traditional!

He hauled himself, dripping, from the bath, towelled off, and dressed hurriedly, pulling on the first suit and shirt he saw. No matter; everything in his wardrobe was bespoke. He looked good, and apart from the damp hair, you would never know there had been any hurry.

He lifted the phone and rang down to the servants' quarters.

'Good evening, M. Massot. Would you like some supper?'

'No thank you, Jacques; could you ask Richard to bring the car round to the drive? I am going to Paris.'

'Very good, monsieur; the chef will await your return.'

'Just ask him to leave me a late supper in the kitchen, would you? I may be some time. And the staff can take the rest of the evening off.'

'Thank you, monsieur.'

The tone, he noted with embarrassment, was much less hostile these days. He supposed he'd become a bit less of an arrogant git.

Maybe, Tom thought, I'm growing up.

Chapter Fifty-Two

Sophie gasped; she flung her head back and clutched at Hugh; waves of pleasure rocked through her. She couldn't see . . . she felt dizzy . . . it was perfect . . .

It washed across her, subsided; she was there in his arms, clutching at him.

'My darling,' she said. 'My darling . . .'

He kissed her, twice, then rolled away.

'I had no idea,' Sophie said.

He lifted a brow; he was bathed in sweat.

'None? I can't believe that . . .'

'It's better – it's so much better now.'

'Guilt-free, eh?' Hugh chuckled.

She blushed. 'Something like that. Yes. And knowing you're all mine now, and you'll stay mine.'

'Well, I will admit that it is rather special,' Hugh said. He breathed in, slowing his racing heart. 'That was a fairly record day.' He pulled Sophie to him, and kissed her again, tasting the salt of perspiration on her lips; she was beautifully flushed, and her skin was mottled.

'Never leave me,' Sophie said.

'Where would I go?' he replied.

'So now,' Stockton said. 'We fire Judy.'

Gregoire Lazard smiled lazily. Finally, it looked like things might be going his way. 'And you can do it in person, my dear Peter. She actually deigned to show up in the building this evening. She's been making calls from her office for the last twenty minutes.'

Stockton grinned. 'Pity, in a way. She's a nice-looking piece of ass . . .'

'We all know you're not the first guy to sit in this office and think that.' Lazard laughed, coarsely.

'Go ahead, get her up here.'

He picked up the phone. 'Judy, it's Gregoire. Could you come up to Pete's office, please?'

Stockton didn't really care that Judy Dean had been an ally; she was as partisan as anybody else. Besides, his last two firings – Hugh and Tom – hadn't gone exactly to plan. He was a bully, and throwing his weight on the little people always made him feel big.

He wanted to see that hard-as-nails little bitch crumple. He'd let her know her secret was coming out, too. So she couldn't just flip him off and run home to the playboy prince. Judy Dean was finished, and he wanted to be there when it happened . . .

A knock on the door.

'Enter,' he said.

There she was. She looked good, but a little flustered.

'Hi, Pete, hi, Gregoire,' she said.

'Judy, I have something to say to you.'

'And I to you. I quit,' she replied instantly, with a bright smile.

Stockton baulked. 'What?'

It couldn't just have happened a third time, could it?

He thought Judy Dean was wedded to this job.

'You heard.' Judy turned up her pert nose. 'And while you're at it, stop eating. Those rolls of flab are just gross.'

'Hey! Just one second!' Stockton roared. 'We called you here to sack you!'

'Don't get excited, Pete, you're obese. You'll probably have a heart attack,' Judy said in a voice of mock-concern. 'And don't wave your hands at me, nobody wants to see the sweat patches under your arms.'

There was a muffled snort from Lazard. Stockton turned on him, enraged.

'Shut the fuck up! And you, you goddamned bitch. You

486

went with the father and the son. And we're going to announce it all over national TV.'

Judy shrugged. 'Who cares? At least I don't have to pay people to fuck me, Pete. Goodbye, Gregoire; you're the world's worst executive and a total waste of skin, but at least you don't stink like Pete. Adieu, losers!'

She pirouetted on one heel and walked out, chuckling.

Later that night, Stockton sat in his suite at the Crillon and wondered where it had all gone wrong. He was homesick. His dream had tanked. Montfort, that bastard, was printing money and Mayberry's stock was sliding down the drain. He wanted to dump his own considerable portfolio, but after Enron, those busybodies on Capitol Hill had put a stop to corporate officers selling . . .

Stockton shuddered. What would happen if this company failed?

It was possible. Jewellery was a nebulous business. You could forget it. It was about design value, like a fashion house or a perfume. Apart from the actual stock of gems, if House Massot, or worse, Mayberry, lost their *cachet* – more fucking French – then the company was worthless. There was no 'there, there', as they said in Brooklyn.

He wished that Sophie bitch hadn't poached his lead designers. That was dumb. He should have wrapped them up in a contract so tight that they could never get out. Ruin them if they tried to double-cross him . . .

Ruin them . . .

He gazed around at the sumptuous suite in the Crillon, with his balcony facing place de la Concord. Shit . . . if he lost his money . . . What *wasn't* in Mayberry stock?

There'd be no more hotels like this. No more limos. No more Claudia – she'd be out the door faster than a hooker after she got paid. Not that he loved her, but she was kind of familiar . . .

The phone rang.

'Lazard, where the fuck are you, you lazy bastard?'

'It's not Gregoire Lazard. It's Tom Massot.'

'And what the hell do you want?'

487

'I have a proposition for you.'

'Go to hell.'

Tom was unfazed. 'One that will make you very rich and rid you of the headache of House Massot.'

Stockton paused.

'OK,' he said. 'I'm listening.'

'This has to be done in person. I'm in the lobby. Would you like me to come to your suite?'

Pete clutched the receiver.

'Sure,' he said heavily. 'Why the fuck not.'

Pete stared at the Massot kid. And he didn't like what he saw. How was it possible the spoilt, petulant little brat he'd gulled into doing the merger looked like this? There was, unmistakably, a young man in front of him, not a boy. He carried himself differently; there was a seriousness to his tone, and a determination in his eyes.

Tom Massot had been a fool.

This was someone to reckon with.

Stockton knew it instantly. Whatever his other faults, he had a sharp appreciation of danger. And Massot spelled trouble.

He was unpleasantly reminded of Hugh Montfort.

'Let's hear this deal you got,' he said. He tried to sound hard, but he worried that Massot could sense his back was against the wall; that he was a cornered animal.

'I want to buy my company back.'

'You don't have that kind of money, kid.'

'Not all of it; just a controlling stake. Mayberry and Massot aren't the fit you thought they'd be.'

'We'll make 'em fit,' said Stockton, unconvincingly.

'I'll be blunt. The deal has been disastrous for you, me, and the stockholders. I've lost my father's company, you've ruined your stock price – I'm sure your board's about to fire you – and there are senior citizens out there who are seeing their retirement fund evaporate.'

Pete tried to think of a comeback. He could only manage a shrug.

'You need to pull something out of the fire. Announce that

you'll divest yourself of Massot, sell it to me. Then quit Mayberry. I'll pay you a separate deal, on the side.'

'On the side?'

Massot nodded. 'A separate deal between you and me. Private payment for services rendered.' His dark eyes swept across the American. 'I'm sure you find it distasteful to be bound to Mayberry for your paycheque. Sell Massot to me before it goes bankrupt, and I'll reward you in the way you deserve.'

'You're bribing me?'

'I certainly am.'

Stockton thought about it for half a second. 'Sounds good. I hate this fucking racket.' He stretched, sighed. 'I'll want six million euros or no deal.'

Tom Massot smiled coldly. 'You're not in a position to argue. I am going to form a company, Bagatelles Incorporated, registered in Switzerland. It will have assets of cash, mostly. I will issue you three million shares. There will be no restriction on your selling them, which you can do immediately. Bagatelles will have a value of ten million euros in ten million shares.'

Stockton closed his eyes; an immense sense of relief washed over him. Of course, this was the end of his little scheme with Lazard. No more dragging the kid's name through the mud. But who the fuck cared about that now; he was going to make about 3.5 US . . . his Mayberry stock might even improve once he dumped the Massot nightmare. Let this punk try to rescue it without the staff and the designers.

'You got it. How quick can we do this thing? I can't let the directors find out.'

'I'll form the company tomorrow; you'll sell the share block to me at eleven a.m., at which time you will receive your shares.'

'I'll say this for you, you don't take nothing personal,' Stockton mumbled. 'I figured you'd get all snotty about losing control in the first place, but I guess you know business is business.'

'Indeed,' Massot said. He turned to leave.

'I fired that tramp Judy Dean tonight,' Stockton said.

Massot turned round again, and his eyes flashed. 'Don't refer to Miss Dean in that manner.'

'Ohhhh.' Stockton smirked. Wow. Was he actually about to put one over on somebody? Sure looked that way. 'But it's an accurate term. You didn't know, kid, I guess, huh?'

'Didn't know what?'

'Long time before she was banging you, she was banging your dad.'

For once, Pete got the satisfaction he was hoping for. Massot's face changed colour. He paled, then flushed a dark red. Rage? Shame? A bit of both.

'Hey, don't shoot the messenger,' he said laconically. 'Ask around if you don't buy it. Anybody at Massot'll tell you. It was an open secret, pretty much. Pierre bought her her apartment, she was his main broad for, like, six years.'

Massot said nothing. Stockton revelled in his obvious pain and embarrassment.

'No wonder your mom didn't like her,' he reflected. 'Wife and girlfriend together in the same office, everybody knowing, and then Judy hooks up with you?' Course, it wasn't like she was your dad's only lay. He was wildcatting with a bunch of other chicks.' Stockton winked. 'Aren't we all, though, right? Guess I did you a favour in slinging her out on her ass –'

Tom Massot's eyes were ice.

'Never speak of my father or mother in my presence again. And never mention Miss Dean again, either. Or I'll come after you. Now, you've got a choice. Sell me the stock tomorrow at eleven a.m. sharp; the documents will be faxed to you by ten. Or sit back as Massot plunges into liquidation and you are ruined.'

Tom turned on his heel and walked out.

Judy tried to hurry home. She was a fast driver, but the traffic was shocking; seven o'clock, and still almost gridlock in the city centre. Her painted nails drummed on the wheel. Damn it! She wanted to get home to Pierre . . .

Divorce; would there be a divorce? Surely there must be. And then, she'd get hers. Finally; Pierre; her love . . .

He didn't even care that she'd slept with his son. Of course, she'd have to call Tom . . . finesse that a bit.

Should Judy confess that there had never been a baby?

Not for want of trying. No contraception, and sex on her most fertile days, but nothing. Every month she tested, every month, negative.

Or should she say she'd had a miscarriage . . .

No; what if he told Pierre? That his woman had been carrying his own grandchild? Of course, Pierre said he wasn't bourgeois, wasn't shockable, but that might just do it . . .

Judy'd need to get Tom off her back. Better to get it over with, to crawl, suck up. To him *and* that witch Katherine . . .

If she was going to be Mrs *Pierre* Massot, finally, she'd better start mending her fences. Tom wouldn't be so hard . . . he was soft inside, not like his dad. And Sophie, she was in love with Hugh Montfort now. She'd be glad if Judy solved the problem of the returning husband, no?

Judy smiled; she was half way to convincing herself that everything was going to be all right. Now if she could only get the fuck home!

This was crazy. She stuck her head out of her window to see what the problem was. Rush hour was over, it shouldn't be like this. There must have been some kind of accident. Yeah – she could just make out flashing lights, a couple of blocks ahead of her, near rue Salopette . . .

Judy turned on her radio. They were playing a cheesy Vanessa Paradis tune from the nineties. She flipped the dial, looking for a news station.

'. . . our top story at this hour, the gruesome murder in rue Salopette of a business executive . . . police have cordoned off a two-block area and traffic is backed up as far as the Seine . . .'

Judy's stomach contracted. Rue Salopette – that was where Gregoire's townhouse was . . . it couldn't be . . .

'. . . formal identification is yet to be released, but sources are telling Radio Cinq that this is Gregoire Lazard, Chief Executive of scandal-hit French jewellers, House Massot. Analysts report that this is turning into a similar situation as the Gucci family murders . . . no word yet on whether there is

491

a connection between this slaying and the bitter takeover battle being fought in the press between Thomas Massot and the new parent company, Mayberry Jewels . . .'

She switched the radio off. It took a second, because Judy's fingers were shaking.

An hour ago she had been faxing all the information the company had on Gregoire Lazard to her own house.

To Pierre.

He couldn't have. Could he? He was weak, skinny . . .

Had he killed Gregoire? Because of what he'd done to Sophie? Was that the reason?

Was Pierre capable of killing? And had Judy helped him?

She was suddenly very cold. Trembling, she pulled the car to the side of the street and parked. Let them tow it. She didn't give a damn. She had to see if Pierre was still in the apartment. There could be no waiting in traffic, not right now . . .

She clambered out of the front seat, turned north, and started to run.

'Hello?' she shouted, as she pushed the front door open. Dear God! There was nobody here! 'Hello?'

The sound of a latch; Judy spun round to see her bathroom door swing open, and Pierre emerge from it, a towel wrapped round his waist.

His body was covered in scars. She winced.

'Judy, be quiet,' he admonished. 'I don't want people to know I have returned.'

She closed the door. He didn't seem to be disturbed.

'Thank you for the documents,' Pierre went on. He walked towards the bedroom, where a new set of men's suits were hanging in her *armoire*. 'I need them. I intend to finish that man.'

'Finish him?' Judy whispered.

'Yes.' He turned round to her, and gestured at the scars across his body. 'I will pay him back for these. Firing him is not enough. He must go to jail for embezzlement. We must ensure it is the worst jail in France. I hope he gets stuck in the ribs with a glass shiv. He would deserve it.'

492

Judy exhaled; her breath was ragged, but she was dizzy with relief.

'No need; there's no need,' she said. 'He's been murdered.'

Pierre ceased ruffling through his suits. 'What?'

'Murdered, tonight. In his apartment . . . he was found gutted . . . his stomach was sliced open.' She blenched. 'Like a trout.'

He stared. 'Are you serious?'

'It was on the news.'

Pierre sighed; his shoulders slumped a little.

'Then he's cheated my vengeance. I wanted to see him disgraced and destroyed.'

'Not literally?'

'Of course not literally, you silly goose.' He came over and ran a hand through her hair; Judy breathed in the scent of his skin, silky with bath oils. 'I'm not a killer.'

She caught herself. 'I know that,' she said, breathlessly.

Pierre kissed her, lightly, possessively, on the lips.

'Let's go to bed. I hunger for more than just food. And afterwards, I will tell you the rest of the story; what happened in Siberia. And you will understand why I hated Gregoire.'

'Yes,' Judy said. Desire, long dormant, almost dead, shuddered through her body. The tension and stress of the last year withered and died; Pierre was alive, with her, touching her . . . hers, not Sophie's . . . hers . . . 'Oh yes, yes, my darling . . .'

Pierre took her hand and led her towards the bed. Women, he thought with contempt; such fools; so easily led; they believe what they want to believe.

When she was younger, and his preferred recreation, he remembered Judy Dean as spirited and adoring; intelligent, and self-reliant. That had all gone; he saw greed, fear, the start of obsession. She had declined.

But she was useful, and she would do. For now.

For one thing, he was going to need an alibi.

'Champagne?' Pierre asked.

Judy nodded, and he solicitously poured the pale golden liquid into her crystal flute, where it frothed lightly. Yes, he approved; while her personality had shifted, unfortunately, the American retained some of her value. She had clawed and scratched at him, excessively, interestingly passionate; and she was providing him with useful cover.

The meal, too, was excellent. He remembered Judy as being a good shopper; she had discriminating taste in food and other luxuries. While he bided his time in rue des Cloches, Pierre was pleased to be doing it in style.

'A good vintage,' he noted. It was Perrier-Jouet '74, and there was a Mouton-Rothschild claret to go with the main dish. An appetiser of goat's cheese and caramelised onion tart with a radicchio and rocket salad – deliciously bitter with the sweetness of the onion; a substantial, rich steak tartare with creamed spinach; and a dark chocolate flourless cake with ginger ice cream. Ah, God – not that he believed in God – the food, the food in France!

He had longed for this, his birthright; imagined it; and it was here. Lazard had died, and horribly. Pierre had no doubts; the bright star of his destiny remained in the ascendant.

Soon House Massot would be his again; he would settle in the château; wife and child would be under his control . . .

'You were going to tell me, darling,' Judy prompted. 'If you feel up to it, of course . . .'

'Yes.' Pierre assumed his most engaging stare, and was rewarded by a loving smile. He took a sip of champagne to cover his disdain.

'You deserve to know. I believe I told you of Lazard's promise to be loyal . . . to take care of my business.'

She nodded.

'I went to Russia that day. I left everything behind. Everything. My family. The houses, my wealth. Everything. You . . .' He ran a finger down her cheek and despite herself, Judy shivered with fear. Pierre looked at her, and continued. 'Briefly. I will omit . . .' He would give her the bowdlerised version. 'I had documents . . . maps of an area in Siberia, where Gregoire said kimberlite was found. You remember, I had been to Russia in my adolescence, and speak the language fluently?'

Judy nodded, her lips parted. She was swallowing that story the same way Lazard had done.

'I made my way to the area. It was very cold, even in summer; they mostly drill for natural gas that far north. There are mining towns.' He paused. 'Bars. I made my way back to a bar I had known once before . . . long ago. It was still standing. The owner is an old man called Pyotr.' He smiled thinly. 'He did not recognise me.'

'And the contacts?'

Pierre sliced off a portion of the goat's cheese tart; it was superb. He enjoyed it, and continued.

'I called them to meet me at the bar. They took me out to the site in a jeep . . . They had guns.' He shrugged. 'This is normal, you understand, in the new Russia. Since the fall of Communism, there is lawlessness everywhere.'

'And was there kimberlite?'

'Oh yes.' Pierre smiled coldly. 'I could see lumps of rough in the ground, glinting under the snow. I got out of the truck, and bent down to pick one up. And the chief of the men slammed the butt of his gun into my neck.'

Judy's hand went to cover her mouth.

'They blindfolded me and drove me north – although I did not know that at the time. Then they flung me into a cell in an abandoned jail. They beat me and whipped me.'

'But why?'

He toyed with his steak; even telling it so simply, it was hard to contain his rage. Pierre ate a mouthful of the rich meat, forcing himself to chew slowly. He must not again lose control.

'Gregoire paid them,' he said.

'But you had more money. So much more money . . .'

'They were not interested. The head of the bandits was a cousin of Lazard's. He had been paid to kill me, not capture me.'

'Gregoire – but – a cousin in Siberia?'

'His real name was Grigoriy Mikhailevitch. He was from Russia, not France. And he had maintained his contact from that netherworld.' Pierre shrugged. 'I was guilty of miscalculation. Since he was such a poor executive . . . I assumed he had no skill at anything. He lied to me.'

Judy digested this. 'But you were away for seven years. Almost eight.'

'And during that time, I never saw the sun, once.'

She was horrified. 'You did not go mad –'

He lifted his head. 'I am not weak. I survive. Lesser men cannot kill me.'

'Why didn't they just shoot you?'

Pierre hesitated. The question took him back to that dark place, where he did not want to go; to the nightly beatings, the sessions with the knife, the rats . . .

'They kept me for their amusement,' he replied, slowly.

'How did you get away?'

'I focused on one guard. He was the poorest of them all; late, otherwise sloppy on his shifts.' Pierre's lip curled. 'I promised him riches, and in the end he believed me. He snuck me food until I was improved in health, enough to travel; and he set aside clothes and boots for me. Eventually, one night, he brought me a gun. His name was Mikhail.' His eyes drifted away. 'We shot the bandits after their evening meal, when they were drunk around the fire.'

Pierre did not elaborate. He recalled the moment with perfect clarity; the satisfaction of aiming multiple rounds in the stomach of each man, so that they would take hours to die, horrible, brutal hours, helpless and terrified.

'And when we were done, I shot Mikhail.'

'But why?' Judy whispered. She had not touched her meal.

'Why do you think?' An indifferent shrug. 'Because for seven years, I had not seen the sun. Do you know what kept me going during that time?'

She shook her head.

'Julius Caesar,' Pierre said. 'He was captured by pirates, who took him to their lair and held him for ransom. He told them he would return and crucify them all. The ransom was paid, and they released him. A year later, he returned, hunted them down, and nailed them to their crosses.' His eyes glittered. 'I had no crosses. But,' he said softly, 'I made do.'

Judy shuddered. 'How did you escape? You were stranded in Siberia . . .'

'I drove south, then west. They had some provisions, a little money. I took it all. It was a dangerous journey.' He smiled. 'But I made it. Once I reached the West, I hitchhiked.'

'But a single phone call – a private jet would have been sent . . .'

'Don't you see?' The smile was more sincere this time. 'I didn't want anybody to know I was alive. Not until my plans were set. When I returned, I would no longer be the victim. I would be in control.'

He poured a good glass of claret; the bright flames hissing and crackling in the grate lit it up, a rich, glossy ruby. Pierre offered Judy a toast.

'And now, my dear, we have dealt with the past,' he said. 'Now, we move on to the future.'

Judy chinked her glass to his, and allowed herself to feel some relief.

'To the future,' she said.

Chapter Fifty-Three

The plane banked and steered above Paris; the wing dipped, and from her first-class seat Sophie could make out the Louvre, its glass pyramid glinting in the thin winter sun. She smiled; Paris was beautiful.

Of course, her current state of happiness made everything appear beautiful. Perhaps that was it.

Hugh, next to her, squeezed her arm.

'This is wonderful,' he said. 'I hope Tom's got his facts right.'

'I believe he has,' Sophie replied, proudly.

'Then I can't begrudge him being the one to do it. Of course, I wanted Stockton for myself. But he has wronged your family more than he's wronged me.'

'Tom is a man.' She could not keep the satisfaction out of her voice. 'He's changed; he's not a boy any more. It's right that he should be the one to take back what was stolen from him. You could have helped, but he wanted to stand on his own two feet.'

'I don't know why I didn't think of it.' Hugh was appreciative. 'In its way, it's rather brilliant; blind him with his own greed. Instead of thinking up some complex solution, Tom has cut the Gordian knot.'

Sophie kissed her husband lingeringly on the lips; her body still echoed from their passion of earlier that morning. It was interesting, what great sex could do; it relaxed her, unwound her tensions and anxieties. Her body was as supple as if she'd spent hours on a masseuse's table.

'The important thing for me is that he wants us to be there.

When he has finished – succeeded – he wants us there to share that moment of triumph.'

'And then will you go back to House Massot?'

Sophie was surprised. 'Of course not. I'm a Montfort now. And don't forget, darling, that the company's half mine.'

He chuckled. 'That would be hard, since you remind me eight times a day.'

Sophie blushed. 'What I mean is that I'm not just your wife . . .'

Hugh stroked her hand. 'Darling, I knew you were competent when I married you; today, I find you inspired. You have nothing to prove to me. I'm not Pierre.'

'Thank God,' Sophie said, and laughed, for the sheer delight of it.

'Mr Stockton.'

The butler – is that what he was? Pete guessed so, fancy suit and all – bowed slightly, with the bare minimum of politeness.

'Would you be so good as to go into the Oak Library? Mr Massot and his party are ready for you now.'

The English was fluent, with just the barest trace of an accent. When he had his safety millions, he'd hire a flunky like this.

'Sure,' Pete said. He mustered up some bravado. OK, this château was a freaking palace, but what the fuck, he preferred the glass and chrome in his place in Bel Air. 'Why don't you just say the library?'

'Because the château has three libraries, sir. The Oak Library, on the ground floor, is the smallest. If you'll just follow me . . .'

Pete tried to think of a comeback, but it failed him. Well, fuck this guy, anyway. He was just a servant. And fuck France, and Montfort, and Massot and all of them. He would take his three million shares and go the fuck home. And if he never saw this frog-eating pile of a nation, it'd be too fucking soon.

The servant opened the heavy door to the library. It was lined in green baize, and Stockton soon got a feel for the wealth of this kid; the room was at least a thousand square feet, lined floor to ceiling with bookshelves crammed with

499

antique volumes, all leather spines and gold lettering. There was a flagstone floor with Persian rugs, a huge fire blazing in the grate, even though it was eleven o'clock in the morning, and furniture that looked as if it came from some stupid museum.

A long oak table had been set up in the centre of the room. There were four mahogany chairs on one side, and a single chair on the other. Massot and three men were standing on their side of the table. He recognised one lawyer; that old bastard Edouard Foche. The other two, no. Lawyers, obviously. Stockton marched up to Massot, and shook his hand.

'Good morning, Mr Stockton,' said Tom Massot, formally. Obviously there would be no reference made to Massot kicking him in the balls, Stockton thought resentfully. He deserved a fucking apology. Little prick. But what the hell, let him be uptight. Maybe it was better that way. Lawyers and everything.

'May I introduce you to John Elgin and Richard Hartford of London? Mr Peter Stockton, Chief Executive of Mayberry.'

They nodded at each other. La di fucking da, thought Pete.

'I take it you have received the bid of Bagatelles Incorporated, for the House Massot division of Mayberry?'

'I have.' Stockton sat down, and the others followed him.

'And you are prepared to sell us the shares. Do you have the documents with you?'

Stockton nodded. He passed over a manila folder to Massot, but the Frog lawyer leaned forward and took it; he read it intently for some minutes.

'Hey.' Pete cleared his throat. He wasn't just here to sit waiting on these Frenchies. 'You give me *my* document about the shares in Bagatelles. Three million shares in Bagatelles,' he repeated, insistently. 'I may not have a law degree but I can read a fucking financial document.'

'Of course.' Tom Massot inclined his head. 'Take all the time you want.'

He handed over the contract; it was already signed, witnessed and dated. Pete read it carefully. Bagatelles Incorporated, S.A. For 'consultancy work' and 'ongoing advice' and 'guidance'. He was made a non-executive director of the company. Nice

500

touch, Stockton thought; giving them a reason to pay him. Board members got gravy gigs like this for doing fuck all all the time.

It was airtight. He'd signed enough shady deals to see that. Three million shares, no restrictions on the sale. Enough to pay off his mortgage . . . enough to cushion his retirement when the Mayberry stock really tanked . . .

Fuck it. He scrawled his signature on the documents. Mayberry's crash and burn would be the Board's problem now.

Edouard Foche silently passed the documents to the limey lawyers. They studied them for an age. Pete just sat there. Two could play that game. He wasn't about to ask them a fucking thing.

'Everything is in order,' the limey, Elgin, said gravely. 'The in-house counsel has appended a memorandum. It is within the power of the Chief Executive to order the sale of any division worth under eighty million dollars. The approval of the Board is suggested, but not strictly necessary in this case.'

'I concur,' said Foche. The other limey nodded.

Fools! Like he'd take a chance the Board could reverse this. He was about to get paid in shares of Bagatelles. It was in his interest to make sure the deal was airtight.

'Very well.' Tom Massot took a heavy gold Mont Blanc pen lying beside him on the burgundy leather of the desk, and signed his name on the contract. He passed it wordlessly to Foche, who witnessed it.

'Mr Hartford . . .'

Tom passed the signed contract to the third lawyer, who folded it crisply and placed it into his jacket pocket. He then said, 'Excuse me', stood up, and left the room.

'Where's he going?' Stockton asked.

'To ensure the transfer of ownership of the shares is registered with the financial authorities. There's an office in the south wing that has a high-speed Internet connection and other modern communications.'

'Well, aren't we perfect,' Stockton sneered. He had his own three million safe and sound in his pocket. He didn't need to suck up to Massot any more.

501

Tom turned to the remaining two suits. 'Would you give us a moment, gentlemen, please? And kindly issue the press release we have prepared.'

They nodded. The Frog lawyer said 'Good day' to him as they left the room. Stockton ignored the old fool. He didn't have time for the hired help.

Massot stood up, and Stockton followed him.

'Would you like a drink?'

He gestured to the decanter of whisky sitting on an oak side-table, with a single cut-glass tumbler next to it.

'I guess it's a bit early for me, son. We're not all drunks like you,' Stockton said rudely.

'Don't call me son.' Massot shrugged. 'I thought you might need it.'

'And why's that?'

There was a knock on the door.

'Come in,' said Tom Massot. And he smiled.

Pete Stockton stared. In walked Hugh Montfort and Sophie Massot. Or Montfort. What the fuck ever. Cool as a freaking cucumber, Montfort in one of his classy dark suits and the Sophie woman in a butterscotch silk skirt, hose, matching shoes and a cream shirt, dripping with pearls and gold bracelets.

'Maman, Hugh, Pete here was just asking me why he'd need a drink at eleven o'clock in the morning.'

Sophie spoke up. He remembered that voice, soft and gentle, English with a Frenchified accent. He'd always laughed at her naivety, but today when she spoke there was a thread of steel to it.

'That would be because Tom has ruined you, Mr Stockton. The way you sought to ruin us, the way you plundered the savings of millions of House Massot shareholders.'

Pete laughed. 'Don't let's get crazy, lady. He got his daddy's company back but he paid plenty to do it. You want to call yourselves the victors? All you did is pay *my* ransom money.' He stared at Tom contemptuously. 'And that'll hurt a lot worse than a kick in the balls – *son*.'

'Tom didn't pay you anything,' Hugh Montfort said. 'Nothing

to speak of, at least. Meanwhile, selling the division at such a discount will certainly get you fired.'

'If you call three million shares in the parent company nothing to speak of.' Pete rolled his eyes. 'You don't give up, Montfort, do you? Whenever he sells a piece, I'll get a cut. Whenever he makes money, *I* make money. Let Mayberry fire me! I don't need those fuckers. I prefer a private income. Work is for losers.'

He tapped his contract, smugly. There it was, against his chest, reassuring in its crisp white envelope with the Massot monogram.

'I didn't grant you three million shares in the parent company,' said Tom Massot.

Stockton stared. 'Yeah, nice try, fucker. I read that sucker eight times over. Three million in Bagatelles Incorporated.'

'I told you that Bagatelles was incorporated in Switzerland. You are the proud owner of three million shares in Bagatelles Incorporated, *S.A.* Bagatelles, South Africa.' The young man shrugged. 'Which has no assets.'

Stockton gasped; a huge wave of nausea rocked through him.

'You little bastard! You cheated me!'

'The same way you cheated me when you promised me the management of House Massot.'

Stockton blundered towards the door. Horribly, he remembered the lawyer saying he was going to rush the deal through. And Tom asking for the press release to be issued . . .

'Fuck you,' he hissed. 'You're not stealing this company!'

'That's right. I'm buying it, for thirty million euros. The discount is deep, but not irrational. It will stand up in any court.' Massot smiled. 'And I'm doing the shareholders a favour. Those who will own shares in the new House Massot will make a large amount of money. Those who own Mayberry may take a short-term hit, but once you are fired, management will improve. In the long run, this will benefit everybody.' He paused. 'Except, of course – you.'

'You asshole!' Stockton screamed. 'And you too, Montfort, and you, you goddamned –'

'I would be very careful how you address my wife,' Hugh Montfort said quietly.

Pete backed away, pulling his mobile from his pocket. 'I'll cancel the deal. Call it off. Say I was threatened . . .'

'Say you accepted a bribe?' Hugh Montfort smiled. 'I don't think so, Pete. You can sell your house, and give back your cars, and sell your wife's jewellery – and then *maybe* there'll be enough left over to rent a two-bedroom apartment in the Valley. But I'm sure you'll agree, that's a hell of a lot better than jail.'

'The deal's done,' Tom Massot informed him. 'By now, it is all over the press. I suggest you try to resign with the shreds of your dignity.'

'Go to hell!' Stockton screamed. 'Go to hell!'

He put his mobile back into his pocket and stumbled, blindly, from the room. Montfort and Sophie stood aside to let him go.

'That was fun.' Tom smiled broadly, watching Stockton's flight. Relief and the vindication washed through him. He had Papa's company back. And this time, he wouldn't mess it up.

'Good work, Tom,' Montfort said.

Sophie walked over to her son and hugged him. 'I'm so proud of you, darling. I'm sure you'll manage House Massot beautifully.'

'I'll certainly try.' He kissed her on the cheek. 'We might do a deal with Montfort Jewels, if you play your cards right. You could do mass-market pieces, and we will make the bespoke.'

'You want to merge?' Sophie asked.

'No. Massot will be Massot. But perhaps we can forge an alliance.'

Montfort said, 'I don't see why not.'

Tom hesitated. 'Hugh, would you mind? I need a few moments alone with my mother.'

'Not at all. You have some splendid grounds; I'll go and take a walk in them.'

Sophie waited until her husband had left and she heard the front door closing. Then she turned to Tom. The triumph had vanished from his face.

'Darling, is this about the baby?'

'Yes. I can't marry her – not properly, anyway.'

Tom recounted, as briefly as he could, the substance of his last conversation with Judy.

'That was two days ago,' he finished, 'and I haven't heard from her since.'

Sophie winced; she had imagined it would be bad, but this . . . Judy seemed to be almost unhinged, coming unglued.

'Do you think she's had an abortion?'

He looked ill. 'My God, I hope not. But then she wouldn't get any money.'

'I suppose that's right.'

'But, Maman, there's something else. Something I didn't want to discuss with you over the phone.' Tom gestured to the velvet-covered couch. 'I think you should sit down . . .'

'I'm perfectly all right, darling. There's nothing you can say to me that I can't handle.' Sophie tried for a reassuring smile. 'Not at this point.'

Tom couldn't hold her gaze. 'Maman, he told me about Papa and Judy. And also, the other women.'

Sophie closed her eyes, briefly.

'Tom,' she said, as firmly as she could, 'Pete Stockton doesn't know what he's talking about. Your father wasn't like that. He was always faithful, and he—'

'I found out.' Tom lifted one hand, to stop her. 'Maman, I didn't want to believe him. But I asked around. Everybody . . . everybody said the same thing.'

Sophie's shoulders slumped; she looked at her son, anxiously. He had always worshipped Pierre.

'It was a different time,' she tried, insincerely.

'It's OK. I don't want to know.' Tom had a look of pain in his eyes. 'It was very wrong of him. But why did you allow it, Maman? And why, why didn't you *tell* me – about Judy?'

She reached out and put a hand on his shoulder; her heart ached to see him hurt. 'My darling,' Sophie said. 'I didn't know about your father. Our marriage was happy.' That was a white lie, but so what? 'He kept it from me . . . it might have been a Gallic thing. I was younger, content to stay home with you. He had an office . . . I never suspected.'

505

'I see.'

'When I first went to Massot, I didn't know they were all talking about me and Judy. Judy befriended me. She wanted a kickback from Gregoire, and she wanted to turn the knife.' Sophie sighed. 'And perhaps she was curious. For what it's worth, I believe that in a sick, obsessive way, she truly loved your father. Or at the very least, was infatuated by him. She was much younger than I am.'

'But she came on to *me*,' Tom cried, agonised. He had tried to hold it in, but his mother's words ripped through his heart. 'I dated her. My father's mistress. Why didn't you tell me?'

'Don't you see that I couldn't?' Sophie asked, her eyes filling with tears. 'Don't you see that, Tom? You love your father so much . . . and you were always accusing me of betraying his wishes, and you . . .'

'I'm sorry, Maman.' Tom turned away so he wouldn't cry. 'I'm so sorry.'

'Don't be. You were loving. You were *loyal*. I tried to warn you not to date Judy, but I couldn't give you the true reason without shattering the past – the way that mine shattered.'

He sat down heavily and put his head in his hands.

'She played me like a violin.'

'And me too.'

'Yes, well, you didn't father her baby.'

Sophie sighed. 'Love, the baby is innocent. It's not the baby's fault.'

'I know. And it won't affect how I feel about the child. But you see why I can't marry her. Not even for the baby's sake.'

Sophie hugged him.

'Yes, darling, I do see that.' She kissed his hair; such a man now, so strong, but still, and always, her baby. 'But we'll fight for that child, and we'll get through this. Our little family is still here.'

She pulled away; outside the lead-paned windows she could see Hugh walking under the willow tree.

'And I'm glad, Tom, in a way. I'm glad you know. Because now everything's out in the open. And at last, there are no more secrets.'

Pierre sat in the warmth of the hired car. And nobody glanced his way. Not one of them. Not his son, not his wife, not the Englishman. They emerged, from his château, laughing and smiling; the fat American had already driven off.

He watched his wife and the Englishman bid farewell to his little son. Of course, Thomas had grown up. Tom bore the stamp of his father on every inch of his face.

But there was no loyalty in his soul.

Rage washed through him. The loss of control, the visceral feelings it evoked, shocked him.

He was back. And all those who had betrayed him would soon know it.

Chapter Fifty-Four

The day started like any other.

Tom woke up in his bed. The alarm was buzzing on the night-stand, incongruously modern in his room full of glorious eighteenth-century antiques. It was still dark; but he was not tired. In barely two seconds he had leapt out of bed.

It felt like it had done when he was very young, on Christmas morning. No matter how broken the night, there was no sleeping after Père Noël had come, at half past five, with his sack of gifts . . .

There was no wake-up call to match sheer joy.

He was going to take over the family firm. And this time, for real.

Tom rushed into his bathroom and climbed straight into the marble shower. The press had gone beserk; he had referred them to a bland, A-list PR agency, the first hire he had made with company funds. No more Judy, sabotaging Massot's press. Doubtless they would gather, looking for a photo or an interview. Tom had no interest in either. If he never saw another paper for as long as he lived, it would be fine with him.

He admired Hugh Montfort's very English restraint. No interviews. No photos. No comment. The Lazard murder was being investigated by the gendarmerie; all questions about that to them. Mr Stockton had been fired by Mayberry and was under investigation for corruption? Call Mayberry. He had nothing to say.

Tom's first order of business was to find a chief executive.

He would get somebody competent; bloody good, in fact.

Somebody with flair, but fiscal conservatism. And when he'd found a name, he would have Hugh check them out.

Tom had discovered something important. He intended to run the greatest fine jewellers in the world. That would take time, and patience. And expertise, which he had to acquire.

He didn't know enough. He could admit that now. He would find a wonderful caretaker.

And then – he was going back to Oxford.

Tom wanted to finish his degree, and then take an M.B.A. He was tired of rushing to grow up. He would learn for the sake of learning, and study business; keep an eye on House Massot from across the Channel; support his child, pay Judy off –

And court Polly.

He dressed, and ran downstairs; the staff were up, and cook had left him a pot of fragrant vanilla coffee and some warm, crumbly croissants. They were delicious, and he tossed the coffee down, black and scalding.

The car was waiting in the driveway, the engine purring, headlights flooding the gravel, steam rising in the pre-dawn chill; Richard, his chauffeur, was silhouetted in the front seat. Tom could see the orange-gold streaks of light breaking in the east.

He felt flooded with possibilities. He would get to the office, and the first call he would place would be to Polly. Whether she'd still be interested in a single dad with this kind of emotional baggage, he didn't know; but there was only one way to find out.

Richard saw him, and got out of the car; he held open the back door.

'Good morning, sir.'

'Please call me Tom, Richard.' He smiled. 'And if you don't mind, I'll ride up front with you.'

The older man smiled, and shook his proffered hand.

Tom slipped in and buckled up.

'The *Wall Street Journal* and the *Financial Times*, sir – I mean Tom.'

'Thanks.' Tom took the papers and flicked through them as

Richard pulled smoothly into the long driveway. 'And Richard, allow me to apologise if I've been an insufferable git.'

Richard glanced at him, then laughed.

'That's quite all right, M. Tom. Most rich people are, you know. Not your mother, though. If you ask me, you'll turn out just like her.'

Tom grinned. 'Thank you. That's quite a compliment.'

It was barely eight o'clock when he got into the office, but many of the staff were already there. They applauded as Tom entered the building, and he thanked them. Mostly, he suspected, it was simple relief not to have to see Stockton again. Winning their trust for real would take time.

Today would be a start.

He moved back into the corner office on the top floor. A beautiful young girl with enormous tits was sitting, simpering, behind the secretary's desk; she looked about nineteen.

'Hello, M. Massot,' she purred, thrusting herself forward.

Ah yes; Stockton's choice of replacement secretary. Celine had demanded an extended leave of absence due to 'ill health'.

'Good morning. What's your name?'

'Lucille, monsieur,' she replied breathlessly.

'How do you do.' He shook hands. 'Lucille, please report to the typing pool for a new assignment. It's nothing personal, but I want a secretary with experience – at least ten years' experience,' he added hastily, before she could say she'd 'worked' for Pete.

She pouted. 'Very good, monsieur.'

He closed the door and called Personnel. 'Get me the best assistant in the company; a mature woman with a track record.'

'Certainly, M. Massot. You do not like Lucille?'

'I'm sure she's very good, but I am looking for competence. Do you understand?'

A note of respect.

'Yes, sir.'

'And tell whomever you select to find me the names of the managing partners of at least six top headhunting firms.'

'Yes, sir.'

Tom hung up. The phone instantly rang again, and he looked at it with irritation. Couldn't they handle a simple request for a good secretary without having their hands held?

'Yes?' he said, annoyed.

'Tom?' A chill shot through him. 'It's Judy.'

OK, he thought. You can handle this. In fact, you have to. It's good that she called.

'Judy,' he said, trying for warmth. 'How are you? You haven't called; I've been concerned.'

'Yes, well, I've been doing a lot of thinking,' she said. He was instantly struck by the change in her tone; it was indifferent, distant. 'I owe you an apology.'

Relief. 'That's fine, Judy – forget about it – we can work this out . . .'

'I can only tell you that I've been under a lot of stress. That's my excuse for my behaviour.'

'Unexpected pregnancy is bound to—'

'There is no baby, Tom.'

He felt sick. 'You had an abortion?'

'No. There never was a baby. When you wanted to break up with me I was hurt, so I pretended I was pregnant.'

Tom's knuckles whitened around the phone. Could it be true?

'Really?' He struggled to keep the exultation from his tone. 'Honestly, Judy, there's no baby?'

'No. And I don't know why I acted that way. We were never serious and never in love. I regret the whole thing.'

Her voice was flat, almost mechanical. Tom instantly decided he believed her about the baby, and need not placate her any more.

'I hope we can part as friends.'

'I very much doubt that,' he said coolly. 'I found out you were my father's mistress. You deceived my mother, and myself.'

There was a pause, but when Judy answered, she did not sound concerned.

'I loved your father, which accounts for all my actions. I don't believe your mother ever did. And you resemble him

511

physically. I was trying to recapture a great love with a man I thought was dead.'

The phrasing didn't strike Tom's ear.

'My parents were married,' he responded. 'Their feelings for each other were none of your concern. And my mother is his widow. That is all you need to know.'

A laugh. 'That's what you think.'

She hung up.

Tom's eyebrows lifted. Weird; but Judy had always been a little weird. He smiled, then laid back in his chair and closed his eyes.

Dear God. It was over. It was over, and he was free! A wave of bliss washed over him; a life with a proper family, a wife who loved him, who wanted to have his children; a wife he could love . . . it was possible now, everything was possible!

He dialled his mother's number from memory.

'Sophie Montfort.'

'I hope I didn't wake you up,' he said. 'But I have some very good news.'

It was time.

Pierre Massot regarded himself in the mirror with approval. He had recovered, in barely a week, sufficiently. The worst part had been on his slow journey home; that was when he had added the basic extra weight he needed for health. Now, with the pliant Judy Dean providing him with whatever he needed – clothes, toiletries, a great deal of excellent food – he looked respectable. His hair was trimmed, his teeth white. The scars were hidden under a beautifully cut Dior suit. And sex with her, daily, multiple times, had offered adequate exercise.

He would not go to a doctor. Nobody knew his body like himself; nobody controlled it. The quack would recommend therapy. He did not need therapy. That was for fat, weak Westerners.

He needed revenge.

Gregoire, first; it had been almost too easy. But he had enjoyed the gibbering terror, the pleading, the muffled scream-ing from the duct-taped mouth. Still, it was over too quickly, for the years of darkness, the long fight against despair. Pierre accepted the consequence of his own moment of weakness. But it would not happen twice.

All that remained was to punish the traitors.

Judy did not count. She had slept with his son, but that was what easy girls like her did. He had no doubt that eventually he would need to kill her; Judy knew too much. But not immediately. She was an alibi, and an albatross. One murder, meticulously planned years in advance, he could get away with; two, close together – he doubted it. She would be bribed and fucked into submission.

It was the others whom he would attend to.

Chiefly, to his darling wife . . .

Who would have thought she had it in her. Quiet, elegant, grateful little Sophie; obedient and maternal. To take the reins, dabble in business, fight her son. Poor conduct. No wife of his should have a public role other than on his arm. He had given her everything, but she had wanted more.

She had declared him dead. She had fucked another man.

The whole world knew that Pierre Massot's woman had lain in the bed of another.

His son, his son had cosied up to Sophie's lover. His son had not chosen to wait for him.

Montfort. Once just an annoyance; now, an enemy. He must be crushed, but again, Pierre would do it slowly. He knew something of the man's war record. Montfort was a soldier, a professional killer. In this case, deception would be necessary.

And . . . Katherine . . .

Katherine. She had been the closest to faithful. But she had flinched in one respect: arranging the sale of her shares to that fool, Stockton. He could not tell if it was a mistake. He knew, of course, that she hated Sophie. Had Katherine allowed her chafing to undermine his wishes? Was her loathing of Sophie so strong that she would sell his trust?

Pierre thought so. Poor, obsessed Tasha, he thought; how completely, how totally he would always own her. He thought with fondness of her little ruse; get Judy to take up with Tom. Perfect! It ruined Sophie, and, she must have thought, would

513

ruin Judy; how could he love the woman that slept with his own son?

Even now, after half a lifetime with him, she did not understand.

He did not *love*. There was approval, and disapproval; fondness at best. I rely upon myself, Pierre thought; it is why I am still alive. And why I will win.

He would manage things perfectly. His wife's new 'marriage' would be destroyed. She was a foolish, credulous Catholic, a believer in a god; she would know her wedding to Montfort was invalid. Let them be torn apart. Sophie would have to come back to him. He would possess her, and do it brutally. He would use her nightly, and she would be under his psychological control. He thought of Sophie with contempt. No way she had changed.

Montfort could pine for his new love; he would lose her like he lost the last one.

Tom would also come to the whip. He would drag him home, in disgrace. No playing at business, no college abroad. If he didn't want to be disinherited, he would do exactly what Papa told him, from now on. Pierre demanded obedience. Tom would learn.

There was no doubt that Katherine would be penitent. She would suffer as she always had; he was not going to give Sophie up. Or, for that matter, Judy.

Wife; mistress; son; all would go on as before. The company would revert to him.

He was going to put everything right.

There was a squeak, and the door opened; Judy had come back from her hair appointment. She looked attractive and fresh. She was wearing the dress he had told her to put on.

'You called them all?'

'They are assembled. The ballroom of the St Louis hotel. TV is there too.' She looked anxious. 'Shall we go? They're waiting.'

Pierre smiled at her benignly. 'Well, they have written about unimportant nonsense for the past year; you, Tom, Sophie, M. Stockton . . . perhaps we should give them a real story?'

Judy walked up to the podium. The room was only half full; there were gaps. Some papers thought the House Massot saga had run its course. She was anxious; would Pierre be angry?

At least two TV cameras were there, though. That would have to do. She knew that the mainstream stations could get their tape. Thankfully, the beauty parlour hadn't let her down; her face was about to be all over the evening news.

She focused. She imagined Sophie, watching this – watching her.

'Good evening, ladies and gentleman. As you know, I am a former director of publicity for House Massot. Some of you may be familiar with events at that company since Mme Massot had her husband legally declared dead.'

Judy arched one plucked eyebrow, and the hacks faked a polite laugh.

'A week ago I received a visitor, who has been staying at my apartment to recuperate from an ordeal. He did not wish to make this announcement until he felt well enough to deal with your questions.'

Now there was a slight murmur in the crowd. She had whetted their appetites; she looked at the newly interested faces.

'Ladies and gentlemen, M. Pierre Massot.'

Silence. They stared at her, mockingly; there was a low hum of derision. Surely the woman had finally lost her mind?

And then the door swung open, and he walked confidently down the aisle to the podium.

For the first second there was nothing but shock. And then, pandemonium.

'Yes, you in the front,' Pierre said. He saw Judy in his peripheral vision, hands folded demurely in her lap. She had done a good job. The thin crowd had filled out, as more and more reporters burst into the conference. He had taken question after question, deftly fielding them all. Kidnap. Imprisonment. Torture. Escape. He had no idea what had happened to poor Gregoire, perhaps it was Russian mafia revenge. Yes, he would cooperate with the gendarmes. He wanted answers as to why they had not protected his dear friend.

Judy smiled softly. It was her Pierre again, the man she had known and worshipped; distinguished, battle-scarred, but utterly in control. He was even enjoying himself.

'Why did you stay at Miss Dean's? Is it true you two were having a relationship?'

'That's a scurrilous rumour. I have been faithful to my wife. There are those who take great pleasure in spreading lies about those who are not there to defend themselves.' He glanced at Judy, sitting there prim as a nun. 'Miss Dean is one of the few people I trust.'

'Why didn't you go back to your château?'

Ah; the moment he had been waiting for. Pierre lowered his head and spoke in a heavy, hopeless tone.

'All that sustained me in those dark years was the thought of my wife and my little boy,' he said. 'I loved and believed in them, and I waited for the day I could be close to them again. I knew they would stay strong for me.' He allowed his eyes to brim, then brushed away a tear as if angry. 'That didn't happen. I discover that my wife had me declared dead, and has married again. My son sold my company. I may wind up in a court battle with my own family. It hurt me so much that at first I didn't know if I could face them again.'

The press went berserk; he could not hear through the shouting match of questions, and he selected one man at the front. 'Yes.'

'Are you going to try to get your wife back?'

'Well, that's up to her, of course. I gather people have told Sophie lies about my conduct while we were married.' Pierre looked soulfully into the camera. 'If you can hear this, darling, it's still true. I pray we can rebuild our family. I married you in the eyes of God, and I am still here. Sophie – it's time to come home.'

He held up one hand through the noise – tried to speak, and couldn't – it was all so easy. Judy, picking up her cue, jumped on the mike.

'Thank you, ladies and gentlemen, that will be all. Please

allow M. Massot some time to get over his grief. I am about to drive him to the château where he will be reunited with his mother.'

'Yes, thank you; yes, I have heard. Goodbye.'
Hugh replaced the receiver and stood up. His face was grey.
'Mrs Percy –'
'Yes, sir.' Elizabeth rushed out. 'I'll close the office.' She hovered by the door. 'Mr Montfort – Hugh – I'm so terribly sorry.'
'Thank you,' he said bleakly. 'Where is . . .?'
He had intended to say 'Mrs Montfort', but the words died on his lips.
'In the studio, with the Brandts.'
'Does she have her mobile with her?'
'No, sir. She left it with me. She didn't want them to be disturbed in a creative session.'
'Thank you.' He glanced at his watch as he walked out of the door; only 9.33 in the morning; her meeting was due to last another hour. He hoped they had not taken a break for coffee. This was something she should hear only from him.
On the street, the traffic was ridiculous; even with the new congestion charge, in rush hour one still could not move. Hugh would not risk being stuck in traffic. Covent Garden was three miles as the crow flies; despite his Savile Row suit and John Lobb shoes, Hugh started to run.
People stared, but he paid no attention. Sophie, his wife – not his wife, his love, his hope, his life – she was all he cared for, now. If he lost her, there was no point in being alive. Hugh made good use of his soldier's training. He ran, as though hell were pursuing him; and after a fashion, it was.

Sophie held the brooch in her hands and sighed for pure pleasure.
Truly, it was a glorious piece of work: a tulip, with folded petals of creamy-white mother-of-pearl spiked with tiny lines of yellow sapphires; the stalk a row of channel-set emeralds, and the three leaves of peridot, Russian chrome diopside, and

517

tsavorite garnet. All cheap gemstones, but the brilliance lay in the variant colours of green; pale, dark, spring – they all gave the flower a delicate verisimilitude that one might expect in a museum piece.

'Fourteen-carat?'

'Yes,' Rachel Greenberg answered her. 'The price point will be 499.'

'No,' Sophie exclaimed. 'You can get it that low?'

'Manufacturing cost will be barely a 110. I expect to sell out the range,' she said proudly. 'There's a red one done using cherry opal and a yellow one done with citrines, they have white and blue spikes in seedpearl and iolite.'

'Fantastic.' Sophie stroked the glittering little thing. 'They're so elegant, so perfect for spring. You could charge thousands for this. What did the Brandts think?'

Rachel blushed. 'They were very kind . . .'

'I bet they were. This is wonderful work.' Sophie looked at the young designer; indeed, it was a hopeful sign that this was being produced by a pupil of Gertrud. The Brandts would not be there for ever, and Montfort must not depend on any one designer; Pete Stockton had learned that the hard way. 'I can't wait to send it out to *Vogue* and *Cosmo*. Congratulations, Rachel. You'll get a bonus.'

Rachel beamed. 'Really?' She was only twenty-four.

'Of course. One per cent of the profits made from this line. It could be quite a lot, if it does as well as I think it will.'

The young girl looked amazed. Sophie smiled; she wanted her to learn. Business was fun, and if you made something commercial, you should benefit. How else would you get people to give you their best work?

There was a sharp knock at the door. Sophie recognised it at once, and thrilled; Hugh. What was he doing here? Come to steal her for lunch – a bit early. Maybe take her to bed. *That* would be nice.

'Tell you what, Rachel, why don't you take the rest of the day off. Come in,' she called out.

The door pushed open, and there he was; panting, sweating. The squirming in her stomach died at once.

'Mr Montfort.' Rachel noticed too. 'Are you OK?'

He looked at her, and she shrank back.

'Give us a moment, please, Miss Greenberg.'

'Yes – of course,' she muttered, and hastily exited the room.

'My God, darling, what's happened?' Sophie exclaimed. Fear flooded her. 'It's not Tom – not my Tom?'

'No; nobody's died.' Hugh grimaced. 'Quite the reverse, in fact.'

Sweat was pouring off him; Sophie saw the stains on his suit.

'My darling – my sweetheart,' she said.

'Don't.' Hugh held up a hand. 'Sophie – don't call me that.'

She stared.

'Sophie.' There was no way to soften it. 'Pierre's alive.'

'What?' she whispered.

'Pierre is alive. He's in Paris.'

'Impossible.'

'He says he was kidnapped and jailed in Russia. He denies having an affair with Judy. He says that the stories about him and other women are just gossip.'

She just stood there. She couldn't take it in.

'You've spoken to Pierre?' she asked numbly.

'He was on television.'

'It's not him. An impostor . . .'

'It is him, Sophie. There's no mistaking it. He looks like Tom, thirty-five years from now. And anyway, I remember him well,' Hugh said, leadenly.

Sophie didn't ask if this was a joke. Hugh would never play with her in that manner. She stared into space.

'Hugh, is it true? That there were no other women?'

'It was common knowledge that there were many other women. I personally did not follow the gossip.' He had agonised as to how to answer this question. 'I believe that there were, but I have no proof.'

'Then why didn't he call me?'

'His answer is that he was so hurt by what he termed your betrayal that he could not face you. He has been staying with Judy Dean, whom he denies is his lover.'

Sophie closed her eyes and tried to cope with the pain.

'He's lying,' she said eventually, and Hugh felt a single one of the iron bands of grief around his heart snap. 'That conversation, in my office – when I found out Judy was his mistress. She was not insane, and she was not lying. He cheated on me for eight years.'

There was a leaden silence in the room.

'Are we married?' Hugh said, eventually.

Sophie shook her head, mutely. A tear rolled down her cheek.

'He's going to the château.'

'Tom will be there. I must go,' she said. 'I must meet him.'

Hugh was silent. Would she say nothing to him? He would not ask her.

'Darling,' she said. 'I am still married to Pierre. I can divorce him, though.'

'I thought Catholics didn't believe in divorce.'

'Civil divorce for a good reason is all right – when it's truly necessary. I think this qualifies, don't you?'

'So we could marry – after that?'

'I would still be married to him in the eyes of God. But I will seek an annulment. I don't think he belicved he'd be faithful when we first got married. I – I *did* intend to love him.' She sounded despairing. 'I would have to prove what he was thinking . . . At the time.'

'And can you?'

She paused.

'I don't know.'

'I love you,' Hugh said.

'I love you, too. I always will.'

'I have nothing to say. No comment,' Tom Massot shouted.

He shoved through the throng of photographers. The bulbs pop-popped in his face; microphones and booms were shoved at him, and the bright lights of the cameras half blinded him.

'Move!' he yelled. He wrenched open the door to his Lamborghini. 'I'm driving out of here. This is private property. As is the château. If I catch you on my land I'll call the police.'

'Isn't it your father's land?' some woman screeched. 'Are you mad you lost your inheritance?'

Tom slammed the door shut. His heart was pounding, he found it hard to breathe. They were banging on the windows, flashbulbs were going off, juddering the light inside the car. The adrenaline had made his palms sweaty, and he wiped them on his trousers. He took a steadying, ragged breath. He didn't want to die in a car crash before he had a chance to see Papa.

Carefully, he eased the car back, the heel of his palm on the horn. Blasting it. It was up to those cockroaches to move. Cursing, they scuttled back. Tom deftly wrenched the wheel to the left, spun the car round; thank God she handled so beautifully. He pulled out of the garage, and wheeled into the streets of Paris. Heading home. Heading to his father.

'They should all be there by now,' Judy said. 'Do you want to head out?'

Pierre looked at his watch. 'No; Sophie will be coming from London. I will wait until this afternoon, when all are assembled. It is better to deal with them together. For now, we can just stay here.'

'Right.' Judy twisted her fingers.

'You want to say something?'

'It's just that . . . in the press conference . . . I didn't expect you to say that about Sophie . . . that you loved her.' Judy looked at him anxiously. 'You love me, right? You're going to marry me . . . get a divorce.'

'Of course I am.' He came over and gently raised her hand to his lips. 'My Judy, who loved me all the time.'

'Then why did you say that?'

He released her hand. The questioning was not good; he frowned, lightly, watching her changed expression. Like all women, she had to be kept on a tight leash.

'I need a year or so, Judy. I intend to break her. To ruin her. She must lose everything. First, that bastard Montfort. I want him to know I'm fucking his wife.' A cruel smile. 'A man like him will never touch her, after that. She needs to be punished.

521

Broken, mentally. Then I will divorce her in disgrace, and you will be the Chatelaine.'

'Your mother . . . won't like that. Nor your son,' Judy dared to say.

Pierre shrugged. 'You know me, beloved. I make the decisions. I am the head of this family. Everybody will learn to respect that.' He smiled. 'And in the meantime, we will have each other. You will found your own PR firm, and Massot will give you contracts that will make you rich beyond your wildest dreams, as the Americans say. You have waited this long, Judy. Can you wait some more?'

She nodded.

Two years, he thought; two years, and then a tragic boating accident on the Seine. As if he would ever marry a whore!

'Good girl.' His fingers splayed, and stroked her ribcage; he enjoyed feeling her shiver. 'Just to show you how much you mean to me, you will accompany me to the château. I will insist that the family accept you as my most trusted friend.'

'Sophie knows we were lovers; Tom, also . . .'

'A youthful indiscretion we both regret. But we intend to stay friends, so I introduce you. It will all be open and above-board; you will dine at the château with the family once a week.'

He smiled. Pitting women against each other was his favourite spectator sport. His mouse of a wife would not object. He knew ways to psychologically break women. In Sophie's case, he would pretend to discover Catholicism.

Guilt was an excellent tool.

'Katherine will hate that,' Judy said, licking her lips.

'Mother, like Sophie and Tom, will obey me.' Pierre shrugged. 'I have had many years to plan this, Judy. I assure you, I have thought every detail through.' His lips twitched at the corners. 'And I intend to enjoy it.'

Darkness had settled across the park. Sophie tugged her sweater tighter around her; through the open doors of the drawing room she could see the stars; there was a three-quarter moon, and the black surface of the lake glittered its reflection, like a flash from a jet bead.

No cloud cover. The night was brilliant, but cold.

She tried to pray. But she could not feel God. Her anger was huge, and hard, inside her chest, a diamond that would cut everything, destroy every feeling. She wanted Hugh, and she might never hold him again. Never feel him inside her. Why had this happened to her?

Pierre must agree – agree that he never intended to marry her, not truly. He must speak the truth and let her go. Or else, she was condemned to a loveless, lonely life. There would never be another man for her but Hugh. Sophie knew it. She had been born to love him. And only him.

She still believed in God. And her faith. She would not go to Hugh, if she were truly married to Pierre. She would live alone, and see only Tom; she would obey God's law.

And she would hate him for it.

The huge fire hissed and crackled in the flagstone hearth. It was the largest one in the whole château; it took some of the chill out of the air, and sent the shadows dancing around the room.

Sophie gazed about; at the portraits on the walls, the fine damasks, the antique firearms, the Roman and Greek statuary. This glorious room had once been one of her favourites. Tonight, she loathed it. It was a prison.

God, how she wanted Hugh.

He had brought her, but he had not stayed. She couldn't allow it. Tom was to meet his father again. This was for the Massots, and no others could be admitted.

'You are not cold, Sophie?' Katherine said, solicitously.

Sophie glanced at her, tiredly. 'No.'

Katherine smiled. 'I am sure', she hissed, 'we are all lit with the fires of love. Especially those of us who had faith.'

Tom said nothing. He was staring into space, and Sophie watched his fingers grip the arm-rest of his chair.

She tried to muster some enthusiasm.

'Thank God Pierre is alive, and well. It is a . . . great mercy.'

He was son, and father, to the two people here. They would always love him, just as she never could.

'There is no need to thank God. Pierre takes care of himself.' Katherine adjusted her collar of gleaming diamonds; they flashed and sparkled in the firelight. Sophie had never seen her dress like this; her appearance at the party had been a mere preamble to tonight.

When Katherine had entered the room, in all the state of a dowager queen, Sophie had gasped. She looked, from a distance, a full twenty years younger. Her hair had been viciously scraped back from her face, pulling the papery skin upwards. Her cheeks and eyes had been professionally made up; the slack folds of the thin neck were completely hidden in the diamond collar, probably, of all her personal pieces, the most expensive; Pierre had explained, long ago, that it had belonged to the Empress Eugénie. Her gown was of a flattering mink-coloured satin, contoured with a whalebone corset and a billowing skirt; her hands wore fingerless ecru lace gloves, to cover the liver spots; and Sophie suspected that under the elegant folds of her hem, Katherine was wearing heels.

On her right hand, she wore a perfect, golden spessartite garnet, eighteen carats, surrounded by flawless diamonds, and a cuff bracelet of intricately worked Russian gold. She might have been attending a ball at the court of the Tsar.

Sophie was amazed; Katherine came close to looking attractive . . . in a certain light, like this one; lit by the dancing flames, not the harsh rays of the sun.

She herself had not changed. She would make no concessions, give nothing but her presence. She wore the suit she had arrived in; a simple, clean Givenchy in cornflower blue, with a sapphire pendant that was a gift from Hugh. Sophie had removed her engagement ring, and her second wedding ring.

The first would go, as well. But – she looked at her son again – not tonight.

There was a sound; the crunch of tyres on gravel. Everybody heard it.

'He's here.' Katherine's voice was a shout of joy; as clear as a forty year old's. 'Pierre! He's here! He's home!'

Sophie felt light-headed, sick, but she didn't care about herself. She walked over to Tom, squeezed him and hugged him.

'I'm happy for you, darling,' she whispered. 'I love you, Tom – I love you so much.'

Tom held her; his grip was so hard it hurt. But she did not care.

The butler came in. His voice trembled.

'Mesdames, monsieur,' he announced. 'The Master of the House is here.'

And then, walking into the room, came her husband.

With Judy Dean, right behind him.

Sophie gasped. She heard Katherine gasp. Tom's grip tightened further, painfully. Judy gave each of them a triumphant smile; she wore a scarlet dress of shimmering silk, and her neck was hung about with rubies.

Pierre was in a suit. And his eyes, reproachfully, swept over the three of them.

'Well,' he said. 'I'm home.'

Chapter Fifty-Five

Pierre turned to the butler. 'Close the door, and make sure that we are not disturbed.'

'Yes, monsieur.'

Sophie looked at Judy. How did he have the nerve to do it? To bring her here? She bit her lip; rage surged in her chest. But her son was gripping her hand. So she said nothing.

Katherine was the first to speak.

'Welcome,' she said, in ringing tones. 'Welcome, welcome, my love – my darling. I never believed you were gone. Never, for one second.'

Pierre walked across the room and took her hand; he gently kissed her cheek.

'My beloved maman,' he said – and Sophie thought she saw a flash of anger in Katherine's eyes. But no. It could not be so.

'And my son. Let me see you.'

Tom relinquished his mother's hand and stood up. He hesitated, then hugged his father.

'My son,' Pierre repeated. 'You look exactly like me.' He kissed him on both cheeks, in the French manner. 'And, finally, Sophie – my beloved wife.'

Sophie was mindful of Tom. She seethed, she wanted to slap him; but instead, she turned a cool cheek to him, and let him kiss her. Then she quickly stood, and moved back a step.

He was not to touch her, beyond that. She would never again be his.

'Pierre – you are well.'

'I am. And I am refreshed in soul to see you. I prayed, day and night, that I would see my family again. I know what has happened.' He moved back, towards the fire. 'And I want you all to know that I forgive you.'

'Why is she here?'

The question burst from Tom. Sophie's head lifted; her son's anger startled her.

'Why is Judy Dean standing like a guest in my mother's parlour?'

Pierre's dark eyes narrowed.

'Because she is a guest. She is my friend.'

'She is your lover.' Tom passed a hand through his hair. 'Do you know, Papa, how often I have dreamed of this day? Do you know how I have prayed – how I have longed for you? How I would have offered my soul just to have this moment? And then, for it to happen, and for you to – to ruin it. To bring that bitch of a woman into our house.' Tom's eyes were full of angry tears. 'You do not know how she has wrecked this family.'

'Tom, Tom.' Pierre glanced over the Massots; they were not reacting quite as he had expected. Perhaps it had not been a good idea to bring the slut. The boy had grown up. The women, of course, were weak; they did not object.

He tinkered with his approach.

'There is an important reason that I bring her, my child. I have prayed, and the good Lord has shown me the way' – that's right, Vladek, lay it on thick – 'our family must heal, and it must know the truth. And the sad truth is that, long ago, I betrayed your mother, the love of my life. Judy and I are both here to beg her forgiveness. Just as I forgive her for giving up all hope of me. We must both live with the fact that another has possessed our spouse. But we can forgive, go on, and be a family again.' He turned to Sophie. 'I am hoping you will introduce me to that old priest – Fr Sabin – I want to start going to church as we rebuild our marriage.'

'I do apologise,' Judy said. 'I was young . . .'

Sophie saw no sincerity in her eyes; the woman was barely suppressing her mirth. A stab of hatred shot through her. Pierre was talking about God? He intended to tie her down.

Still, she said nothing.

'But Judy and I are friends. We have fifteen years as close friends, before we ever slipped as lovers, and I will not betray that. When you are alone in a prison cell you learn what's important. We'll remain friendly, and Judy will be a guest of this family.' Pierre's eyes, confident, commanding, settled on Tom. 'You will resign from the firm tomorrow and give up your place at Oxford. I will select a position where you can work, under me – nothing too senior, you understand. You must learn from your error in selling the shares. Maman – my dear.' He turned to Katherine. 'You must give up all the shares I had allocated to you, for you see, I can no longer trust your judgement. Since your grasp of financial matters seems a little hazy, I will start to have the accounts of the dower house audited. For your own good. And you, Sophie.' He turned to her last. 'I love you, and you know we are obliged to forgive each other's infidelities. I expect you to stay home and to try to repair your reputation . . .' He reached out, and traced a fingertip across her collarbone. 'I intend that we shall regain our marital passion.'

Pierre smiled. 'You see? It is as if no time had passed. Everything shall be what it was.'

'No,' Sophie said.

She surprised herself; her voice was clear, and calm.

'What do you mean, no?' he asked, with soft malice.

It didn't impress Sophie. To his fury, she ignored him and turned to their son.

'Tom,' Sophie said, 'I am sorry, dearest, but I think we should get some things straight at the outset. It will be better for the family that way.'

'It's all right, Maman.' Tom had brushed off the tears, and nodded at her. 'I agree.'

'Pierre, I am not prepared to live as your wife. I thank God you are well, but I want to apply for an annulment.'

He could not believe it. 'I just told you, that God's law . . .'

'I don't believe you care about God's law,' Sophie said coldly. 'I believe you never intended fidelity. I know there were countless women. We have a son together, so I hope we will be courteous. Even friendly. But I shall file for civil divorce tomorrow and I will seek to have this marriage annulled.'

'And I will resign my job; the new company probably belongs to you anyway.' Tom stood up. 'But I will go back to Oxford, Papa. And I will never speak to Judy Dean again. If you bring her into any place where I am, I will leave. This point is not negotiable.'

Pierre stared.

He could not believe it. It simply did not compute. His clingy son and his mouse-like wife. Defying him. Refusing his authority. Sophie, who he had been so sure would jump at the first bit of religious trash he tossed at her . . .

'I will not give you an annulment,' he said, with ice-cold tones. 'I will fight you all the way to the Vatican. You will never get to marry that English bastard. You will love *me*, be with *me*, or be a lonely old maid for the rest of your life.'

Sophie could not stop herself.

'No contest,' she said, with contempt.

Tom bristled. 'Do not speak to Maman that way, Papa. The fault was yours, not hers. You don't own her. She was a good wife to you.'

A red mist, a pure, bright rage, rose up in his gorge, choking him.

'You dare to side with her,' he said. Intimidation, all the icy command of his personality, now bore down on his son. 'You are my *blood*.'

'Yes, but hers too.'

'I can disinherit you. I can reduce you to poverty.'

'I love you, Papa,' said Tom, standing and backing away. 'But don't threaten me.'

'Darling.' Sophie put a hand on his shoulder. 'Your father is not himself. He's been through a terrible ordeal . . .'

'Don't patronise me!' Pierre roared. 'Don't you *dare*! You are my woman, Sophie, and you will stay in my home!'

He was shaking. Never in all his years had he been so utterly defied. Not to his face. That was his magic, the magic of Pierre Massot, of Pyotr Vladekvitch, of Vladek the nameless

– he manipulated; he commanded; he enslaved. And of all the creatures in the world, were not these two most utterly his?

But then there came another noise.

'Pierre, Pierre.'

His head lashed round in annoyance. Katherine – there she was – his Natasha, and she was speaking out of place. She had glided up to him in her rich robes . . . And there was a ghost of her former beauty. 'She is not your woman, Pierre! You do not need her!'

He missed the feverish brightness in Katherine's eyes: he gave her a little push – out of his way.

'Be quiet,' he hissed.

But she was still there. Pawing at him, demanding his attention.

'You're mine.' Katherine – Natasha – smiled; there was an intensity to her stare he could not miss. 'After it all! After everything.' She moved towards him, her old eyes fiery. 'I was true to you. I obeyed you. I won! Didn't I? Now you're mine, for ever – for ever! The way I always knew it would be. None of them ever meant anything to you. Only me!'

He shook his head, furiously. 'Calm yourself!'

'And the whore. Why is the whore here? Send her away. She is not for you,' Katherine murmured. 'I am here – I am here, at last – I am here, who believed in you, my darling, my Pierre . . .'

'Grandmother.' Tom found his voice at last. 'This is between Maman and Papa. You should stay out of it.'

'Did you not hear her?' Katherine cried. 'She doesn't love you! She never did! She cannot be your woman!'

'Grand—'

'You be silent,' she hissed at Tom, with sudden, spiteful venom. 'You betrayed him! You are nothing! You are hers, hers, all hers!'

Pierre stared at Katherine.

'Maman, be still.'

But she was on him; under the lace gloves, he could feel the old, withered hands, clutching, insistent.

'I don't want the whore . . . I don't want her in our house . . .'

'It's his house!' Judy shouted, unable to bear it. 'Not yours! You're sick! You don't want *any* woman to have him! If not Sophie, then me! Me! I love him!'

Pierre's red mist of anger was pierced with another feeling. Fear. He turned to Katherine. Fool, old fool!

'Maman!' he said, sharply.

But she turned to him, her rheumy eyes glowing and intense. 'Tell them, Pierre – Pyotr – tell them. It's time – it's our time – she's nothing, she's a traitor!'

'You've gone mad,' he said coldly.

'No. I've waited long enough. Now, now is the time!' Katherine laughed, wild and high, in a maddened triumph. 'You love me, tell them you love me! Send them away!' She waved at Sophie and Judy. 'They aren't for you! You choose me, only me!'

'You're his mother!' Judy shouted.

'No!' Katherine stepped back, and too late, too late, he saw that the madness, the obsession, had boiled over, and was brilliant in her gaze. 'I am not his mother! I am his woman! I am his woman, Natasha! I have loved him! I have killed for him! You are nothing, nothing, whore! And you – you are nothing, too! You were never worthy to be his wife!'

'My mother is unwell,' Pierre said.

And then Katherine turned, slowly, to face him.

'I have kept the faith,' she said. 'I – only I. This one left for the Englishman. The whore screwed your son. I, I am faithful. Tell them you love me, Pyotr. Tell them about us. Tell them I am your woman. Not Sophie. I, Natasha. Natasha Vladekvitch. Your true wife.'

Sophie clutched at Tom. They were both silent.

'Mother – stop. You are unbalanced.'

'Noooo,' she crooned, and now there was something else. Terrible, slow-burning rage. 'Nooooo. You will not betray me. *You will choose me.*'

'We should call a hospital,' Pierre said. 'Maman has gone insane.'

Katherine turned to Sophie, hatred written bright across her

531

face. 'His name is Pyotr. Mine is Natasha. He found me in Estonia. We were in love, we escaped to Finland. He killed my niece to get here, her name was Aud—'

'Stop!' Pierre shouted.

'There is no House Massot,' Katherine screamed. 'There is a dead watchmaker – Giles – and his wife. He killed them both. I was to pretend to be his mother – I loved him, loved him so! You never did! And he gave you a son! But I, I am the one he has been with all his life!'

'My God.' Tom found his voice. 'Is that true, Papa?'

Judy, at the door, crumpled; her legs buckled, and she clutched at a table.

'You killed Gregoire,' she said. 'You did, you killed him –'

Pierre felt the red mist thicken, and bubble, until the fury, the rage consumed him. He turned to Natasha.

'You are a traitor! You are a liar! You are not worthy of me! You do not even know my name! I was never Pyotr . . .'

Sophie gave a little shriek; Tom shoved his mother behind him, and clutched at a poker . . .

And Pierre suddenly realised . . . he'd screamed in Russian.

And now Katherine was screaming, in Russian, back at him –

'You are mine, you are mine, you are mine! I am your woman!' She rushed at him. 'I am your woman . . .'

He started to swear that he would kill her, that he would choke the life from her . . .

But nothing came out. There was a hissing. Just a hissing. And then he saw the first spatters of red.

Sophie screamed. Tom lunged for Natasha. And then the pain . . .

Pierre, Pyotr, Vladek . . . he reached up . . . he felt the hole in his neck, saw the stiletto in her hand. Long, sharp . . . it was made of gold, and sparkled with diamonds . . .

Katherine had used the knife as a hairpin. In his agony, Pierre wondered wildly just how long she'd waited. Had she always known this moment was going to come?

He tried to scream. No sound came out. He thought of Giles, Mathilde. Aud. His father . . .

Blood, blood. It hurt. So bad –

'Papa!' Tom yelled. 'Papa, Papa!'

His son caught him; he felt Tom's fingers on the wound, his palm . . . desperately, fruitlessly trying to patch a cut throat . . . held Tom's eyes –

And in his last seconds, he registered, with surprise, that there was love – real love. And for one moment, Vladek was sorry –

He could not speak. But he looked into Tom's eyes.

For that one moment, Vladek returned his love, and asked for his forgiveness.

And then he died.

Katherine, Natasha, wrenched herself free from Sophie's grip; covered in Pierre's blood, she wailed, keened, like the cry of an animal in pain, floating up from her very soul.

And then, before anyone could stop her, she took the knife, and her hands, in their last moment of strength, drove the slender blade straight into her heart.

When the police finally left, it was past three in the morning. Hugh had raced over, and had stayed by Sophie's side. Tom did not want to be parted from her. They had sat, in a knot, at the end of the room, watching the medical examiners come, watching the corpses go out, answering the endless questions.

Judy hovered in a corner of the room, by herself. She occasionally brushed her hand over her eyes; obviously weeping.

Sophie kissed her son on the cheek.

'Are you all right for a moment, darling?'

'I'm fine.' Tom struggled to smile; he was hollow-eyed with grief, but Sophie knew that in the end, he would be OK. He had come to the last few months a boy, and left them a man. He would survive this, too. 'I'll go to bed soon. And in the morning I'll call Polly.'

'All right.' She hugged him. 'I'll be back.'

Sophie walked across the polished oak floorboards to Judy.

'I'll be out of your hair in just a minute,' Judy said courageously, tilting her chin upwards. 'I've got a mobile. The police impounded his car – I'll call for a cab.'

533

'No need. Richard will drive you wherever you want to go.' Sophie gestured towards the French doors. 'Would you like to get some air for a moment? It's not too cold outside.'

Judy looked at her, surprised; Sophie saw the tear-streaks down her chin.

'Yes. Thank you.'

She followed Sophie out on to the terrace, and sat with her on the Victorian wrought-iron bench, piled with tapestry cushions, which they kept under the loggia. The harvest moon was low now, but still bright; it shone through the clouds.

Judy spoke first.

'I know I owe you an apology.' She sighed, bitterly. 'I really thought I loved him, if it makes any difference.'

'So did I, at one time. The difference is you truly did love him. So did Katherine – or whoever she was.'

Judy shook her head.

'No,' she answered. 'We never knew him. I never did, anyway. I loved an idea. He wasn't that idea. But by the time I discovered the truth it was far too late. I clung on to that romantic ideal so long that I utterly lost myself. Katherine might have known him better, but she just had the same disease, worse. It's not love; it's obsession.' She sighed. 'You and your husband have love.'

'Yes, we do.' Sophie smiled, and blinked away tears. 'I understand, you know. I forgive you – for what that's worth. There's no bitterness here. I think we've all had enough of hate and rage.'

'Oh, God, yes,' Judy said. She drew her shoulders back. 'I think I guessed he'd killed Gregoire – even when he was acting. I just didn't want to admit it to myself. It had been so long. By then, Pierre was the focus of my life. A goal, not a real person.' She shivered. 'He's gone, and it's like waking up . . . coming out of a fog.'

'What will you do?'

For the first time, a slight smile appeared on the younger woman's face.

'Start fresh,' she replied. 'I've learned a lot. Sell the apartment, go back to New York. Now I don't have this weighing me down, I feel like I could do – almost anything. I'm going to start my own business.' She grinned. 'Maybe even fall in love – with a nice single guy.'

'I think we can do anything we put our minds to.' Sophie smiled back at her. 'I really do.'

'Me too. Something else we have in common.' Judy stood, straight and confident. She extended her hand to Sophie, who shook it. 'I wish you well.'

'And I you. If you're ready, Richard's waiting on the drive. He'll take you home.'

'Thanks. Goodbye,' Judy said.

'Goodbye.' Sophie watched as Judy, her old rival, left, head held high. Suddenly she felt a great sense of peace.

She sat there, alone, looking down towards the lake under the moonlight. Sophie wasn't sure how long; after a while, a strong hand descended on her shoulder. She turned round; it was Hugh.

'How are you, sweetheart?'

'I'm fine,' she said.

'Tom went to bed.'

'He'll recover. He's strong; I know him.'

Hugh sat down next to her and put his arm around her.

'You know I love you,' he said. 'I didn't want it to end like this.'

'None of us did. But it was Pierre's choice. And Katherine's.'

'Shall I drive us back to the hotel?'

'No; I'll stay here tonight.' She kissed him, lingeringly, on the lips. 'I don't believe in ghosts. I believe in forgiveness, and mercy, and love – and our family.'

Something in her tone caught Hugh's ear. He pulled away from her, his eyes searching her face.

'Maybe it's a strange time to tell you.' Sophie passed a hand over her belly, gently, caressing it. 'But this is an end, of sorts – and now it's a beginning, too.'

'My God – you don't mean . . .'

'Yes I do. I'm pregnant,' she said, and leaned in to him. She kissed him again, deeply, and Hugh's arms enfolded her.

'Let's not move,' he said, after a minute. 'This is the greatest moment of my life. Let's just sit here for ever. What do you say?'

'There'll be even better ones, soon. From now on. Everything is going to be wonderful.' Sophie sighed with sheer joy. 'Although I do love the moonshine on the lake. I love how it sparkles.'

Hugh kissed her again, and led her back into the house.